Wings of Fire

OF

Fire

THE HIDDEN KINGDOM
THE GRAPHIC NOVEL

For Elliot, who is as snuggly as a
sloth, as funny as Kinkajou, as charming as
Deathbringer, and as awesome as Glory.
—T.T.S.

For my friends in Halifax, who
supported me and my dumb art for years.
—M.H.

Story and text copyright © 2019 by Tui T. Sutherland
Adaptation by Barry Deutsch and Rachel Swirsky
Map and border design © 2012 by Mike Schley
Art by Mike Holmes © 2019 by Scholastic Inc.

Library of Congress Control Number Available

ISBN 978-1-338-34406-6 (hardcover)
ISBN 978-1-338-34405-9 (paperback)

10 9 8 7 6 5 4 3 2 1   19 20 21 22 23

Printed in China   62
First edition, October 2019
Edited by Amanda Maciel
Coloring by Maarta Laiho
Lettering by E.K. Weaver
Book design by Phil Falco
Publisher: David Saylor

WINGS OF FIRE

THE HIDDEN KINGDOM
THE GRAPHIC NOVEL

BY **TUI T. SUTHERLAND**

ADAPTED BY **BARRY DEUTSCH**
AND **RACHEL SWIRSKY**

ART BY **MIKE HOLMES**
COLOR BY **MAARTA LAIHO**

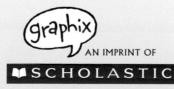

graphix

AN IMPRINT OF

■ SCHOLASTIC

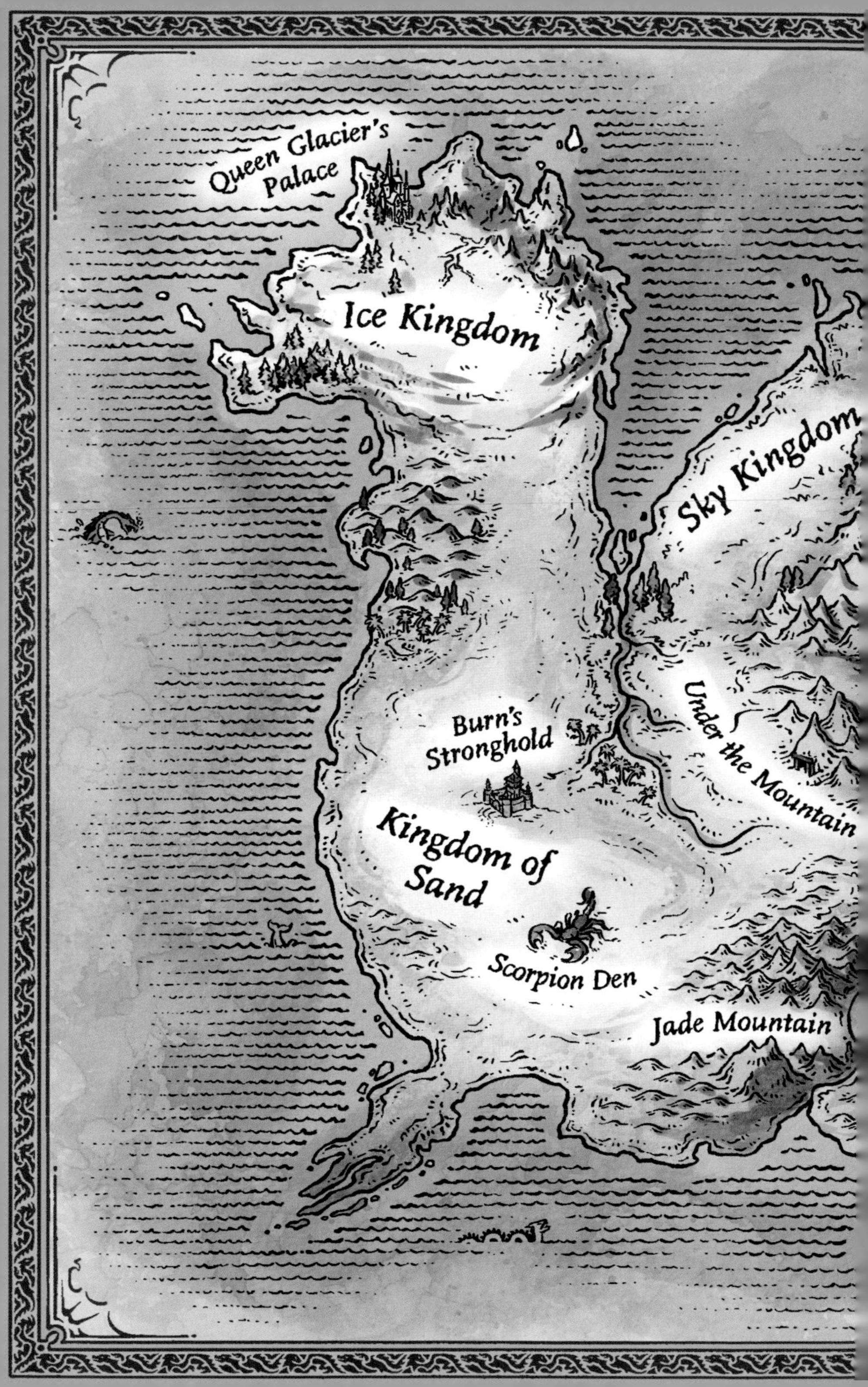

Queen Glacier's Palace
Ice Kingdom
Sky Kingdom
Burn's Stronghold
Under the Mountain
Kingdom of Sand
Scorpion Den
Jade Mountain

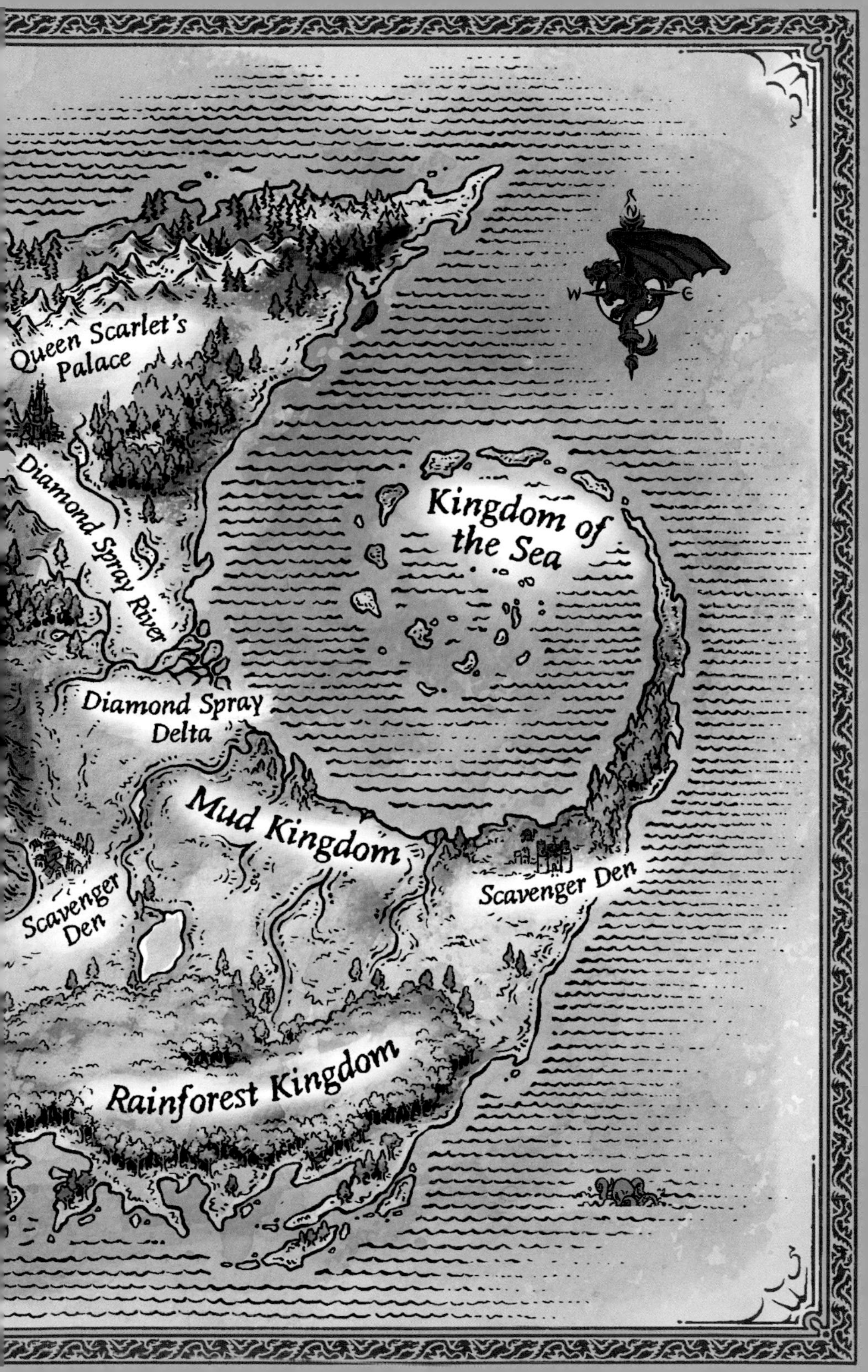

N
W
E
Queen Scarlet's Palace
Diamond Spray River
Kingdom of the Sea
Diamond Spray Delta
Mud Kingdom
Scavenger Den
Scavenger Den
Rainforest Kingdom

THE HIDDEN KINGDOM

THE DRAGONET
PROPHECY

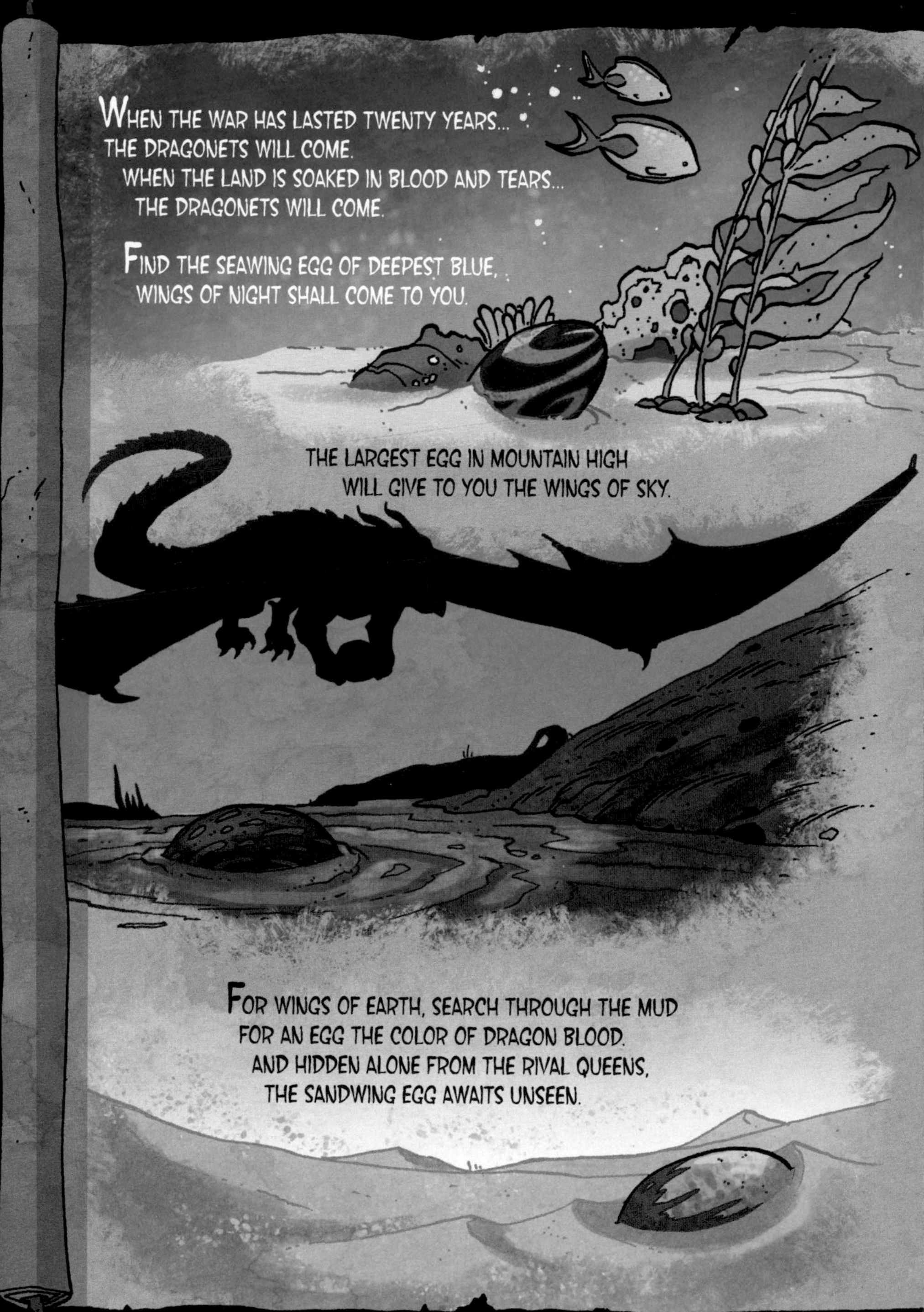
WHEN THE WAR HAS LASTED TWENTY YEARS...
THE DRAGONETS WILL COME.
WHEN THE LAND IS SOAKED IN BLOOD AND TEARS...
THE DRAGONETS WILL COME.
FIND THE SEAWING EGG OF DEEPEST BLUE,
WINGS OF NIGHT SHALL COME TO YOU.
THE LARGEST EGG IN MOUNTAIN HIGH
WILL GIVE TO YOU THE WINGS OF SKY.
FOR WINGS OF EARTH, SEARCH THROUGH THE MUD
FOR AN EGG THE COLOR OF DRAGON BLOOD.
AND HIDDEN ALONE FROM THE RIVAL QUEENS,
THE SANDWING EGG AWAITS UNSEEN.

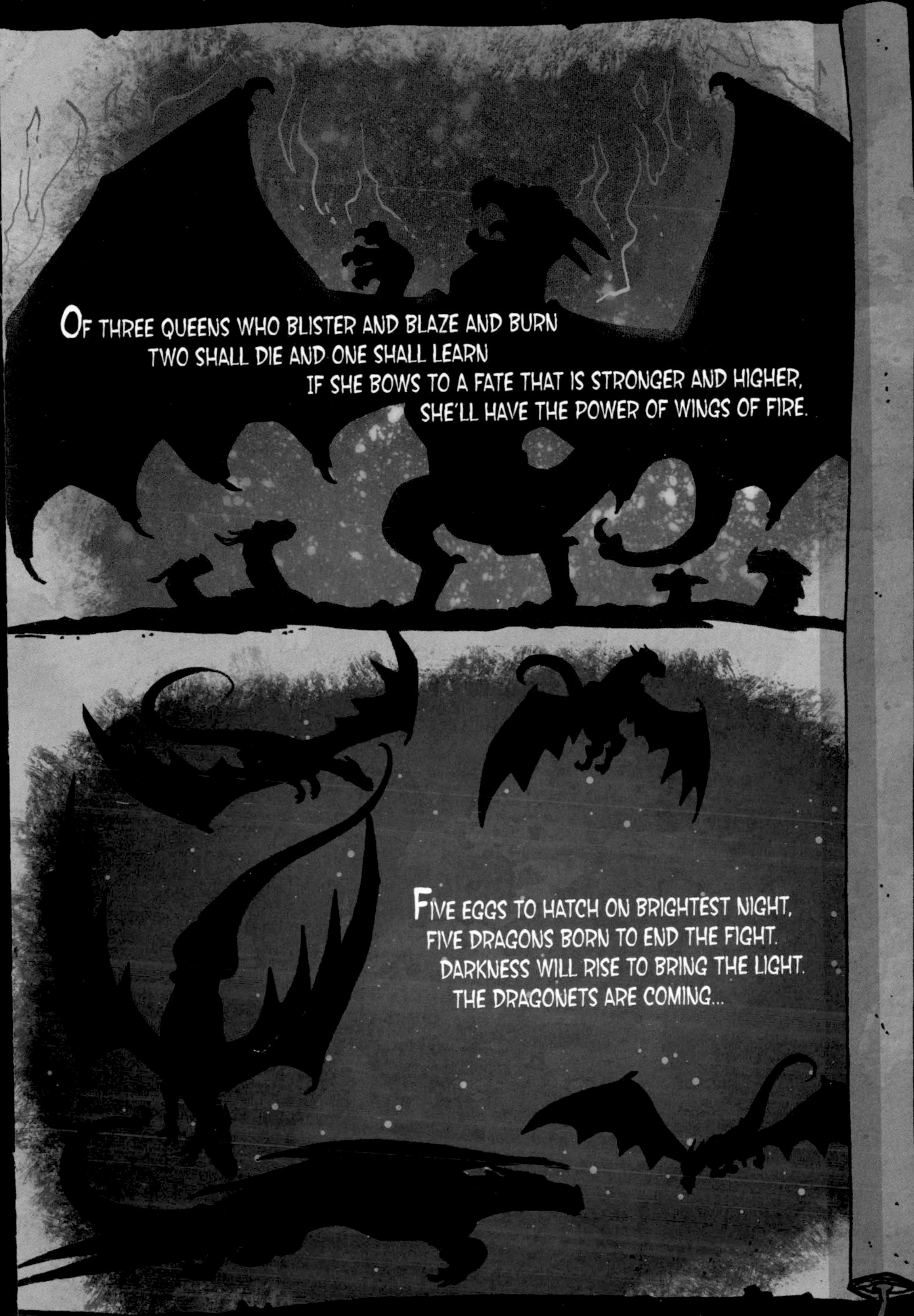
Of three queens who blister and blaze and burn
two shall die and one shall learn
if she bows to a fate that is stronger and higher,
she'll have the power of wings of fire.
Five eggs to hatch on brightest night,
five dragons born to end the fight.
Darkness will rise to bring the light.
The dragonets are coming...

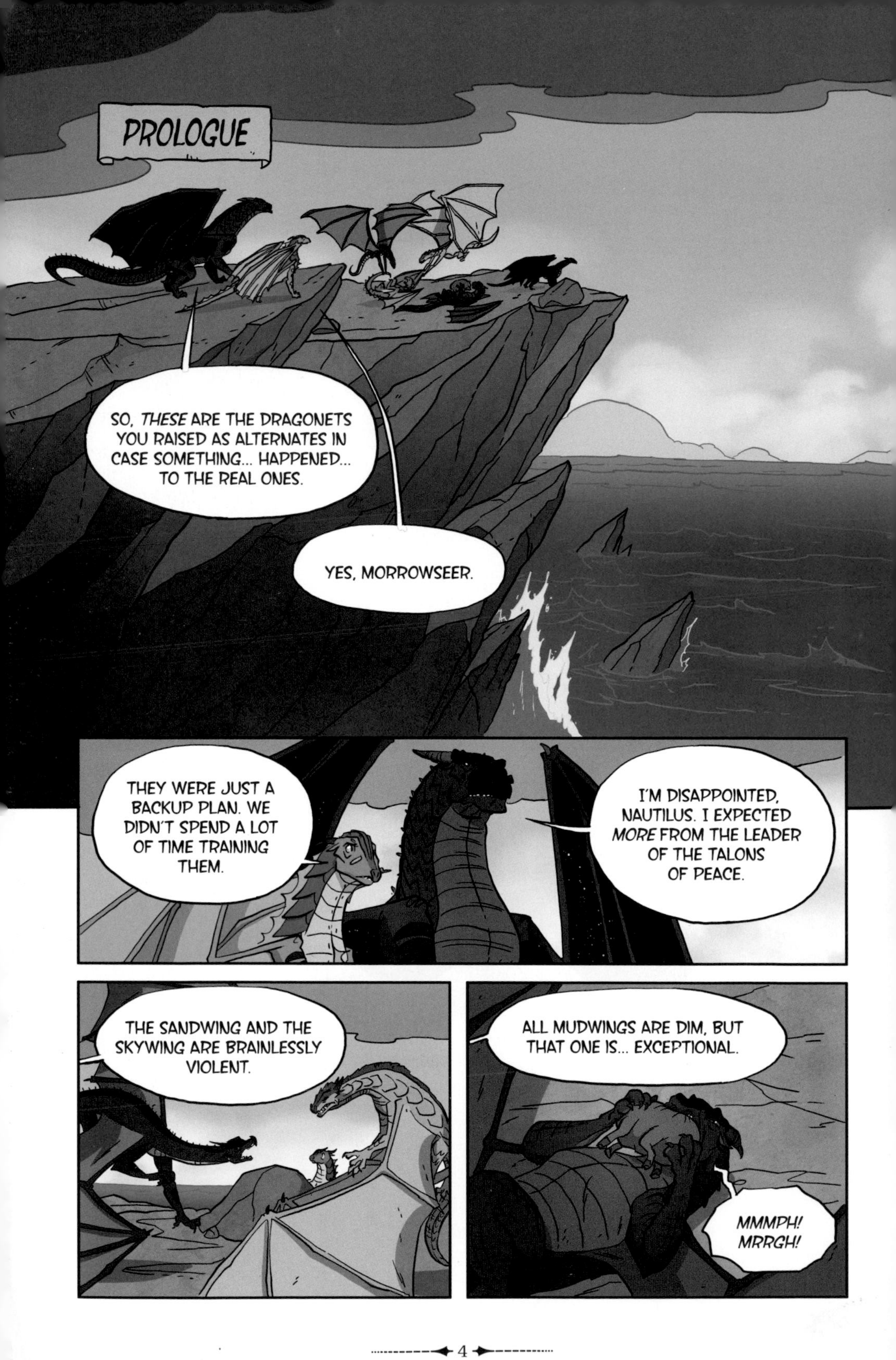
PROLOGUE
SO, *THESE* ARE THE DRAGONETS YOU RAISED AS ALTERNATES IN CASE SOMETHING... HAPPENED... TO THE REAL ONES.
YES, MORROWSEER.
THEY WERE JUST A BACKUP PLAN. WE DIDN'T SPEND A LOT OF TIME TRAINING THEM.
I'M DISAPPOINTED, NAUTILUS. I EXPECTED *MORE* FROM THE LEADER OF THE TALONS OF PEACE.
THE SANDWING AND THE SKYWING ARE BRAINLESSLY VIOLENT.
ALL MUDWINGS ARE DIM, BUT THAT ONE IS... EXCEPTIONAL.
MMMPH! MRRGH!

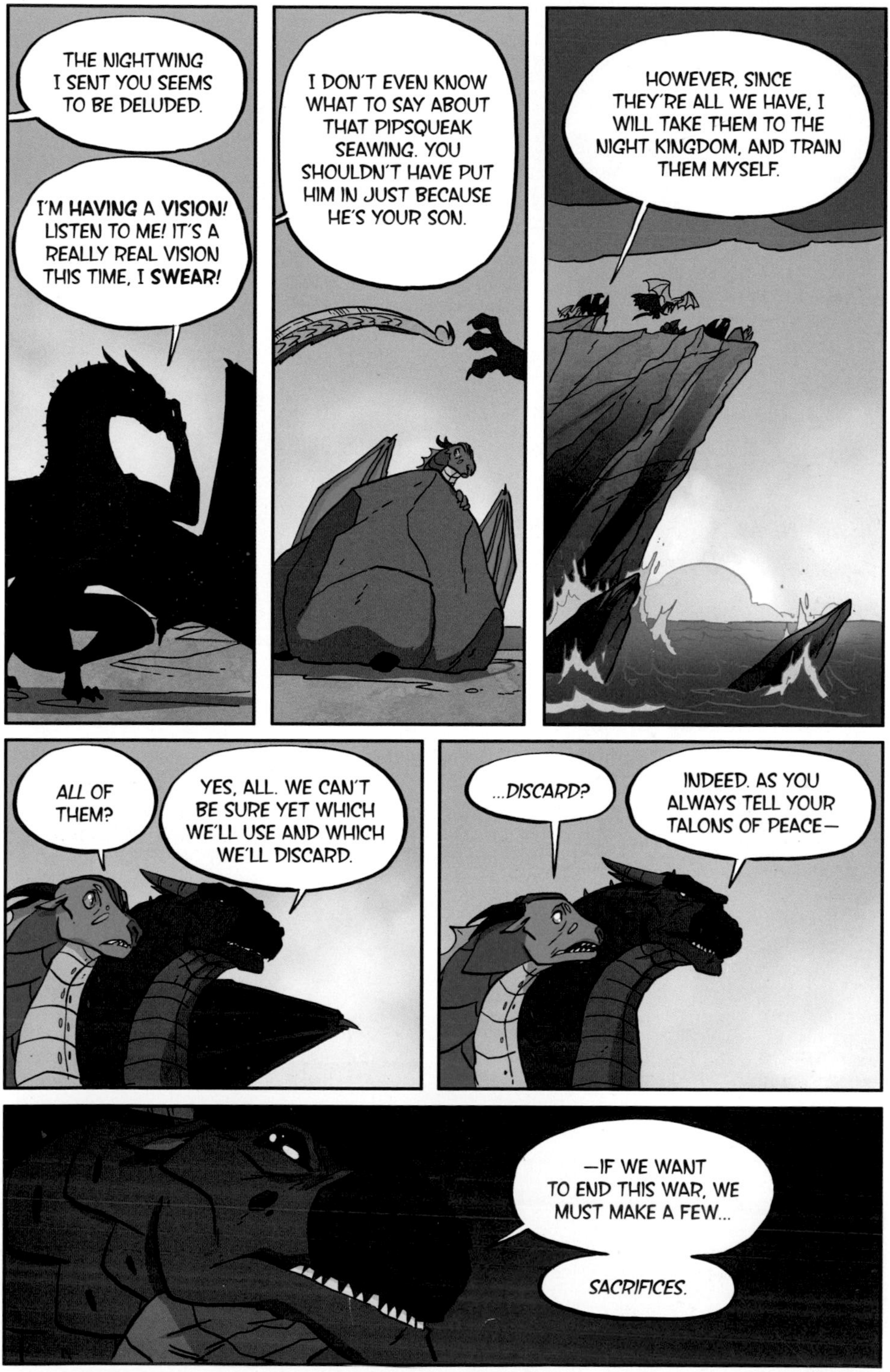
THE NIGHTWING I SENT YOU SEEMS TO BE DELUDED.
I'M **HAVING** A **VISION!** LISTEN TO ME! IT'S A REALLY REAL VISION THIS TIME, I **SWEAR!**
I DON'T EVEN KNOW WHAT TO SAY ABOUT THAT PIPSQUEAK SEAWING. YOU SHOULDN'T HAVE PUT HIM IN JUST BECAUSE HE'S YOUR SON.
HOWEVER, SINCE THEY'RE ALL WE HAVE, I WILL TAKE THEM TO THE NIGHT KINGDOM, AND TRAIN THEM MYSELF.
ALL OF THEM?
YES, ALL. WE CAN'T BE SURE YET WHICH WE'LL USE AND WHICH WE'LL DISCARD.
...*DISCARD?*
INDEED. AS YOU ALWAYS TELL YOUR TALONS OF PEACE—
—IF WE WANT TO END THIS WAR, WE MUST MAKE A FEW...
SACRIFICES.

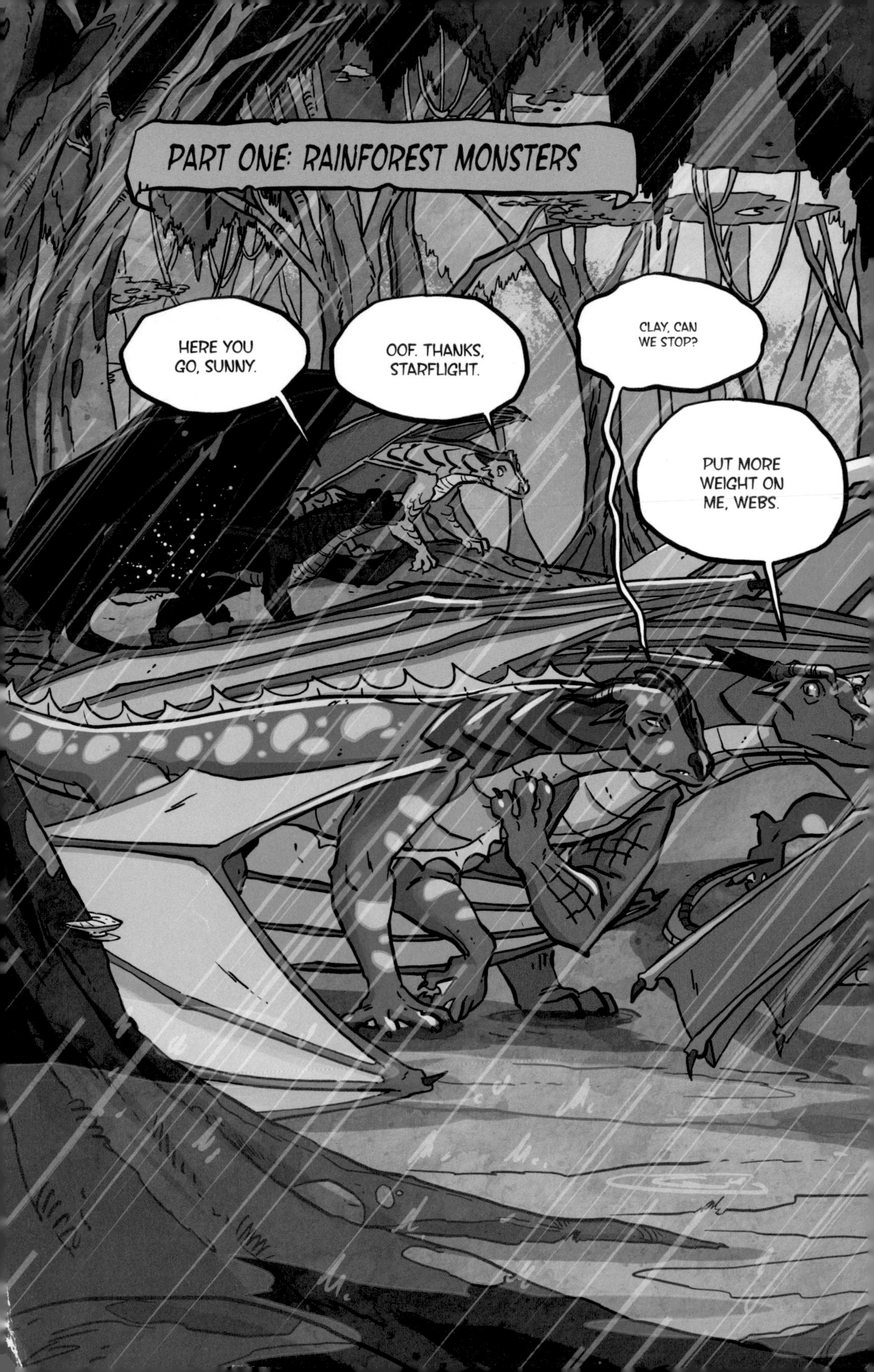
PART ONE: RAINFOREST MONSTERS
HERE YOU GO, SUNNY.
OOF. THANKS, STARFLIGHT.
CLAY, CAN WE STOP?
PUT MORE WEIGHT ON ME, WEBS.

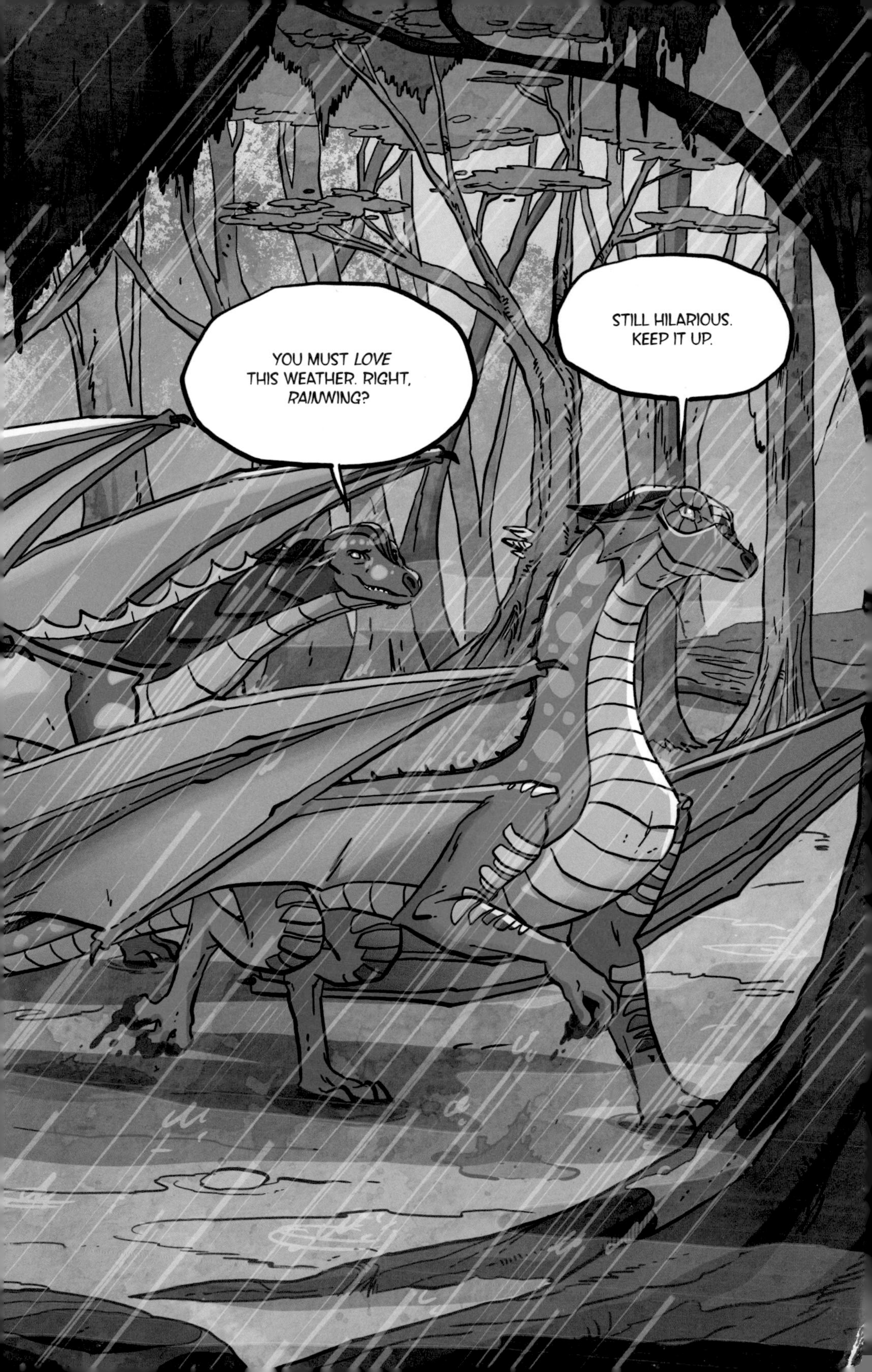
YOU MUST *LOVE* THIS WEATHER. RIGHT, *RAINWING*?
STILL HILARIOUS. KEEP IT UP.

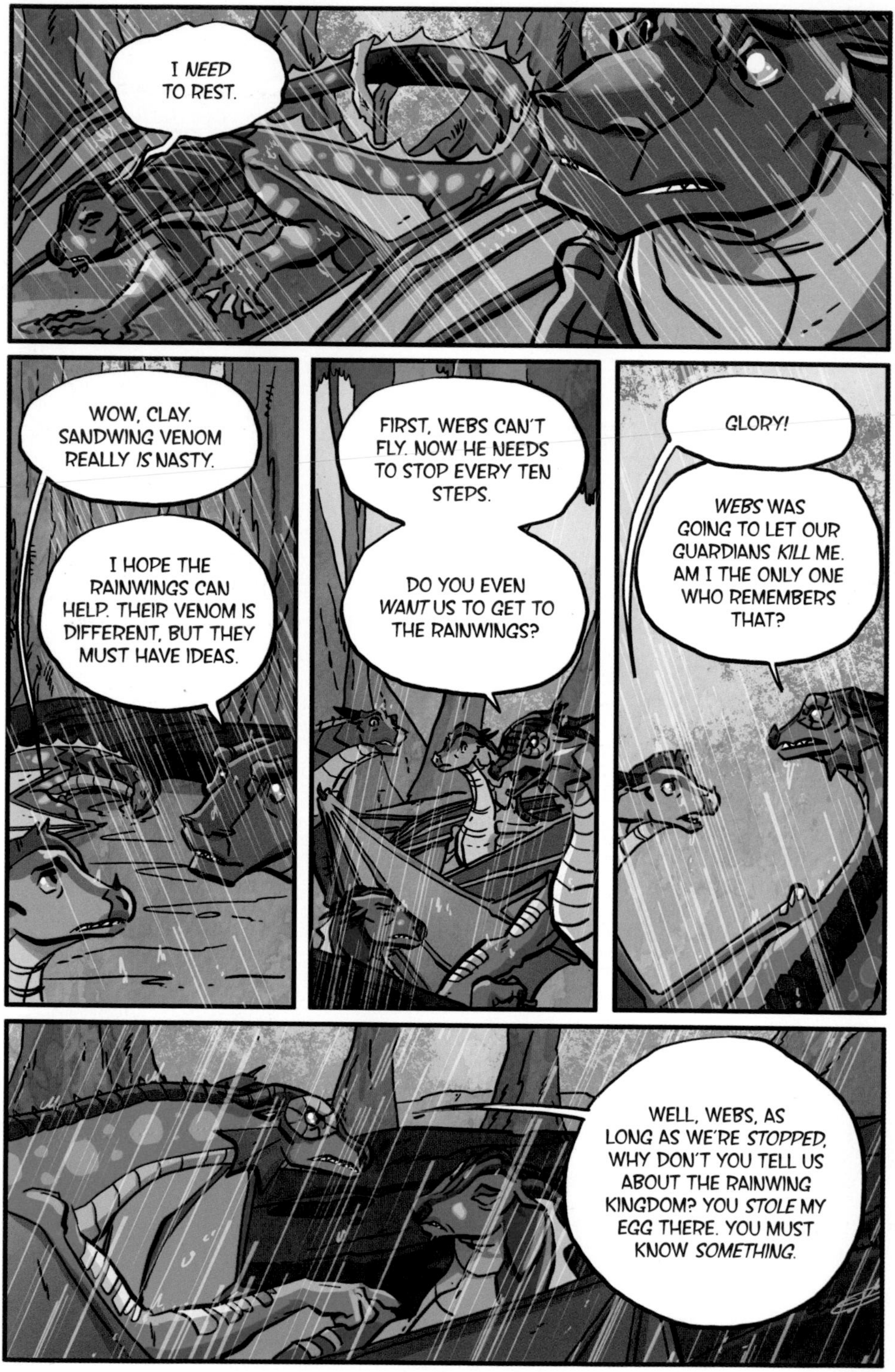
I *NEED* TO REST.
WOW, CLAY. SANDWING VENOM REALLY *IS* NASTY.
I HOPE THE RAINWINGS CAN HELP. THEIR VENOM IS DIFFERENT, BUT THEY MUST HAVE IDEAS.
FIRST, WEBS CAN'T FLY. NOW HE NEEDS TO STOP EVERY TEN STEPS.
DO YOU EVEN *WANT* US TO GET TO THE RAINWINGS?
GLORY!
WEBS WAS GOING TO LET OUR GUARDIANS *KILL* ME. AM I THE ONLY ONE WHO REMEMBERS THAT?
WELL, WEBS, AS LONG AS WE'RE *STOPPED*, WHY DON'T YOU TELL US ABOUT THE RAINWING KINGDOM? YOU *STOLE* MY EGG THERE. YOU MUST KNOW *SOMETHING*.

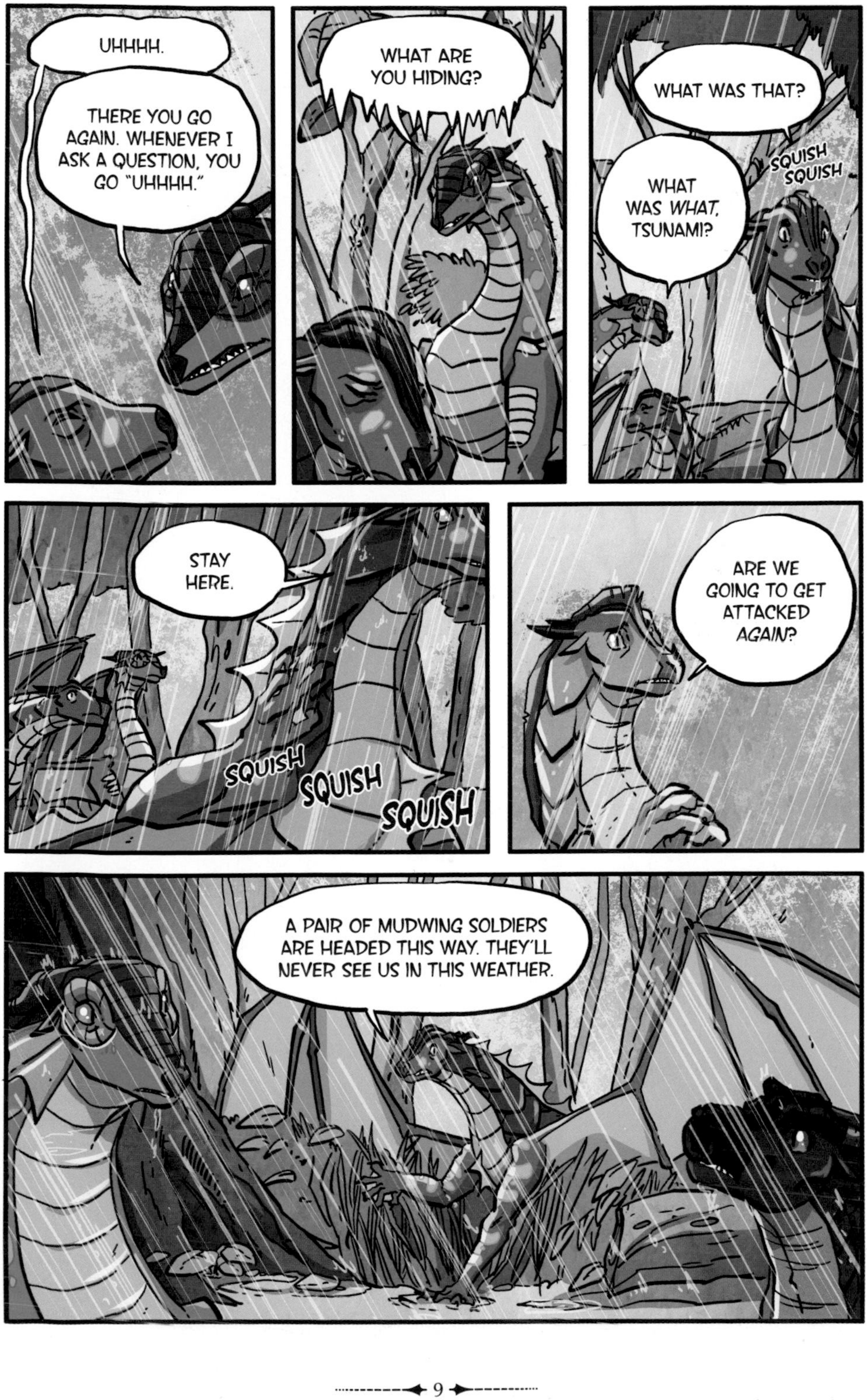
UHHHH.
THERE YOU GO AGAIN. WHENEVER I ASK A QUESTION, YOU GO "UHHHH."
WHAT ARE YOU HIDING?
WHAT WAS THAT?
SQUISH SQUISH
WHAT WAS *WHAT*, TSUNAMI?
STAY HERE.
SQUISH
SQUISH
SQUISH
ARE WE GOING TO GET ATTACKED AGAIN?
A PAIR OF MUDWING SOLDIERS ARE HEADED THIS WAY. THEY'LL NEVER SEE US IN THIS WEATHER.

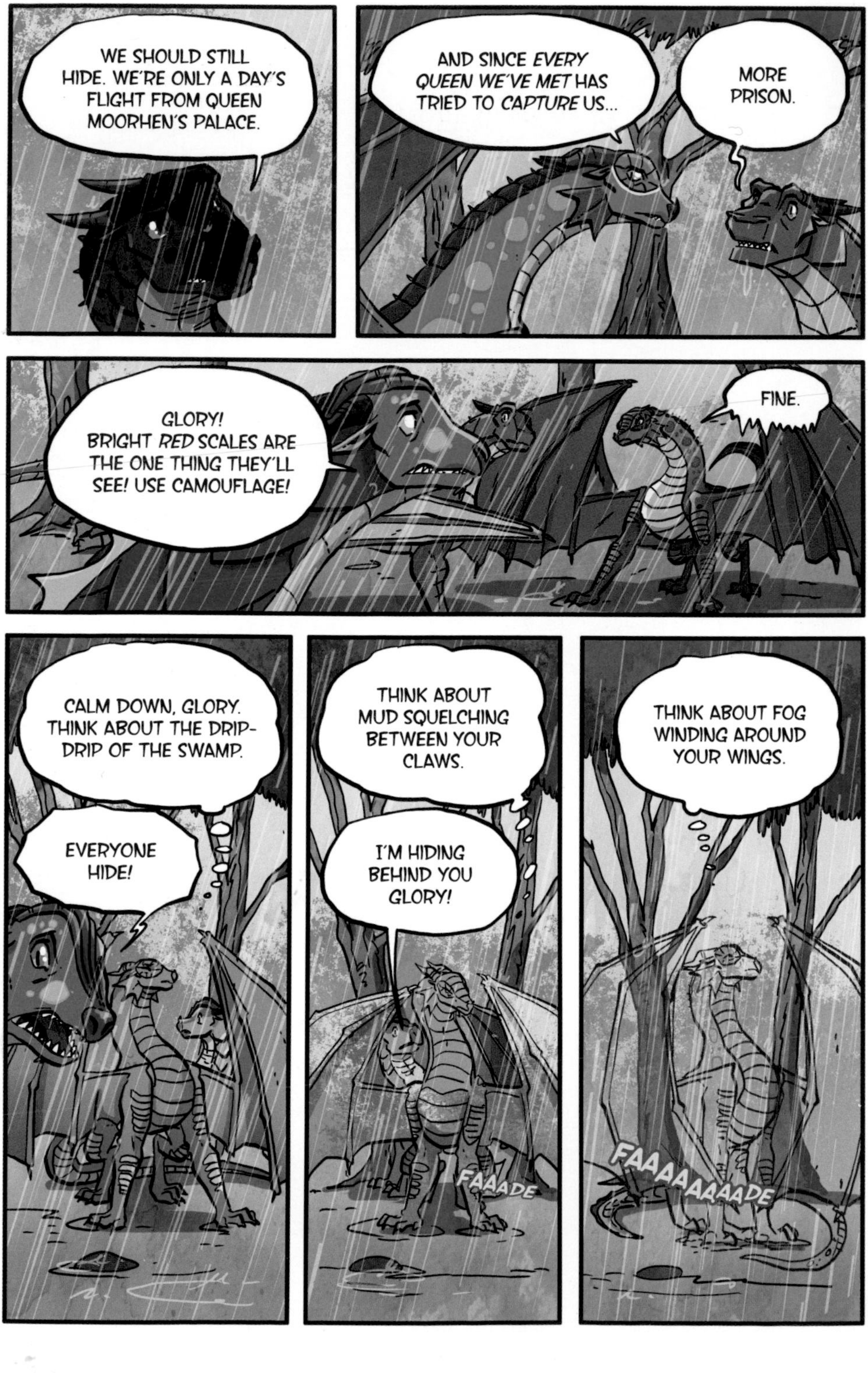
WE SHOULD STILL HIDE. WE'RE ONLY A DAY'S FLIGHT FROM QUEEN MOORHEN'S PALACE.
AND SINCE EVERY QUEEN WE'VE MET HAS TRIED TO CAPTURE US...
MORE PRISON.
GLORY! BRIGHT RED SCALES ARE THE ONE THING THEY'LL SEE! USE CAMOUFLAGE!
FINE.
CALM DOWN, GLORY. THINK ABOUT THE DRIP-DRIP OF THE SWAMP.
EVERYONE HIDE!
THINK ABOUT MUD SQUELCHING BETWEEN YOUR CLAWS.
I'M HIDING BEHIND YOU GLORY!
FAAADE
THINK ABOUT FOG WINDING AROUND YOUR WINGS.
FAAAAAAAADE

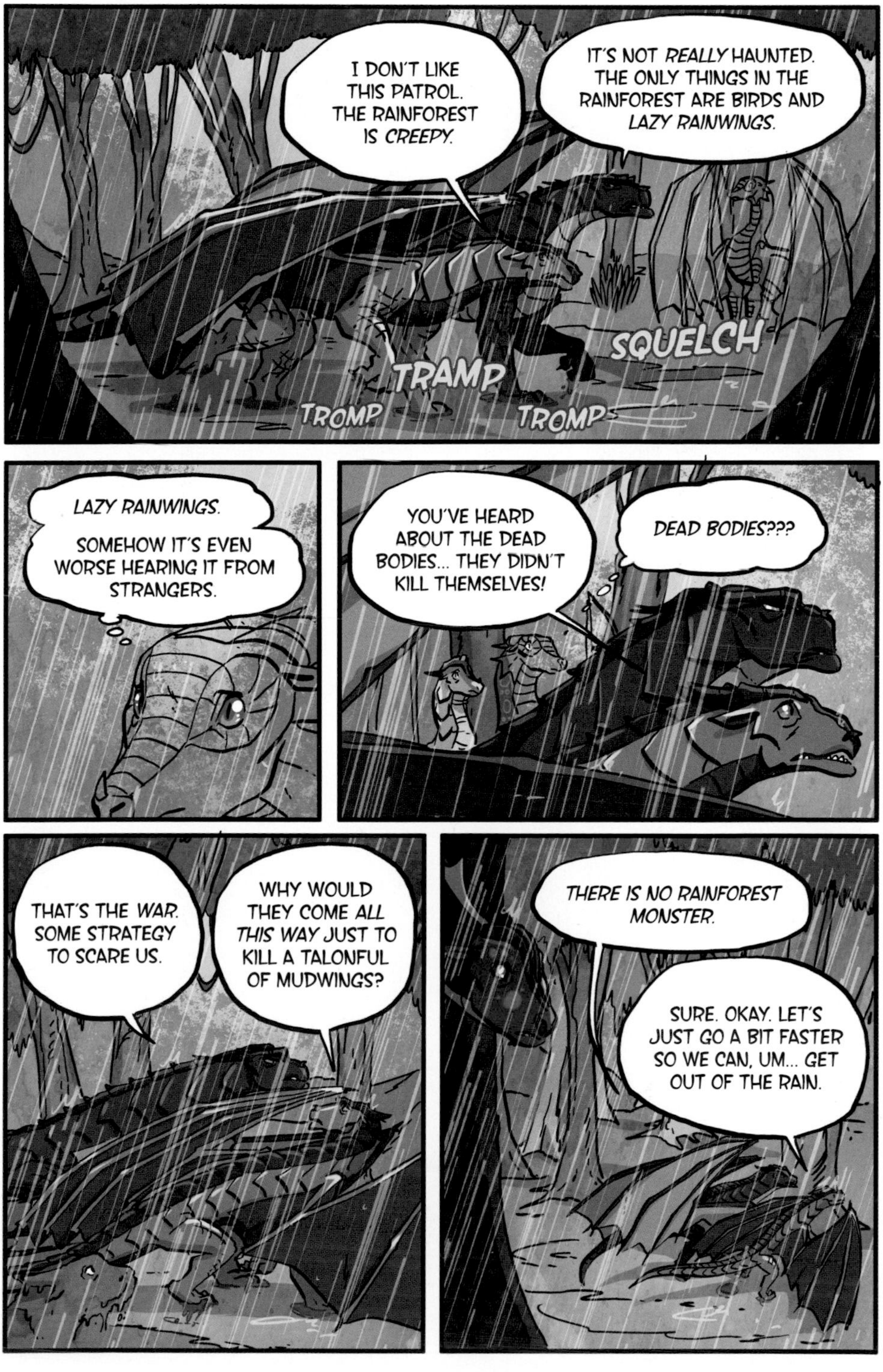
I DON'T LIKE THIS PATROL. THE RAINFOREST IS CREEPY.
IT'S NOT REALLY HAUNTED. THE ONLY THINGS IN THE RAINFOREST ARE BIRDS AND LAZY RAINWINGS.
SQUELCH
TRAMP
TROMP
TROMP
LAZY RAINWINGS.
SOMEHOW IT'S EVEN WORSE HEARING IT FROM STRANGERS.
YOU'VE HEARD ABOUT THE DEAD BODIES... THEY DIDN'T KILL THEMSELVES!
DEAD BODIES???
THAT'S THE WAR. SOME STRATEGY TO SCARE US.
WHY WOULD THEY COME ALL THIS WAY JUST TO KILL A TALONFUL OF MUDWINGS?
THERE IS NO RAINFOREST MONSTER.
SURE. OKAY. LET'S JUST GO A BIT FASTER SO WE CAN, UM... GET OUT OF THE RAIN.

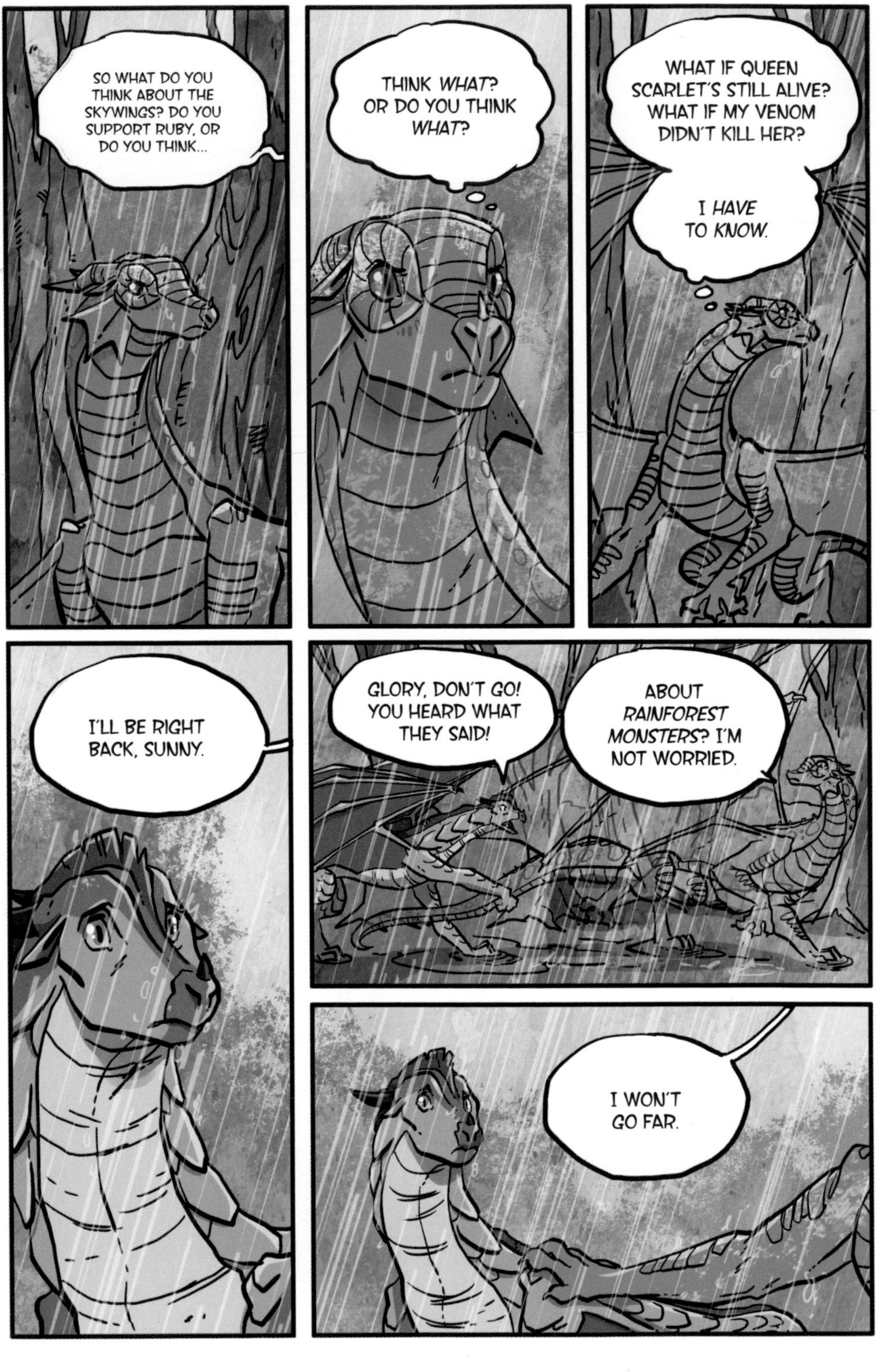
SO WHAT DO YOU THINK ABOUT THE SKYWINGS? DO YOU SUPPORT RUBY, OR DO YOU THINK...
THINK *WHAT*? OR DO YOU THINK *WHAT*?
WHAT IF QUEEN SCARLET'S STILL ALIVE? WHAT IF MY VENOM DIDN'T KILL HER?
I *HAVE* TO *KNOW*.
I'LL BE RIGHT BACK, SUNNY.
GLORY, DON'T GO! YOU HEARD WHAT THEY SAID!
ABOUT *RAINFOREST MONSTERS*? I'M NOT WORRIED.
I WON'T GO FAR.

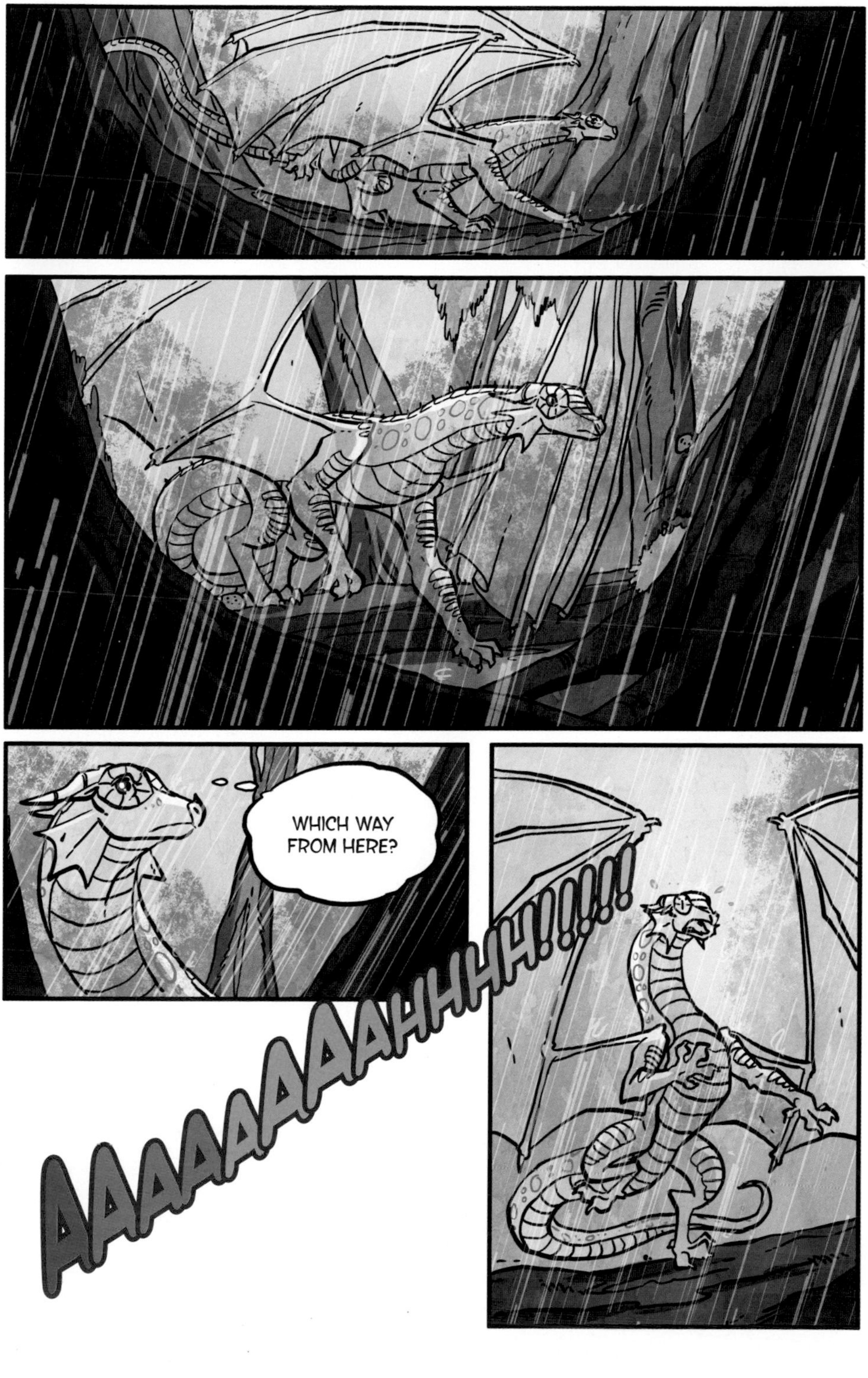
WHICH WAY FROM HERE?
AAAAAAAAAHHHH!!!!!

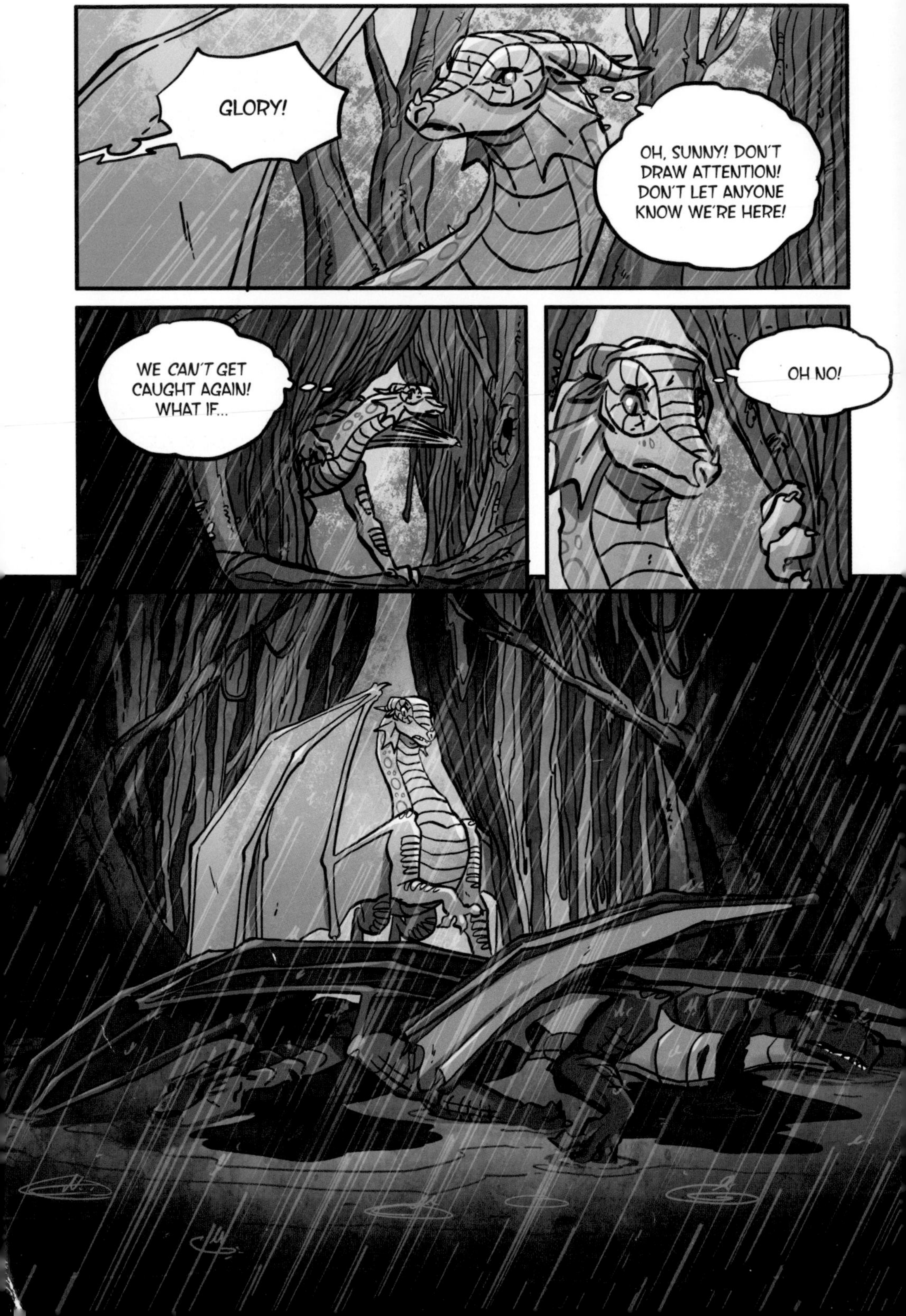
GLORY!
OH, SUNNY! DON'T DRAW ATTENTION! DON'T LET ANYONE KNOW WE'RE HERE!
WE *CAN'T* GET CAUGHT AGAIN! WHAT IF...
OH NO!

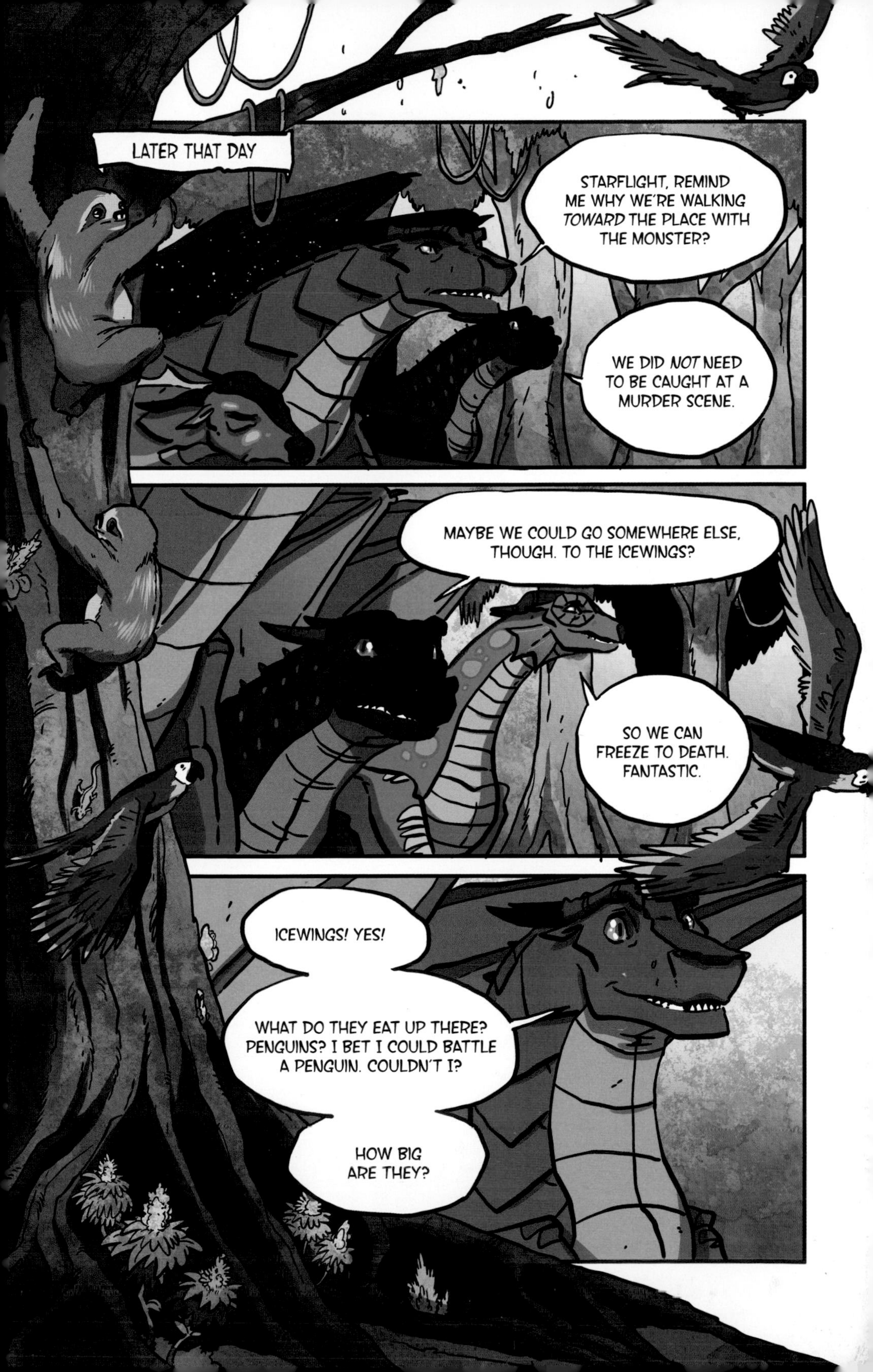
LATER THAT DAY
STARFLIGHT, REMIND ME WHY WE'RE WALKING *TOWARD* THE PLACE WITH THE MONSTER?
WE DID *NOT* NEED TO BE CAUGHT AT A MURDER SCENE.
MAYBE WE COULD GO SOMEWHERE ELSE, THOUGH. TO THE ICEWINGS?
SO WE CAN FREEZE TO DEATH. FANTASTIC.
ICEWINGS! YES!
WHAT DO THEY EAT UP THERE? PENGUINS? I BET I COULD BATTLE A PENGUIN. COULDN'T I?
HOW BIG ARE THEY?

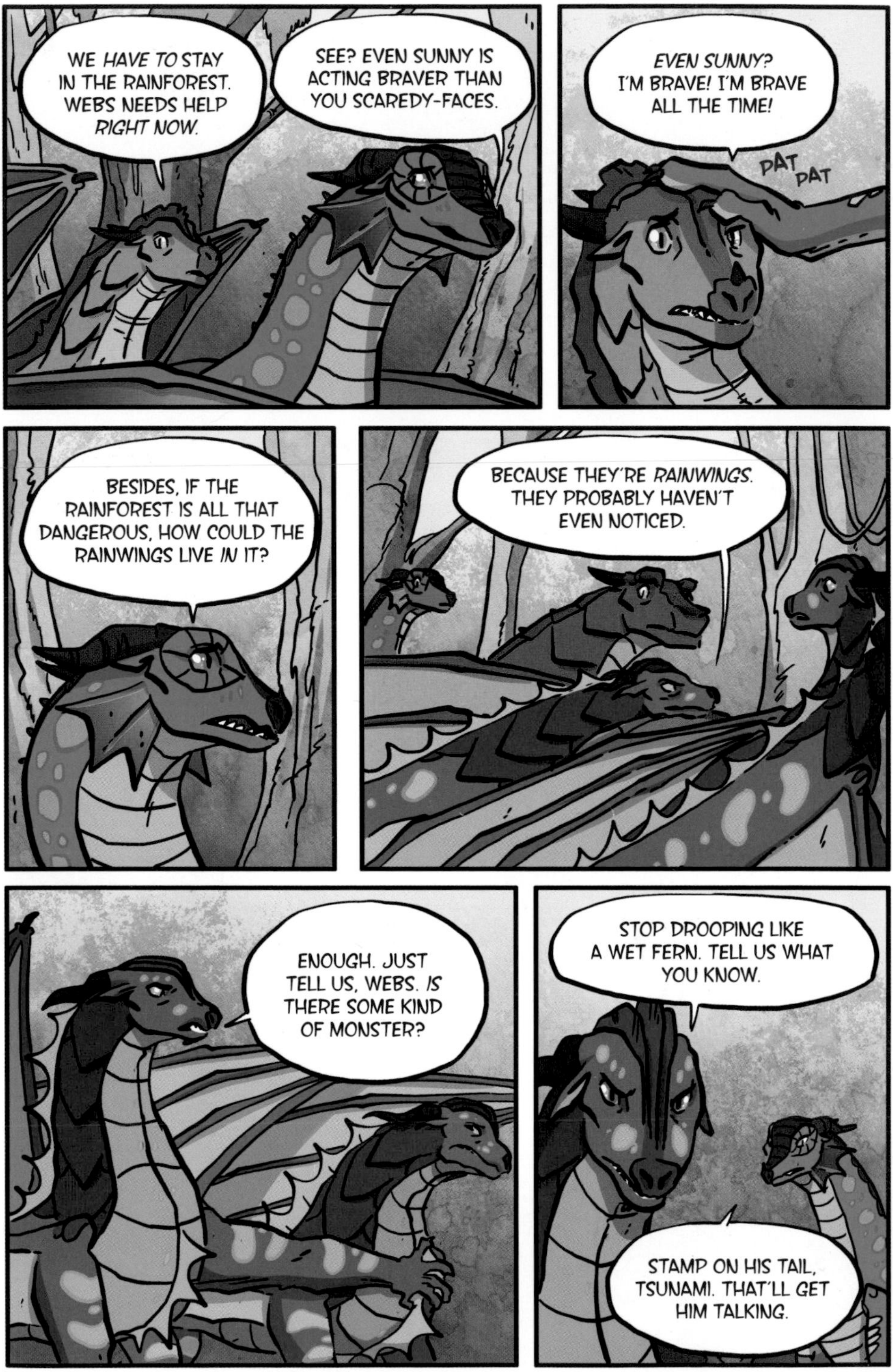
WE *HAVE TO* STAY IN THE RAINFOREST. WEBS NEEDS HELP *RIGHT NOW.*
SEE? EVEN SUNNY IS ACTING BRAVER THAN YOU SCAREDY-FACES.
EVEN SUNNY? I'M BRAVE! I'M BRAVE ALL THE TIME!
PAT PAT
BESIDES, IF THE RAINFOREST IS ALL THAT DANGEROUS, HOW COULD THE RAINWINGS LIVE *IN* IT?
BECAUSE THEY'RE *RAINWINGS.* THEY PROBABLY HAVEN'T EVEN NOTICED.
ENOUGH. JUST TELL US, WEBS. *IS* THERE SOME KIND OF MONSTER?
STOP DROOPING LIKE A WET FERN. TELL US WHAT YOU KNOW.
STAMP ON HIS TAIL, TSUNAMI. THAT'LL GET HIM TALKING.

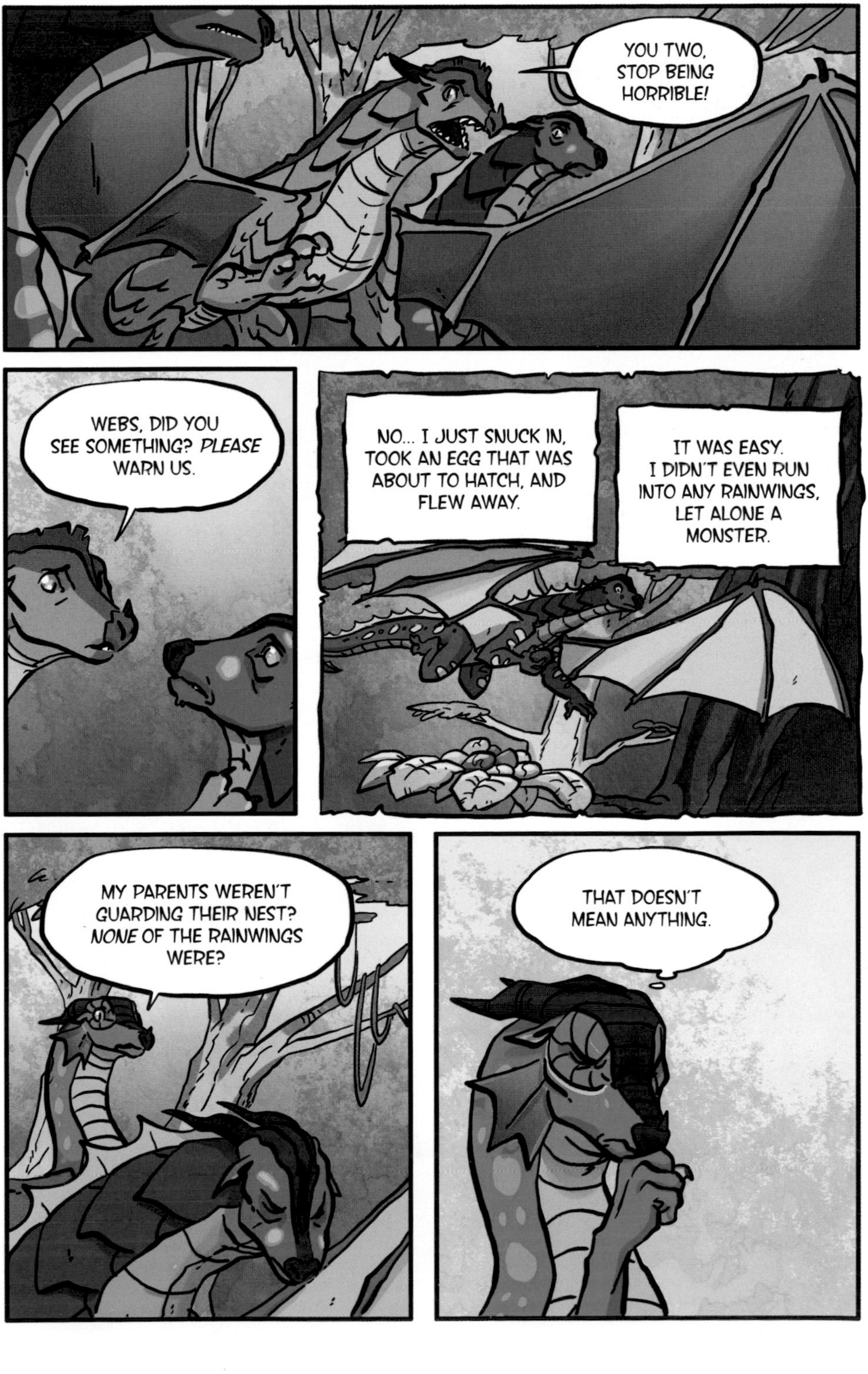
YOU TWO, STOP BEING HORRIBLE!
WEBS, DID YOU SEE SOMETHING? *PLEASE* WARN US.
NO... I JUST SNUCK IN, TOOK AN EGG THAT WAS ABOUT TO HATCH, AND FLEW AWAY.
IT WAS EASY. I DIDN'T EVEN RUN INTO ANY RAINWINGS, LET ALONE A MONSTER.
MY PARENTS WEREN'T GUARDING THEIR NEST? *NONE* OF THE RAINWINGS WERE?
THAT DOESN'T MEAN ANYTHING.

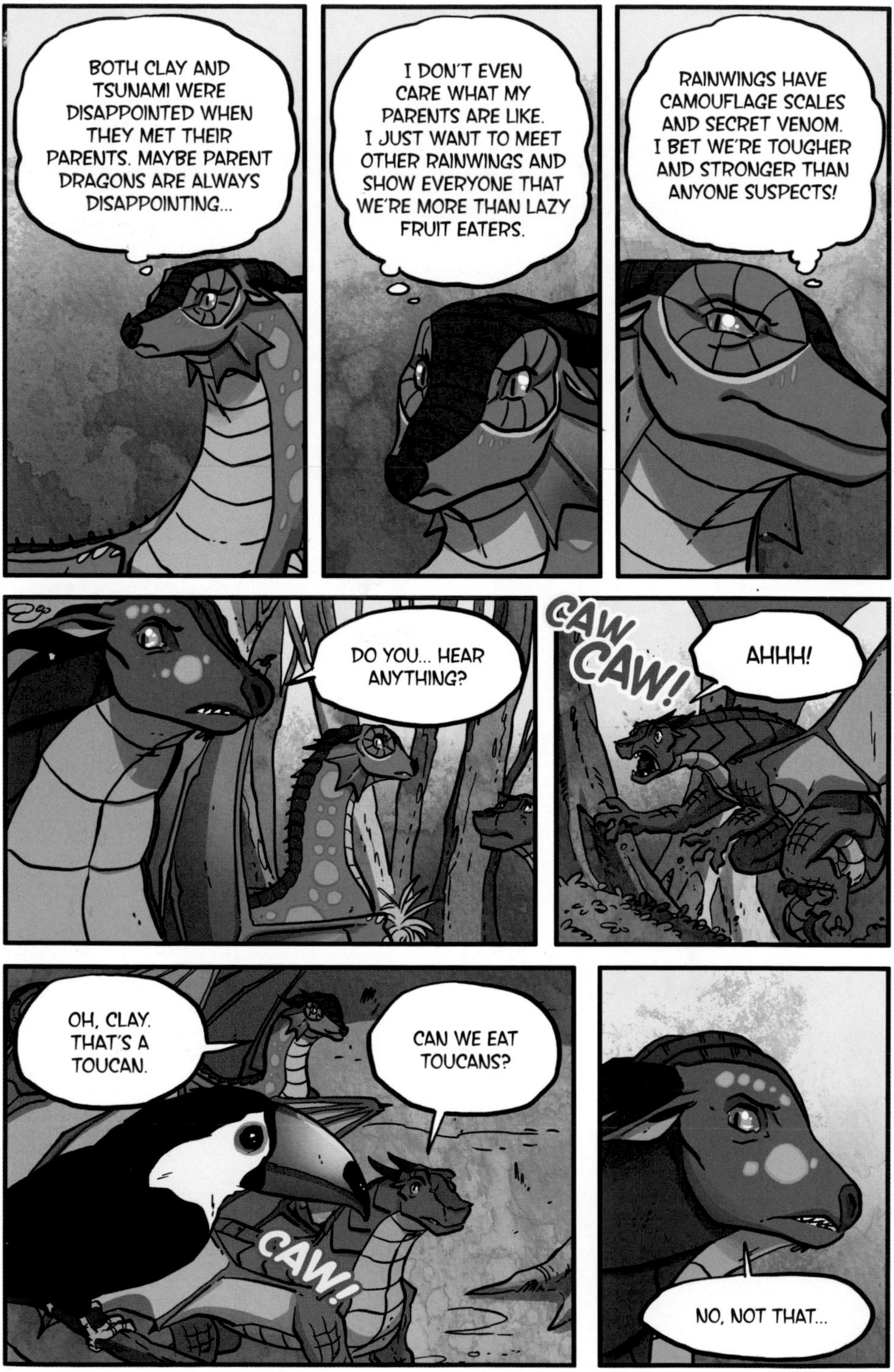
BOTH CLAY AND TSUNAMI WERE DISAPPOINTED WHEN THEY MET THEIR PARENTS. MAYBE PARENT DRAGONS ARE ALWAYS DISAPPOINTING...
I DON'T EVEN CARE WHAT MY PARENTS ARE LIKE. I JUST WANT TO MEET OTHER RAINWINGS AND SHOW EVERYONE THAT WE'RE MORE THAN LAZY FRUIT EATERS.
RAINWINGS HAVE CAMOUFLAGE SCALES AND SECRET VENOM. I BET WE'RE TOUGHER AND STRONGER THAN ANYONE SUSPECTS!
DO YOU... HEAR ANYTHING?
CAW CAW!
AHHH!
OH, CLAY. THAT'S A TOUCAN.
CAN WE EAT TOUCANS?
CAW!
NO, NOT THAT...

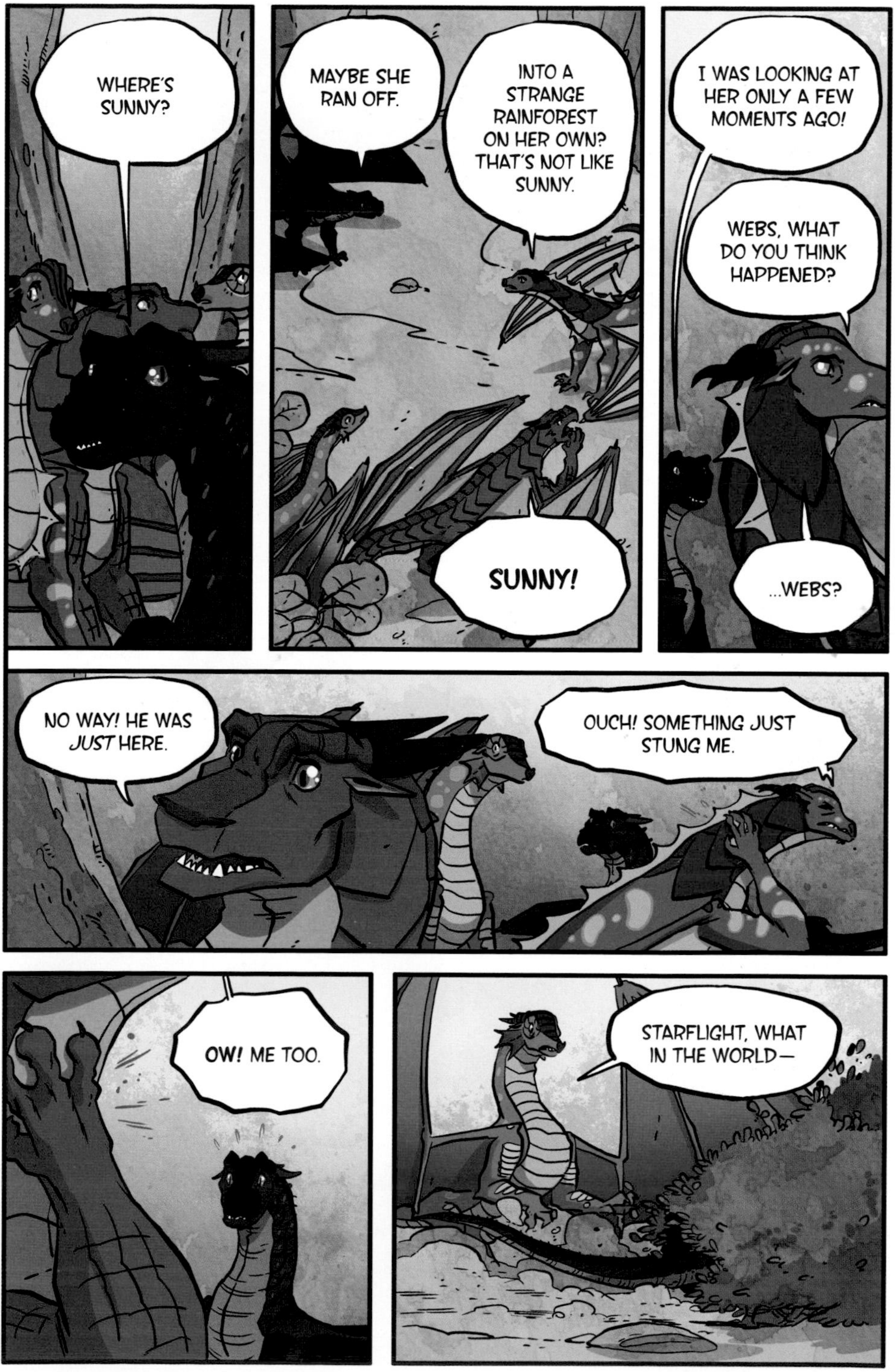
WHERE'S SUNNY?
MAYBE SHE RAN OFF.
INTO A STRANGE RAINFOREST ON HER OWN? THAT'S NOT LIKE SUNNY.
SUNNY!
I WAS LOOKING AT HER ONLY A FEW MOMENTS AGO!
WEBS, WHAT DO YOU THINK HAPPENED?
...WEBS?
NO WAY! HE WAS JUST HERE.
OUCH! SOMETHING JUST STUNG ME.
OW! ME TOO.
STARFLIGHT, WHAT IN THE WORLD—

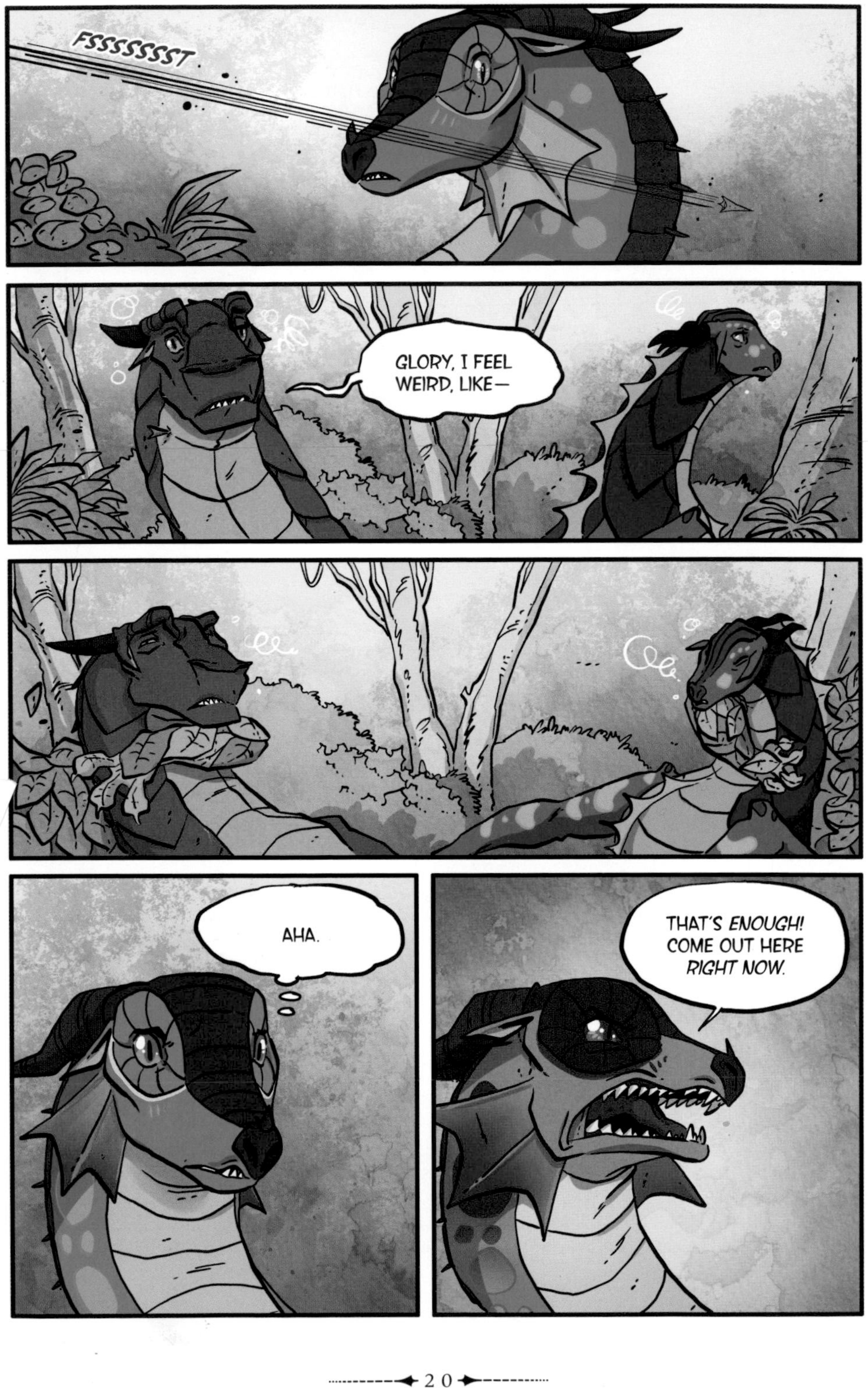
FSSSSSSST
GLORY, I FEEL WEIRD, LIKE—
...
AHA.
THAT'S *ENOUGH!* COME OUT HERE *RIGHT NOW.*

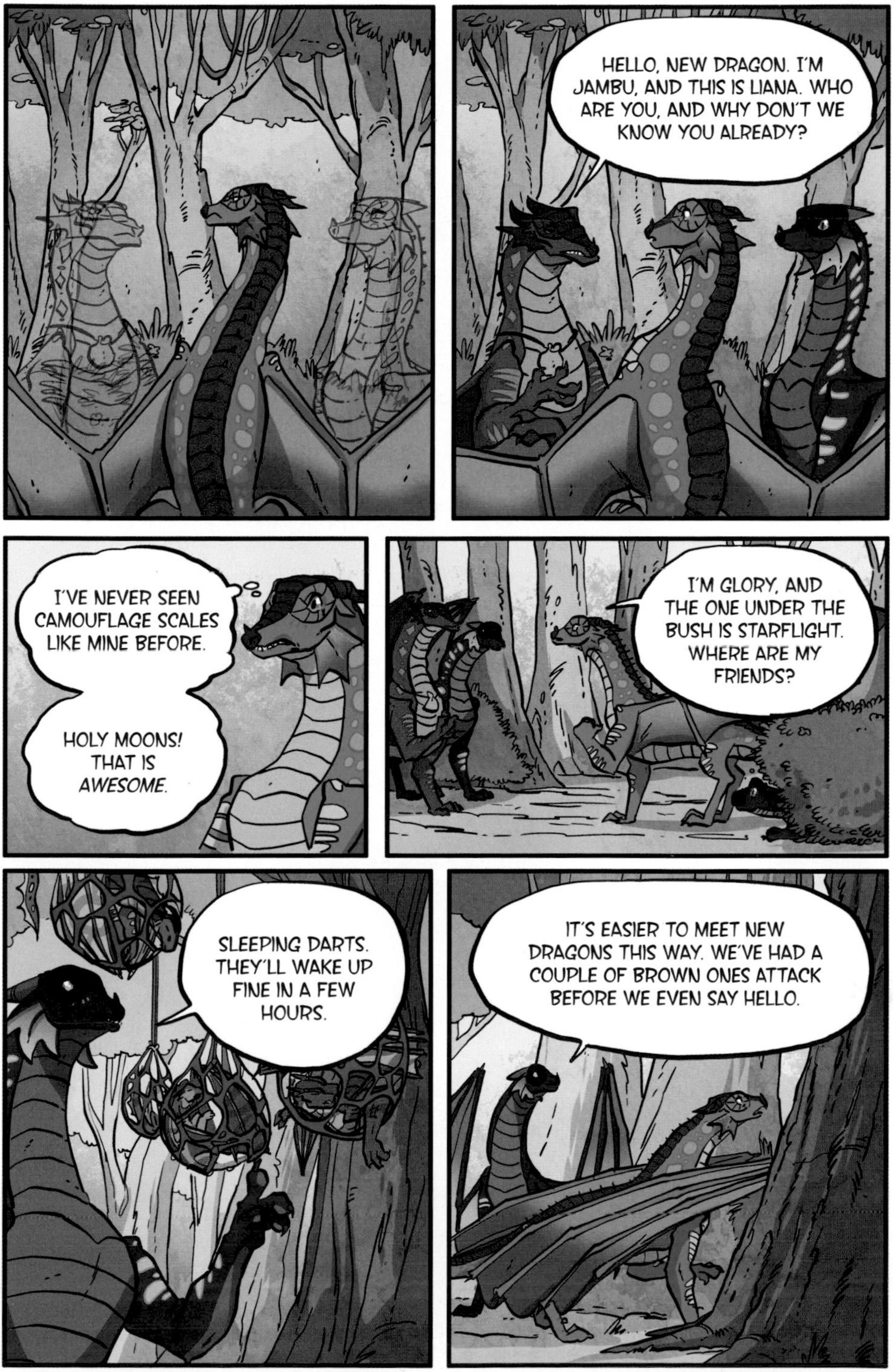
HELLO, NEW DRAGON. I'M JAMBU, AND THIS IS LIANA. WHO ARE YOU, AND WHY DON'T WE KNOW YOU ALREADY?
I'VE NEVER SEEN CAMOUFLAGE SCALES LIKE MINE BEFORE.
HOLY MOONS! THAT IS *AWESOME*.
I'M GLORY, AND THE ONE UNDER THE BUSH IS STARFLIGHT. WHERE ARE MY FRIENDS?
SLEEPING DARTS. THEY'LL WAKE UP FINE IN A FEW HOURS.
IT'S EASIER TO MEET NEW DRAGONS THIS WAY. WE'VE HAD A COUPLE OF BROWN ONES ATTACK BEFORE WE EVEN SAY HELLO.

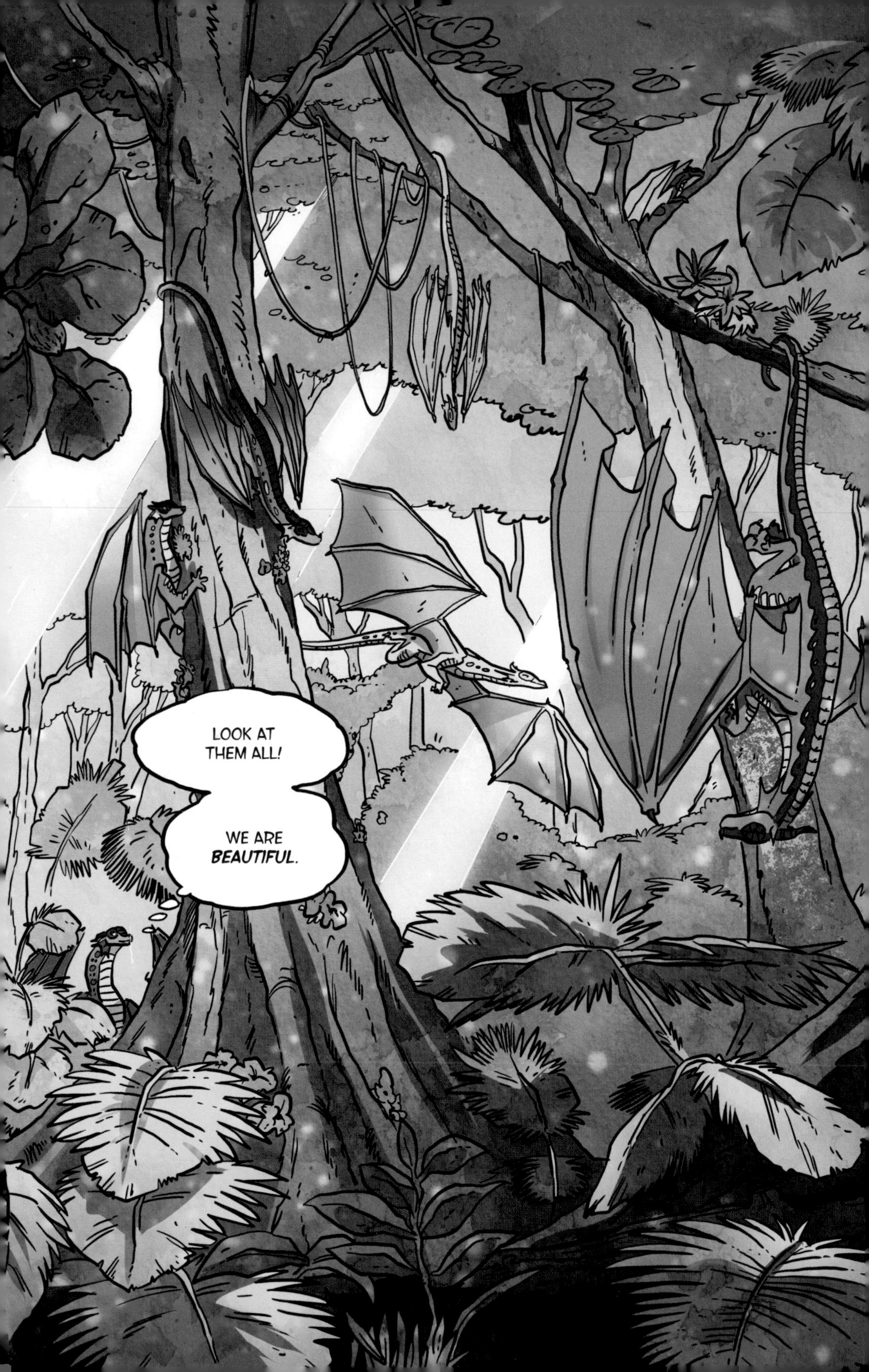
LOOK AT THEM ALL!
WE ARE *BEAUTIFUL.*

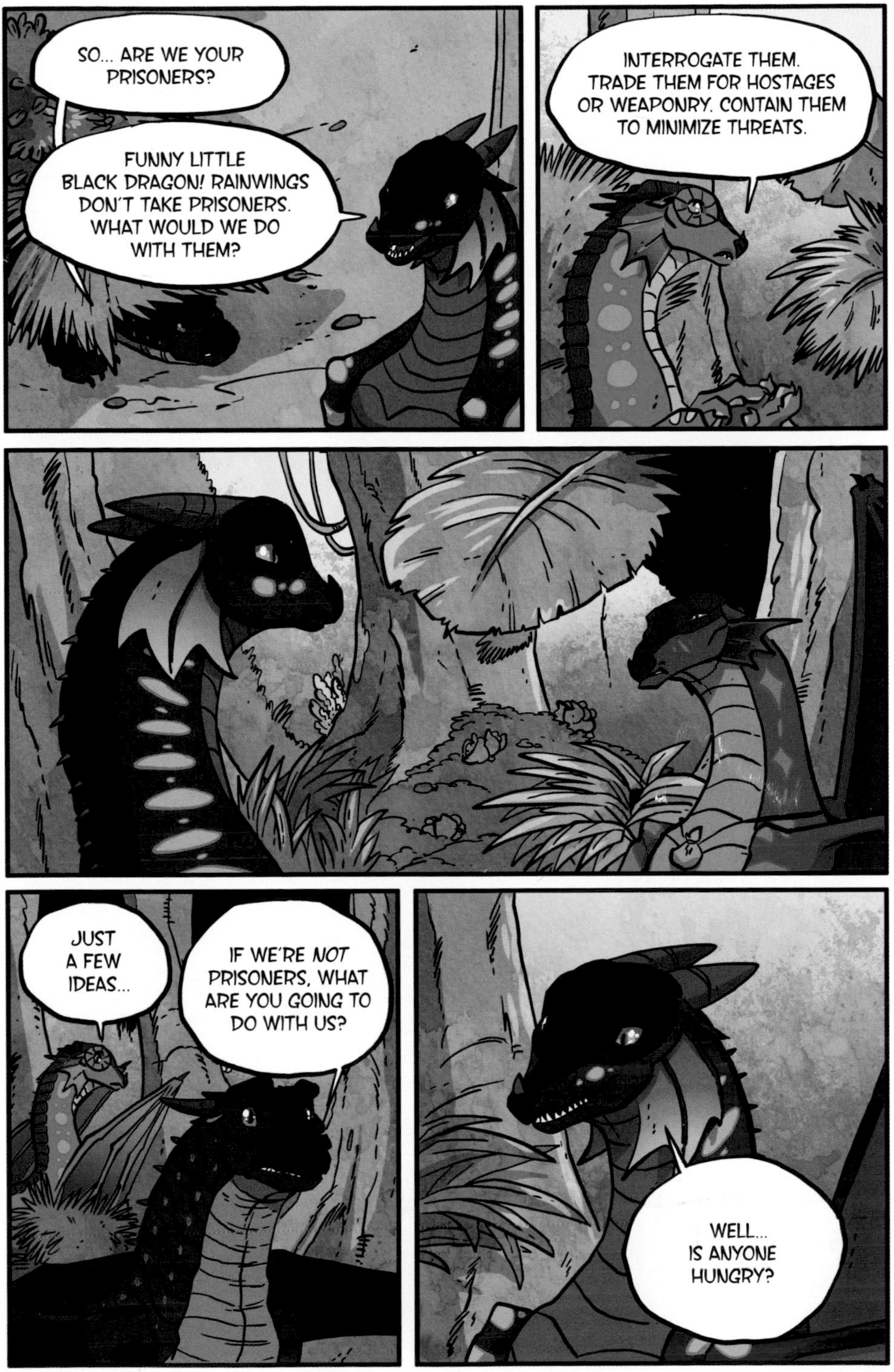
SO... ARE WE YOUR PRISONERS?
FUNNY LITTLE BLACK DRAGON! RAINWINGS DON'T TAKE PRISONERS. WHAT WOULD WE DO WITH THEM?
INTERROGATE THEM. TRADE THEM FOR HOSTAGES OR WEAPONRY. CONTAIN THEM TO MINIMIZE THREATS.
JUST A FEW IDEAS...
IF WE'RE *NOT* PRISONERS, WHAT ARE YOU GOING TO DO WITH US?
WELL... IS ANYONE HUNGRY?

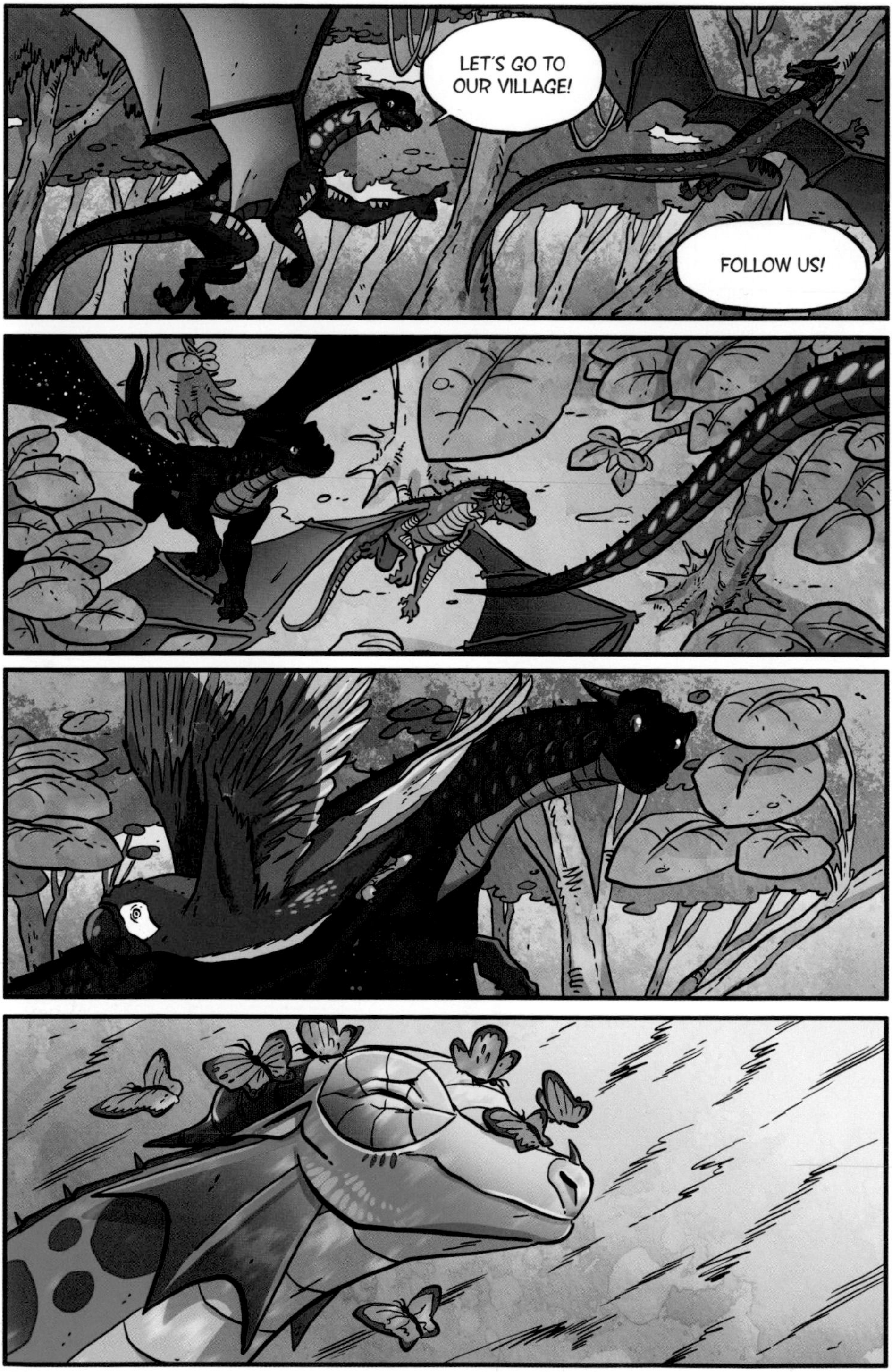
LET'S GO TO OUR VILLAGE!
FOLLOW US!

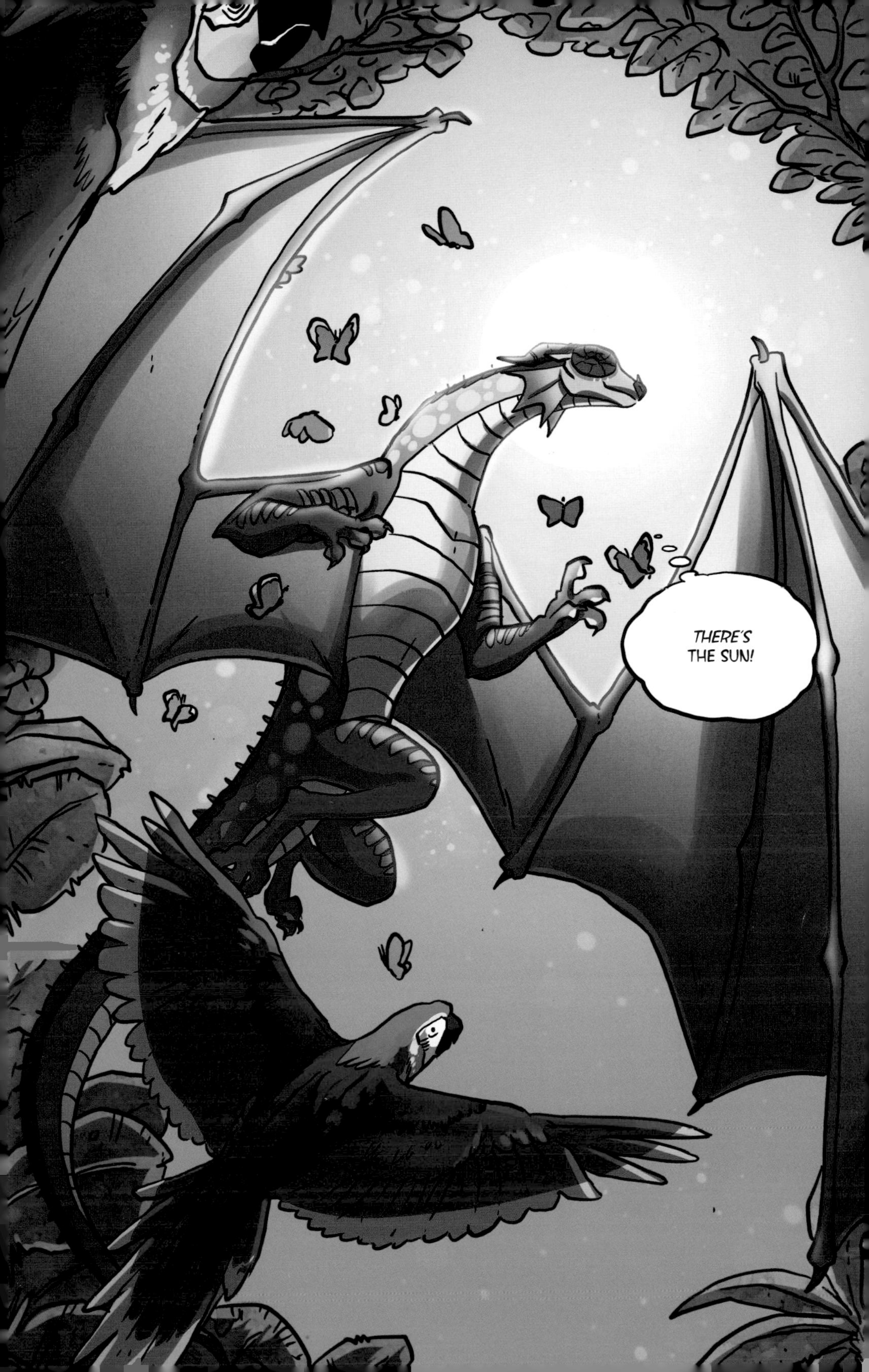
THERE'S THE SUN!

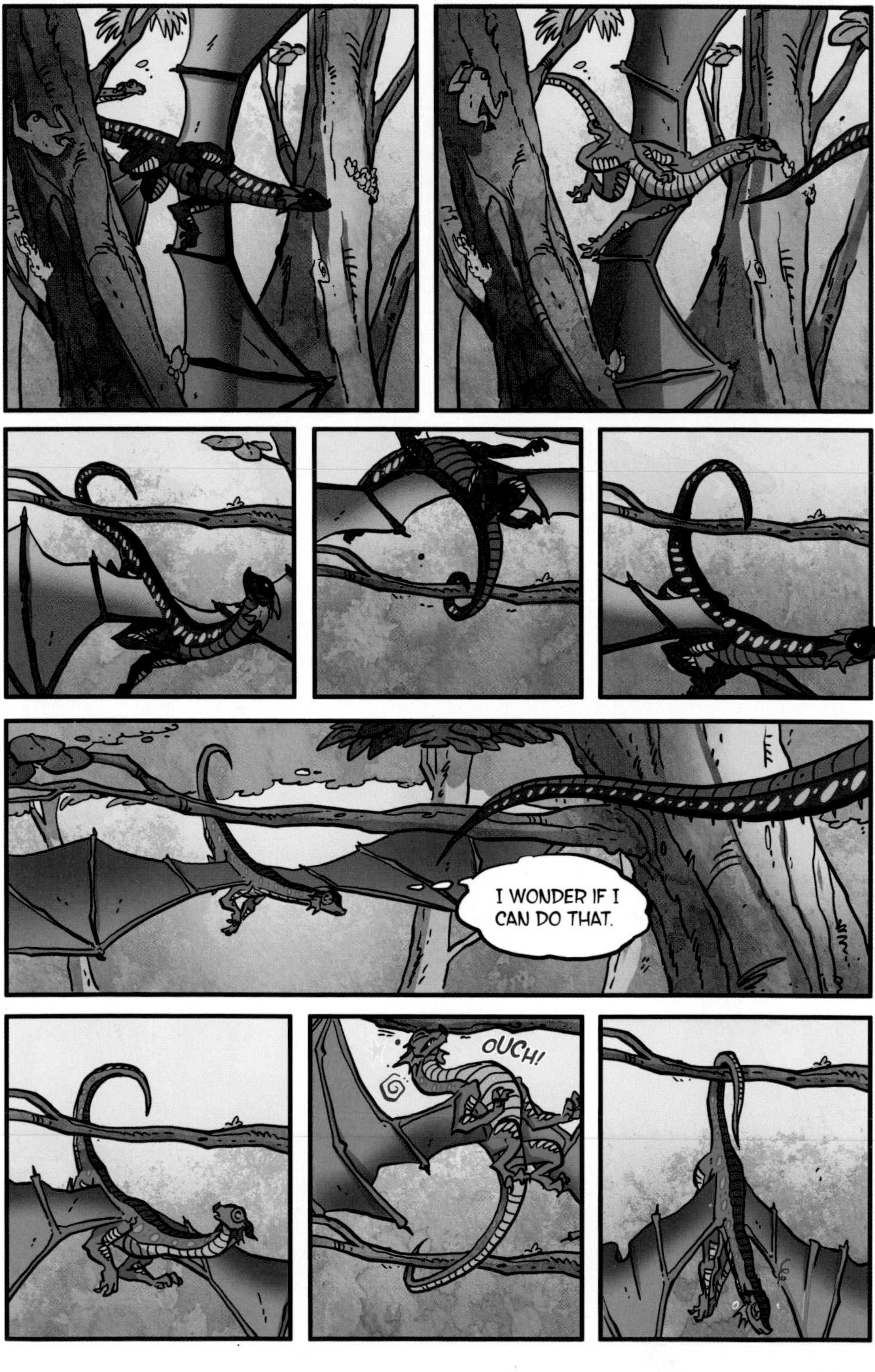
I WONDER IF I CAN DO THAT.
OUCH!

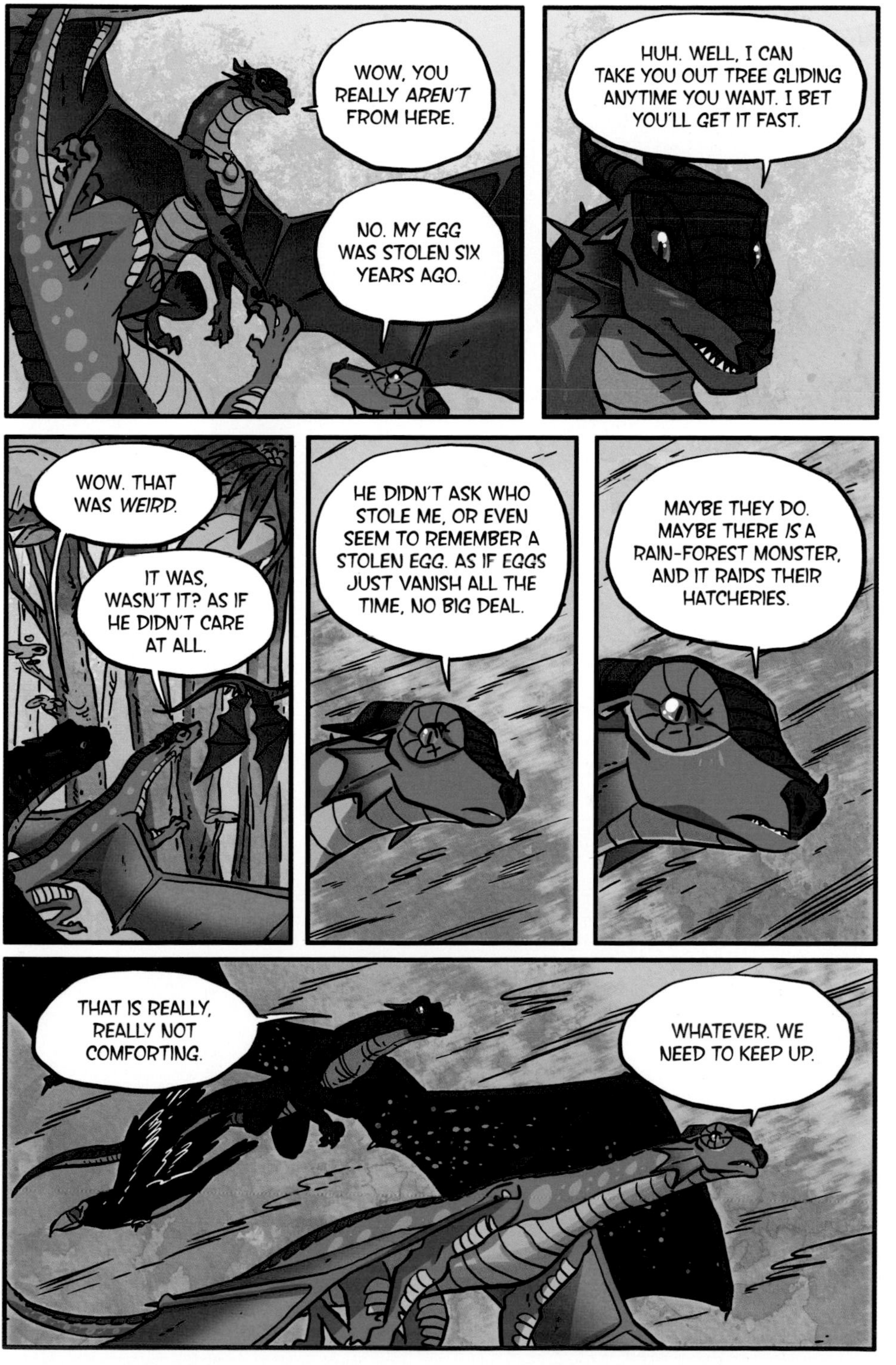
WOW, YOU REALLY *AREN'T* FROM HERE.
NO. MY EGG WAS STOLEN SIX YEARS AGO.
HUH. WELL, I CAN TAKE YOU OUT TREE GLIDING ANYTIME YOU WANT. I BET YOU'LL GET IT FAST.
WOW. THAT WAS *WEIRD*.
IT WAS, WASN'T IT? AS IF HE DIDN'T CARE AT ALL.
HE DIDN'T ASK WHO STOLE ME, OR EVEN SEEM TO REMEMBER A STOLEN EGG. AS IF EGGS JUST VANISH ALL THE TIME, NO BIG DEAL.
MAYBE THEY DO. MAYBE THERE *IS* A RAIN-FOREST MONSTER, AND IT RAIDS THEIR HATCHERIES.
THAT IS REALLY, REALLY NOT COMFORTING.
WHATEVER. WE NEED TO KEEP UP.

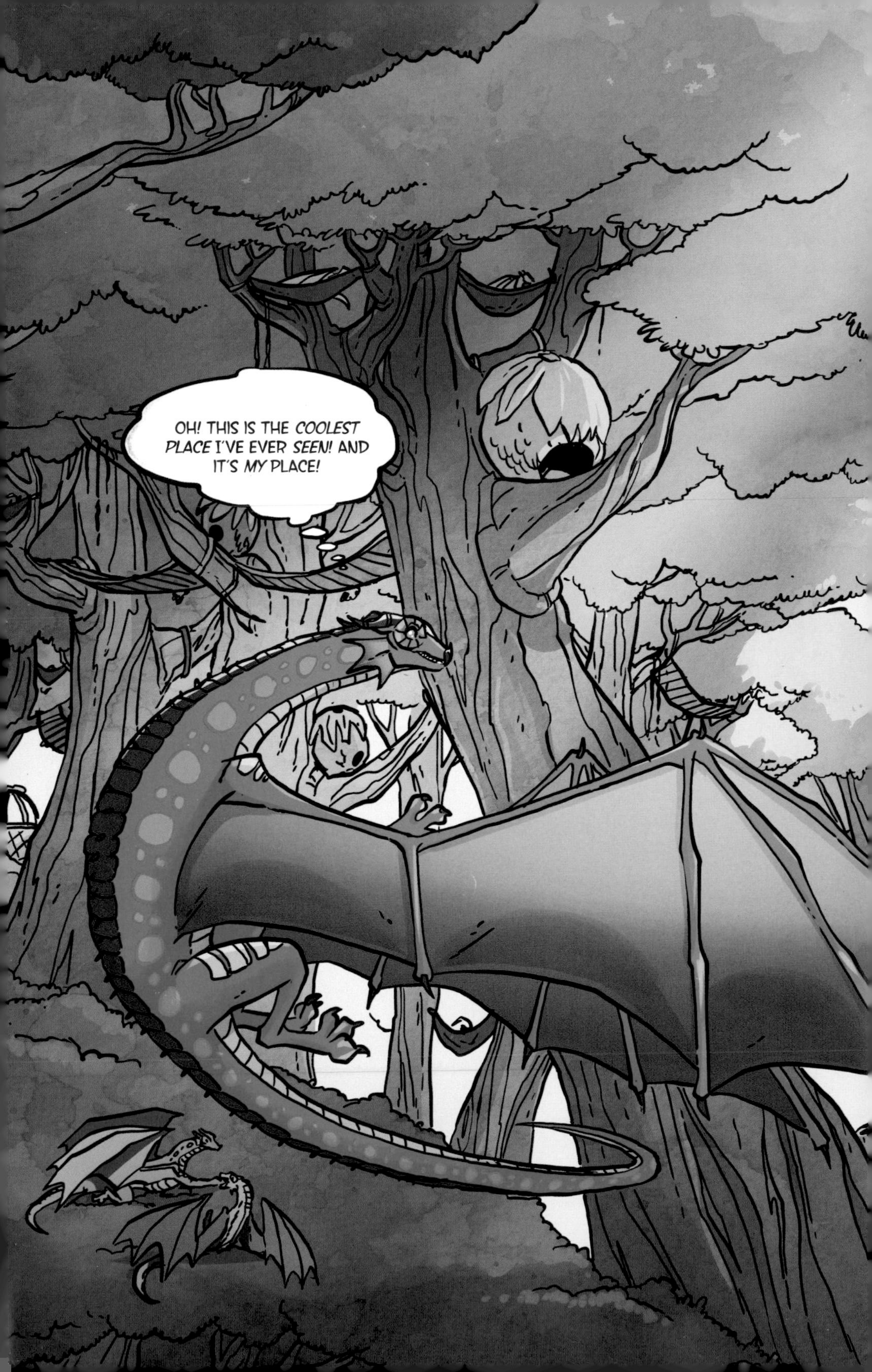
OH! THIS IS THE *COOLEST PLACE* I'VE EVER *SEEN!* AND IT'S *MY* PLACE!

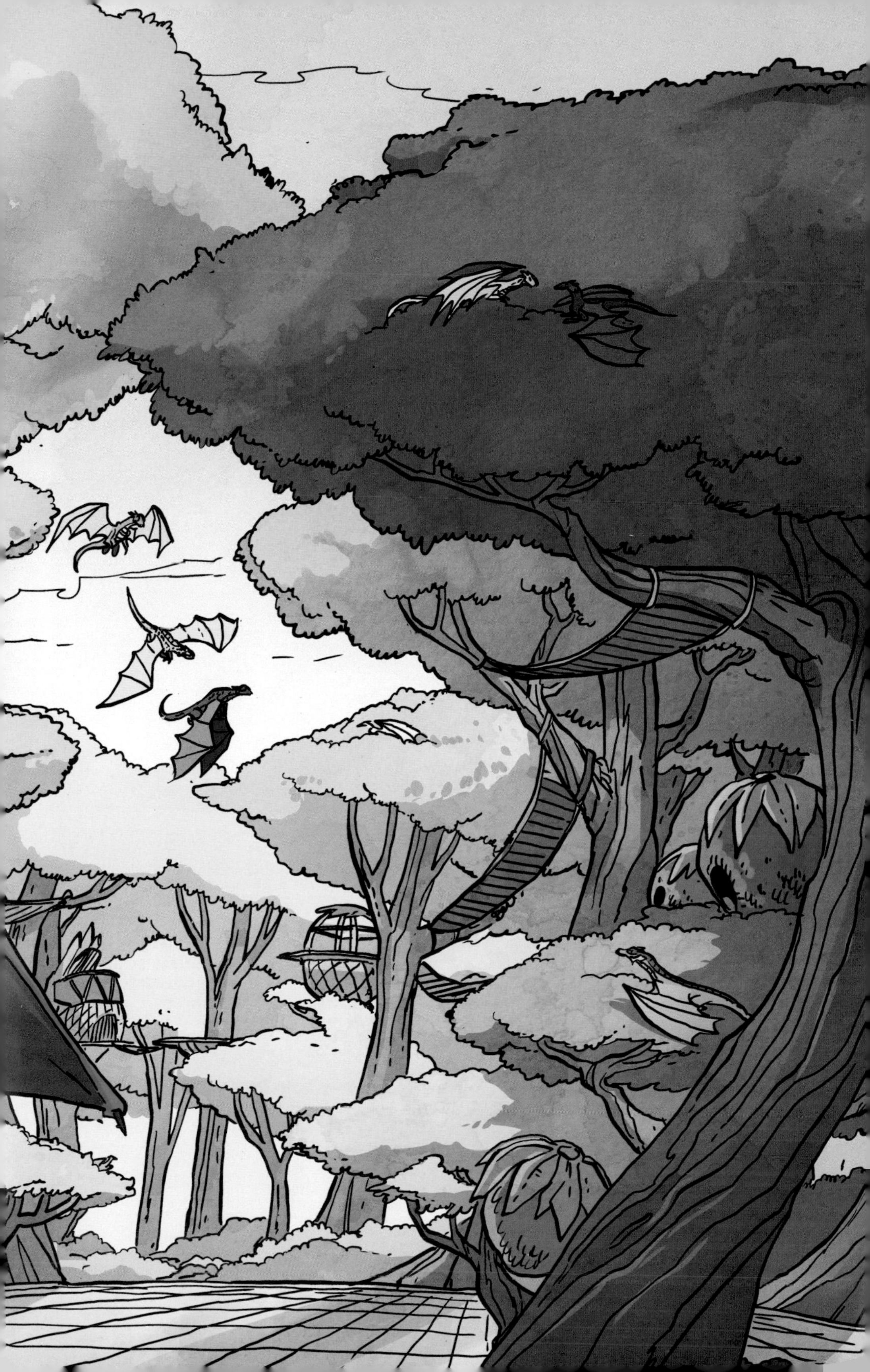

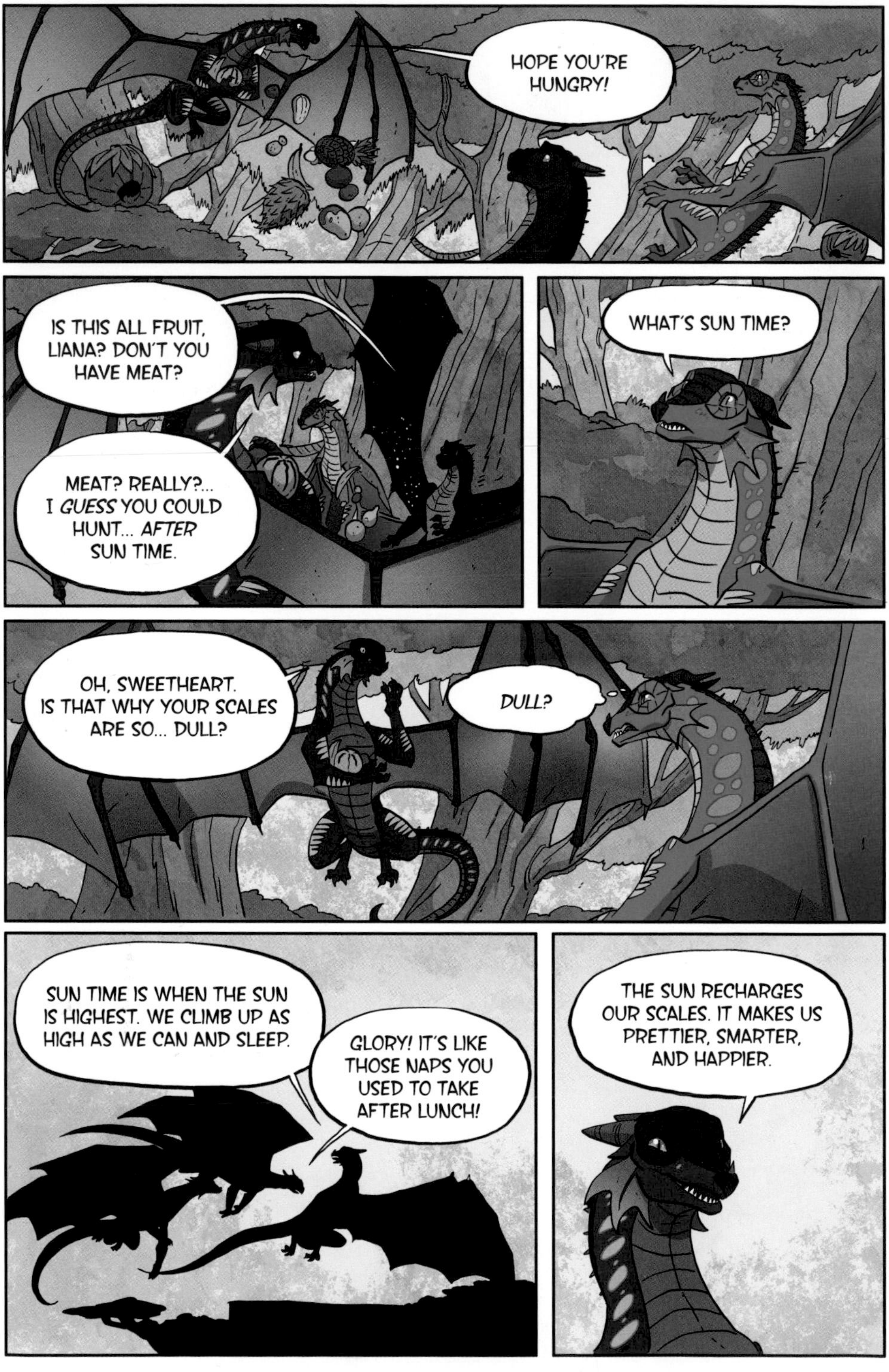
HOPE YOU'RE HUNGRY!
IS THIS ALL FRUIT, LIANA? DON'T YOU HAVE MEAT?
MEAT? REALLY?... I *GUESS* YOU COULD HUNT... *AFTER* SUN TIME.
WHAT'S SUN TIME?
OH, SWEETHEART. IS THAT WHY YOUR SCALES ARE SO... DULL?
DULL?
SUN TIME IS WHEN THE SUN IS HIGHEST. WE CLIMB UP AS HIGH AS WE CAN AND SLEEP.
GLORY! IT'S LIKE THOSE NAPS YOU USED TO TAKE AFTER LUNCH!
THE SUN RECHARGES OUR SCALES. IT MAKES US PRETTIER, SMARTER, AND HAPPIER.

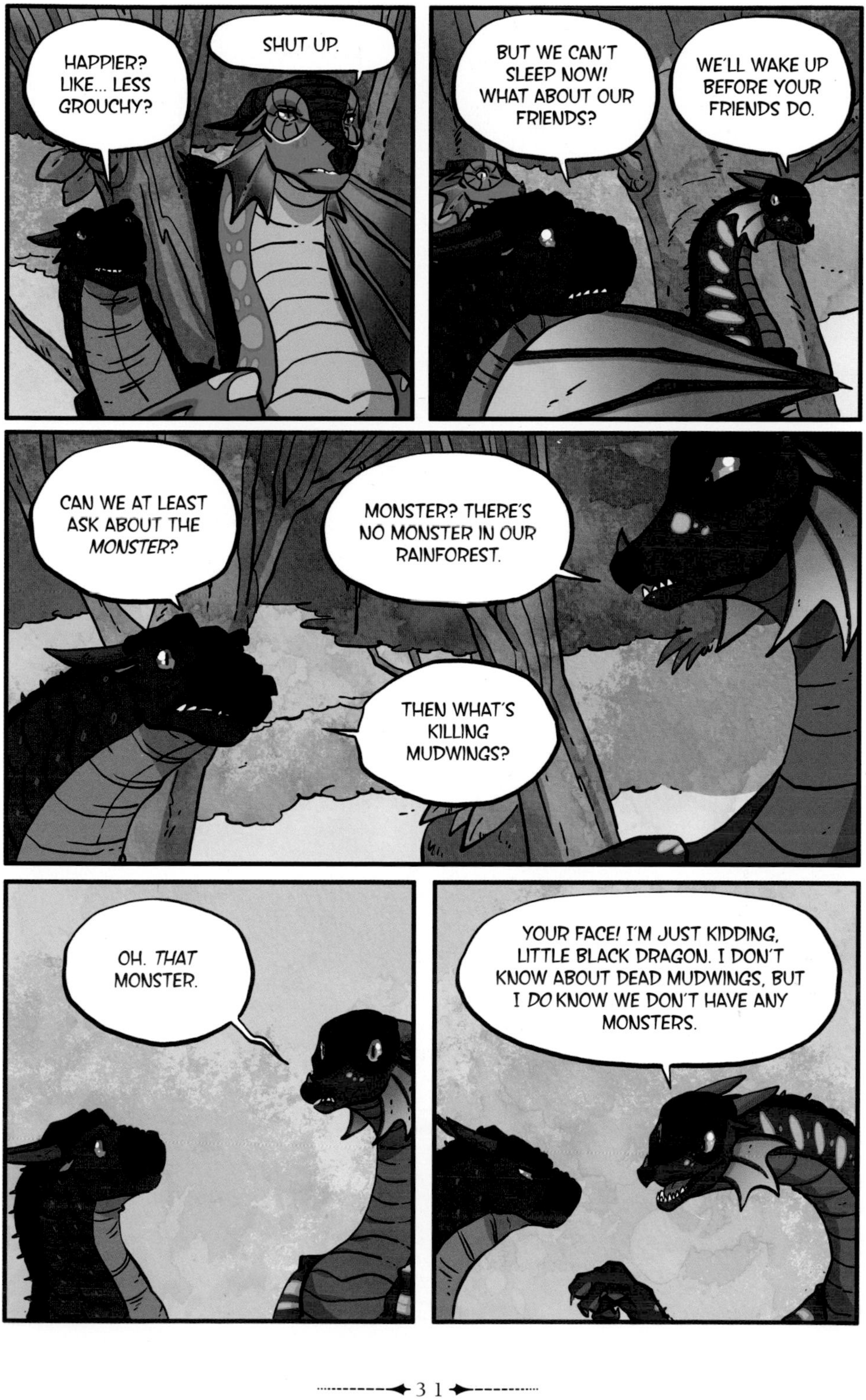
HAPPIER? LIKE... LESS GROUCHY?
SHUT UP.
BUT WE CAN'T SLEEP NOW! WHAT ABOUT OUR FRIENDS?
WE'LL WAKE UP BEFORE YOUR FRIENDS DO.
CAN WE AT LEAST ASK ABOUT THE *MONSTER*?
MONSTER? THERE'S NO MONSTER IN OUR RAINFOREST.
THEN WHAT'S KILLING MUDWINGS?
OH. *THAT* MONSTER.
YOUR FACE! I'M JUST KIDDING, LITTLE BLACK DRAGON. I DON'T KNOW ABOUT DEAD MUDWINGS, BUT I *DO* KNOW WE DON'T HAVE ANY MONSTERS.

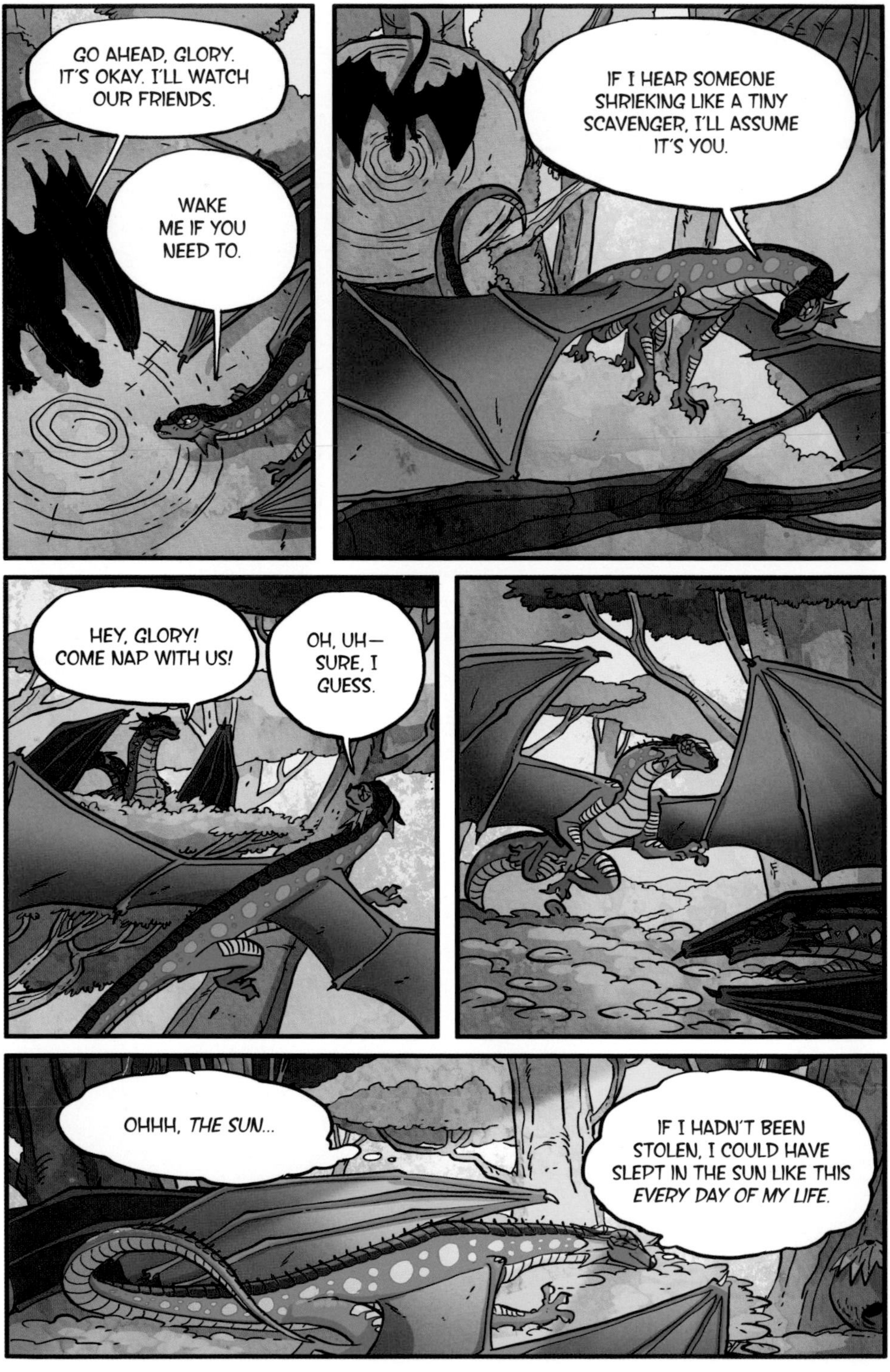
GO AHEAD, GLORY. IT'S OKAY. I'LL WATCH OUR FRIENDS.
WAKE ME IF YOU NEED TO.
IF I HEAR SOMEONE SHRIEKING LIKE A TINY SCAVENGER, I'LL ASSUME IT'S YOU.
HEY, GLORY! COME NAP WITH US!
OH, UH— SURE, I GUESS.
OHHH, *THE SUN*...
IF I HADN'T BEEN STOLEN, I COULD HAVE SLEPT IN THE SUN LIKE THIS *EVERY DAY OF MY LIFE.*

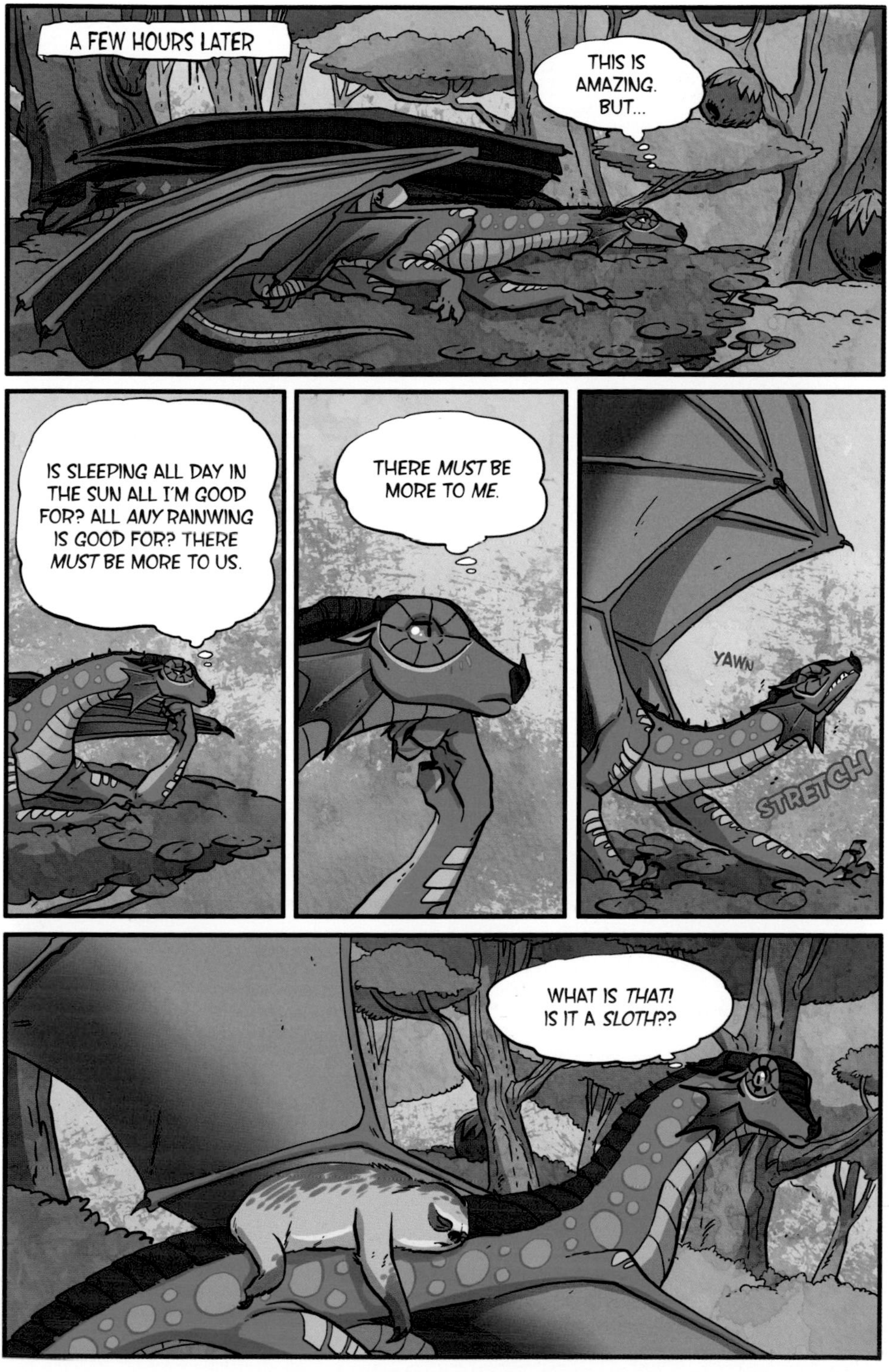
A FEW HOURS LATER
THIS IS AMAZING. BUT...
IS SLEEPING ALL DAY IN THE SUN ALL I'M GOOD FOR? ALL *ANY* RAINWING IS GOOD FOR? THERE *MUST* BE MORE TO US.
THERE *MUST* BE MORE TO *ME*.
YAWN
STRETCH
WHAT IS *THAT!* IS IT A *SLOTH*??

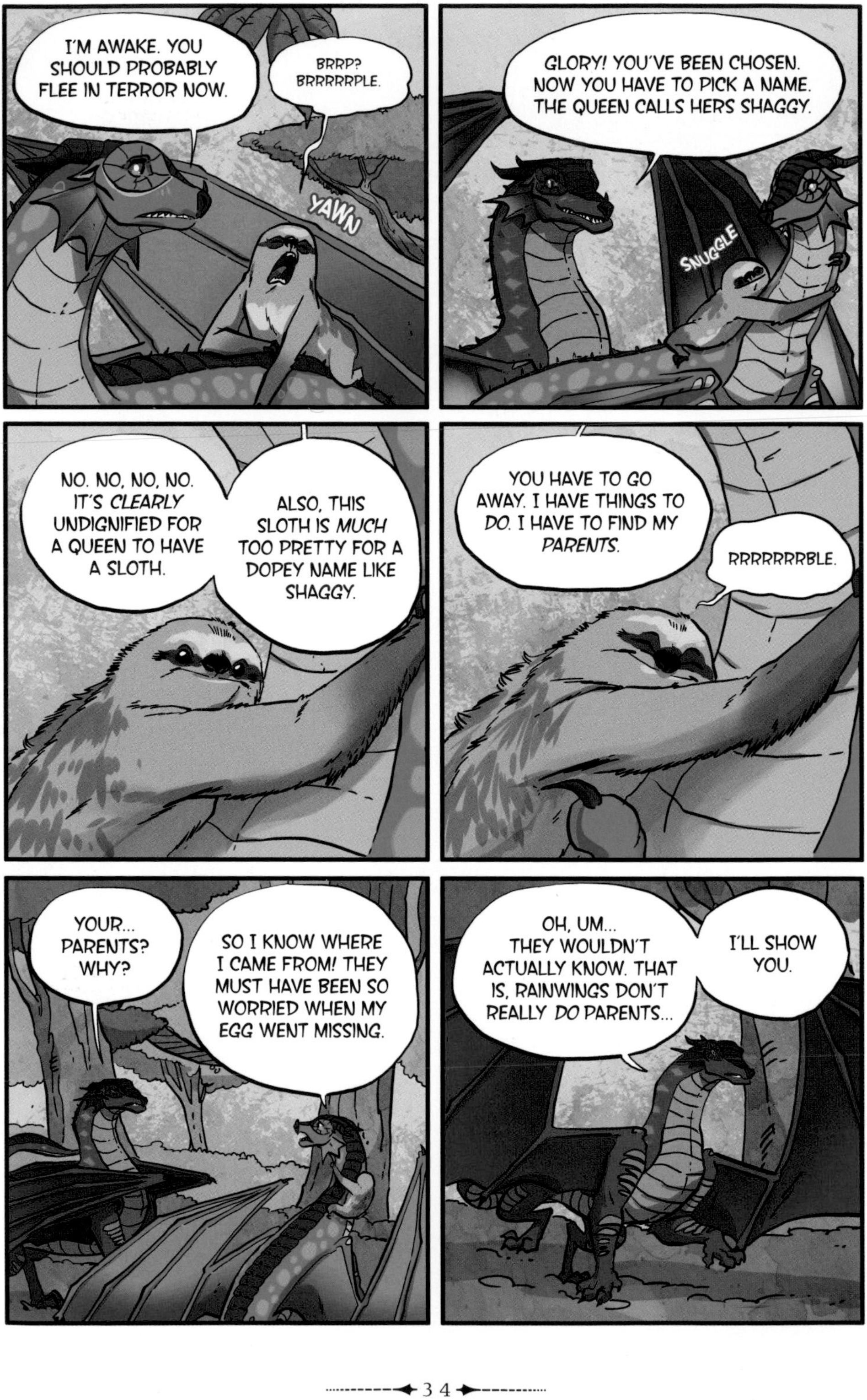
I'M AWAKE. YOU SHOULD PROBABLY FLEE IN TERROR NOW.
BRRP? BRRRRRPLE.
YAWN
GLORY! YOU'VE BEEN CHOSEN. NOW YOU HAVE TO PICK A NAME. THE QUEEN CALLS HERS SHAGGY.
SNUGGLE
NO. NO, NO, NO. IT'S *CLEARLY* UNDIGNIFIED FOR A QUEEN TO HAVE A SLOTH.
ALSO, THIS SLOTH IS *MUCH* TOO PRETTY FOR A DOPEY NAME LIKE SHAGGY.
YOU HAVE TO GO AWAY. I HAVE THINGS TO *DO*. I HAVE TO FIND MY *PARENTS*.
RRRRRRRBLE.
YOUR... PARENTS? WHY?
SO I KNOW WHERE I CAME FROM! THEY MUST HAVE BEEN SO WORRIED WHEN MY EGG WENT MISSING.
OH, UM... THEY WOULDN'T ACTUALLY KNOW. THAT IS, RAINWINGS DON'T REALLY *DO* PARENTS...
I'LL SHOW YOU.

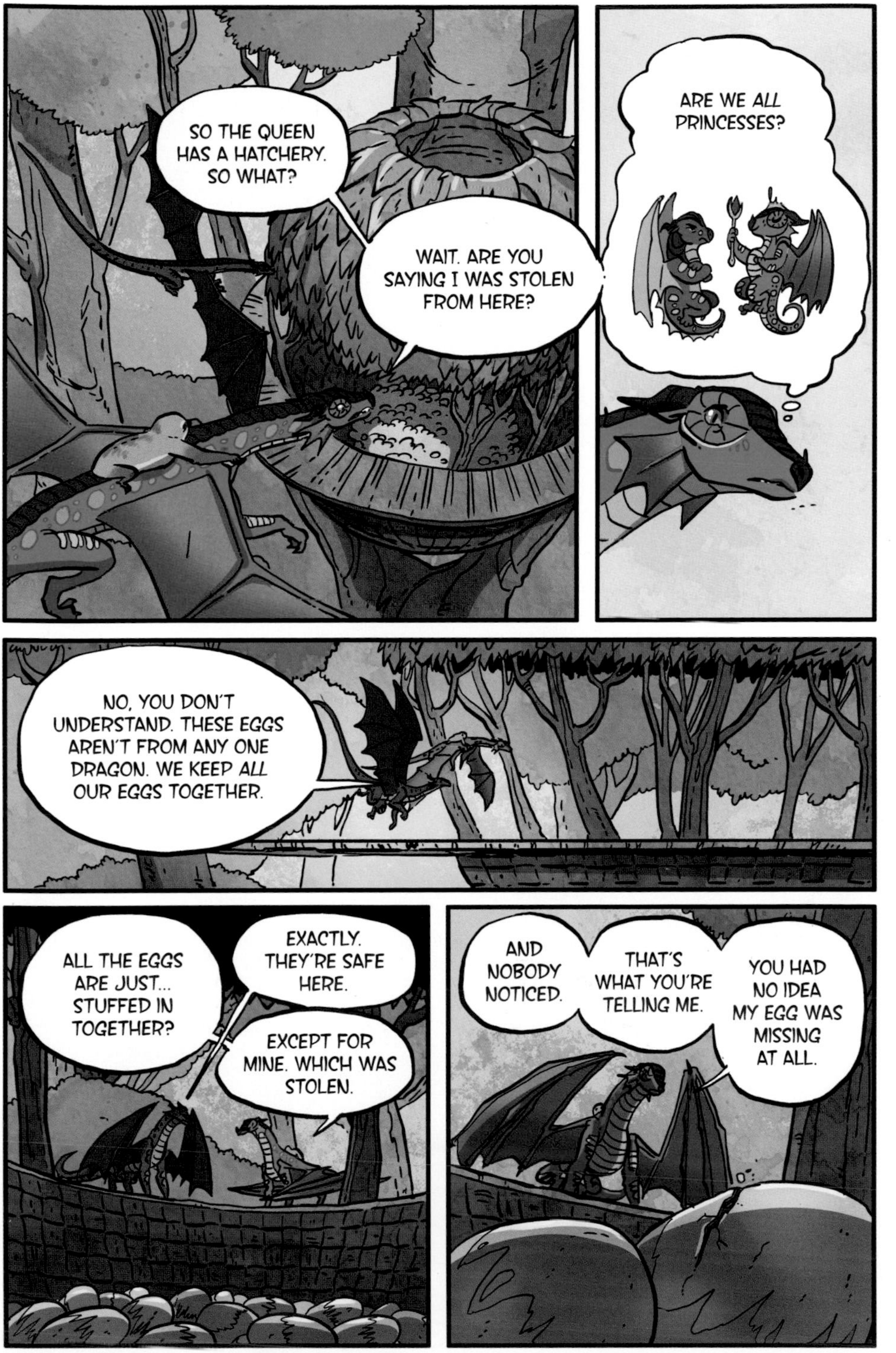
SO THE QUEEN HAS A HATCHERY. SO WHAT?
WAIT. ARE YOU SAYING I WAS STOLEN FROM HERE?
ARE WE ALL PRINCESSES?
NO, YOU DON'T UNDERSTAND. THESE EGGS AREN'T FROM ANY ONE DRAGON. WE KEEP ALL OUR EGGS TOGETHER.
ALL THE EGGS ARE JUST... STUFFED IN TOGETHER?
EXACTLY. THEY'RE SAFE HERE.
EXCEPT FOR MINE. WHICH WAS STOLEN.
AND NOBODY NOTICED.
THAT'S WHAT YOU'RE TELLING ME.
YOU HAD NO IDEA MY EGG WAS MISSING AT ALL.

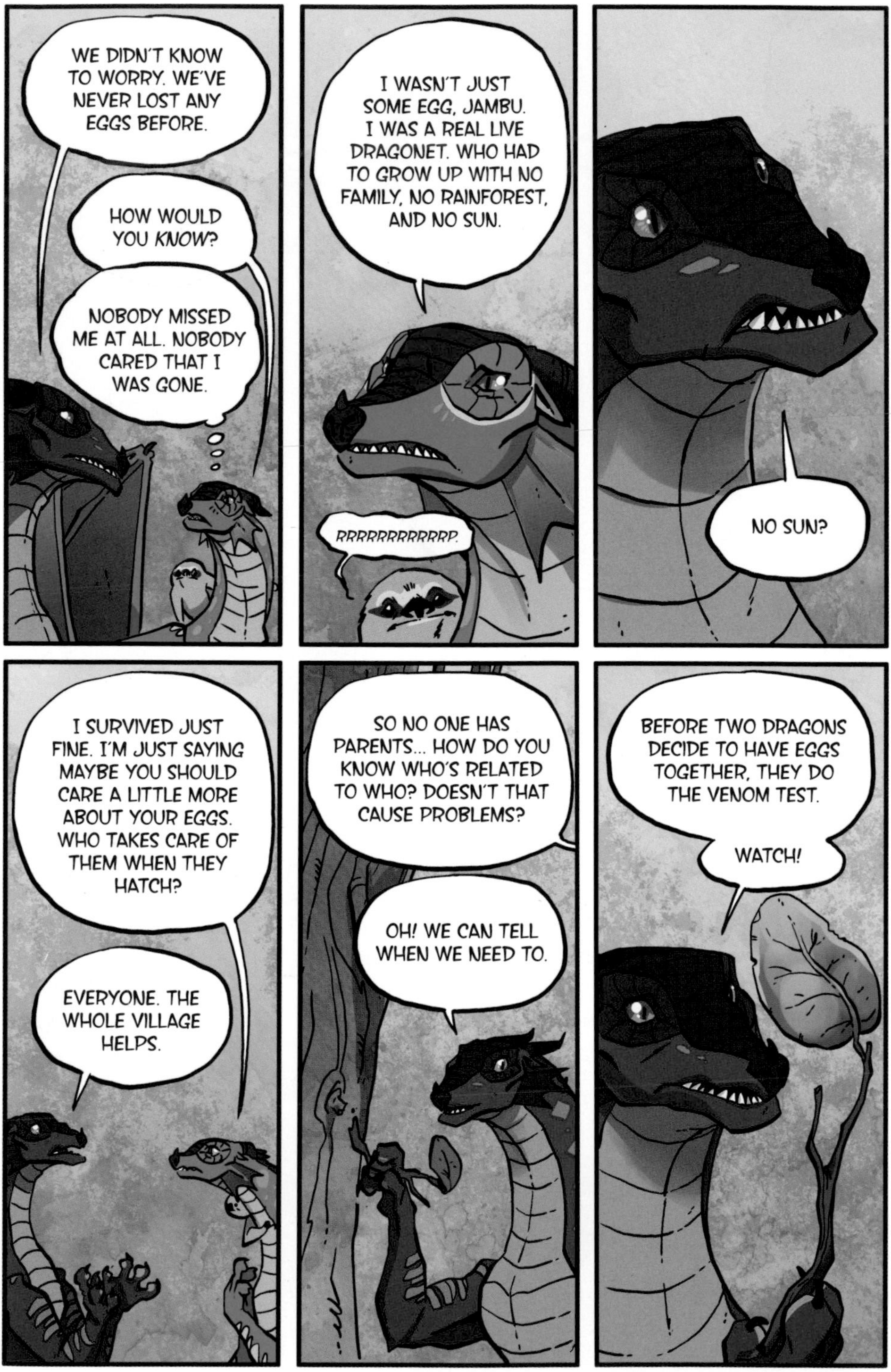

WE DIDN'T KNOW TO WORRY. WE'VE NEVER LOST ANY EGGS BEFORE.
HOW WOULD YOU *KNOW*?
NOBODY MISSED ME AT ALL. NOBODY CARED THAT I WAS GONE.
I WASN'T JUST SOME EGG, JAMBU. I WAS A REAL LIVE DRAGONET. WHO HAD TO GROW UP WITH NO FAMILY, NO RAINFOREST, AND NO SUN.
RRRRRRRRRRRP.
NO SUN?
I SURVIVED JUST FINE. I'M JUST SAYING MAYBE YOU SHOULD CARE A LITTLE MORE ABOUT YOUR EGGS. WHO TAKES CARE OF THEM WHEN THEY HATCH?
EVERYONE. THE WHOLE VILLAGE HELPS.
SO NO ONE HAS PARENTS... HOW DO YOU KNOW WHO'S RELATED TO WHO? DOESN'T THAT CAUSE PROBLEMS?
OH! WE CAN TELL WHEN WE NEED TO.
BEFORE TWO DRAGONS DECIDE TO HAVE EGGS TOGETHER, THEY DO THE VENOM TEST.
WATCH!

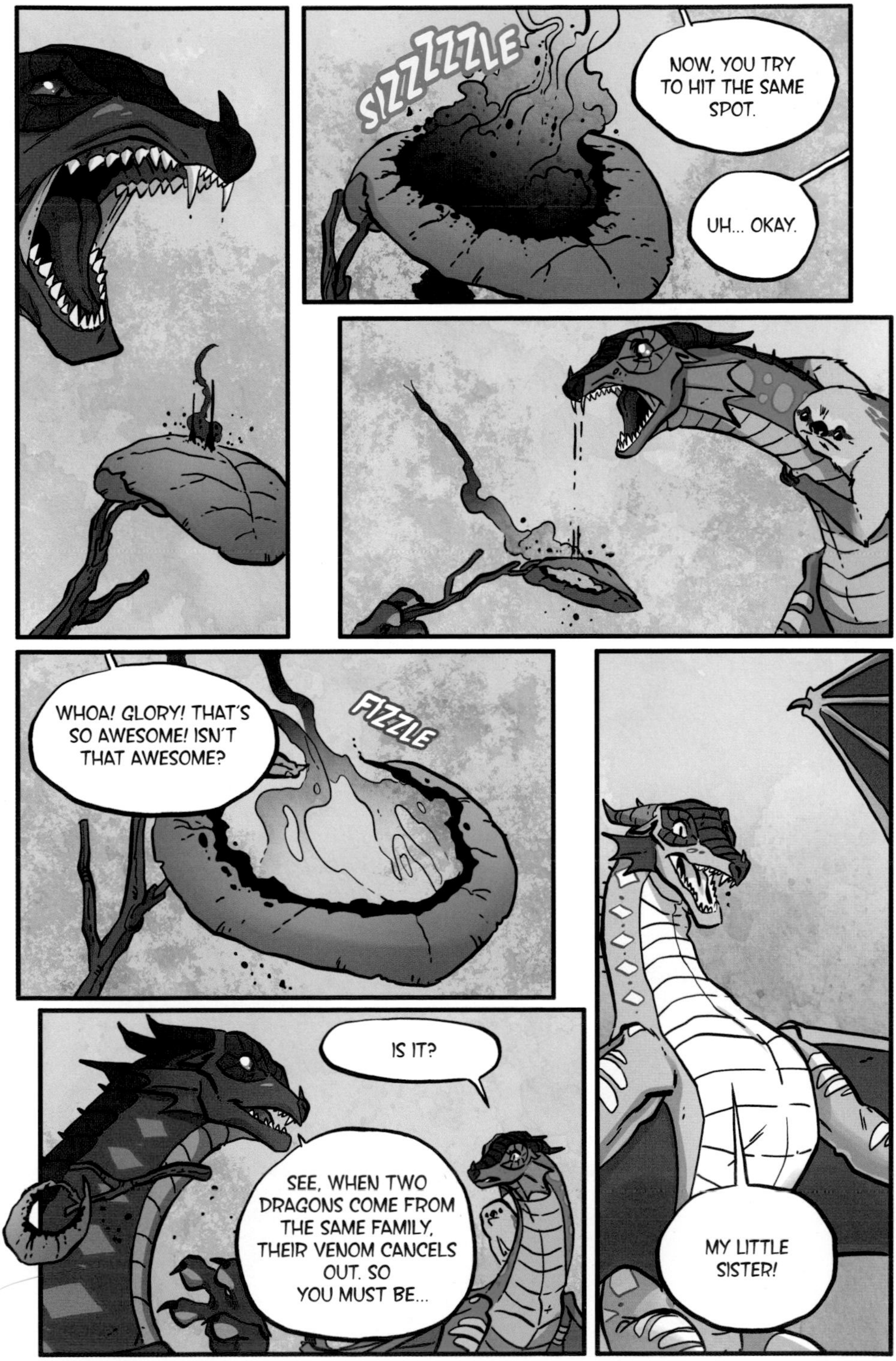
SIZZZZZLE
NOW, YOU TRY TO HIT THE SAME SPOT.
UH... OKAY.
WHOA! GLORY! THAT'S SO AWESOME! ISN'T THAT AWESOME?
FIZZLE
IS IT?
SEE, WHEN TWO DRAGONS COME FROM THE SAME FAMILY, THEIR VENOM CANCELS OUT. SO YOU MUST BE...
MY LITTLE SISTER!

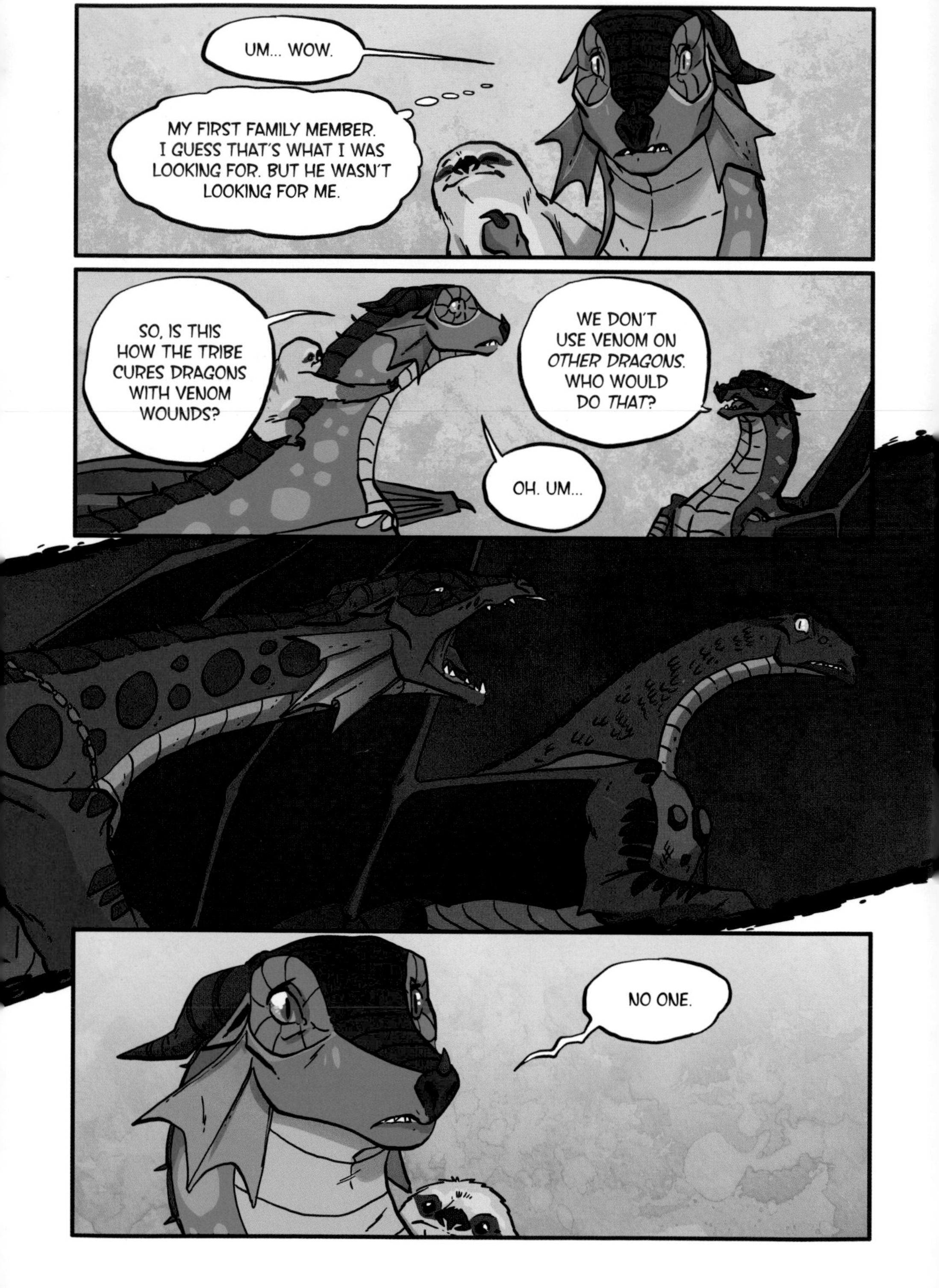
UM... WOW.
MY FIRST FAMILY MEMBER. I GUESS THAT'S WHAT I WAS LOOKING FOR. BUT HE WASN'T LOOKING FOR ME.
SO, IS THIS HOW THE TRIBE CURES DRAGONS WITH VENOM WOUNDS?
WE DON'T USE VENOM ON *OTHER DRAGONS*. WHO WOULD DO *THAT*?
OH. UM...
NO ONE.

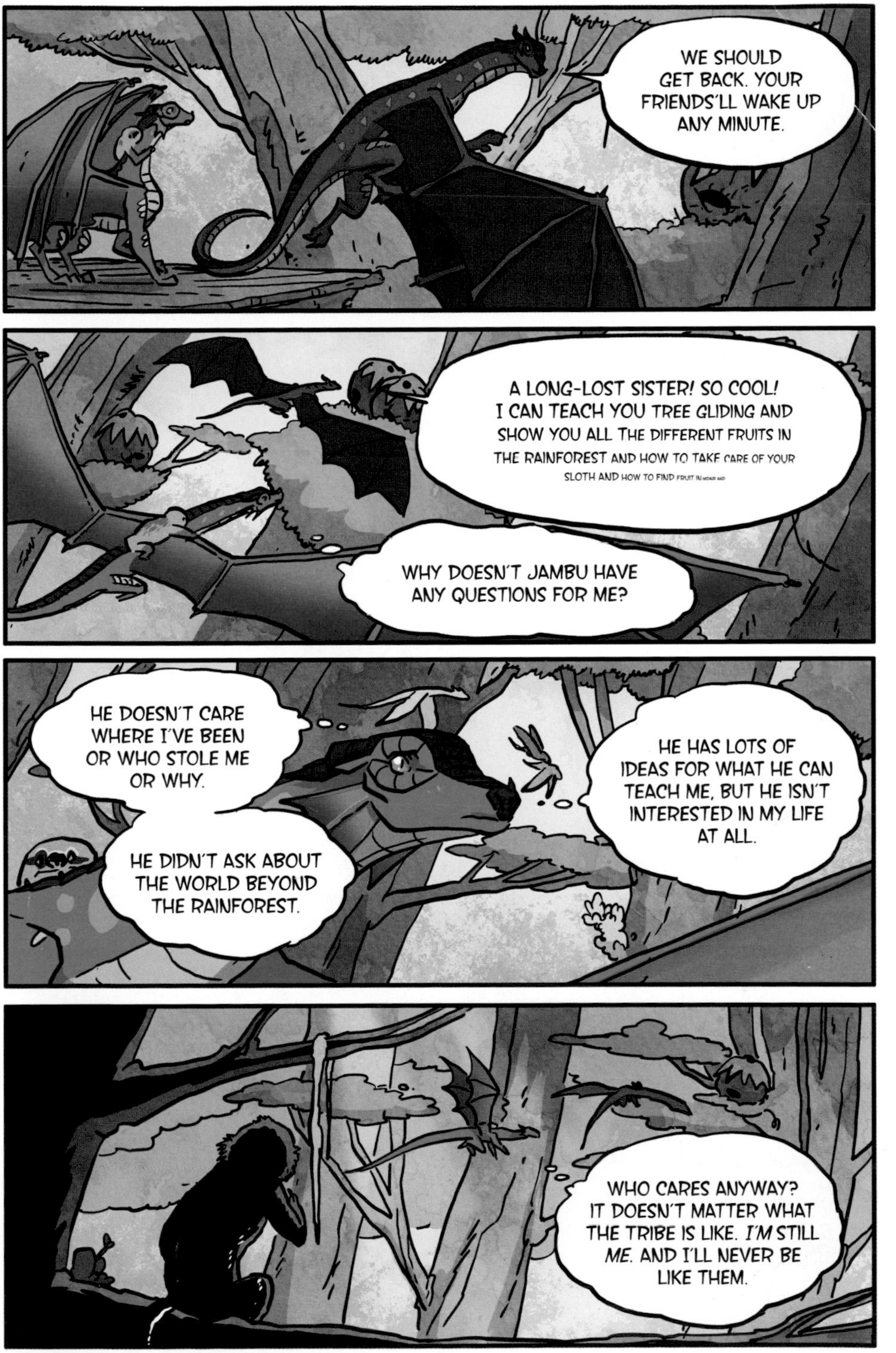
WE SHOULD GET BACK. YOUR FRIENDS'LL WAKE UP ANY MINUTE.
A LONG-LOST SISTER! SO COOL! I CAN TEACH YOU TREE GLIDING AND SHOW YOU ALL THE DIFFERENT FRUITS IN THE RAINFOREST AND HOW TO TAKE CARE OF YOUR SLOTH AND HOW TO FIND FRUIT IN
WHY DOESN'T JAMBU HAVE ANY QUESTIONS FOR ME?
HE DOESN'T CARE WHERE I'VE BEEN OR WHO STOLE ME OR WHY.
HE DIDN'T ASK ABOUT THE WORLD BEYOND THE RAINFOREST.
HE HAS LOTS OF IDEAS FOR WHAT HE CAN TEACH ME, BUT HE ISN'T INTERESTED IN MY LIFE AT ALL.
WHO CARES ANYWAY? IT DOESN'T MATTER WHAT THE TRIBE IS LIKE. *I'M* STILL *ME*. AND I'LL NEVER BE LIKE THEM.

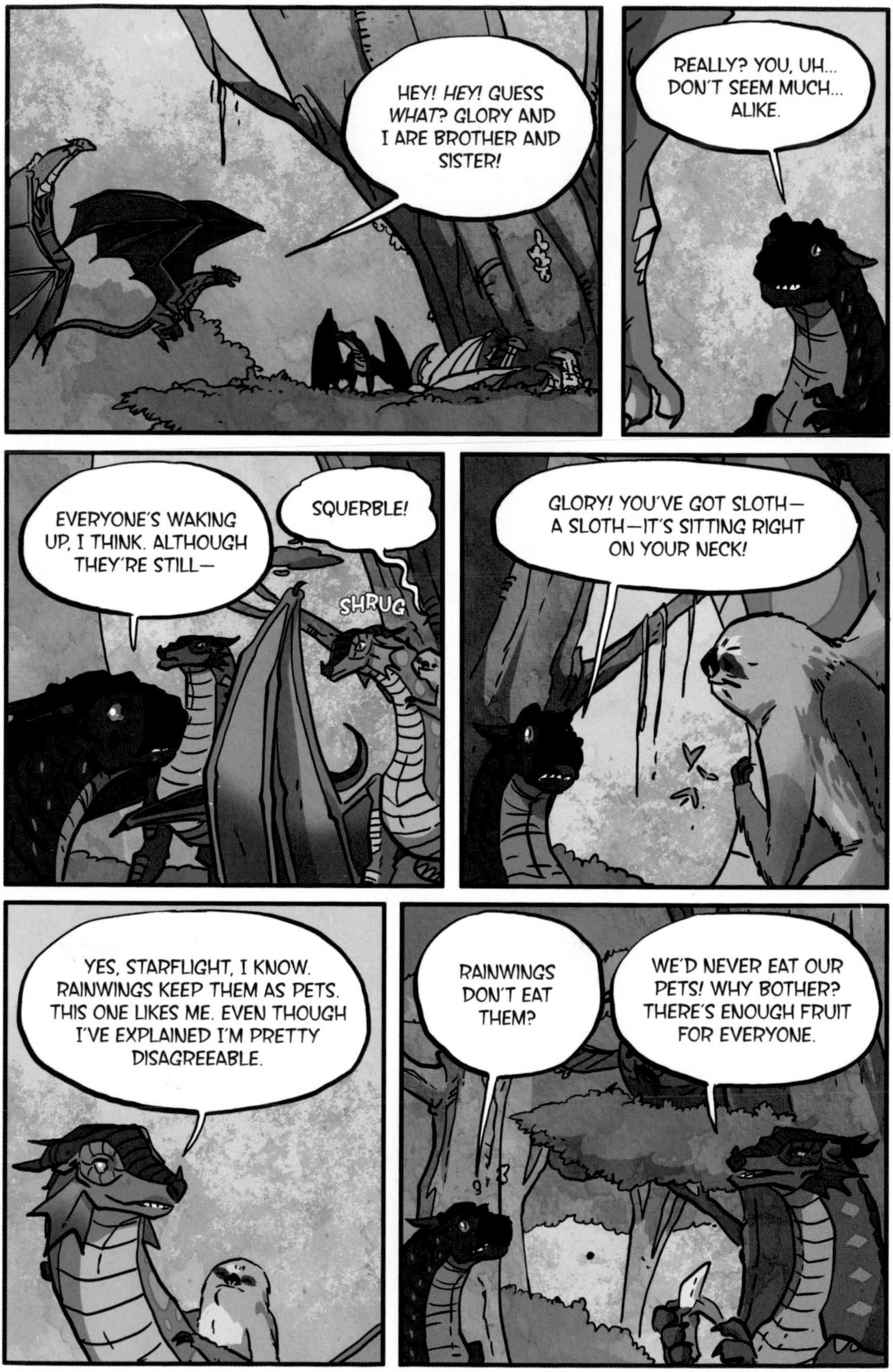
HEY! HEY! GUESS WHAT? GLORY AND I ARE BROTHER AND SISTER!
REALLY? YOU, UH... DON'T SEEM MUCH... ALIKE.
EVERYONE'S WAKING UP, I THINK. ALTHOUGH THEY'RE STILL—
SQUERBLE!
SHRUG
GLORY! YOU'VE GOT SLOTH— A SLOTH—IT'S SITTING RIGHT ON YOUR NECK!
YES, STARFLIGHT, I KNOW. RAINWINGS KEEP THEM AS PETS. THIS ONE LIKES ME. EVEN THOUGH I'VE EXPLAINED I'M PRETTY DISAGREEABLE.
RAINWINGS DON'T EAT THEM?
WE'D NEVER EAT OUR PETS! WHY BOTHER? THERE'S ENOUGH FRUIT FOR EVERYONE.

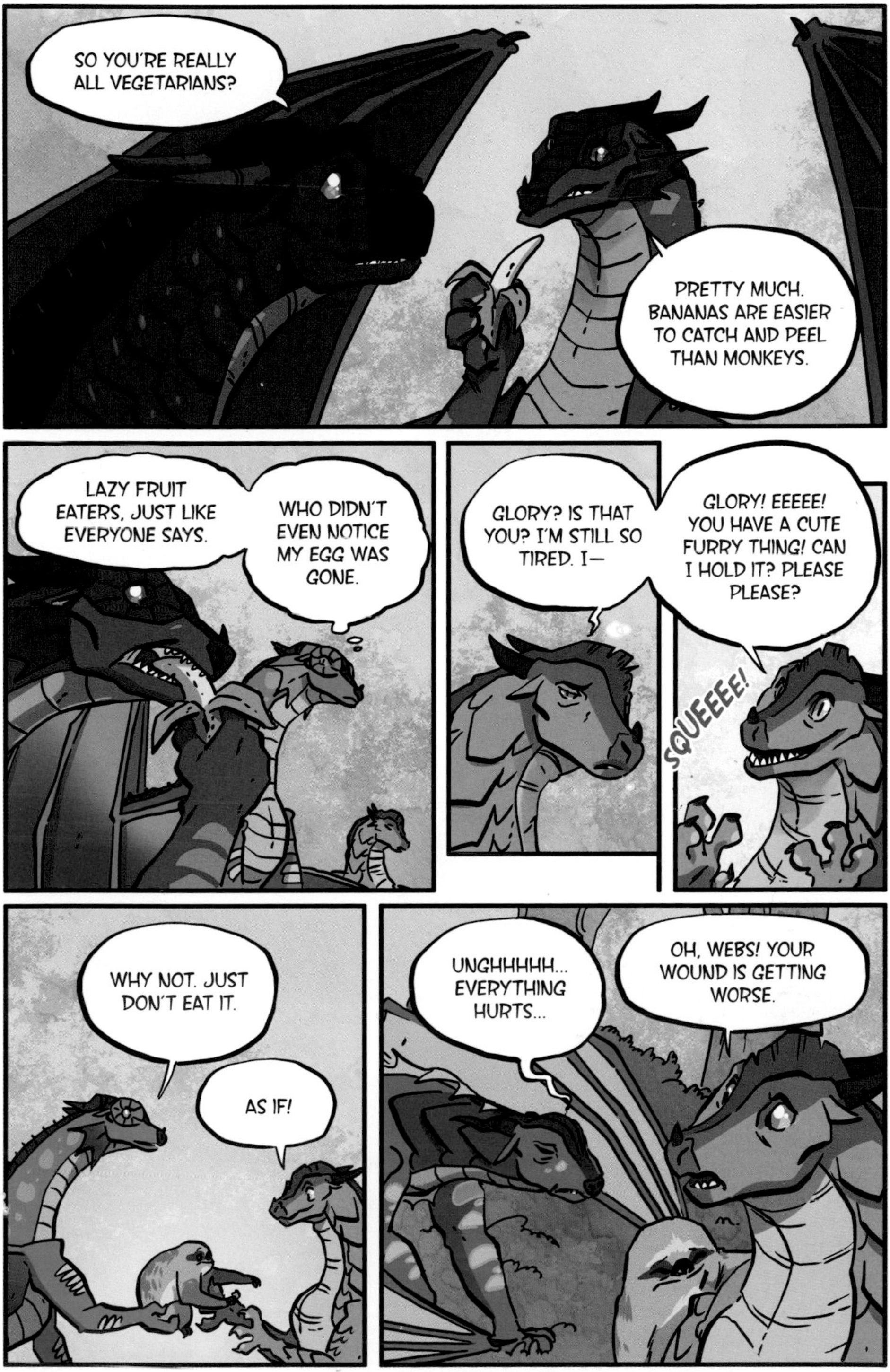
SO YOU'RE REALLY ALL VEGETARIANS?
PRETTY MUCH. BANANAS ARE EASIER TO CATCH AND PEEL THAN MONKEYS.
LAZY FRUIT EATERS, JUST LIKE EVERYONE SAYS.
WHO DIDN'T EVEN NOTICE MY EGG WAS GONE.
GLORY? IS THAT YOU? I'M STILL SO TIRED. I—
GLORY! EEEEE! YOU HAVE A CUTE FURRY THING! CAN I HOLD IT? PLEASE PLEASE?
SQUEEEE!
WHY NOT. JUST DON'T EAT IT.
AS IF!
UNGHHHHH... EVERYTHING HURTS...
OH, WEBS! YOUR WOUND IS GETTING WORSE.

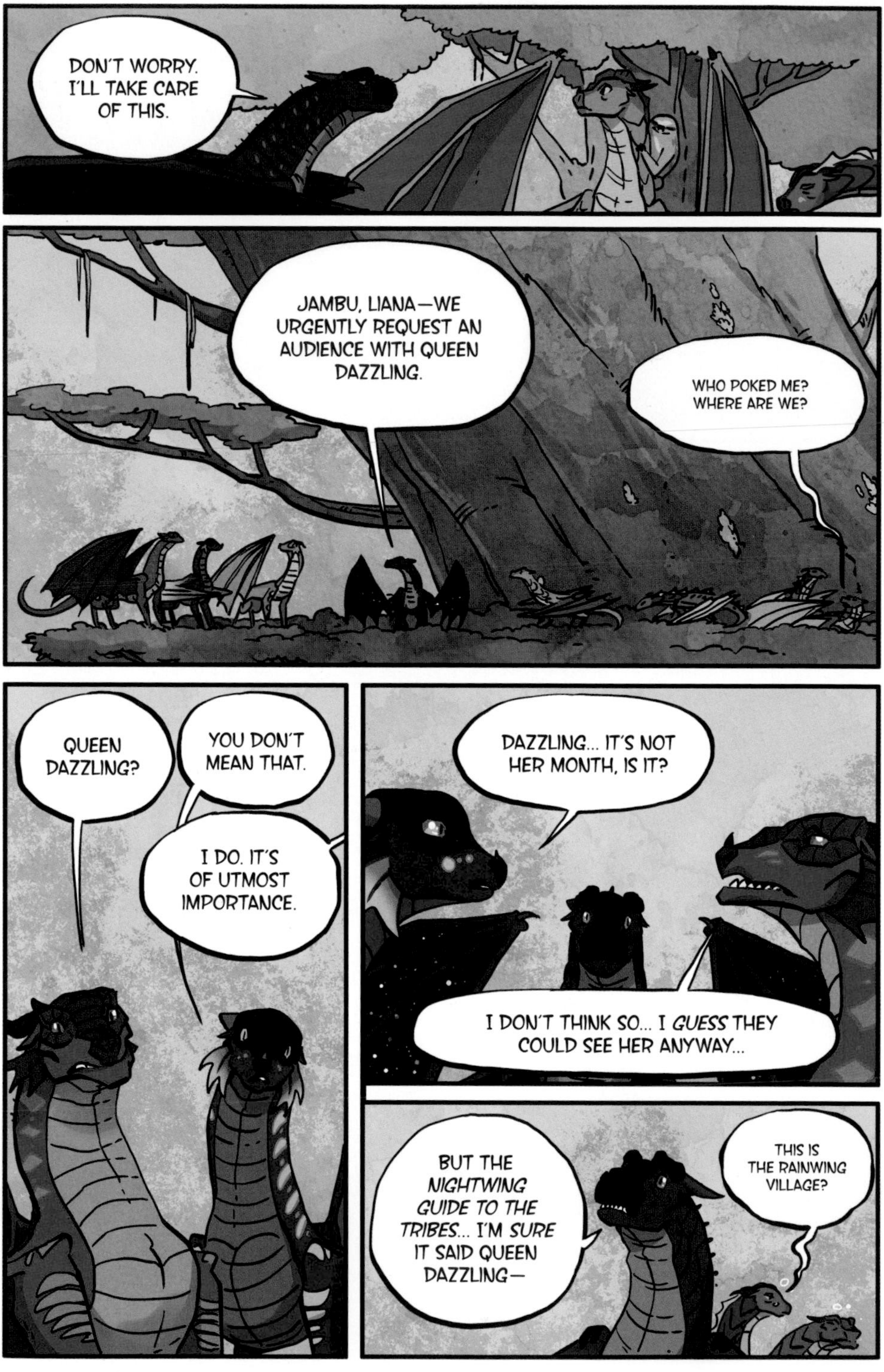
DON'T WORRY. I'LL TAKE CARE OF THIS.
JAMBU, LIANA—WE URGENTLY REQUEST AN AUDIENCE WITH QUEEN DAZZLING.
WHO POKED ME? WHERE ARE WE?
QUEEN DAZZLING?
YOU DON'T MEAN THAT.
I DO. IT'S OF UTMOST IMPORTANCE.
DAZZLING... IT'S NOT HER MONTH, IS IT?
I DON'T THINK SO... I *GUESS* THEY COULD SEE HER ANYWAY...
BUT THE *NIGHTWING GUIDE TO THE TRIBES*... I'M *SURE* IT SAID QUEEN DAZZLING—
THIS IS THE RAINWING VILLAGE?

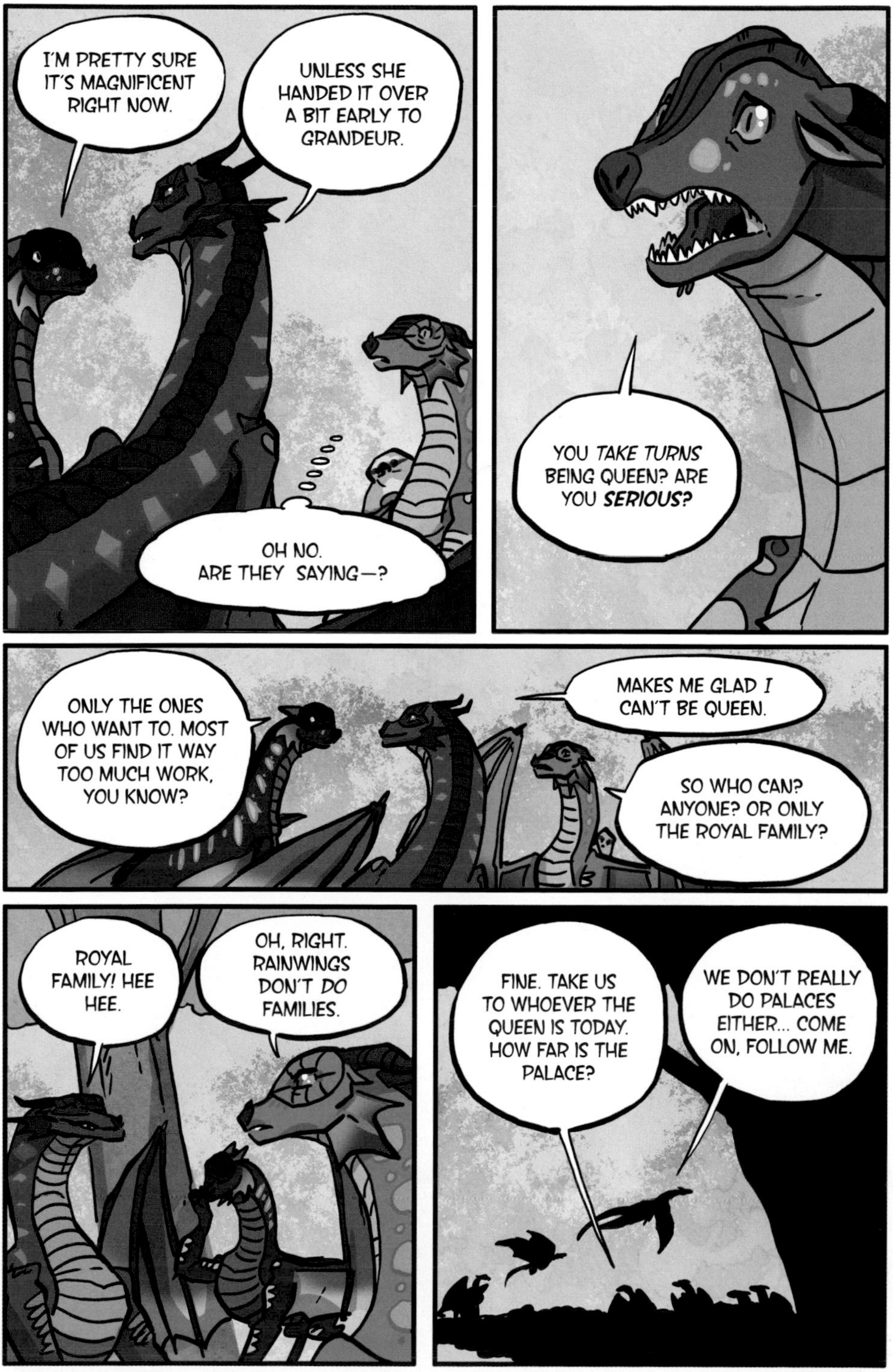
I'M PRETTY SURE IT'S MAGNIFICENT RIGHT NOW.
UNLESS SHE HANDED IT OVER A BIT EARLY TO GRANDEUR.
OH NO. ARE THEY SAYING—?
YOU *TAKE TURNS* BEING QUEEN? ARE YOU ***SERIOUS?***
ONLY THE ONES WHO WANT TO. MOST OF US FIND IT WAY TOO MUCH WORK, YOU KNOW?
MAKES ME GLAD *I* CAN'T BE QUEEN.
SO WHO CAN? ANYONE? OR ONLY THE ROYAL FAMILY?
ROYAL FAMILY! HEE HEE.
OH, RIGHT. RAINWINGS DON'T *DO* FAMILIES.
FINE. TAKE US TO WHOEVER THE QUEEN IS TODAY. HOW FAR IS THE PALACE?
WE DON'T REALLY DO PALACES EITHER... COME ON, FOLLOW ME.

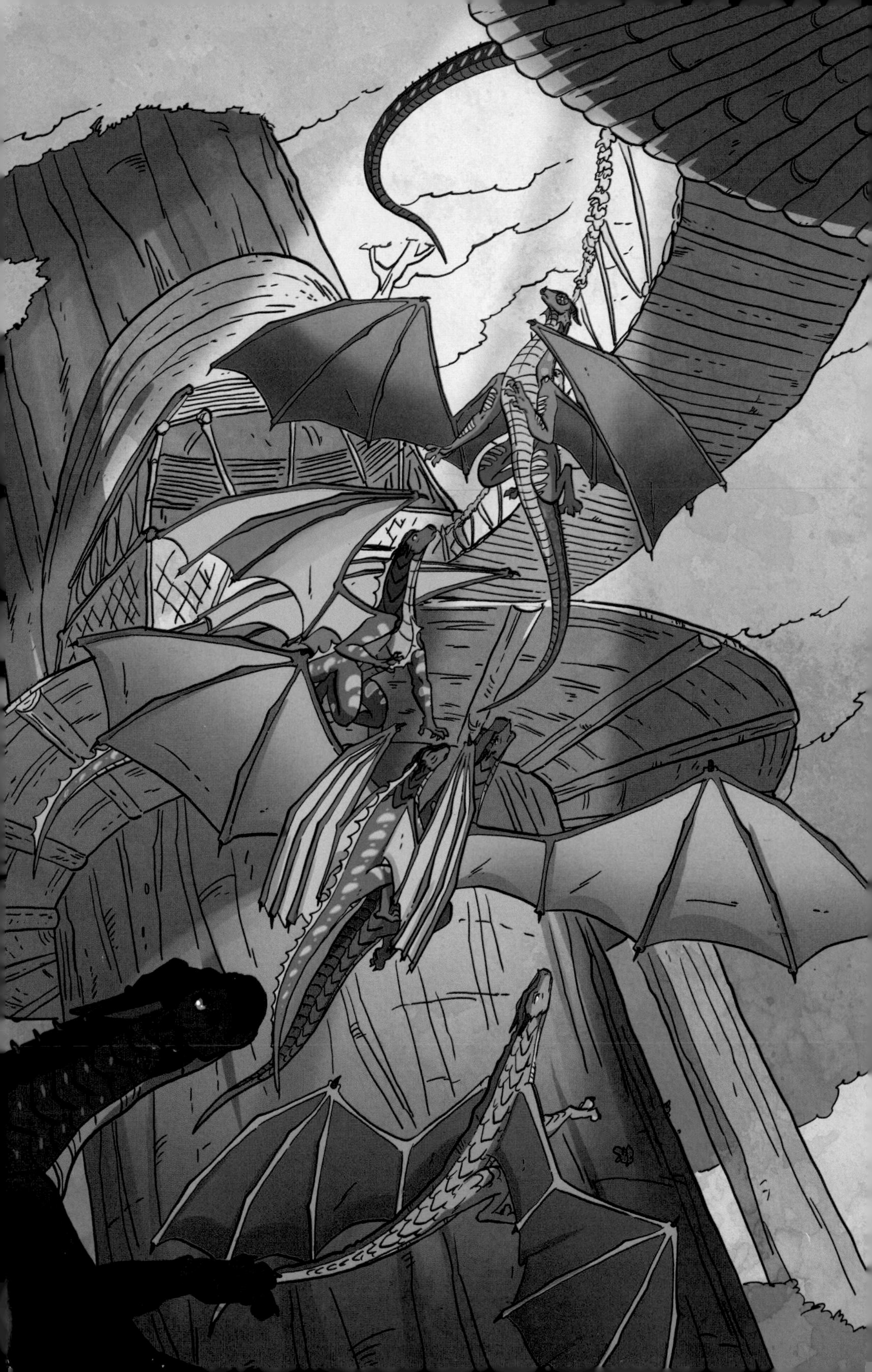

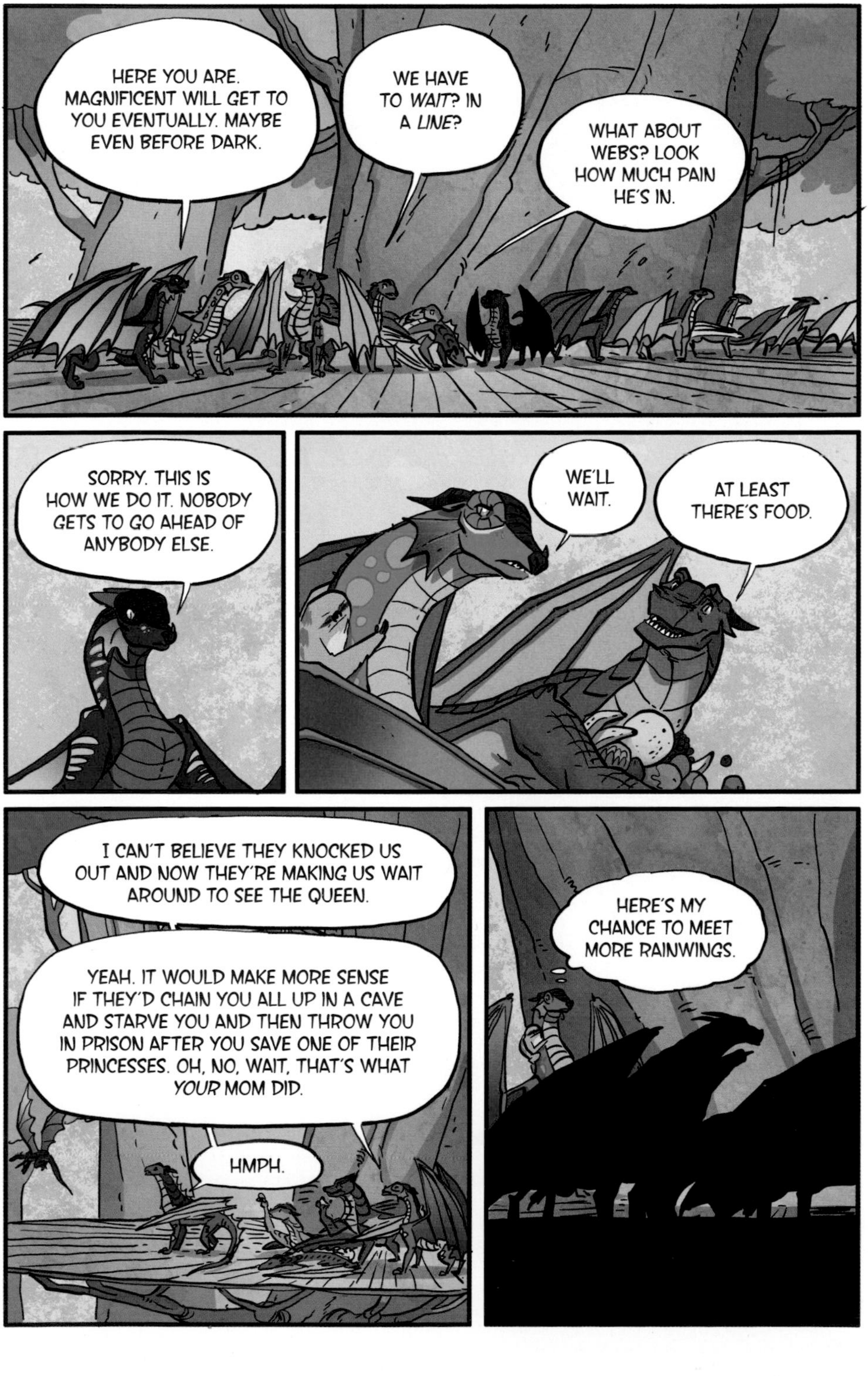
HERE YOU ARE. MAGNIFICENT WILL GET TO YOU EVENTUALLY. MAYBE EVEN BEFORE DARK.
WE HAVE TO *WAIT*? IN A *LINE*?
WHAT ABOUT WEBS? LOOK HOW MUCH PAIN HE'S IN.
SORRY. THIS IS HOW WE DO IT. NOBODY GETS TO GO AHEAD OF ANYBODY ELSE.
WE'LL WAIT.
AT LEAST THERE'S FOOD.
I CAN'T BELIEVE THEY KNOCKED US OUT AND NOW THEY'RE MAKING US WAIT AROUND TO SEE THE QUEEN.
YEAH. IT WOULD MAKE MORE SENSE IF THEY'D CHAIN YOU ALL UP IN A CAVE AND STARVE YOU AND THEN THROW YOU IN PRISON AFTER YOU SAVE ONE OF THEIR PRINCESSES. OH, NO, WAIT, THAT'S WHAT *YOUR* MOM DID.
HMPH.
HERE'S MY CHANCE TO MEET MORE RAINWINGS.

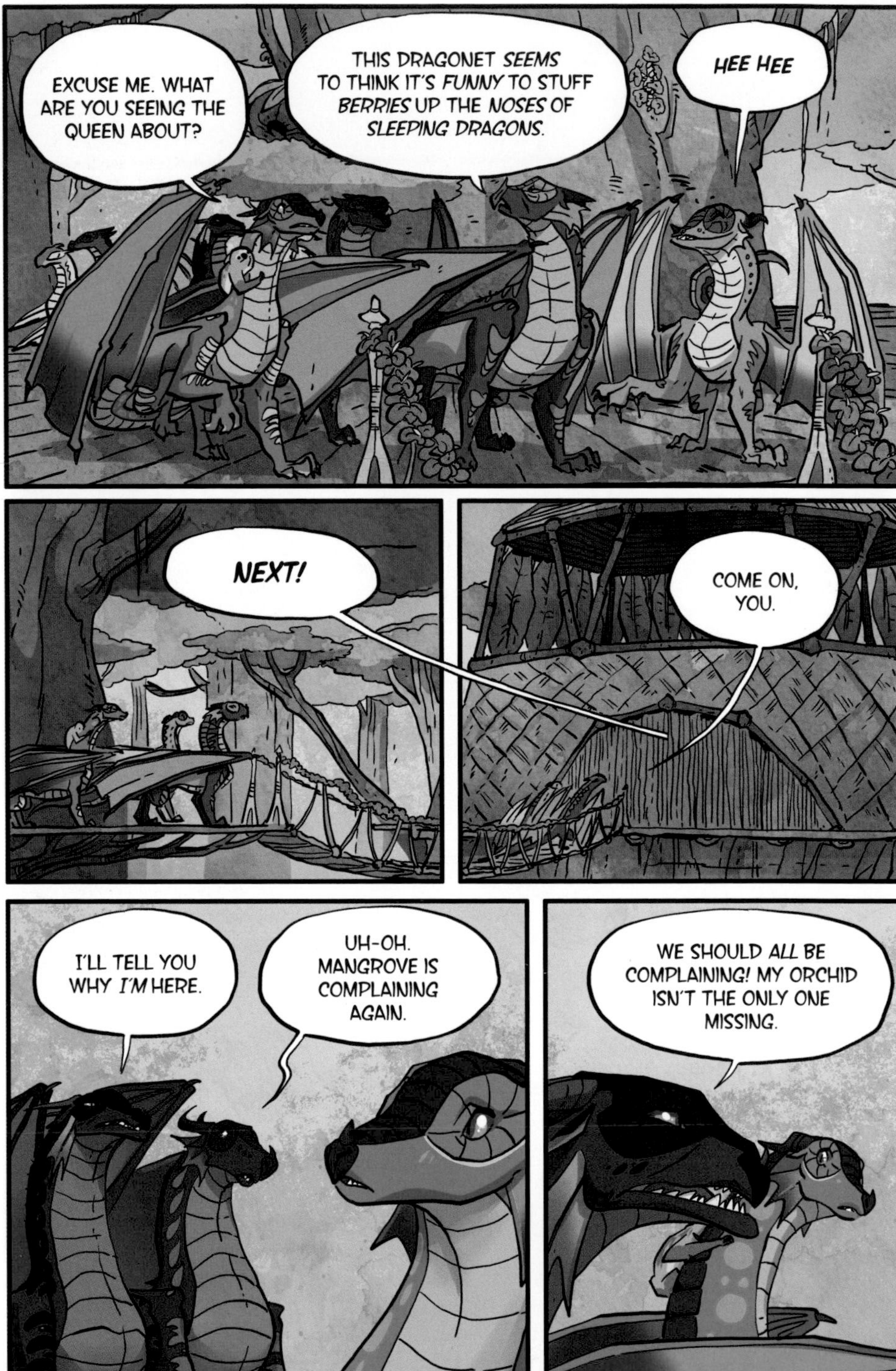
EXCUSE ME. WHAT ARE YOU SEEING THE QUEEN ABOUT?
THIS DRAGONET *SEEMS* TO THINK IT'S *FUNNY* TO STUFF *BERRIES* UP THE *NOSES* OF *SLEEPING DRAGONS.*
HEE HEE
NEXT!
COME ON, YOU.
I'LL TELL YOU WHY *I'M* HERE.
UH-OH. MANGROVE IS COMPLAINING AGAIN.
WE SHOULD *ALL* BE COMPLAINING! MY ORCHID ISN'T THE ONLY ONE MISSING.

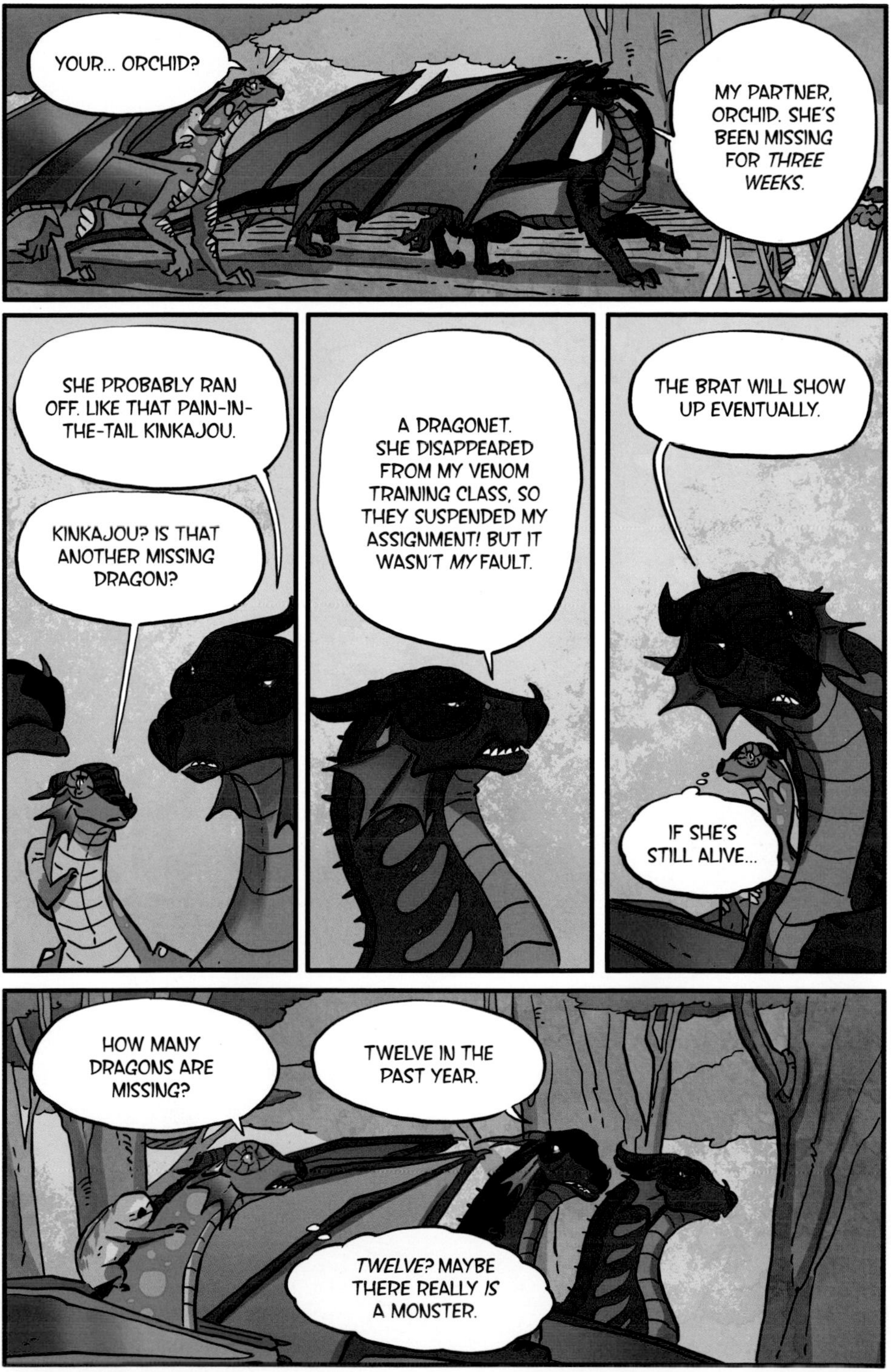
YOUR... ORCHID?
MY PARTNER, ORCHID. SHE'S BEEN MISSING FOR *THREE WEEKS.*
SHE PROBABLY RAN OFF. LIKE THAT PAIN-IN-THE-TAIL KINKAJOU.
KINKAJOU? IS THAT ANOTHER MISSING DRAGON?
A DRAGONET. SHE DISAPPEARED FROM MY VENOM TRAINING CLASS, SO THEY SUSPENDED MY ASSIGNMENT! BUT IT WASN'T *MY* FAULT.
THE BRAT WILL SHOW UP EVENTUALLY.
IF SHE'S STILL ALIVE...
HOW MANY DRAGONS ARE MISSING?
TWELVE IN THE PAST YEAR.
TWELVE? MAYBE THERE REALLY *IS* A MONSTER.

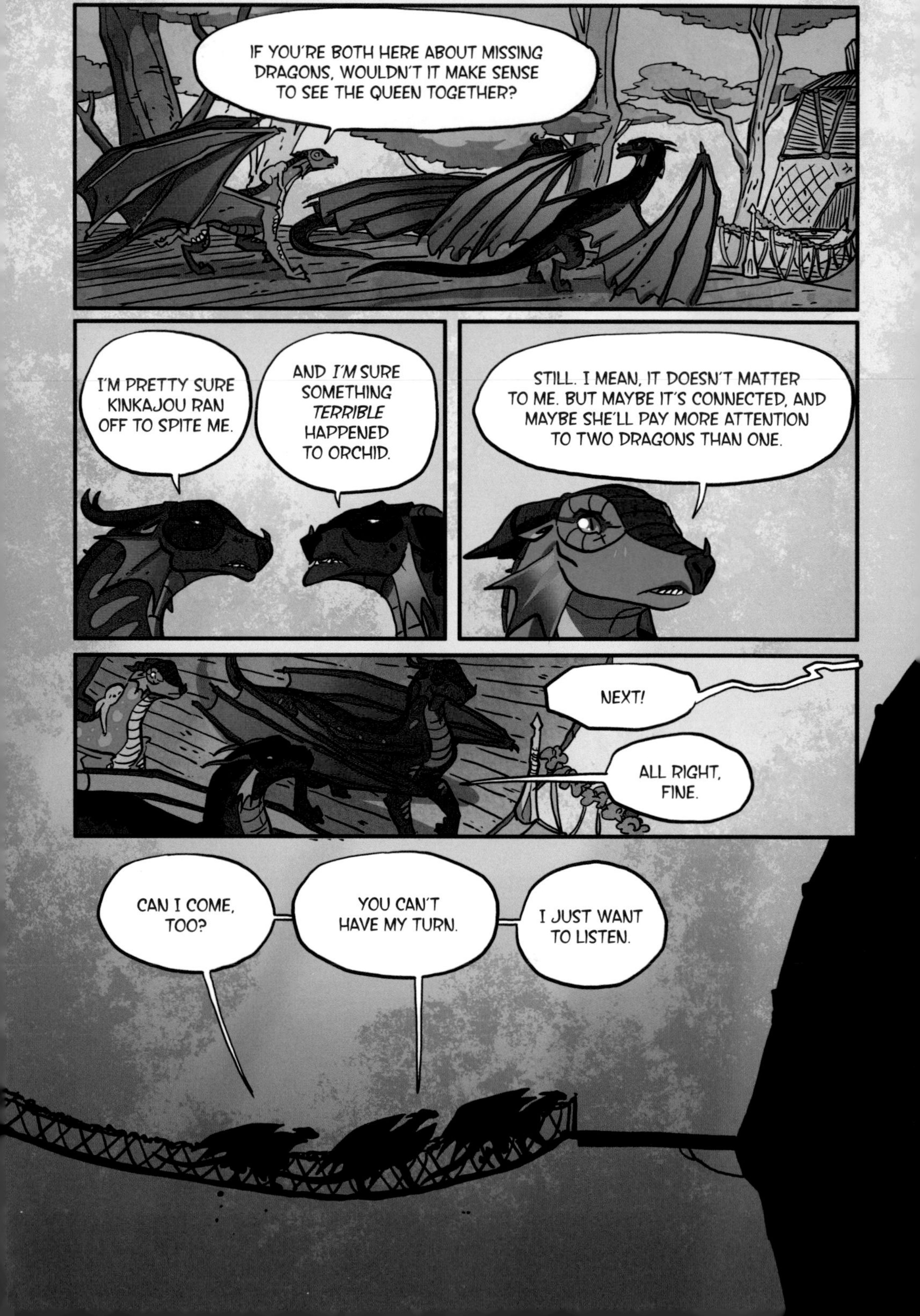
IF YOU'RE BOTH HERE ABOUT MISSING DRAGONS, WOULDN'T IT MAKE SENSE TO SEE THE QUEEN TOGETHER?
I'M PRETTY SURE KINKAJOU RAN OFF TO SPITE ME.
AND *I'M* SURE SOMETHING *TERRIBLE* HAPPENED TO ORCHID.
STILL. I MEAN, IT DOESN'T MATTER TO ME. BUT MAYBE IT'S CONNECTED, AND MAYBE SHE'LL PAY MORE ATTENTION TO TWO DRAGONS THAN ONE.
NEXT!
ALL RIGHT, FINE.
CAN I COME, TOO?
YOU CAN'T HAVE MY TURN.
I JUST WANT TO LISTEN.

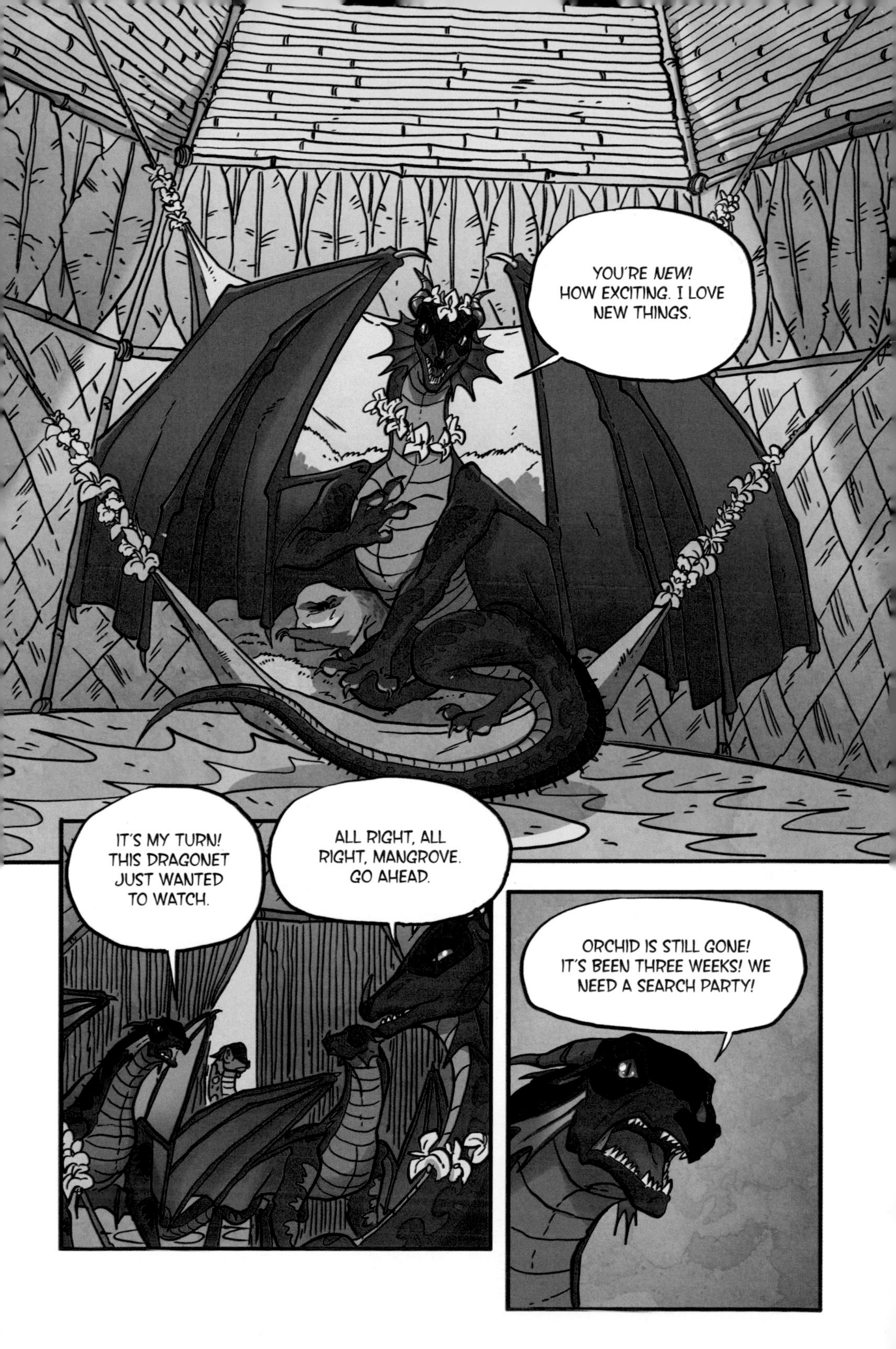
YOU'RE *NEW*! HOW EXCITING. I LOVE NEW THINGS.
IT'S MY TURN! THIS DRAGONET JUST WANTED TO WATCH.
ALL RIGHT, ALL RIGHT, MANGROVE. GO AHEAD.
ORCHID IS STILL GONE! IT'S BEEN THREE WEEKS! WE NEED A SEARCH PARTY!

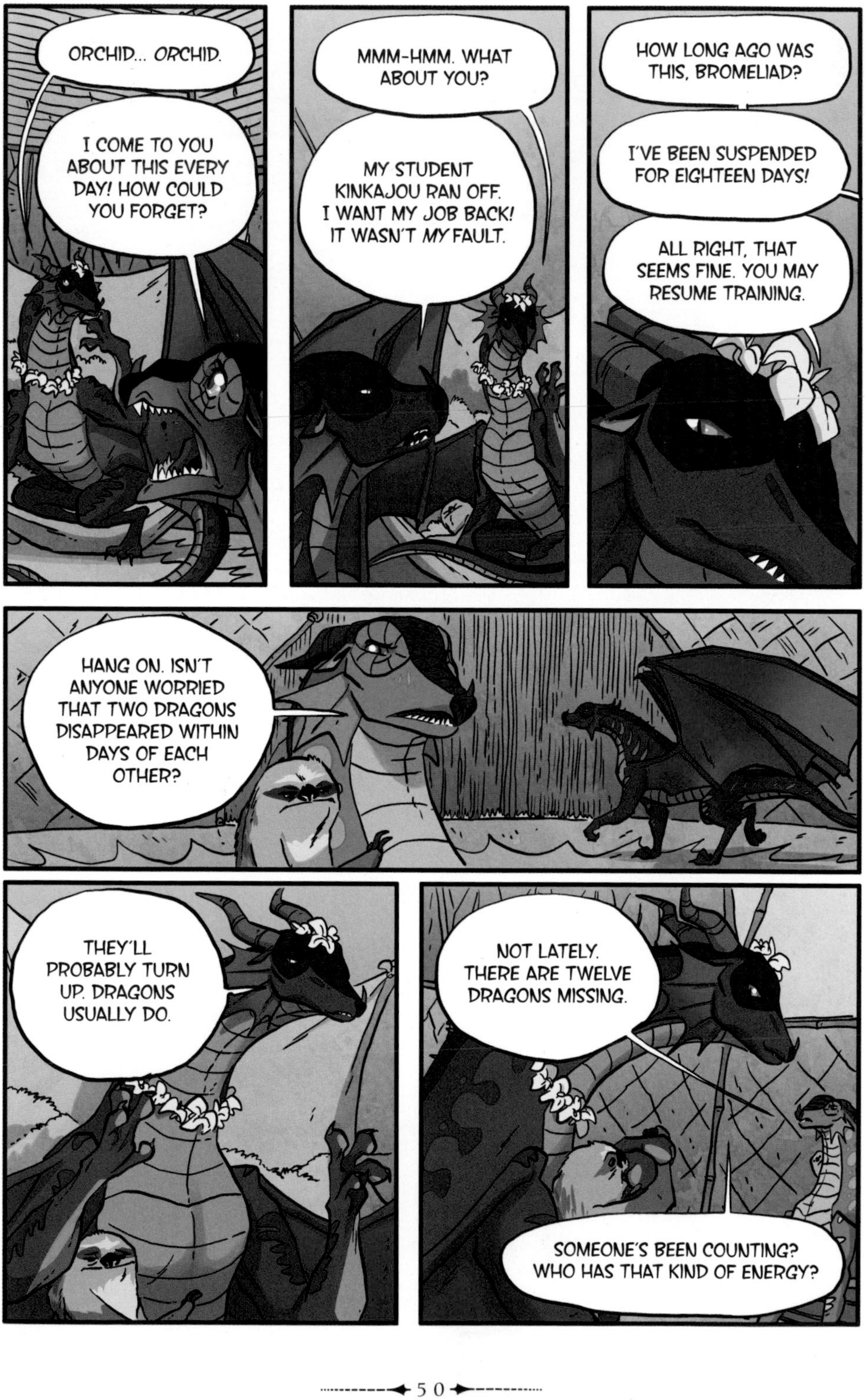
ORCHID... *ORCHID*.
I COME TO YOU ABOUT THIS EVERY DAY! HOW COULD YOU FORGET?
MMM-HMM. WHAT ABOUT YOU?
MY STUDENT KINKAJOU RAN OFF. I WANT MY JOB BACK! IT WASN'T *MY* FAULT.
HOW LONG AGO WAS THIS, BROMELIAD?
I'VE BEEN SUSPENDED FOR EIGHTEEN DAYS!
ALL RIGHT, THAT SEEMS FINE. YOU MAY RESUME TRAINING.
HANG ON. ISN'T ANYONE WORRIED THAT TWO DRAGONS DISAPPEARED WITHIN DAYS OF EACH OTHER?
THEY'LL PROBABLY TURN UP. DRAGONS USUALLY DO.
NOT LATELY. THERE ARE TWELVE DRAGONS MISSING.
SOMEONE'S BEEN COUNTING? WHO HAS THAT KIND OF ENERGY?

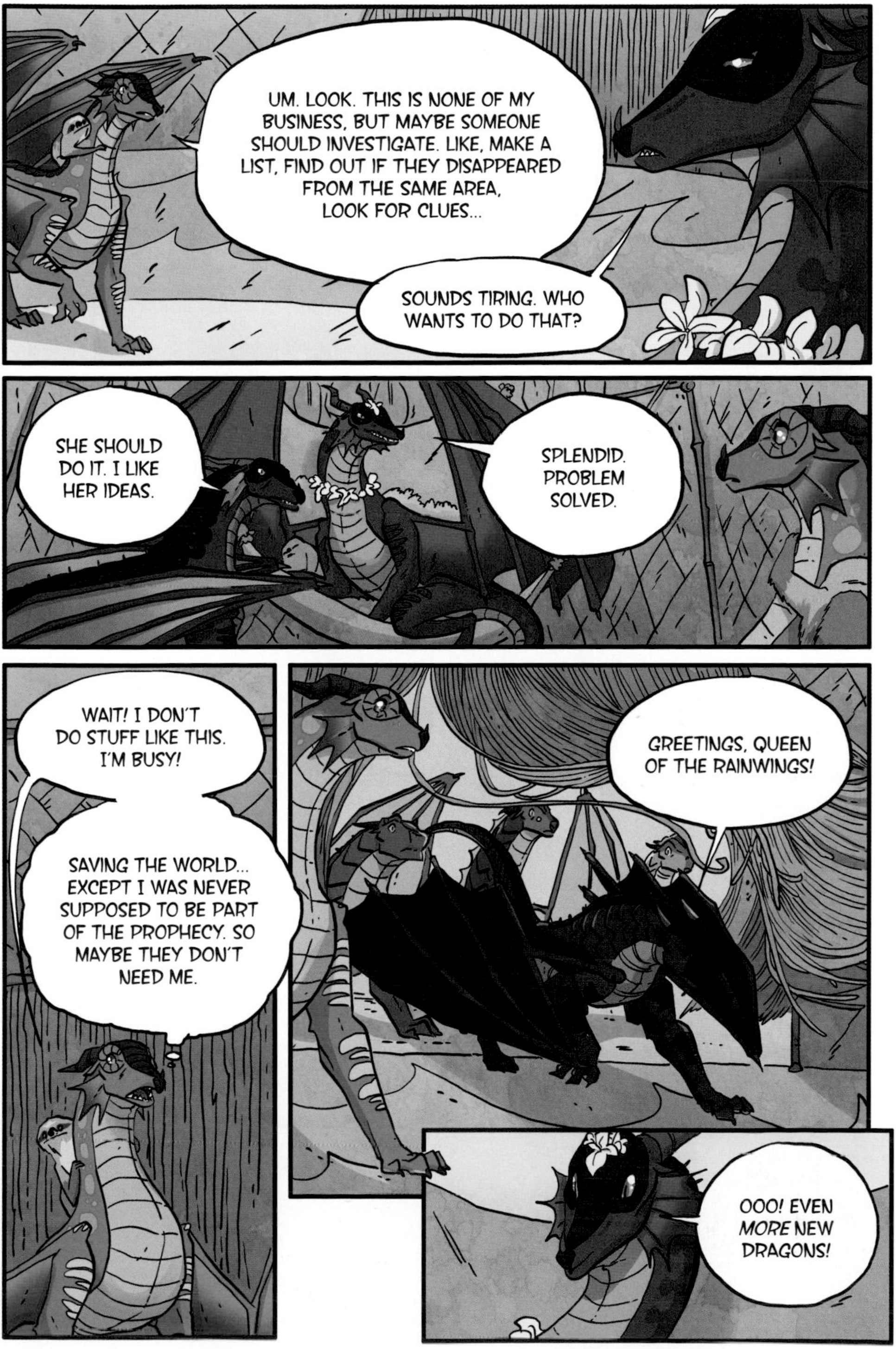
UM. LOOK. THIS IS NONE OF MY BUSINESS, BUT MAYBE SOMEONE SHOULD INVESTIGATE. LIKE, MAKE A LIST, FIND OUT IF THEY DISAPPEARED FROM THE SAME AREA, LOOK FOR CLUES...
SOUNDS TIRING. WHO WANTS TO DO THAT?
SHE SHOULD DO IT. I LIKE HER IDEAS.
SPLENDID. PROBLEM SOLVED.
WAIT! I DON'T DO STUFF LIKE THIS. I'M BUSY!
SAVING THE WORLD... EXCEPT I WAS NEVER SUPPOSED TO BE PART OF THE PROPHECY. SO MAYBE THEY DON'T NEED ME.
GREETINGS, QUEEN OF THE RAINWINGS!
OOO! EVEN *MORE* NEW DRAGONS!

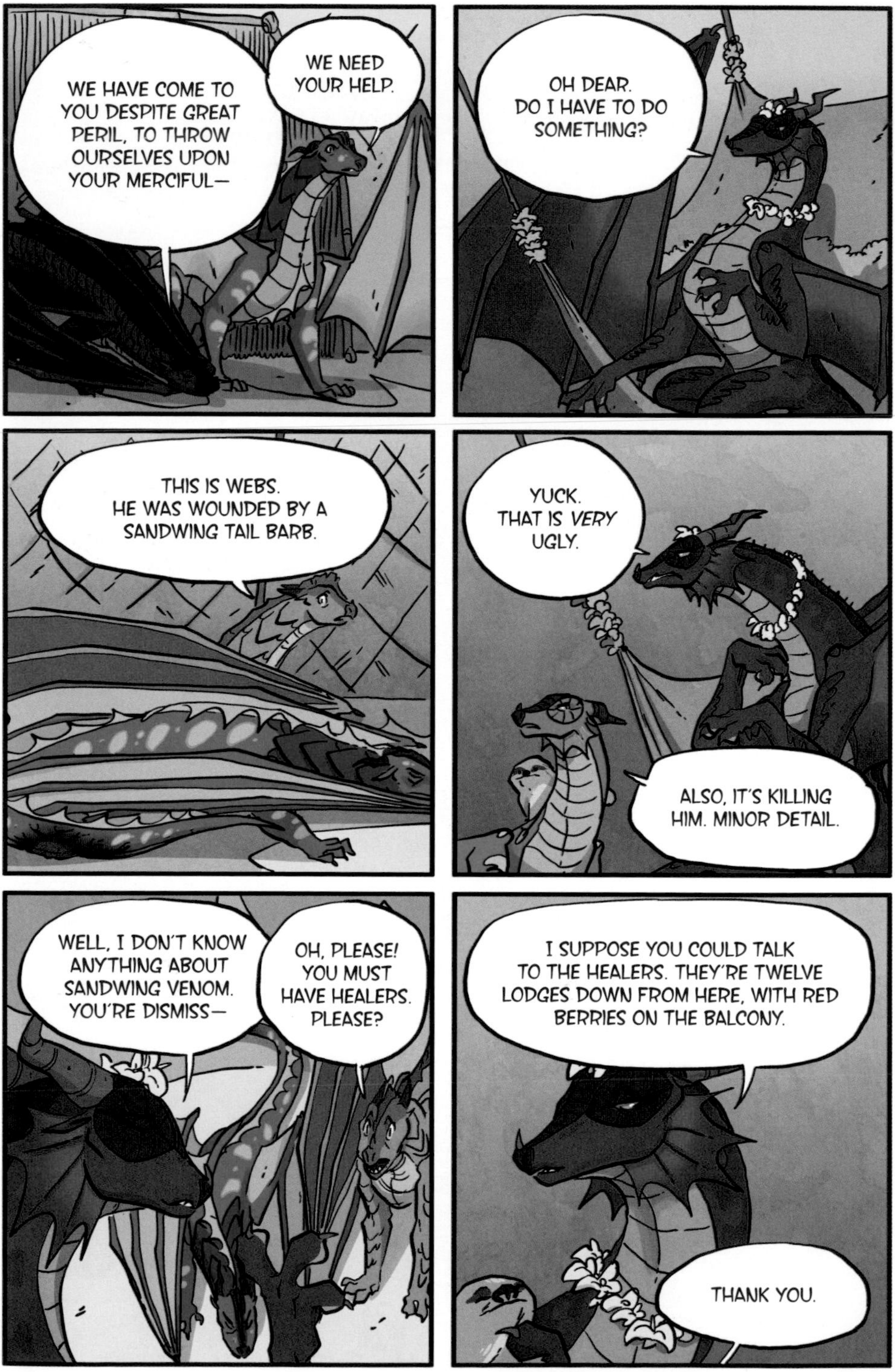
WE HAVE COME TO YOU DESPITE GREAT PERIL, TO THROW OURSELVES UPON YOUR MERCIFUL—
WE NEED YOUR HELP.
OH DEAR. DO I HAVE TO DO SOMETHING?
THIS IS WEBS. HE WAS WOUNDED BY A SANDWING TAIL BARB.
YUCK. THAT IS *VERY* UGLY.
ALSO, IT'S KILLING HIM. MINOR DETAIL.
WELL, I DON'T KNOW ANYTHING ABOUT SANDWING VENOM. YOU'RE DISMISS—
OH, PLEASE! YOU MUST HAVE HEALERS. PLEASE?
I SUPPOSE YOU COULD TALK TO THE HEALERS. THEY'RE TWELVE LODGES DOWN FROM HERE, WITH RED BERRIES ON THE BALCONY.
THANK YOU.

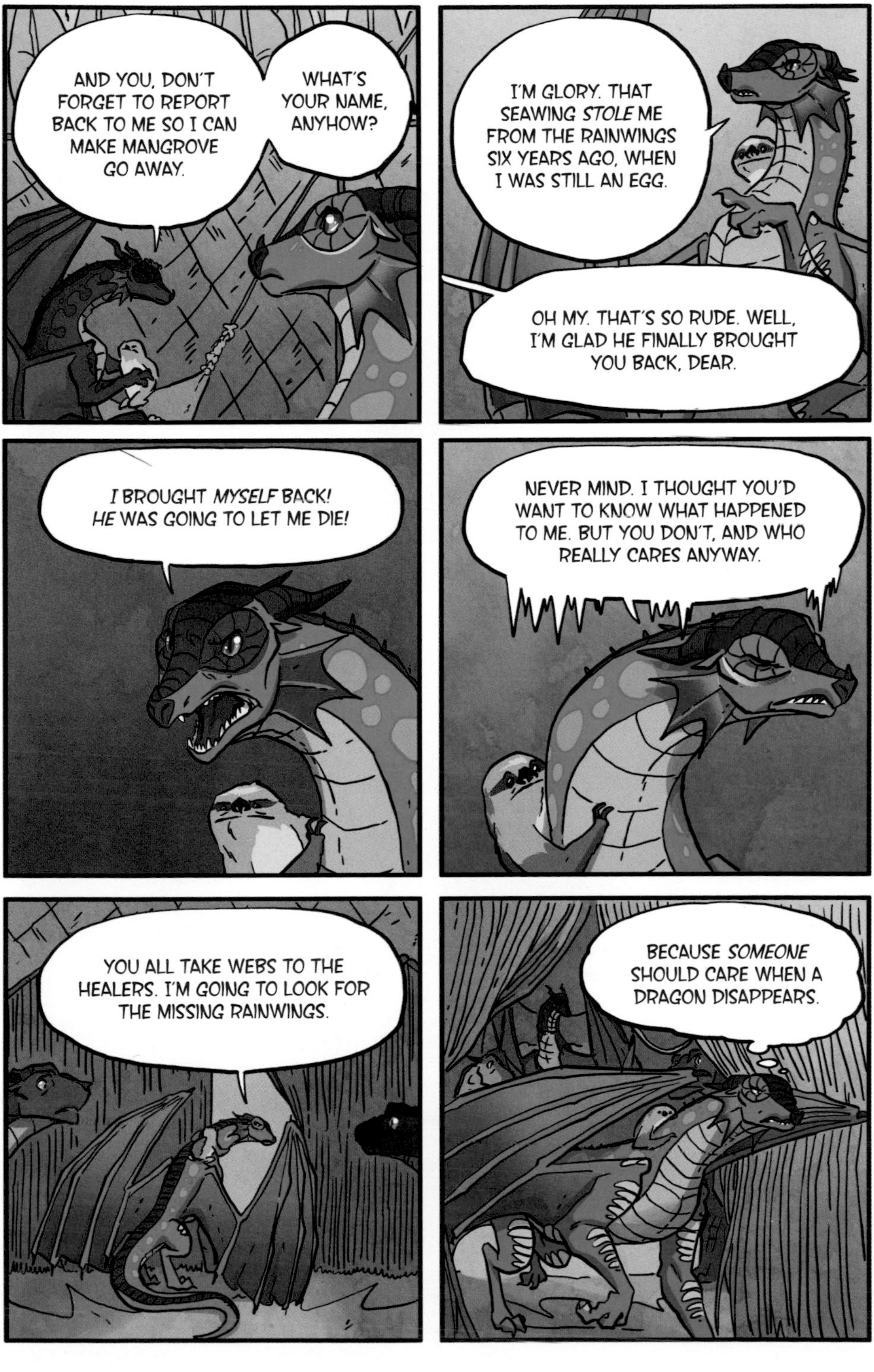
AND YOU, DON'T FORGET TO REPORT BACK TO ME SO I CAN MAKE MANGROVE GO AWAY.
WHAT'S YOUR NAME, ANYHOW?
I'M GLORY. THAT SEAWING *STOLE* ME FROM THE RAINWINGS SIX YEARS AGO, WHEN I WAS STILL AN EGG.
OH MY. THAT'S SO RUDE. WELL, I'M GLAD HE FINALLY BROUGHT YOU BACK, DEAR.
I BROUGHT *MYSELF* BACK! *HE* WAS GOING TO LET ME DIE!
NEVER MIND. I THOUGHT YOU'D WANT TO KNOW WHAT HAPPENED TO ME. BUT YOU DON'T, AND WHO REALLY CARES ANYWAY.
YOU ALL TAKE WEBS TO THE HEALERS. I'M GOING TO LOOK FOR THE MISSING RAINWINGS.
BECAUSE *SOMEONE* SHOULD CARE WHEN A DRAGON DISAPPEARS.

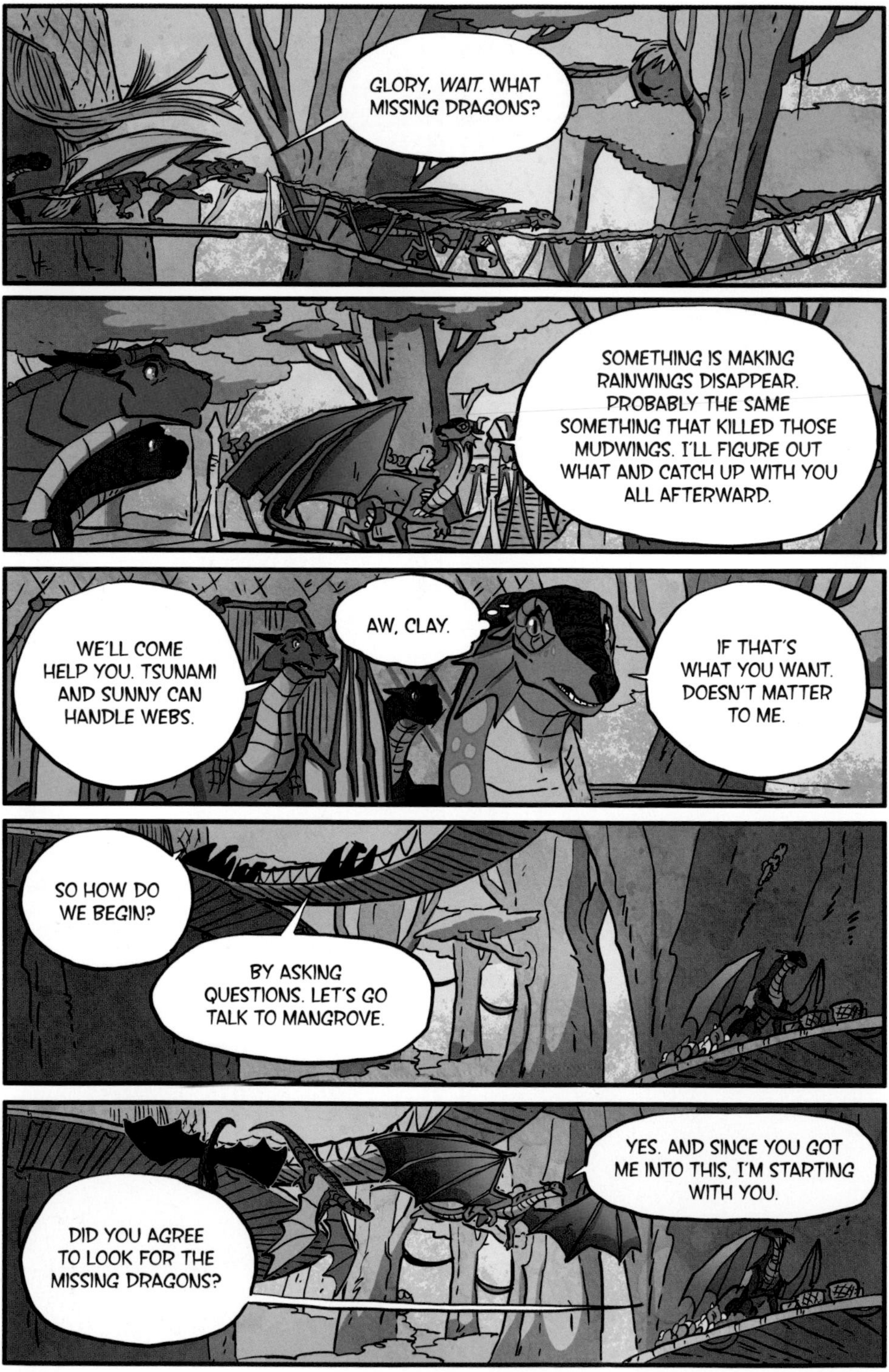
GLORY, WAIT. WHAT MISSING DRAGONS?
SOMETHING IS MAKING RAINWINGS DISAPPEAR. PROBABLY THE SAME SOMETHING THAT KILLED THOSE MUDWINGS. I'LL FIGURE OUT WHAT AND CATCH UP WITH YOU ALL AFTERWARD.
WE'LL COME HELP YOU. TSUNAMI AND SUNNY CAN HANDLE WEBS.
AW, CLAY.
IF THAT'S WHAT YOU WANT. DOESN'T MATTER TO ME.
SO HOW DO WE BEGIN?
BY ASKING QUESTIONS. LET'S GO TALK TO MANGROVE.
DID YOU AGREE TO LOOK FOR THE MISSING DRAGONS?
YES. AND SINCE YOU GOT ME INTO THIS, I'M STARTING WITH YOU.

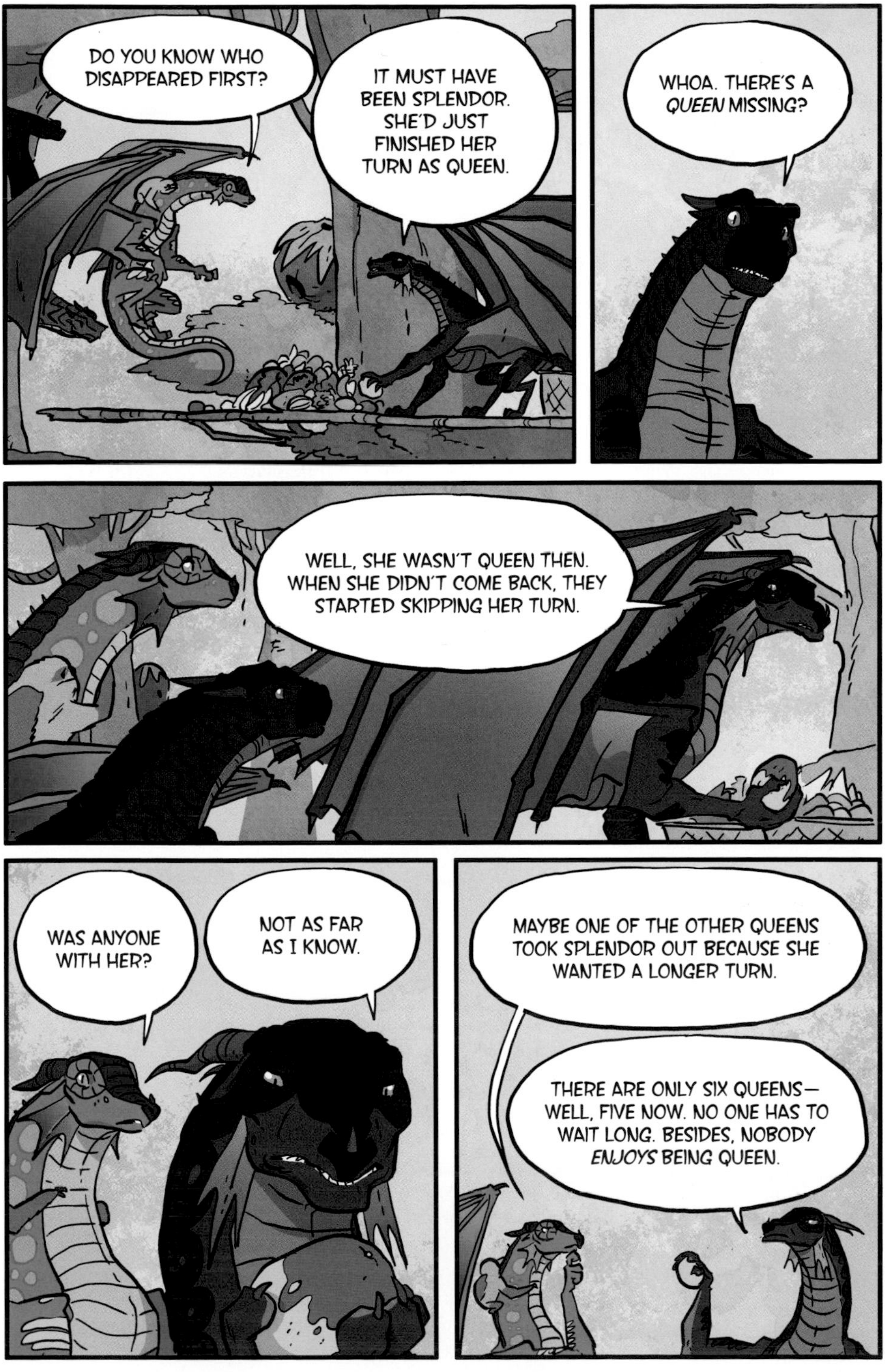
DO YOU KNOW WHO DISAPPEARED FIRST?
IT MUST HAVE BEEN SPLENDOR. SHE'D JUST FINISHED HER TURN AS QUEEN.
WHOA. THERE'S A *QUEEN* MISSING?
WELL, SHE WASN'T QUEEN THEN. WHEN SHE DIDN'T COME BACK, THEY STARTED SKIPPING HER TURN.
WAS ANYONE WITH HER?
NOT AS FAR AS I KNOW.
MAYBE ONE OF THE OTHER QUEENS TOOK SPLENDOR OUT BECAUSE SHE WANTED A LONGER TURN.
THERE ARE ONLY SIX QUEENS—WELL, FIVE NOW. NO ONE HAS TO WAIT LONG. BESIDES, NOBODY *ENJOYS* BEING QUEEN.

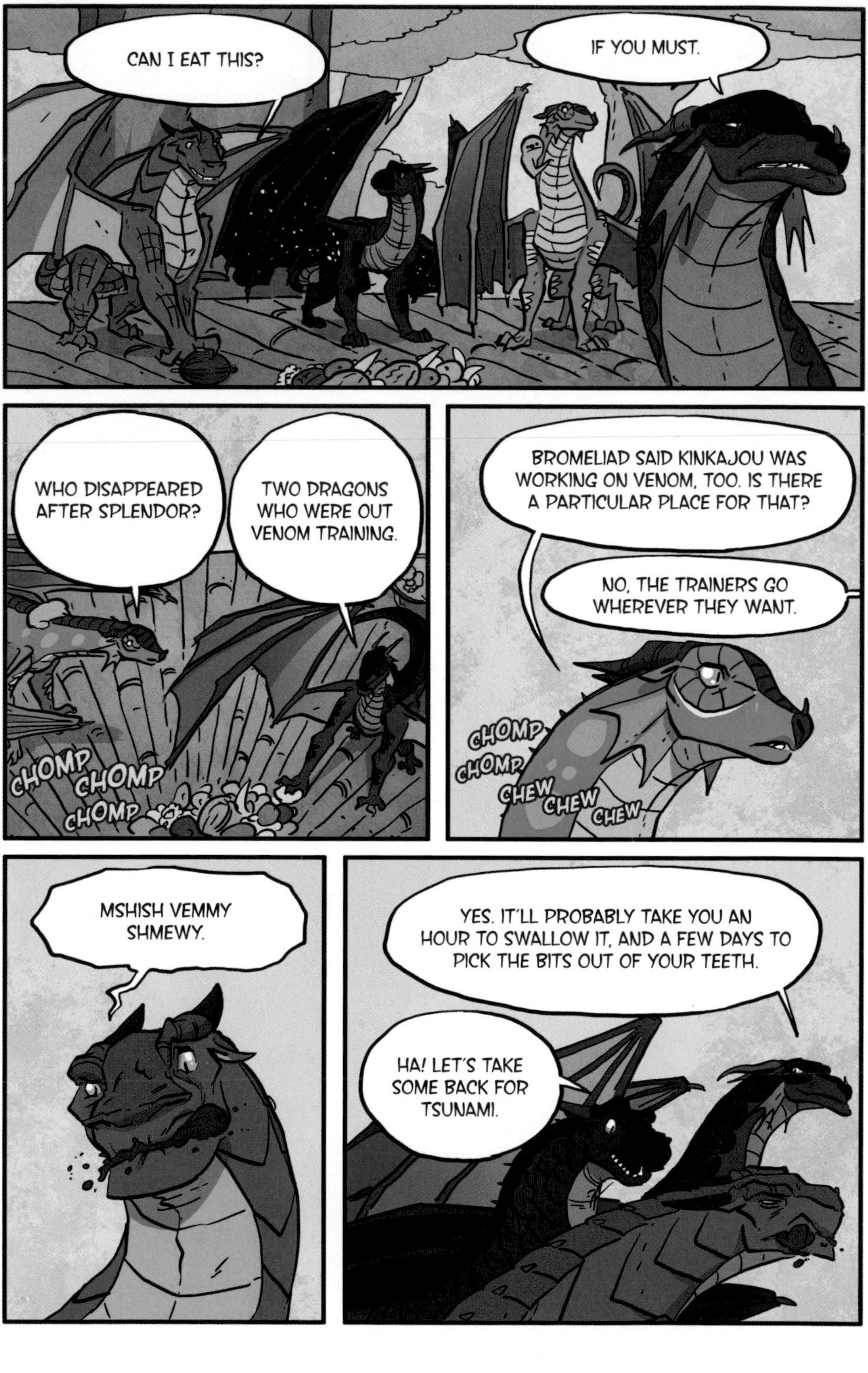
CAN I EAT THIS?
IF YOU MUST.
WHO DISAPPEARED AFTER SPLENDOR?
TWO DRAGONS WHO WERE OUT VENOM TRAINING.
CHOMP CHOMP CHOMP
BROMELIAD SAID KINKAJOU WAS WORKING ON VENOM, TOO. IS THERE A PARTICULAR PLACE FOR THAT?
NO, THE TRAINERS GO WHEREVER THEY WANT.
CHOMP CHOMP CHEW CHEW CHEW
MSHISH VEMMY SHMEWY.
YES. IT'LL PROBABLY TAKE YOU AN HOUR TO SWALLOW IT, AND A FEW DAYS TO PICK THE BITS OUT OF YOUR TEETH.
HA! LET'S TAKE SOME BACK FOR TSUNAMI.

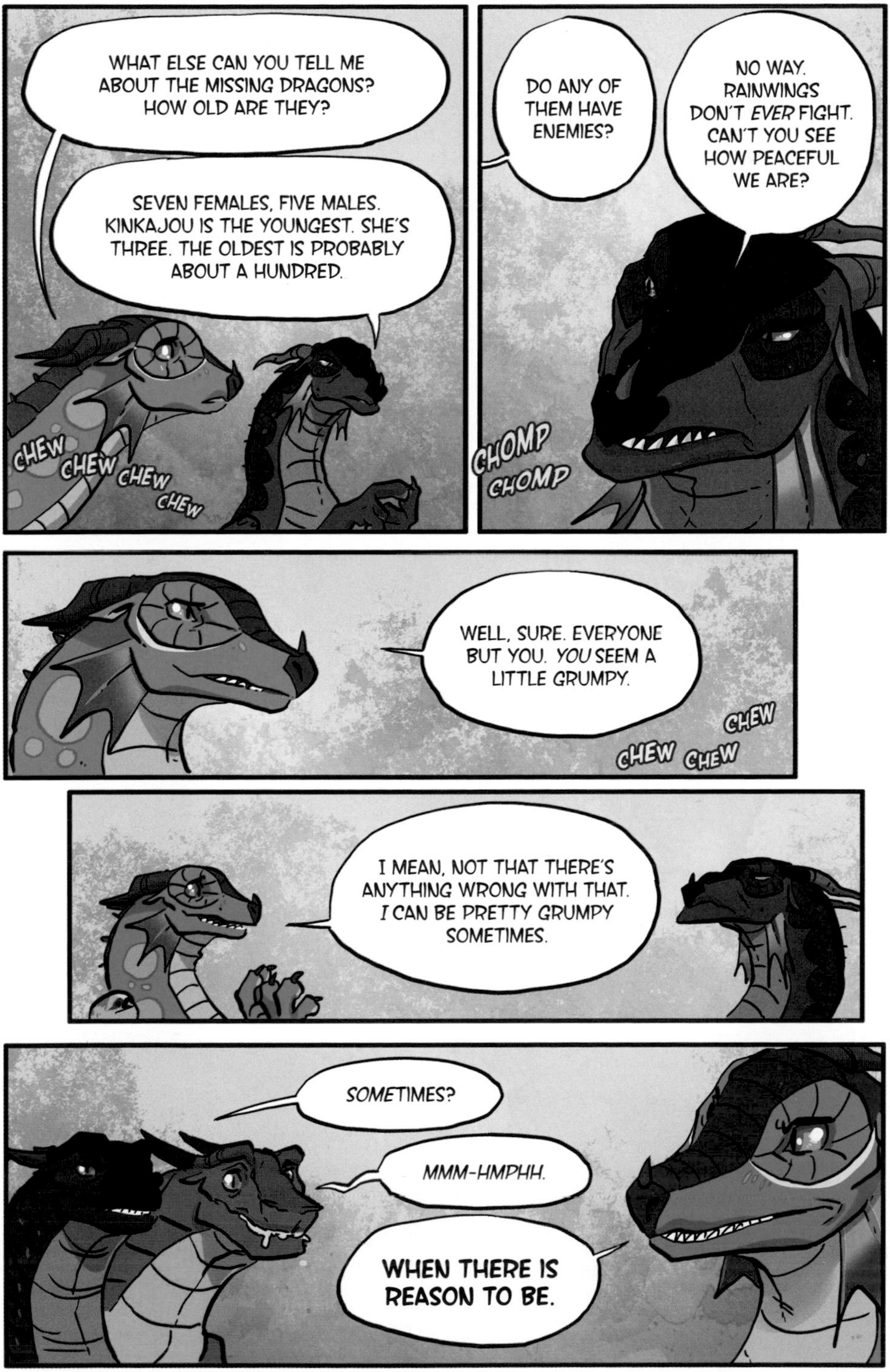
WHAT ELSE CAN YOU TELL ME ABOUT THE MISSING DRAGONS? HOW OLD ARE THEY?
SEVEN FEMALES, FIVE MALES. KINKAJOU IS THE YOUNGEST. SHE'S THREE. THE OLDEST IS PROBABLY ABOUT A HUNDRED.
CHEW CHEW CHEW CHEW
DO ANY OF THEM HAVE ENEMIES?
NO WAY. RAINWINGS DON'T *EVER* FIGHT. CAN'T YOU SEE HOW PEACEFUL WE ARE?
CHOMP CHOMP
WELL, SURE. EVERYONE BUT YOU. *YOU* SEEM A LITTLE GRUMPY.
CHEW CHEW CHEW
I MEAN, NOT THAT THERE'S ANYTHING WRONG WITH THAT. *I* CAN BE PRETTY GRUMPY SOMETIMES.
SOMETIMES?
MMM-HMPHH.
WHEN THERE IS REASON TO BE.

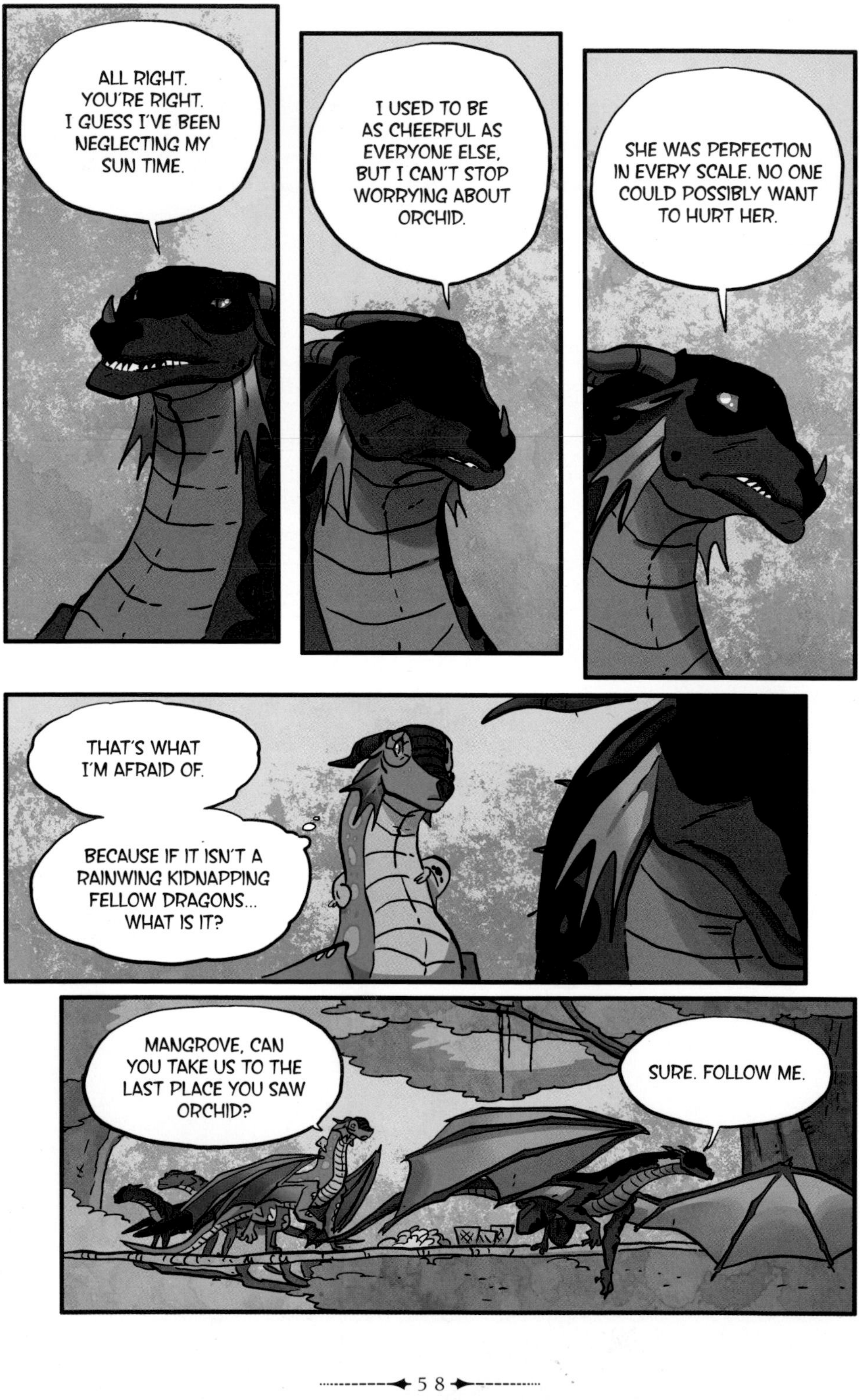
ALL RIGHT. YOU'RE RIGHT. I GUESS I'VE BEEN NEGLECTING MY SUN TIME.
I USED TO BE AS CHEERFUL AS EVERYONE ELSE, BUT I CAN'T STOP WORRYING ABOUT ORCHID.
SHE WAS PERFECTION IN EVERY SCALE. NO ONE COULD POSSIBLY WANT TO HURT HER.
THAT'S WHAT I'M AFRAID OF.
BECAUSE IF IT ISN'T A RAINWING KIDNAPPING FELLOW DRAGONS... WHAT IS IT?
MANGROVE, CAN YOU TAKE US TO THE LAST PLACE YOU SAW ORCHID?
SURE. FOLLOW ME.

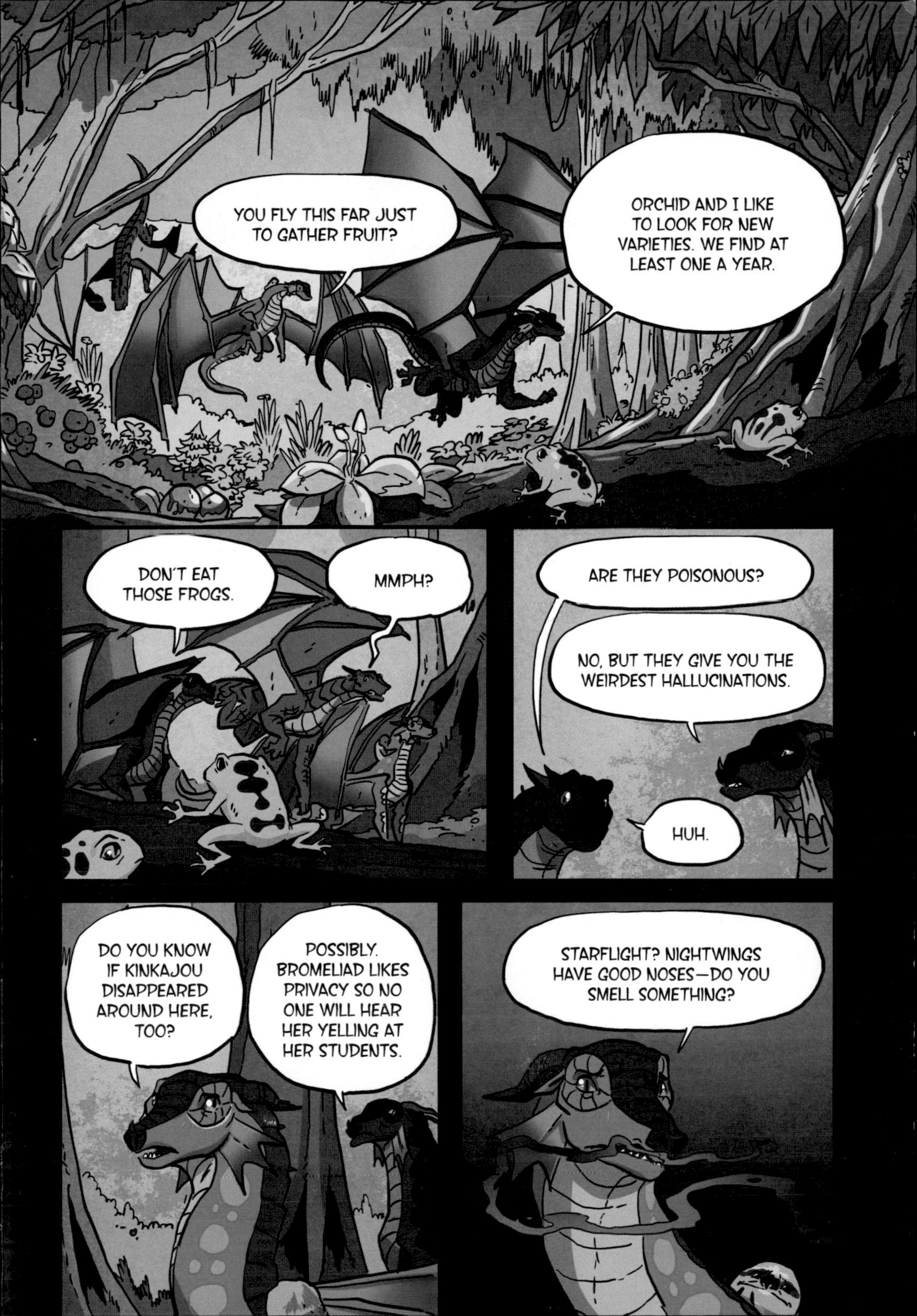
YOU FLY THIS FAR JUST TO GATHER FRUIT?
ORCHID AND I LIKE TO LOOK FOR NEW VARIETIES. WE FIND AT LEAST ONE A YEAR.
DON'T EAT THOSE FROGS.
MMPH?
ARE THEY POISONOUS?
NO, BUT THEY GIVE YOU THE WEIRDEST HALLUCINATIONS.
HUH.
DO YOU KNOW IF KINKAJOU DISAPPEARED AROUND HERE, TOO?
POSSIBLY. BROMELIAD LIKES PRIVACY SO NO ONE WILL HEAR HER YELLING AT HER STUDENTS.
STARFLIGHT? NIGHTWINGS HAVE GOOD NOSES—DO YOU SMELL SOMETHING?

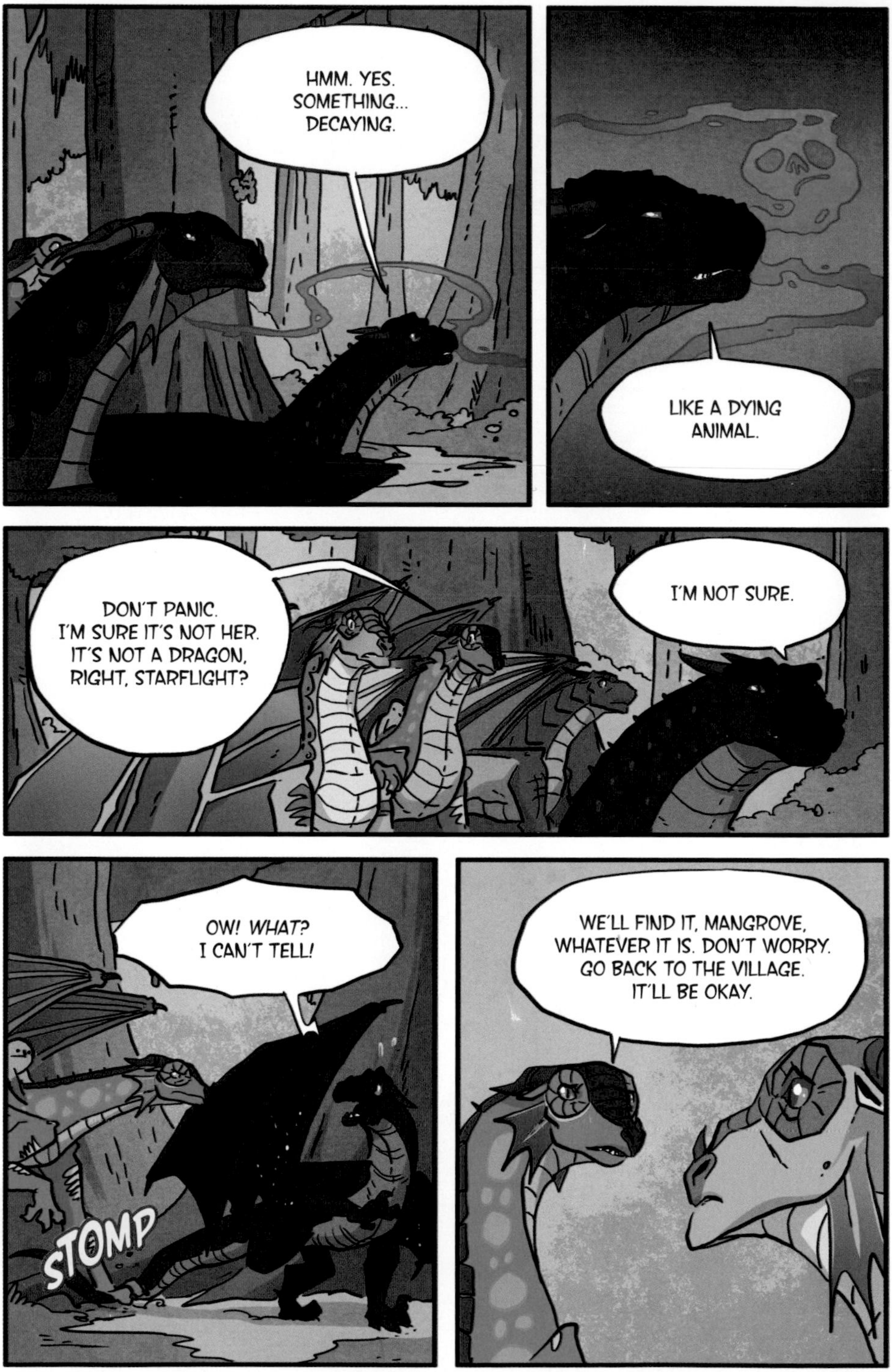
HMM. YES. SOMETHING... DECAYING.
LIKE A DYING ANIMAL.
DON'T PANIC. I'M SURE IT'S NOT HER. IT'S NOT A DRAGON, RIGHT, STARFLIGHT?
I'M NOT SURE.
OW! WHAT? I CAN'T TELL!
STOMP
WE'LL FIND IT, MANGROVE, WHATEVER IT IS. DON'T WORRY. GO BACK TO THE VILLAGE. IT'LL BE OKAY.

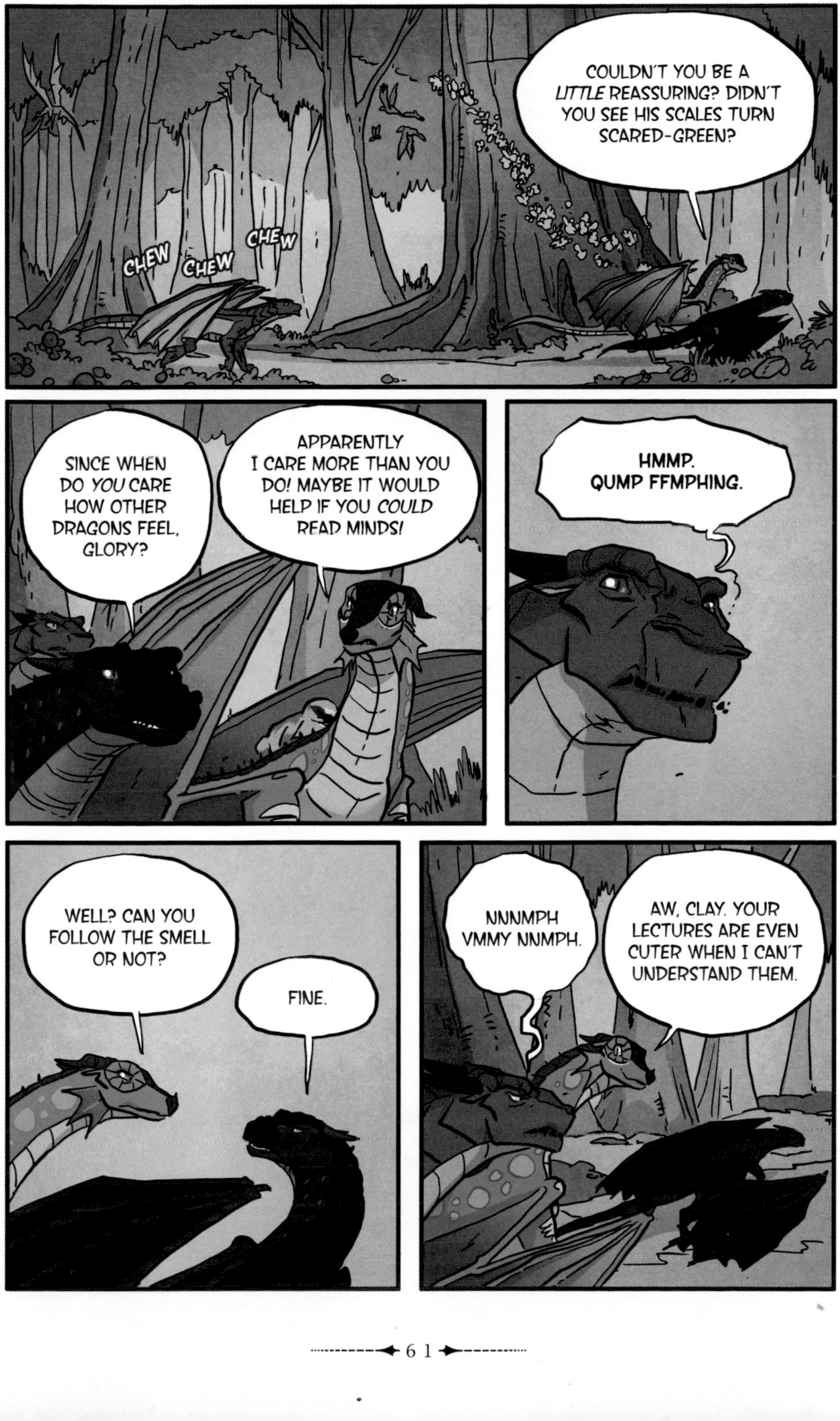
COULDN'T YOU BE A *LITTLE* REASSURING? DIDN'T YOU SEE HIS SCALES TURN SCARED-GREEN?
CHEW
CHEW
CHEW
SINCE WHEN DO *YOU* CARE HOW OTHER DRAGONS FEEL, GLORY?
APPARENTLY I CARE MORE THAN YOU DO! MAYBE IT WOULD HELP IF YOU *COULD* READ MINDS!
HMMP. QUMP FFMPHING.
WELL? CAN YOU FOLLOW THE SMELL OR NOT?
FINE.
NNNMPH VMMY NNMPH.
AW, CLAY. YOUR LECTURES ARE EVEN CUTER WHEN I CAN'T UNDERSTAND THEM.

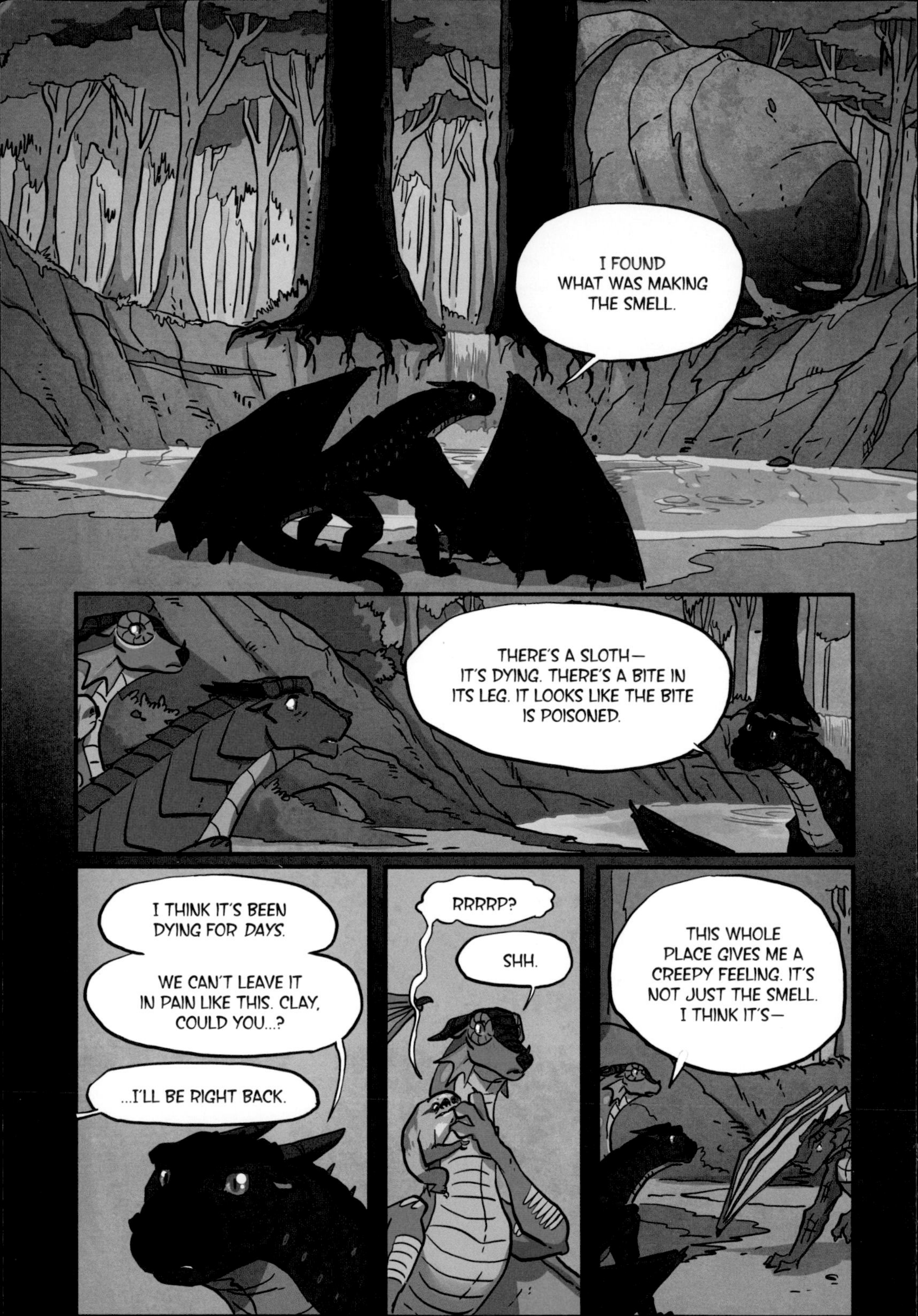
I FOUND WHAT WAS MAKING THE SMELL.
THERE'S A SLOTH— IT'S DYING. THERE'S A BITE IN ITS LEG. IT LOOKS LIKE THE BITE IS POISONED.
I THINK IT'S BEEN DYING FOR *DAYS.*
WE CAN'T LEAVE IT IN PAIN LIKE THIS. CLAY, COULD YOU...?
...I'LL BE RIGHT BACK.
RRRRP?
SHH.
THIS WHOLE PLACE GIVES ME A CREEPY FEELING. IT'S NOT JUST THE SMELL. I THINK IT'S—

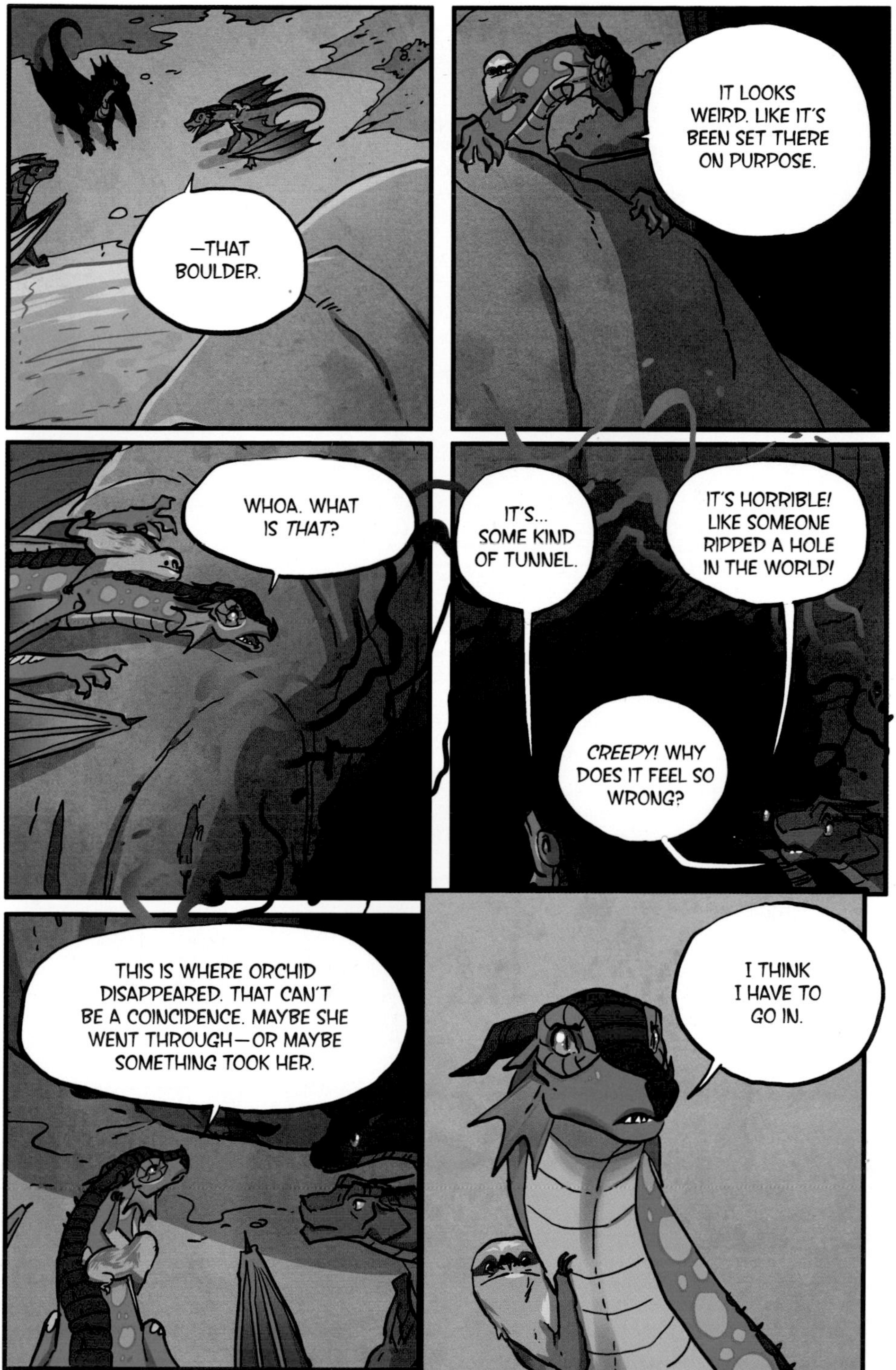
—THAT BOULDER.
IT LOOKS WEIRD. LIKE IT'S BEEN SET THERE ON PURPOSE.
WHOA. WHAT IS *THAT*?
IT'S... SOME KIND OF TUNNEL.
IT'S HORRIBLE! LIKE SOMEONE RIPPED A HOLE IN THE WORLD!
CREEPY! WHY DOES IT FEEL SO WRONG?
THIS IS WHERE ORCHID DISAPPEARED. THAT CAN'T BE A COINCIDENCE. MAYBE SHE WENT THROUGH—OR MAYBE SOMETHING TOOK HER.
I THINK I HAVE TO GO IN.

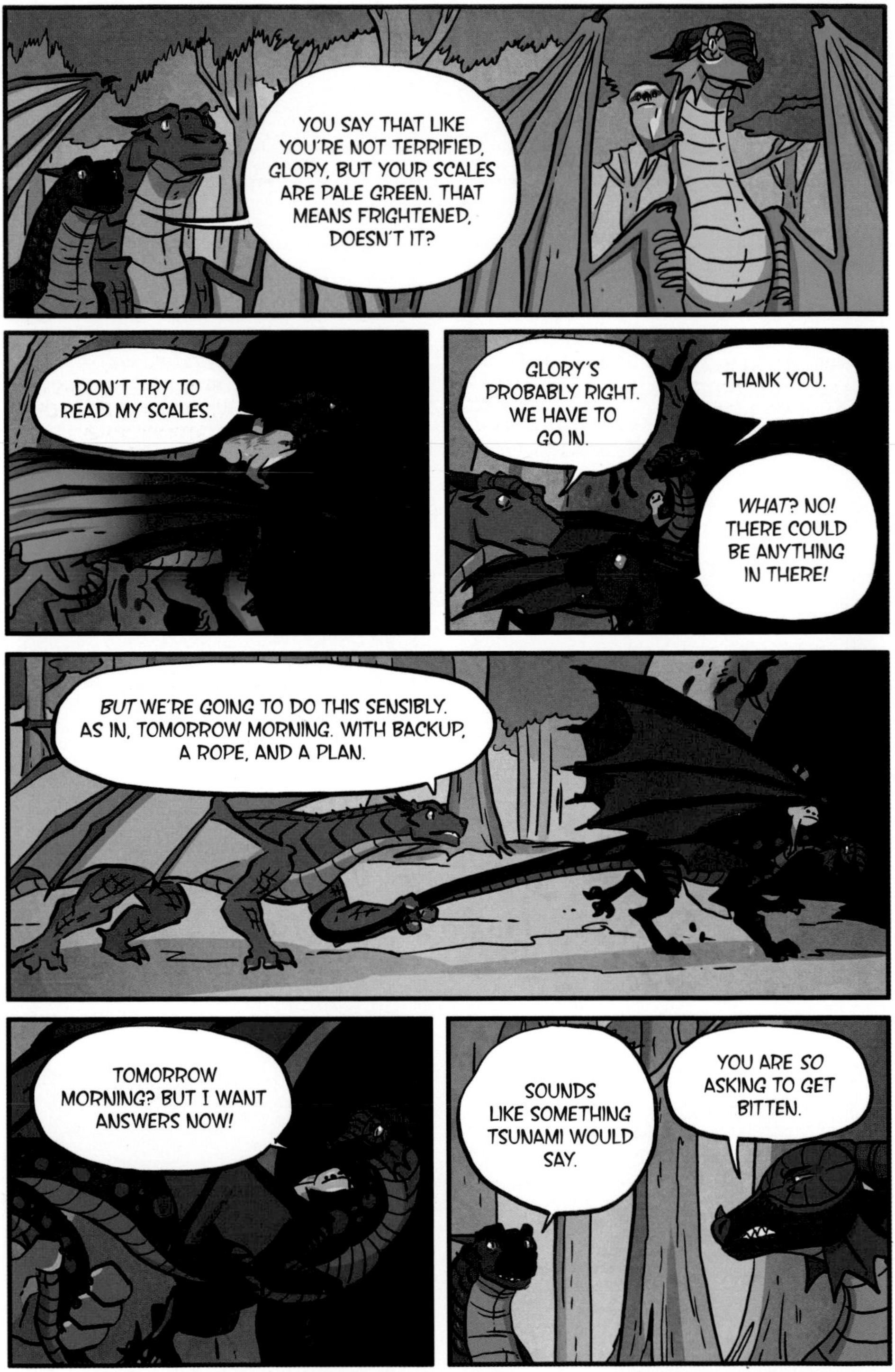
YOU SAY THAT LIKE YOU'RE NOT TERRIFIED, GLORY, BUT YOUR SCALES ARE PALE GREEN. THAT MEANS FRIGHTENED, DOESN'T IT?
DON'T TRY TO READ MY SCALES.
GLORY'S PROBABLY RIGHT. WE HAVE TO GO IN.
THANK YOU.
WHAT? NO! THERE COULD BE ANYTHING IN THERE!
BUT WE'RE GOING TO DO THIS SENSIBLY. AS IN, TOMORROW MORNING. WITH BACKUP, A ROPE, AND A PLAN.
TOMORROW MORNING? BUT I WANT ANSWERS NOW!
SOUNDS LIKE SOMETHING TSUNAMI WOULD SAY.
YOU ARE *SO* ASKING TO GET BITTEN.

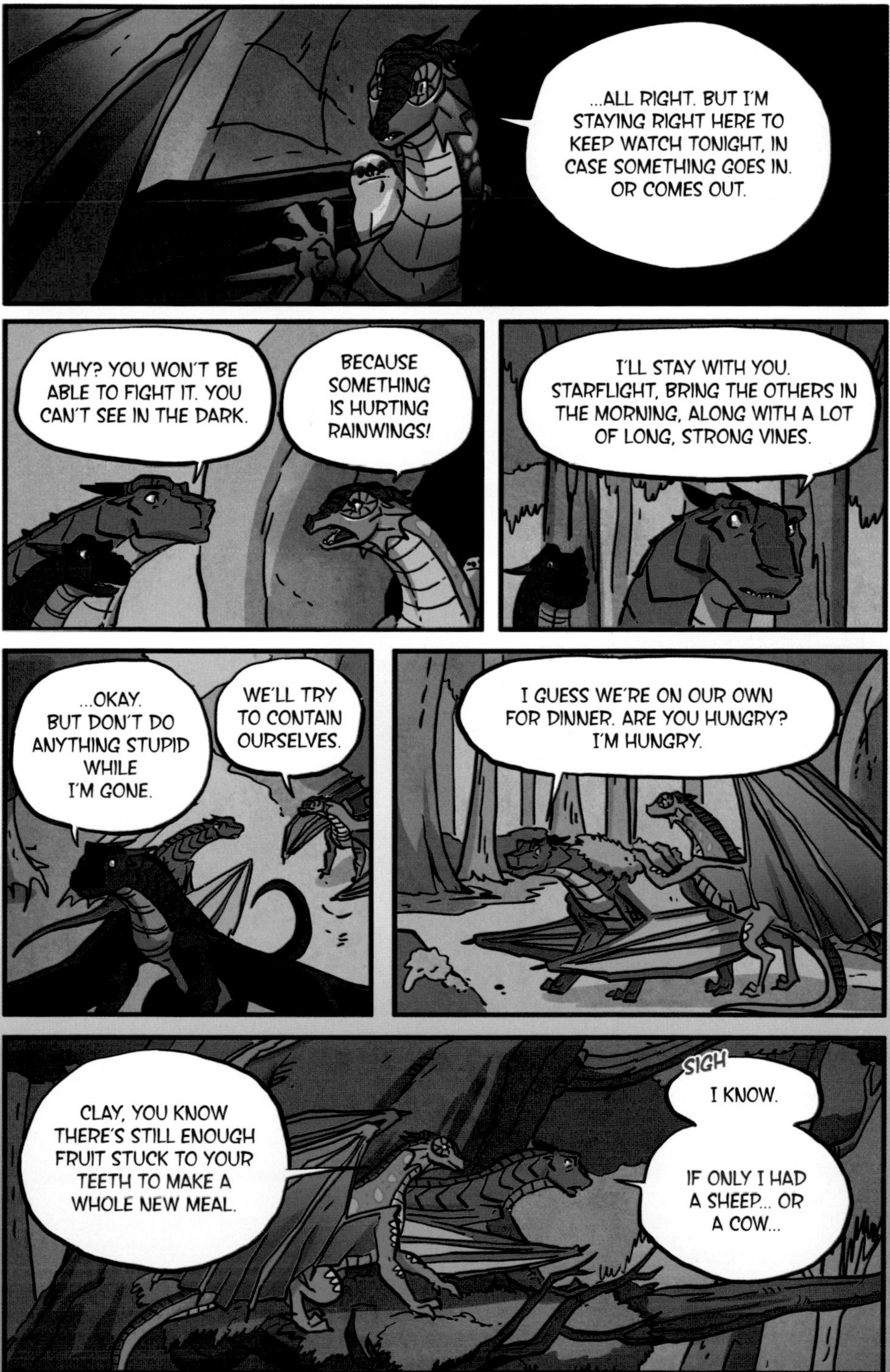
...ALL RIGHT. BUT I'M STAYING RIGHT HERE TO KEEP WATCH TONIGHT, IN CASE SOMETHING GOES IN. OR COMES OUT.
WHY? YOU WON'T BE ABLE TO FIGHT IT. YOU CAN'T SEE IN THE DARK.
BECAUSE SOMETHING IS HURTING RAINWINGS!
I'LL STAY WITH YOU. STARFLIGHT, BRING THE OTHERS IN THE MORNING, ALONG WITH A LOT OF LONG, STRONG VINES.
...OKAY. BUT DON'T DO ANYTHING STUPID WHILE I'M GONE.
WE'LL TRY TO CONTAIN OURSELVES.
I GUESS WE'RE ON OUR OWN FOR DINNER. ARE YOU HUNGRY? I'M HUNGRY.
CLAY, YOU KNOW THERE'S STILL ENOUGH FRUIT STUCK TO YOUR TEETH TO MAKE A WHOLE NEW MEAL.
SIGH
I KNOW.
IF ONLY I HAD A SHEEP... OR A COW...

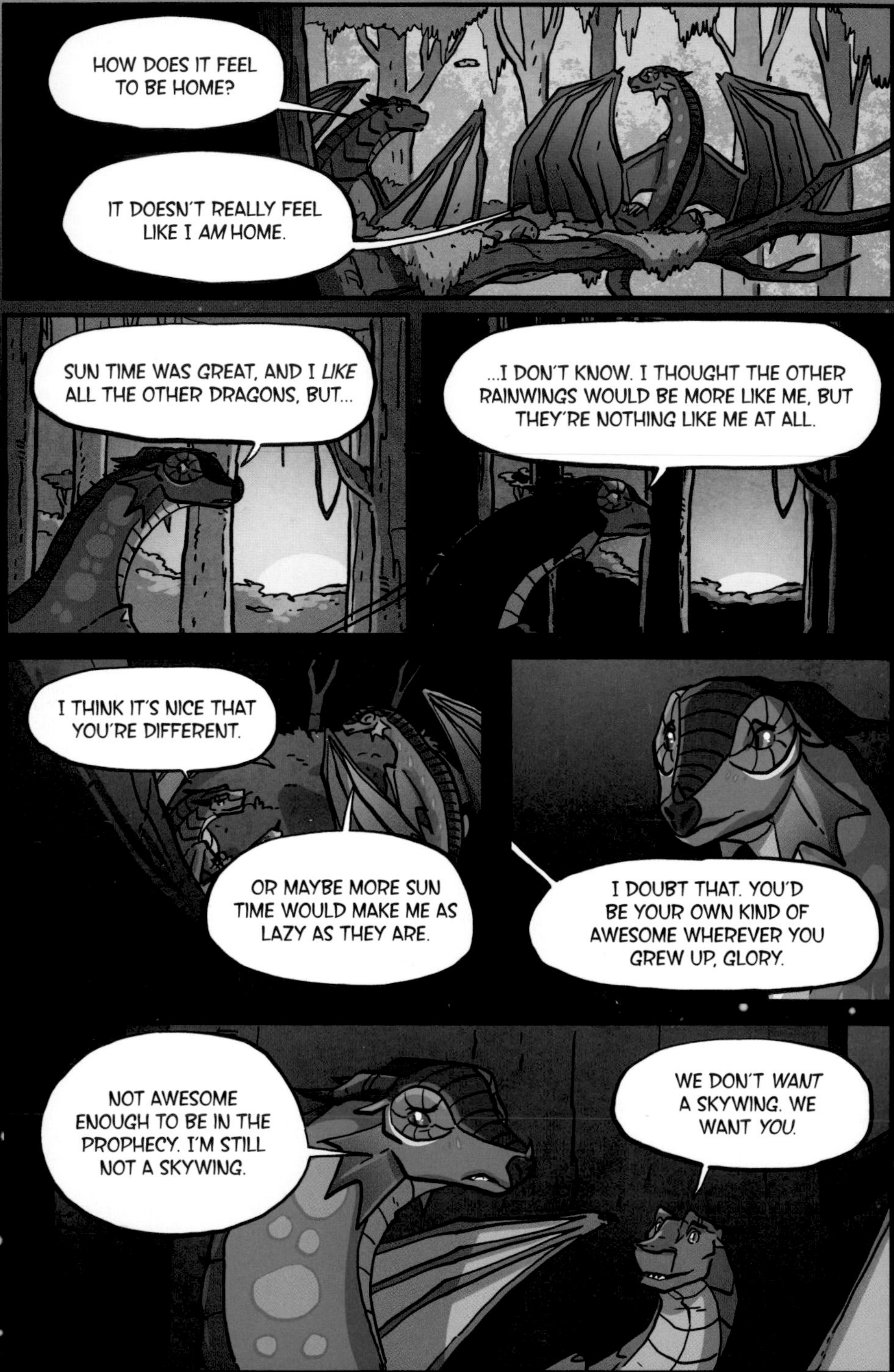
HOW DOES IT FEEL TO BE HOME?
IT DOESN'T REALLY FEEL LIKE I *AM* HOME.
SUN TIME WAS GREAT, AND I *LIKE* ALL THE OTHER DRAGONS, BUT...
...I DON'T KNOW. I THOUGHT THE OTHER RAINWINGS WOULD BE MORE LIKE ME, BUT THEY'RE NOTHING LIKE ME AT ALL.
I THINK IT'S NICE THAT YOU'RE DIFFERENT.
OR MAYBE MORE SUN TIME WOULD MAKE ME AS LAZY AS THEY ARE.
I DOUBT THAT. YOU'D BE YOUR OWN KIND OF AWESOME WHEREVER YOU GREW UP, GLORY.
NOT AWESOME ENOUGH TO BE IN THE PROPHECY. I'M STILL NOT A SKYWING.
WE DON'T *WANT* A SKYWING. WE WANT *YOU*.

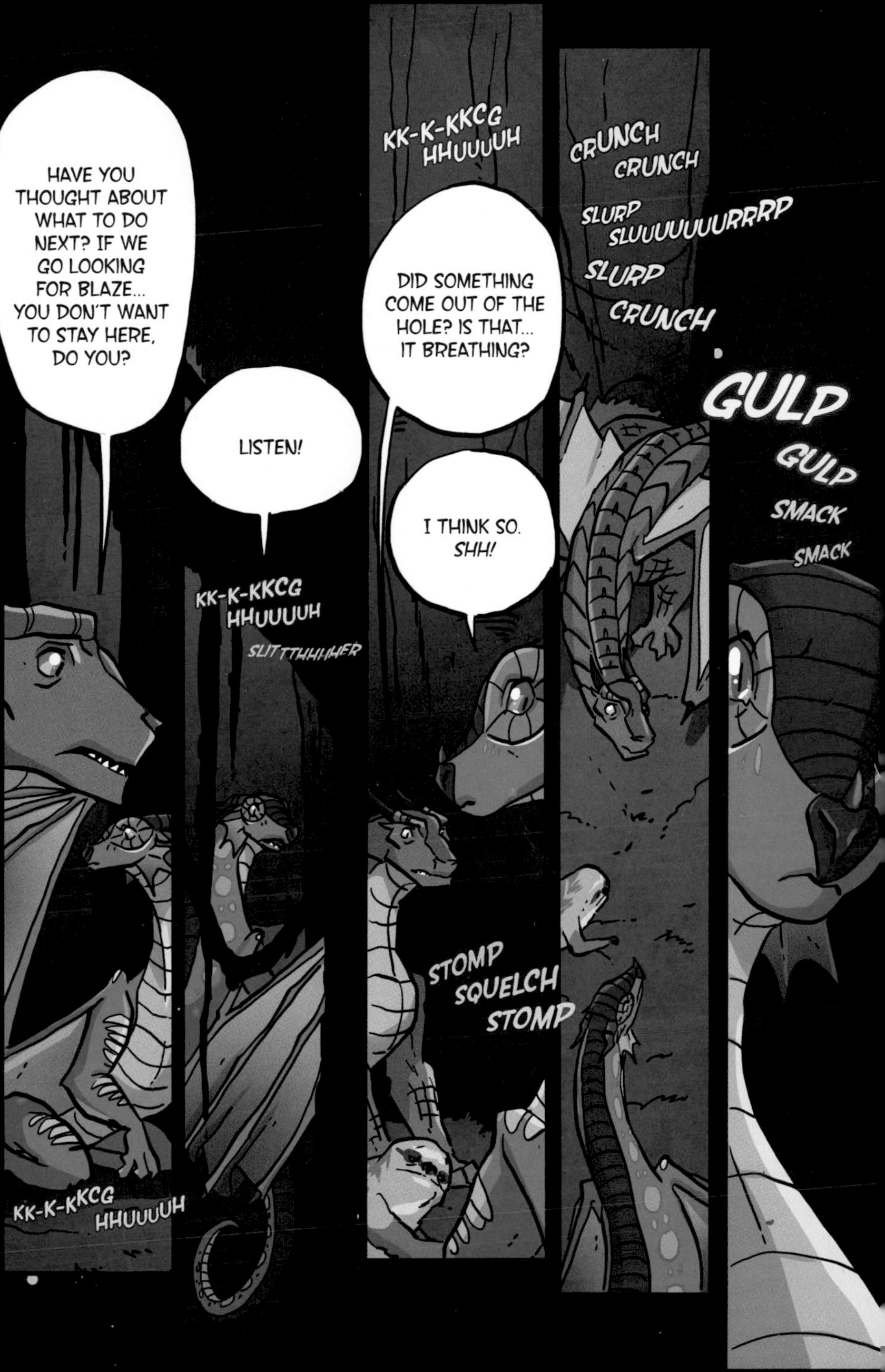
HAVE YOU THOUGHT ABOUT WHAT TO DO NEXT? IF WE GO LOOKING FOR BLAZE... YOU DON'T WANT TO STAY HERE, DO YOU?
KK-K-KKCG HHUUUUH
LISTEN!
KK-K-KKCG HHUUUUH
SLITTTHHHHER
KK-K-KKCG HHUUUUH
DID SOMETHING COME OUT OF THE HOLE? IS THAT... IT BREATHING?
I THINK SO. *SHH!*
STOMP
SQUELCH
STOMP
CRUNCH
CRUNCH
SLURP
SLUUUUUUURRRP
SLURP
CRUNCH
GULP
GULP
SMACK
SMACK

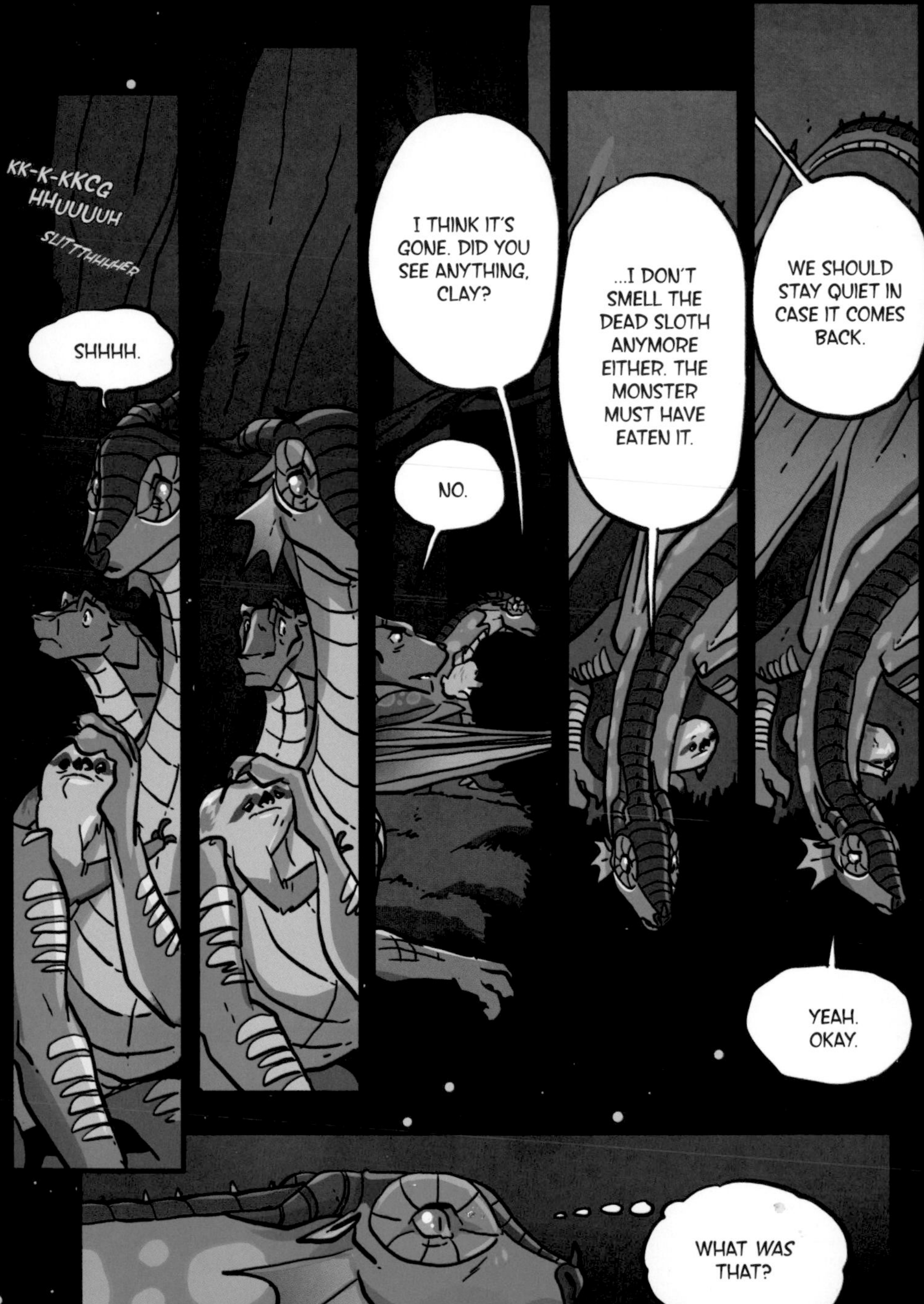
KK-K-KKCG
HHUUUUH
SLITTTHHHHER
SHHHH.
I THINK IT'S GONE. DID YOU SEE ANYTHING, CLAY?
NO.
...I DON'T SMELL THE DEAD SLOTH ANYMORE EITHER. THE MONSTER MUST HAVE EATEN IT.
WE SHOULD STAY QUIET IN CASE IT COMES BACK.
YEAH. OKAY.
WHAT *WAS* THAT?

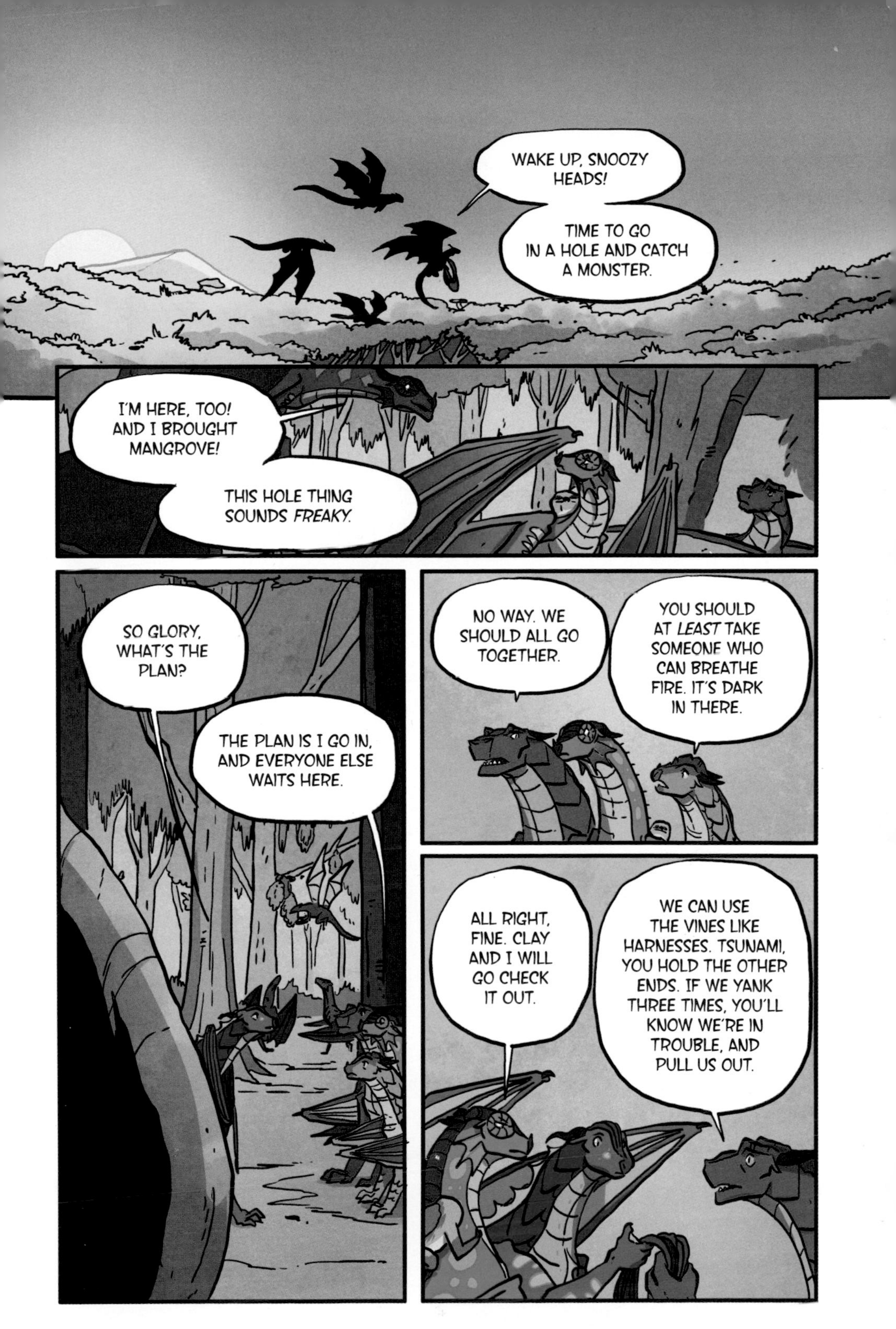
WAKE UP, SNOOZY HEADS!
TIME TO GO IN A HOLE AND CATCH A MONSTER.
I'M HERE, TOO! AND I BROUGHT MANGROVE!
THIS HOLE THING SOUNDS *FREAKY.*
SO GLORY, WHAT'S THE PLAN?
THE PLAN IS I GO IN, AND EVERYONE ELSE WAITS HERE.
NO WAY. WE SHOULD ALL GO TOGETHER.
YOU SHOULD AT *LEAST* TAKE SOMEONE WHO CAN BREATHE FIRE. IT'S DARK IN THERE.
ALL RIGHT, FINE. CLAY AND I WILL GO CHECK IT OUT.
WE CAN USE THE VINES LIKE HARNESSES. TSUNAMI, YOU HOLD THE OTHER ENDS. IF WE YANK THREE TIMES, YOU'LL KNOW WE'RE IN TROUBLE, AND PULL US OUT.

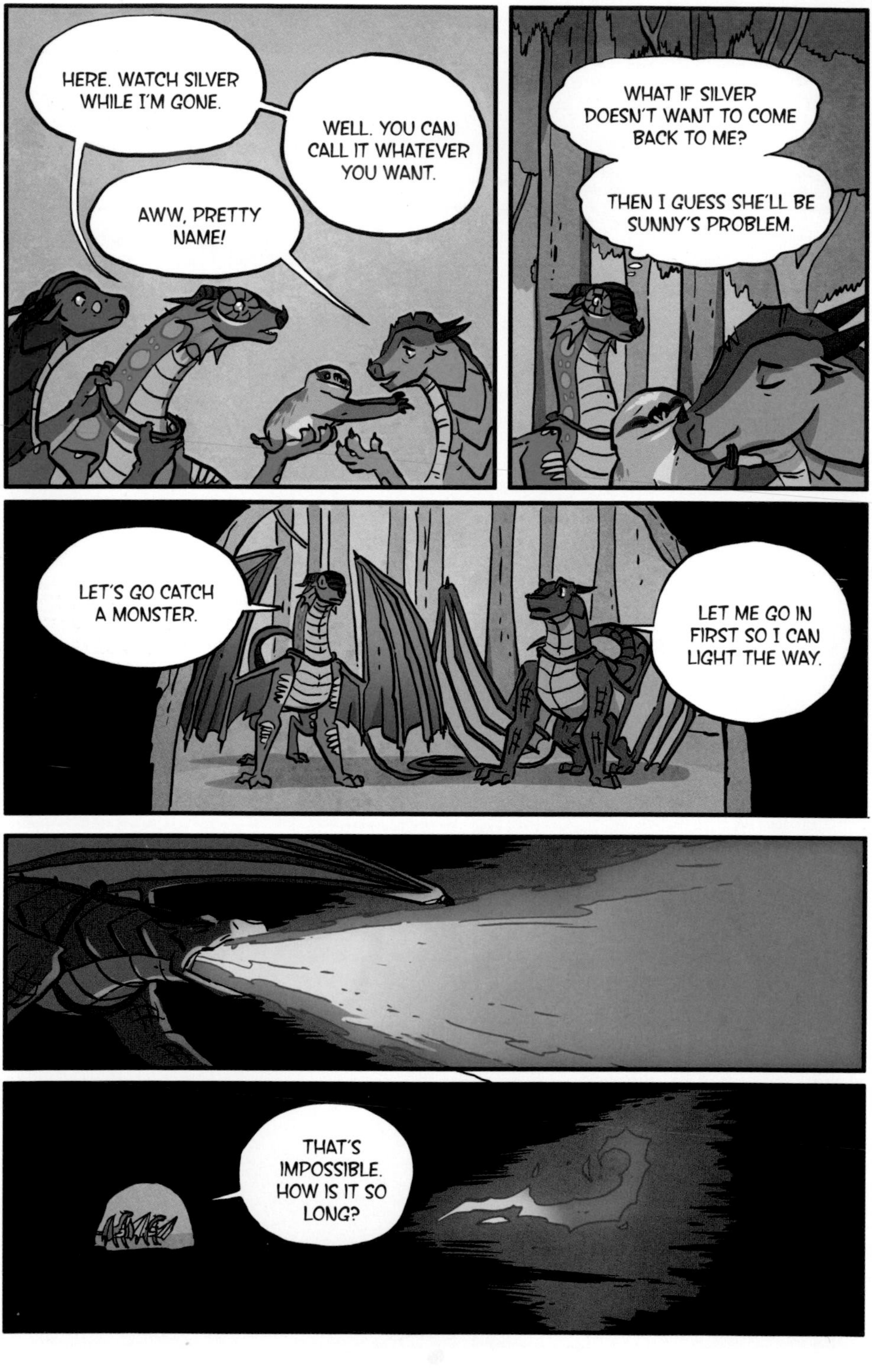
HERE. WATCH SILVER WHILE I'M GONE.
WELL. YOU CAN CALL IT WHATEVER YOU WANT.
AWW, PRETTY NAME!
WHAT IF SILVER DOESN'T WANT TO COME BACK TO ME?
THEN I GUESS SHE'LL BE SUNNY'S PROBLEM.
LET'S GO CATCH A MONSTER.
LET ME GO IN FIRST SO I CAN LIGHT THE WAY.
THAT'S IMPOSSIBLE. HOW IS IT SO LONG?

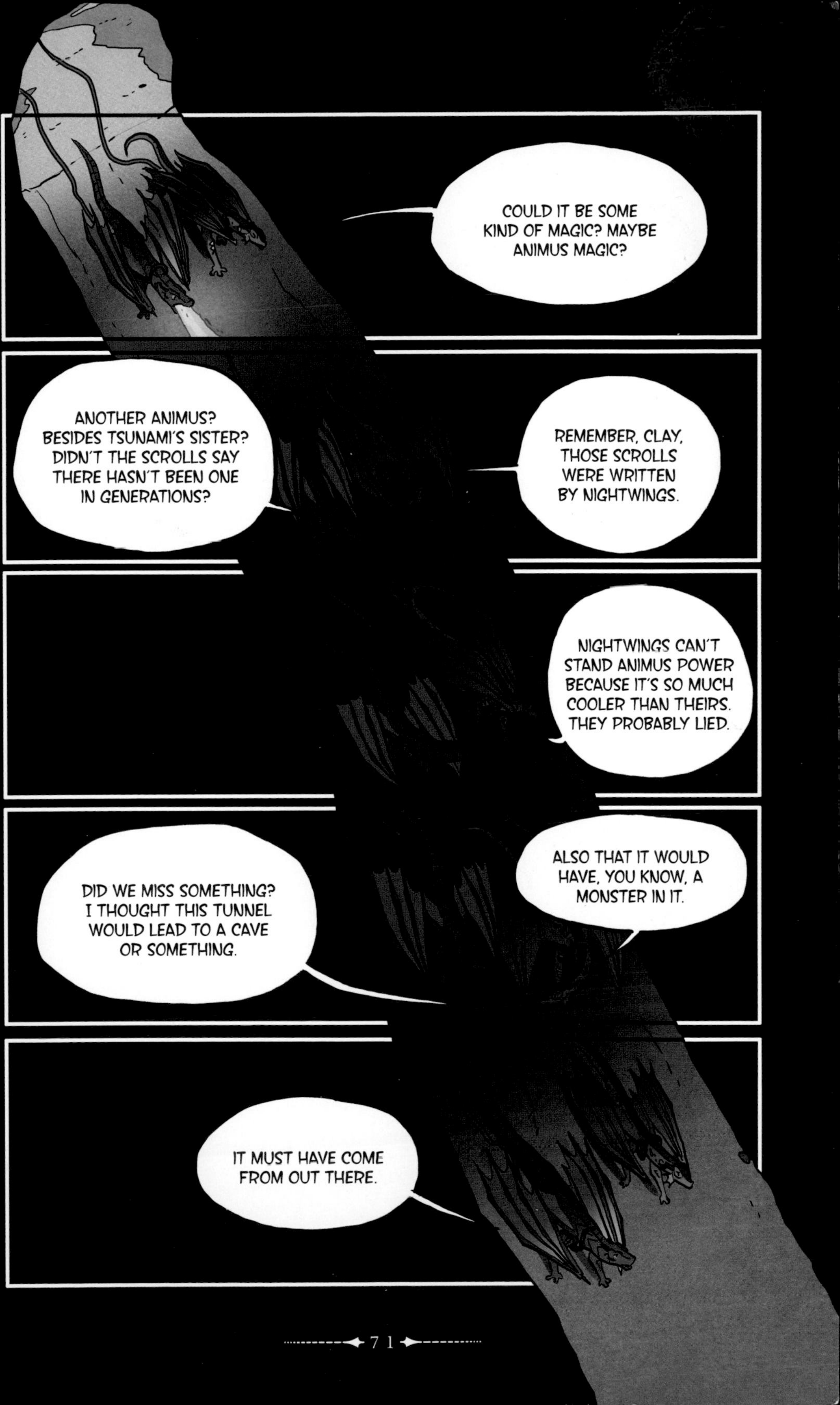
COULD IT BE SOME KIND OF MAGIC? MAYBE ANIMUS MAGIC?
ANOTHER ANIMUS? BESIDES TSUNAMI'S SISTER? DIDN'T THE SCROLLS SAY THERE HASN'T BEEN ONE IN GENERATIONS?
REMEMBER, CLAY, THOSE SCROLLS WERE WRITTEN BY NIGHTWINGS.
NIGHTWINGS CAN'T STAND ANIMUS POWER BECAUSE IT'S SO MUCH COOLER THAN THEIRS. THEY PROBABLY LIED.
DID WE MISS SOMETHING? I THOUGHT THIS TUNNEL WOULD LEAD TO A CAVE OR SOMETHING.
ALSO THAT IT WOULD HAVE, YOU KNOW, A MONSTER IN IT.
IT MUST HAVE COME FROM OUT THERE.

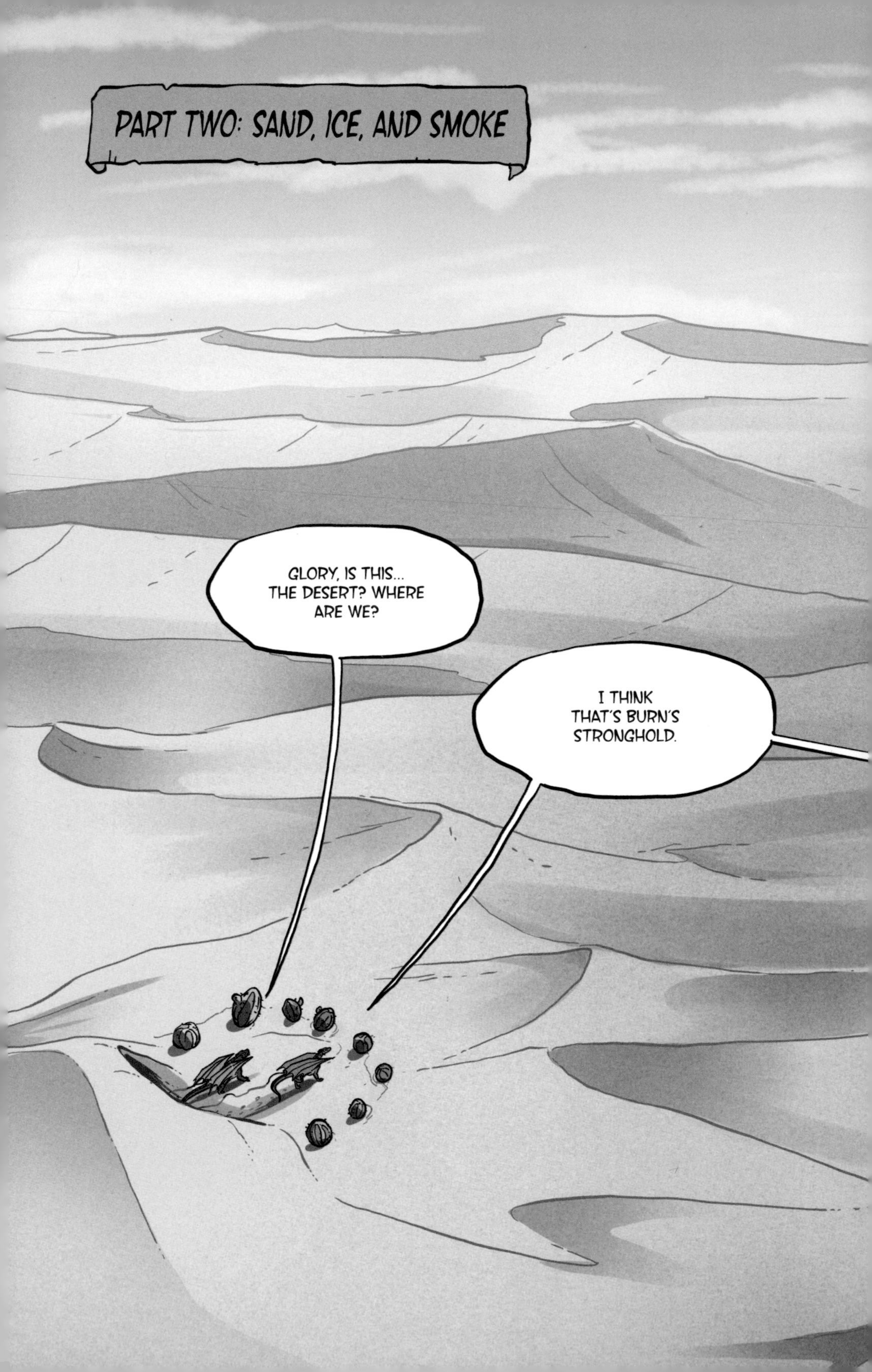
PART TWO: SAND, ICE, AND SMOKE
GLORY, IS THIS... THE DESERT? WHERE ARE WE?
I THINK THAT'S BURN'S STRONGHOLD.

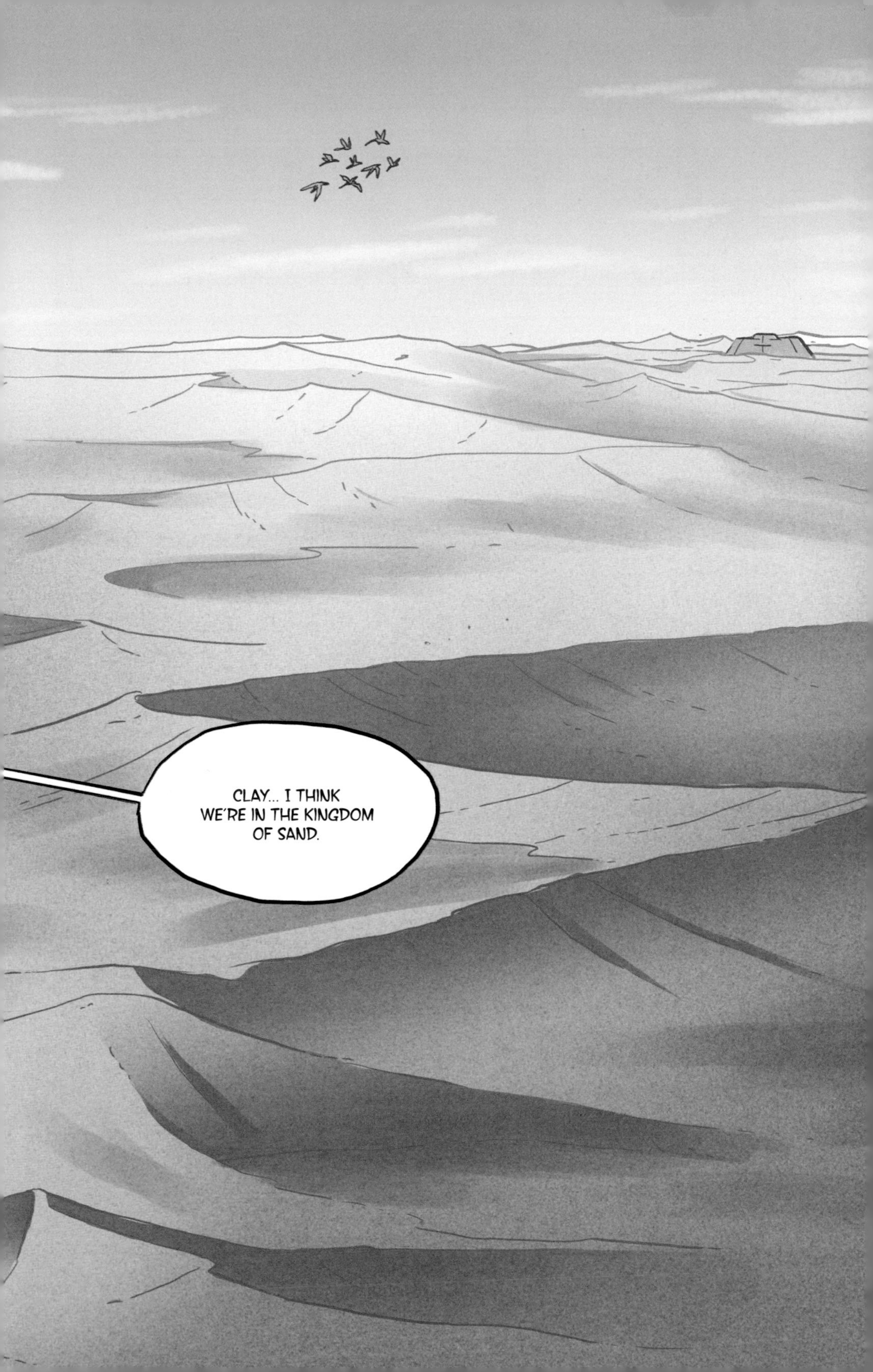
CLAY... I THINK WE'RE IN THE KINGDOM OF SAND.

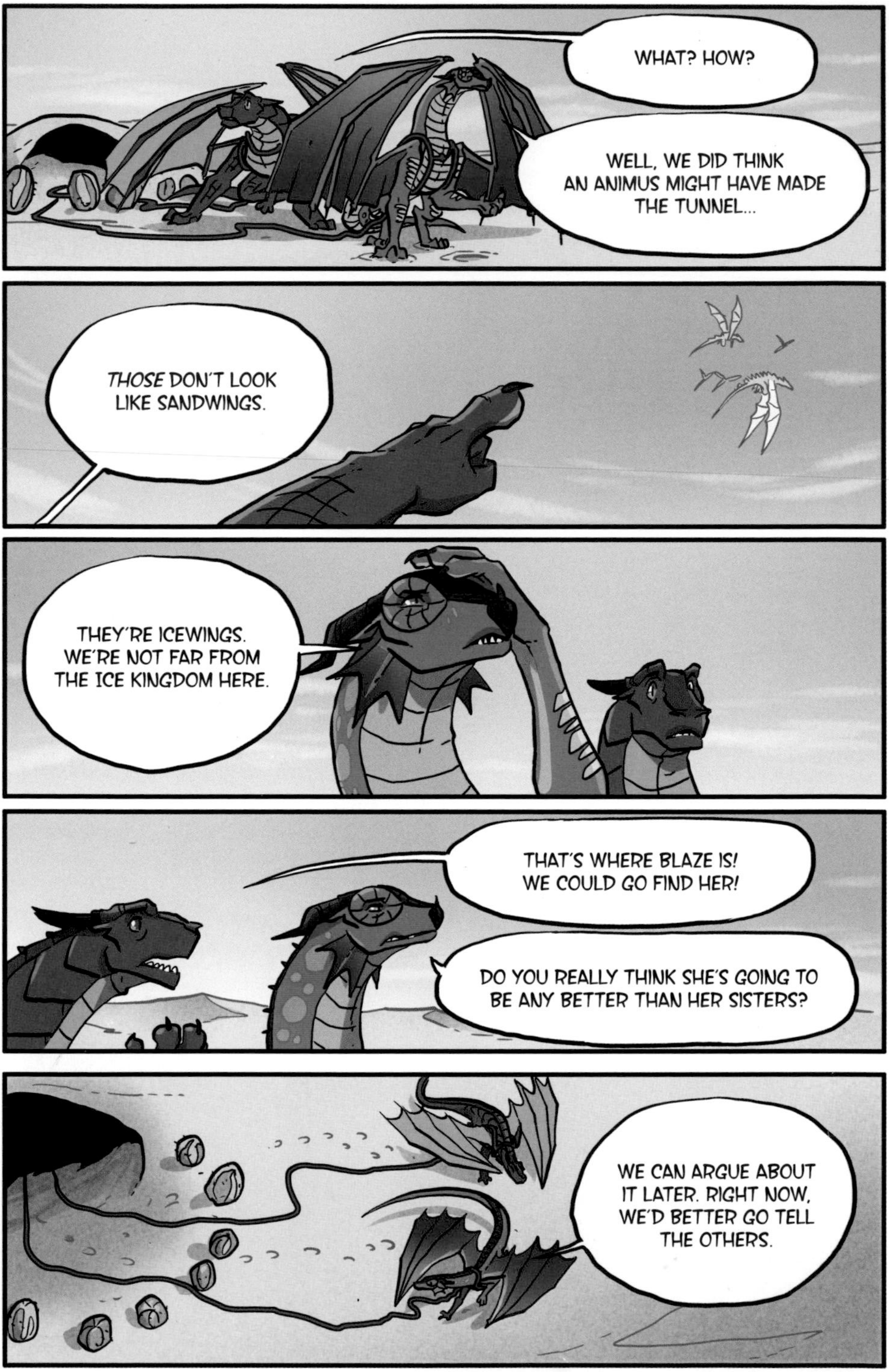
WHAT? HOW?
WELL, WE DID THINK AN ANIMUS MIGHT HAVE MADE THE TUNNEL...
THOSE DON'T LOOK LIKE SANDWINGS.
THEY'RE ICEWINGS. WE'RE NOT FAR FROM THE ICE KINGDOM HERE.
THAT'S WHERE BLAZE IS! WE COULD GO FIND HER!
DO YOU REALLY THINK SHE'S GOING TO BE ANY BETTER THAN HER SISTERS?
WE CAN ARGUE ABOUT IT LATER. RIGHT NOW, WE'D BETTER GO TELL THE OTHERS.

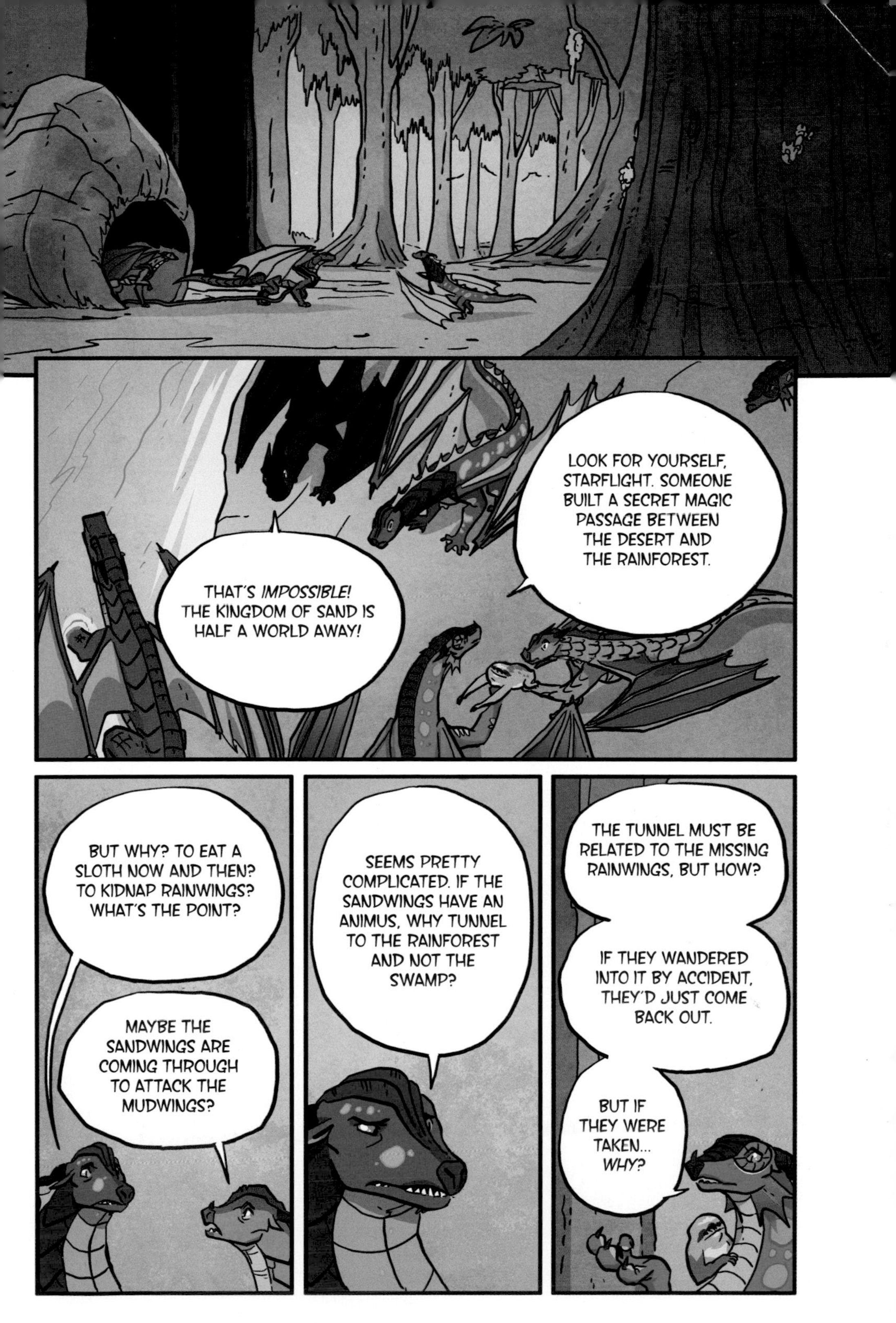
THAT'S IMPOSSIBLE! THE KINGDOM OF SAND IS HALF A WORLD AWAY!
LOOK FOR YOURSELF, STARFLIGHT. SOMEONE BUILT A SECRET MAGIC PASSAGE BETWEEN THE DESERT AND THE RAINFOREST.
BUT WHY? TO EAT A SLOTH NOW AND THEN? TO KIDNAP RAINWINGS? WHAT'S THE POINT?
MAYBE THE SANDWINGS ARE COMING THROUGH TO ATTACK THE MUDWINGS?
SEEMS PRETTY COMPLICATED. IF THE SANDWINGS HAVE AN ANIMUS, WHY TUNNEL TO THE RAINFOREST AND NOT THE SWAMP?
THE TUNNEL MUST BE RELATED TO THE MISSING RAINWINGS, BUT HOW?
IF THEY WANDERED INTO IT BY ACCIDENT, THEY'D JUST COME BACK OUT.
BUT IF THEY WERE TAKEN... WHY?

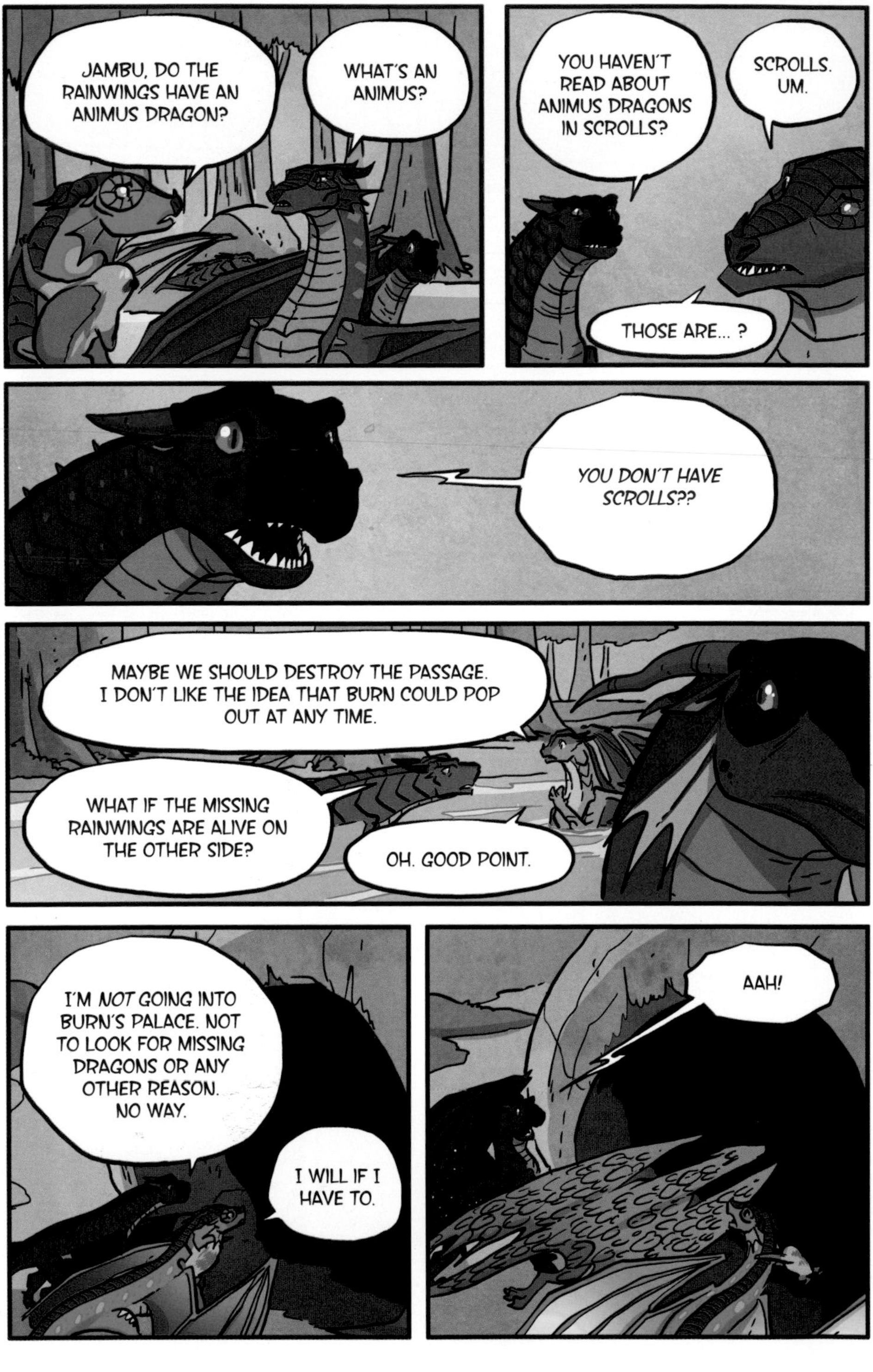
JAMBU, DO THE RAINWINGS HAVE AN ANIMUS DRAGON?
WHAT'S AN ANIMUS?
YOU HAVEN'T READ ABOUT ANIMUS DRAGONS IN SCROLLS?
SCROLLS. UM.
THOSE ARE... ?
YOU DON'T HAVE SCROLLS??
MAYBE WE SHOULD DESTROY THE PASSAGE. I DON'T LIKE THE IDEA THAT BURN COULD POP OUT AT ANY TIME.
WHAT IF THE MISSING RAINWINGS ARE ALIVE ON THE OTHER SIDE?
OH. GOOD POINT.
I'M *NOT* GOING INTO BURN'S PALACE. NOT TO LOOK FOR MISSING DRAGONS OR ANY OTHER REASON. NO WAY.
I WILL IF I HAVE TO.
AAH!

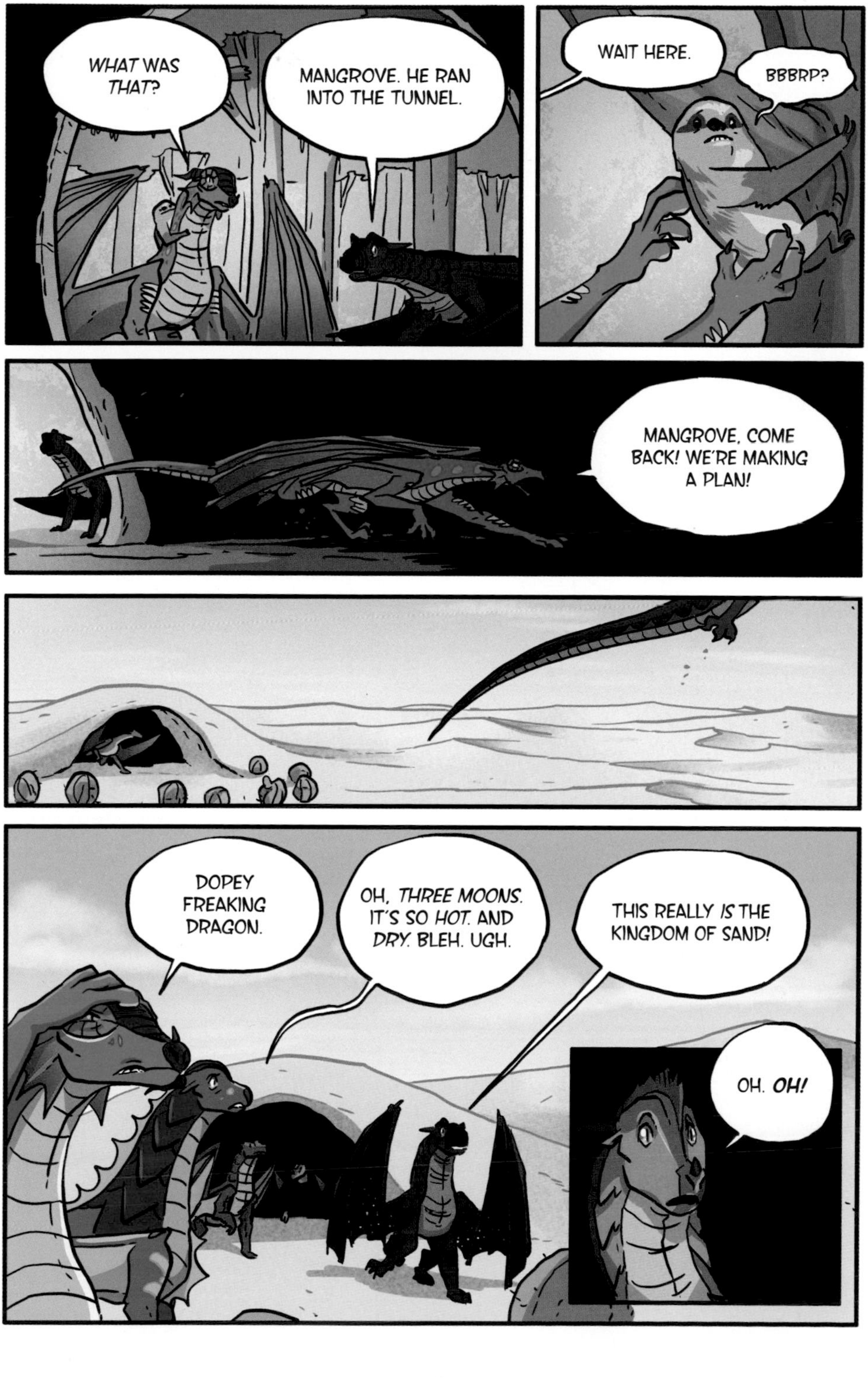
WHAT WAS THAT?
MANGROVE. HE RAN INTO THE TUNNEL.
WAIT HERE.
BBBRP?
MANGROVE, COME BACK! WE'RE MAKING A PLAN!
DOPEY FREAKING DRAGON.
OH, *THREE MOONS*. IT'S SO *HOT*. AND *DRY*. BLEH. UGH.
THIS REALLY *IS* THE KINGDOM OF SAND!
OH. ***OH!***

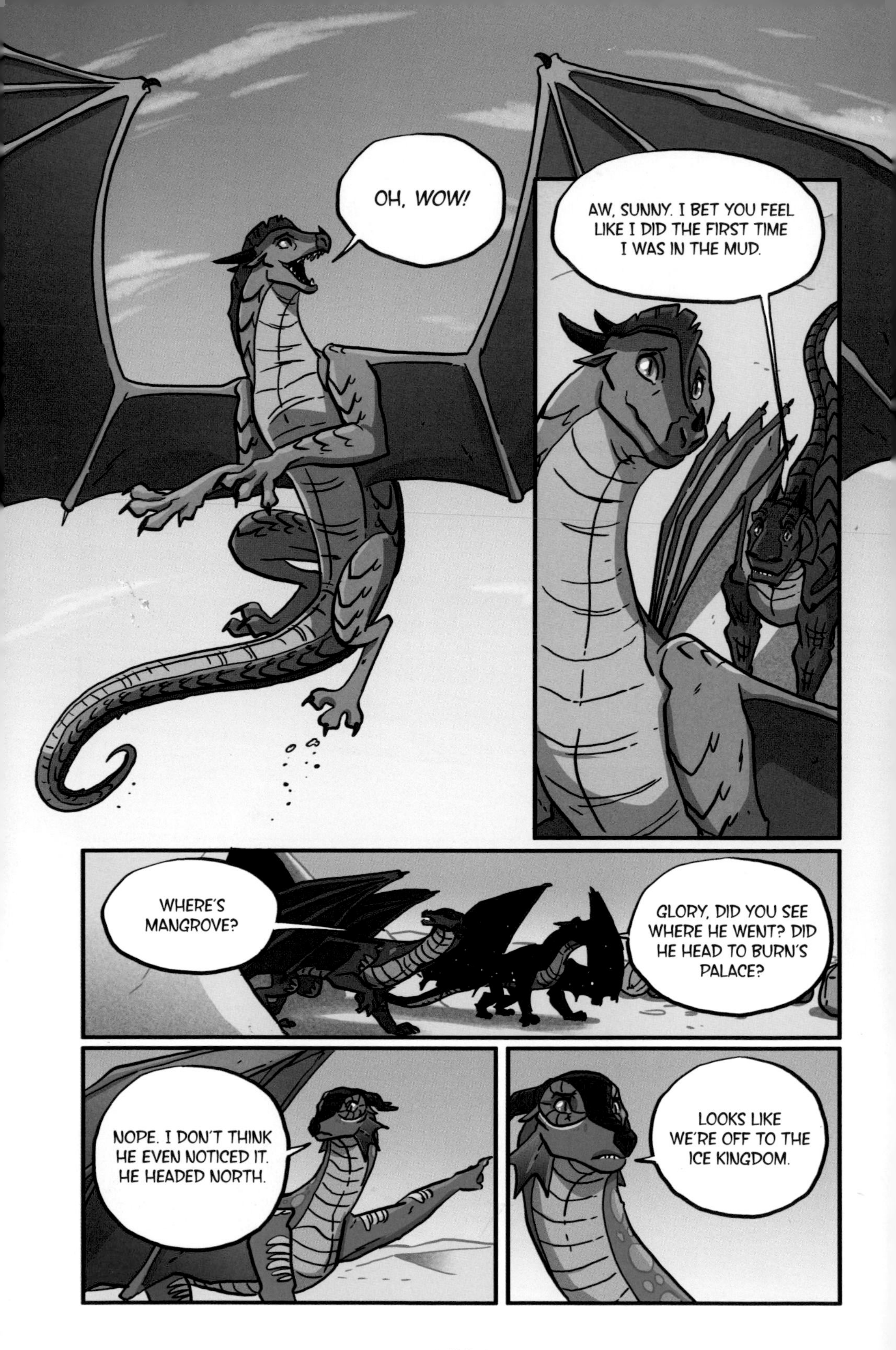
OH, WOW!
AW, SUNNY. I BET YOU FEEL LIKE I DID THE FIRST TIME I WAS IN THE MUD.
WHERE'S MANGROVE?
GLORY, DID YOU SEE WHERE HE WENT? DID HE HEAD TO BURN'S PALACE?
NOPE. I DON'T THINK HE EVEN NOTICED IT. HE HEADED NORTH.
LOOKS LIKE WE'RE OFF TO THE ICE KINGDOM.

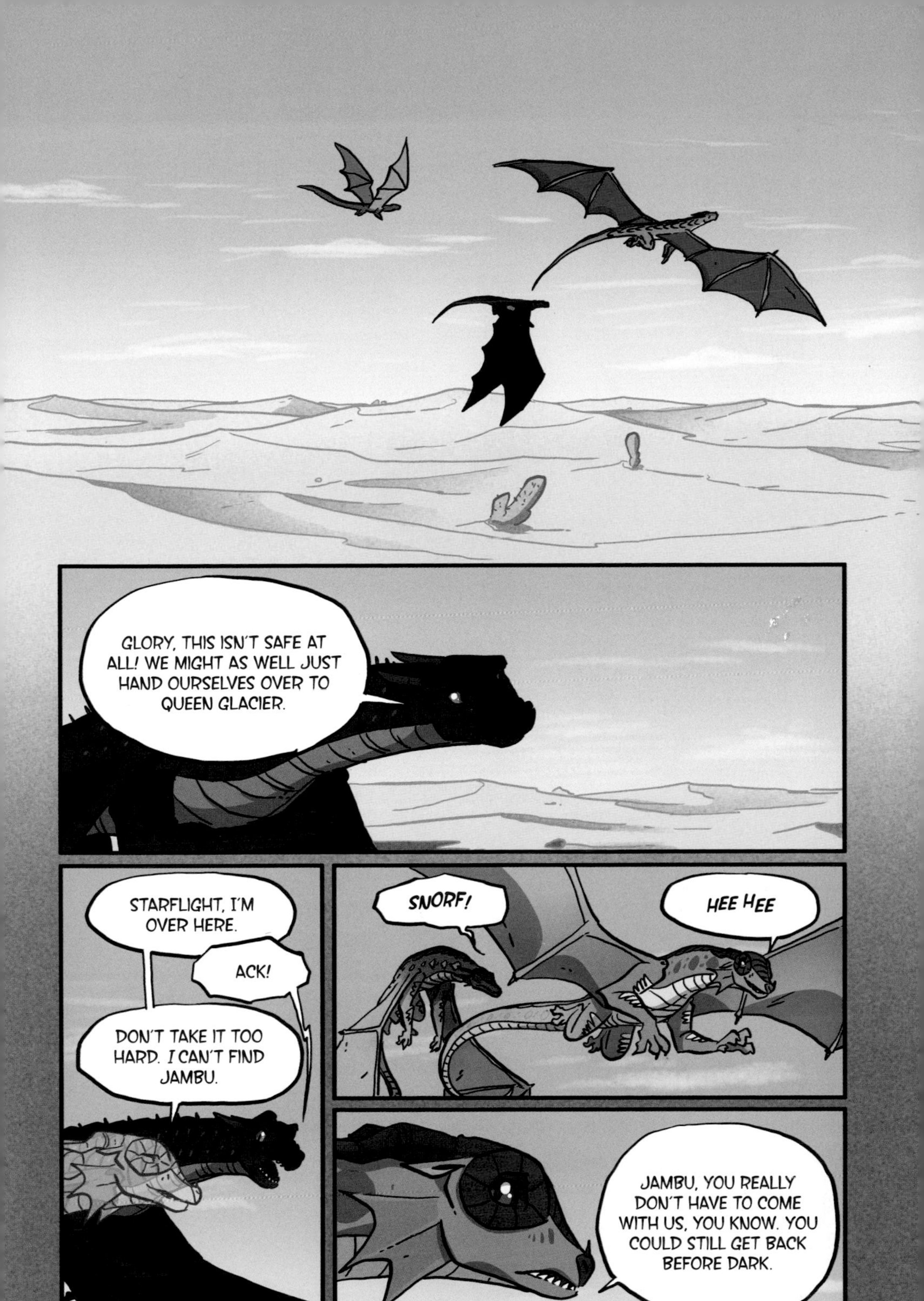
GLORY, THIS ISN'T SAFE AT ALL! WE MIGHT AS WELL JUST HAND OURSELVES OVER TO QUEEN GLACIER.
STARFLIGHT, I'M OVER HERE.
ACK!
DON'T TAKE IT TOO HARD. I CAN'T FIND JAMBU.
SNORF!
HEE HEE
JAMBU, YOU REALLY DON'T HAVE TO COME WITH US, YOU KNOW. YOU COULD STILL GET BACK BEFORE DARK.

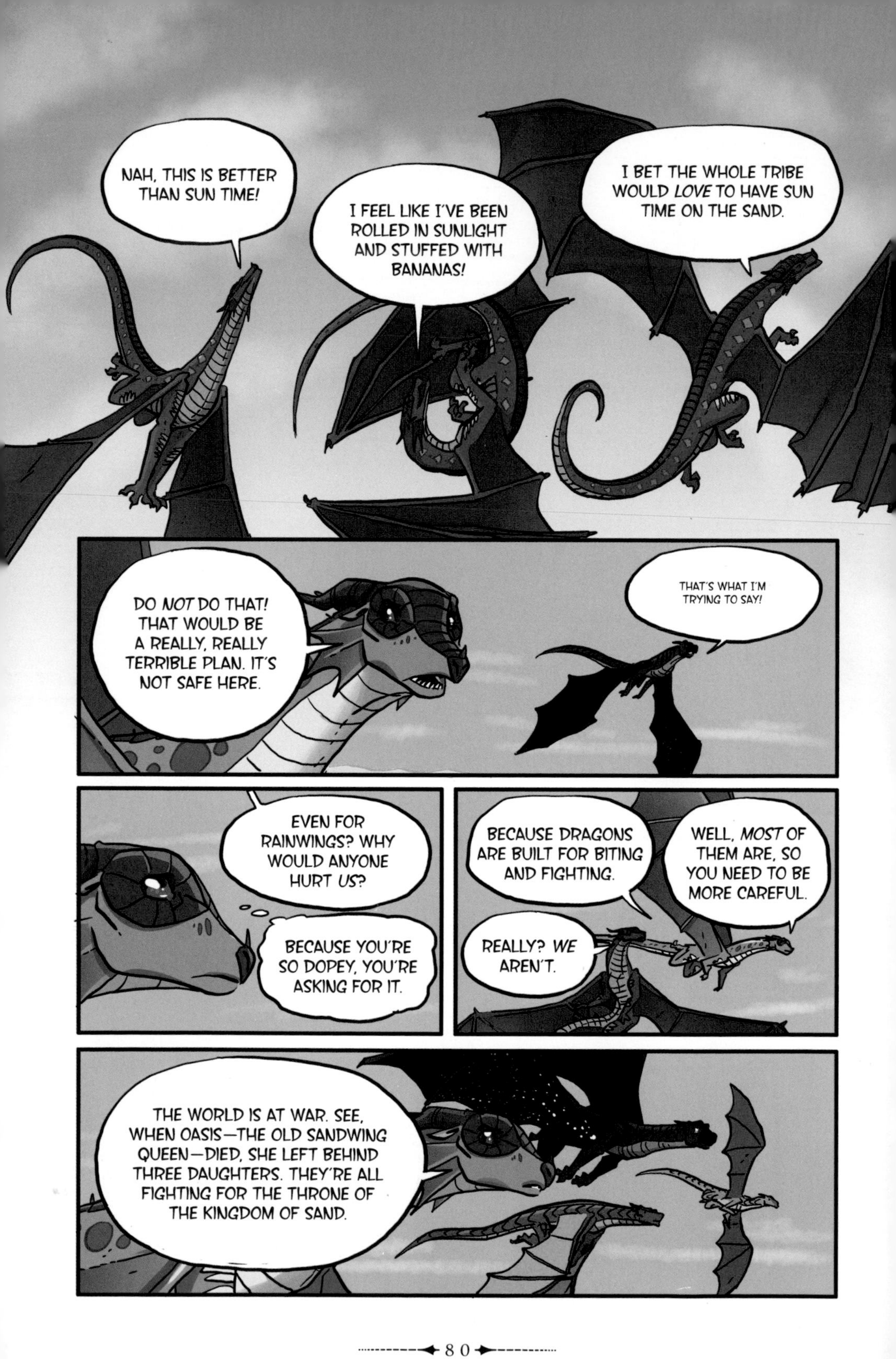
NAH, THIS IS BETTER THAN SUN TIME!
I FEEL LIKE I'VE BEEN ROLLED IN SUNLIGHT AND STUFFED WITH BANANAS!
I BET THE WHOLE TRIBE WOULD *LOVE* TO HAVE SUN TIME ON THE SAND.
DO *NOT* DO THAT! THAT WOULD BE A REALLY, REALLY TERRIBLE PLAN. IT'S NOT SAFE HERE.
THAT'S WHAT I'M TRYING TO SAY!
EVEN FOR RAINWINGS? WHY WOULD ANYONE HURT *US*?
BECAUSE YOU'RE SO DOPEY, YOU'RE ASKING FOR IT.
BECAUSE DRAGONS ARE BUILT FOR BITING AND FIGHTING.
WELL, *MOST* OF THEM ARE, SO YOU NEED TO BE MORE CAREFUL.
REALLY? *WE* AREN'T.
THE WORLD IS AT WAR. SEE, WHEN OASIS—THE OLD SANDWING QUEEN—DIED, SHE LEFT BEHIND THREE DAUGHTERS. THEY'RE ALL FIGHTING FOR THE THRONE OF THE KINGDOM OF SAND.

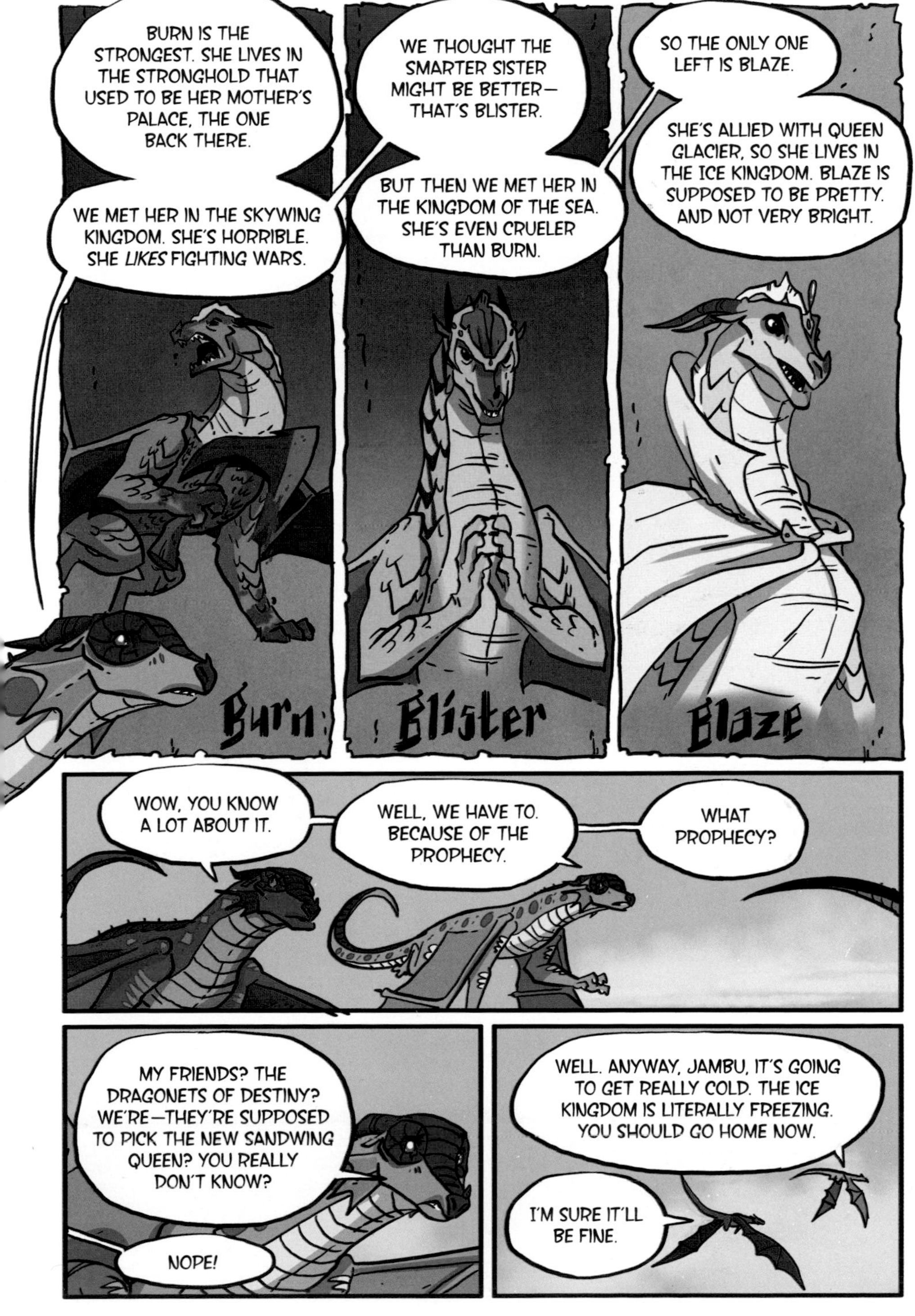
BURN IS THE STRONGEST. SHE LIVES IN THE STRONGHOLD THAT USED TO BE HER MOTHER'S PALACE, THE ONE BACK THERE.
WE MET HER IN THE SKYWING KINGDOM. SHE'S HORRIBLE. SHE *LIKES* FIGHTING WARS.
Burn
WE THOUGHT THE SMARTER SISTER MIGHT BE BETTER— THAT'S BLISTER.
BUT THEN WE MET HER IN THE KINGDOM OF THE SEA. SHE'S EVEN CRUELER THAN BURN.
Blister
SO THE ONLY ONE LEFT IS BLAZE.
SHE'S ALLIED WITH QUEEN GLACIER, SO SHE LIVES IN THE ICE KINGDOM. BLAZE IS SUPPOSED TO BE PRETTY. AND NOT VERY BRIGHT.
Blaze
WOW, YOU KNOW A LOT ABOUT IT.
WELL, WE HAVE TO. BECAUSE OF THE PROPHECY.
WHAT PROPHECY?
MY FRIENDS? THE DRAGONETS OF DESTINY? WE'RE—THEY'RE SUPPOSED TO PICK THE NEW SANDWING QUEEN? YOU REALLY DON'T KNOW?
NOPE!
WELL. ANYWAY, JAMBU, IT'S GOING TO GET REALLY COLD. THE ICE KINGDOM IS LITERALLY FREEZING. YOU SHOULD GO HOME NOW.
I'M SURE IT'LL BE FINE.

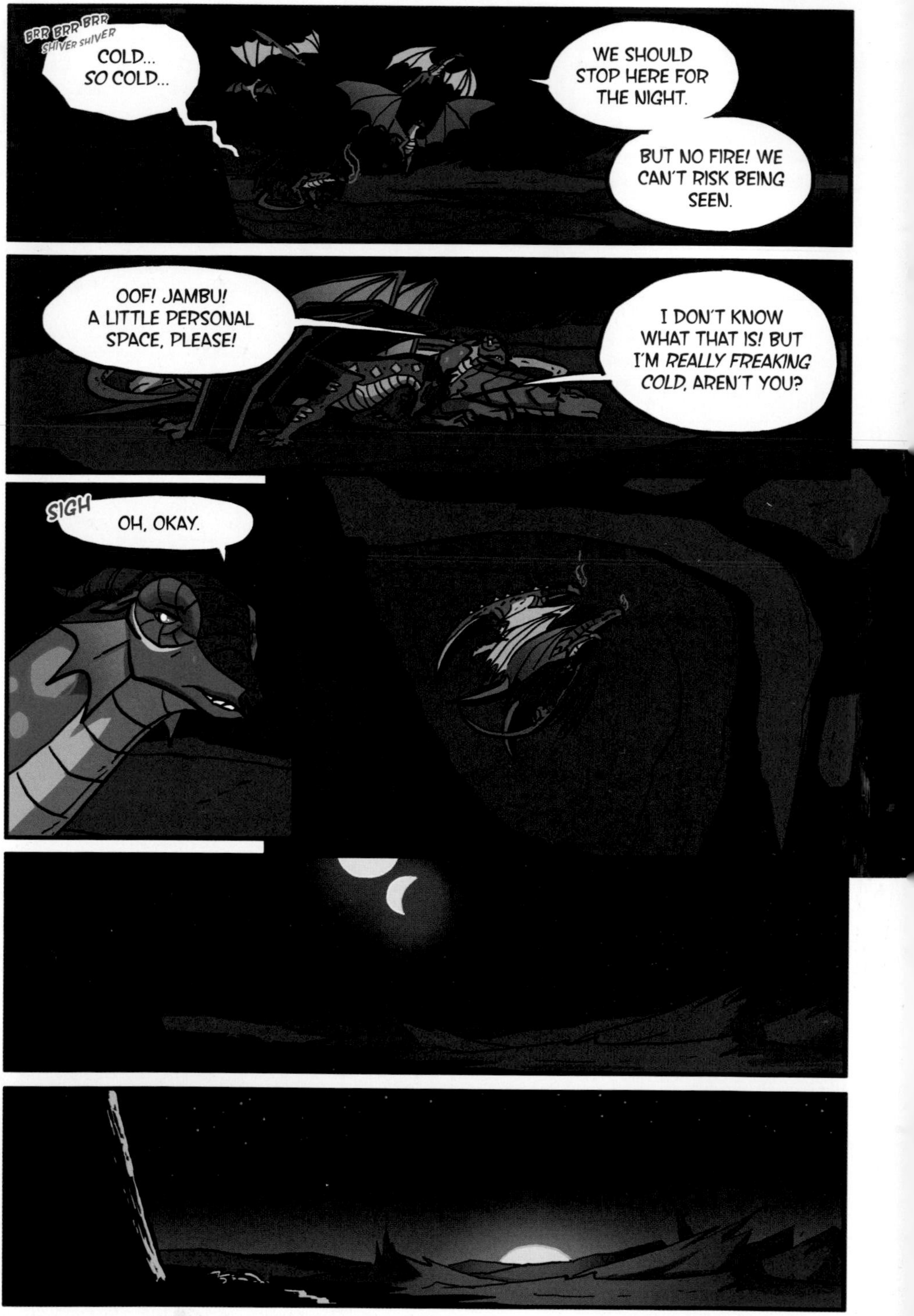
BRR BRR BRR
SHIVER SHIVER
COLD... SO COLD...
WE SHOULD STOP HERE FOR THE NIGHT.
BUT NO FIRE! WE CAN'T RISK BEING SEEN.
OOF! JAMBU! A LITTLE PERSONAL SPACE, PLEASE!
I DON'T KNOW WHAT THAT IS! BUT I'M *REALLY FREAKING COLD*, AREN'T YOU?
SIGH
OH, OKAY.

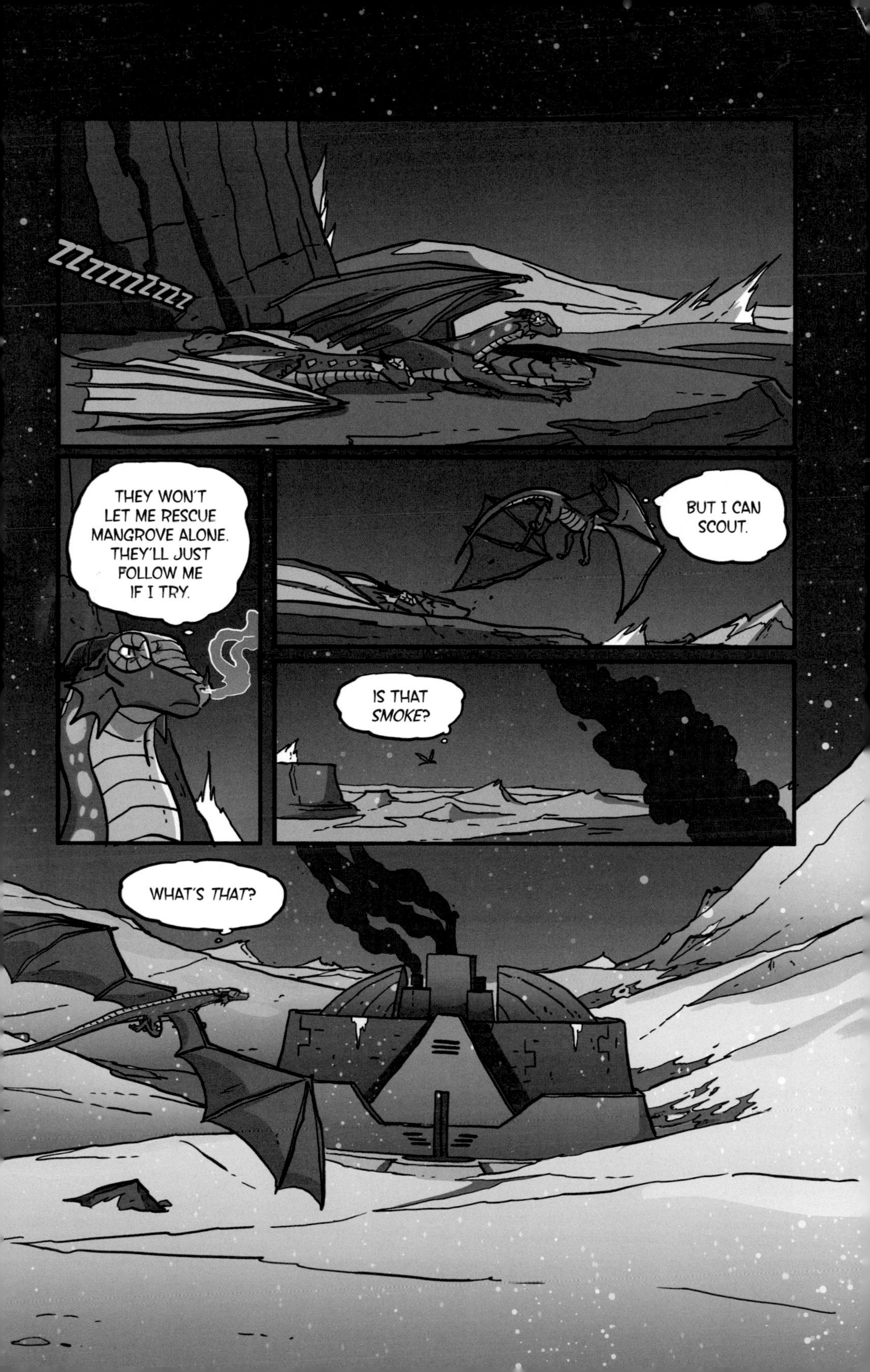
ZZZZZZZZZZ
THEY WON'T LET ME RESCUE MANGROVE ALONE. THEY'LL JUST FOLLOW ME IF I TRY.
BUT I CAN SCOUT.
IS THAT *SMOKE*?
WHAT'S *THAT*?

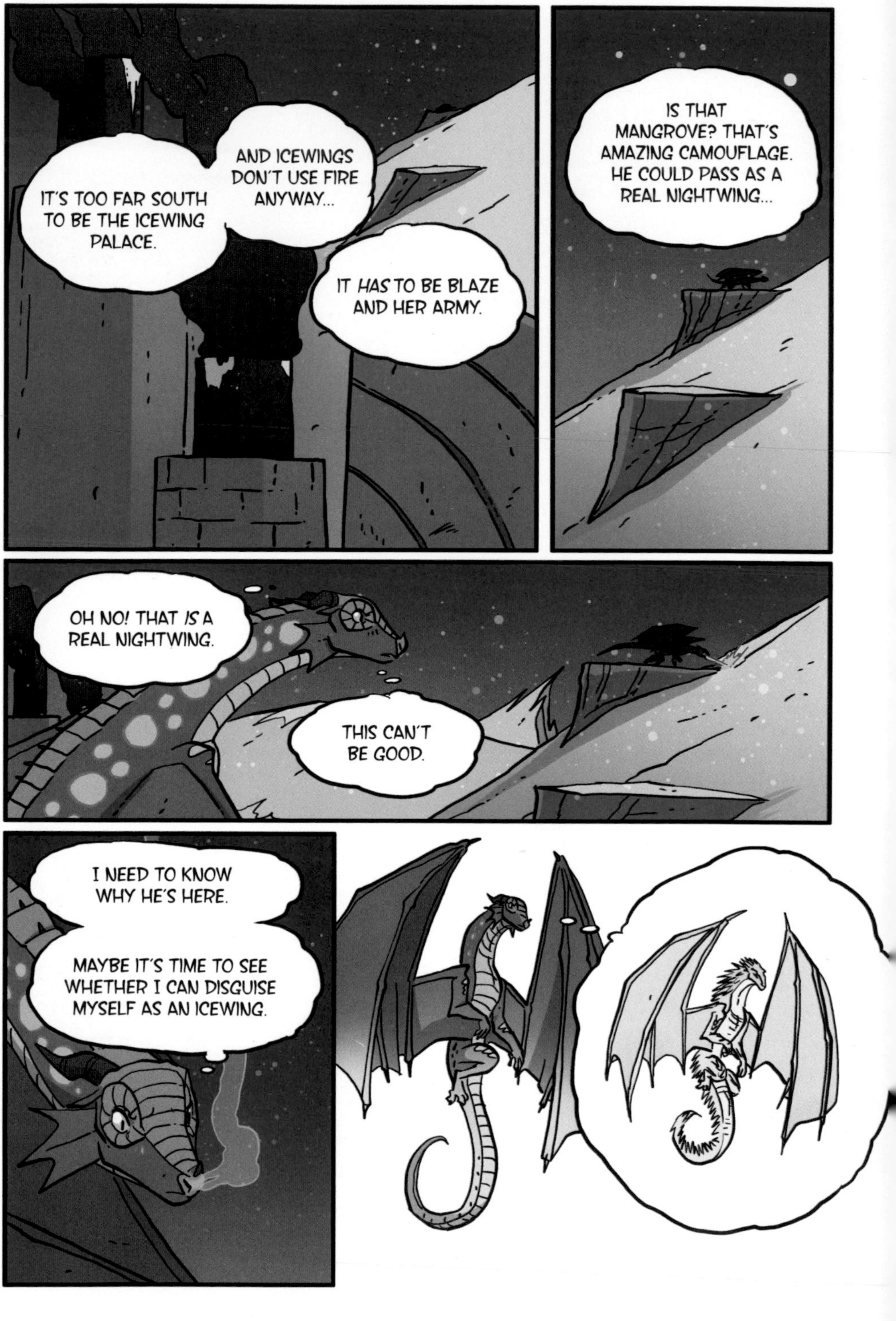
IT'S TOO FAR SOUTH TO BE THE ICEWING PALACE.
AND ICEWINGS DON'T USE FIRE ANYWAY...
IT HAS TO BE BLAZE AND HER ARMY.
IS THAT MANGROVE? THAT'S AMAZING CAMOUFLAGE. HE COULD PASS AS A REAL NIGHTWING...
OH NO! THAT IS A REAL NIGHTWING.
THIS CAN'T BE GOOD.
I NEED TO KNOW WHY HE'S HERE.
MAYBE IT'S TIME TO SEE WHETHER I CAN DISGUISE MYSELF AS AN ICEWING.

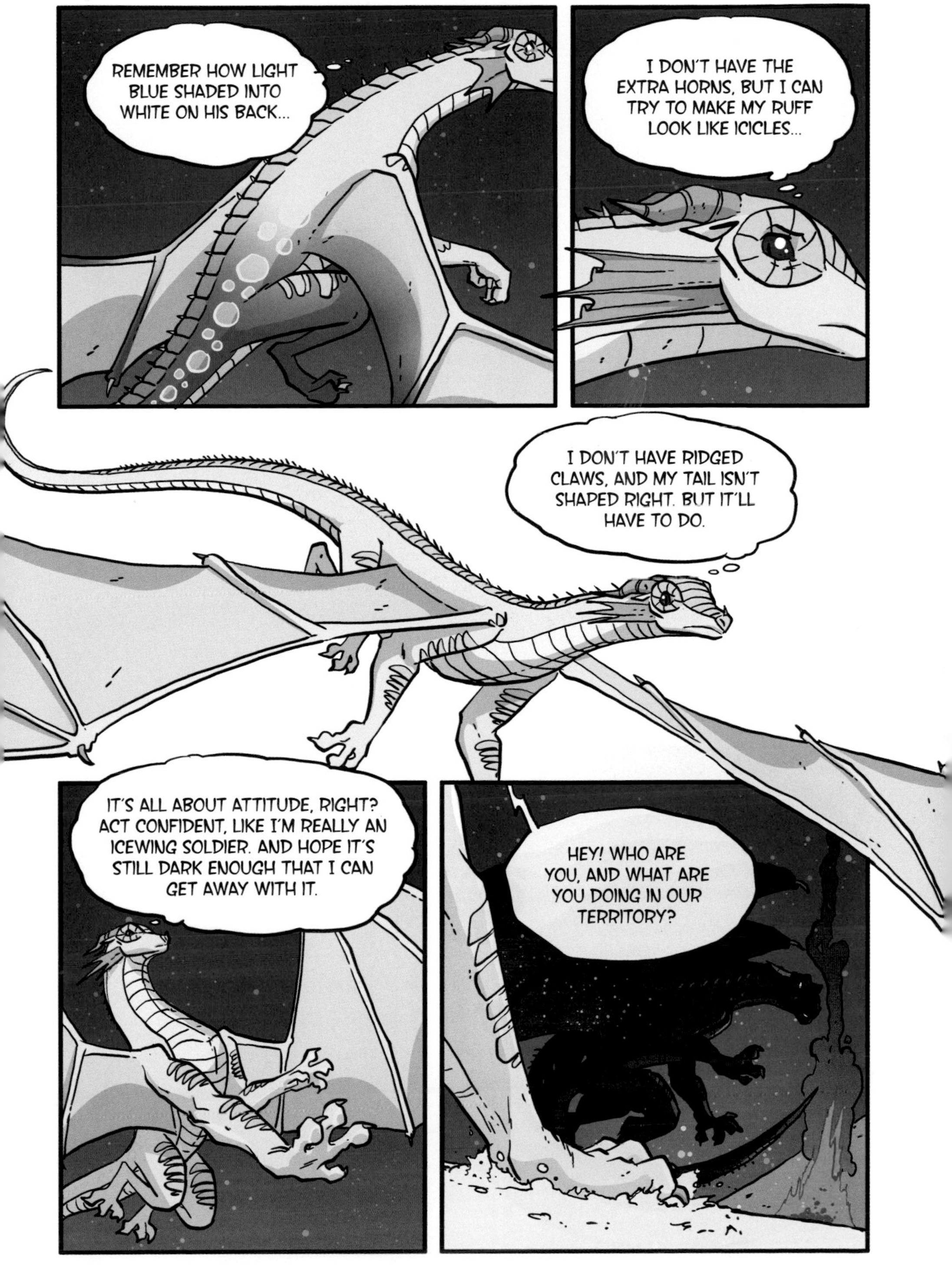
REMEMBER HOW LIGHT BLUE SHADED INTO WHITE ON HIS BACK...
I DON'T HAVE THE EXTRA HORNS, BUT I CAN TRY TO MAKE MY RUFF LOOK LIKE ICICLES...
I DON'T HAVE RIDGED CLAWS, AND MY TAIL ISN'T SHAPED RIGHT. BUT IT'LL HAVE TO DO.
IT'S ALL ABOUT ATTITUDE, RIGHT? ACT CONFIDENT, LIKE I'M REALLY AN ICEWING SOLDIER. AND HOPE IT'S STILL DARK ENOUGH THAT I CAN GET AWAY WITH IT.
HEY! WHO ARE YOU, AND WHAT ARE YOU DOING IN OUR TERRITORY?

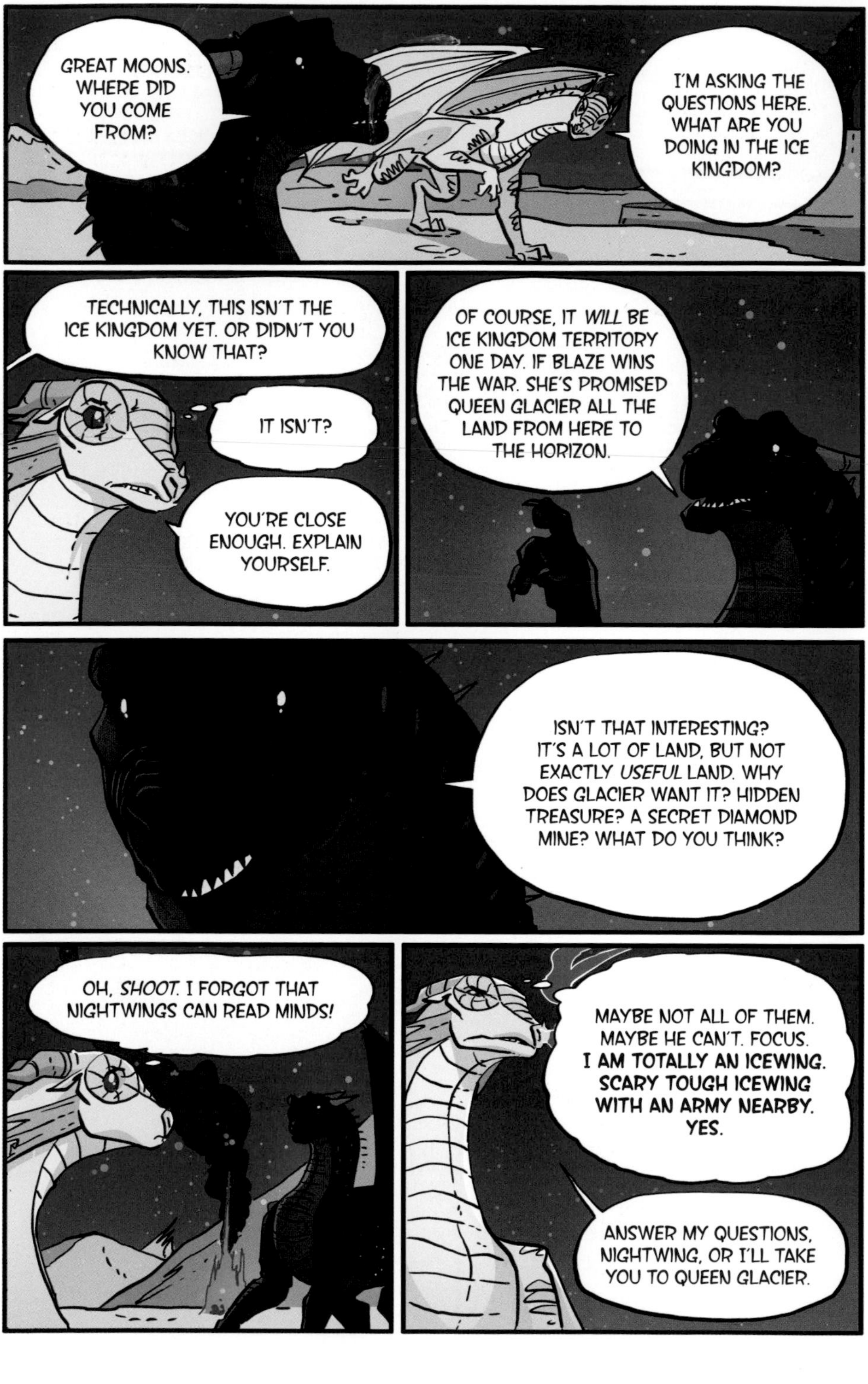
GREAT MOONS. WHERE DID YOU COME FROM?
I'M ASKING THE QUESTIONS HERE. WHAT ARE YOU DOING IN THE ICE KINGDOM?
TECHNICALLY, THIS ISN'T THE ICE KINGDOM YET. OR DIDN'T YOU KNOW THAT?
IT ISN'T?
YOU'RE CLOSE ENOUGH. EXPLAIN YOURSELF.
OF COURSE, IT *WILL* BE ICE KINGDOM TERRITORY ONE DAY. IF BLAZE WINS THE WAR. SHE'S PROMISED QUEEN GLACIER ALL THE LAND FROM HERE TO THE HORIZON.
ISN'T THAT INTERESTING? IT'S A LOT OF LAND, BUT NOT EXACTLY *USEFUL* LAND. WHY DOES GLACIER WANT IT? HIDDEN TREASURE? A SECRET DIAMOND MINE? WHAT DO YOU THINK?
OH, *SHOOT*. I FORGOT THAT NIGHTWINGS CAN READ MINDS!
MAYBE NOT ALL OF THEM. MAYBE HE CAN'T. FOCUS. **I AM TOTALLY AN ICEWING. SCARY TOUGH ICEWING WITH AN ARMY NEARBY. YES.**
ANSWER MY QUESTIONS, NIGHTWING, OR I'LL TAKE YOU TO QUEEN GLACIER.

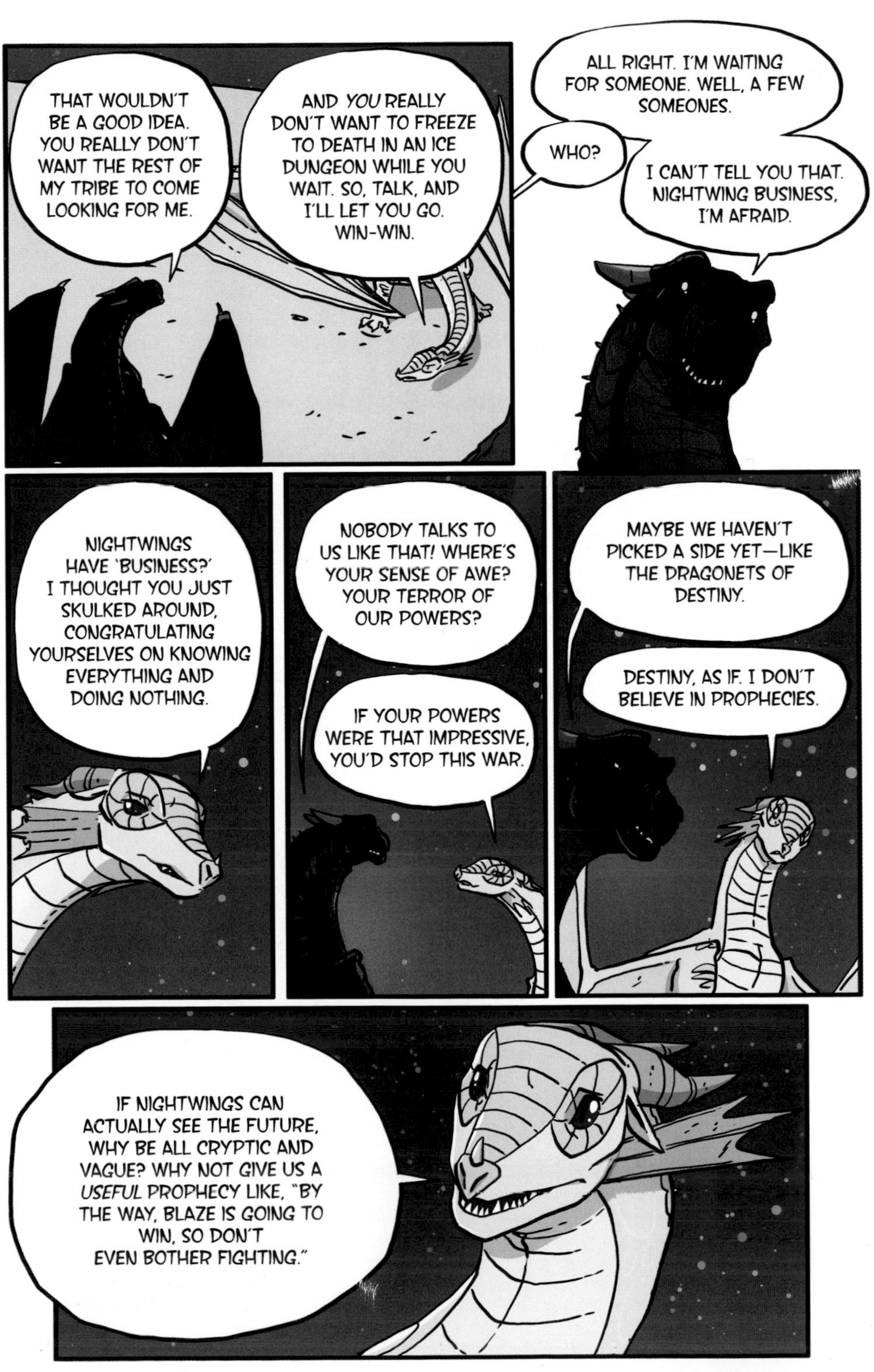
THAT WOULDN'T BE A GOOD IDEA. YOU REALLY DON'T WANT THE REST OF MY TRIBE TO COME LOOKING FOR ME.
AND *YOU* REALLY DON'T WANT TO FREEZE TO DEATH IN AN ICE DUNGEON WHILE YOU WAIT. SO, TALK, AND I'LL LET YOU GO. WIN-WIN.
ALL RIGHT. I'M WAITING FOR SOMEONE. WELL, A FEW SOMEONES.
WHO?
I CAN'T TELL YOU THAT. NIGHTWING BUSINESS, I'M AFRAID.
NIGHTWINGS HAVE 'BUSINESS?' I THOUGHT YOU JUST SKULKED AROUND, CONGRATULATING YOURSELVES ON KNOWING EVERYTHING AND DOING NOTHING.
NOBODY TALKS TO US LIKE THAT! WHERE'S YOUR SENSE OF AWE? YOUR TERROR OF OUR POWERS?
IF YOUR POWERS WERE THAT IMPRESSIVE, YOU'D STOP THIS WAR.
MAYBE WE HAVEN'T PICKED A SIDE YET—LIKE THE DRAGONETS OF DESTINY.
DESTINY, AS IF. I DON'T BELIEVE IN PROPHECIES.
IF NIGHTWINGS CAN ACTUALLY SEE THE FUTURE, WHY BE ALL CRYPTIC AND VAGUE? WHY NOT GIVE US A *USEFUL* PROPHECY LIKE, "BY THE WAY, BLAZE IS GOING TO WIN, SO DON'T EVEN BOTHER FIGHTING."

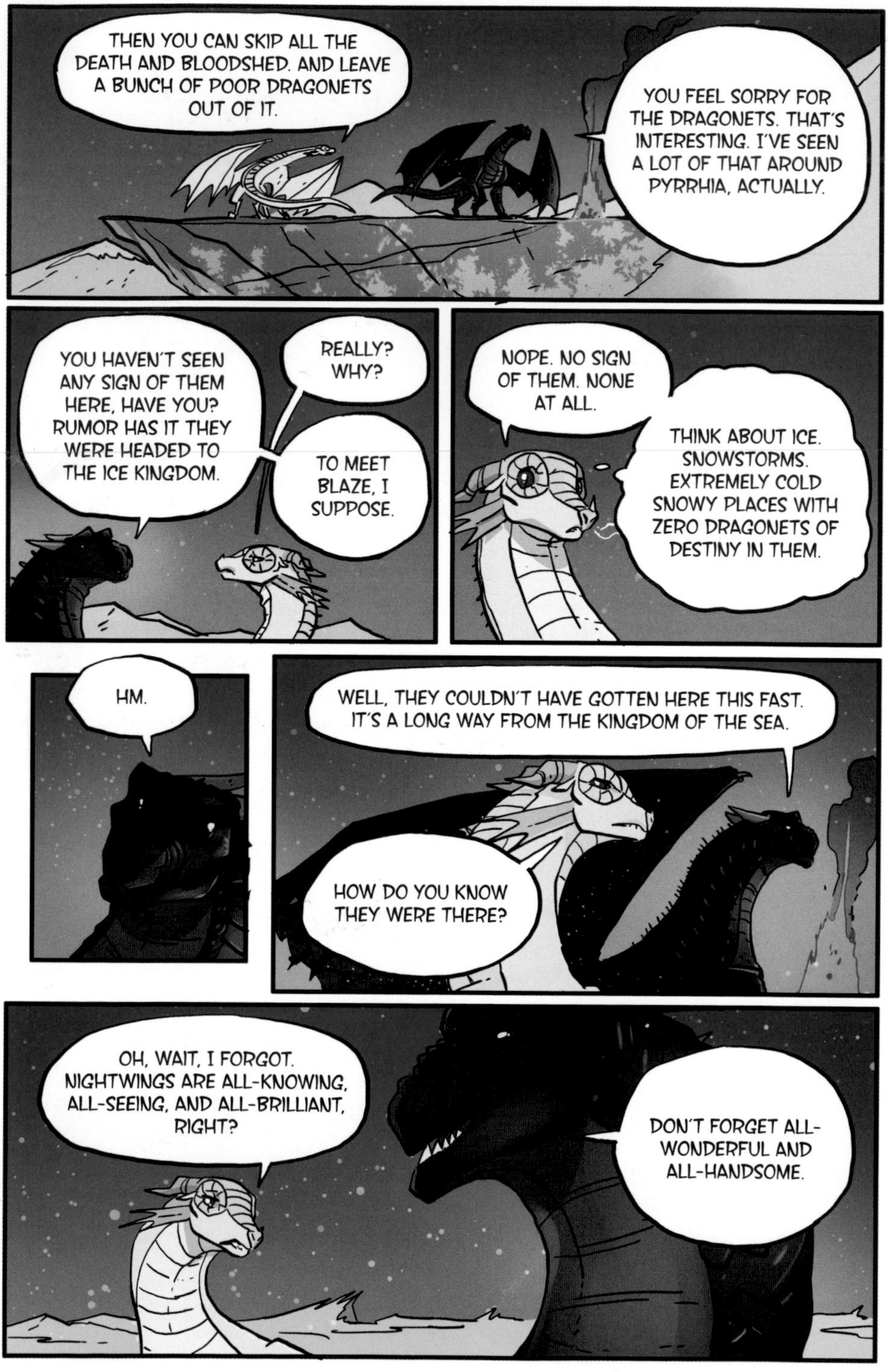
THEN YOU CAN SKIP ALL THE DEATH AND BLOODSHED. AND LEAVE A BUNCH OF POOR DRAGONETS OUT OF IT.
YOU FEEL SORRY FOR THE DRAGONETS. THAT'S INTERESTING. I'VE SEEN A LOT OF THAT AROUND PYRRHIA, ACTUALLY.
YOU HAVEN'T SEEN ANY SIGN OF THEM HERE, HAVE YOU? RUMOR HAS IT THEY WERE HEADED TO THE ICE KINGDOM.
REALLY? WHY?
TO MEET BLAZE, I SUPPOSE.
NOPE. NO SIGN OF THEM. NONE AT ALL.
THINK ABOUT ICE. SNOWSTORMS. EXTREMELY COLD SNOWY PLACES WITH ZERO DRAGONETS OF DESTINY IN THEM.
HM.
WELL, THEY COULDN'T HAVE GOTTEN HERE THIS FAST. IT'S A LONG WAY FROM THE KINGDOM OF THE SEA.
HOW DO YOU KNOW THEY WERE THERE?
OH, WAIT, I FORGOT. NIGHTWINGS ARE ALL-KNOWING, ALL-SEEING, AND ALL-BRILLIANT, RIGHT?
DON'T FORGET ALL-WONDERFUL AND ALL-HANDSOME.

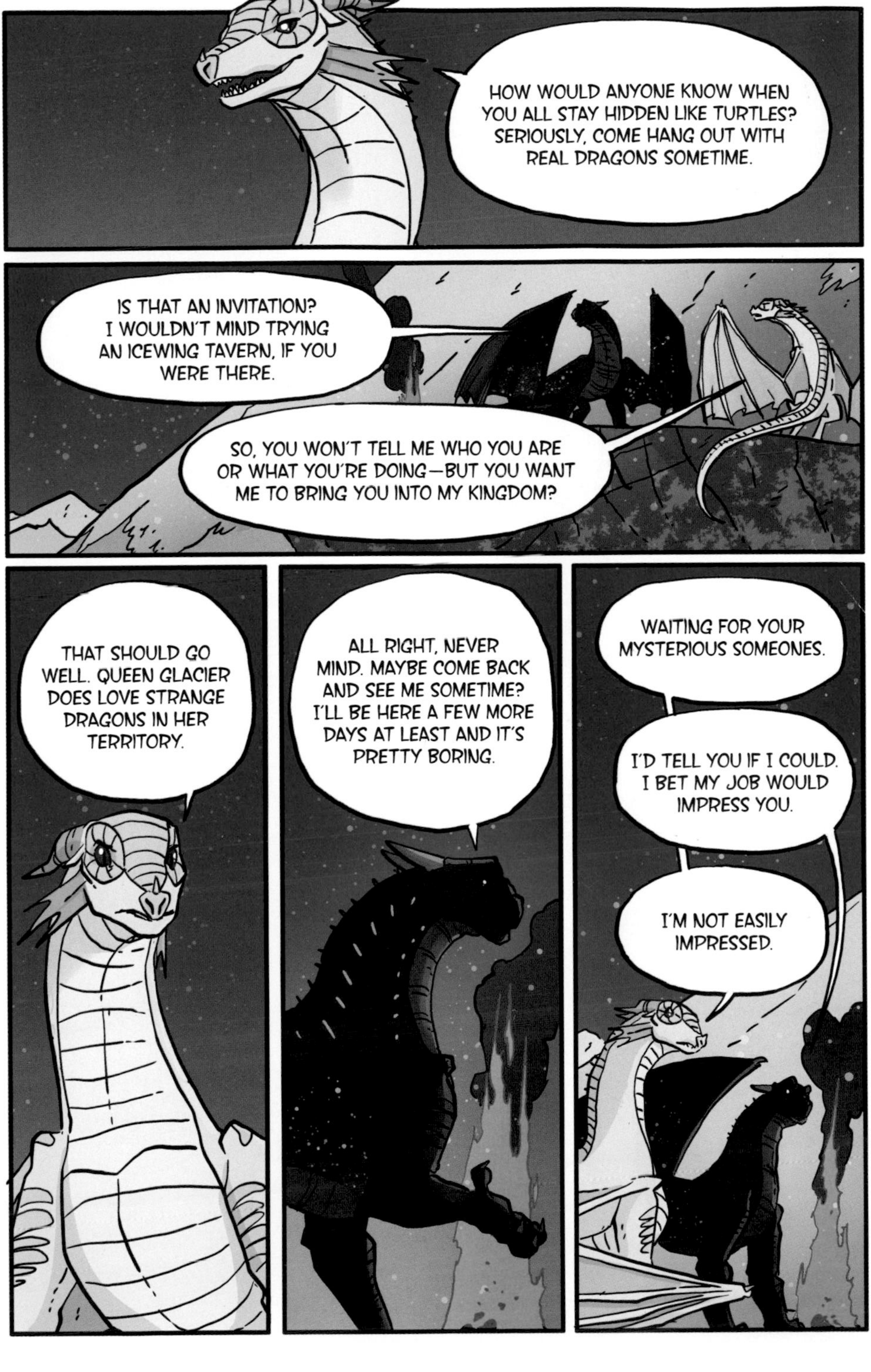
HOW WOULD ANYONE KNOW WHEN YOU ALL STAY HIDDEN LIKE TURTLES? SERIOUSLY, COME HANG OUT WITH REAL DRAGONS SOMETIME.
IS THAT AN INVITATION? I WOULDN'T MIND TRYING AN ICEWING TAVERN, IF YOU WERE THERE.
SO, YOU WON'T TELL ME WHO YOU ARE OR WHAT YOU'RE DOING—BUT YOU WANT ME TO BRING YOU INTO MY KINGDOM?
THAT SHOULD GO WELL. QUEEN GLACIER DOES LOVE STRANGE DRAGONS IN HER TERRITORY.
ALL RIGHT, NEVER MIND. MAYBE COME BACK AND SEE ME SOMETIME? I'LL BE HERE A FEW MORE DAYS AT LEAST AND IT'S PRETTY BORING.
WAITING FOR YOUR MYSTERIOUS SOMEONES.
I'D TELL YOU IF I COULD. I BET MY JOB WOULD IMPRESS YOU.
I'M NOT EASILY IMPRESSED.

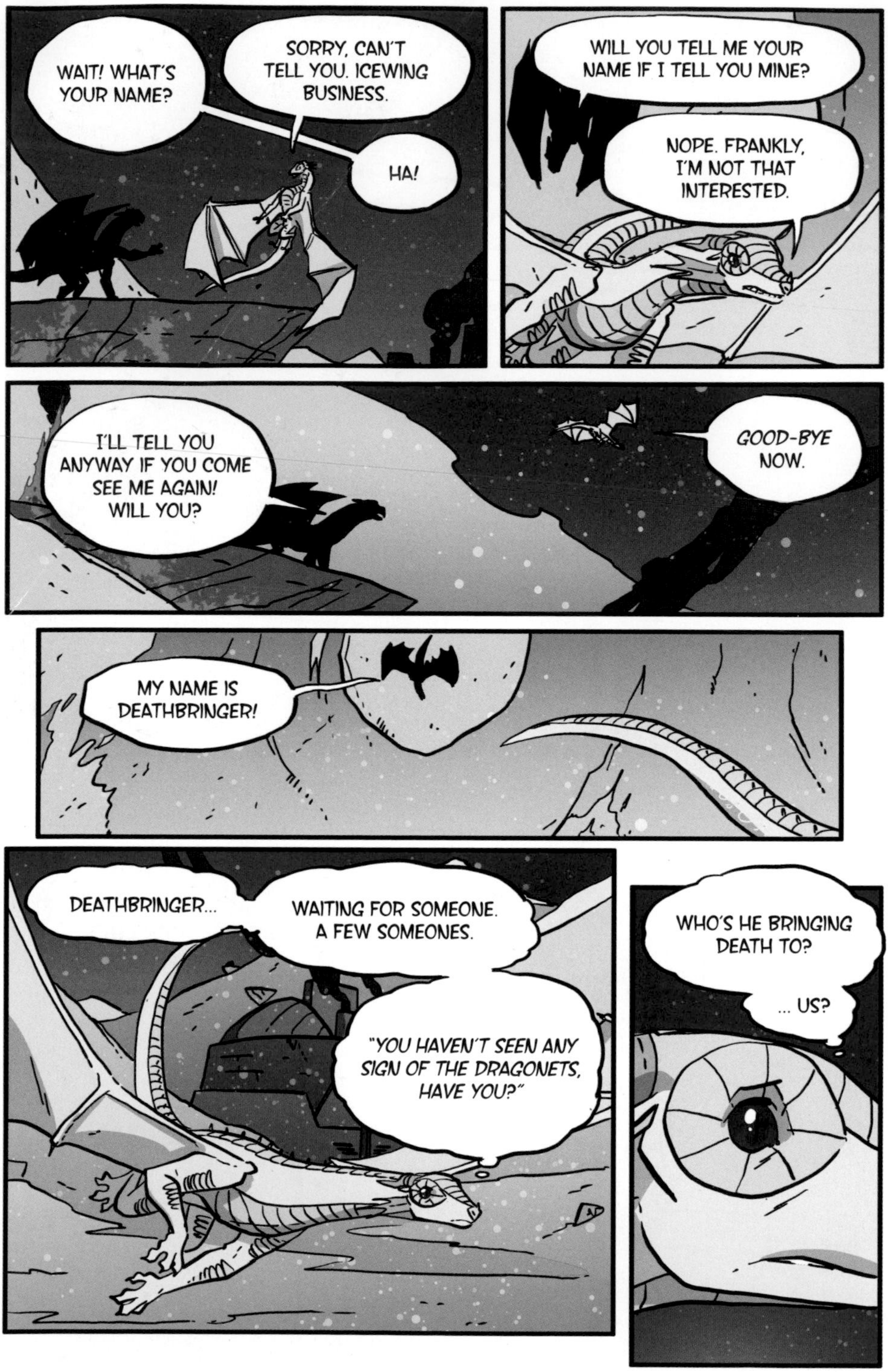
WAIT! WHAT'S YOUR NAME?
SORRY, CAN'T TELL YOU. ICEWING BUSINESS.
HA!
WILL YOU TELL ME YOUR NAME IF I TELL YOU MINE?
NOPE. FRANKLY, I'M NOT THAT INTERESTED.
I'LL TELL YOU ANYWAY IF YOU COME SEE ME AGAIN! WILL YOU?
GOOD-BYE NOW.
MY NAME IS DEATHBRINGER!
DEATHBRINGER...
WAITING FOR SOMEONE. A FEW SOMEONES.
"YOU HAVEN'T SEEN ANY SIGN OF THE DRAGONETS, HAVE YOU?"
WHO'S HE BRINGING DEATH TO?
... US?

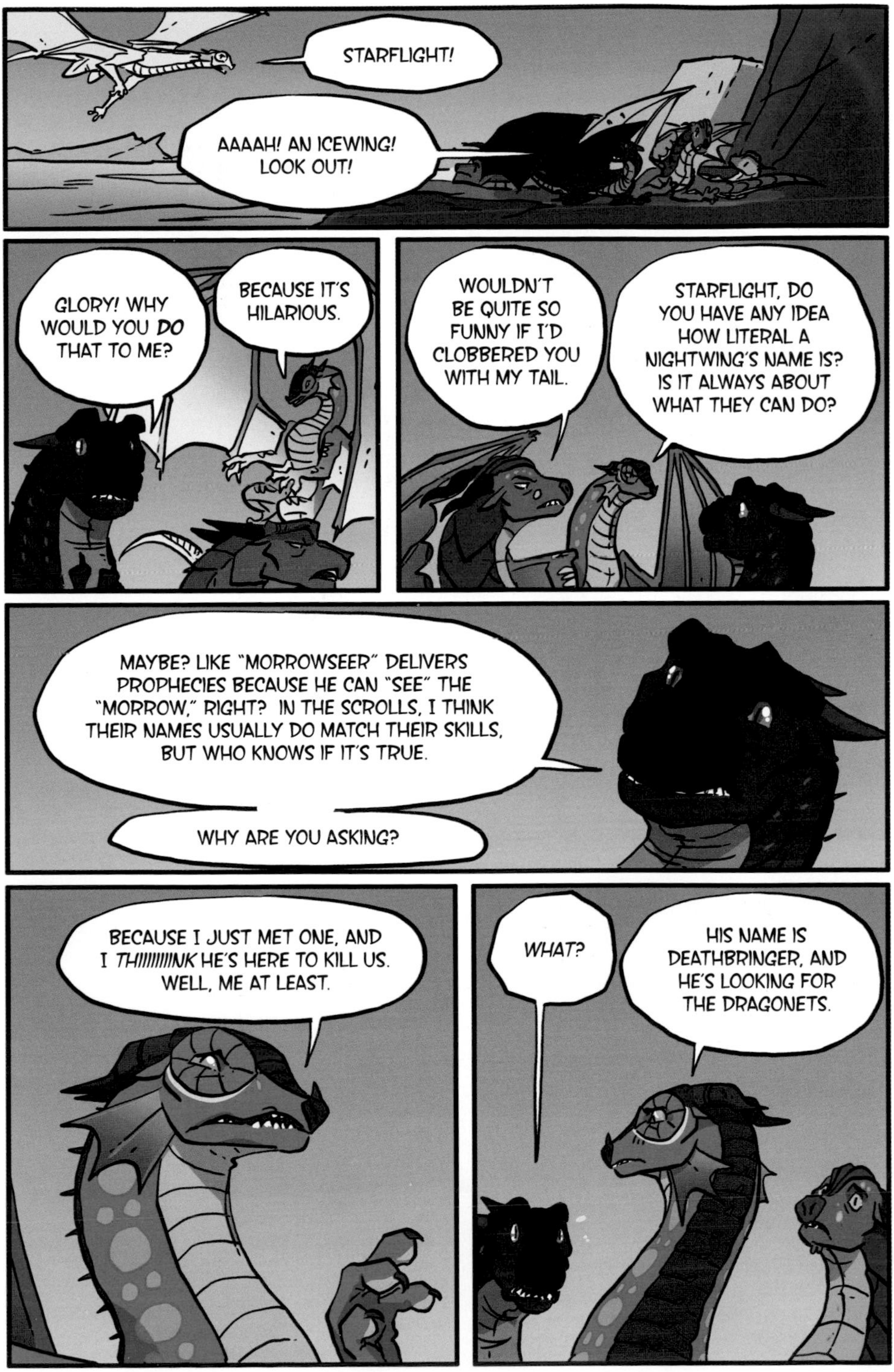
STARFLIGHT!
AAAAH! AN ICEWING! LOOK OUT!
GLORY! WHY WOULD YOU *DO* THAT TO ME?
BECAUSE IT'S HILARIOUS.
WOULDN'T BE QUITE SO FUNNY IF I'D CLOBBERED YOU WITH MY TAIL.
STARFLIGHT, DO YOU HAVE ANY IDEA HOW LITERAL A NIGHTWING'S NAME IS? IS IT ALWAYS ABOUT WHAT THEY CAN DO?
MAYBE? LIKE "MORROWSEER" DELIVERS PROPHECIES BECAUSE HE CAN "SEE" THE "MORROW," RIGHT? IN THE SCROLLS, I THINK THEIR NAMES USUALLY DO MATCH THEIR SKILLS, BUT WHO KNOWS IF IT'S TRUE.
WHY ARE YOU ASKING?
BECAUSE I JUST MET ONE, AND I *THIIIIIIIINK* HE'S HERE TO KILL US. WELL, ME AT LEAST.
WHAT?
HIS NAME IS DEATHBRINGER, AND HE'S LOOKING FOR THE DRAGONETS.

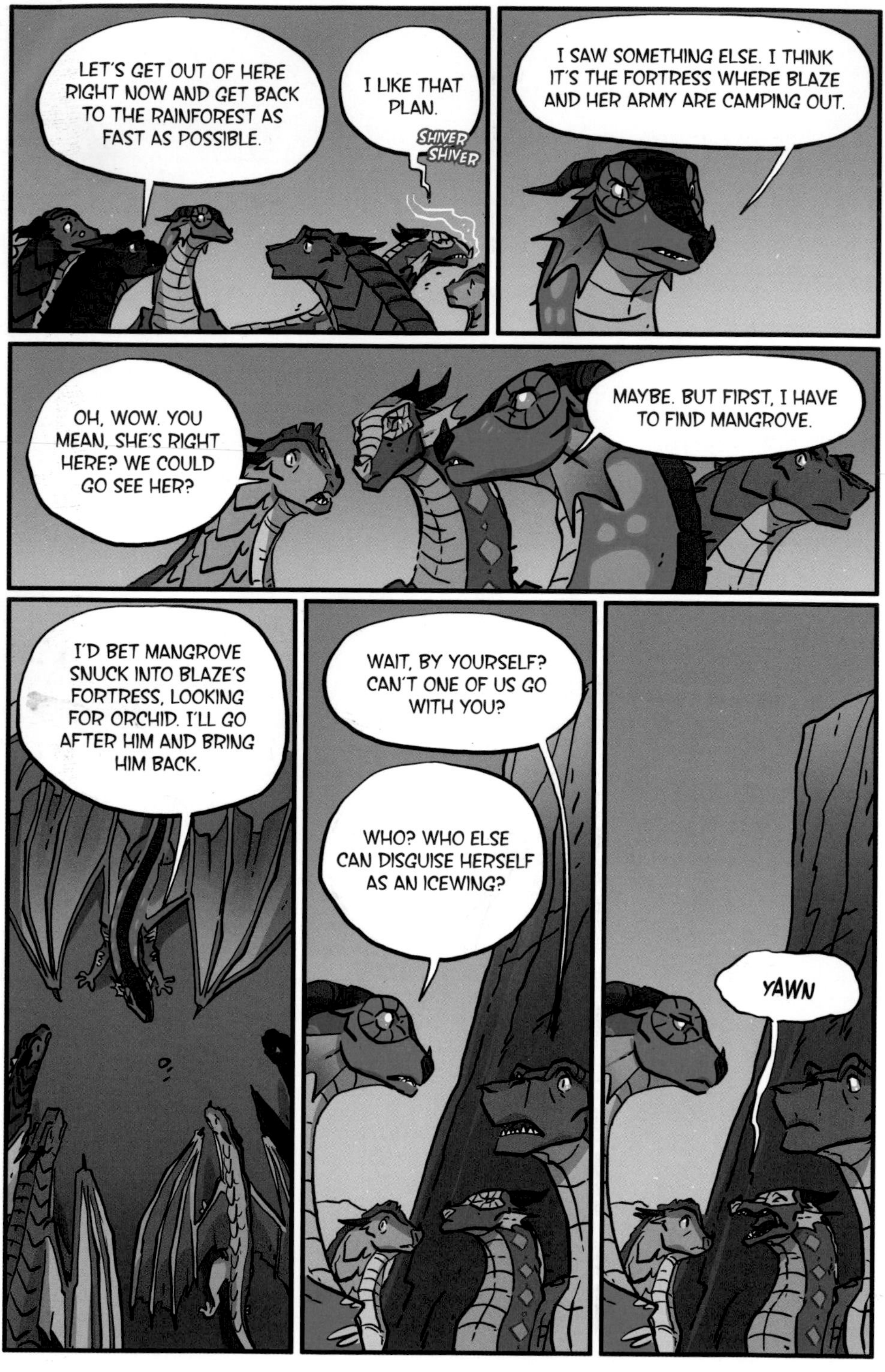

LET'S GET OUT OF HERE RIGHT NOW AND GET BACK TO THE RAINFOREST AS FAST AS POSSIBLE.
I LIKE THAT PLAN.
SHIVER SHIVER
I SAW SOMETHING ELSE. I THINK IT'S THE FORTRESS WHERE BLAZE AND HER ARMY ARE CAMPING OUT.
OH, WOW. YOU MEAN, SHE'S RIGHT HERE? WE COULD GO SEE HER?
MAYBE. BUT FIRST, I HAVE TO FIND MANGROVE.
I'D BET MANGROVE SNUCK INTO BLAZE'S FORTRESS, LOOKING FOR ORCHID. I'LL GO AFTER HIM AND BRING HIM BACK.
WAIT, BY YOURSELF? CAN'T ONE OF US GO WITH YOU?
WHO? WHO ELSE CAN DISGUISE HERSELF AS AN ICEWING?
YAWN

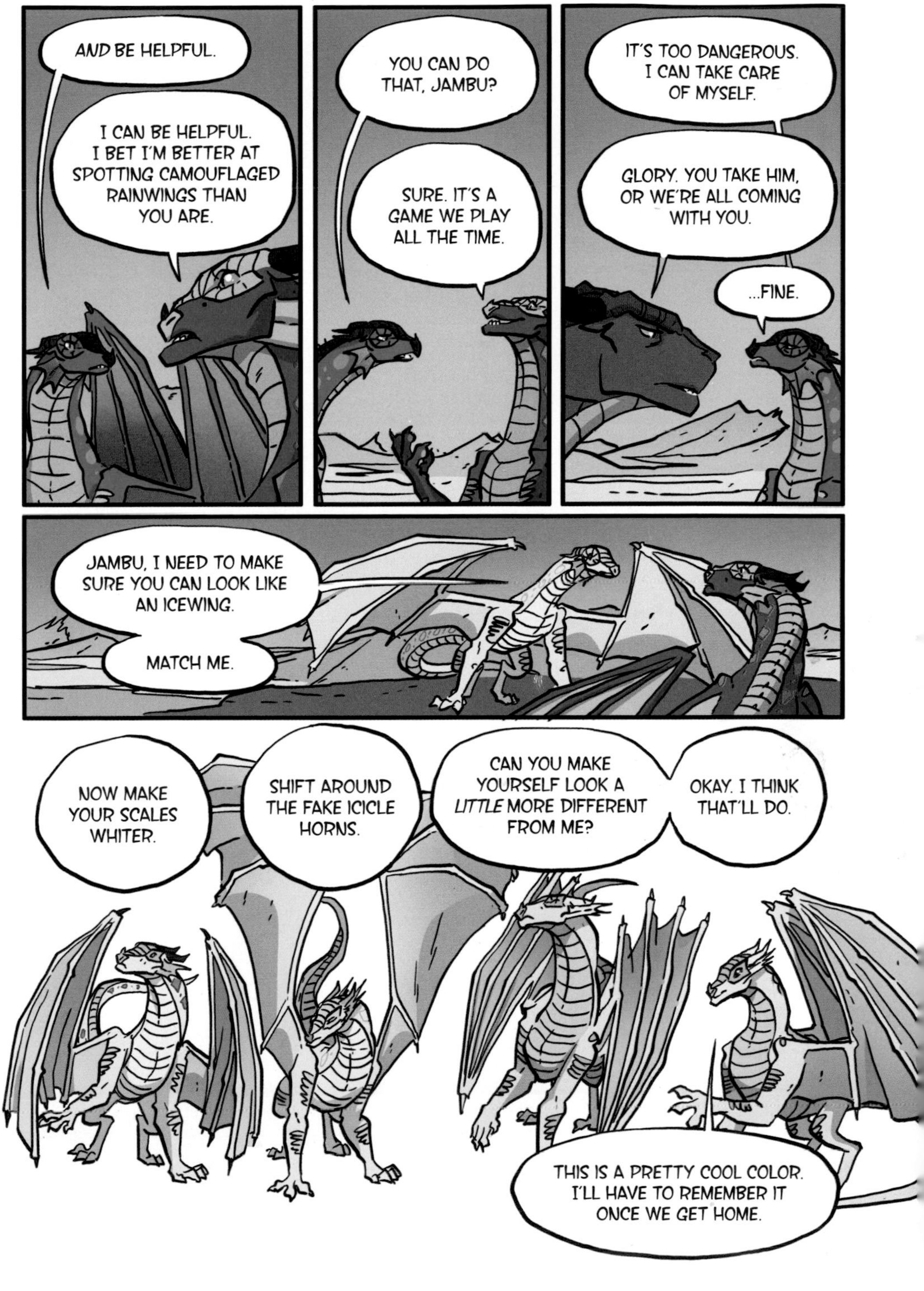
AND BE HELPFUL.
I CAN BE HELPFUL. I BET I'M BETTER AT SPOTTING CAMOUFLAGED RAINWINGS THAN YOU ARE.
YOU CAN DO THAT, JAMBU?
SURE. IT'S A GAME WE PLAY ALL THE TIME.
IT'S TOO DANGEROUS. I CAN TAKE CARE OF MYSELF.
GLORY. YOU TAKE HIM, OR WE'RE ALL COMING WITH YOU.
...FINE.
JAMBU, I NEED TO MAKE SURE YOU CAN LOOK LIKE AN ICEWING.
MATCH ME.
NOW MAKE YOUR SCALES WHITER.
SHIFT AROUND THE FAKE ICICLE HORNS.
CAN YOU MAKE YOURSELF LOOK A *LITTLE* MORE DIFFERENT FROM ME?
OKAY. I THINK THAT'LL DO.
THIS IS A PRETTY COOL COLOR. I'LL HAVE TO REMEMBER IT ONCE WE GET HOME.

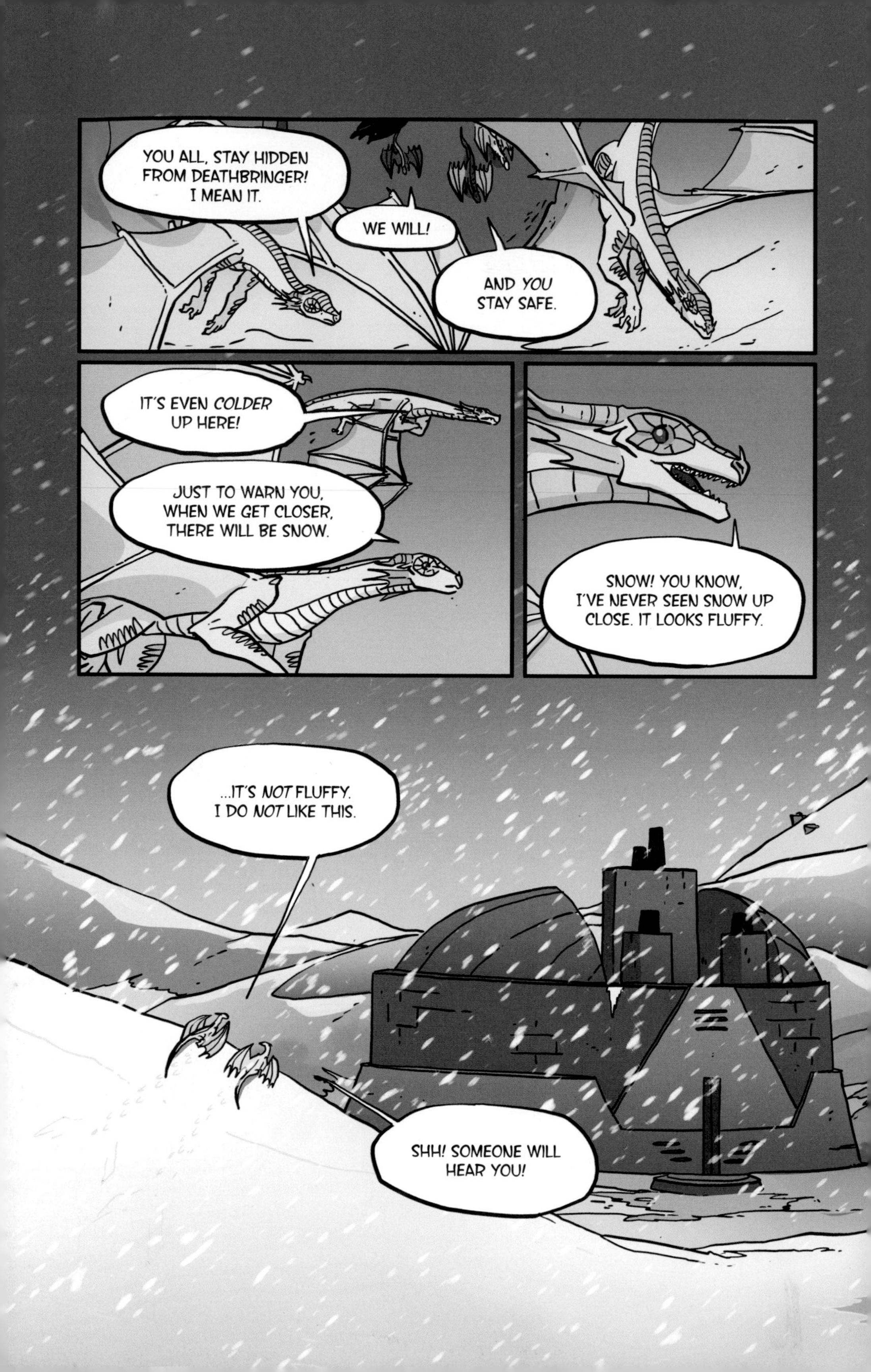
YOU ALL, STAY HIDDEN FROM DEATHBRINGER! I MEAN IT.
WE WILL!
AND *YOU* STAY SAFE.
IT'S EVEN *COLDER* UP HERE!
JUST TO WARN YOU, WHEN WE GET CLOSER, THERE WILL BE SNOW.
SNOW! YOU KNOW, I'VE NEVER SEEN SNOW UP CLOSE. IT LOOKS FLUFFY.
...IT'S *NOT* FLUFFY. I DO *NOT* LIKE THIS.
SHH! SOMEONE WILL HEAR YOU!

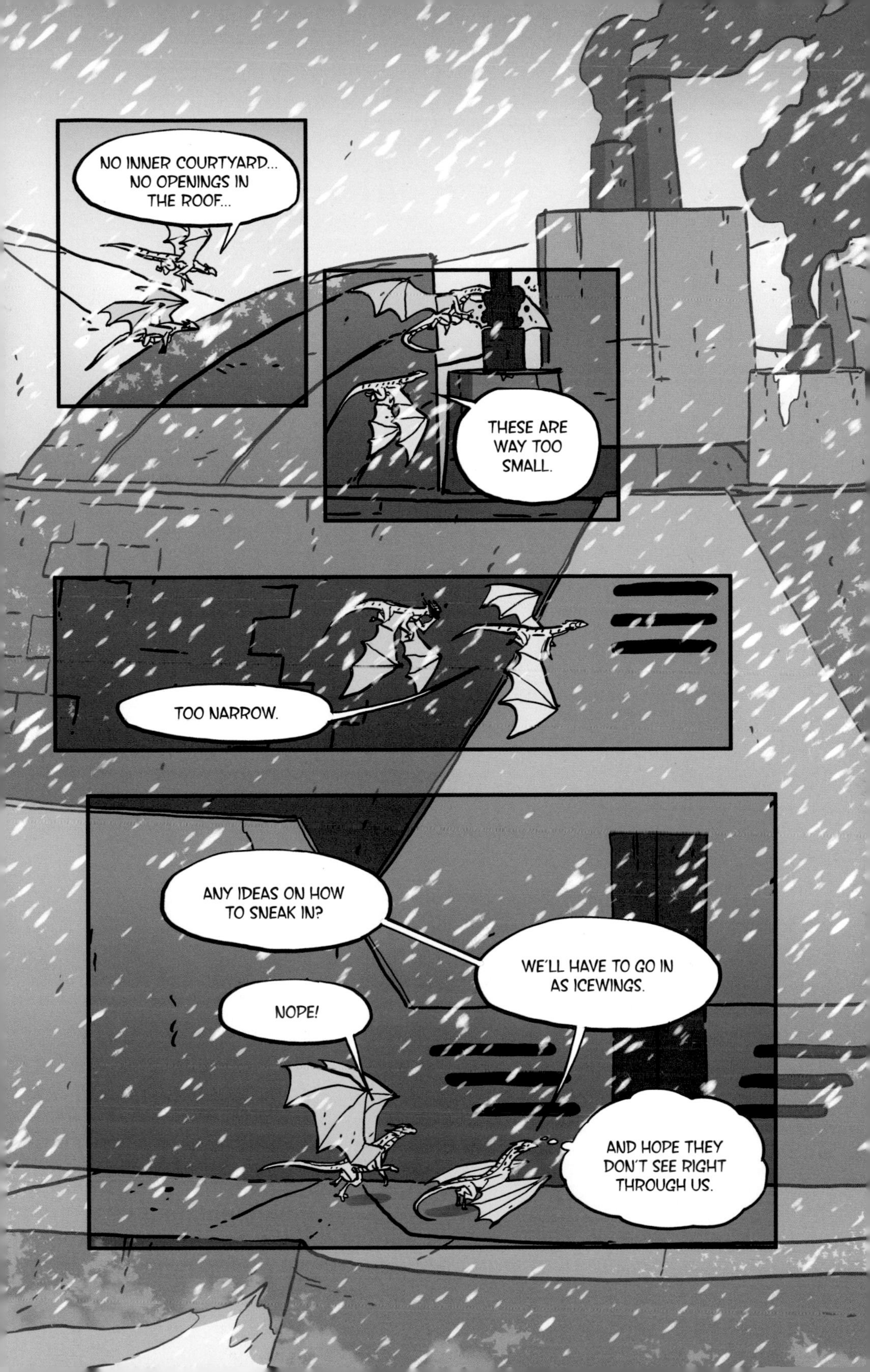

NO INNER COURTYARD... NO OPENINGS IN THE ROOF...
THESE ARE WAY TOO SMALL.
TOO NARROW.
ANY IDEAS ON HOW TO SNEAK IN?
WE'LL HAVE TO GO IN AS ICEWINGS.
NOPE!
AND HOPE THEY DON'T SEE RIGHT THROUGH US.

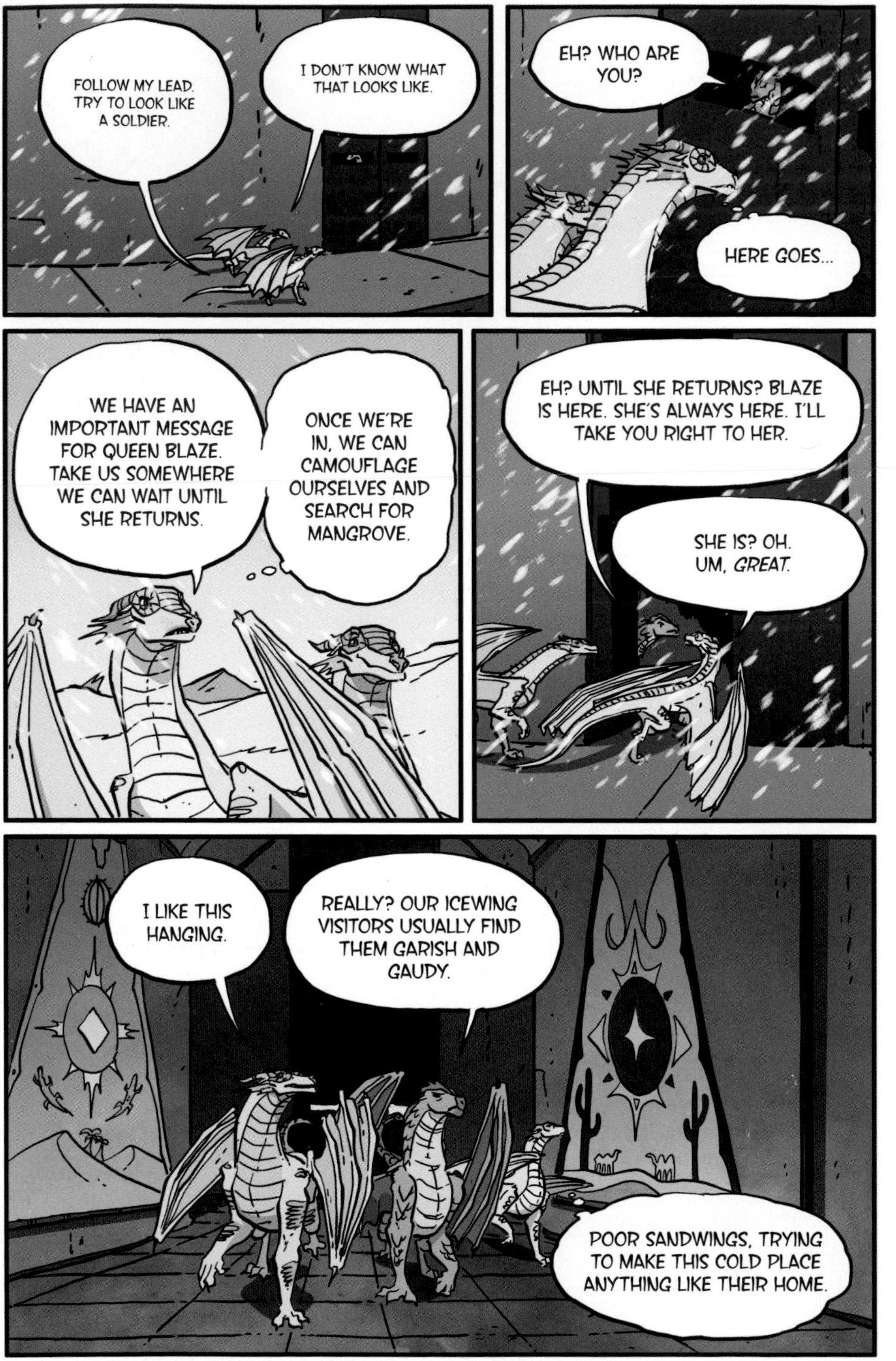
FOLLOW MY LEAD. TRY TO LOOK LIKE A SOLDIER.
I DON'T KNOW WHAT THAT LOOKS LIKE.
EH? WHO ARE YOU?
HERE GOES...
WE HAVE AN IMPORTANT MESSAGE FOR QUEEN BLAZE. TAKE US SOMEWHERE WE CAN WAIT UNTIL SHE RETURNS.
ONCE WE'RE IN, WE CAN CAMOUFLAGE OURSELVES AND SEARCH FOR MANGROVE.
EH? UNTIL SHE RETURNS? BLAZE IS HERE. SHE'S ALWAYS HERE. I'LL TAKE YOU RIGHT TO HER.
SHE IS? OH. UM, *GREAT.*
I LIKE THIS HANGING.
REALLY? OUR ICEWING VISITORS USUALLY FIND THEM GARISH AND GAUDY.
POOR SANDWINGS, TRYING TO MAKE THIS COLD PLACE ANYTHING LIKE THEIR HOME.

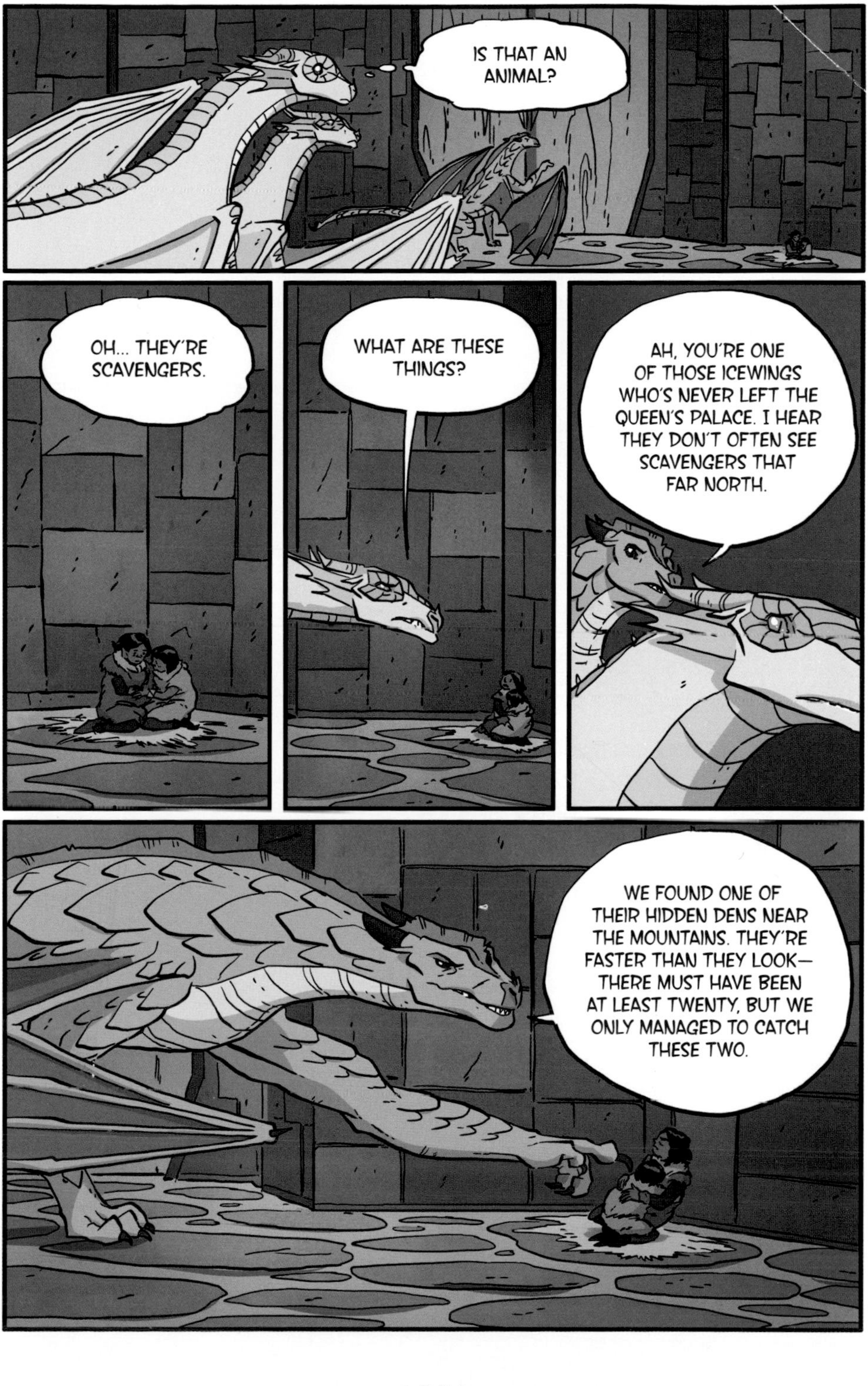

IS THAT AN ANIMAL?
OH... THEY'RE SCAVENGERS.
WHAT ARE THESE THINGS?
AH, YOU'RE ONE OF THOSE ICEWINGS WHO'S NEVER LEFT THE QUEEN'S PALACE. I HEAR THEY DON'T OFTEN SEE SCAVENGERS THAT FAR NORTH.
WE FOUND ONE OF THEIR HIDDEN DENS NEAR THE MOUNTAINS. THEY'RE FASTER THAN THEY LOOK— THERE MUST HAVE BEEN AT LEAST TWENTY, BUT WE ONLY MANAGED TO CATCH THESE TWO.

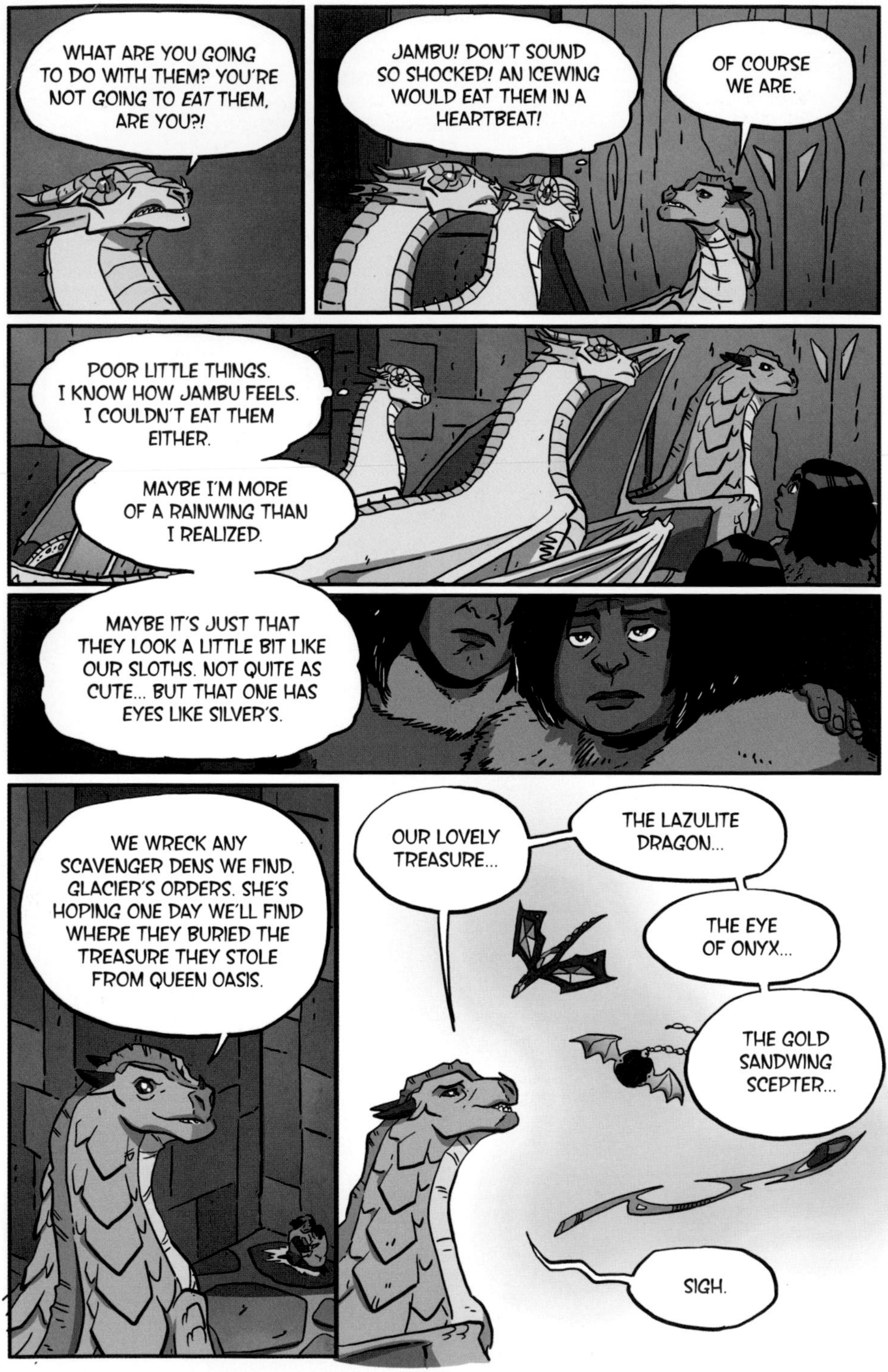
WHAT ARE YOU GOING TO DO WITH THEM? YOU'RE NOT GOING TO *EAT* THEM, ARE YOU?!
JAMBU! DON'T SOUND SO SHOCKED! AN ICEWING WOULD EAT THEM IN A HEARTBEAT!
OF COURSE WE ARE.
POOR LITTLE THINGS. I KNOW HOW JAMBU FEELS. I COULDN'T EAT THEM EITHER.
MAYBE I'M MORE OF A RAINWING THAN I REALIZED.
MAYBE IT'S JUST THAT THEY LOOK A LITTLE BIT LIKE OUR SLOTHS. NOT QUITE AS CUTE... BUT THAT ONE HAS EYES LIKE SILVER'S.
WE WRECK ANY SCAVENGER DENS WE FIND. GLACIER'S ORDERS. SHE'S HOPING ONE DAY WE'LL FIND WHERE THEY BURIED THE TREASURE THEY STOLE FROM QUEEN OASIS.
OUR LOVELY TREASURE...
THE LAZULITE DRAGON...
THE EYE OF ONYX...
THE GOLD SANDWING SCEPTER...
SIGH.

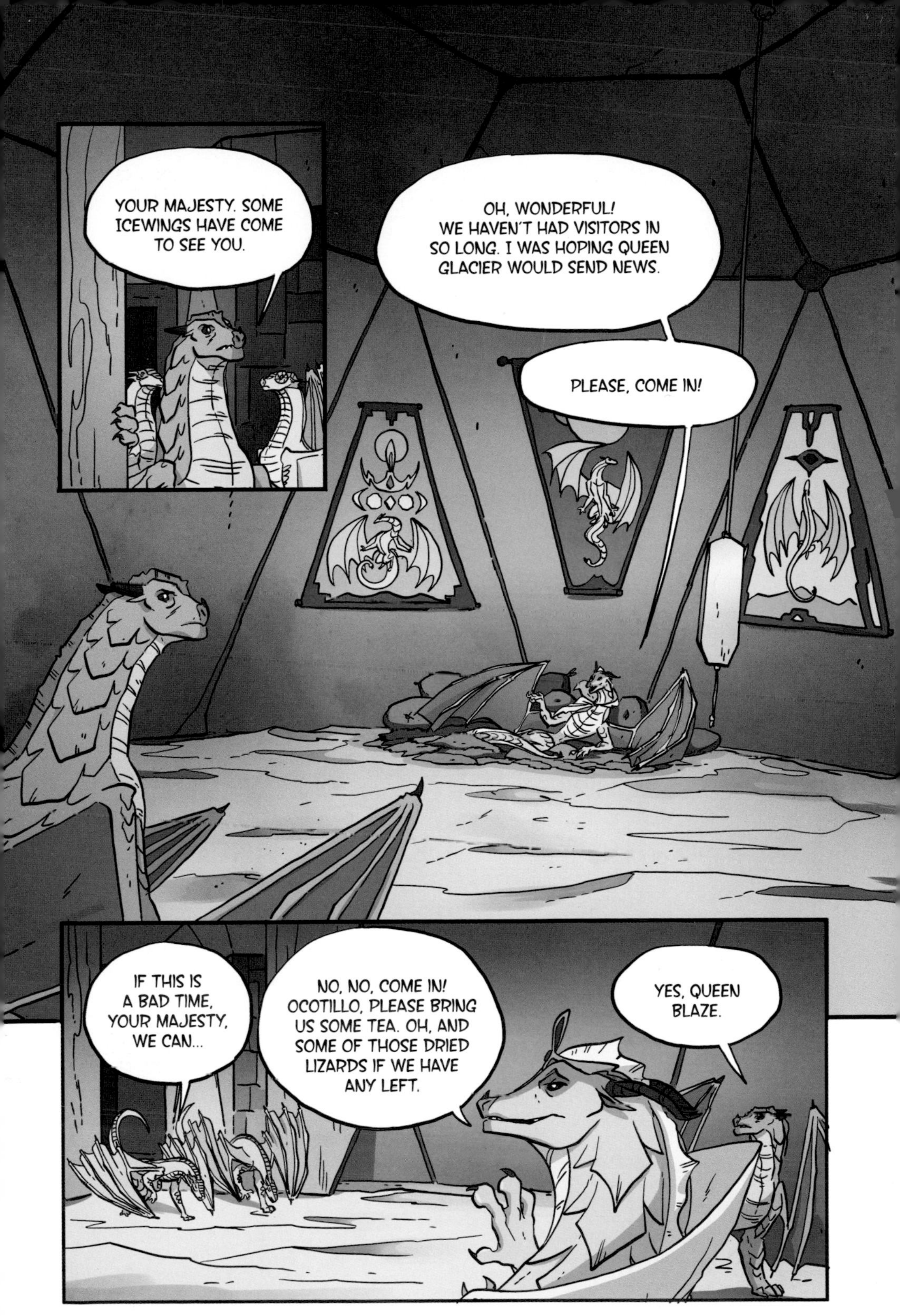
YOUR MAJESTY. SOME ICEWINGS HAVE COME TO SEE YOU.
OH, WONDERFUL! WE HAVEN'T HAD VISITORS IN SO LONG. I WAS HOPING QUEEN GLACIER WOULD SEND NEWS.
PLEASE, COME IN!
IF THIS IS A BAD TIME, YOUR MAJESTY, WE CAN...
NO, NO, COME IN! OCOTILLO, PLEASE BRING US SOME TEA. OH, AND SOME OF THOSE DRIED LIZARDS IF WE HAVE ANY LEFT.
YES, QUEEN BLAZE.

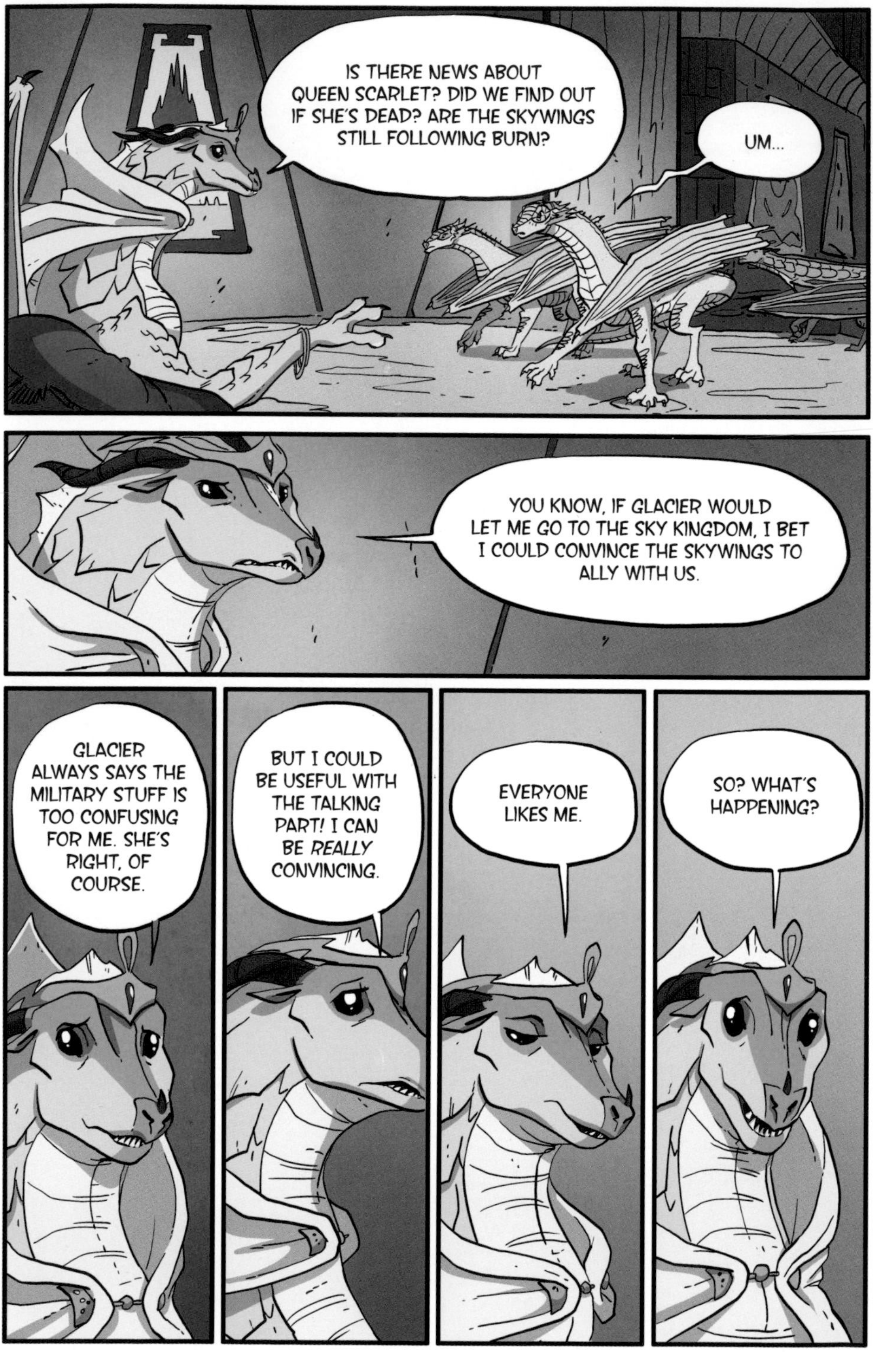
IS THERE NEWS ABOUT QUEEN SCARLET? DID WE FIND OUT IF SHE'S DEAD? ARE THE SKYWINGS STILL FOLLOWING BURN?
UM...
YOU KNOW, IF GLACIER WOULD LET ME GO TO THE SKY KINGDOM, I BET I COULD CONVINCE THE SKYWINGS TO ALLY WITH US.
GLACIER ALWAYS SAYS THE MILITARY STUFF IS TOO CONFUSING FOR ME. SHE'S RIGHT, OF COURSE.
BUT I COULD BE USEFUL WITH THE TALKING PART! I CAN BE *REALLY* CONVINCING.
EVERYONE LIKES ME.
SO? WHAT'S HAPPENING?

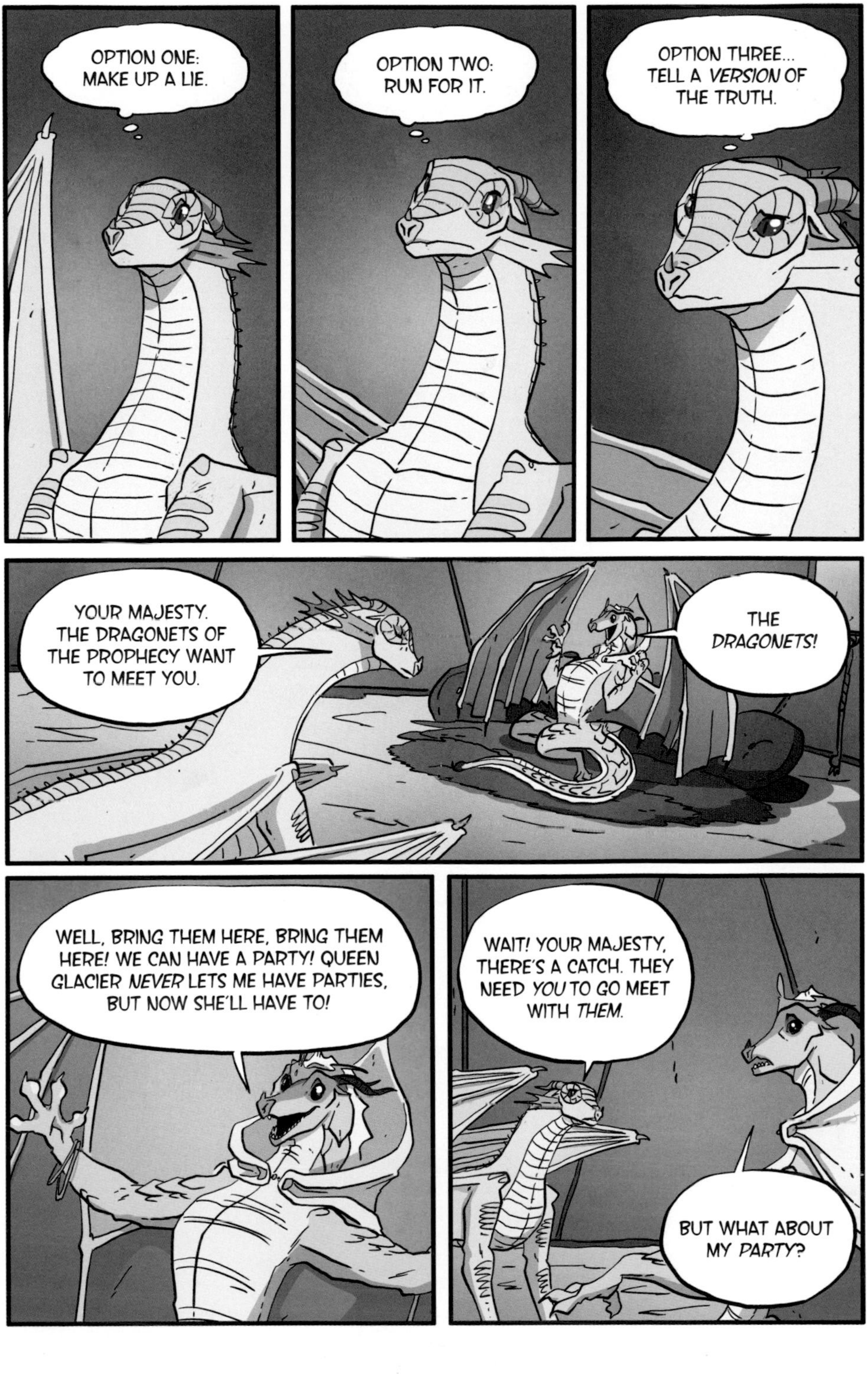
OPTION ONE: MAKE UP A LIE.
OPTION TWO: RUN FOR IT.
OPTION THREE... TELL A *VERSION* OF THE TRUTH.
YOUR MAJESTY. THE DRAGONETS OF THE PROPHECY WANT TO MEET YOU.
THE *DRAGONETS!*
WELL, BRING THEM HERE, BRING THEM HERE! WE CAN HAVE A PARTY! QUEEN GLACIER *NEVER* LETS ME HAVE PARTIES, BUT NOW SHE'LL HAVE TO!
WAIT! YOUR MAJESTY, THERE'S A CATCH. THEY NEED *YOU* TO GO MEET WITH *THEM*.
BUT WHAT ABOUT MY *PARTY*?

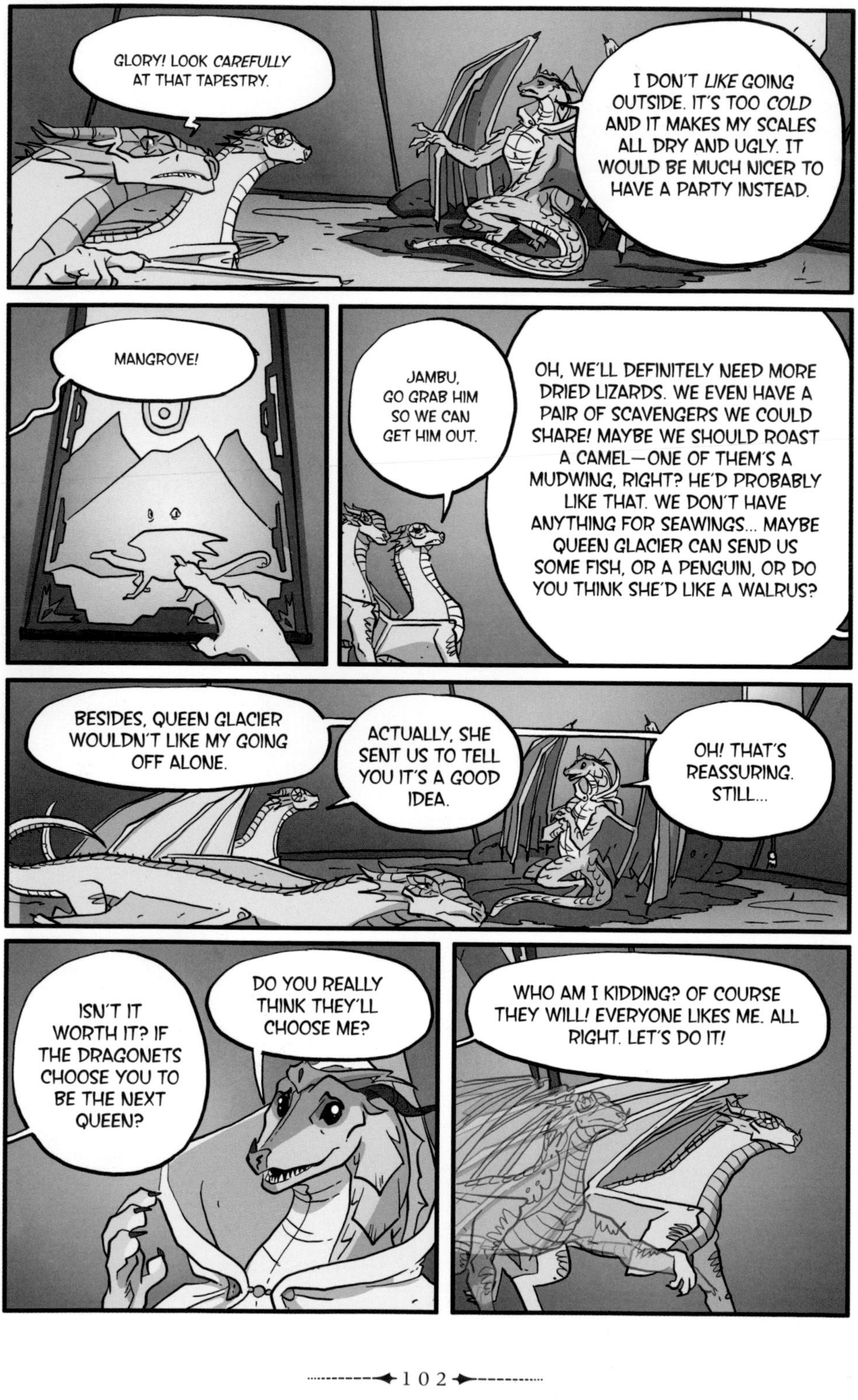
GLORY! LOOK CAREFULLY AT THAT TAPESTRY.
I DON'T LIKE GOING OUTSIDE. IT'S TOO COLD AND IT MAKES MY SCALES ALL DRY AND UGLY. IT WOULD BE MUCH NICER TO HAVE A PARTY INSTEAD.
MANGROVE!
JAMBU, GO GRAB HIM SO WE CAN GET HIM OUT.
OH, WE'LL DEFINITELY NEED MORE DRIED LIZARDS. WE EVEN HAVE A PAIR OF SCAVENGERS WE COULD SHARE! MAYBE WE SHOULD ROAST A CAMEL—ONE OF THEM'S A MUDWING, RIGHT? HE'D PROBABLY LIKE THAT. WE DON'T HAVE ANYTHING FOR SEAWINGS... MAYBE QUEEN GLACIER CAN SEND US SOME FISH, OR A PENGUIN, OR DO YOU THINK SHE'D LIKE A WALRUS?
BESIDES, QUEEN GLACIER WOULDN'T LIKE MY GOING OFF ALONE.
ACTUALLY, SHE SENT US TO TELL YOU IT'S A GOOD IDEA.
OH! THAT'S REASSURING. STILL...
ISN'T IT WORTH IT? IF THE DRAGONETS CHOOSE YOU TO BE THE NEXT QUEEN?
DO YOU REALLY THINK THEY'LL CHOOSE ME?
WHO AM I KIDDING? OF COURSE THEY WILL! EVERYONE LIKES ME. ALL RIGHT. LET'S DO IT!

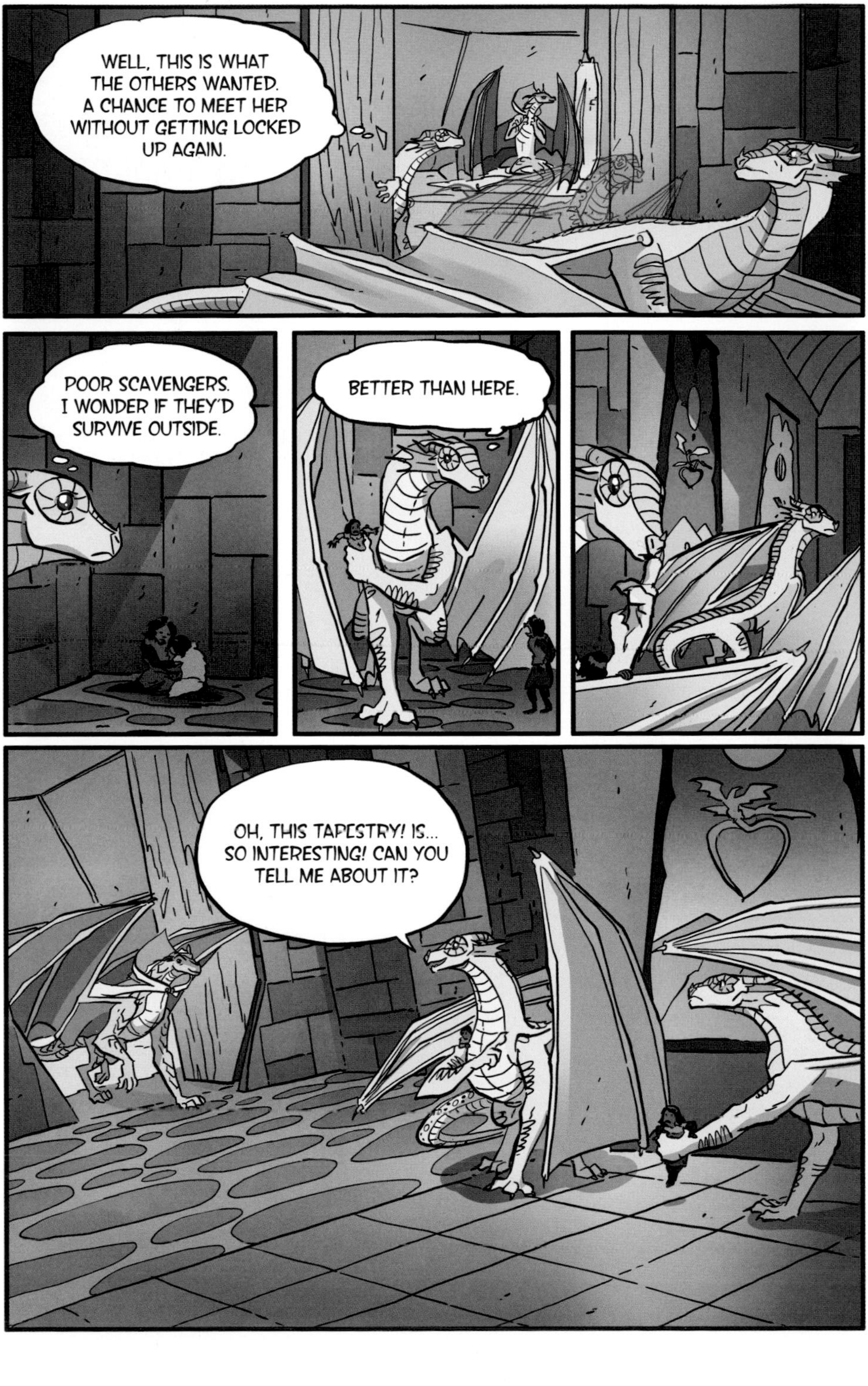
WELL, THIS IS WHAT THE OTHERS WANTED. A CHANCE TO MEET HER WITHOUT GETTING LOCKED UP AGAIN.
POOR SCAVENGERS. I WONDER IF THEY'D SURVIVE OUTSIDE.
BETTER THAN HERE.
OH, THIS TAPESTRY! IS... SO INTERESTING! CAN YOU TELL ME ABOUT IT?

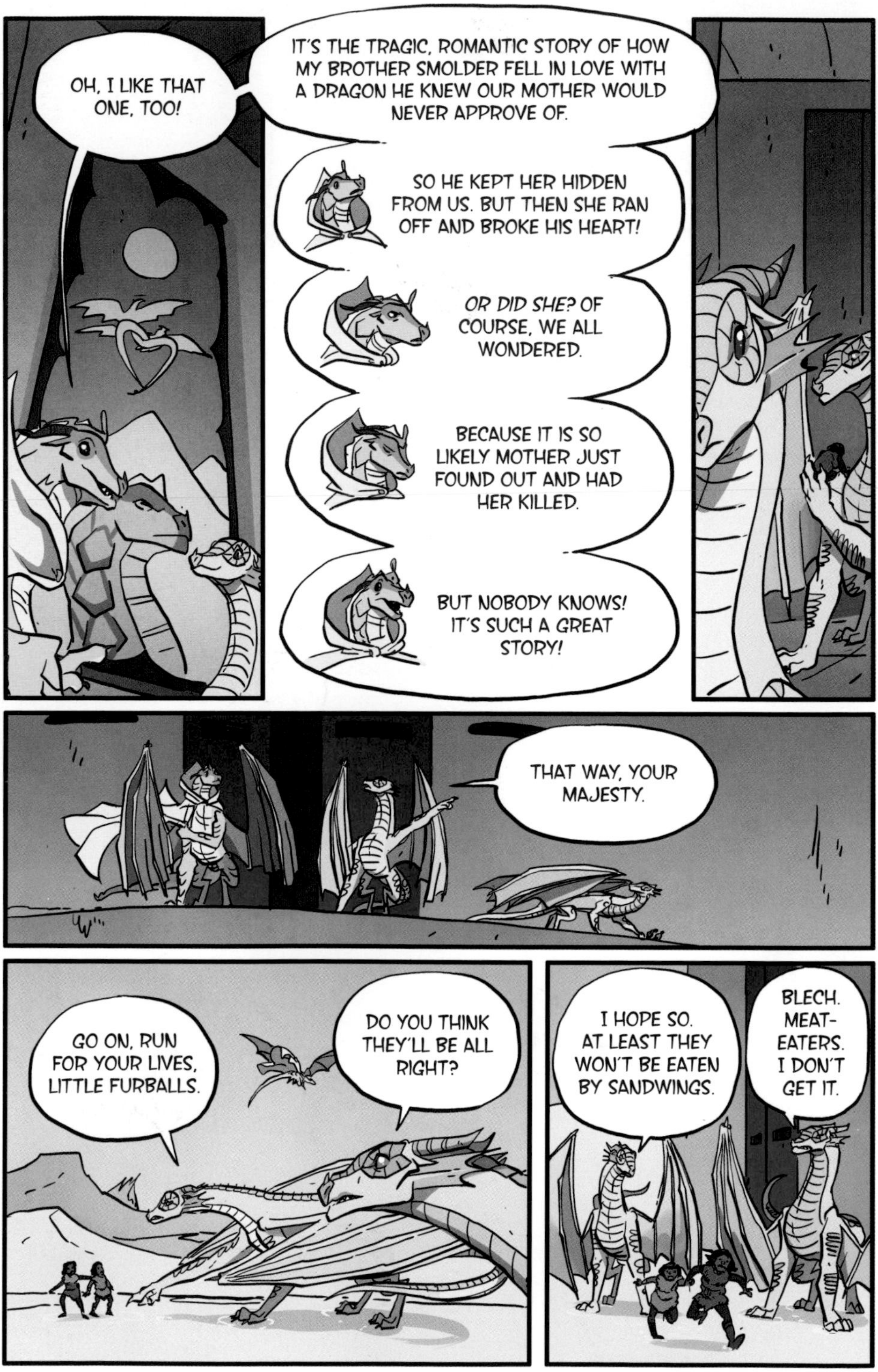
OH, I LIKE THAT ONE, TOO!
IT'S THE TRAGIC, ROMANTIC STORY OF HOW MY BROTHER SMOLDER FELL IN LOVE WITH A DRAGON HE KNEW OUR MOTHER WOULD NEVER APPROVE OF.
SO HE KEPT HER HIDDEN FROM US. BUT THEN SHE RAN OFF AND BROKE HIS HEART!
OR DID SHE? OF COURSE, WE ALL WONDERED.
BECAUSE IT IS SO LIKELY MOTHER JUST FOUND OUT AND HAD HER KILLED.
BUT NOBODY KNOWS! IT'S SUCH A GREAT STORY!
THAT WAY, YOUR MAJESTY.
GO ON, RUN FOR YOUR LIVES, LITTLE FURBALLS.
DO YOU THINK THEY'LL BE ALL RIGHT?
I HOPE SO. AT LEAST THEY WON'T BE EATEN BY SANDWINGS.
BLECH. MEAT-EATERS. I DON'T GET IT.

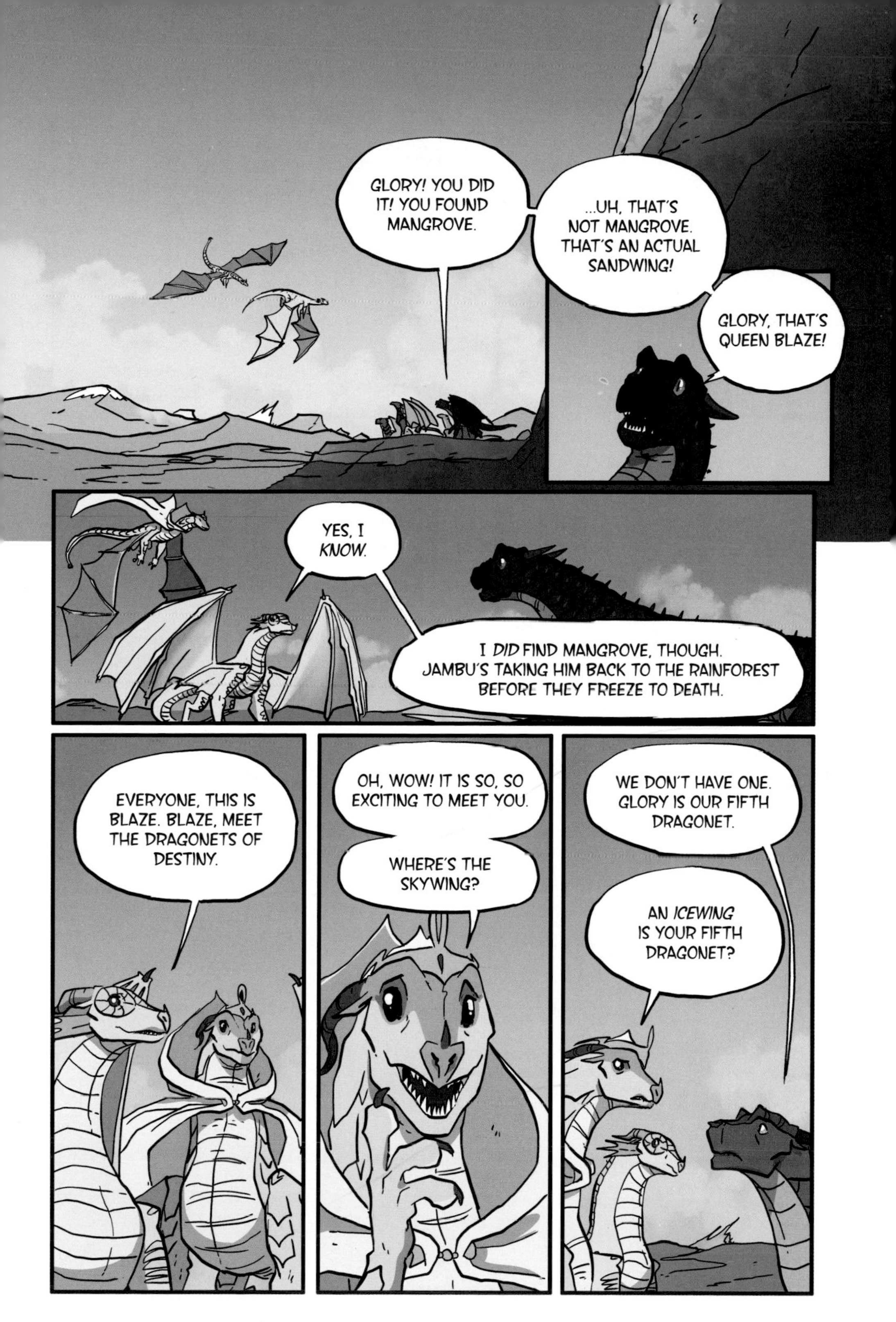
GLORY! YOU DID IT! YOU FOUND MANGROVE.
...UH, THAT'S NOT MANGROVE. THAT'S AN ACTUAL SANDWING!
GLORY, THAT'S QUEEN BLAZE!
YES, I KNOW.
I *DID* FIND MANGROVE, THOUGH. JAMBU'S TAKING HIM BACK TO THE RAINFOREST BEFORE THEY FREEZE TO DEATH.
EVERYONE, THIS IS BLAZE. BLAZE, MEET THE DRAGONETS OF DESTINY.
OH, WOW! IT IS SO, SO EXCITING TO MEET YOU.
WHERE'S THE SKYWING?
WE DON'T HAVE ONE. GLORY IS OUR FIFTH DRAGONET.
AN *ICEWING* IS YOUR FIFTH DRAGONET?

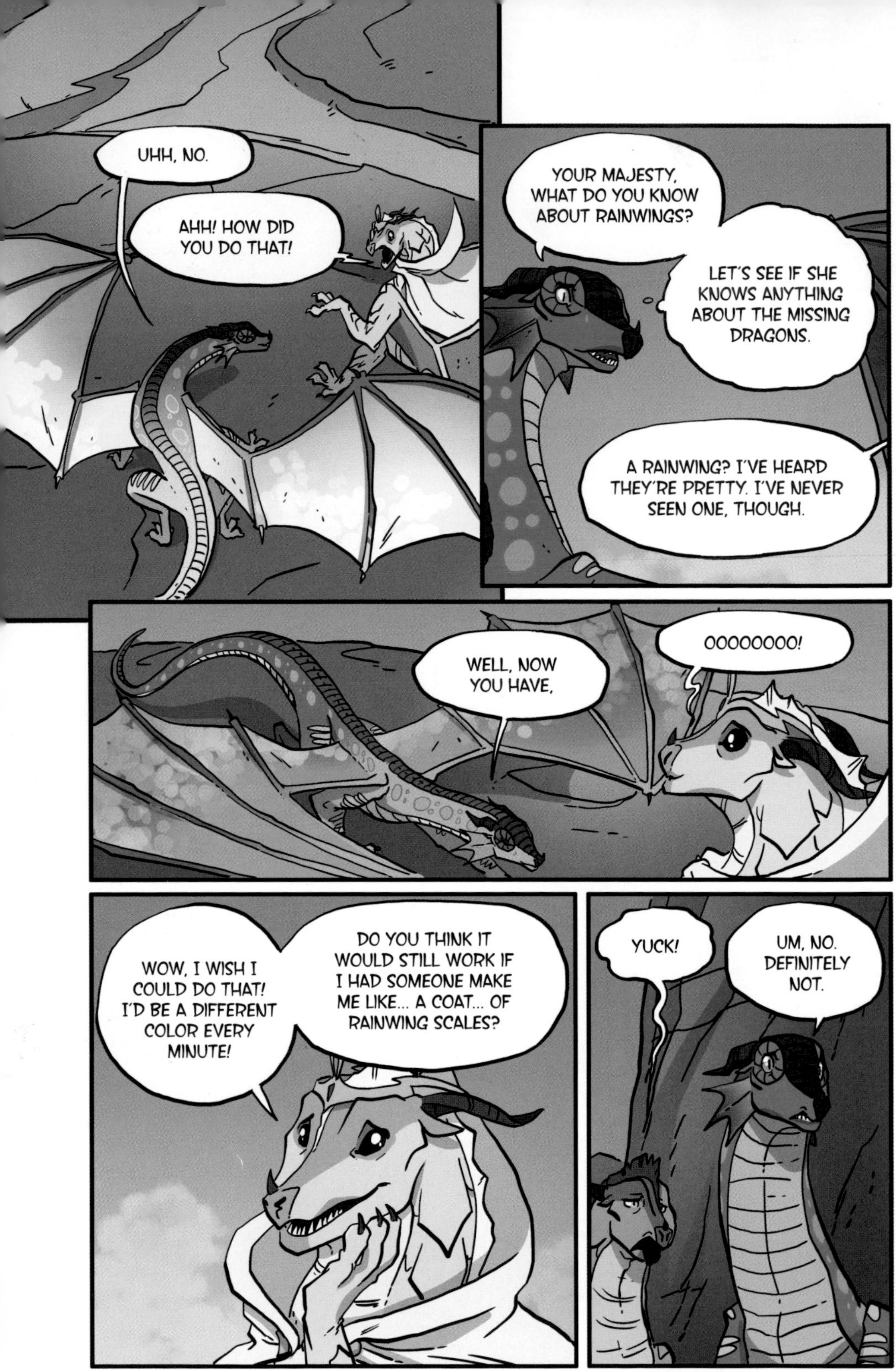
UHH, NO.
AHH! HOW DID YOU DO THAT!
YOUR MAJESTY, WHAT DO YOU KNOW ABOUT RAINWINGS?
LET'S SEE IF SHE KNOWS ANYTHING ABOUT THE MISSING DRAGONS.
A RAINWING? I'VE HEARD THEY'RE PRETTY. I'VE NEVER SEEN ONE, THOUGH.
WELL, NOW YOU HAVE,
OOOOOOOO!
WOW, I WISH I COULD DO THAT! I'D BE A DIFFERENT COLOR EVERY MINUTE!
DO YOU THINK IT WOULD STILL WORK IF I HAD SOMEONE MAKE ME LIKE... A COAT... OF RAINWING SCALES?
YUCK!
UM, NO. DEFINITELY NOT.

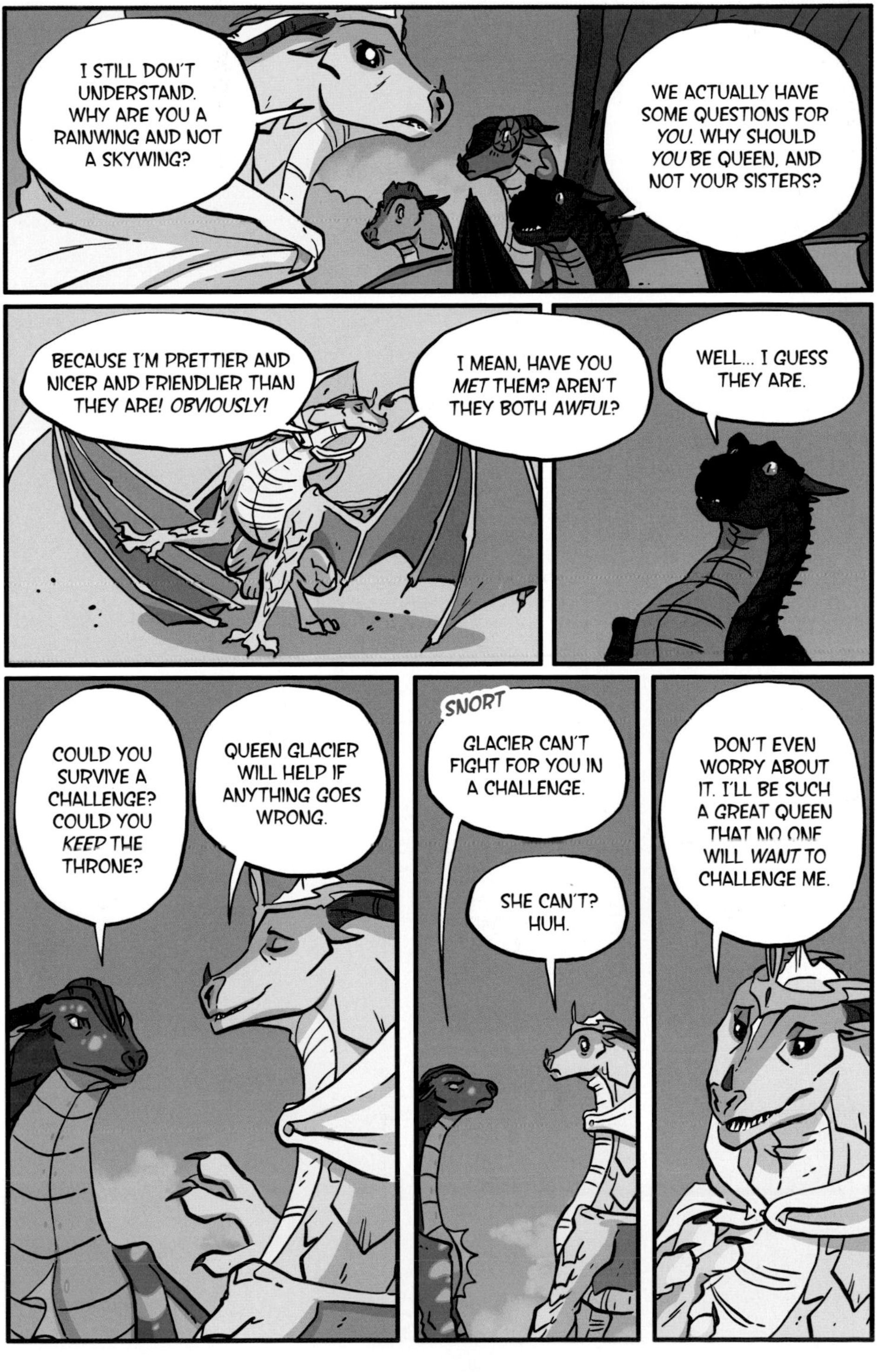
I STILL DON'T UNDERSTAND. WHY ARE YOU A RAINWING AND NOT A SKYWING?
WE ACTUALLY HAVE SOME QUESTIONS FOR *YOU.* WHY SHOULD *YOU* BE QUEEN, AND NOT YOUR SISTERS?
BECAUSE I'M PRETTIER AND NICER AND FRIENDLIER THAN THEY ARE! *OBVIOUSLY!*
I MEAN, HAVE YOU *MET* THEM? AREN'T THEY BOTH *AWFUL?*
WELL... I GUESS THEY ARE.
COULD YOU SURVIVE A CHALLENGE? COULD YOU *KEEP* THE THRONE?
QUEEN GLACIER WILL HELP IF ANYTHING GOES WRONG.
SNORT
GLACIER CAN'T FIGHT FOR YOU IN A CHALLENGE.
SHE CAN'T? HUH.
DON'T EVEN WORRY ABOUT IT. I'LL BE SUCH A GREAT QUEEN THAT NO ONE WILL *WANT* TO CHALLENGE ME.

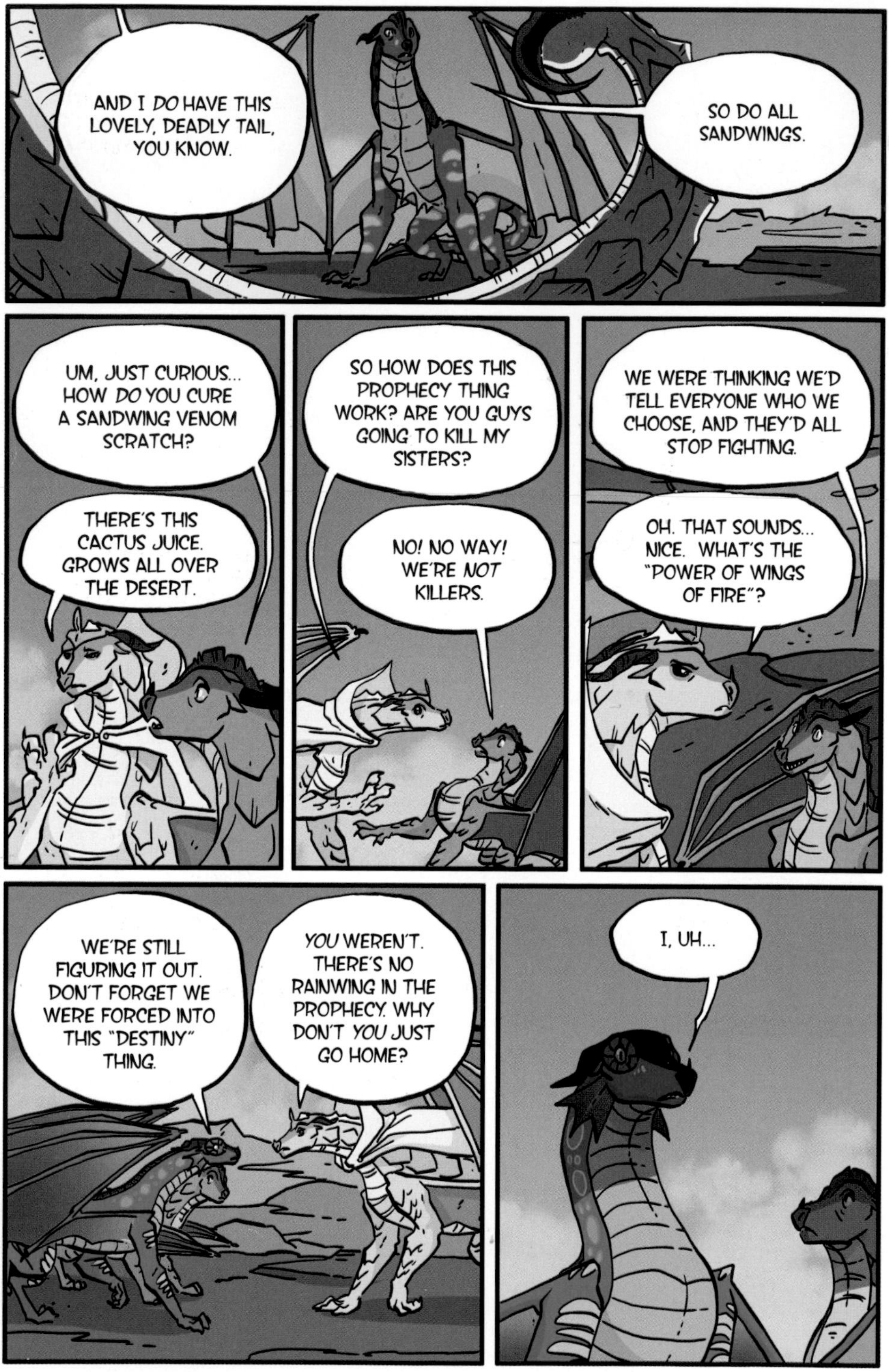
AND I *DO* HAVE THIS LOVELY, DEADLY TAIL, YOU KNOW.
SO DO ALL SANDWINGS.
UM, JUST CURIOUS... HOW *DO* YOU CURE A SANDWING VENOM SCRATCH?
THERE'S THIS CACTUS JUICE. GROWS ALL OVER THE DESERT.
SO HOW DOES THIS PROPHECY THING WORK? ARE YOU GUYS GOING TO KILL MY SISTERS?
NO! NO WAY! WE'RE *NOT* KILLERS.
WE WERE THINKING WE'D TELL EVERYONE WHO WE CHOOSE, AND THEY'D ALL STOP FIGHTING.
OH. THAT SOUNDS... NICE. WHAT'S THE "POWER OF WINGS OF FIRE"?
WE'RE STILL FIGURING IT OUT. DON'T FORGET WE WERE FORCED INTO THIS "DESTINY" THING.
YOU WEREN'T. THERE'S NO RAINWING IN THE PROPHECY. WHY DON'T *YOU* JUST GO HOME?
I, UH...

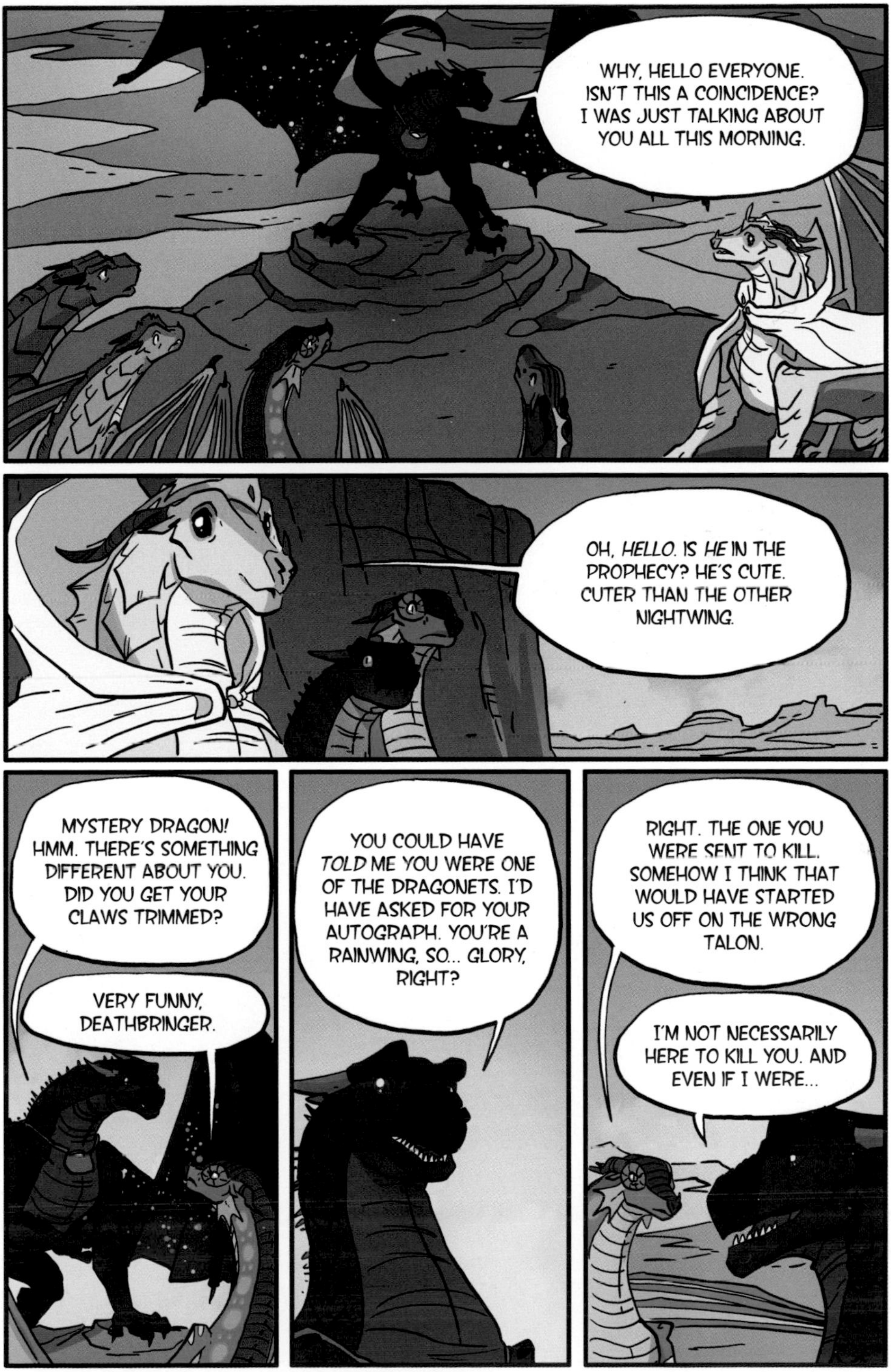
WHY, HELLO EVERYONE. ISN'T THIS A COINCIDENCE? I WAS JUST TALKING ABOUT YOU ALL THIS MORNING.
OH, *HELLO*. IS *HE* IN THE PROPHECY? HE'S CUTE. CUTER THAN THE OTHER NIGHTWING.
MYSTERY DRAGON! HMM. THERE'S SOMETHING DIFFERENT ABOUT YOU. DID YOU GET YOUR CLAWS TRIMMED?
VERY FUNNY, DEATHBRINGER.
YOU COULD HAVE *TOLD* ME YOU WERE ONE OF THE DRAGONETS. I'D HAVE ASKED FOR YOUR AUTOGRAPH. YOU'RE A RAINWING, SO... GLORY, RIGHT?
RIGHT. THE ONE YOU WERE SENT TO KILL. SOMEHOW I THINK THAT WOULD HAVE STARTED US OFF ON THE WRONG TALON.
I'M NOT NECESSARILY HERE TO KILL YOU. AND EVEN IF I WERE...

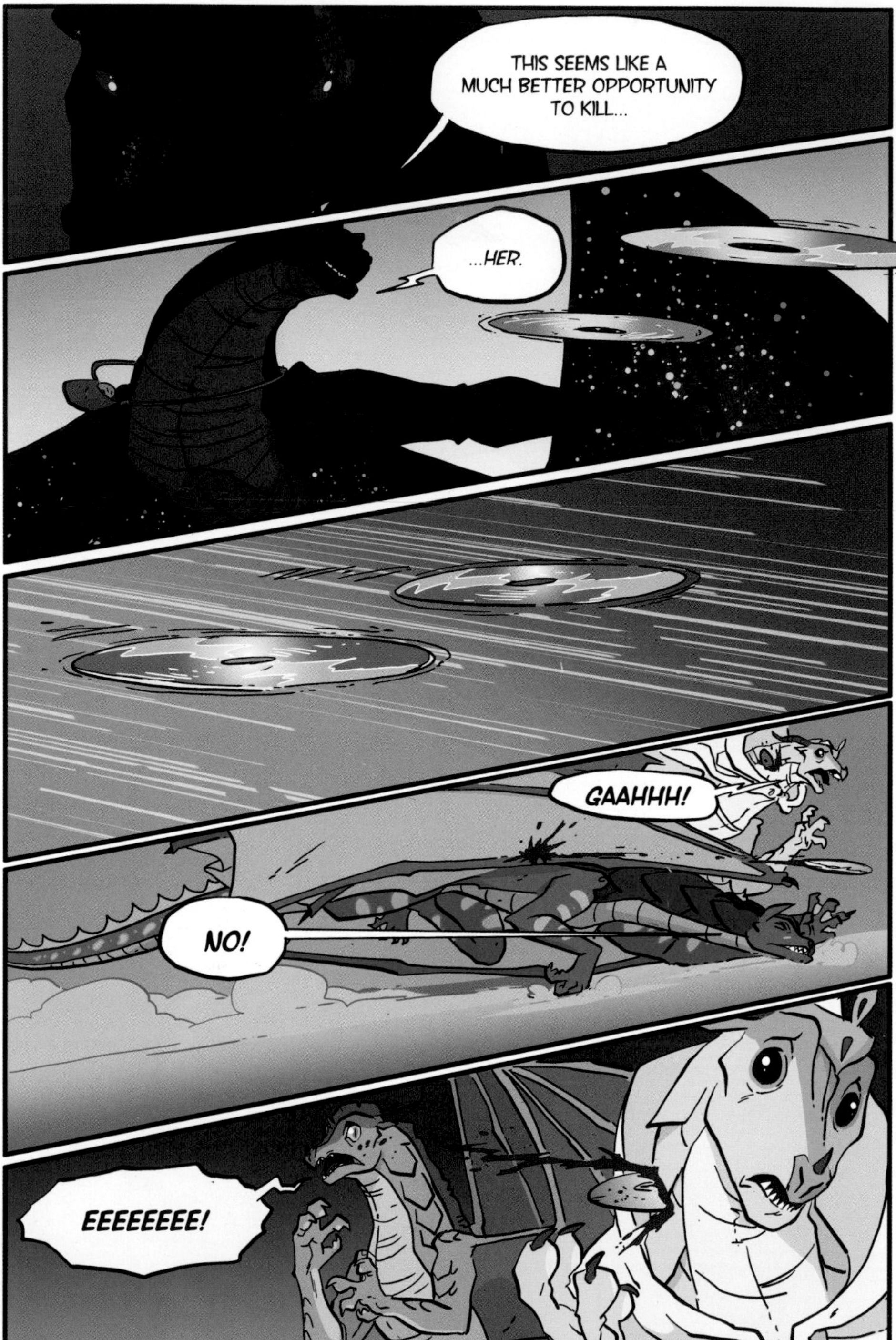
THIS SEEMS LIKE A MUCH BETTER OPPORTUNITY TO KILL...
...HER.
GAAHHH!
NO!
EEEEEEEE!

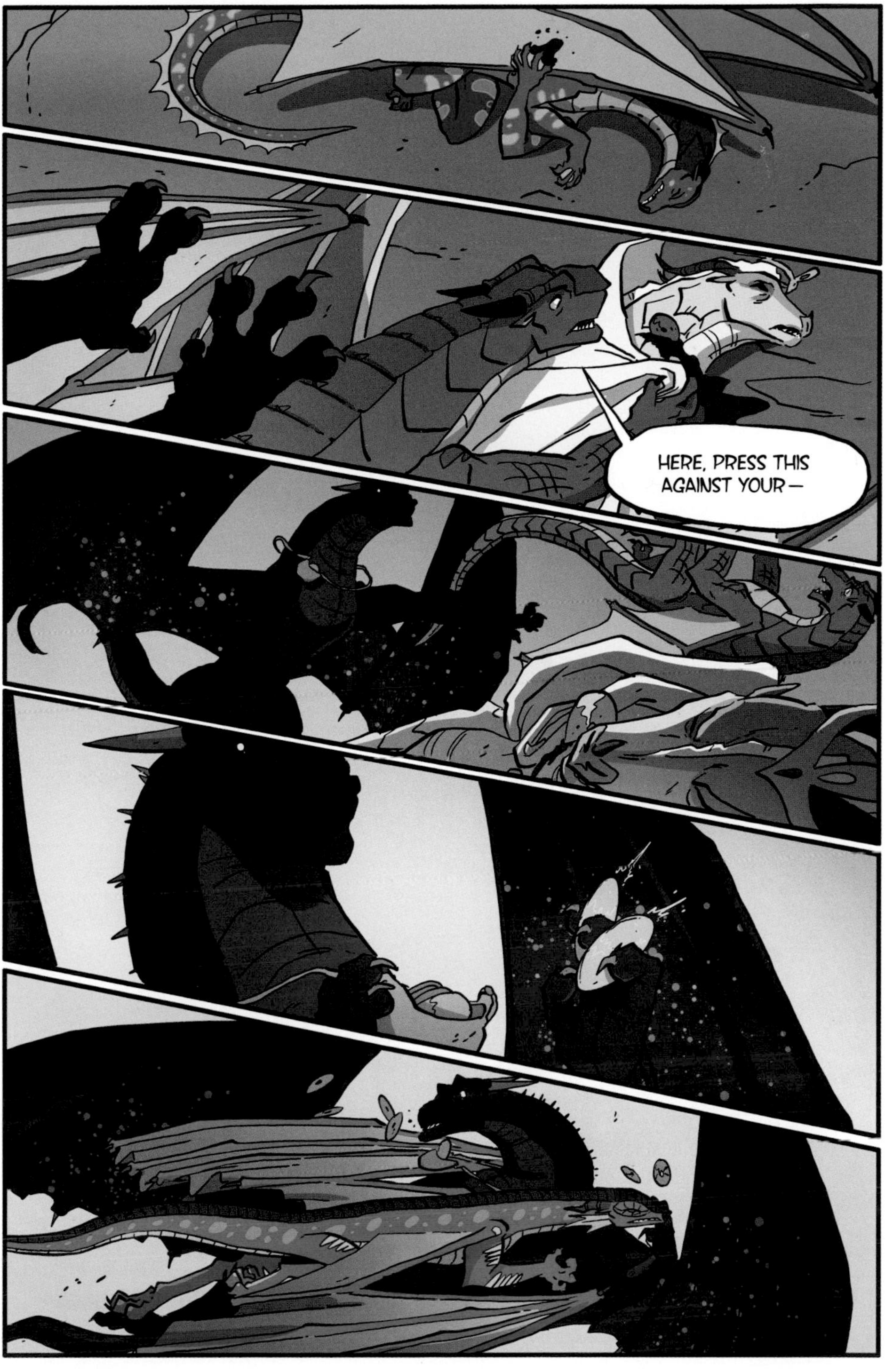
HERE, PRESS THIS AGAINST YOUR—

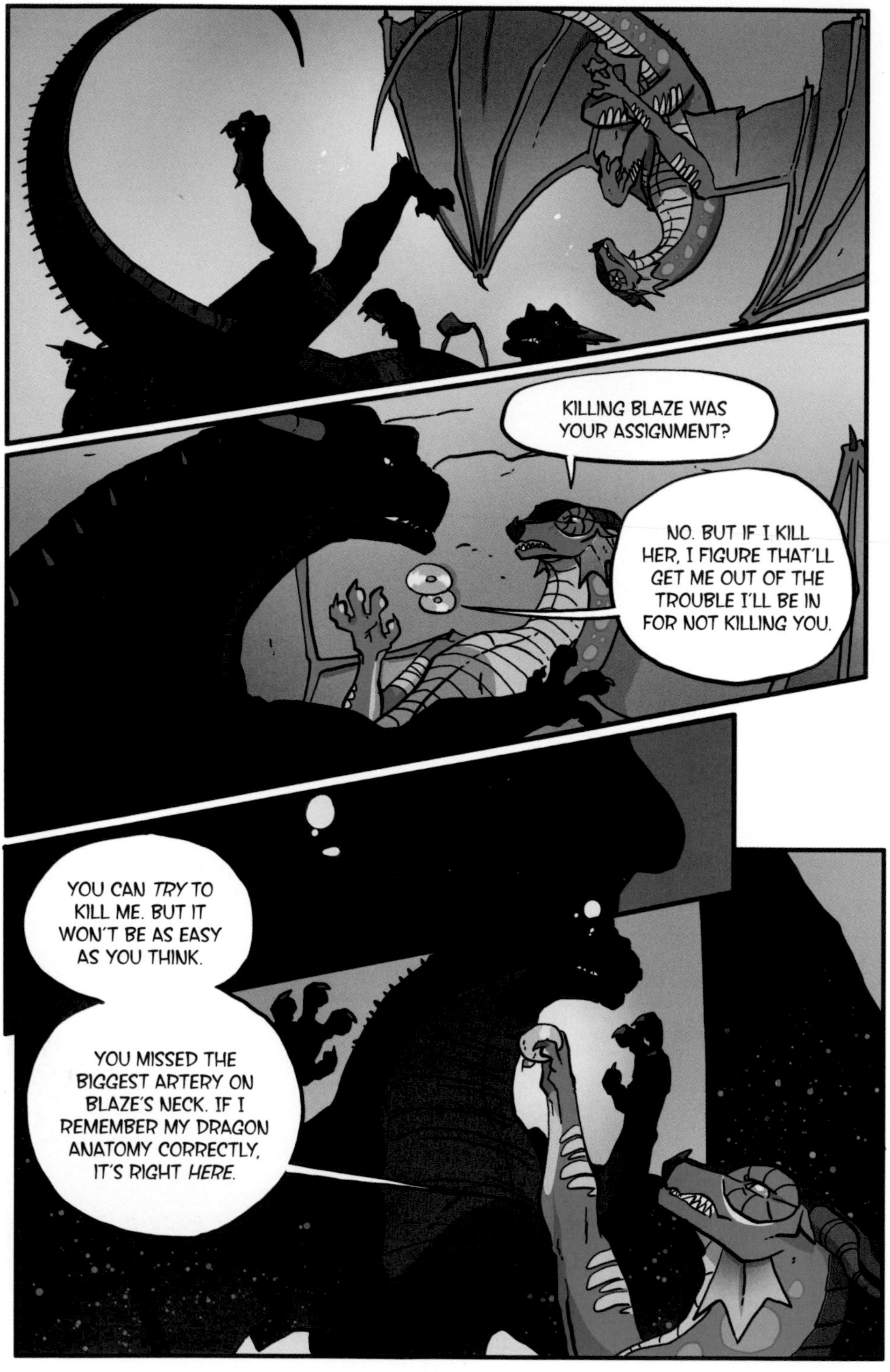

KILLING BLAZE WAS YOUR ASSIGNMENT?
NO. BUT IF I KILL HER, I FIGURE THAT'LL GET ME OUT OF THE TROUBLE I'LL BE IN FOR NOT KILLING YOU.
YOU CAN *TRY* TO KILL ME. BUT IT WON'T BE AS EASY AS YOU THINK.
YOU MISSED THE BIGGEST ARTERY ON BLAZE'S NECK. IF I REMEMBER MY DRAGON ANATOMY CORRECTLY, IT'S RIGHT *HERE*.

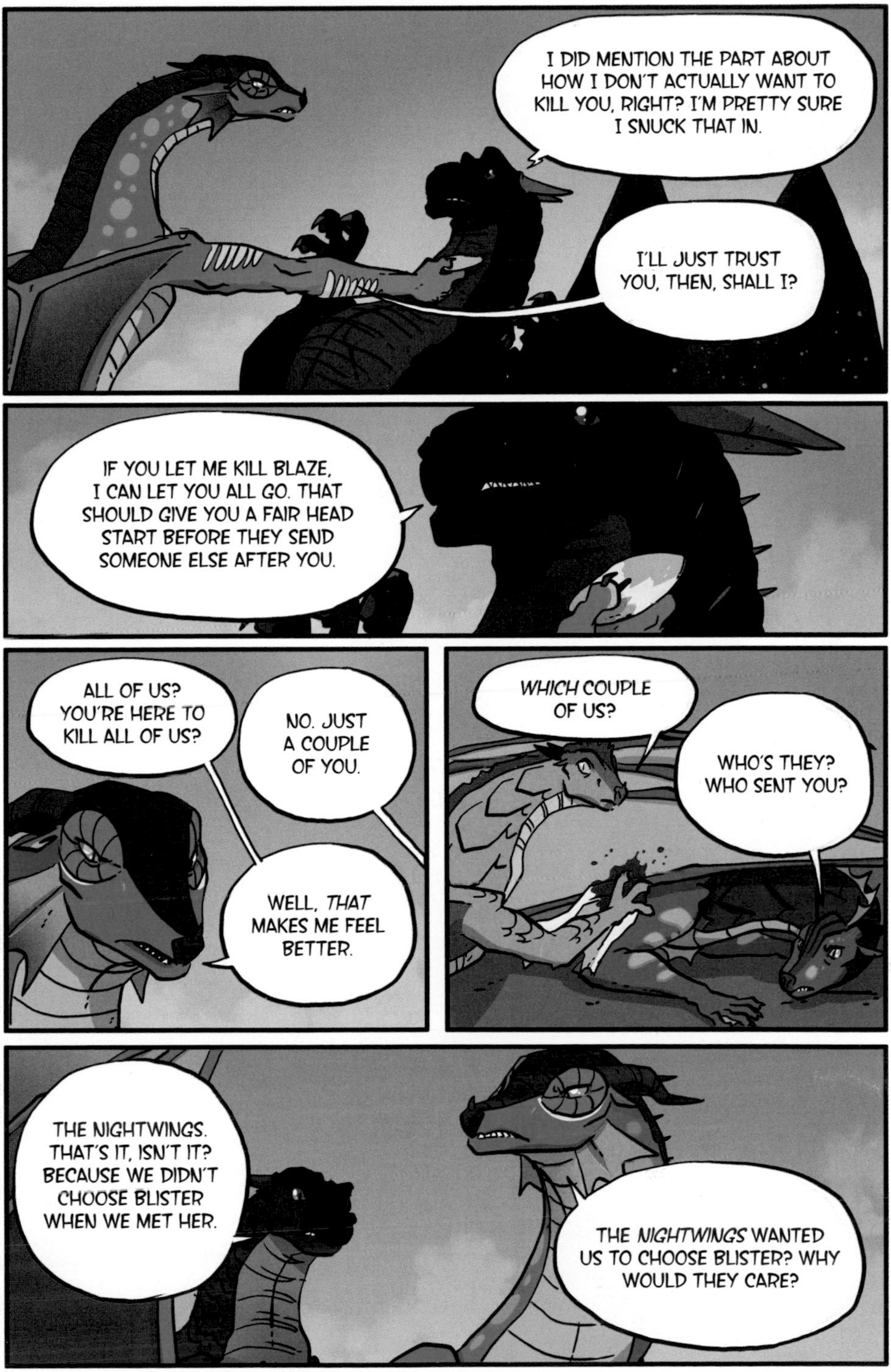
I DID MENTION THE PART ABOUT HOW I DON'T ACTUALLY WANT TO KILL YOU, RIGHT? I'M PRETTY SURE I SNUCK THAT IN.
I'LL JUST TRUST YOU, THEN, SHALL I?
IF YOU LET ME KILL BLAZE, I CAN LET YOU ALL GO. THAT SHOULD GIVE YOU A FAIR HEAD START BEFORE THEY SEND SOMEONE ELSE AFTER YOU.
ALL OF US? YOU'RE HERE TO KILL ALL OF US?
NO. JUST A COUPLE OF YOU.
WELL, *THAT* MAKES ME FEEL BETTER.
WHICH COUPLE OF US?
WHO'S THEY? WHO SENT YOU?
THE NIGHTWINGS. THAT'S IT, ISN'T IT? BECAUSE WE DIDN'T CHOOSE BLISTER WHEN WE MET HER.
THE *NIGHTWINGS* WANTED US TO CHOOSE BLISTER? WHY WOULD THEY CARE?

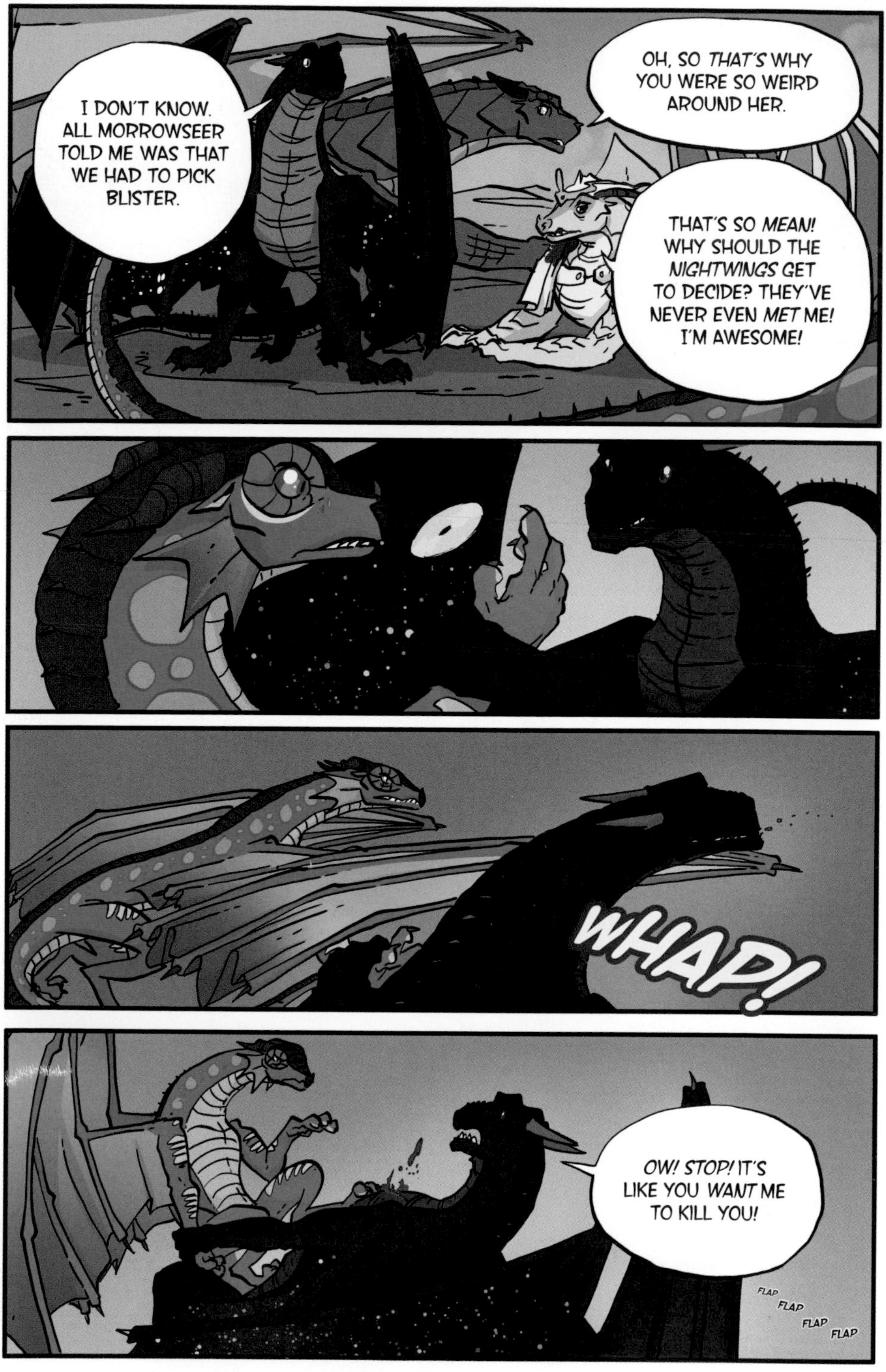
I DON'T KNOW. ALL MORROWSEER TOLD ME WAS THAT WE HAD TO PICK BLISTER.
OH, SO *THAT'S* WHY YOU WERE SO WEIRD AROUND HER.
THAT'S SO *MEAN!* WHY SHOULD THE *NIGHTWINGS* GET TO DECIDE? THEY'VE NEVER EVEN *MET* ME! I'M AWESOME!
WHAP!
OW! STOP! IT'S LIKE YOU *WANT* ME TO KILL YOU!
FLAP
FLAP
FLAP
FLAP

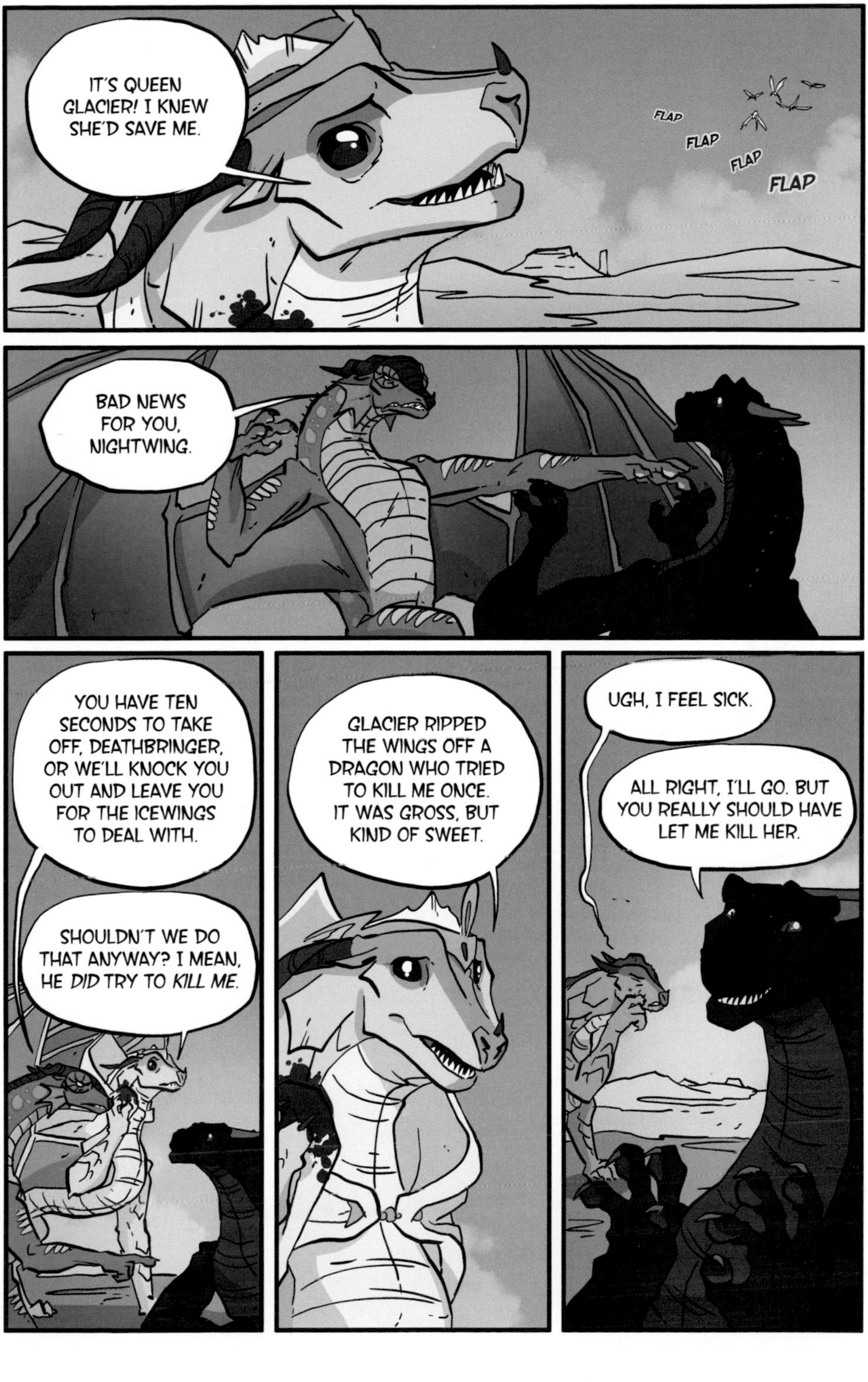
IT'S QUEEN GLACIER! I KNEW SHE'D SAVE ME.
FLAP
FLAP
FLAP
FLAP
BAD NEWS FOR YOU, NIGHTWING.
YOU HAVE TEN SECONDS TO TAKE OFF, DEATHBRINGER, OR WE'LL KNOCK YOU OUT AND LEAVE YOU FOR THE ICEWINGS TO DEAL WITH.
SHOULDN'T WE DO THAT ANYWAY? I MEAN, HE *DID* TRY TO *KILL ME.*
GLACIER RIPPED THE WINGS OFF A DRAGON WHO TRIED TO KILL ME ONCE. IT WAS GROSS, BUT KIND OF SWEET.
UGH, I FEEL SICK.
ALL RIGHT, I'LL GO. BUT YOU REALLY SHOULD HAVE LET ME KILL HER.

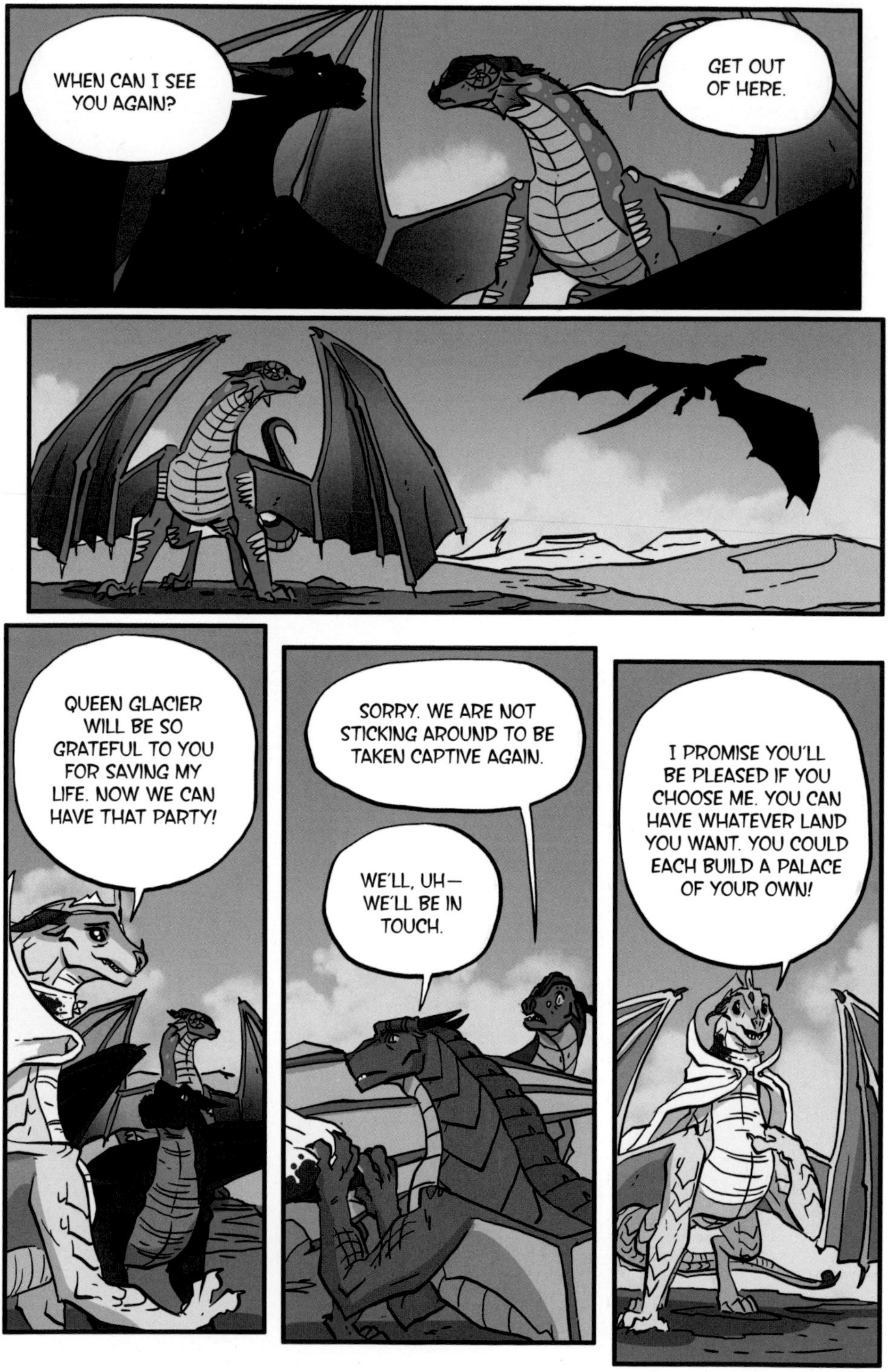
WHEN CAN I SEE YOU AGAIN?
GET OUT OF HERE.
QUEEN GLACIER WILL BE SO GRATEFUL TO YOU FOR SAVING MY LIFE. NOW WE CAN HAVE THAT PARTY!
SORRY. WE ARE NOT STICKING AROUND TO BE TAKEN CAPTIVE AGAIN.
WE'LL, UH— WE'LL BE IN TOUCH.
I PROMISE YOU'LL BE PLEASED IF YOU CHOOSE ME. YOU CAN HAVE WHATEVER LAND YOU WANT. YOU COULD EACH BUILD A PALACE OF YOUR OWN!

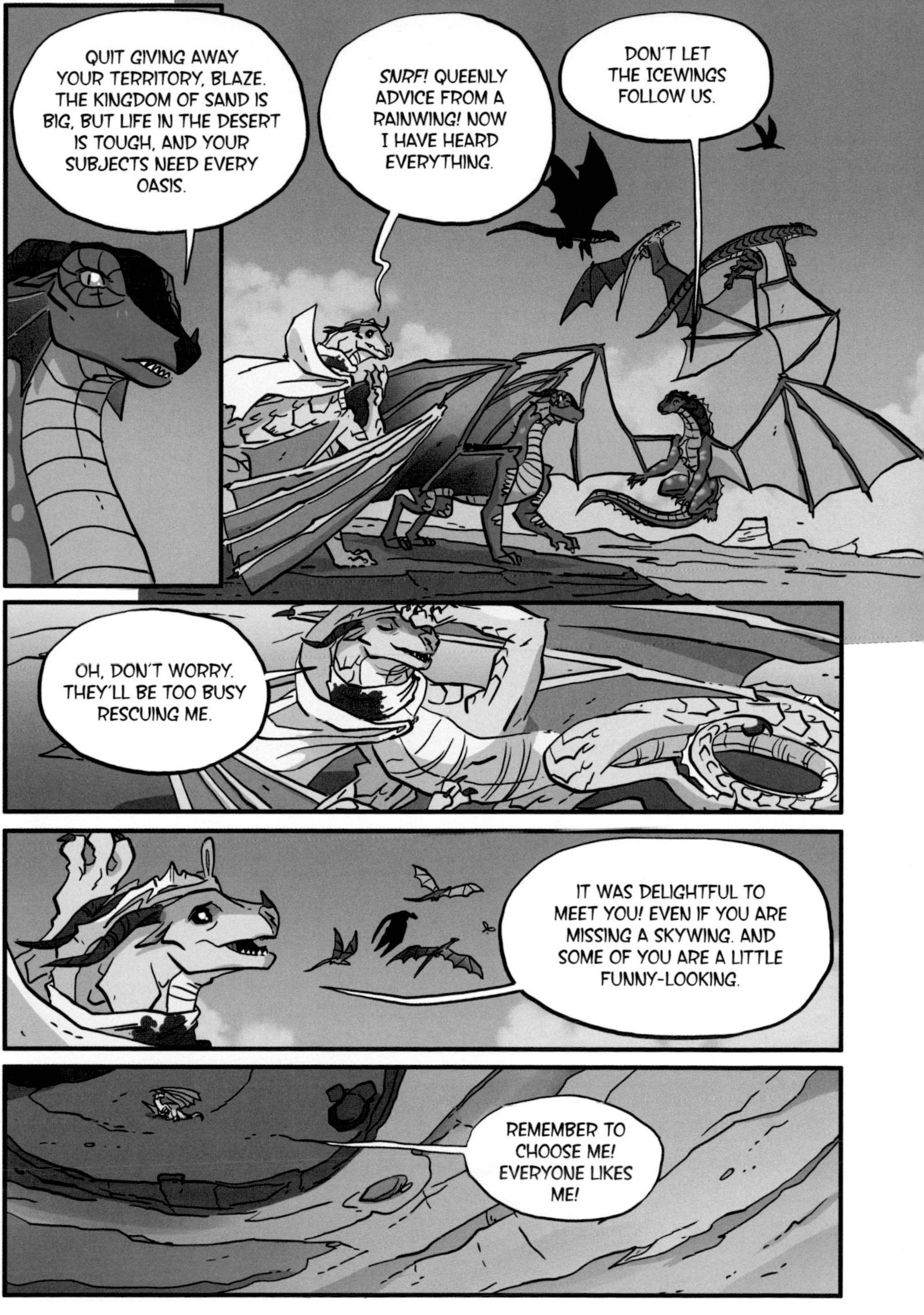
QUIT GIVING AWAY YOUR TERRITORY, BLAZE. THE KINGDOM OF SAND IS BIG, BUT LIFE IN THE DESERT IS TOUGH, AND YOUR SUBJECTS NEED EVERY OASIS.
SNRF! QUEENLY ADVICE FROM A RAINWING! NOW I HAVE HEARD EVERYTHING.
DON'T LET THE ICEWINGS FOLLOW US.
OH, DON'T WORRY. THEY'LL BE TOO BUSY RESCUING ME.
IT WAS DELIGHTFUL TO MEET YOU! EVEN IF YOU ARE MISSING A SKYWING. AND SOME OF YOU ARE A LITTLE FUNNY-LOOKING.
REMEMBER TO CHOOSE ME! EVERYONE LIKES ME!

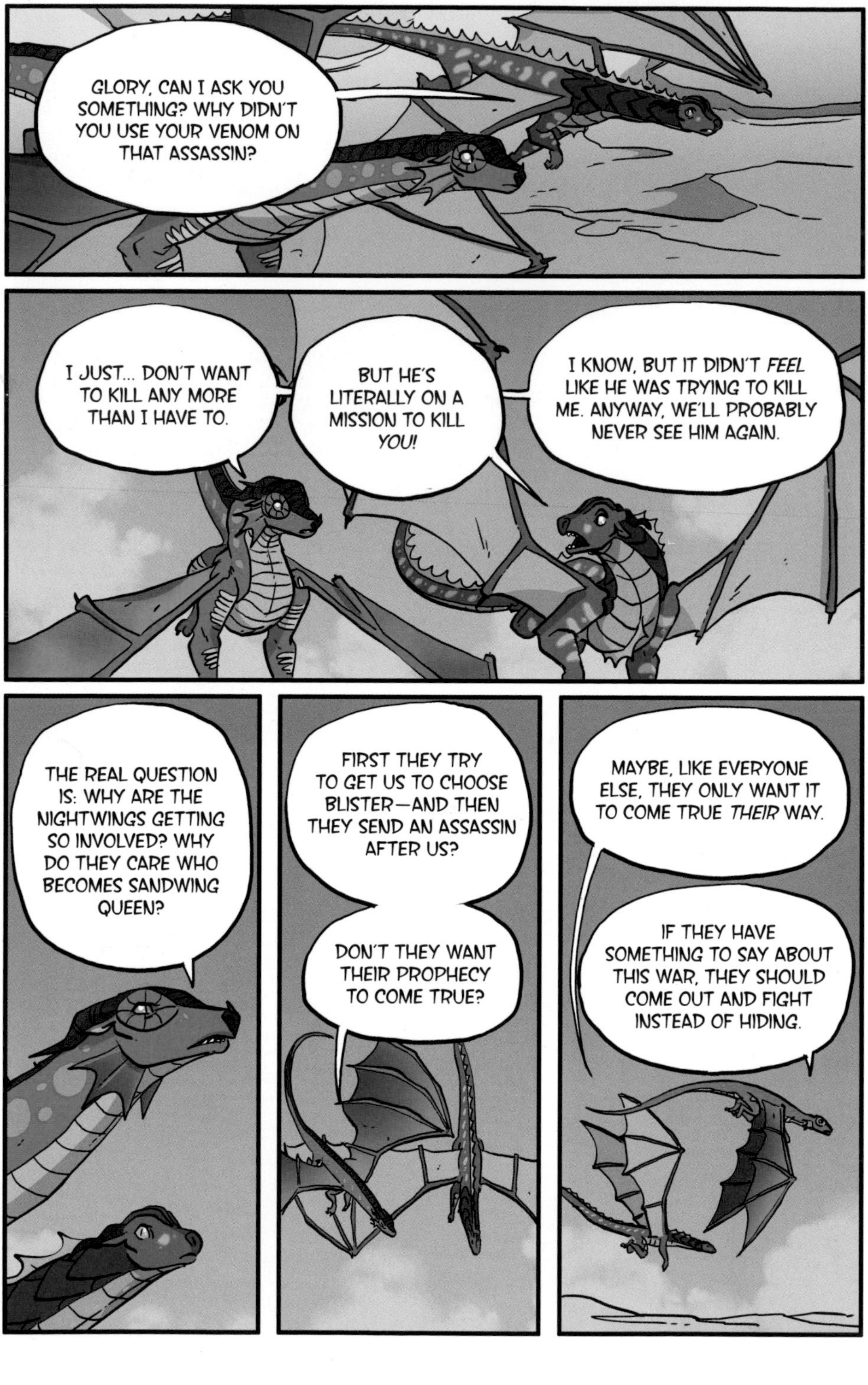
GLORY, CAN I ASK YOU SOMETHING? WHY DIDN'T YOU USE YOUR VENOM ON THAT ASSASSIN?
I JUST... DON'T WANT TO KILL ANY MORE THAN I HAVE TO.
BUT HE'S LITERALLY ON A MISSION TO KILL *YOU!*
I KNOW, BUT IT DIDN'T *FEEL* LIKE HE WAS TRYING TO KILL ME. ANYWAY, WE'LL PROBABLY NEVER SEE HIM AGAIN.
THE REAL QUESTION IS: WHY ARE THE NIGHTWINGS GETTING SO INVOLVED? WHY DO THEY CARE WHO BECOMES SANDWING QUEEN?
FIRST THEY TRY TO GET US TO CHOOSE BLISTER—AND THEN THEY SEND AN ASSASSIN AFTER US?
DON'T THEY WANT THEIR PROPHECY TO COME TRUE?
MAYBE, LIKE EVERYONE ELSE, THEY ONLY WANT IT TO COME TRUE *THEIR* WAY.
IF THEY HAVE SOMETHING TO SAY ABOUT THIS WAR, THEY SHOULD COME OUT AND FIGHT INSTEAD OF HIDING.

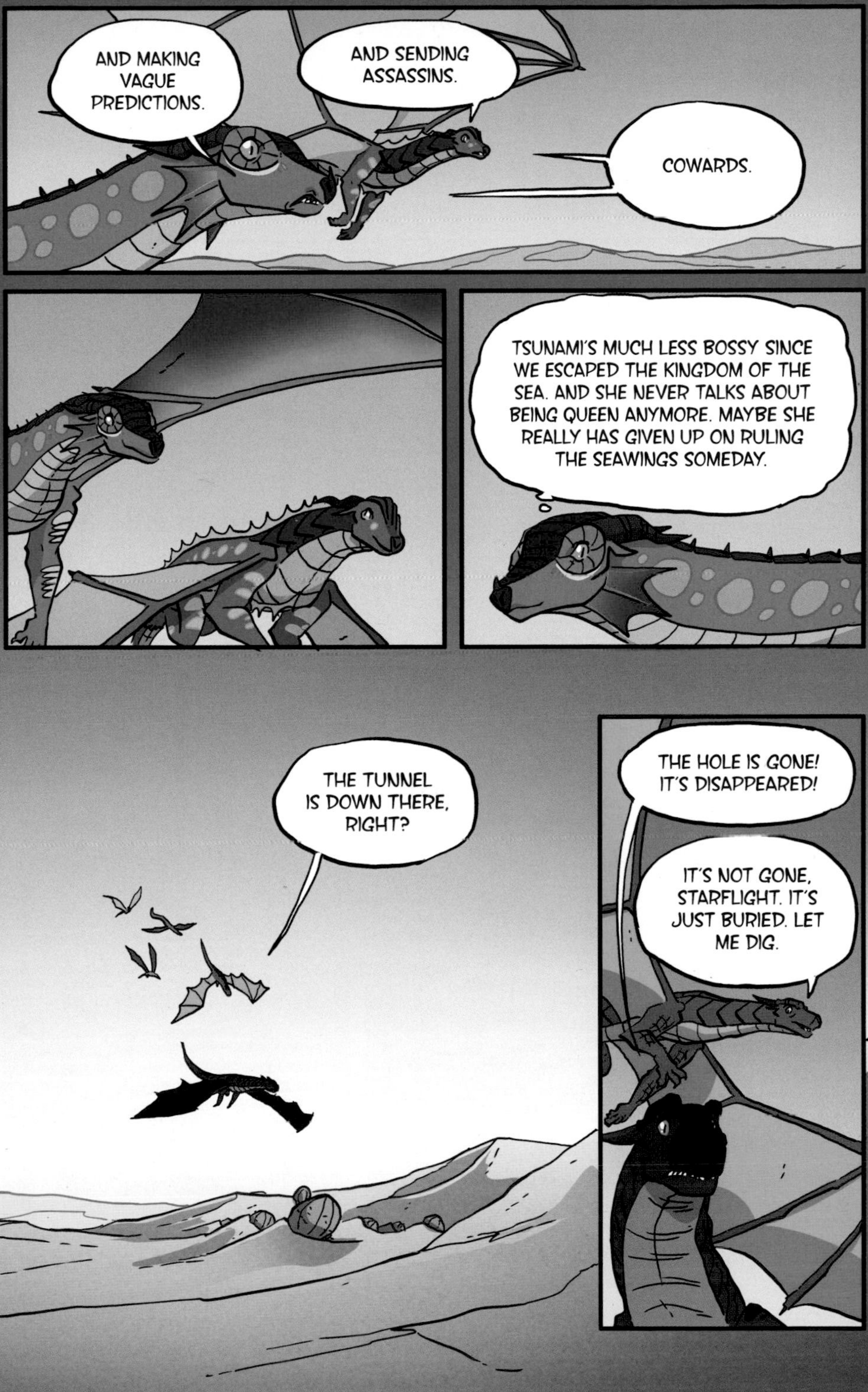
AND MAKING VAGUE PREDICTIONS.
AND SENDING ASSASSINS.
COWARDS.
TSUNAMI'S MUCH LESS BOSSY SINCE WE ESCAPED THE KINGDOM OF THE SEA. AND SHE NEVER TALKS ABOUT BEING QUEEN ANYMORE. MAYBE SHE REALLY HAS GIVEN UP ON RULING THE SEAWINGS SOMEDAY.
THE TUNNEL IS DOWN THERE, RIGHT?
THE HOLE IS GONE! IT'S DISAPPEARED!
IT'S NOT GONE, STARFLIGHT. IT'S JUST BURIED. LET ME DIG.

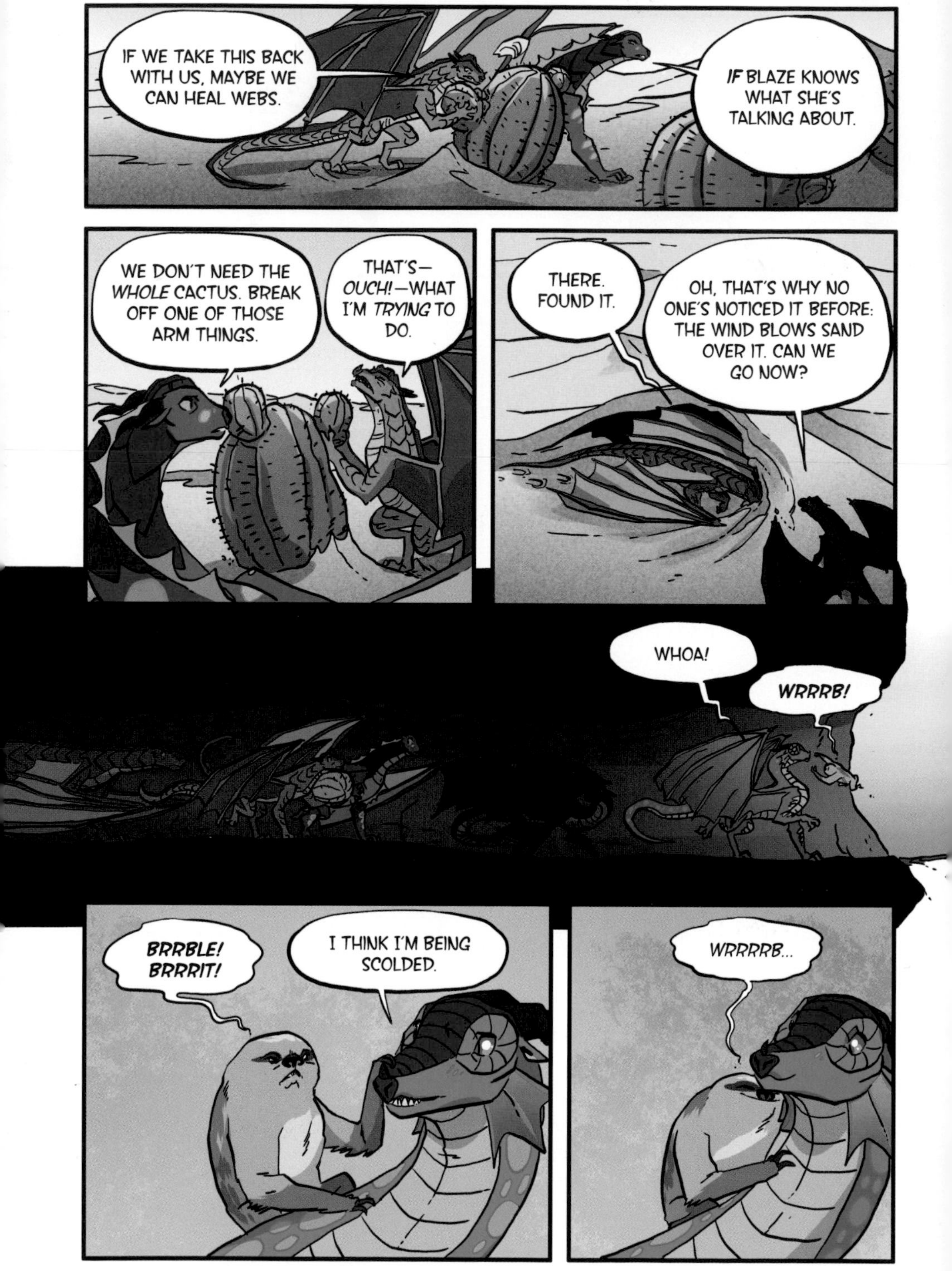

IF WE TAKE THIS BACK WITH US, MAYBE WE CAN HEAL WEBS.
IF BLAZE KNOWS WHAT SHE'S TALKING ABOUT.
WE DON'T NEED THE *WHOLE* CACTUS. BREAK OFF ONE OF THOSE ARM THINGS.
THAT'S— *OUCH!*—WHAT I'M *TRYING* TO DO.
THERE. FOUND IT.
OH, THAT'S WHY NO ONE'S NOTICED IT BEFORE: THE WIND BLOWS SAND OVER IT. CAN WE GO NOW?
WHOA!
WRRRB!
BRRBLE! BRRRIT!
I THINK I'M BEING SCOLDED.
WRRRRB...

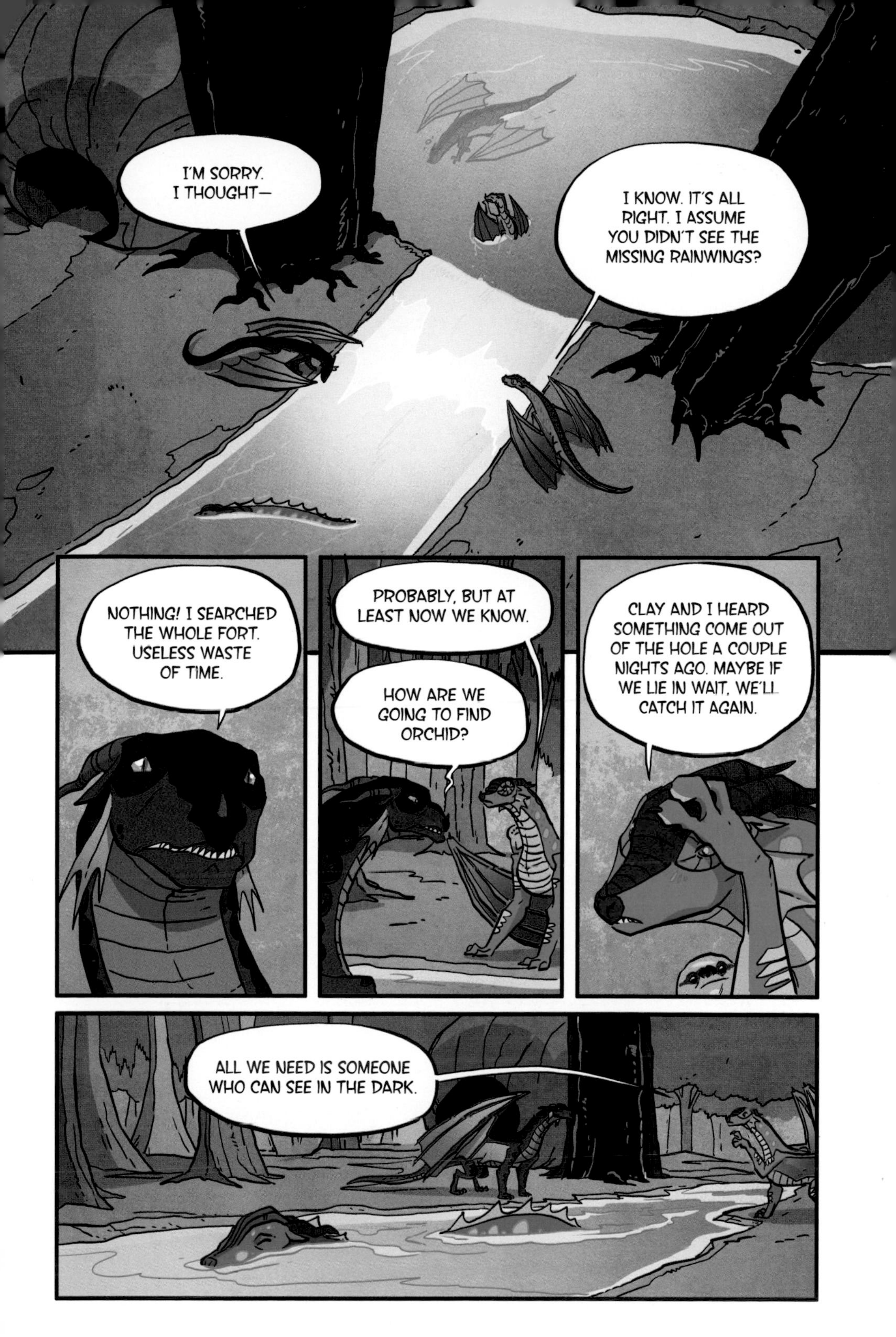
I'M SORRY. I THOUGHT—
I KNOW. IT'S ALL RIGHT. I ASSUME YOU DIDN'T SEE THE MISSING RAINWINGS?
NOTHING! I SEARCHED THE WHOLE FORT. USELESS WASTE OF TIME.
PROBABLY, BUT AT LEAST NOW WE KNOW.
HOW ARE WE GOING TO FIND ORCHID?
CLAY AND I HEARD SOMETHING COME OUT OF THE HOLE A COUPLE NIGHTS AGO. MAYBE IF WE LIE IN WAIT, WE'LL CATCH IT AGAIN.
ALL WE NEED IS SOMEONE WHO CAN SEE IN THE DARK.

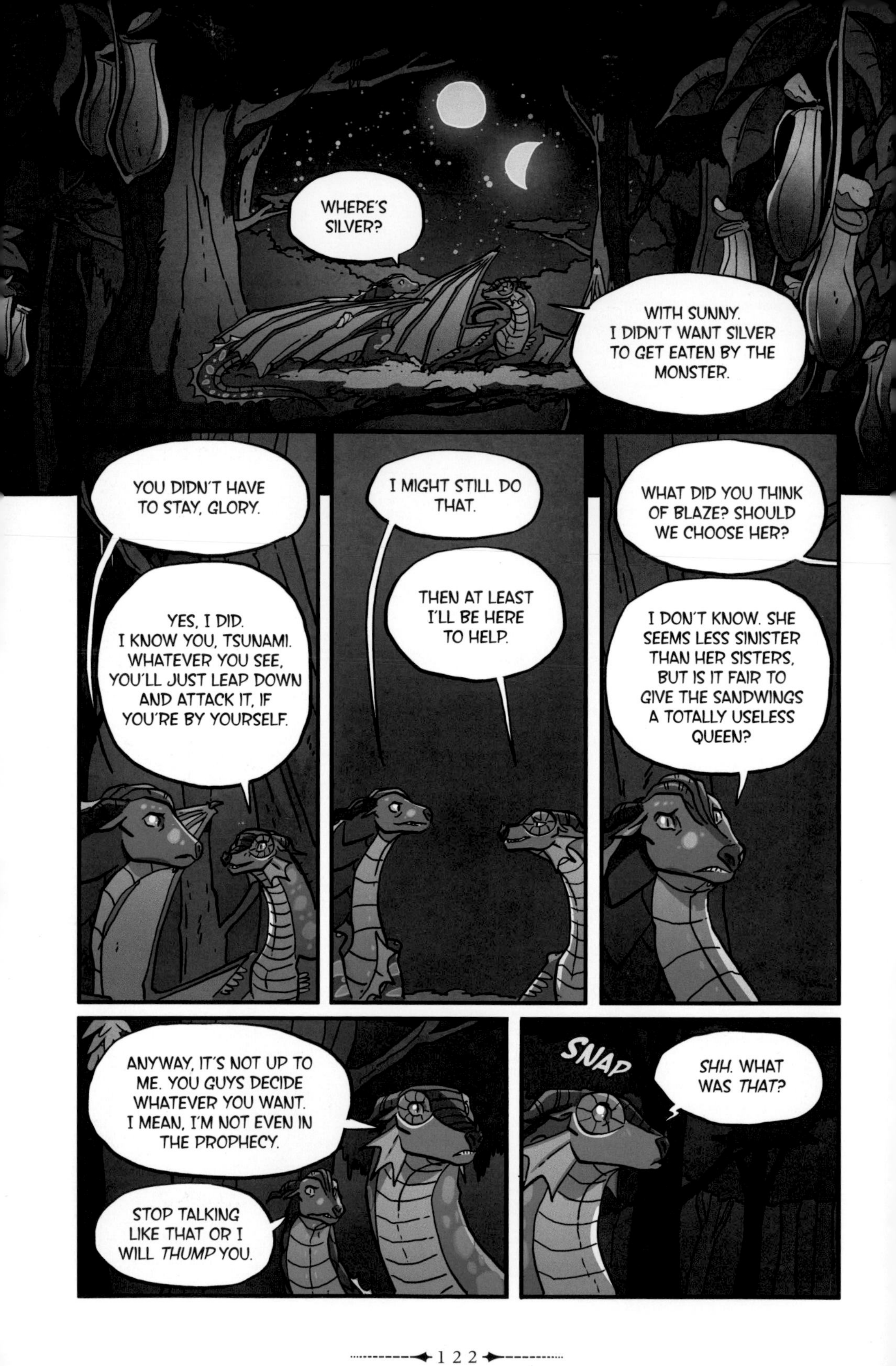
WHERE'S SILVER?
WITH SUNNY. I DIDN'T WANT SILVER TO GET EATEN BY THE MONSTER.
YOU DIDN'T HAVE TO STAY, GLORY.
YES, I DID. I KNOW YOU, TSUNAMI. WHATEVER YOU SEE, YOU'LL JUST LEAP DOWN AND ATTACK IT, IF YOU'RE BY YOURSELF.
I MIGHT STILL DO THAT.
THEN AT LEAST I'LL BE HERE TO HELP.
WHAT DID YOU THINK OF BLAZE? SHOULD WE CHOOSE HER?
I DON'T KNOW. SHE SEEMS LESS SINISTER THAN HER SISTERS, BUT IS IT FAIR TO GIVE THE SANDWINGS A TOTALLY USELESS QUEEN?
ANYWAY, IT'S NOT UP TO ME. YOU GUYS DECIDE WHATEVER YOU WANT. I MEAN, I'M NOT EVEN IN THE PROPHECY.
STOP TALKING LIKE THAT OR I WILL *THUMP* YOU.
SNAP
SHH. WHAT WAS *THAT*?

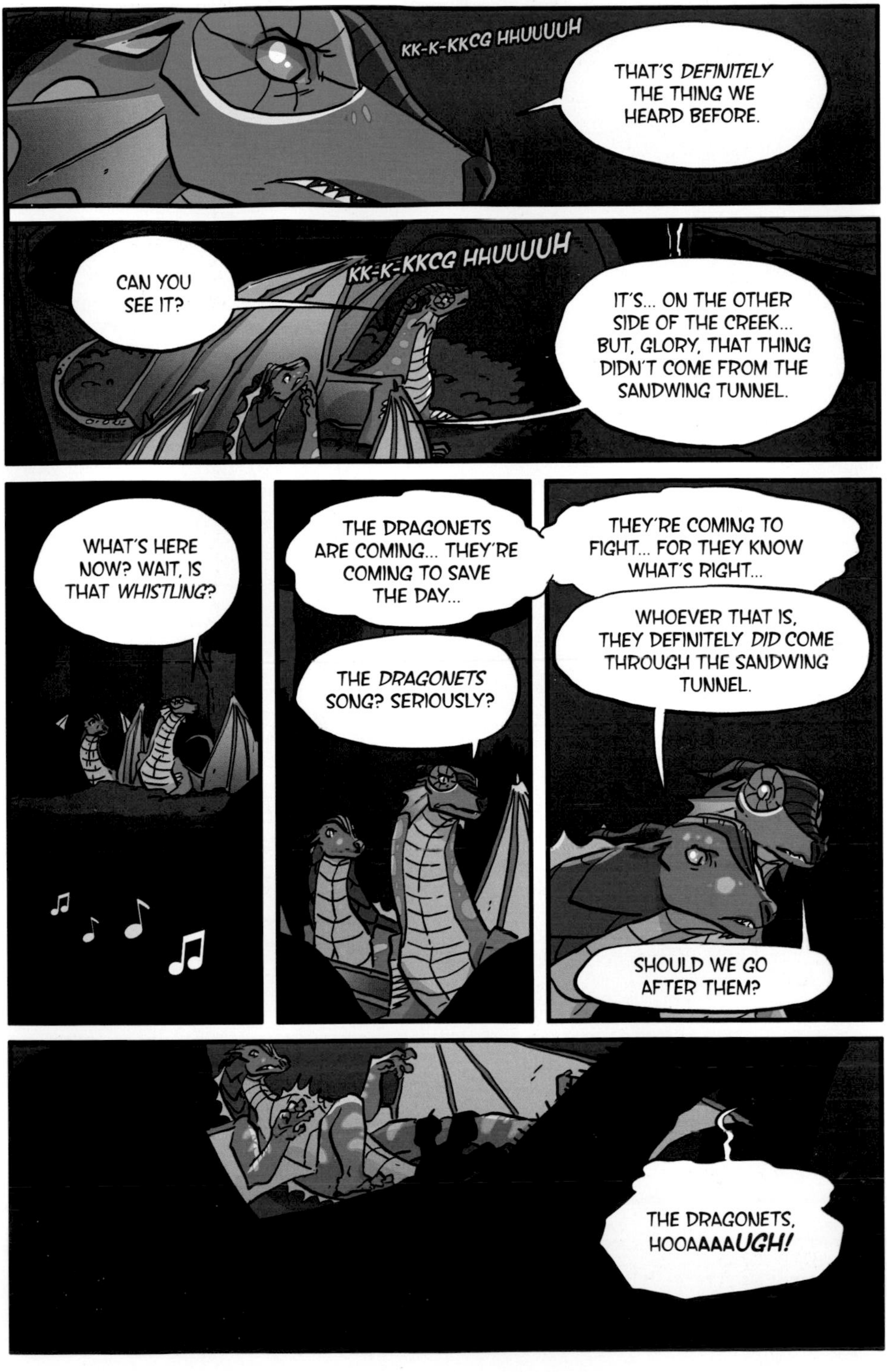

KK-K-KKCG HHUUUUH
THAT'S *DEFINITELY* THE THING WE HEARD BEFORE.
KK-K-KKCG HHUUUUH
CAN YOU SEE IT?
IT'S... ON THE OTHER SIDE OF THE CREEK... BUT, GLORY, THAT THING DIDN'T COME FROM THE SANDWING TUNNEL.
WHAT'S HERE NOW? WAIT, IS THAT *WHISTLING*?
THE DRAGONETS ARE COMING... THEY'RE COMING TO SAVE THE DAY...
THE *DRAGONETS* SONG? SERIOUSLY?
THEY'RE COMING TO FIGHT... FOR THEY KNOW WHAT'S RIGHT...
WHOEVER THAT IS, THEY DEFINITELY *DID* COME THROUGH THE SANDWING TUNNEL.
SHOULD WE GO AFTER THEM?
THE DRAGONETS, HOOAAAA**UGH!**

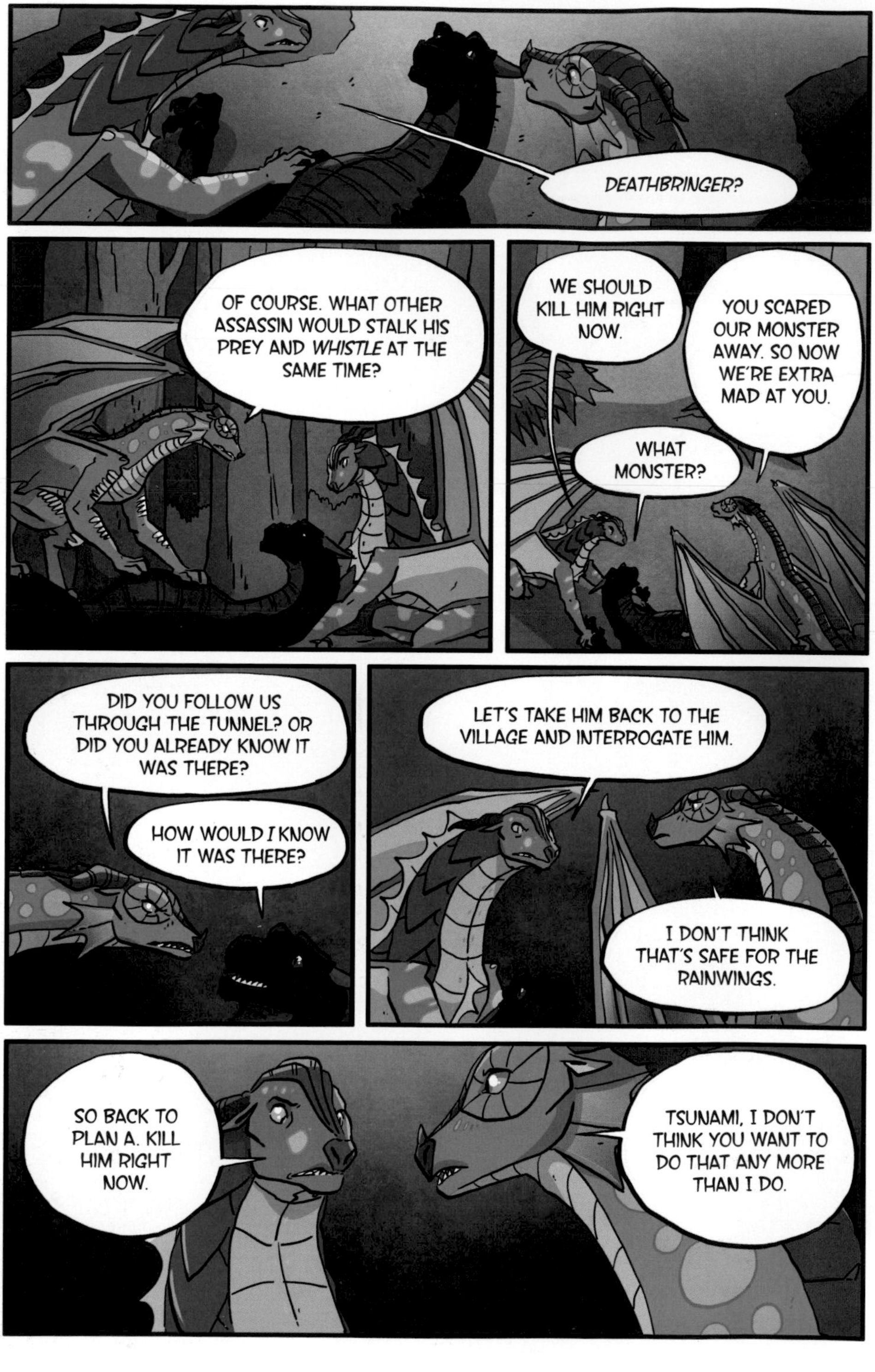
DEATHBRINGER?
OF COURSE. WHAT OTHER ASSASSIN WOULD STALK HIS PREY AND *WHISTLE* AT THE SAME TIME?
WE SHOULD KILL HIM RIGHT NOW.
YOU SCARED OUR MONSTER AWAY. SO NOW WE'RE EXTRA MAD AT YOU.
WHAT MONSTER?
DID YOU FOLLOW US THROUGH THE TUNNEL? OR DID YOU ALREADY KNOW IT WAS THERE?
HOW WOULD *I* KNOW IT WAS THERE?
LET'S TAKE HIM BACK TO THE VILLAGE AND INTERROGATE HIM.
I DON'T THINK THAT'S SAFE FOR THE RAINWINGS.
SO BACK TO PLAN A. KILL HIM RIGHT NOW.
TSUNAMI, I DON'T THINK YOU WANT TO DO THAT ANY MORE THAN I DO.

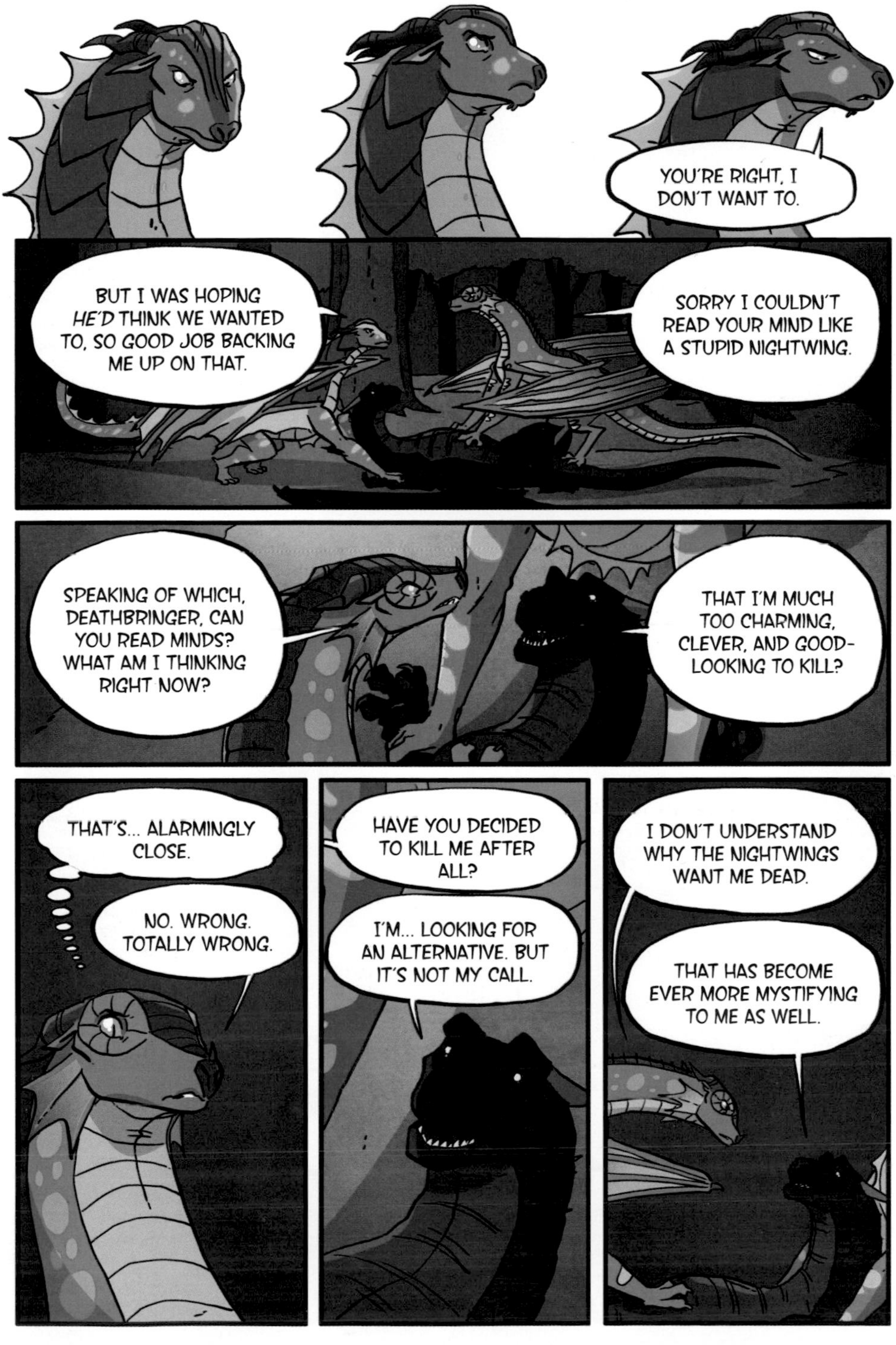
YOU'RE RIGHT, I DON'T WANT TO.
BUT I WAS HOPING *HE'D* THINK WE WANTED TO, SO GOOD JOB BACKING ME UP ON THAT.
SORRY I COULDN'T READ YOUR MIND LIKE A STUPID NIGHTWING.
SPEAKING OF WHICH, DEATHBRINGER, CAN YOU READ MINDS? WHAT AM I THINKING RIGHT NOW?
THAT I'M MUCH TOO CHARMING, CLEVER, AND GOOD-LOOKING TO KILL?
THAT'S... ALARMINGLY CLOSE.
NO. WRONG. TOTALLY WRONG.
HAVE YOU DECIDED TO KILL ME AFTER ALL?
I'M... LOOKING FOR AN ALTERNATIVE. BUT IT'S NOT MY CALL.
I DON'T UNDERSTAND WHY THE NIGHTWINGS WANT ME DEAD.
THAT HAS BECOME EVER MORE MYSTIFYING TO ME AS WELL.

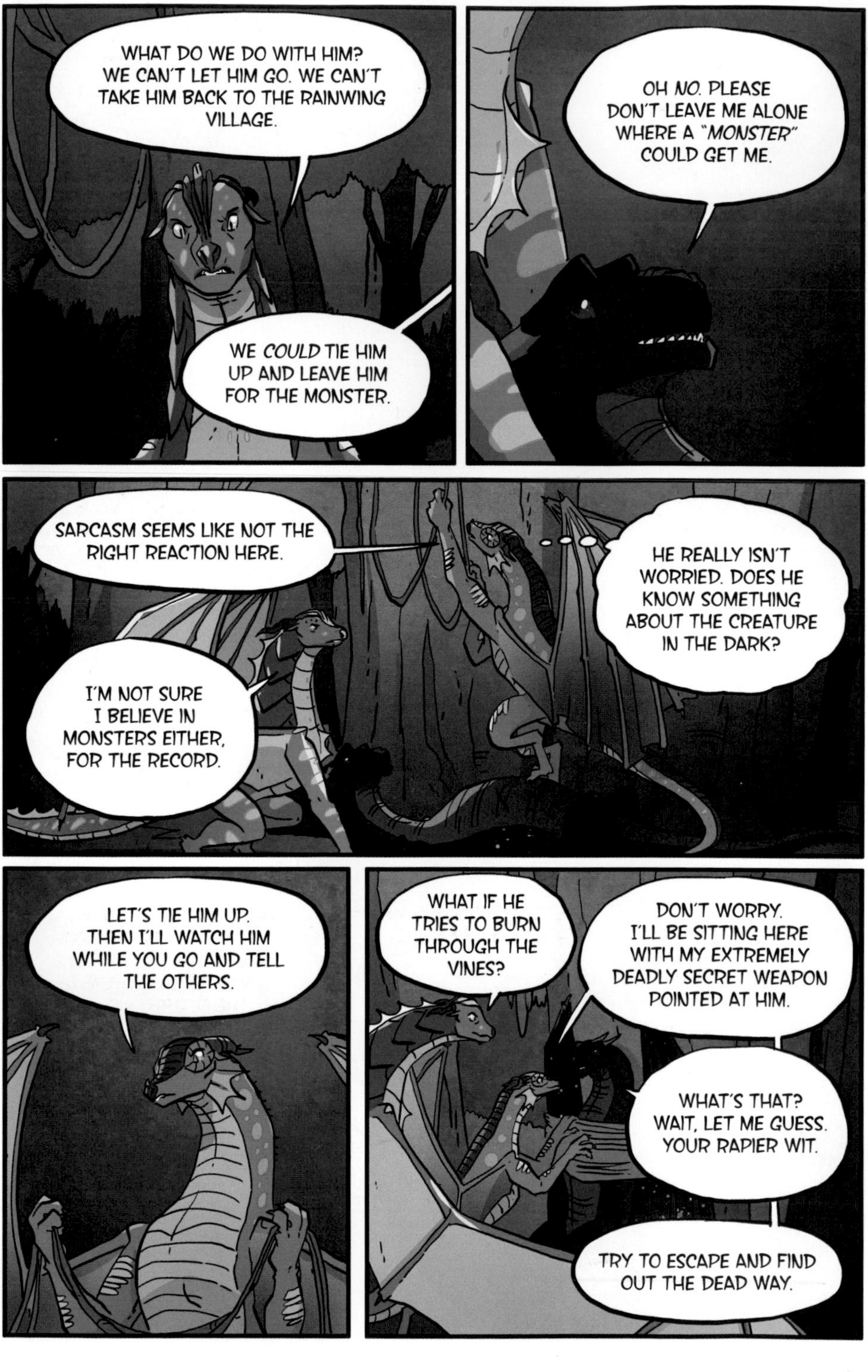
WHAT DO WE DO WITH HIM? WE CAN'T LET HIM GO. WE CAN'T TAKE HIM BACK TO THE RAINWING VILLAGE.
WE *COULD* TIE HIM UP AND LEAVE HIM FOR THE MONSTER.
OH *NO*. PLEASE DON'T LEAVE ME ALONE WHERE A "*MONSTER*" COULD GET ME.
SARCASM SEEMS LIKE NOT THE RIGHT REACTION HERE.
HE REALLY ISN'T WORRIED. DOES HE KNOW SOMETHING ABOUT THE CREATURE IN THE DARK?
I'M NOT SURE I BELIEVE IN MONSTERS EITHER, FOR THE RECORD.
LET'S TIE HIM UP. THEN I'LL WATCH HIM WHILE YOU GO AND TELL THE OTHERS.
WHAT IF HE TRIES TO BURN THROUGH THE VINES?
DON'T WORRY. I'LL BE SITTING HERE WITH MY EXTREMELY DEADLY SECRET WEAPON POINTED AT HIM.
WHAT'S THAT? WAIT, LET ME GUESS. YOUR RAPIER WIT.
TRY TO ESCAPE AND FIND OUT THE DEAD WAY.

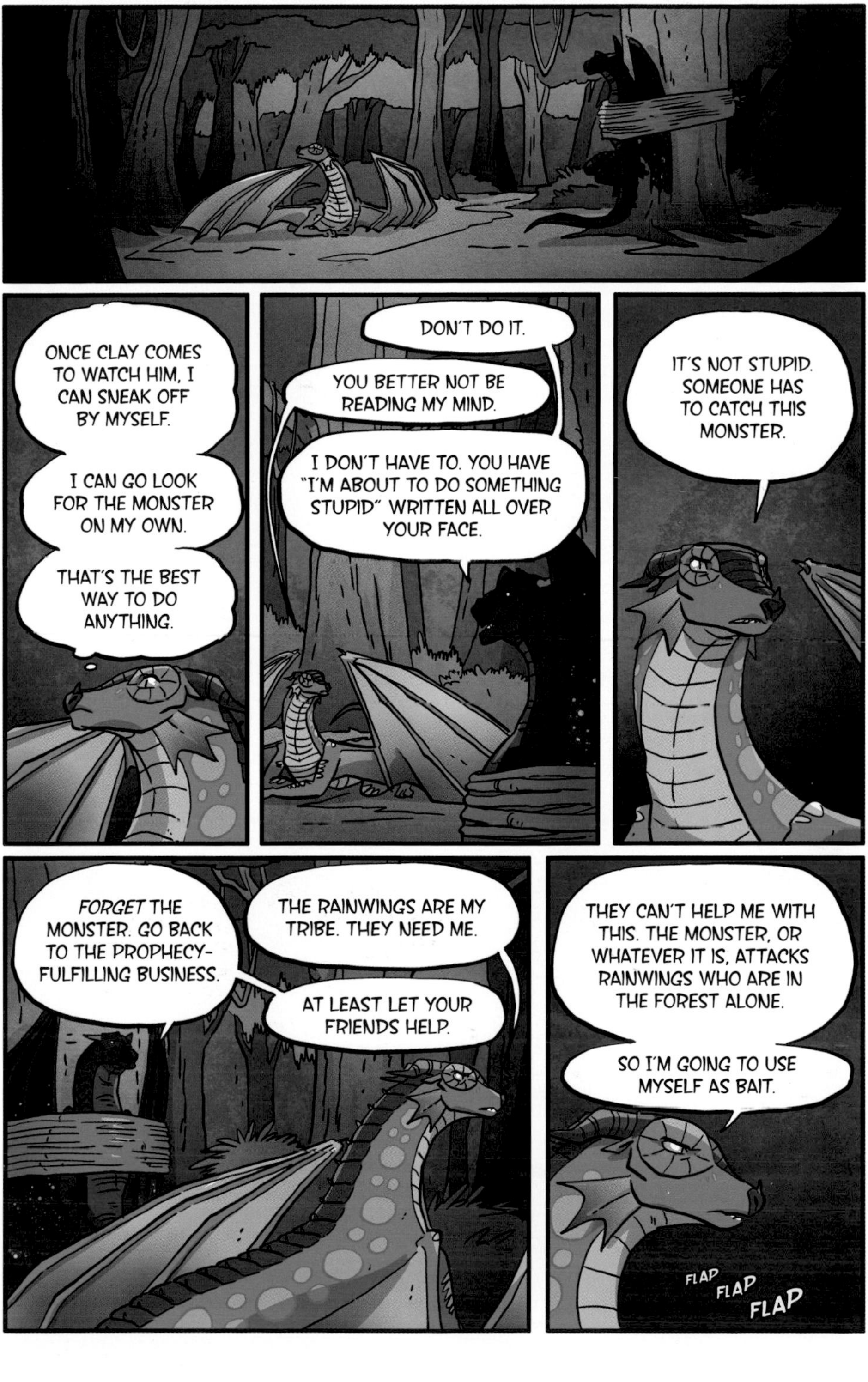
ONCE CLAY COMES TO WATCH HIM, I CAN SNEAK OFF BY MYSELF.
I CAN GO LOOK FOR THE MONSTER ON MY OWN.
THAT'S THE BEST WAY TO DO ANYTHING.
DON'T DO IT.
YOU BETTER NOT BE READING MY MIND.
I DON'T HAVE TO. YOU HAVE "I'M ABOUT TO DO SOMETHING STUPID" WRITTEN ALL OVER YOUR FACE.
IT'S NOT STUPID. SOMEONE HAS TO CATCH THIS MONSTER.
FORGET THE MONSTER. GO BACK TO THE PROPHECY-FULFILLING BUSINESS.
THE RAINWINGS ARE MY TRIBE. THEY NEED ME.
AT LEAST LET YOUR FRIENDS HELP.
THEY CAN'T HELP ME WITH THIS. THE MONSTER, OR WHATEVER IT IS, ATTACKS RAINWINGS WHO ARE IN THE FOREST ALONE.
SO I'M GOING TO USE MYSELF AS BAIT.
FLAP FLAP FLAP

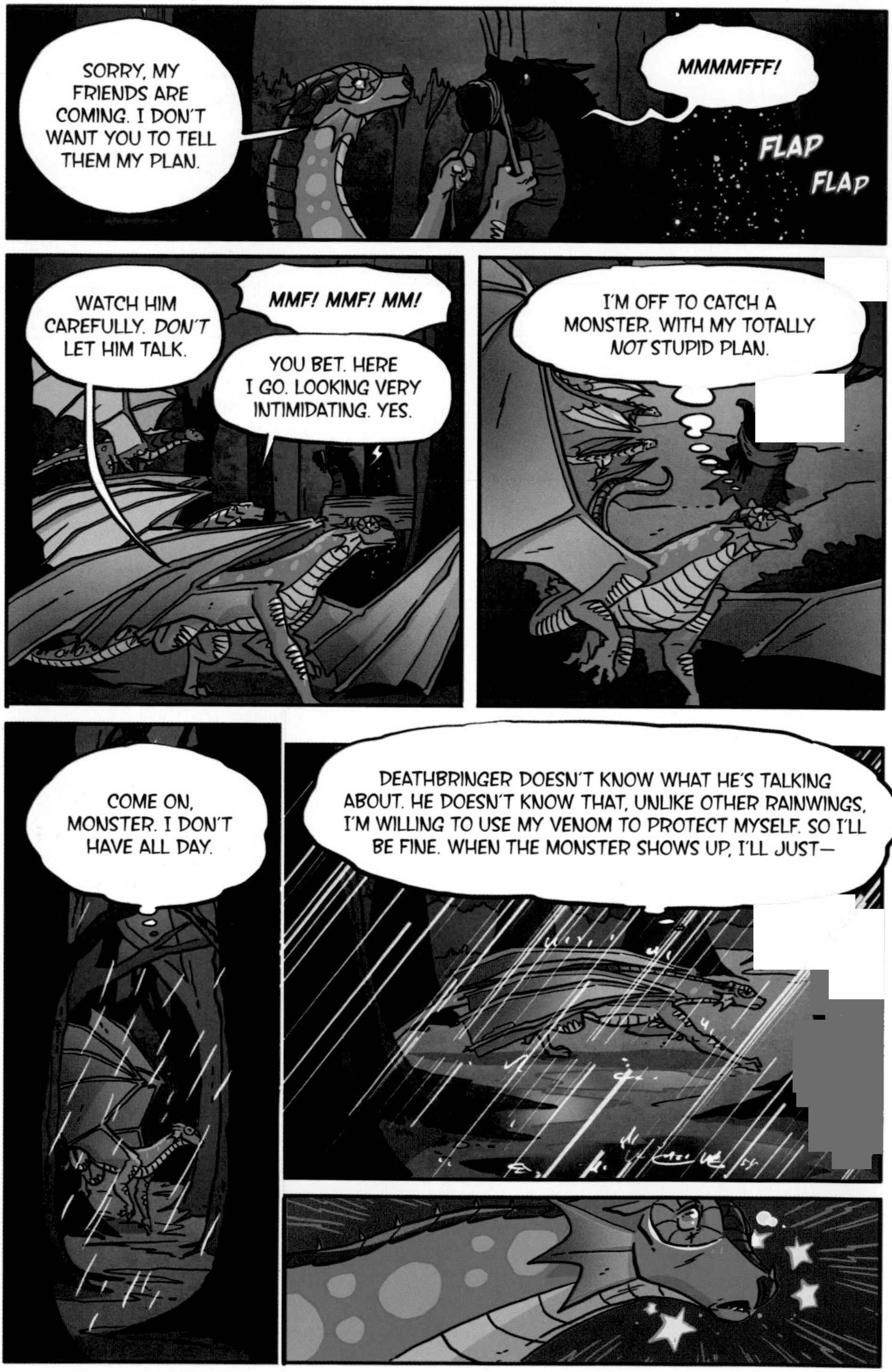
SORRY, MY FRIENDS ARE COMING. I DON'T WANT YOU TO TELL THEM MY PLAN.
MMMMFFF!
FLAP
FLAP
WATCH HIM CAREFULLY. *DON'T* LET HIM TALK.
MMF! MMF! MM!
YOU BET. HERE I GO. LOOKING VERY INTIMIDATING. YES.
I'M OFF TO CATCH A MONSTER. WITH MY TOTALLY *NOT* STUPID PLAN.
COME ON, MONSTER. I DON'T HAVE ALL DAY.
DEATHBRINGER DOESN'T KNOW WHAT HE'S TALKING ABOUT. HE DOESN'T KNOW THAT, UNLIKE OTHER RAINWINGS, I'M WILLING TO USE MY VENOM TO PROTECT MYSELF. SO I'LL BE FINE. WHEN THE MONSTER SHOWS UP, I'LL JUST—

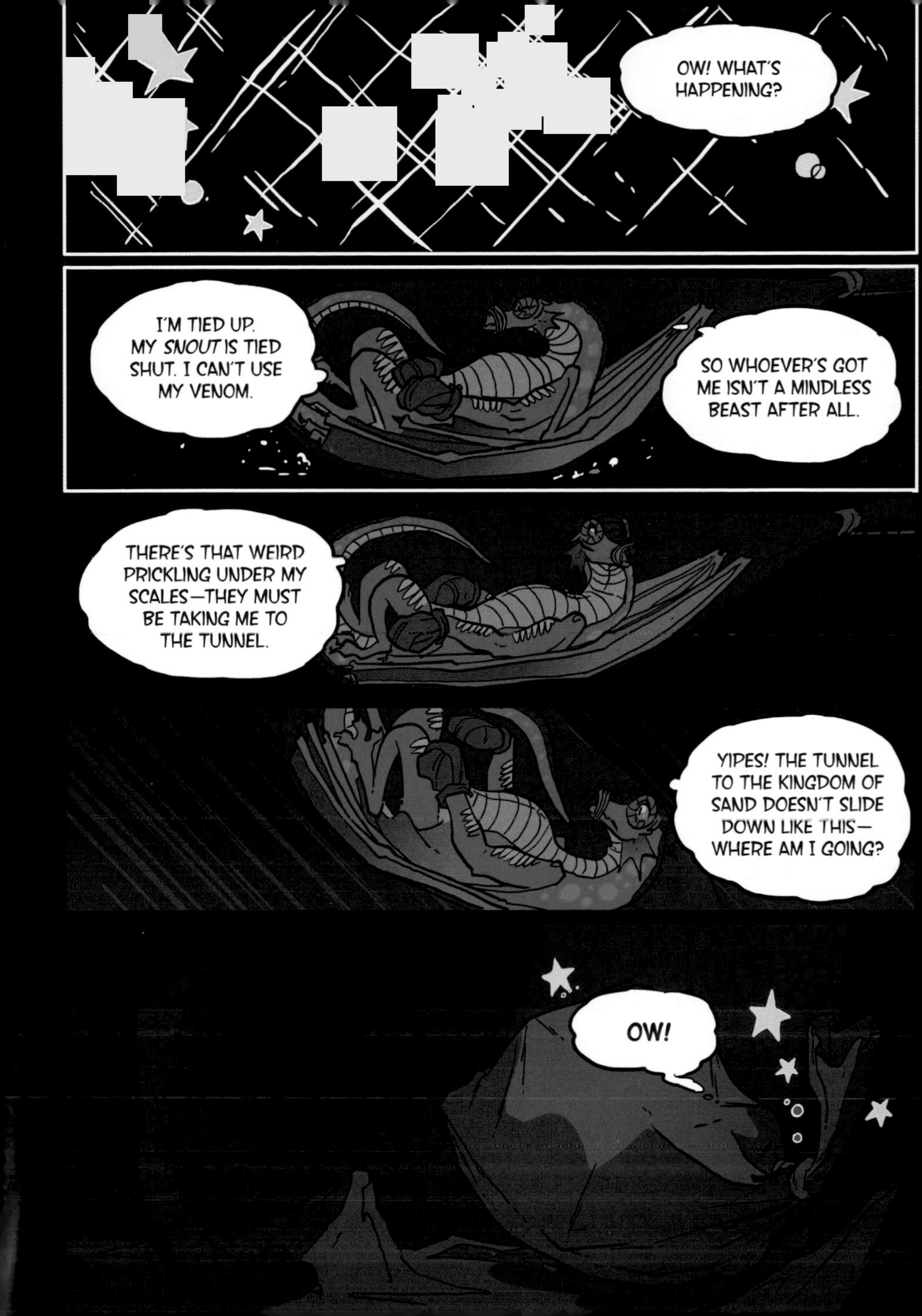
OW! WHAT'S HAPPENING?
I'M TIED UP. MY *SNOUT* IS TIED SHUT. I CAN'T USE MY VENOM.
SO WHOEVER'S GOT ME ISN'T A MINDLESS BEAST AFTER ALL.
THERE'S THAT WEIRD PRICKLING UNDER MY SCALES—THEY MUST BE TAKING ME TO THE TUNNEL.
YIPES! THE TUNNEL TO THE KINGDOM OF SAND DOESN'T SLIDE DOWN LIKE THIS—WHERE AM I GOING?
OW!

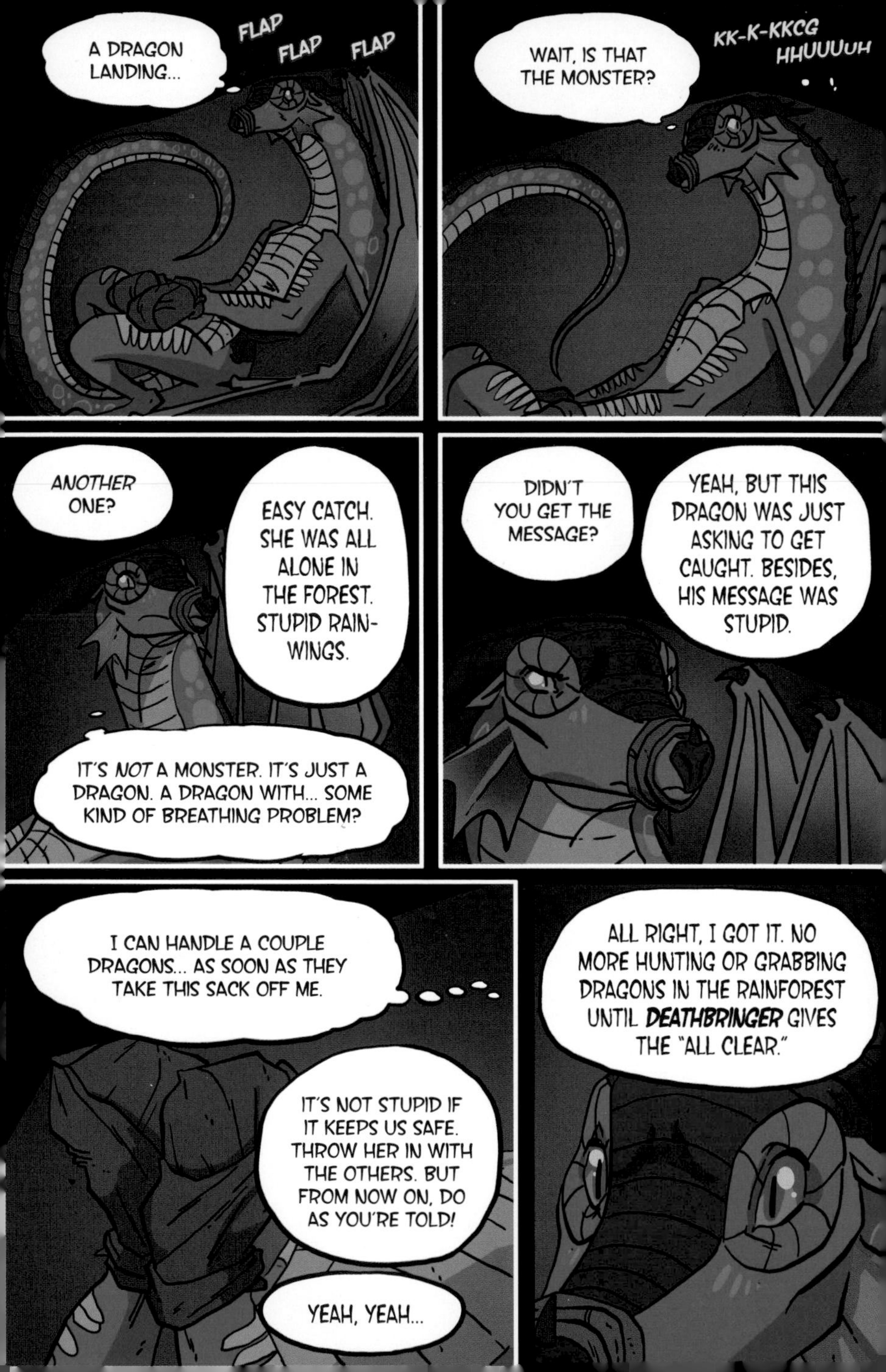

A DRAGON LANDING...
FLAP FLAP FLAP
WAIT, IS THAT THE MONSTER?
KK-K-KKCG HHUUUUH
ANOTHER ONE?
EASY CATCH. SHE WAS ALL ALONE IN THE FOREST. STUPID RAIN-WINGS.
IT'S *NOT* A MONSTER. IT'S JUST A DRAGON. A DRAGON WITH... SOME KIND OF BREATHING PROBLEM?
DIDN'T YOU GET THE MESSAGE?
YEAH, BUT THIS DRAGON WAS JUST ASKING TO GET CAUGHT. BESIDES, HIS MESSAGE WAS STUPID.
I CAN HANDLE A COUPLE DRAGONS... AS SOON AS THEY TAKE THIS SACK OFF ME.
IT'S NOT STUPID IF IT KEEPS US SAFE. THROW HER IN WITH THE OTHERS. BUT FROM NOW ON, DO AS YOU'RE TOLD!
YEAH, YEAH...
ALL RIGHT, I GOT IT. NO MORE HUNTING OR GRABBING DRAGONS IN THE RAINFOREST UNTIL ***DEATHBRINGER*** GIVES THE "ALL CLEAR."

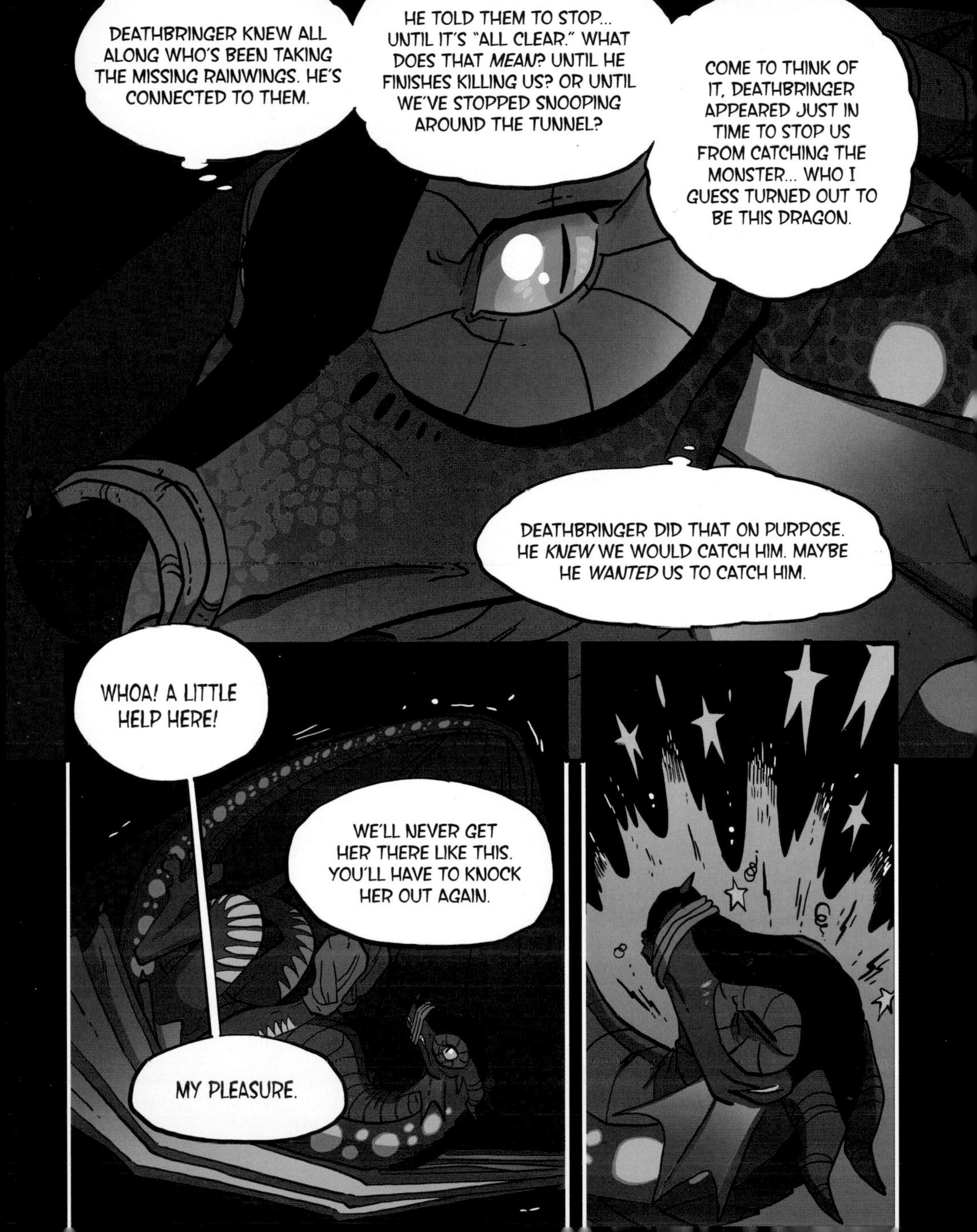
DEATHBRINGER KNEW ALL ALONG WHO'S BEEN TAKING THE MISSING RAINWINGS. HE'S CONNECTED TO THEM.
HE TOLD THEM TO STOP... UNTIL IT'S "ALL CLEAR." WHAT DOES THAT *MEAN*? UNTIL HE FINISHES KILLING US? OR UNTIL WE'VE STOPPED SNOOPING AROUND THE TUNNEL?
COME TO THINK OF IT, DEATHBRINGER APPEARED JUST IN TIME TO STOP US FROM CATCHING THE MONSTER... WHO I GUESS TURNED OUT TO BE THIS DRAGON.
DEATHBRINGER DID THAT ON PURPOSE. HE *KNEW* WE WOULD CATCH HIM. MAYBE HE *WANTED* US TO CATCH HIM.
WHOA! A LITTLE HELP HERE!
WE'LL NEVER GET HER THERE LIKE THIS. YOU'LL HAVE TO KNOCK HER OUT AGAIN.
MY PLEASURE.

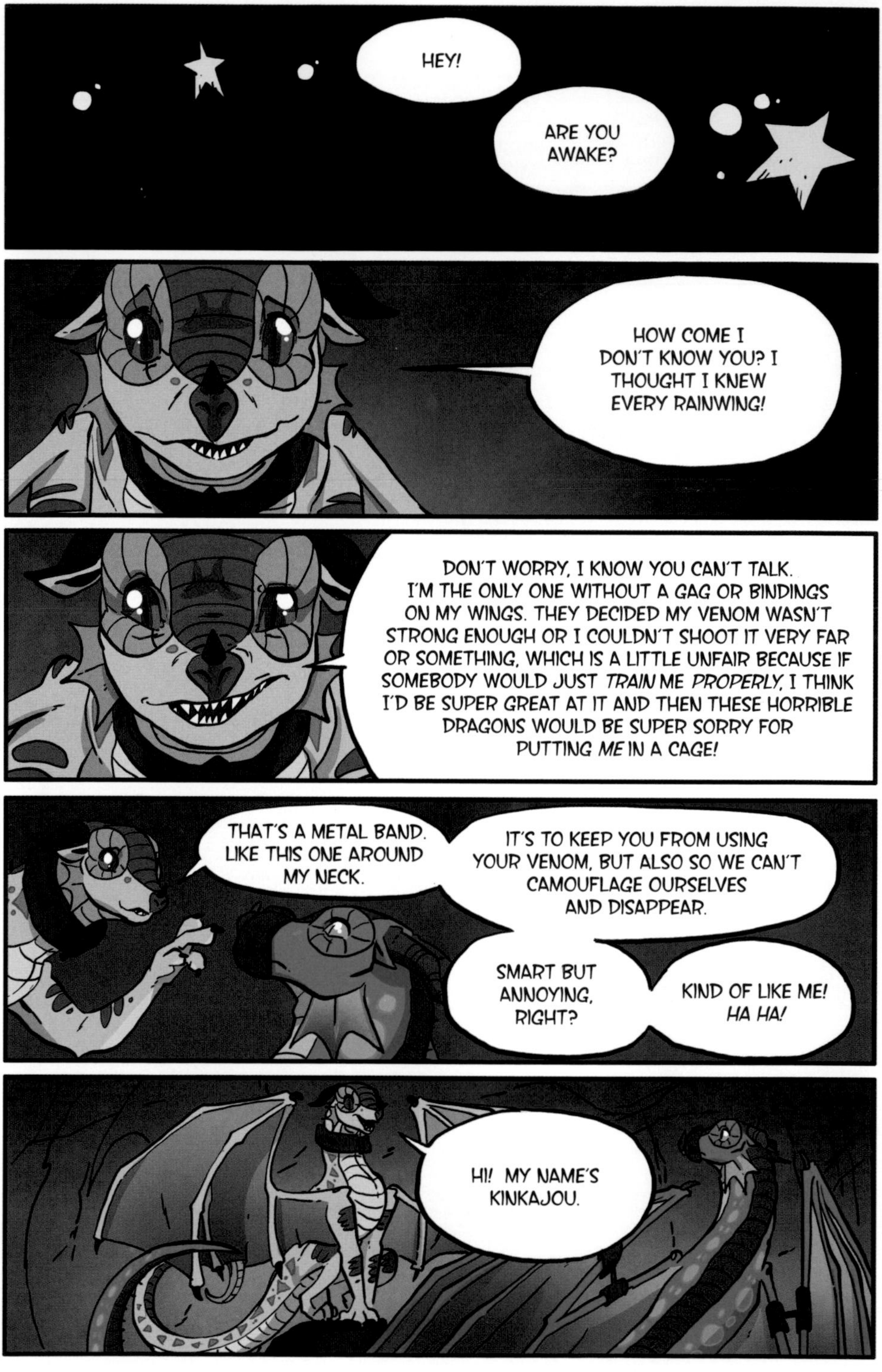
HEY!
ARE YOU AWAKE?
HOW COME I DON'T KNOW YOU? I THOUGHT I KNEW EVERY RAINWING!
DON'T WORRY, I KNOW YOU CAN'T TALK. I'M THE ONLY ONE WITHOUT A GAG OR BINDINGS ON MY WINGS. THEY DECIDED MY VENOM WASN'T STRONG ENOUGH OR I COULDN'T SHOOT IT VERY FAR OR SOMETHING, WHICH IS A LITTLE UNFAIR BECAUSE IF SOMEBODY WOULD JUST *TRAIN* ME *PROPERLY*, I THINK I'D BE SUPER GREAT AT IT AND THEN THESE HORRIBLE DRAGONS WOULD BE SUPER SORRY FOR PUTTING *ME* IN A CAGE!
THAT'S A METAL BAND. LIKE THIS ONE AROUND MY NECK.
IT'S TO KEEP YOU FROM USING YOUR VENOM, BUT ALSO SO WE CAN'T CAMOUFLAGE OURSELVES AND DISAPPEAR.
SMART BUT ANNOYING, RIGHT?
KIND OF LIKE ME! *HA HA!*
HI! MY NAME'S KINKAJOU.

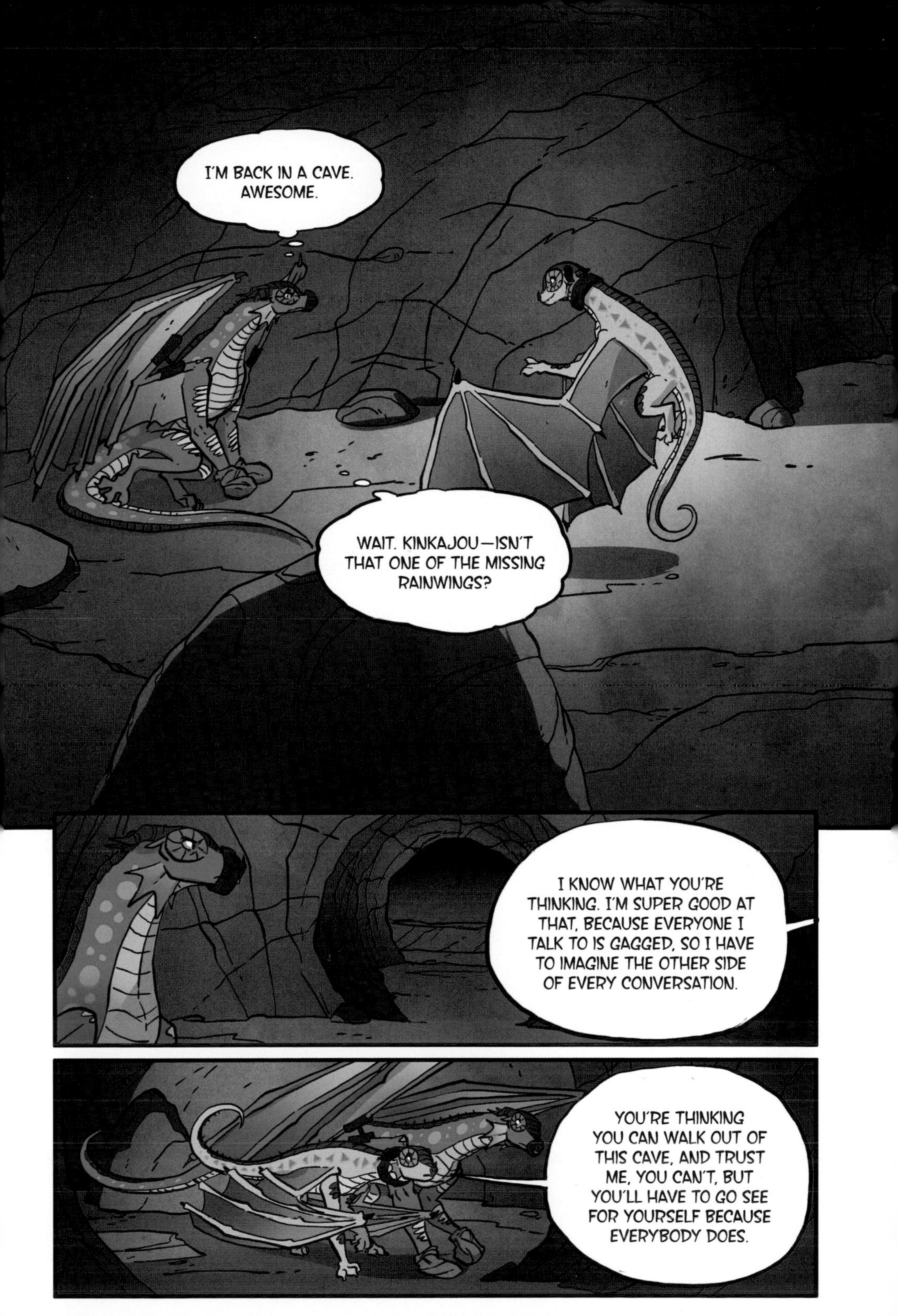
I'M BACK IN A CAVE. AWESOME.
WAIT. KINKAJOU—ISN'T THAT ONE OF THE MISSING RAINWINGS?
I KNOW WHAT YOU'RE THINKING. I'M SUPER GOOD AT THAT, BECAUSE EVERYONE I TALK TO IS GAGGED, SO I HAVE TO IMAGINE THE OTHER SIDE OF EVERY CONVERSATION.
YOU'RE THINKING YOU CAN WALK OUT OF THIS CAVE, AND TRUST ME, YOU CAN'T, BUT YOU'LL HAVE TO GO SEE FOR YOURSELF BECAUSE EVERYBODY DOES.

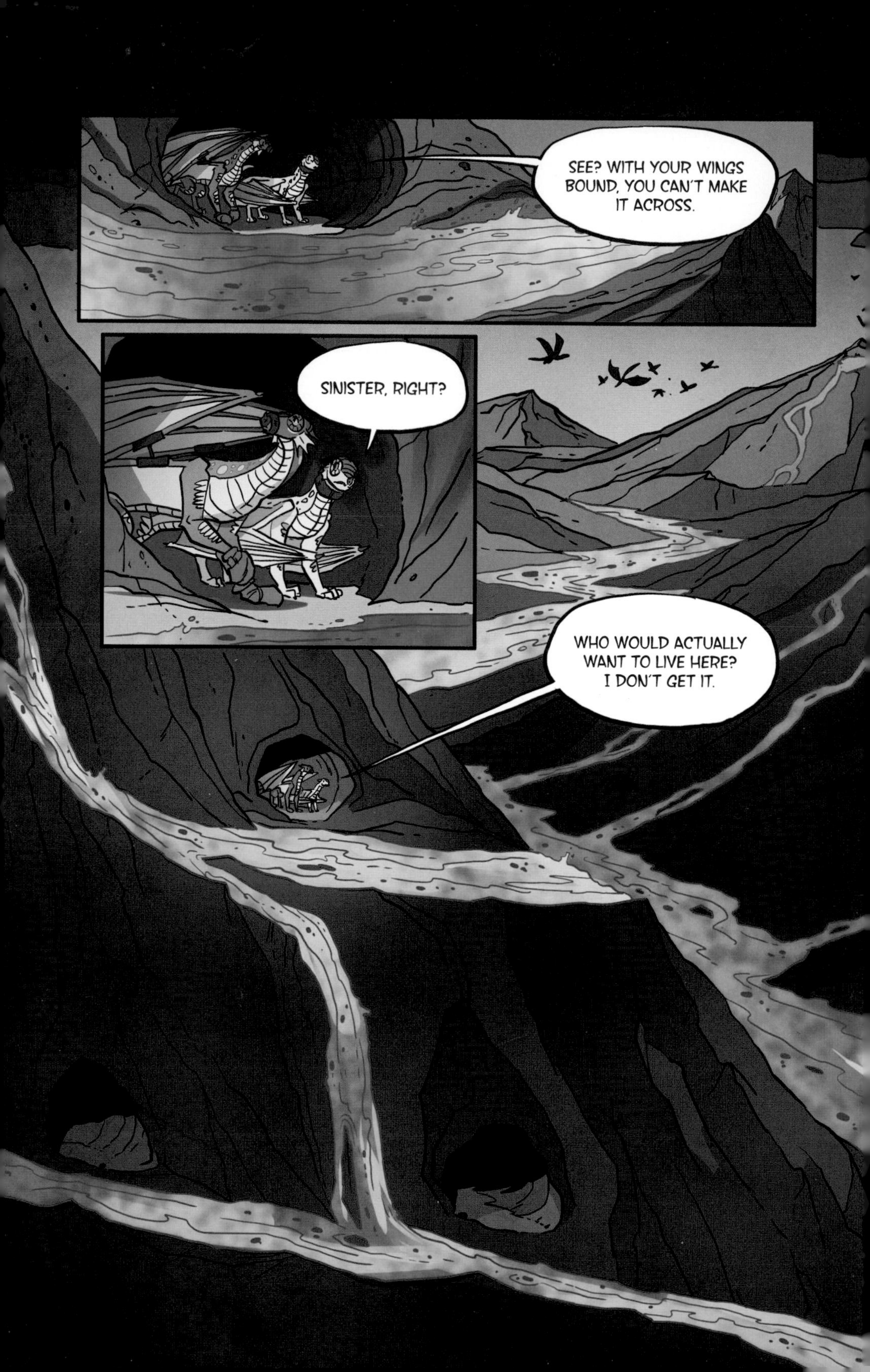
SEE? WITH YOUR WINGS BOUND, YOU CAN'T MAKE IT ACROSS.
SINISTER, RIGHT?
WHO WOULD ACTUALLY WANT TO LIVE HERE? I DON'T GET IT.

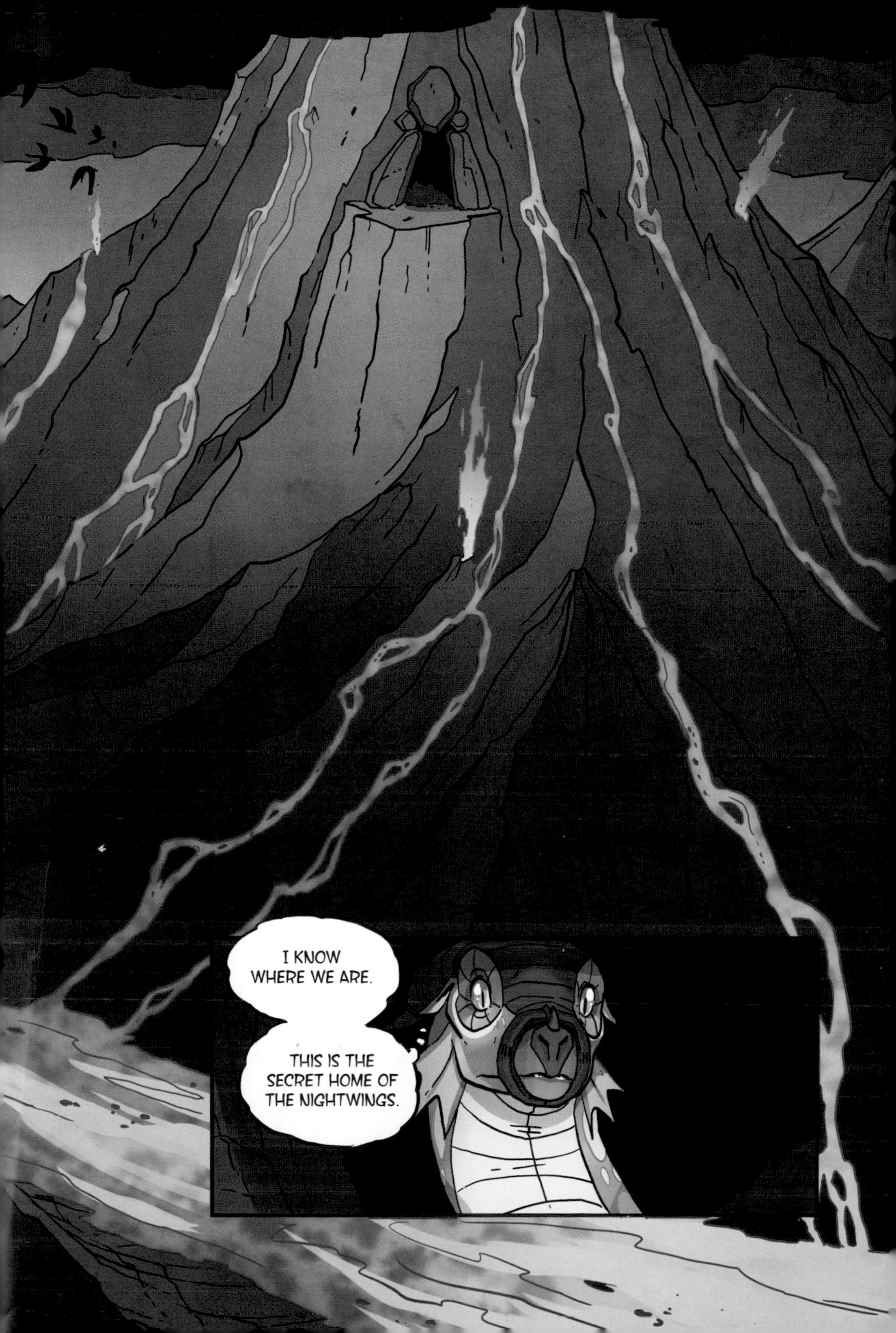
I KNOW WHERE WE ARE.
THIS IS THE SECRET HOME OF THE NIGHTWINGS.

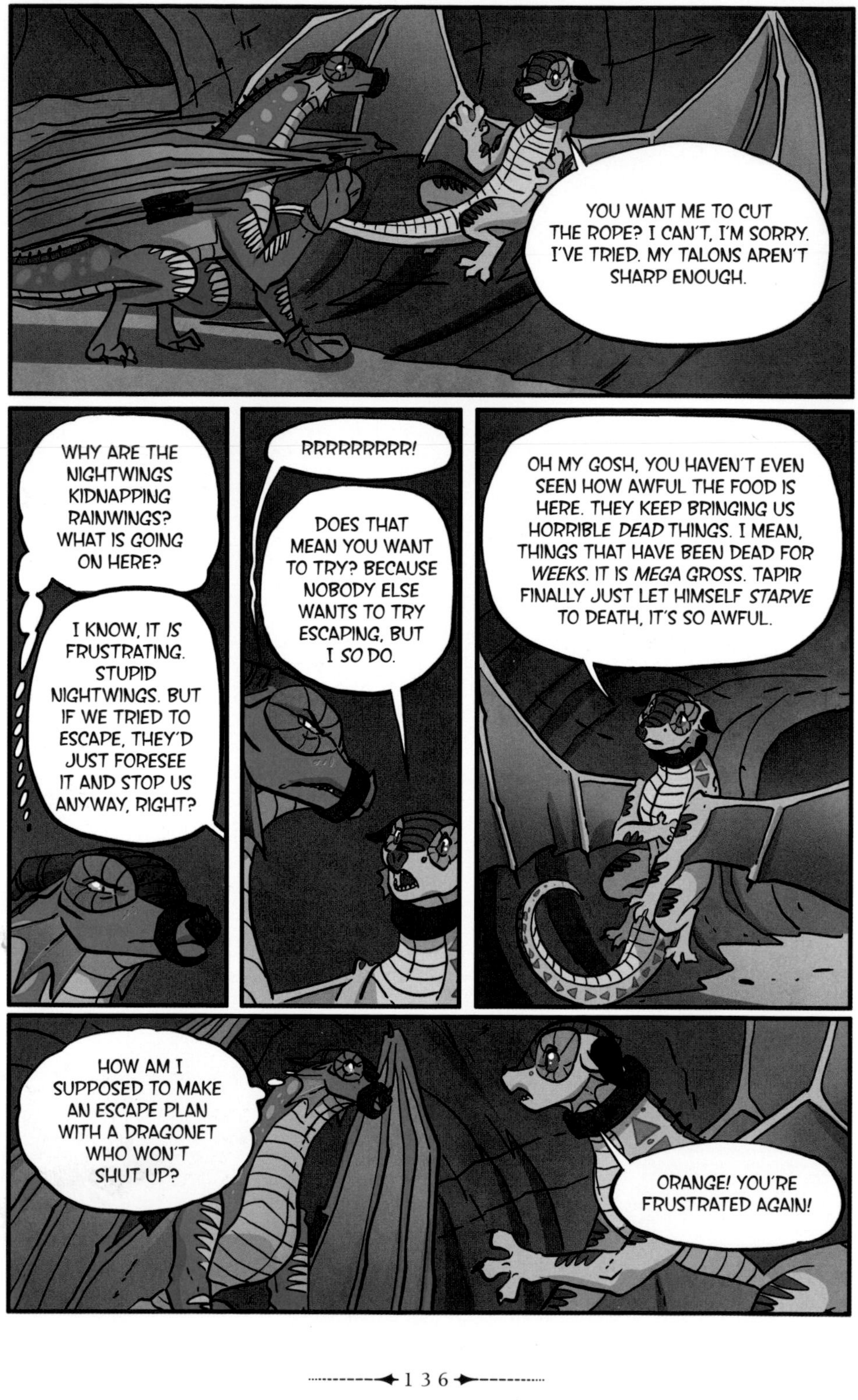
YOU WANT ME TO CUT THE ROPE? I CAN'T, I'M SORRY. I'VE TRIED. MY TALONS AREN'T SHARP ENOUGH.
WHY ARE THE NIGHTWINGS KIDNAPPING RAINWINGS? WHAT IS GOING ON HERE?
I KNOW, IT *IS* FRUSTRATING. STUPID NIGHTWINGS. BUT IF WE TRIED TO ESCAPE, THEY'D JUST FORESEE IT AND STOP US ANYWAY, RIGHT?
RRRRRRRRR!
DOES THAT MEAN YOU WANT TO TRY? BECAUSE NOBODY ELSE WANTS TO TRY ESCAPING, BUT I *SO* DO.
OH MY GOSH, YOU HAVEN'T EVEN SEEN HOW AWFUL THE FOOD IS HERE. THEY KEEP BRINGING US HORRIBLE *DEAD* THINGS. I MEAN, THINGS THAT HAVE BEEN DEAD FOR *WEEKS*. IT IS *MEGA GROSS*. TAPIR FINALLY JUST LET HIMSELF *STARVE* TO DEATH, IT'S SO AWFUL.
HOW AM I SUPPOSED TO MAKE AN ESCAPE PLAN WITH A DRAGONET WHO WON'T SHUT UP?
ORANGE! YOU'RE FRUSTRATED AGAIN!

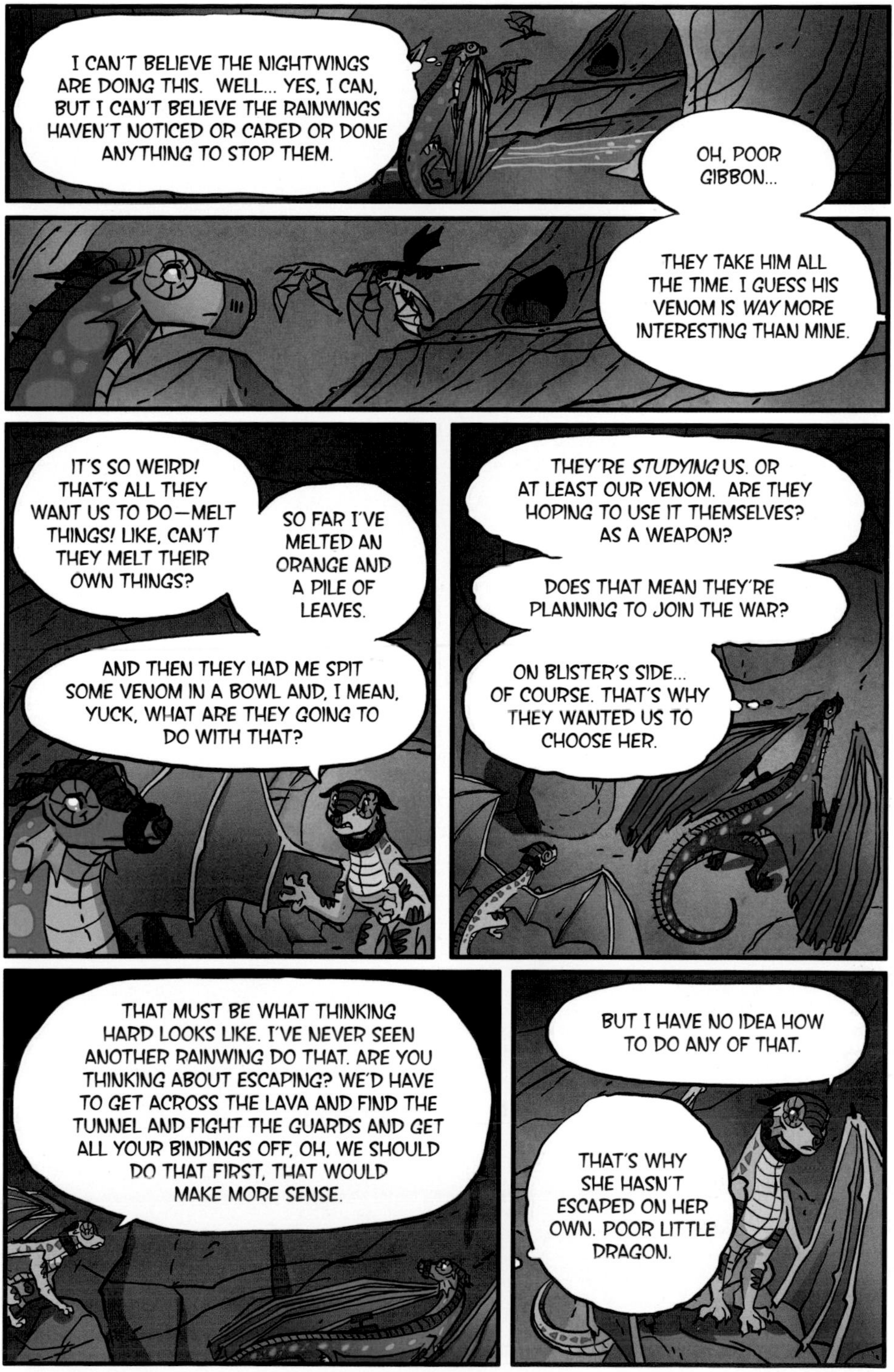
I CAN'T BELIEVE THE NIGHTWINGS ARE DOING THIS. WELL... YES, I CAN, BUT I CAN'T BELIEVE THE RAINWINGS HAVEN'T NOTICED OR CARED OR DONE ANYTHING TO STOP THEM.
OH, POOR GIBBON...
THEY TAKE HIM ALL THE TIME. I GUESS HIS VENOM IS *WAY* MORE INTERESTING THAN MINE.
IT'S SO WEIRD! THAT'S ALL THEY WANT US TO DO—MELT THINGS! LIKE, CAN'T THEY MELT THEIR OWN THINGS?
SO FAR I'VE MELTED AN ORANGE AND A PILE OF LEAVES.
AND THEN THEY HAD ME SPIT SOME VENOM IN A BOWL AND, I MEAN, YUCK, WHAT ARE THEY GOING TO DO WITH THAT?
THEY'RE *STUDYING* US. OR AT LEAST OUR VENOM. ARE THEY HOPING TO USE IT THEMSELVES? AS A WEAPON?
DOES THAT MEAN THEY'RE PLANNING TO JOIN THE WAR?
ON BLISTER'S SIDE... OF COURSE. THAT'S WHY THEY WANTED US TO CHOOSE HER.
THAT MUST BE WHAT THINKING HARD LOOKS LIKE. I'VE NEVER SEEN ANOTHER RAINWING DO THAT. ARE YOU THINKING ABOUT ESCAPING? WE'D HAVE TO GET ACROSS THE LAVA AND FIND THE TUNNEL AND FIGHT THE GUARDS AND GET ALL YOUR BINDINGS OFF. OH, WE SHOULD DO THAT FIRST, THAT WOULD MAKE MORE SENSE.
BUT I HAVE NO IDEA HOW TO DO ANY OF THAT.
THAT'S WHY SHE HASN'T ESCAPED ON HER OWN. POOR LITTLE DRAGON.

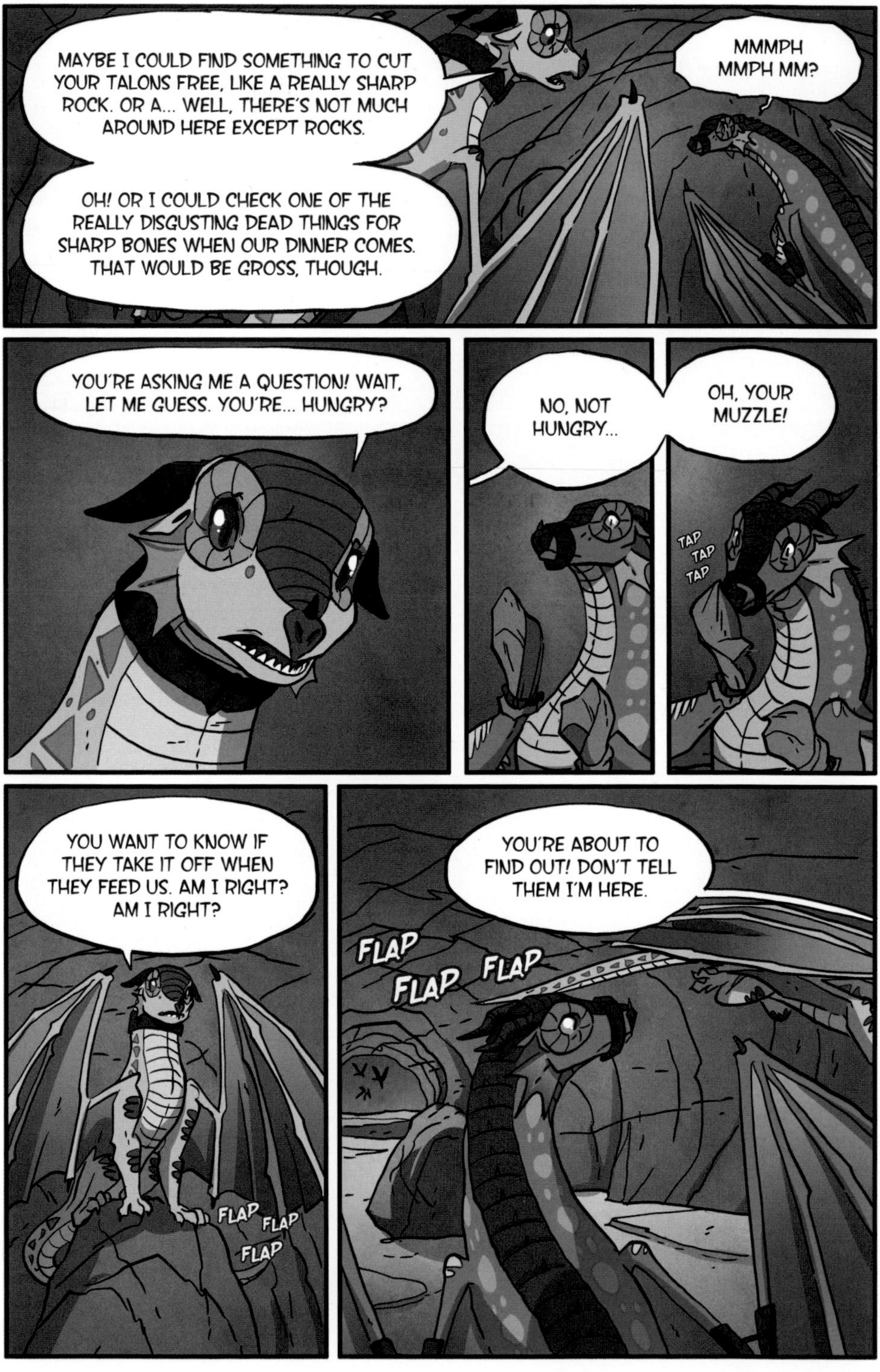
MAYBE I COULD FIND SOMETHING TO CUT YOUR TALONS FREE, LIKE A REALLY SHARP ROCK. OR A... WELL, THERE'S NOT MUCH AROUND HERE EXCEPT ROCKS.
OH! OR I COULD CHECK ONE OF THE REALLY DISGUSTING DEAD THINGS FOR SHARP BONES WHEN OUR DINNER COMES. THAT WOULD BE GROSS, THOUGH.
MMMPH MMPH MM?
YOU'RE ASKING ME A QUESTION! WAIT, LET ME GUESS. YOU'RE... HUNGRY?
NO, NOT HUNGRY...
OH, YOUR MUZZLE!
TAP TAP TAP
YOU WANT TO KNOW IF THEY TAKE IT OFF WHEN THEY FEED US. AM I RIGHT? AM I RIGHT?
FLAP FLAP FLAP
YOU'RE ABOUT TO FIND OUT! DON'T TELL THEM I'M HERE.
FLAP FLAP FLAP

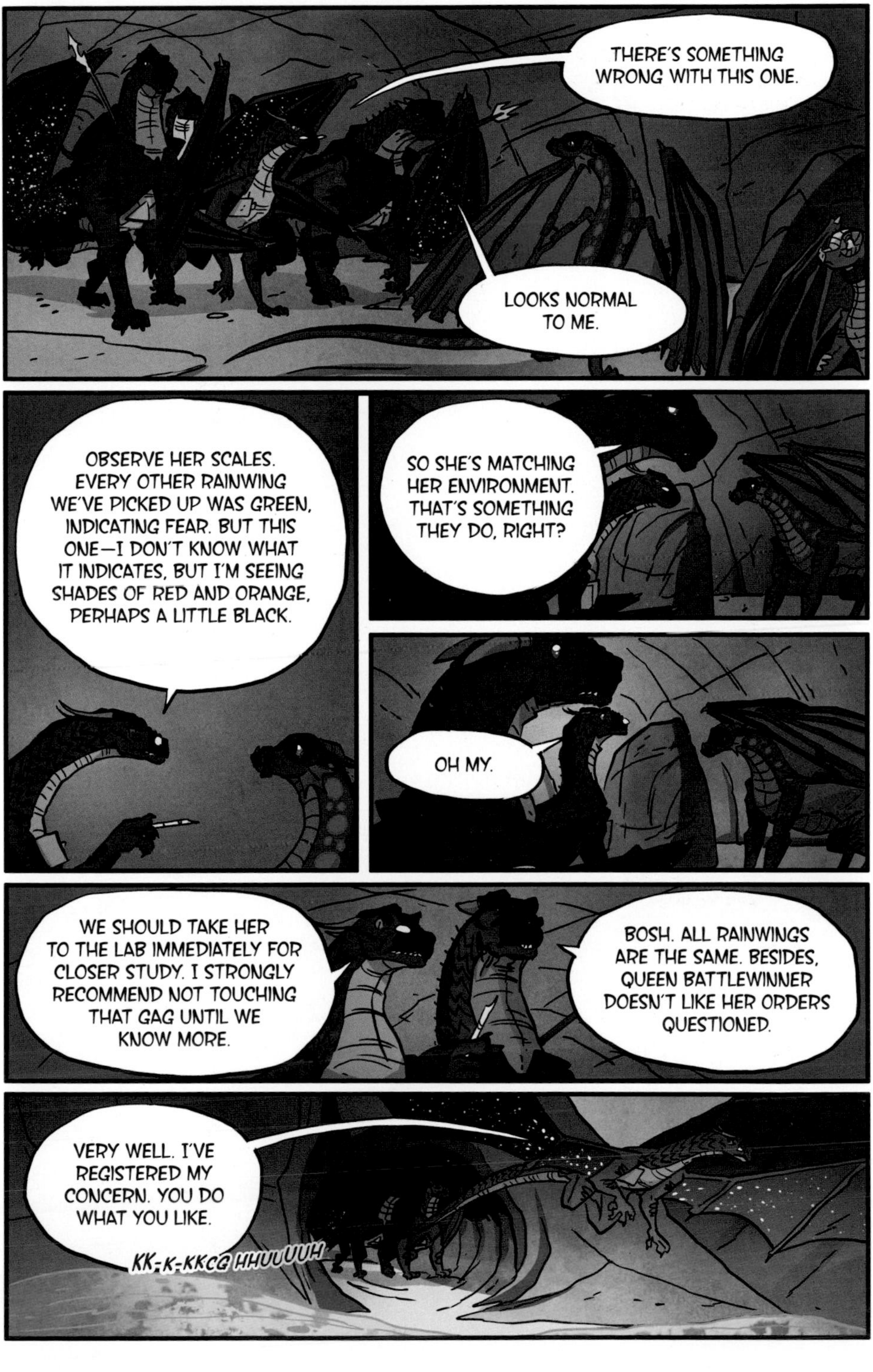
THERE'S SOMETHING WRONG WITH THIS ONE.
LOOKS NORMAL TO ME.
OBSERVE HER SCALES. EVERY OTHER RAINWING WE'VE PICKED UP WAS GREEN, INDICATING FEAR. BUT THIS ONE—I DON'T KNOW WHAT IT INDICATES, BUT I'M SEEING SHADES OF RED AND ORANGE, PERHAPS A LITTLE BLACK.
SO SHE'S MATCHING HER ENVIRONMENT. THAT'S SOMETHING THEY DO, RIGHT?
OH MY.
WE SHOULD TAKE HER TO THE LAB IMMEDIATELY FOR CLOSER STUDY. I STRONGLY RECOMMEND NOT TOUCHING THAT GAG UNTIL WE KNOW MORE.
BOSH. ALL RAINWINGS ARE THE SAME. BESIDES, QUEEN BATTLEWINNER DOESN'T LIKE HER ORDERS QUESTIONED.
VERY WELL. I'VE REGISTERED MY CONCERN. YOU DO WHAT YOU LIKE.
KK-K-KKCG HHUUUUH

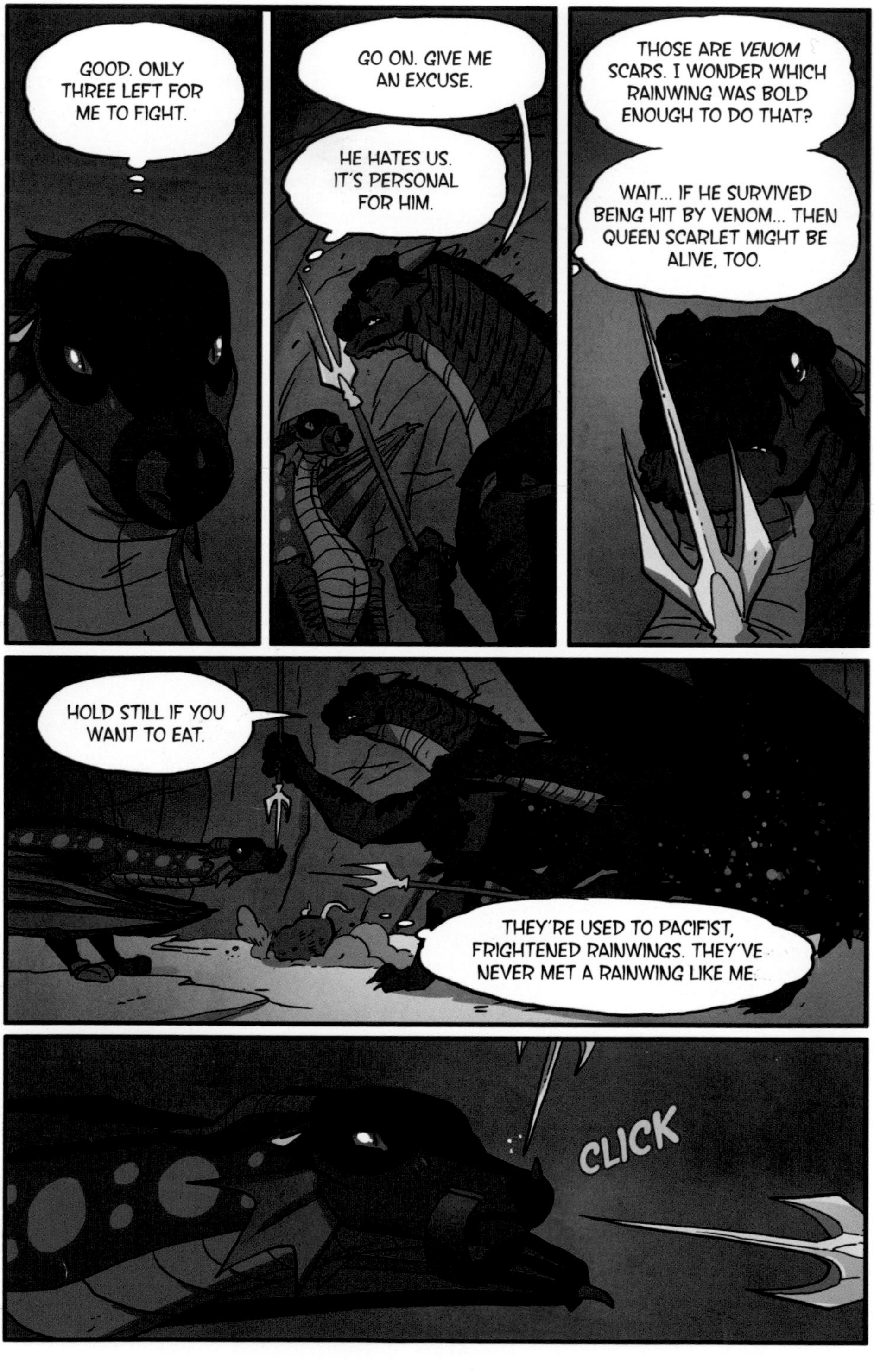
GOOD. ONLY THREE LEFT FOR ME TO FIGHT.
GO ON. GIVE ME AN EXCUSE.
HE HATES US. IT'S PERSONAL FOR HIM.
THOSE ARE *VENOM* SCARS. I WONDER WHICH RAINWING WAS BOLD ENOUGH TO DO THAT?
WAIT... IF HE SURVIVED BEING HIT BY VENOM... THEN QUEEN SCARLET MIGHT BE ALIVE, TOO.
HOLD STILL IF YOU WANT TO EAT.
THEY'RE USED TO PACIFIST, FRIGHTENED RAINWINGS. THEY'VE NEVER MET A RAINWING LIKE ME.
CLICK

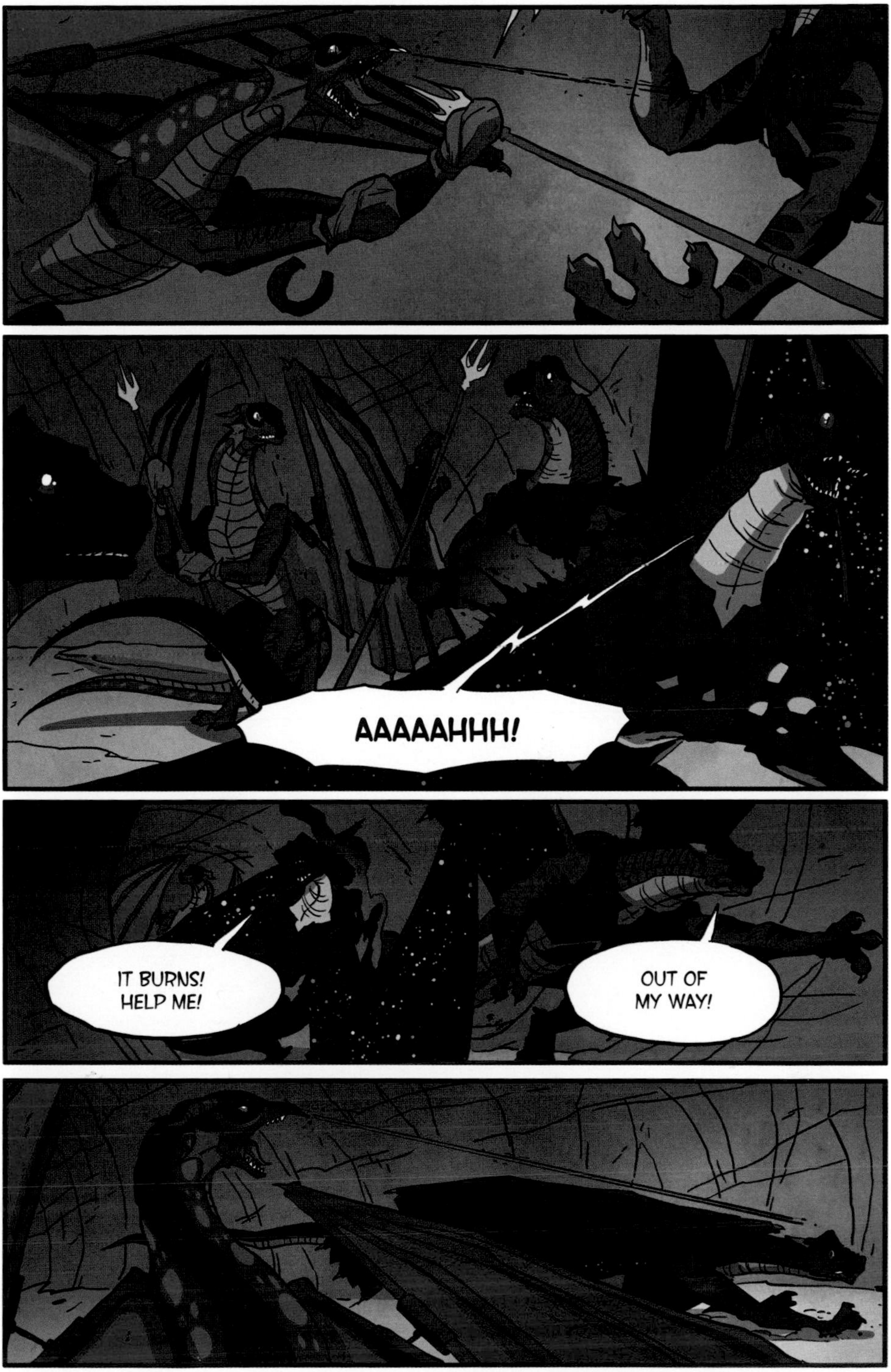
AAAAAHHH!
IT BURNS! HELP ME!
OUT OF MY WAY!

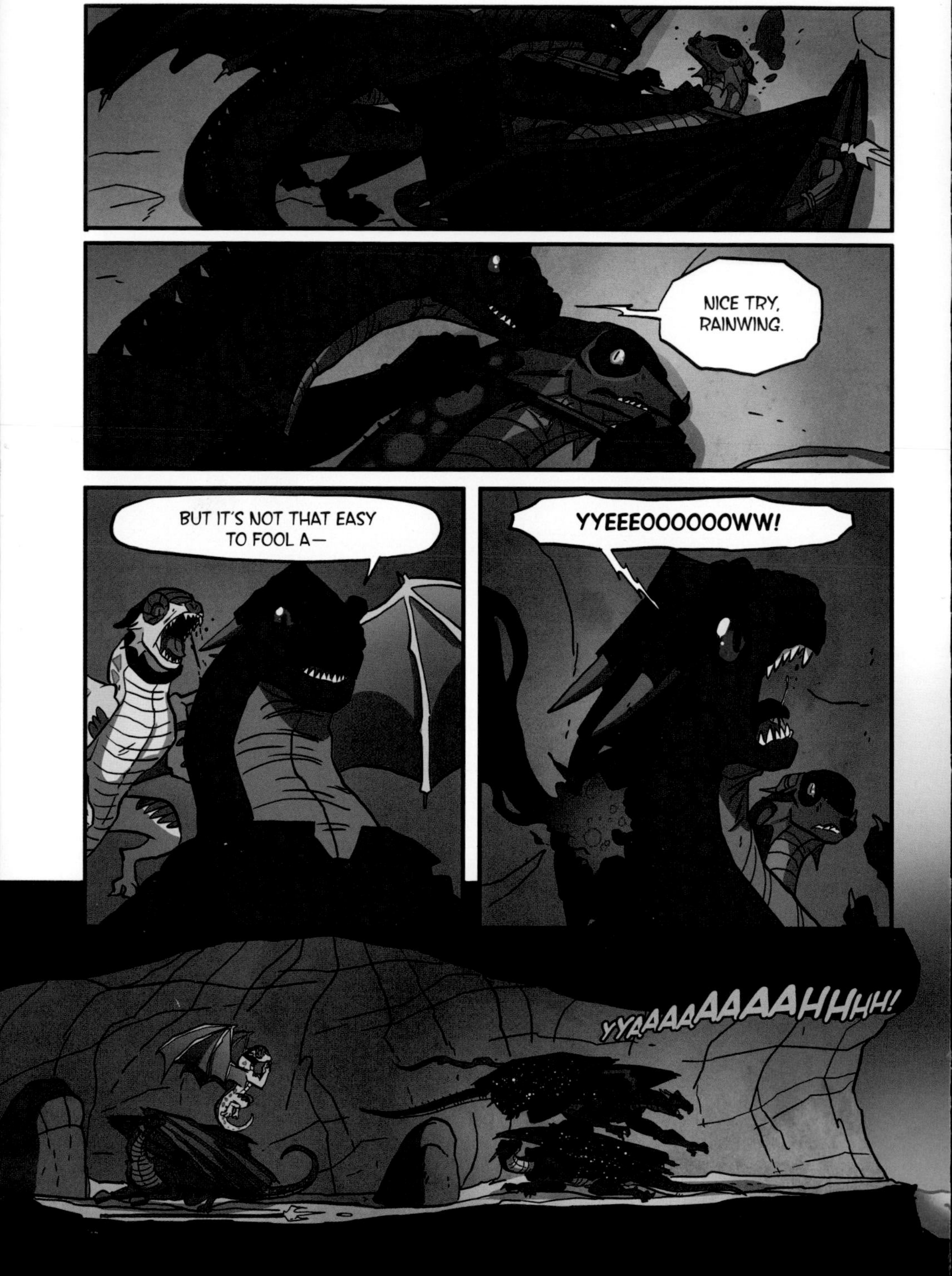
NICE TRY, RAINWING.
BUT IT'S NOT THAT EASY TO FOOL A—
YYEEEOOOOOOWW!
YYAAAAAAAAHHHH!

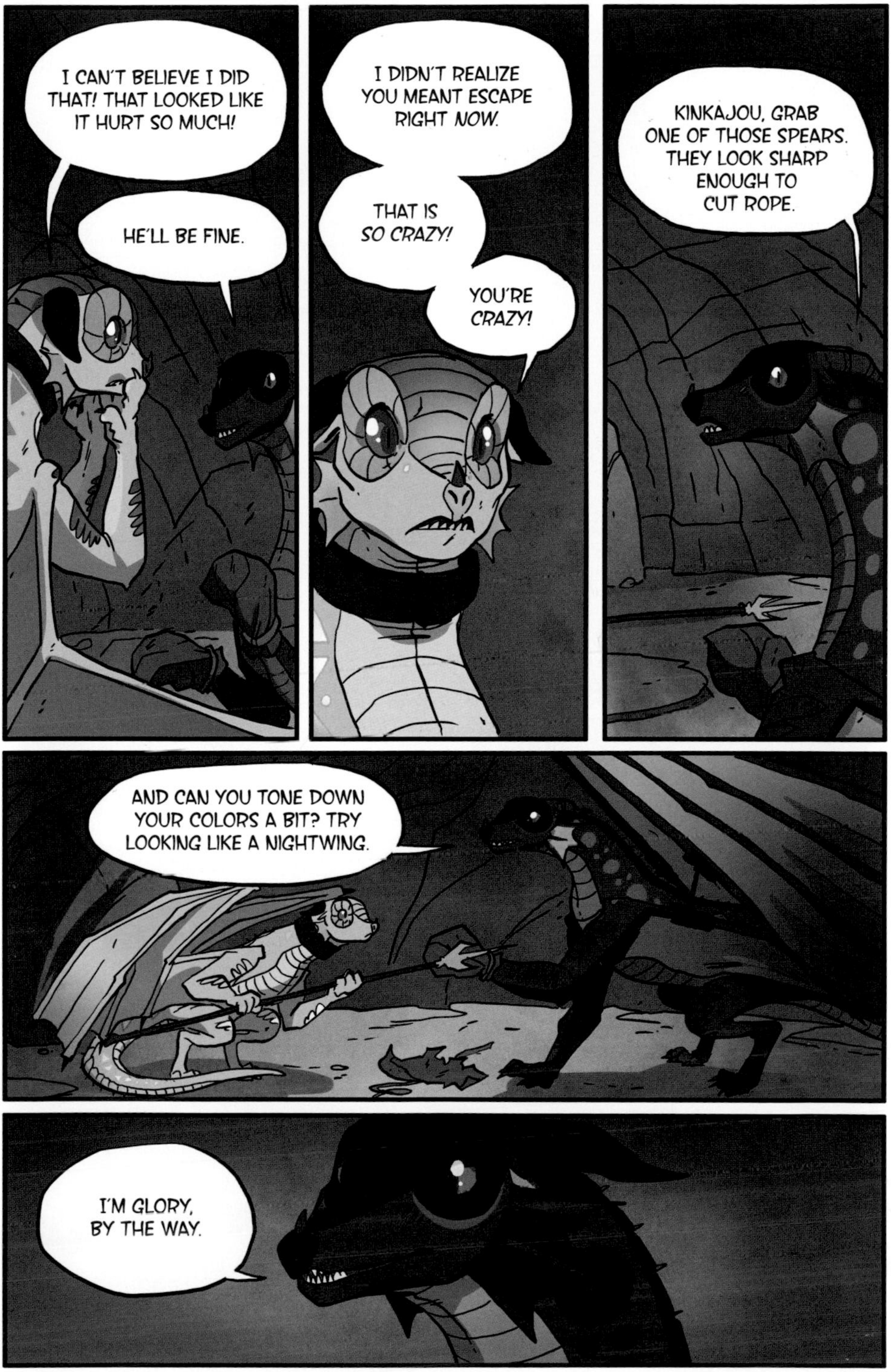
I CAN'T BELIEVE I DID THAT! THAT LOOKED LIKE IT HURT SO MUCH!
HE'LL BE FINE.
I DIDN'T REALIZE YOU MEANT ESCAPE RIGHT *NOW*.
THAT IS *SO CRAZY!*
YOU'RE *CRAZY!*
KINKAJOU, GRAB ONE OF THOSE SPEARS. THEY LOOK SHARP ENOUGH TO CUT ROPE.
AND CAN YOU TONE DOWN YOUR COLORS A BIT? TRY LOOKING LIKE A NIGHTWING.
I'M GLORY, BY THE WAY.

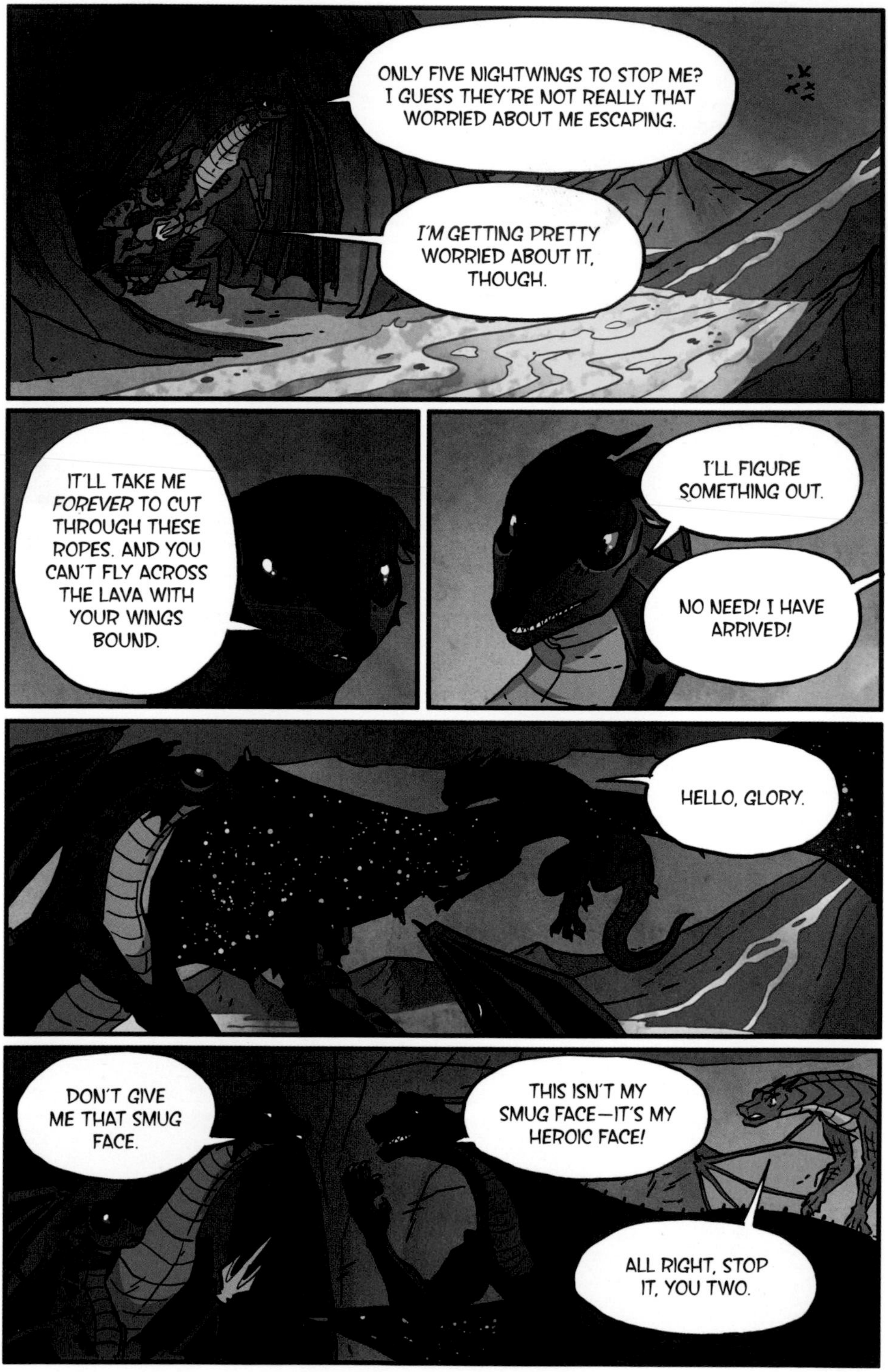
ONLY FIVE NIGHTWINGS TO STOP ME? I GUESS THEY'RE NOT REALLY THAT WORRIED ABOUT ME ESCAPING.
I'M GETTING PRETTY WORRIED ABOUT IT, THOUGH.
IT'LL TAKE ME *FOREVER* TO CUT THROUGH THESE ROPES. AND YOU CAN'T FLY ACROSS THE LAVA WITH YOUR WINGS BOUND.
I'LL FIGURE SOMETHING OUT.
NO NEED! I HAVE ARRIVED!
HELLO, GLORY.
DON'T GIVE ME THAT SMUG FACE.
THIS ISN'T MY SMUG FACE—IT'S MY HEROIC FACE!
ALL RIGHT, STOP IT, YOU TWO.

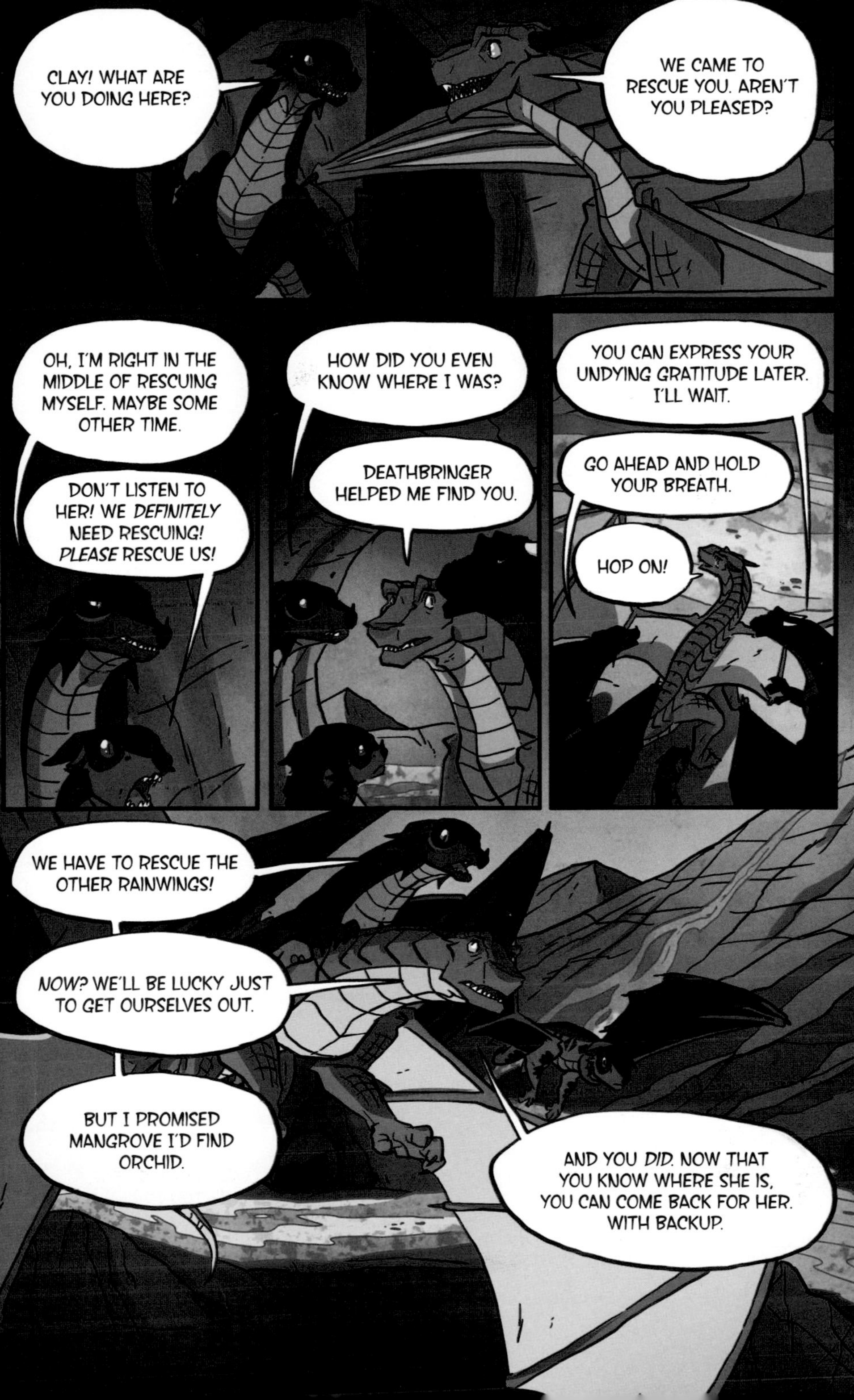
CLAY! WHAT ARE YOU DOING HERE?
WE CAME TO RESCUE YOU. AREN'T YOU PLEASED?
OH, I'M RIGHT IN THE MIDDLE OF RESCUING MYSELF. MAYBE SOME OTHER TIME.
DON'T LISTEN TO HER! WE *DEFINITELY* NEED RESCUING! *PLEASE* RESCUE US!
HOW DID YOU EVEN KNOW WHERE I WAS?
DEATHBRINGER HELPED ME FIND YOU.
YOU CAN EXPRESS YOUR UNDYING GRATITUDE LATER. I'LL WAIT.
GO AHEAD AND HOLD YOUR BREATH.
HOP ON!
WE HAVE TO RESCUE THE OTHER RAINWINGS!
NOW? WE'LL BE LUCKY JUST TO GET OURSELVES OUT.
BUT I PROMISED MANGROVE I'D FIND ORCHID.
AND YOU *DID*. NOW THAT YOU KNOW WHERE SHE IS, YOU CAN COME BACK FOR HER. WITH BACKUP.

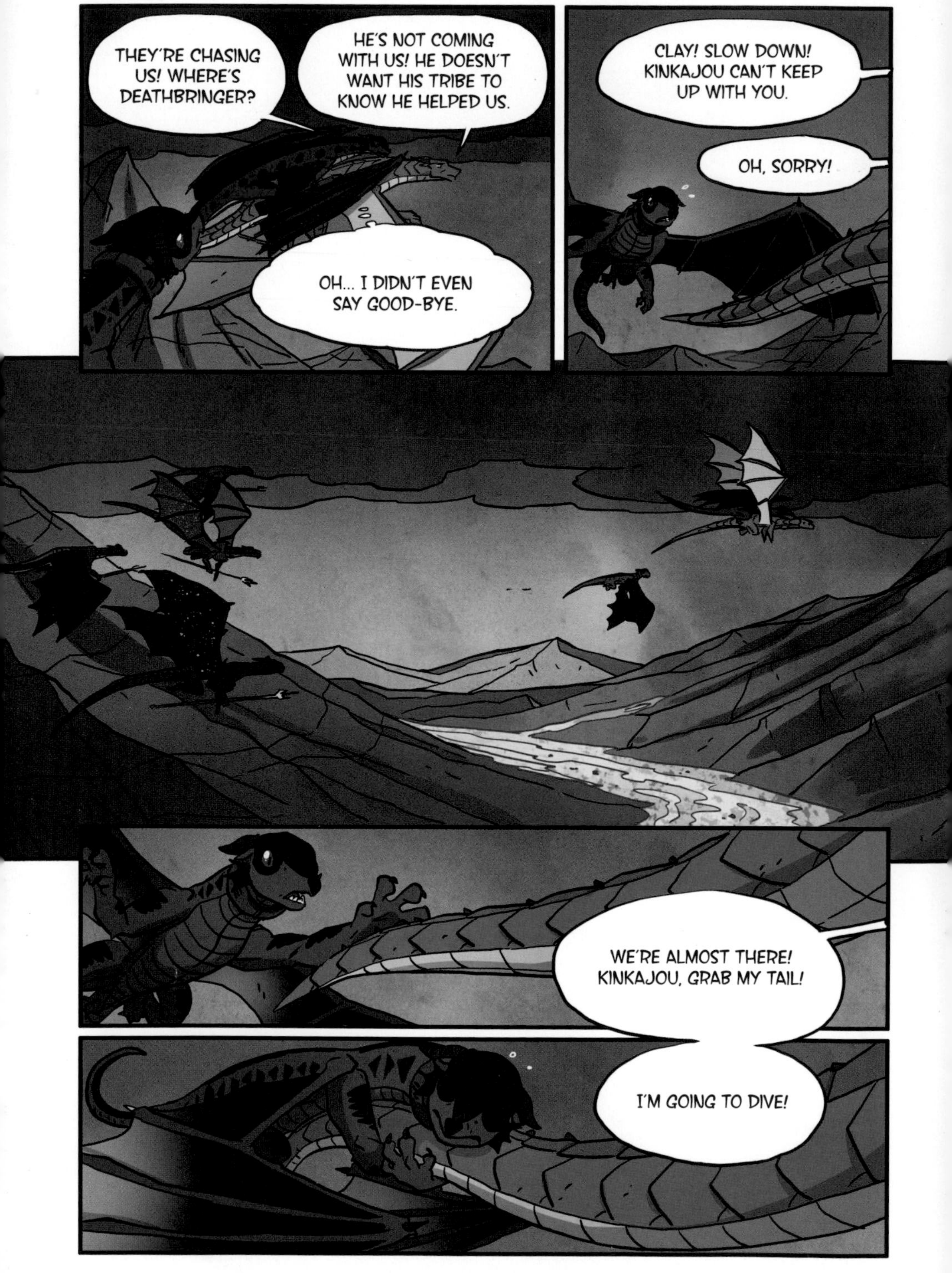
THEY'RE CHASING US! WHERE'S DEATHBRINGER?
HE'S NOT COMING WITH US! HE DOESN'T WANT HIS TRIBE TO KNOW HE HELPED US.
OH... I DIDN'T EVEN SAY GOOD-BYE.
CLAY! SLOW DOWN! KINKAJOU CAN'T KEEP UP WITH YOU.
OH, SORRY!
WE'RE ALMOST THERE! KINKAJOU, GRAB MY TAIL!
I'M GOING TO DIVE!

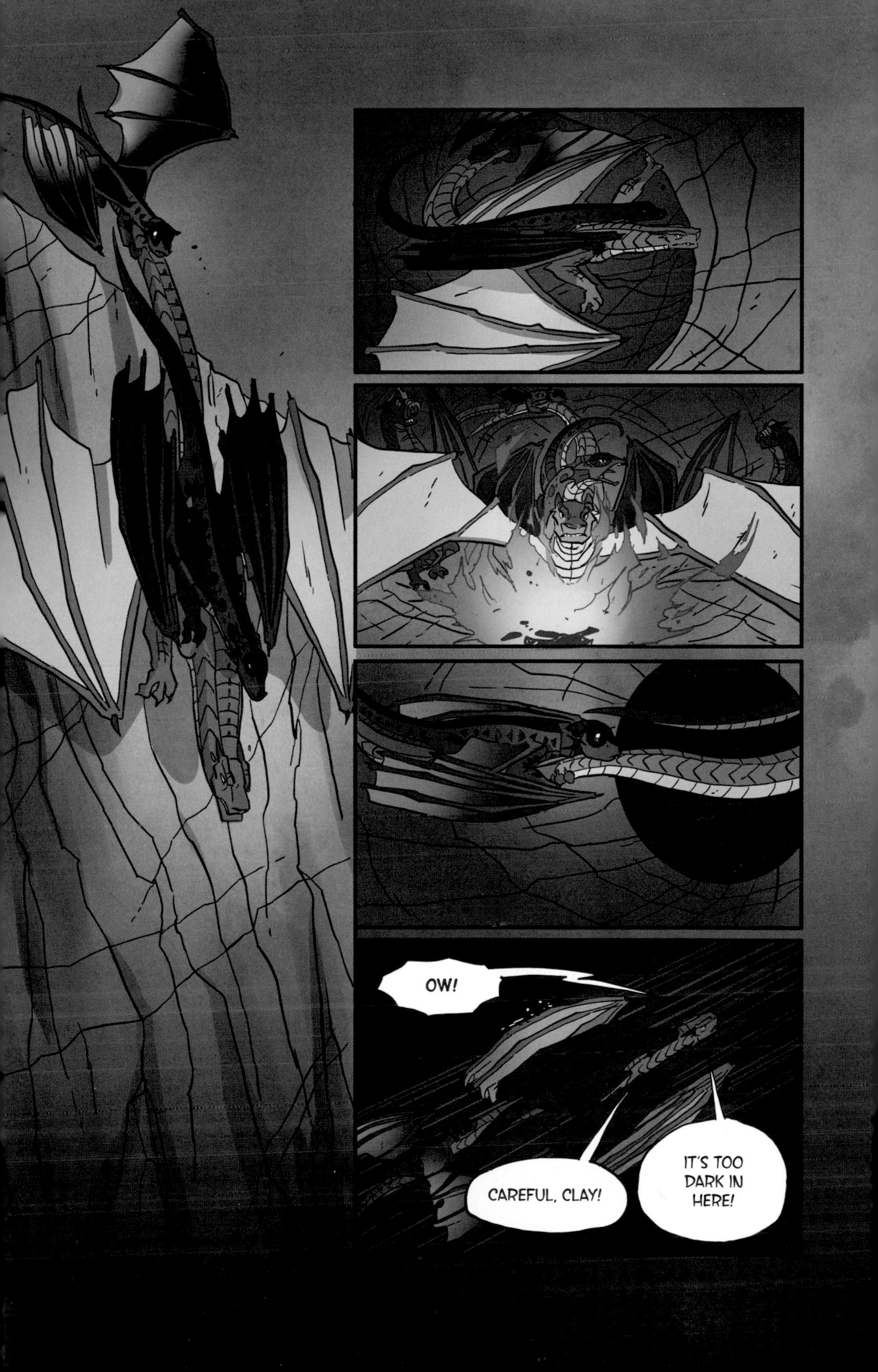
OW!
CAREFUL, CLAY!
IT'S TOO DARK IN HERE!

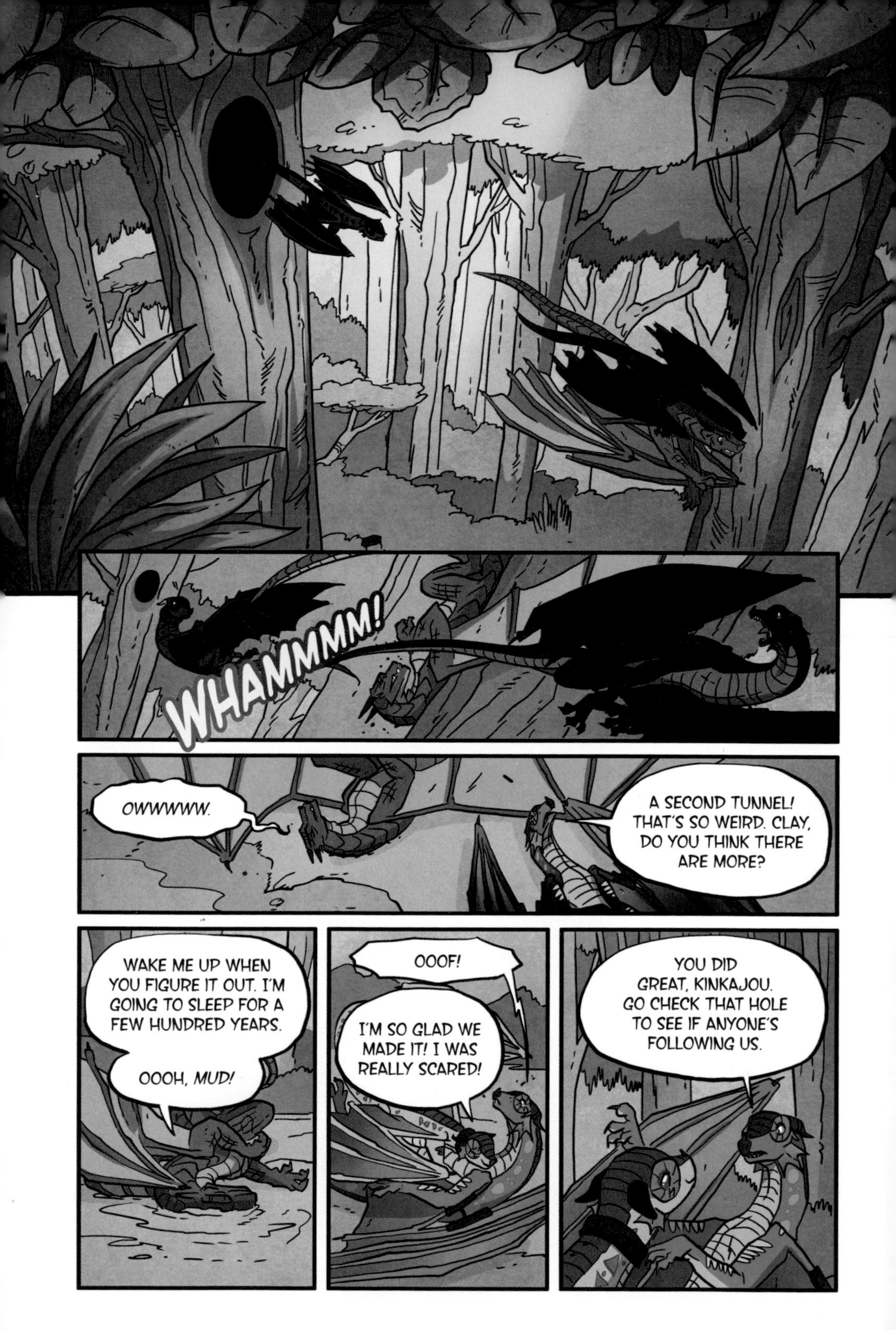
WHAMMMMM!
OWWWWW.
A SECOND TUNNEL! THAT'S SO WEIRD. CLAY, DO YOU THINK THERE ARE MORE?
WAKE ME UP WHEN YOU FIGURE IT OUT. I'M GOING TO SLEEP FOR A FEW HUNDRED YEARS.
OOOH, MUD!
OOOF!
I'M SO GLAD WE MADE IT! I WAS REALLY SCARED!
YOU DID GREAT, KINKAJOU. GO CHECK THAT HOLE TO SEE IF ANYONE'S FOLLOWING US.

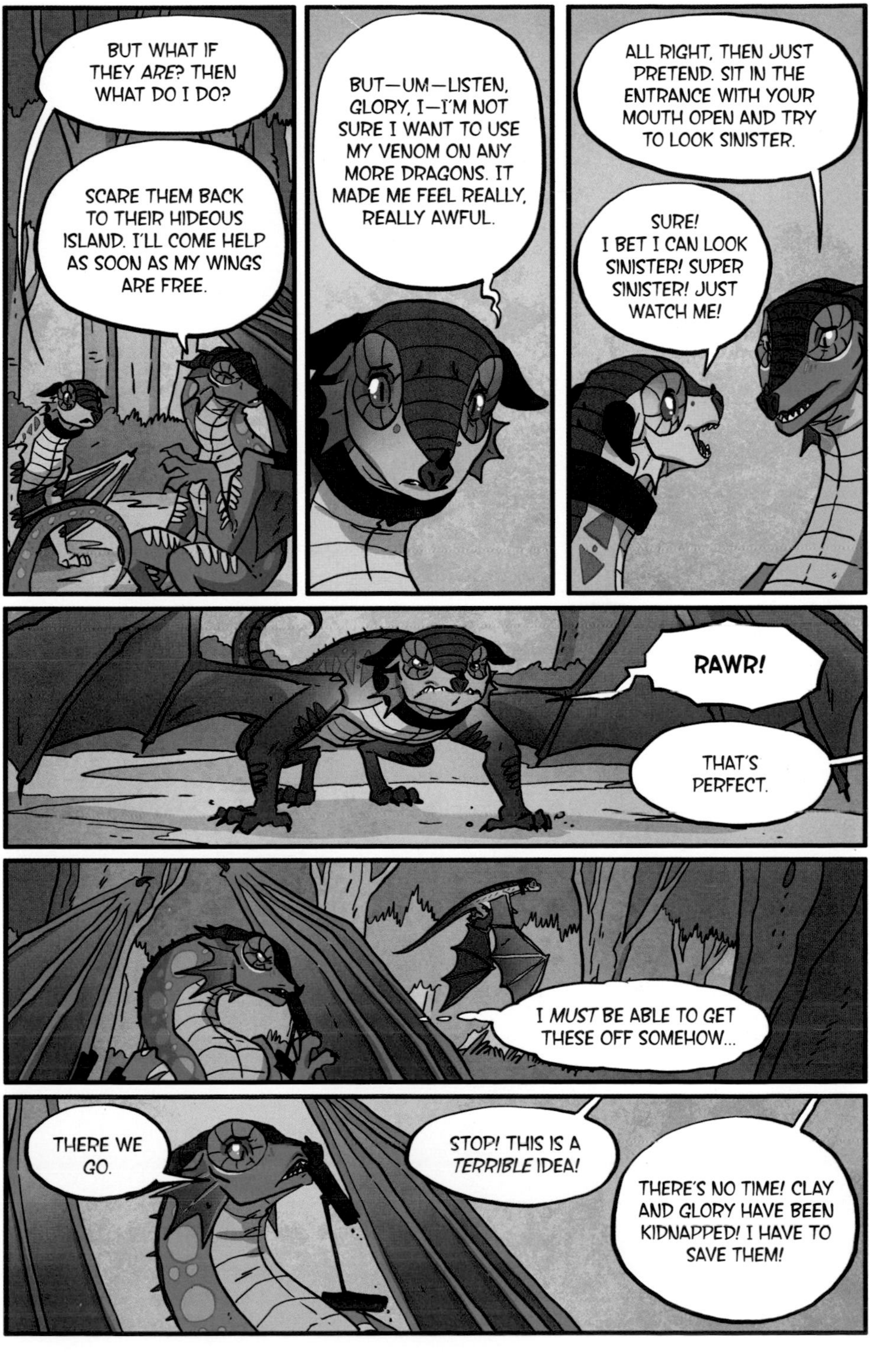
BUT WHAT IF THEY *ARE*? THEN WHAT DO I DO?
SCARE THEM BACK TO THEIR HIDEOUS ISLAND. I'LL COME HELP AS SOON AS MY WINGS ARE FREE.
BUT—UM—LISTEN, GLORY, I—I'M NOT SURE I WANT TO USE MY VENOM ON ANY MORE DRAGONS. IT MADE ME FEEL REALLY, REALLY AWFUL.
ALL RIGHT, THEN JUST PRETEND. SIT IN THE ENTRANCE WITH YOUR MOUTH OPEN AND TRY TO LOOK SINISTER.
SURE! I BET I CAN LOOK SINISTER! SUPER SINISTER! JUST WATCH ME!
RAWR!
THAT'S PERFECT.
I *MUST* BE ABLE TO GET THESE OFF SOMEHOW...
THERE WE GO.
STOP! THIS IS A *TERRIBLE* IDEA!
THERE'S NO TIME! CLAY AND GLORY HAVE BEEN KIDNAPPED! I HAVE TO SAVE THEM!

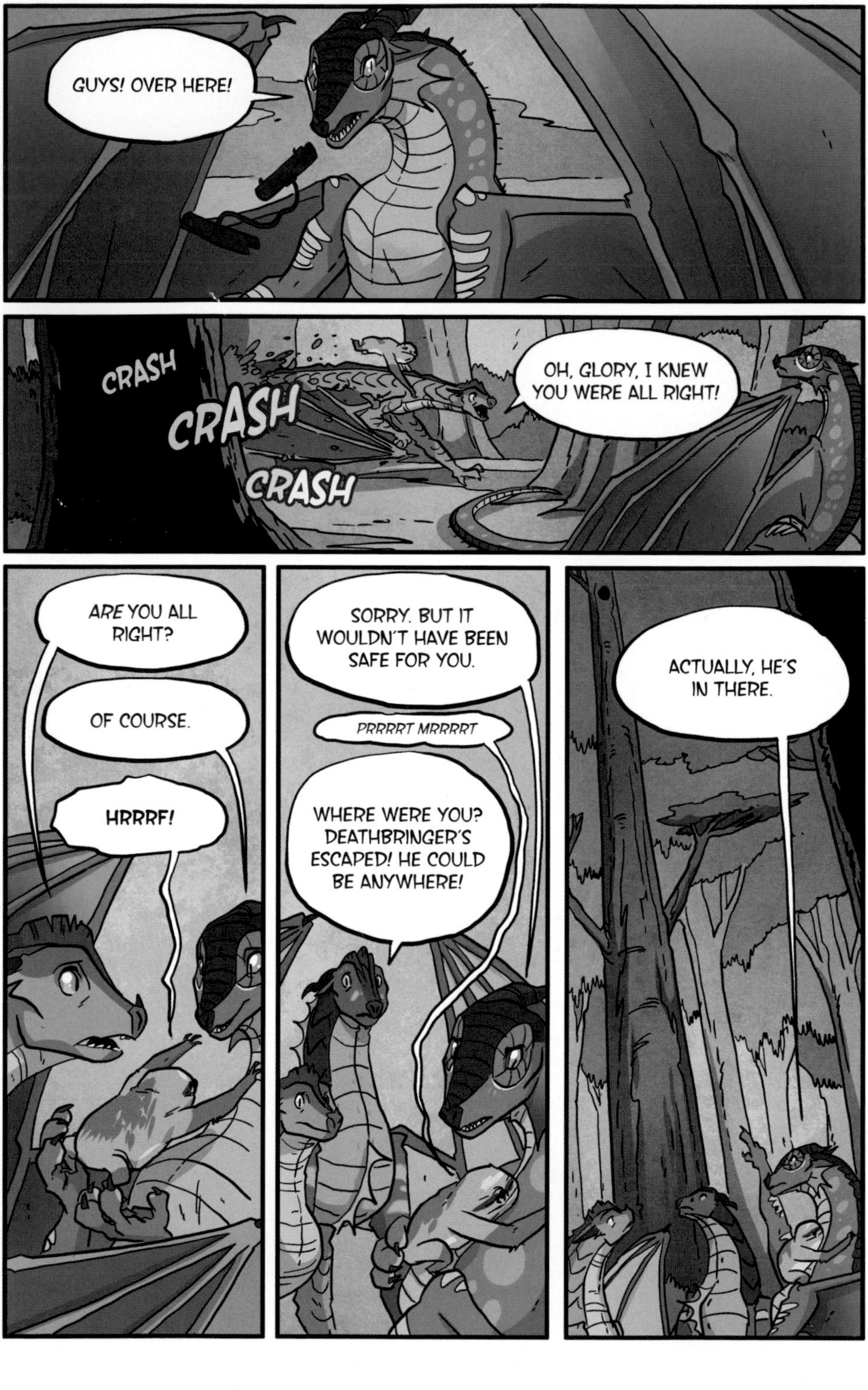
GUYS! OVER HERE!
CRASH
CRASH
CRASH
OH, GLORY, I KNEW YOU WERE ALL RIGHT!
ARE YOU ALL RIGHT?
OF COURSE.
HRRRF!
SORRY. BUT IT WOULDN'T HAVE BEEN SAFE FOR YOU.
PRRRRT MRRRRT
WHERE WERE YOU? DEATHBRINGER'S ESCAPED! HE COULD BE ANYWHERE!
ACTUALLY, HE'S IN THERE.

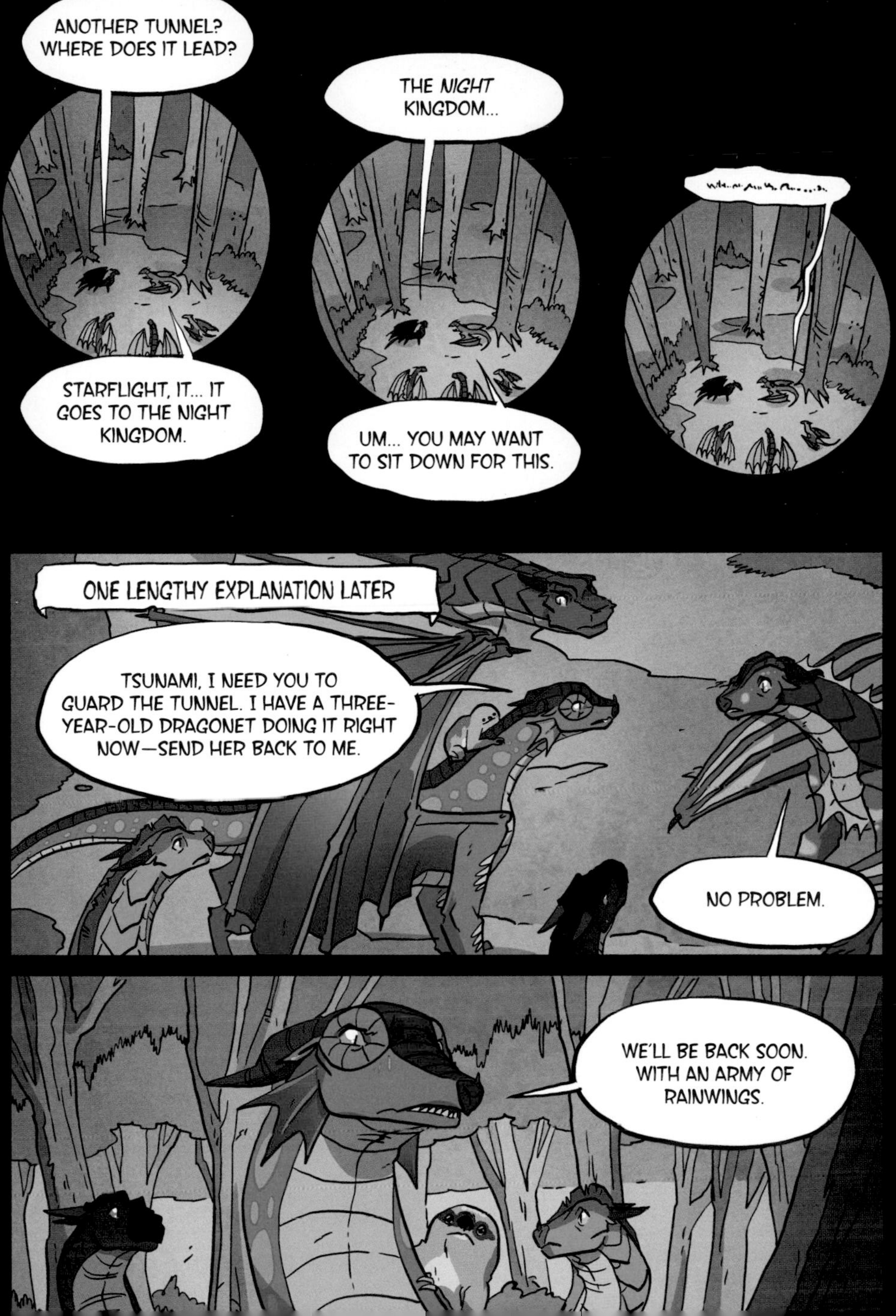
ANOTHER TUNNEL? WHERE DOES IT LEAD?
STARFLIGHT, IT... IT GOES TO THE NIGHT KINGDOM.
THE *NIGHT* KINGDOM...
UM... YOU MAY WANT TO SIT DOWN FOR THIS.
ONE LENGTHY EXPLANATION LATER
TSUNAMI, I NEED YOU TO GUARD THE TUNNEL. I HAVE A THREE-YEAR-OLD DRAGONET DOING IT RIGHT NOW—SEND HER BACK TO ME.
NO PROBLEM.
WE'LL BE BACK SOON. WITH AN ARMY OF RAINWINGS.

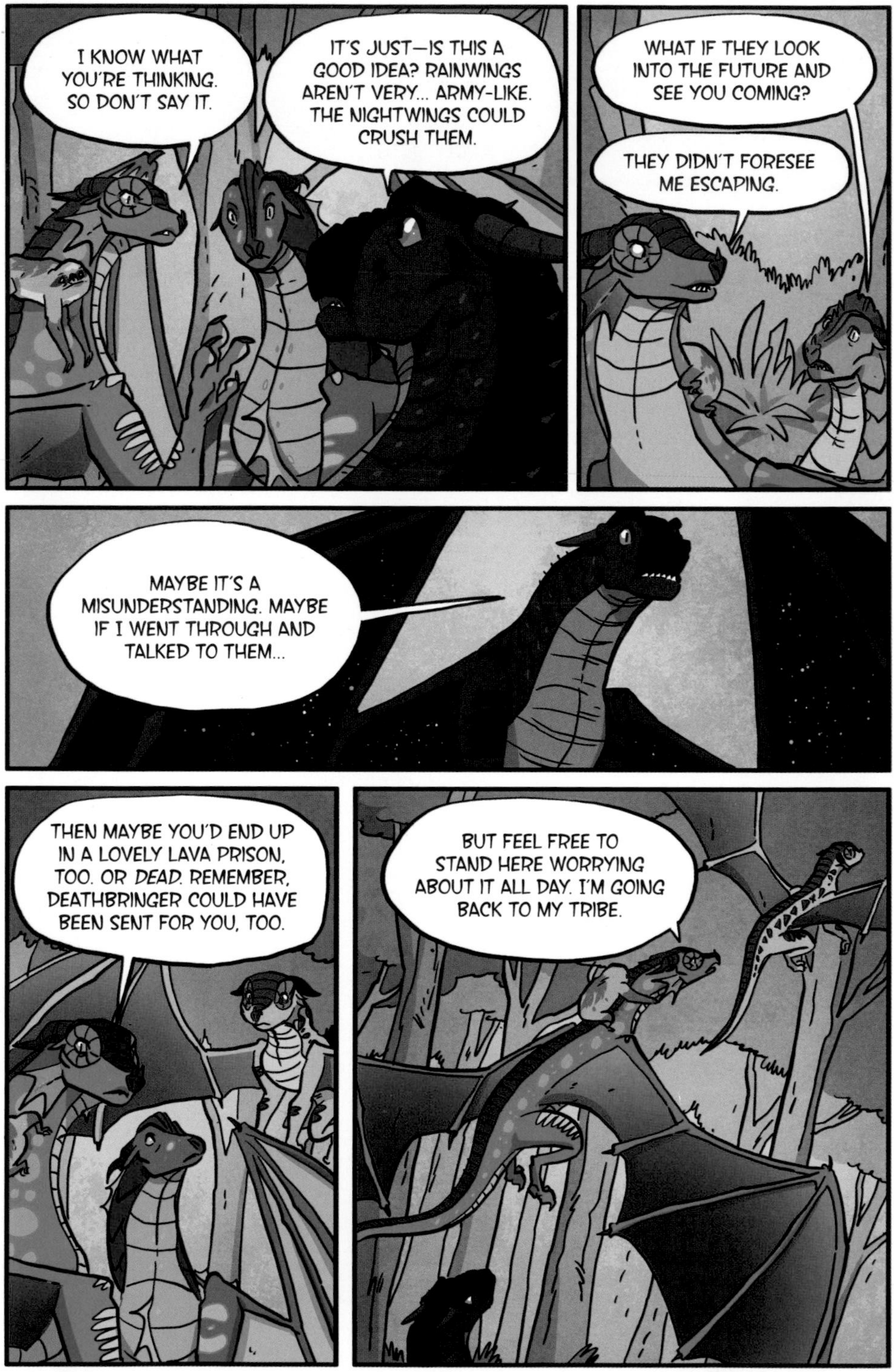
I KNOW WHAT YOU'RE THINKING. SO DON'T SAY IT.
IT'S JUST—IS THIS A GOOD IDEA? RAINWINGS AREN'T VERY... ARMY-LIKE. THE NIGHTWINGS COULD CRUSH THEM.
WHAT IF THEY LOOK INTO THE FUTURE AND SEE YOU COMING?
THEY DIDN'T FORESEE ME ESCAPING.
MAYBE IT'S A MISUNDERSTANDING. MAYBE IF I WENT THROUGH AND TALKED TO THEM...
THEN MAYBE YOU'D END UP IN A LOVELY LAVA PRISON, TOO. OR *DEAD*. REMEMBER, DEATHBRINGER COULD HAVE BEEN SENT FOR YOU, TOO.
BUT FEEL FREE TO STAND HERE WORRYING ABOUT IT ALL DAY. I'M GOING BACK TO MY TRIBE.

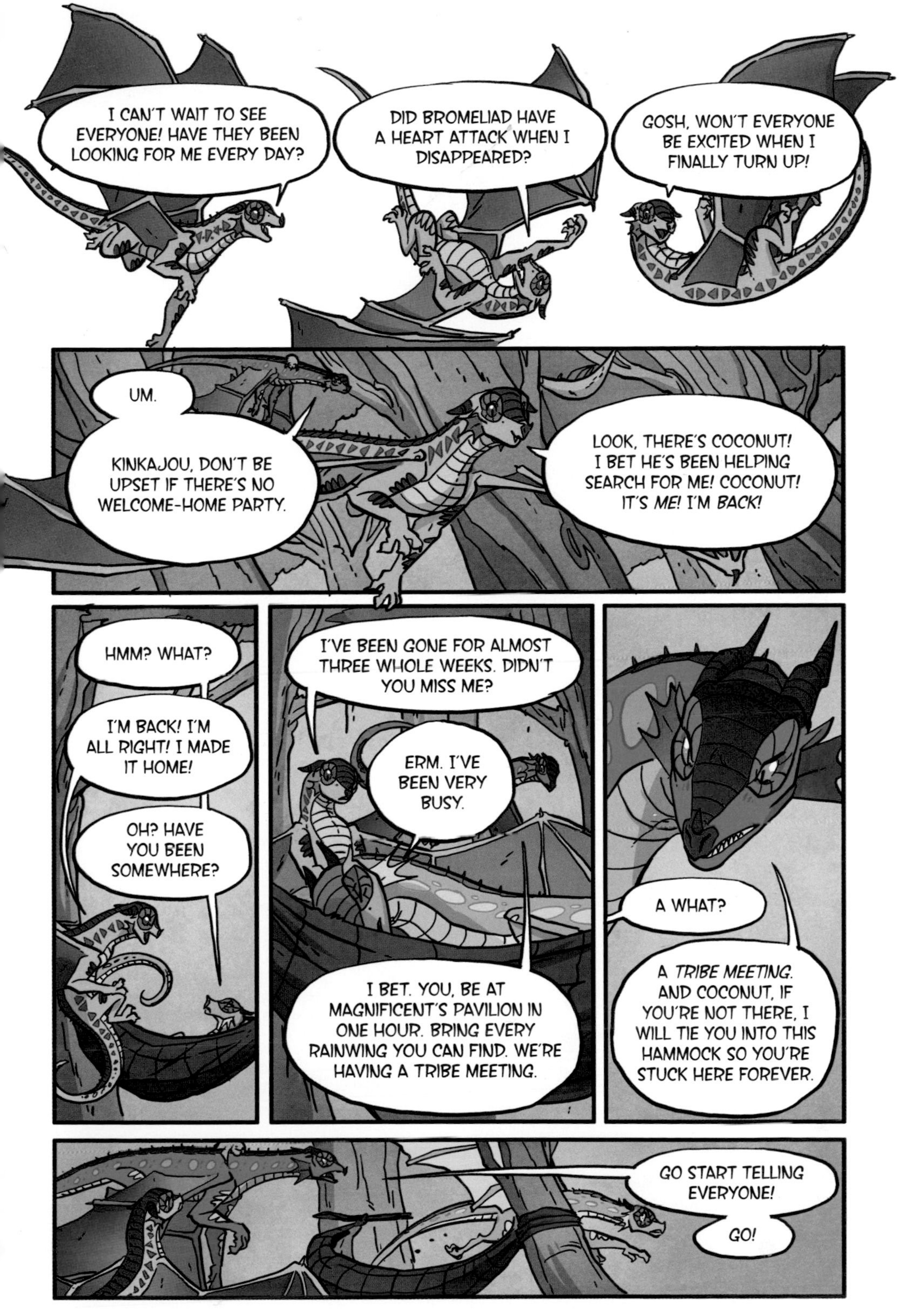
I CAN'T WAIT TO SEE EVERYONE! HAVE THEY BEEN LOOKING FOR ME EVERY DAY?
DID BROMELIAD HAVE A HEART ATTACK WHEN I DISAPPEARED?
GOSH, WON'T EVERYONE BE EXCITED WHEN I FINALLY TURN UP!
UM.
KINKAJOU, DON'T BE UPSET IF THERE'S NO WELCOME-HOME PARTY.
LOOK, THERE'S COCONUT! I BET HE'S BEEN HELPING SEARCH FOR ME! COCONUT! IT'S *ME!* I'M *BACK!*
HMM? WHAT?
I'M BACK! I'M ALL RIGHT! I MADE IT HOME!
OH? HAVE YOU BEEN SOMEWHERE?
I'VE BEEN GONE FOR ALMOST THREE WHOLE WEEKS. DIDN'T YOU MISS ME?
ERM. I'VE BEEN VERY BUSY.
I BET. YOU, BE AT MAGNIFICENT'S PAVILION IN ONE HOUR. BRING EVERY RAINWING YOU CAN FIND. WE'RE HAVING A TRIBE MEETING.
A WHAT?
A *TRIBE MEETING.* AND COCONUT, IF YOU'RE NOT THERE, I WILL TIE YOU INTO THIS HAMMOCK SO YOU'RE STUCK HERE FOREVER.
GO START TELLING EVERYONE!
GO!

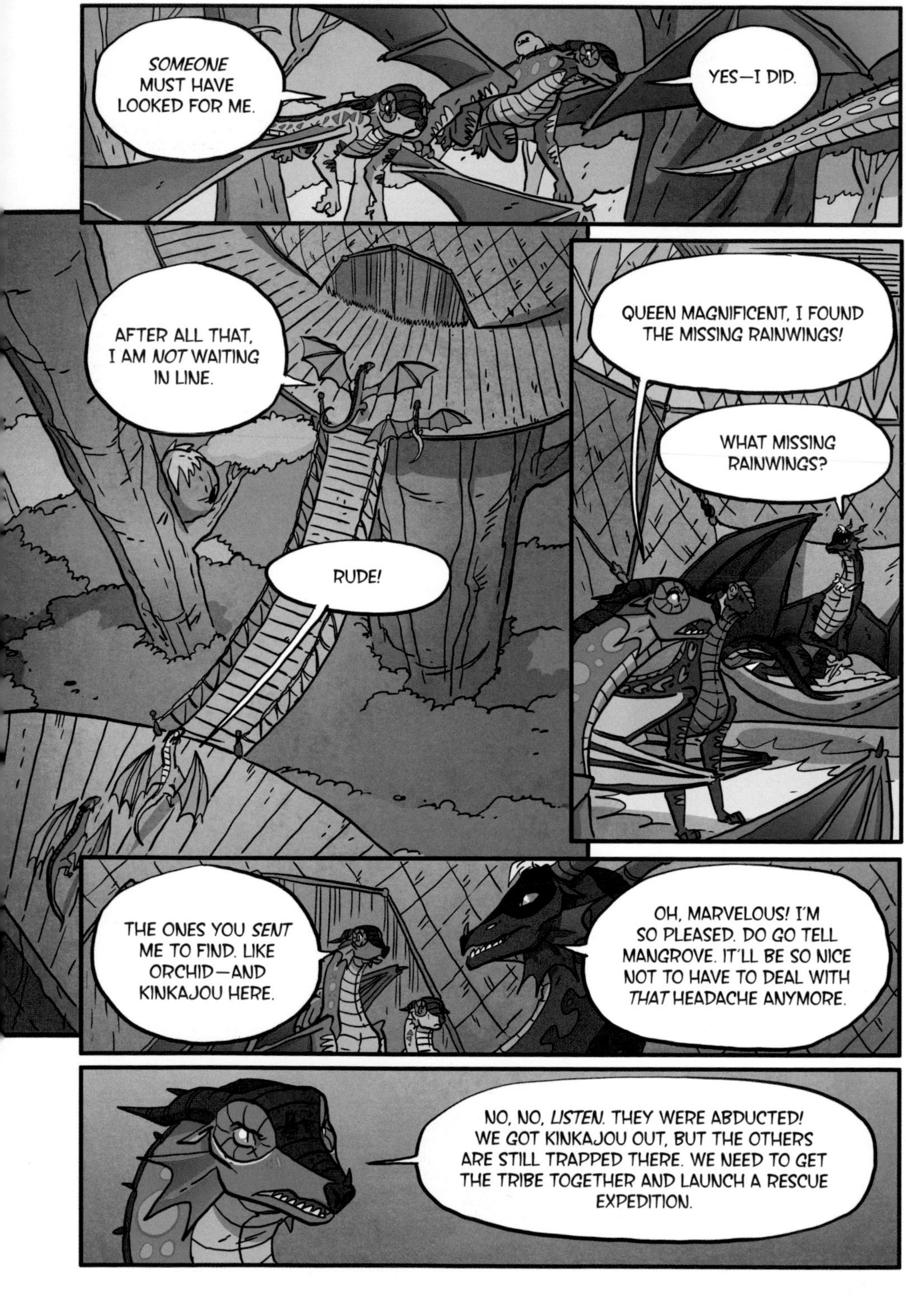

SOMEONE MUST HAVE LOOKED FOR ME.
YES—I DID.
AFTER ALL THAT, I AM *NOT* WAITING IN LINE.
RUDE!
QUEEN MAGNIFICENT, I FOUND THE MISSING RAINWINGS!
WHAT MISSING RAINWINGS?
THE ONES YOU *SENT* ME TO FIND. LIKE ORCHID—AND KINKAJOU HERE.
OH, MARVELOUS! I'M SO PLEASED. DO GO TELL MANGROVE. IT'LL BE SO NICE NOT TO HAVE TO DEAL WITH *THAT* HEADACHE ANYMORE.
NO, NO, *LISTEN*. THEY WERE ABDUCTED! WE GOT KINKAJOU OUT, BUT THE OTHERS ARE STILL TRAPPED THERE. WE NEED TO GET THE TRIBE TOGETHER AND LAUNCH A RESCUE EXPEDITION.

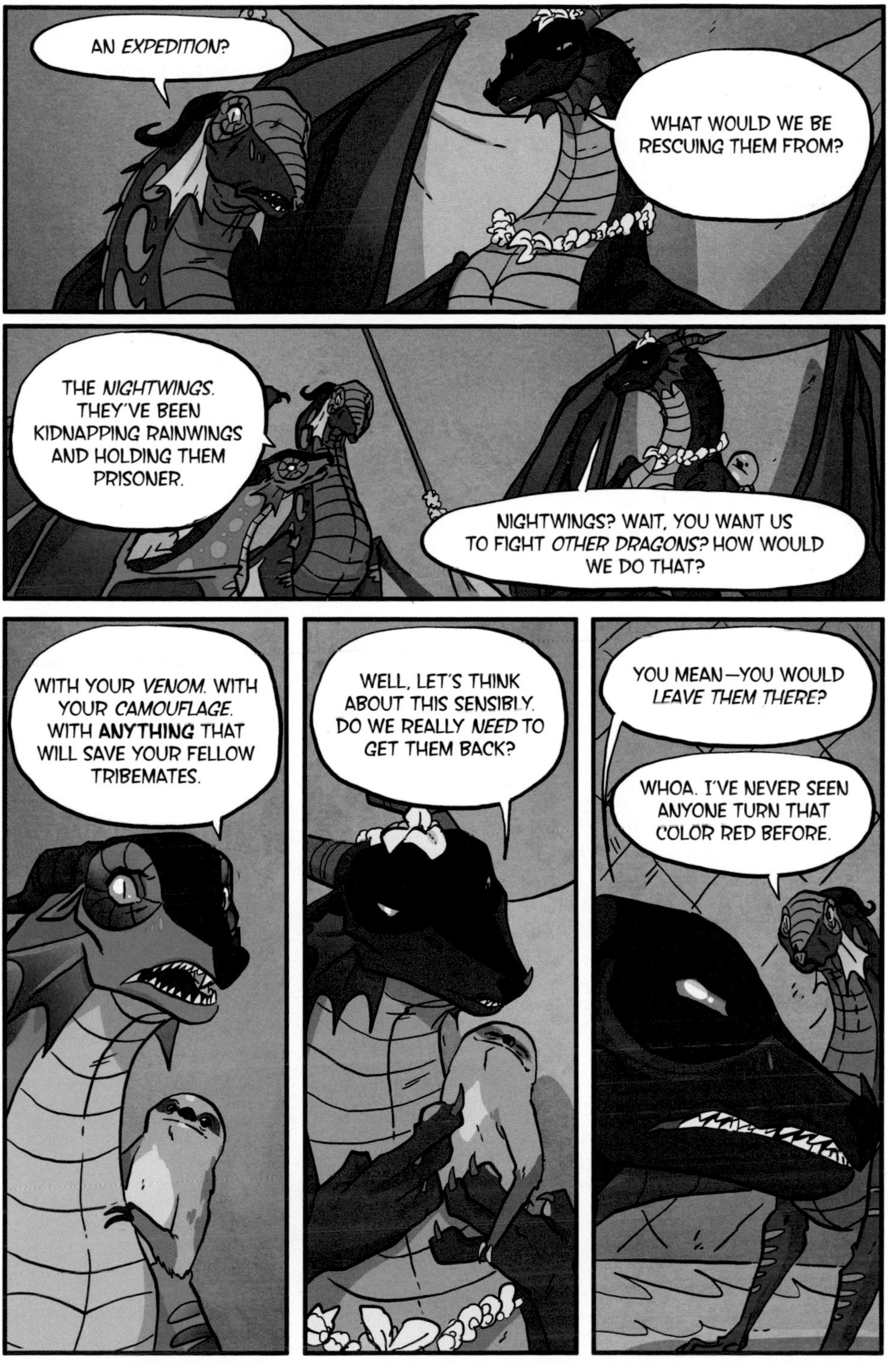
AN *EXPEDITION*?
WHAT WOULD WE BE RESCUING THEM FROM?
THE *NIGHTWINGS*. THEY'VE BEEN KIDNAPPING RAINWINGS AND HOLDING THEM PRISONER.
NIGHTWINGS? WAIT, YOU WANT US TO FIGHT *OTHER DRAGONS*? HOW WOULD WE DO THAT?
WITH YOUR *VENOM*. WITH YOUR *CAMOUFLAGE*. WITH **ANYTHING** THAT WILL SAVE YOUR FELLOW TRIBEMATES.
WELL, LET'S THINK ABOUT THIS SENSIBLY. DO WE REALLY *NEED* TO GET THEM BACK?
YOU MEAN—YOU WOULD *LEAVE THEM THERE?*
WHOA. I'VE NEVER SEEN ANYONE TURN THAT COLOR RED BEFORE.

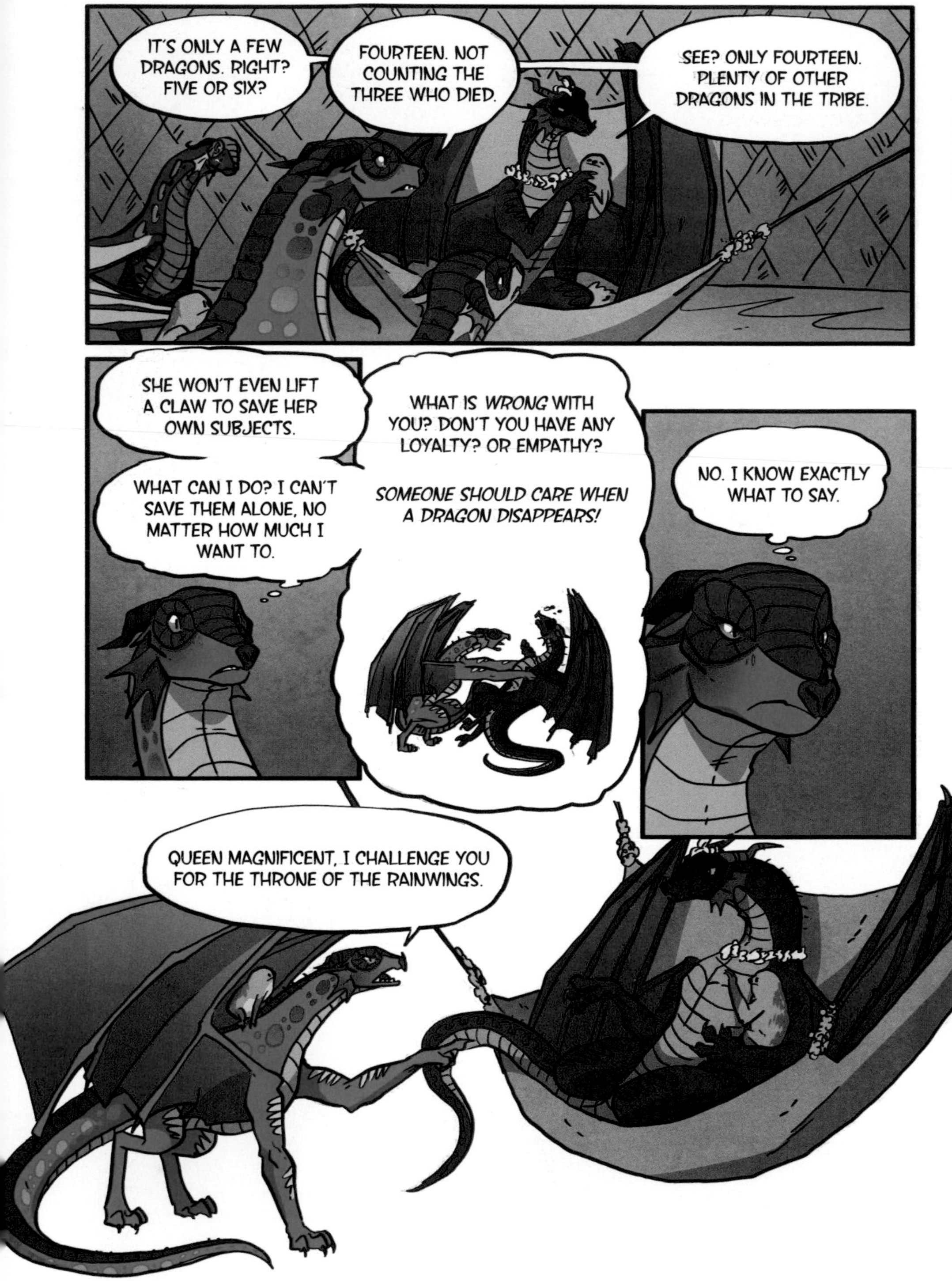
IT'S ONLY A FEW DRAGONS. RIGHT? FIVE OR SIX?
FOURTEEN. NOT COUNTING THE THREE WHO DIED.
SEE? ONLY FOURTEEN. PLENTY OF OTHER DRAGONS IN THE TRIBE.
SHE WON'T EVEN LIFT A CLAW TO SAVE HER OWN SUBJECTS.
WHAT CAN I DO? I CAN'T SAVE THEM ALONE, NO MATTER HOW MUCH I WANT TO.
WHAT IS *WRONG* WITH YOU? DON'T YOU HAVE ANY LOYALTY? OR EMPATHY?
SOMEONE SHOULD CARE WHEN A DRAGON DISAPPEARS!
NO. I KNOW EXACTLY WHAT TO SAY.
QUEEN MAGNIFICENT, I CHALLENGE YOU FOR THE THRONE OF THE RAINWINGS.

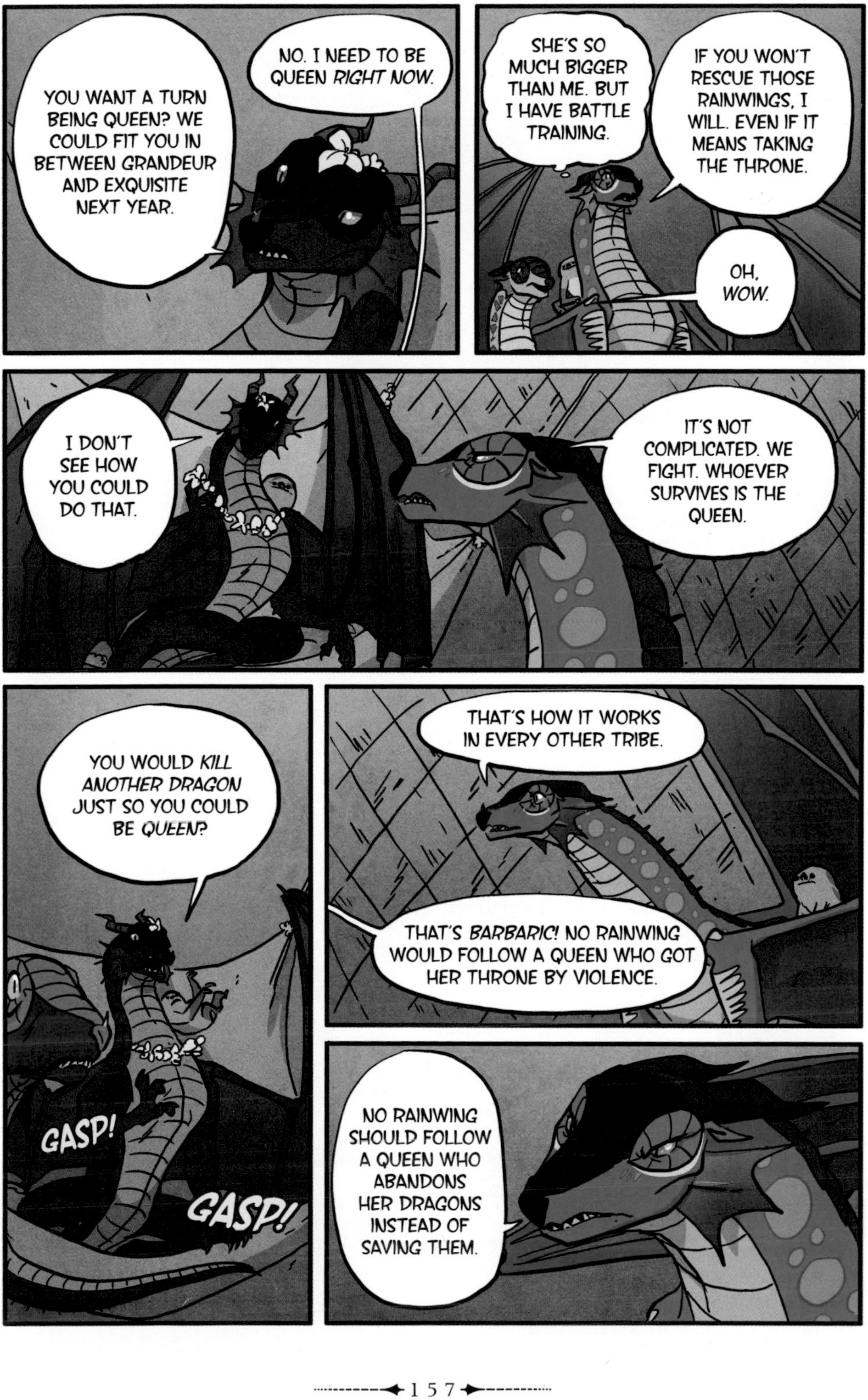
YOU WANT A TURN BEING QUEEN? WE COULD FIT YOU IN BETWEEN GRANDEUR AND EXQUISITE NEXT YEAR.
NO. I NEED TO BE QUEEN *RIGHT NOW.*
SHE'S SO MUCH BIGGER THAN ME. BUT I HAVE BATTLE TRAINING.
IF YOU WON'T RESCUE THOSE RAINWINGS, I WILL. EVEN IF IT MEANS TAKING THE THRONE.
OH, *WOW.*
I DON'T SEE HOW YOU COULD DO THAT.
IT'S NOT COMPLICATED. WE FIGHT. WHOEVER SURVIVES IS THE QUEEN.
YOU WOULD *KILL ANOTHER DRAGON* JUST SO YOU COULD BE *QUEEN*?
GASP!
GASP!
THAT'S HOW IT WORKS IN EVERY OTHER TRIBE.
THAT'S *BARBARIC!* NO RAINWING WOULD FOLLOW A QUEEN WHO GOT HER THRONE BY VIOLENCE.
NO RAINWING SHOULD FOLLOW A QUEEN WHO ABANDONS HER DRAGONS INSTEAD OF SAVING THEM.

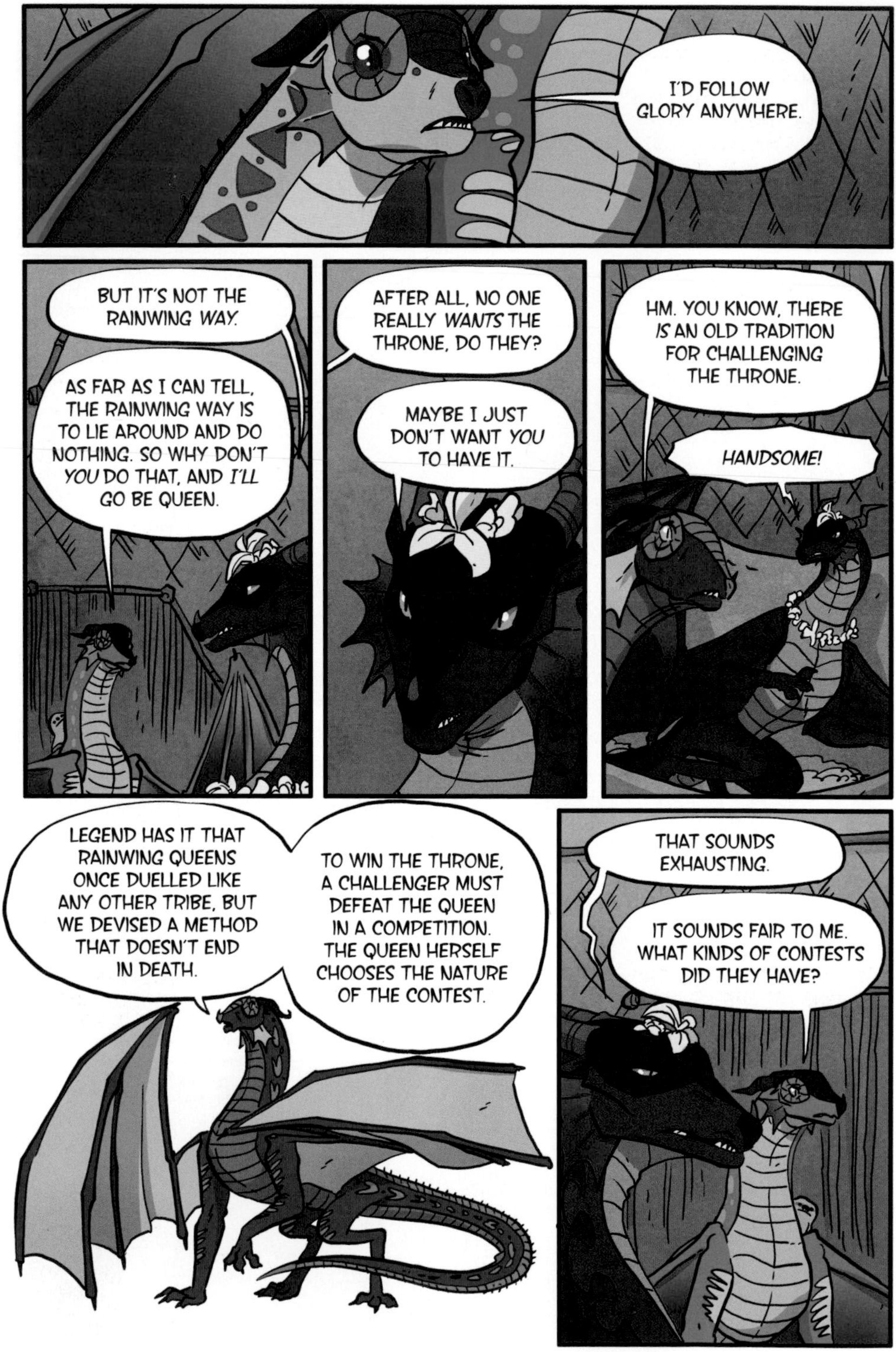
I'D FOLLOW GLORY ANYWHERE.
BUT IT'S NOT THE RAINWING *WAY.*
AS FAR AS I CAN TELL, THE RAINWING WAY IS TO LIE AROUND AND DO NOTHING. SO WHY DON'T *YOU* DO THAT, AND *I'LL* GO BE QUEEN.
AFTER ALL, NO ONE REALLY *WANTS* THE THRONE, DO THEY?
MAYBE I JUST DON'T WANT *YOU* TO HAVE IT.
HM. YOU KNOW, THERE *IS* AN OLD TRADITION FOR CHALLENGING THE THRONE.
HANDSOME!
LEGEND HAS IT THAT RAINWING QUEENS ONCE DUELLED LIKE ANY OTHER TRIBE, BUT WE DEVISED A METHOD THAT DOESN'T END IN DEATH.
TO WIN THE THRONE, A CHALLENGER MUST DEFEAT THE QUEEN IN A COMPETITION. THE QUEEN HERSELF CHOOSES THE NATURE OF THE CONTEST.
THAT SOUNDS EXHAUSTING.
IT SOUNDS FAIR TO ME. WHAT KINDS OF CONTESTS DID THEY HAVE?

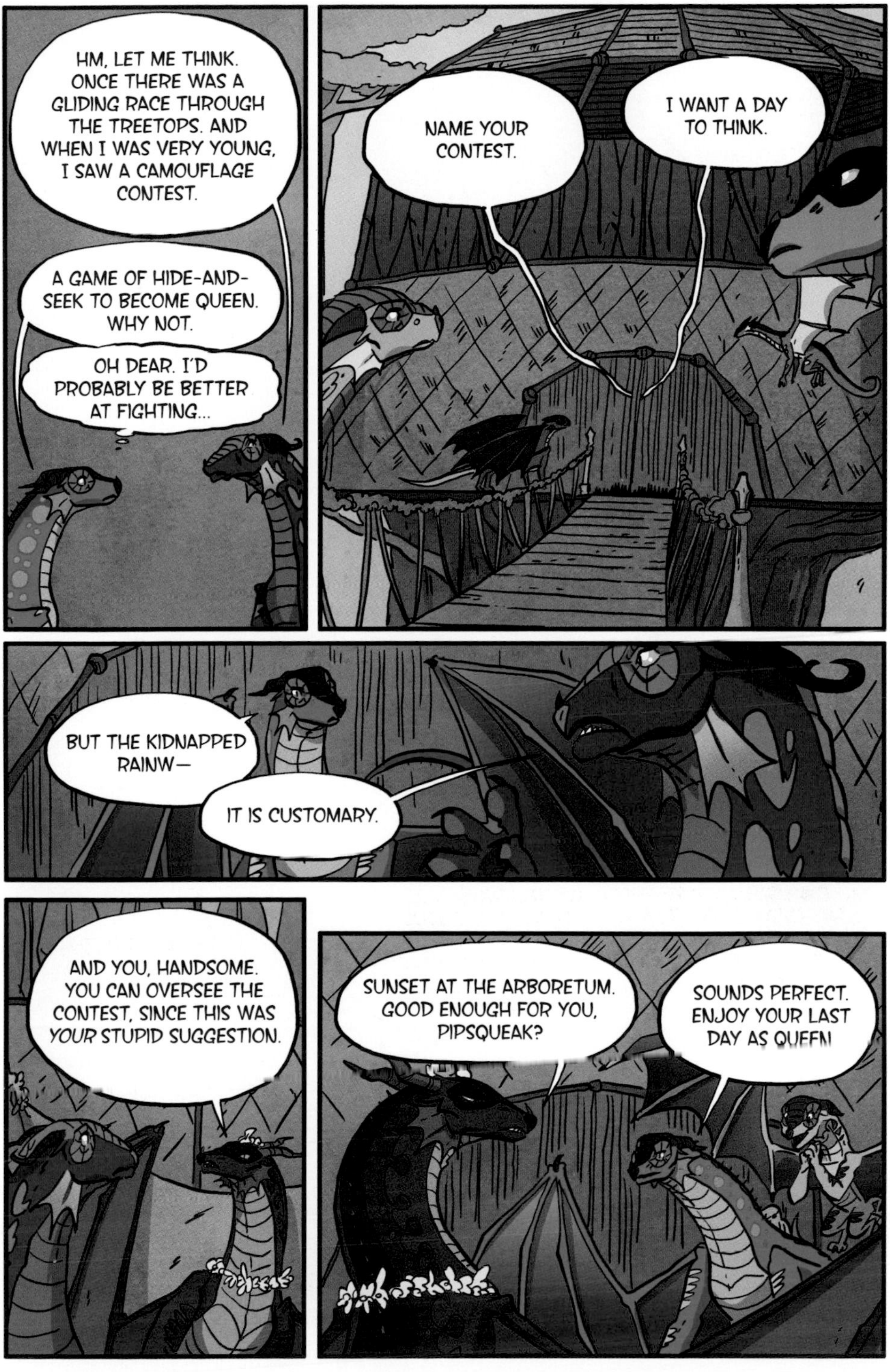
HM, LET ME THINK. ONCE THERE WAS A GLIDING RACE THROUGH THE TREETOPS. AND WHEN I WAS VERY YOUNG, I SAW A CAMOUFLAGE CONTEST.
A GAME OF HIDE-AND-SEEK TO BECOME QUEEN. WHY NOT.
OH DEAR. I'D PROBABLY BE BETTER AT FIGHTING...
NAME YOUR CONTEST.
I WANT A DAY TO THINK.
BUT THE KIDNAPPED RAINW—
IT IS CUSTOMARY.
AND YOU, HANDSOME. YOU CAN OVERSEE THE CONTEST, SINCE THIS WAS *YOUR* STUPID SUGGESTION.
SUNSET AT THE ARBORETUM. GOOD ENOUGH FOR YOU, PIPSQUEAK?
SOUNDS PERFECT. ENJOY YOUR LAST DAY AS QUEEN.

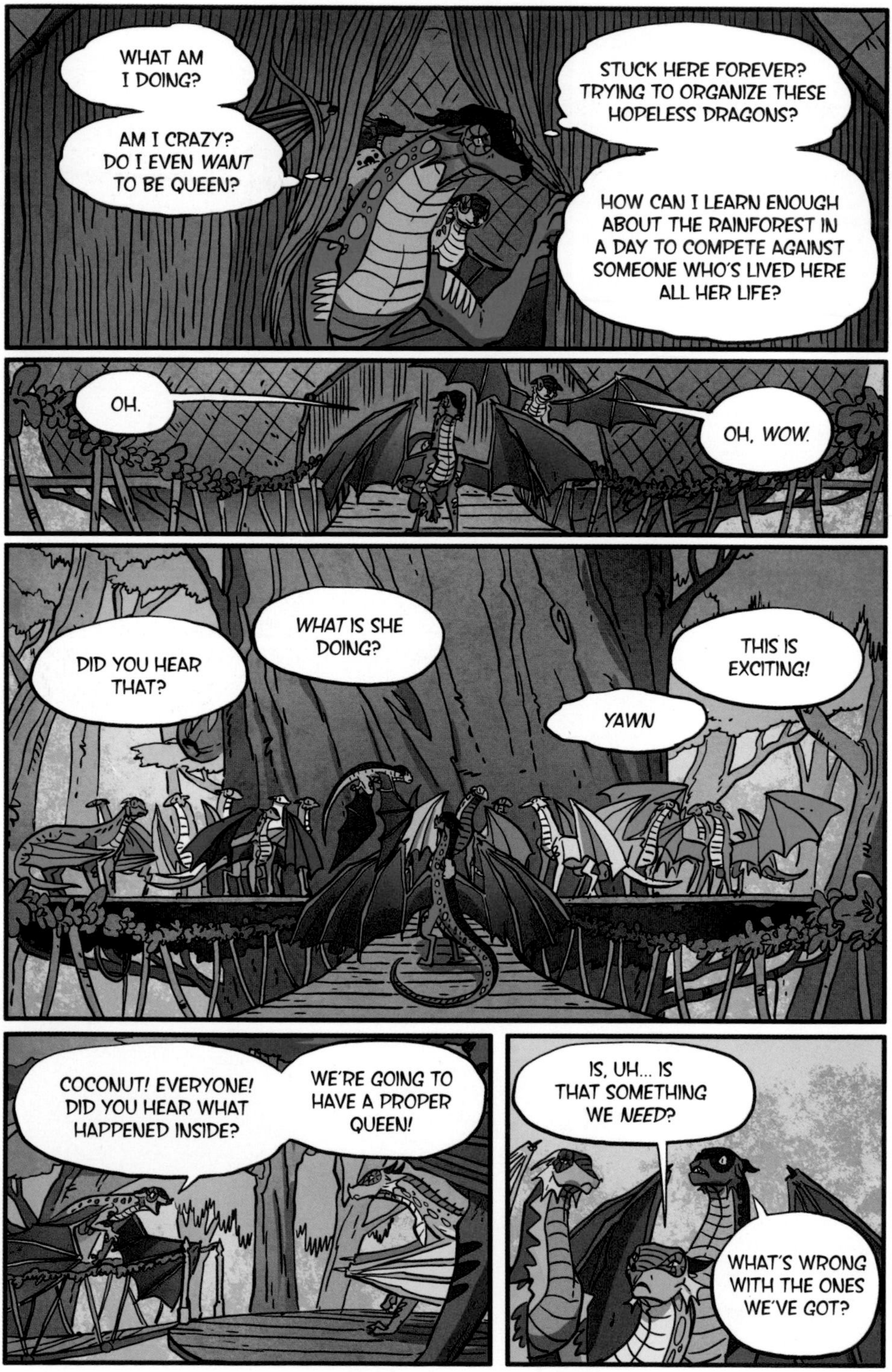
WHAT AM I DOING?
AM I CRAZY? DO I EVEN *WANT* TO BE QUEEN?
STUCK HERE FOREVER? TRYING TO ORGANIZE THESE HOPELESS DRAGONS?
HOW CAN I LEARN ENOUGH ABOUT THE RAINFOREST IN A DAY TO COMPETE AGAINST SOMEONE WHO'S LIVED HERE ALL HER LIFE?
OH.
OH, *WOW.*
DID YOU HEAR THAT?
WHAT IS SHE DOING?
THIS IS EXCITING!
YAWN
COCONUT! EVERYONE! DID YOU HEAR WHAT HAPPENED INSIDE?
WE'RE GOING TO HAVE A PROPER QUEEN!
IS, UH... IS THAT SOMETHING WE *NEED*?
WHAT'S WRONG WITH THE ONES WE'VE GOT?

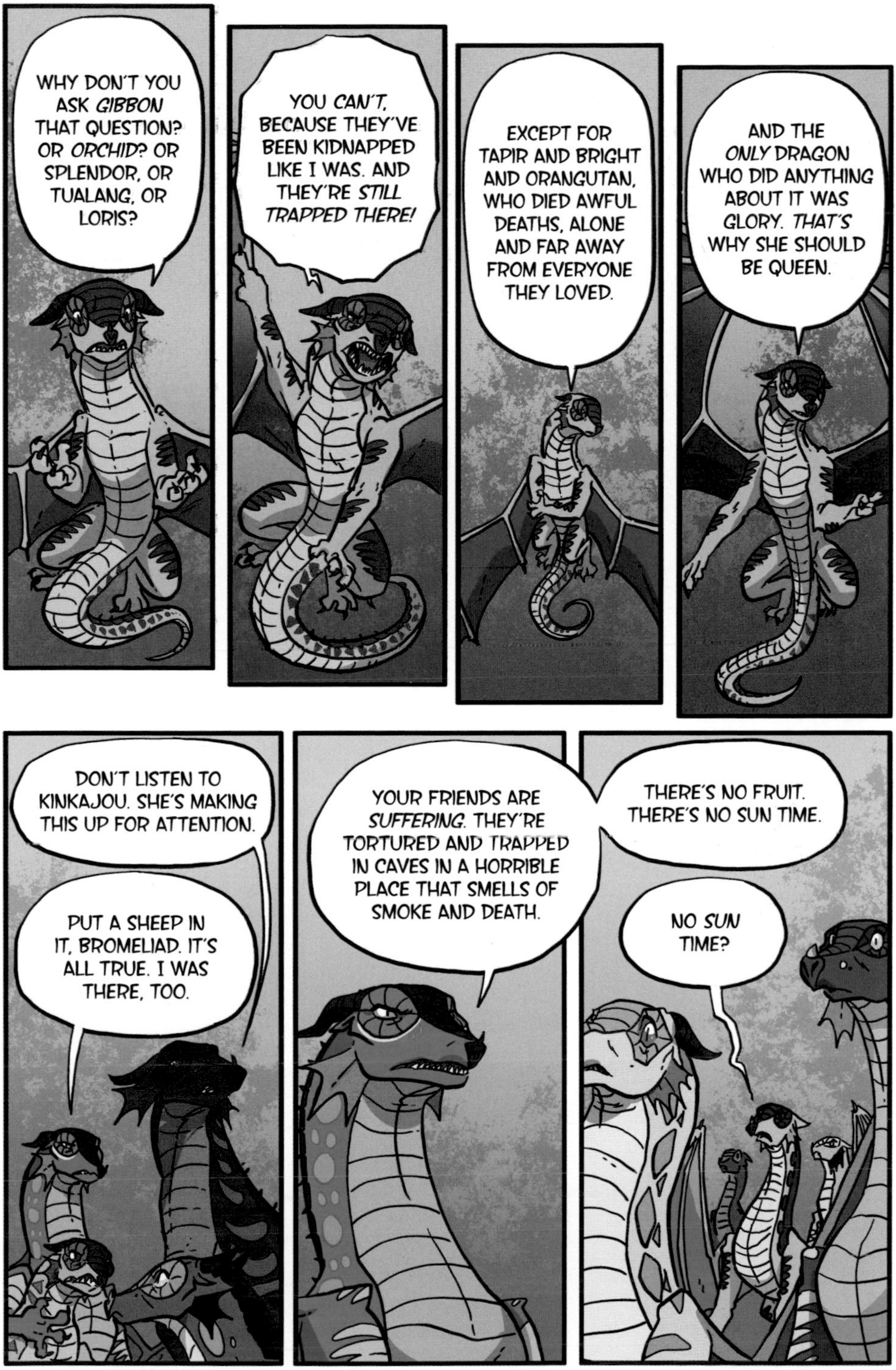
WHY DON'T YOU ASK *GIBBON* THAT QUESTION? OR *ORCHID*? OR SPLENDOR, OR TUALANG, OR LORIS?
YOU *CAN'T*, BECAUSE THEY'VE BEEN KIDNAPPED LIKE I WAS. AND THEY'RE *STILL TRAPPED THERE!*
EXCEPT FOR TAPIR AND BRIGHT AND ORANGUTAN, WHO DIED AWFUL DEATHS, ALONE AND FAR AWAY FROM EVERYONE THEY LOVED.
AND THE *ONLY* DRAGON WHO DID ANYTHING ABOUT IT WAS GLORY. *THAT'S* WHY SHE SHOULD BE QUEEN.
DON'T LISTEN TO KINKAJOU. SHE'S MAKING THIS UP FOR ATTENTION.
PUT A SHEEP IN IT, BROMELIAD. IT'S ALL TRUE. I WAS THERE, TOO.
YOUR FRIENDS ARE *SUFFERING*. THEY'RE TORTURED AND TRAPPED IN CAVES IN A HORRIBLE PLACE THAT SMELLS OF SMOKE AND DEATH.
THERE'S NO FRUIT. THERE'S NO SUN TIME.
NO *SUN* TIME?

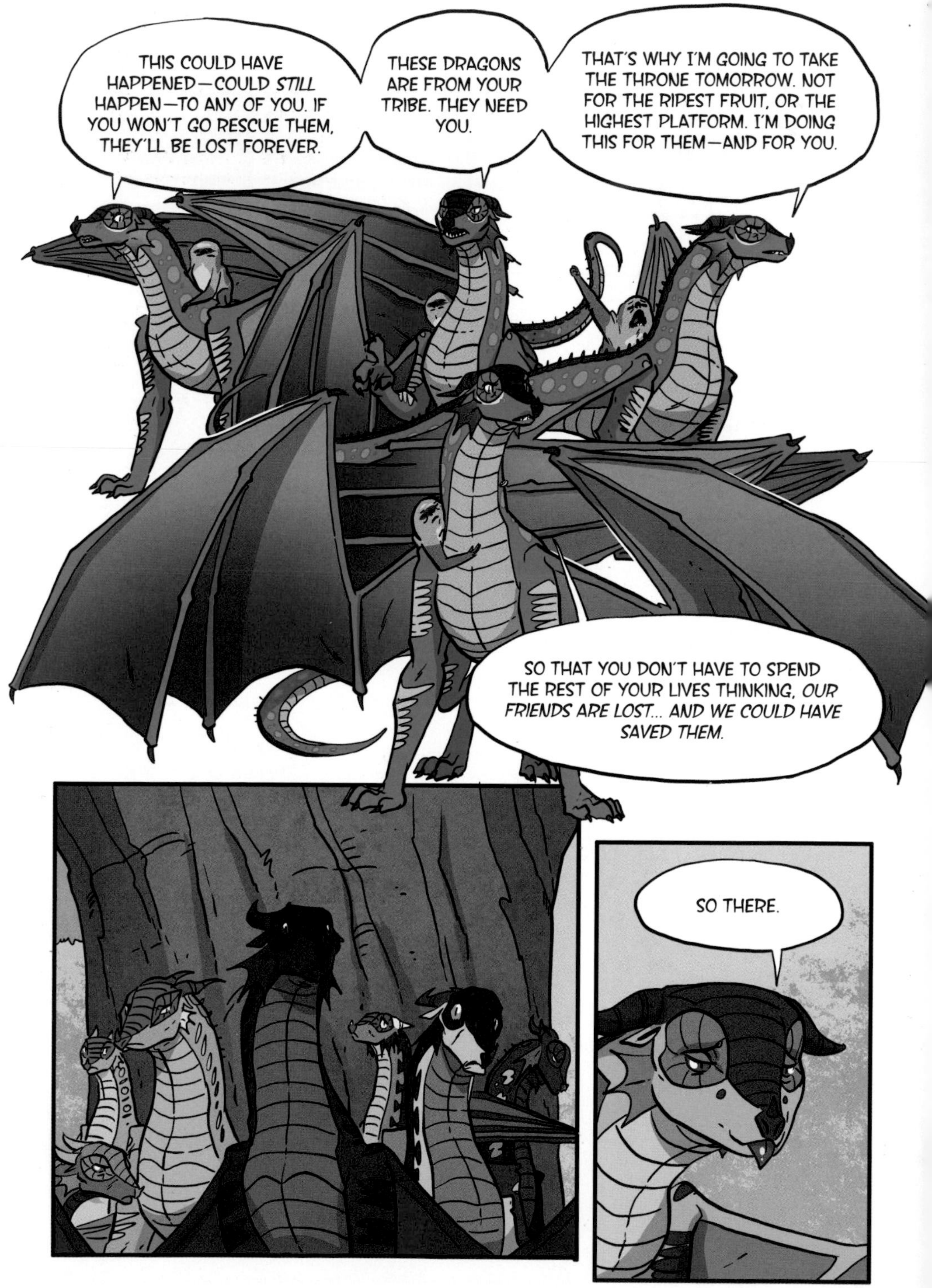
THIS COULD HAVE HAPPENED—COULD *STILL* HAPPEN—TO ANY OF YOU. IF YOU WON'T GO RESCUE THEM, THEY'LL BE LOST FOREVER.
THESE DRAGONS ARE FROM YOUR TRIBE. THEY NEED YOU.
THAT'S WHY I'M GOING TO TAKE THE THRONE TOMORROW. NOT FOR THE RIPEST FRUIT, OR THE HIGHEST PLATFORM. I'M DOING THIS FOR THEM—AND FOR YOU.
SO THAT YOU DON'T HAVE TO SPEND THE REST OF YOUR LIVES THINKING, *OUR FRIENDS ARE LOST... AND WE COULD HAVE SAVED THEM.*
SO THERE.

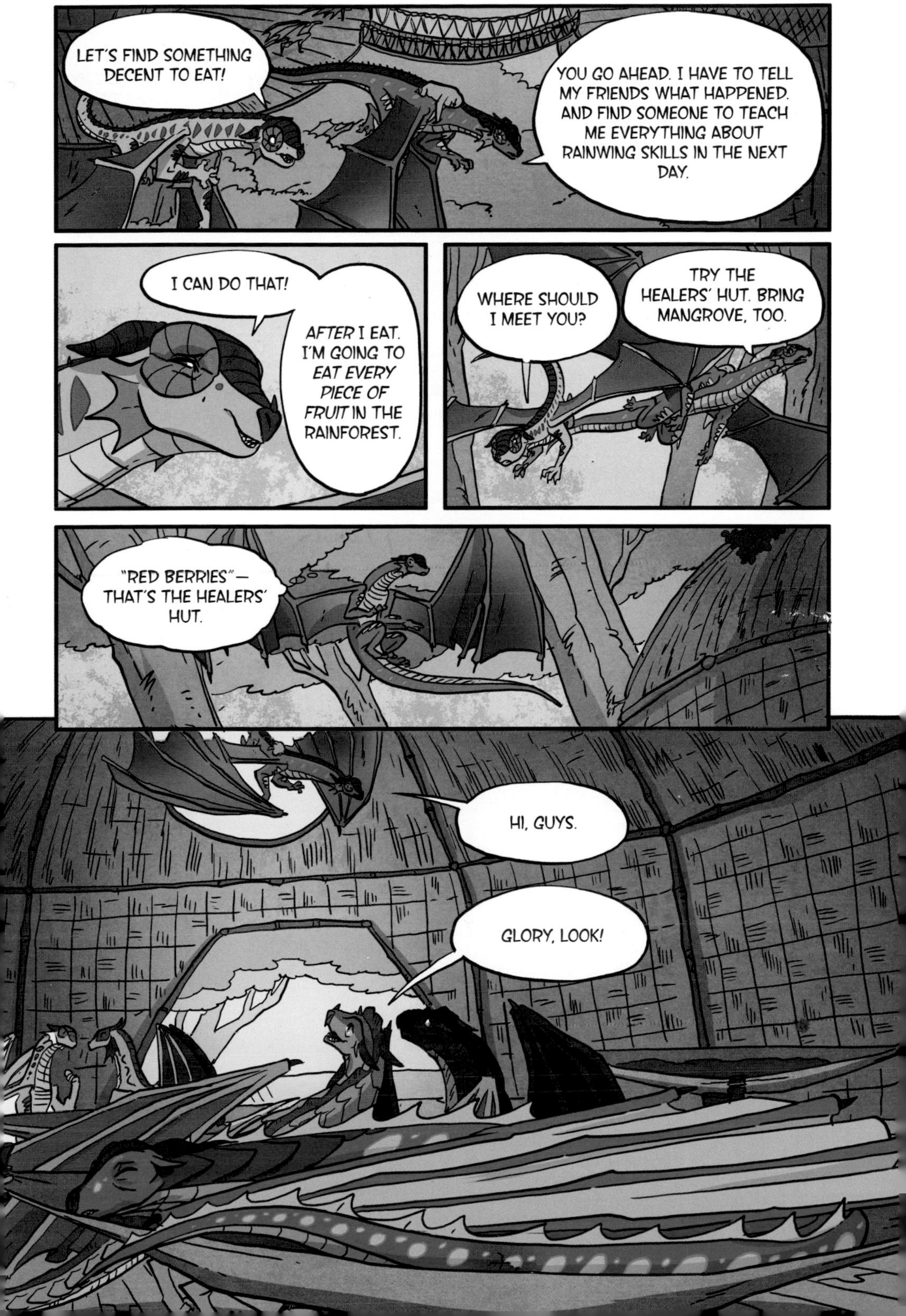
LET'S FIND SOMETHING DECENT TO EAT!
YOU GO AHEAD. I HAVE TO TELL MY FRIENDS WHAT HAPPENED. AND FIND SOMEONE TO TEACH ME EVERYTHING ABOUT RAINWING SKILLS IN THE NEXT DAY.
I CAN DO THAT!
AFTER I EAT. I'M GOING TO *EAT EVERY PIECE OF FRUIT* IN THE RAINFOREST.
WHERE SHOULD I MEET YOU?
TRY THE HEALERS' HUT. BRING MANGROVE, TOO.
"RED BERRIES"— THAT'S THE HEALERS' HUT.
HI, GUYS.
GLORY, LOOK!

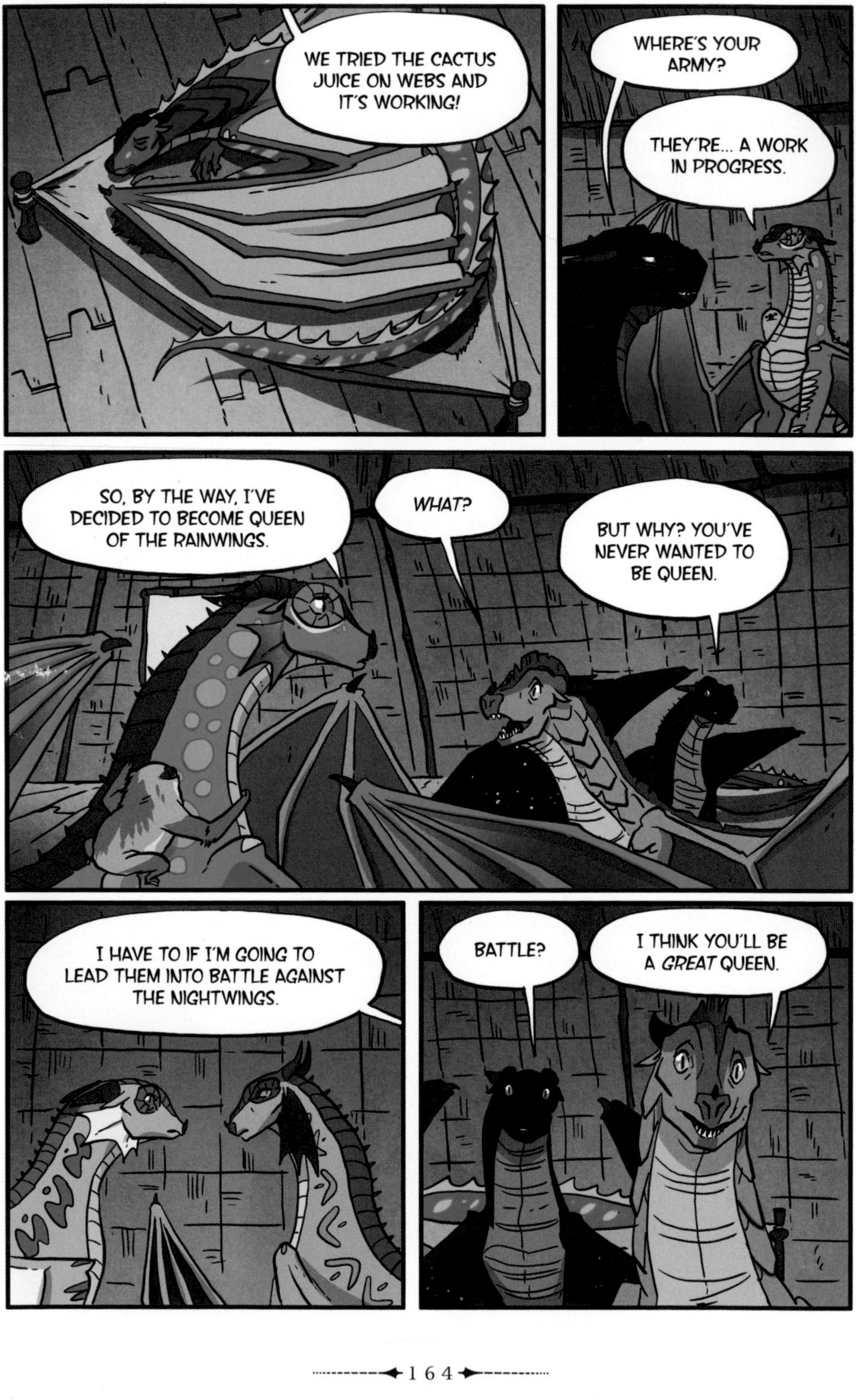

WE TRIED THE CACTUS JUICE ON WEBS AND IT'S WORKING!
WHERE'S YOUR ARMY?
THEY'RE... A WORK IN PROGRESS.
SO, BY THE WAY, I'VE DECIDED TO BECOME QUEEN OF THE RAINWINGS.
WHAT?
BUT WHY? YOU'VE NEVER WANTED TO BE QUEEN.
I HAVE TO IF I'M GOING TO LEAD THEM INTO BATTLE AGAINST THE NIGHTWINGS.
BATTLE?
I THINK YOU'LL BE A *GREAT* QUEEN.

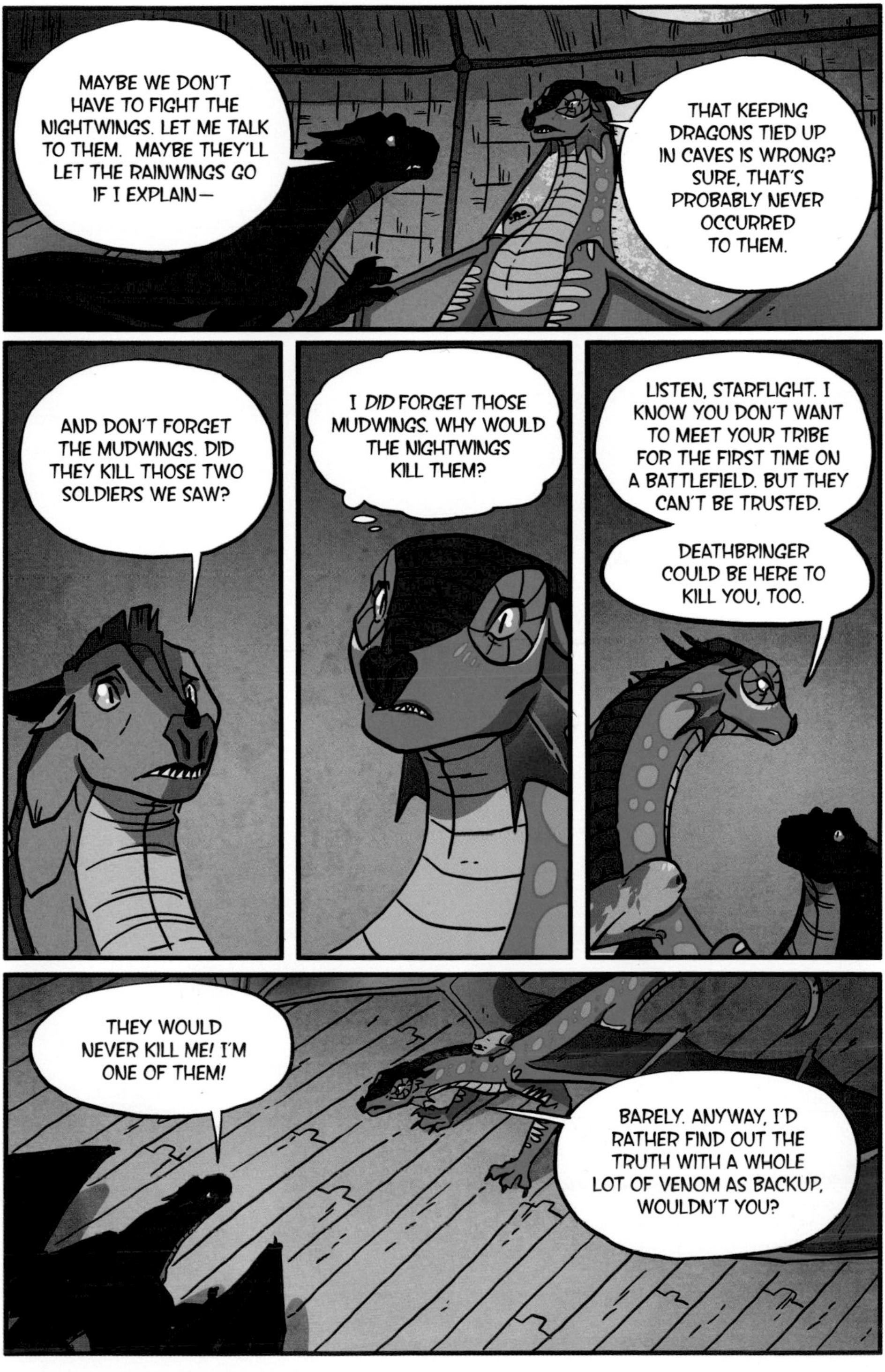
MAYBE WE DON'T HAVE TO FIGHT THE NIGHTWINGS. LET ME TALK TO THEM. MAYBE THEY'LL LET THE RAINWINGS GO IF I EXPLAIN—
THAT KEEPING DRAGONS TIED UP IN CAVES IS WRONG? SURE, THAT'S PROBABLY NEVER OCCURRED TO THEM.
AND DON'T FORGET THE MUDWINGS. DID THEY KILL THOSE TWO SOLDIERS WE SAW?
I *DID* FORGET THOSE MUDWINGS. WHY WOULD THE NIGHTWINGS KILL THEM?
LISTEN, STARFLIGHT. I KNOW YOU DON'T WANT TO MEET YOUR TRIBE FOR THE FIRST TIME ON A BATTLEFIELD. BUT THEY CAN'T BE TRUSTED.
DEATHBRINGER COULD BE HERE TO KILL YOU, TOO.
THEY WOULD NEVER KILL ME! I'M ONE OF THEM!
BARELY. ANYWAY, I'D RATHER FIND OUT THE TRUTH WITH A WHOLE LOT OF VENOM AS BACKUP, WOULDN'T YOU?

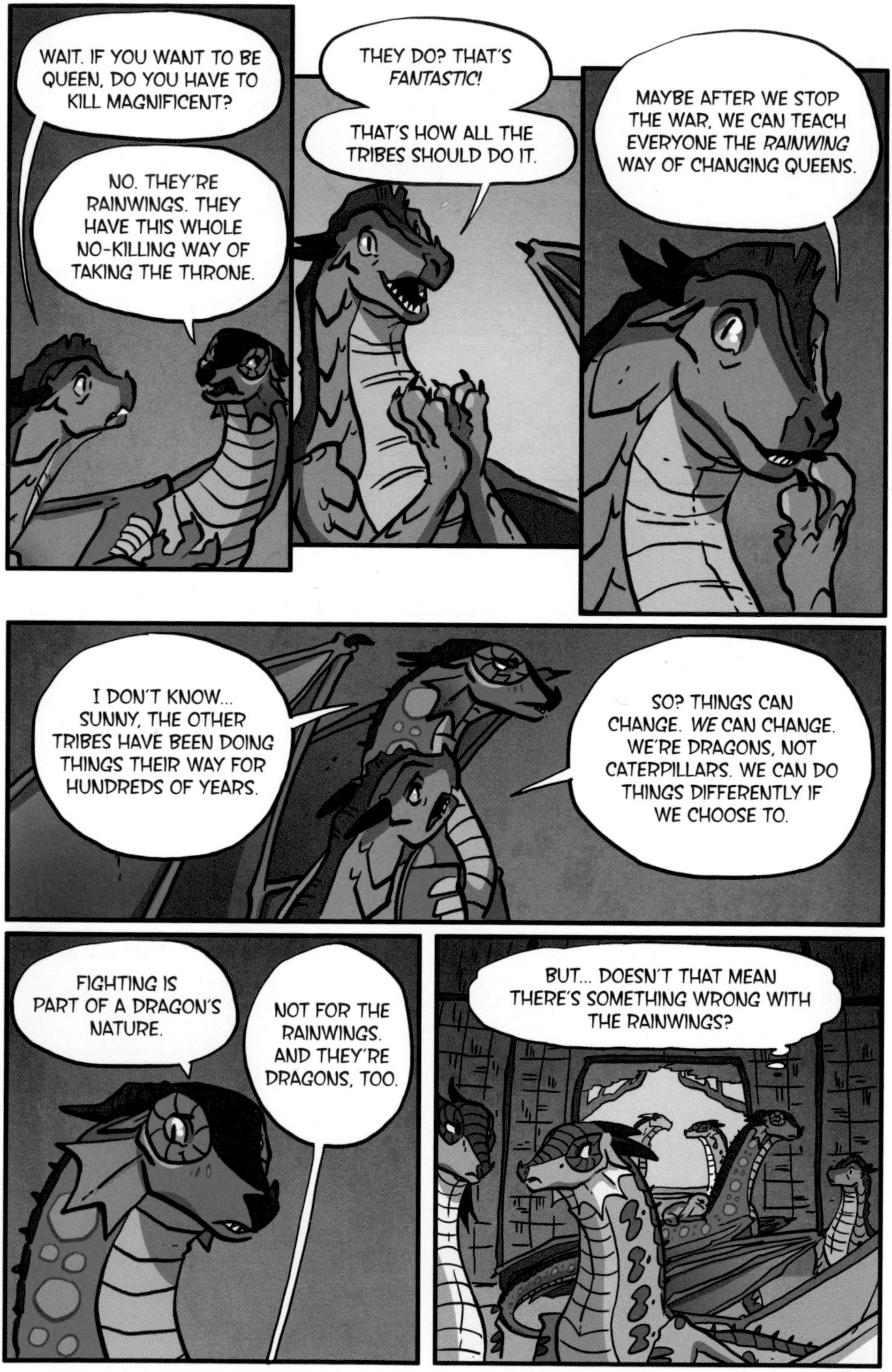
WAIT. IF YOU WANT TO BE QUEEN, DO YOU HAVE TO KILL MAGNIFICENT?
NO. THEY'RE RAINWINGS. THEY HAVE THIS WHOLE NO-KILLING WAY OF TAKING THE THRONE.
THEY DO? THAT'S *FANTASTIC!*
THAT'S HOW ALL THE TRIBES SHOULD DO IT.
MAYBE AFTER WE STOP THE WAR, WE CAN TEACH EVERYONE THE *RAINWING* WAY OF CHANGING QUEENS.
I DON'T KNOW... SUNNY, THE OTHER TRIBES HAVE BEEN DOING THINGS THEIR WAY FOR HUNDREDS OF YEARS.
SO? THINGS CAN CHANGE. *WE* CAN CHANGE. WE'RE DRAGONS, NOT CATERPILLARS. WE CAN DO THINGS DIFFERENTLY IF WE CHOOSE TO.
FIGHTING IS PART OF A DRAGON'S NATURE.
NOT FOR THE RAINWINGS. AND THEY'RE DRAGONS, TOO.
BUT... DOESN'T THAT MEAN THERE'S SOMETHING WRONG WITH THE RAINWINGS?

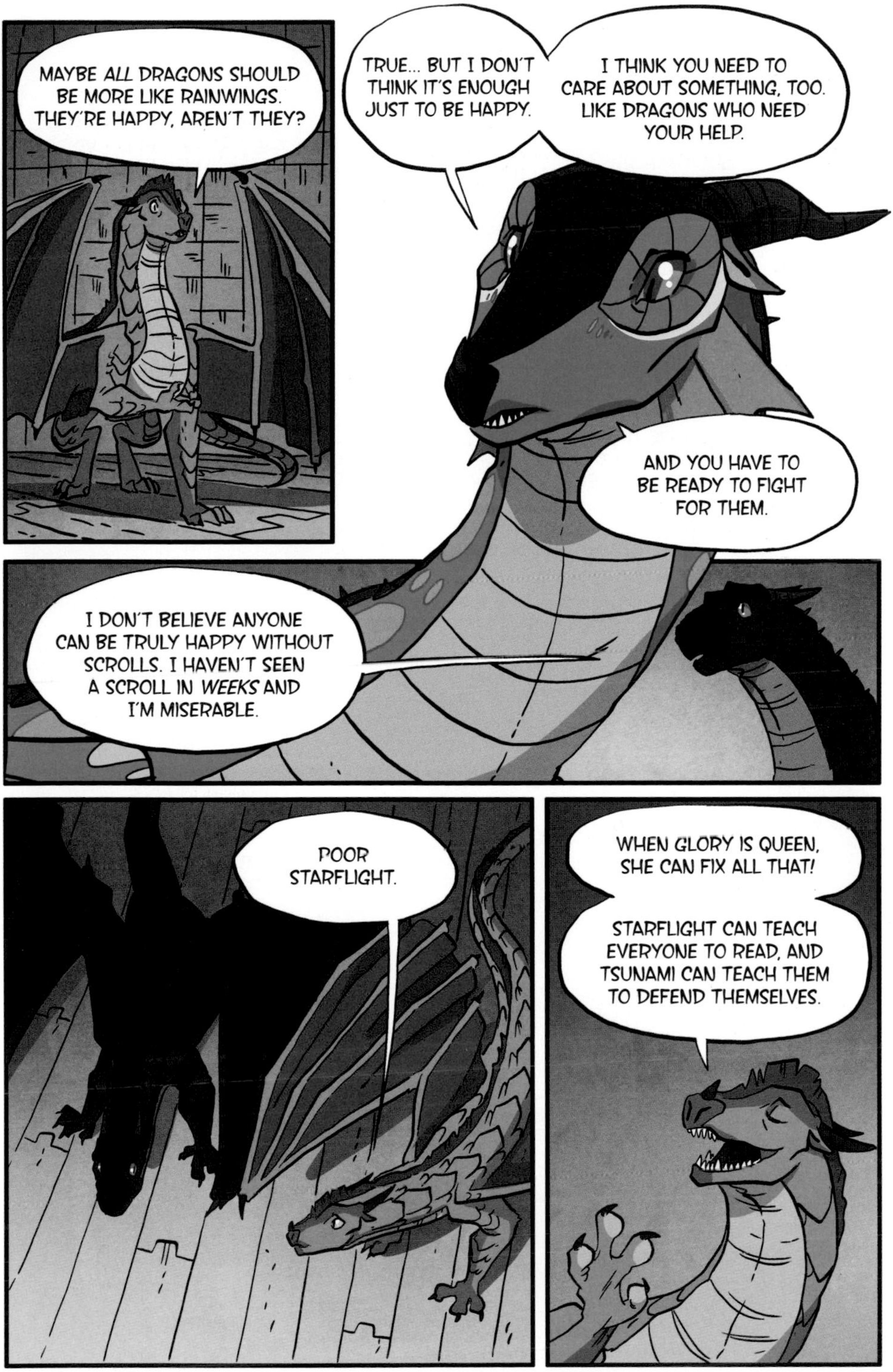
MAYBE ALL DRAGONS SHOULD BE MORE LIKE RAINWINGS. THEY'RE HAPPY, AREN'T THEY?
TRUE... BUT I DON'T THINK IT'S ENOUGH JUST TO BE HAPPY.
I THINK YOU NEED TO CARE ABOUT SOMETHING, TOO. LIKE DRAGONS WHO NEED YOUR HELP.
AND YOU HAVE TO BE READY TO FIGHT FOR THEM.
I DON'T BELIEVE ANYONE CAN BE TRULY HAPPY WITHOUT SCROLLS. I HAVEN'T SEEN A SCROLL IN WEEKS AND I'M MISERABLE.
POOR STARFLIGHT.
WHEN GLORY IS QUEEN, SHE CAN FIX ALL THAT!
STARFLIGHT CAN TEACH EVERYONE TO READ, AND TSUNAMI CAN TEACH THEM TO DEFEND THEMSELVES.

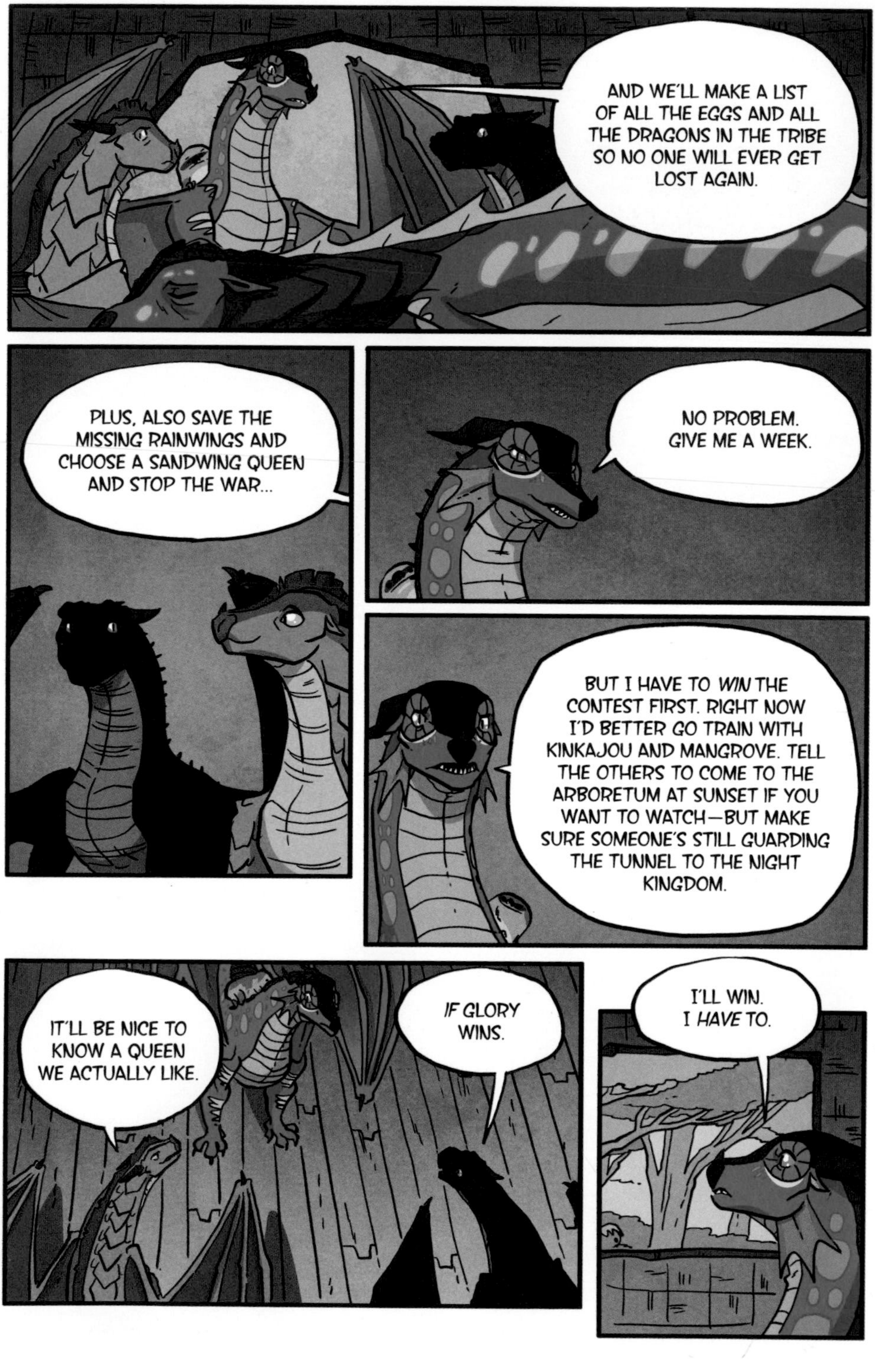
AND WE'LL MAKE A LIST OF ALL THE EGGS AND ALL THE DRAGONS IN THE TRIBE SO NO ONE WILL EVER GET LOST AGAIN.
PLUS, ALSO SAVE THE MISSING RAINWINGS AND CHOOSE A SANDWING QUEEN AND STOP THE WAR...
NO PROBLEM. GIVE ME A WEEK.
BUT I HAVE TO *WIN* THE CONTEST FIRST. RIGHT NOW I'D BETTER GO TRAIN WITH KINKAJOU AND MANGROVE. TELL THE OTHERS TO COME TO THE ARBORETUM AT SUNSET IF YOU WANT TO WATCH—BUT MAKE SURE SOMEONE'S STILL GUARDING THE TUNNEL TO THE NIGHT KINGDOM.
IT'LL BE NICE TO KNOW A QUEEN WE ACTUALLY LIKE.
IF GLORY WINS.
I'LL WIN. I *HAVE* TO.

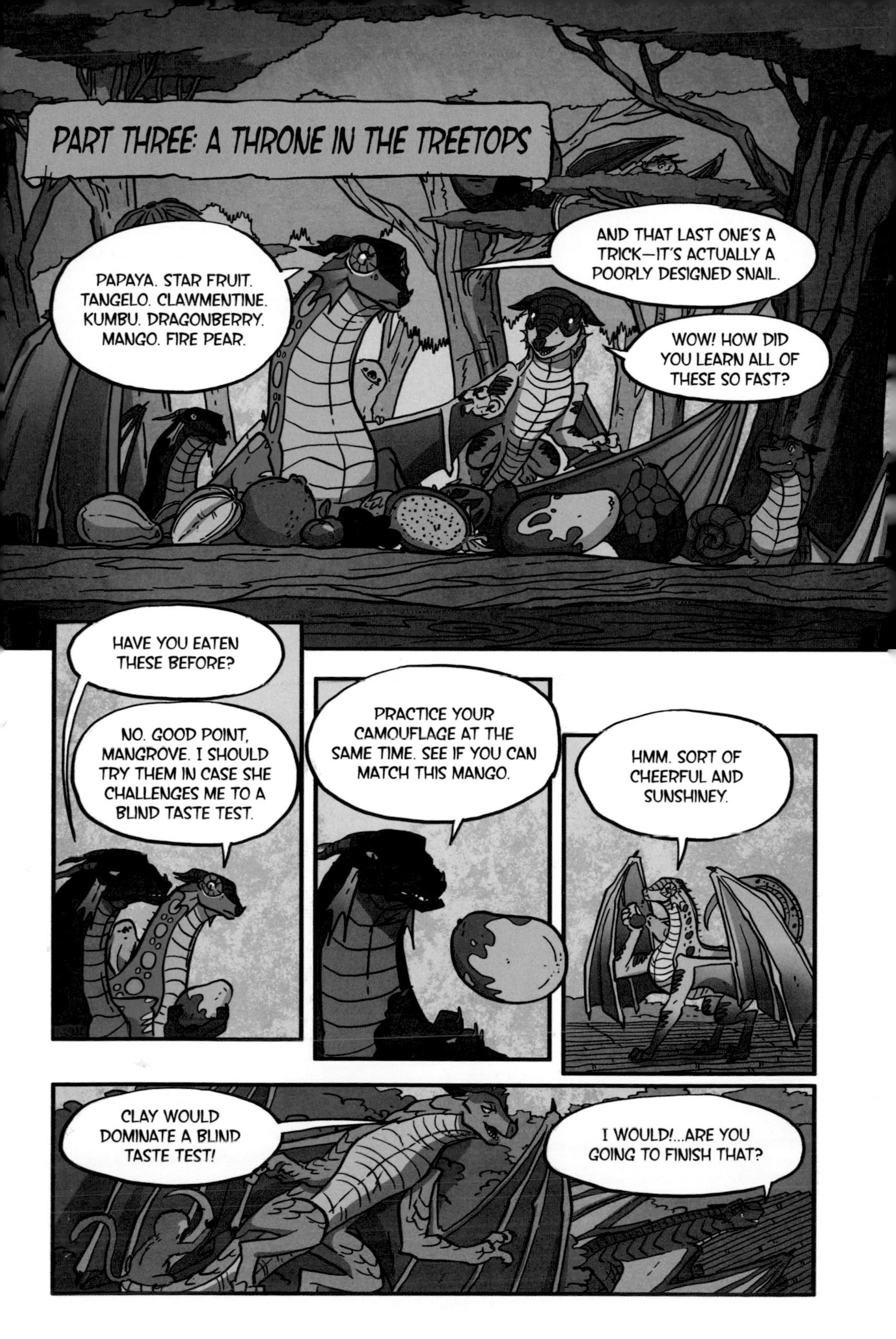
PART THREE: A THRONE IN THE TREETOPS
PAPAYA. STAR FRUIT. TANGELO. CLAWMENTINE. KUMBU. DRAGONBERRY. MANGO. FIRE PEAR.
AND THAT LAST ONE'S A TRICK—IT'S ACTUALLY A POORLY DESIGNED SNAIL.
WOW! HOW DID YOU LEARN ALL OF THESE SO FAST?
HAVE YOU EATEN THESE BEFORE?
NO. GOOD POINT, MANGROVE. I SHOULD TRY THEM IN CASE SHE CHALLENGES ME TO A BLIND TASTE TEST.
PRACTICE YOUR CAMOUFLAGE AT THE SAME TIME. SEE IF YOU CAN MATCH THIS MANGO.
HMM. SORT OF CHEERFUL AND SUNSHINEY.
CLAY WOULD DOMINATE A BLIND TASTE TEST!
I WOULD!...ARE YOU GOING TO FINISH THAT?

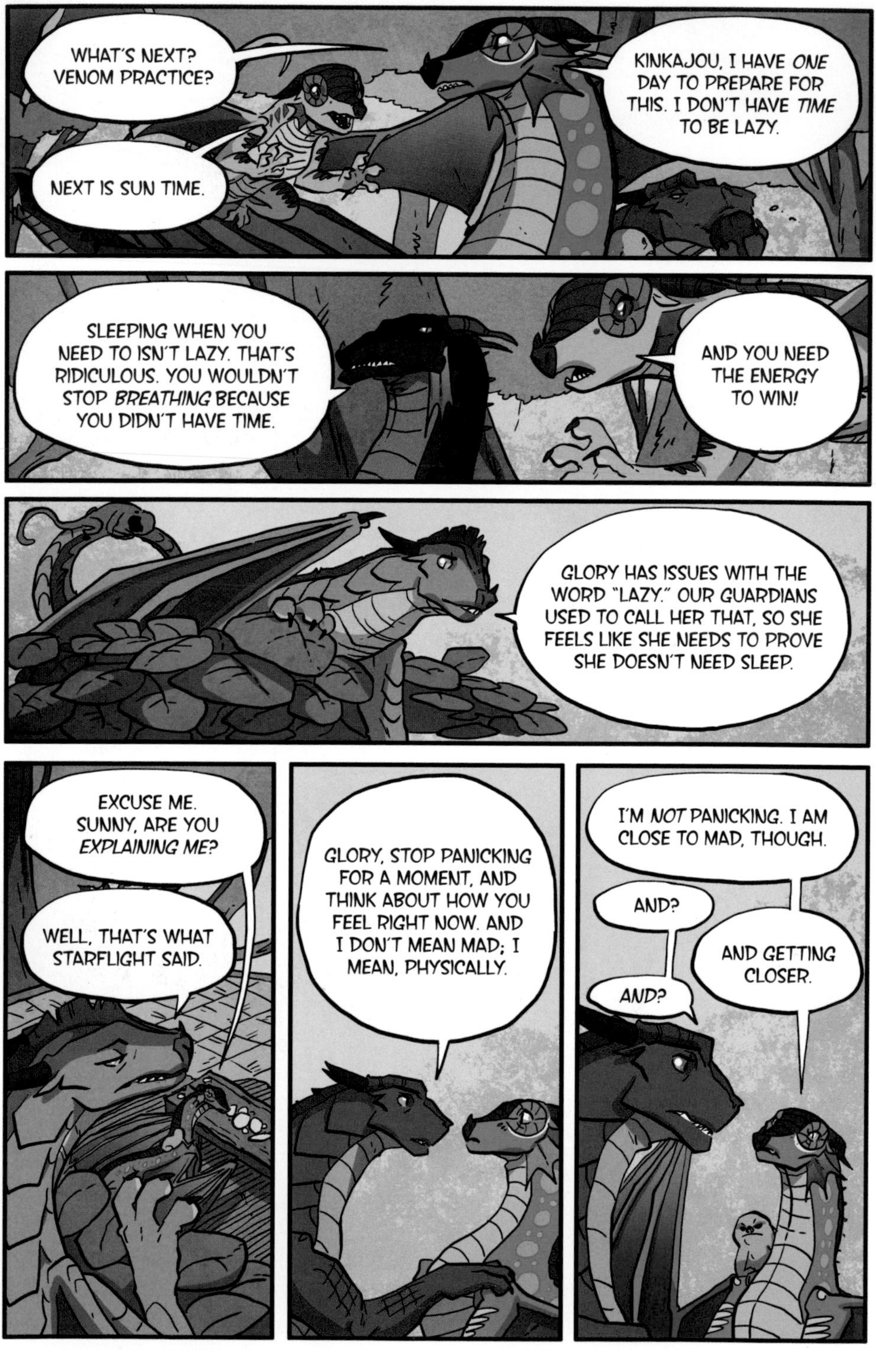
WHAT'S NEXT? VENOM PRACTICE?
NEXT IS SUN TIME.
KINKAJOU, I HAVE *ONE* DAY TO PREPARE FOR THIS. I DON'T HAVE *TIME* TO BE LAZY.
SLEEPING WHEN YOU NEED TO ISN'T LAZY. THAT'S RIDICULOUS. YOU WOULDN'T STOP *BREATHING* BECAUSE YOU DIDN'T HAVE TIME.
AND YOU NEED THE ENERGY TO WIN!
GLORY HAS ISSUES WITH THE WORD "LAZY." OUR GUARDIANS USED TO CALL HER THAT, SO SHE FEELS LIKE SHE NEEDS TO PROVE SHE DOESN'T NEED SLEEP.
EXCUSE ME. SUNNY, ARE YOU *EXPLAINING ME?*
WELL, THAT'S WHAT STARFLIGHT SAID.
GLORY, STOP PANICKING FOR A MOMENT, AND THINK ABOUT HOW YOU FEEL RIGHT NOW. AND I DON'T MEAN MAD; I MEAN, PHYSICALLY.
I'M *NOT* PANICKING. I AM CLOSE TO MAD, THOUGH.
AND?
AND GETTING CLOSER.
AND?

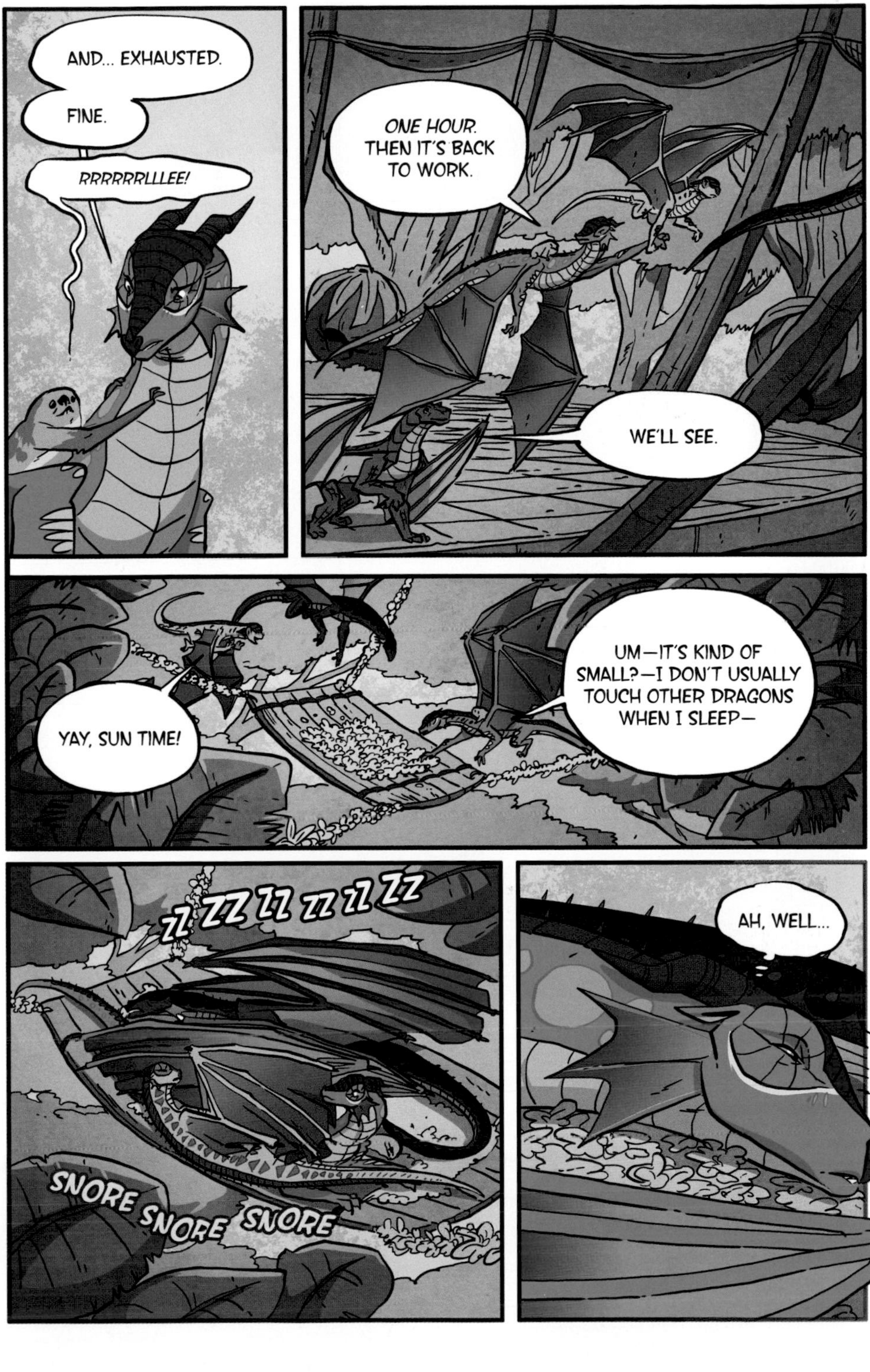
AND... EXHAUSTED.
FINE.
RRRRRRLLLEE!
ONE HOUR. THEN IT'S BACK TO WORK.
WE'LL SEE.
YAY, SUN TIME!
UM—IT'S KIND OF SMALL?—I DON'T USUALLY TOUCH OTHER DRAGONS WHEN I SLEEP—
ZZ ZZ ZZ ZZ ZZ ZZ
SNORE SNORE SNORE
AH, WELL...

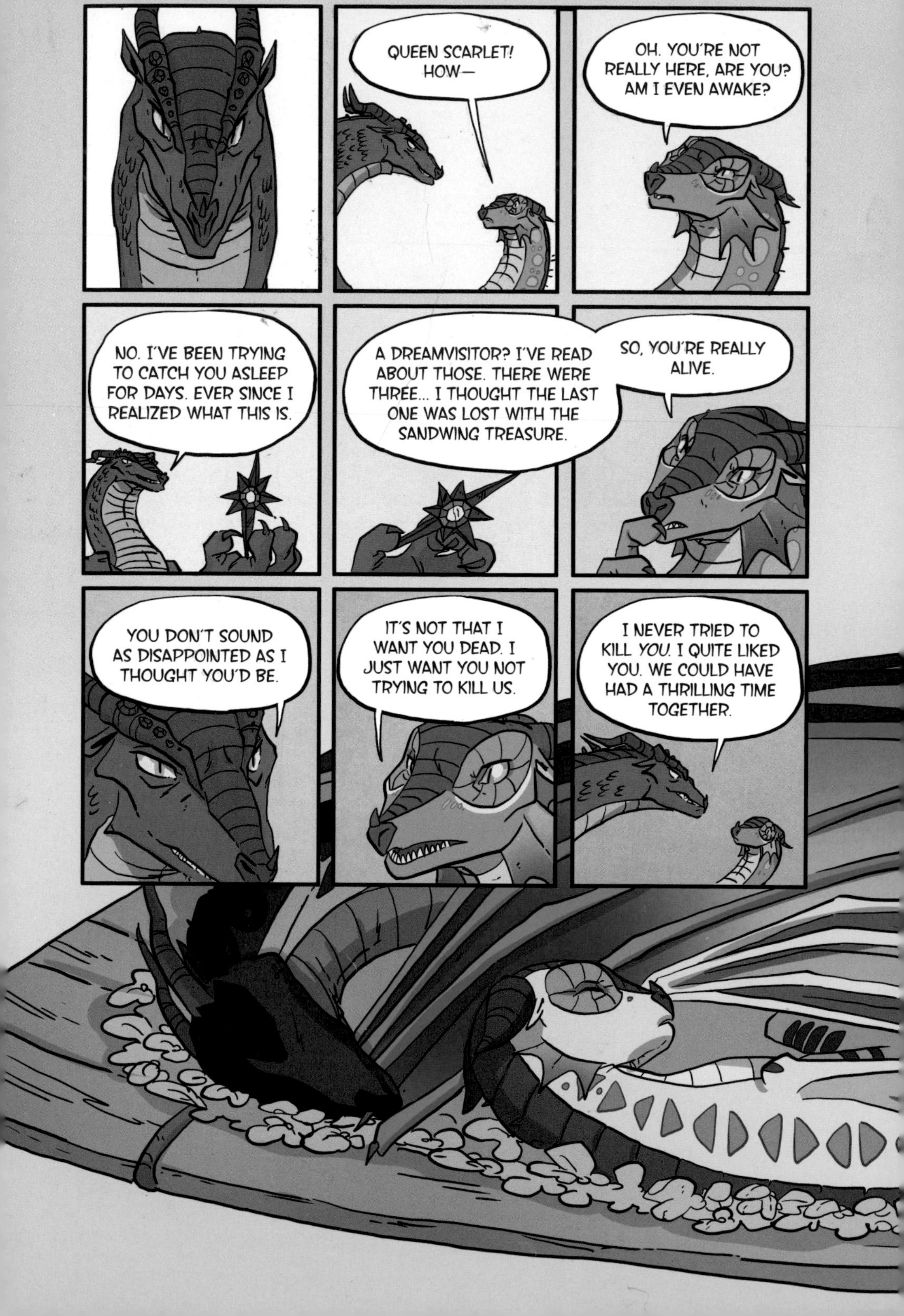
QUEEN SCARLET! HOW—
OH. YOU'RE NOT REALLY HERE, ARE YOU? AM I EVEN AWAKE?
NO. I'VE BEEN TRYING TO CATCH YOU ASLEEP FOR DAYS. EVER SINCE I REALIZED WHAT THIS IS.
A DREAMVISITOR? I'VE READ ABOUT THOSE. THERE WERE THREE... I THOUGHT THE LAST ONE WAS LOST WITH THE SANDWING TREASURE.
SO, YOU'RE REALLY ALIVE.
YOU DON'T SOUND AS DISAPPOINTED AS I THOUGHT YOU'D BE.
IT'S NOT THAT I WANT YOU DEAD. I JUST WANT YOU NOT TRYING TO KILL US.
I NEVER TRIED TO KILL *YOU*. I QUITE LIKED YOU. WE COULD HAVE HAD A THRILLING TIME TOGETHER.

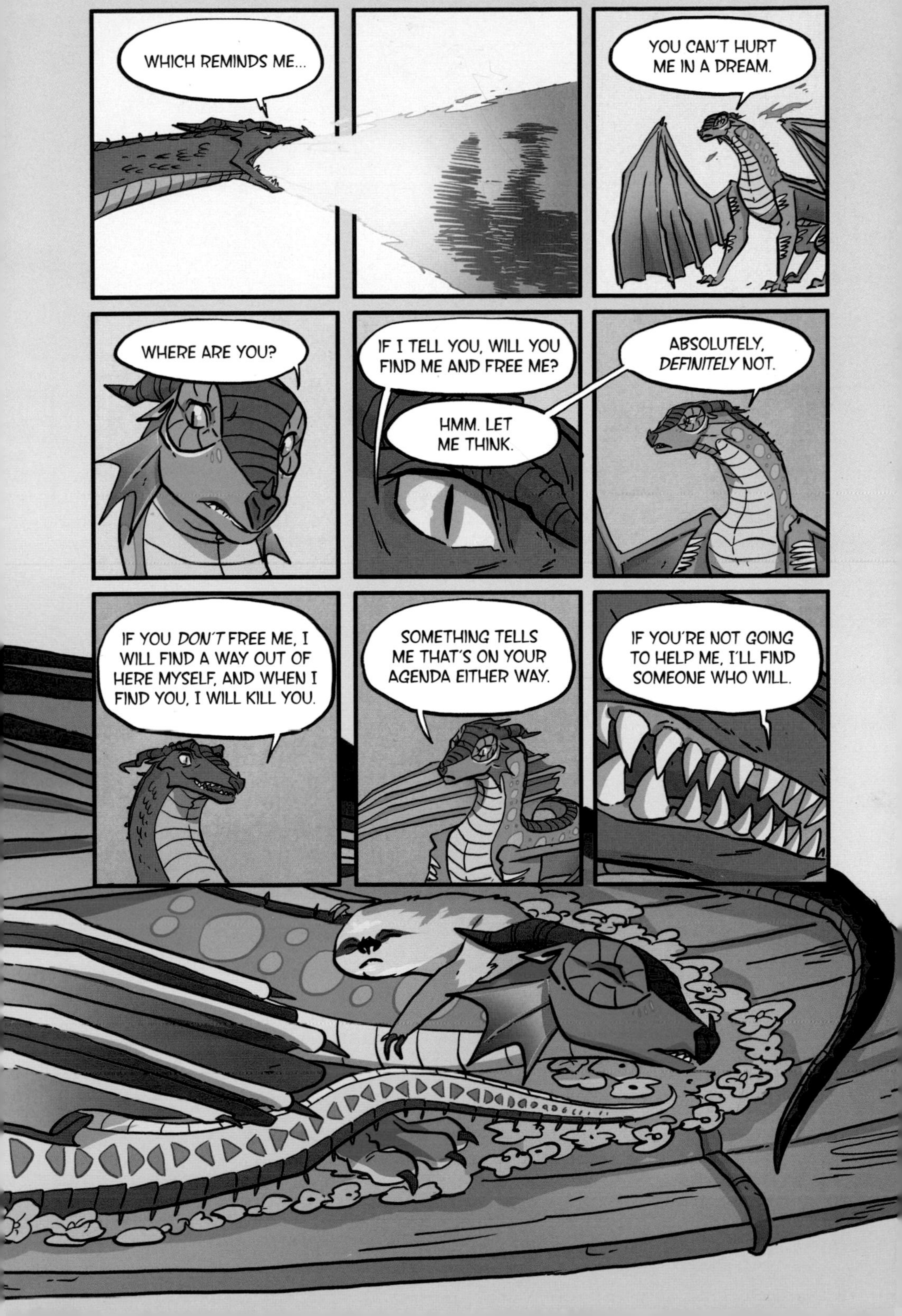
WHICH REMINDS ME...
YOU CAN'T HURT ME IN A DREAM.
WHERE ARE YOU?
IF I TELL YOU, WILL YOU FIND ME AND FREE ME?
HMM. LET ME THINK.
ABSOLUTELY, *DEFINITELY* NOT.
IF YOU *DON'T* FREE ME, I WILL FIND A WAY OUT OF HERE MYSELF, AND WHEN I FIND YOU, I WILL KILL YOU.
SOMETHING TELLS ME THAT'S ON YOUR AGENDA EITHER WAY.
IF YOU'RE NOT GOING TO HELP ME, I'LL FIND SOMEONE WHO WILL.

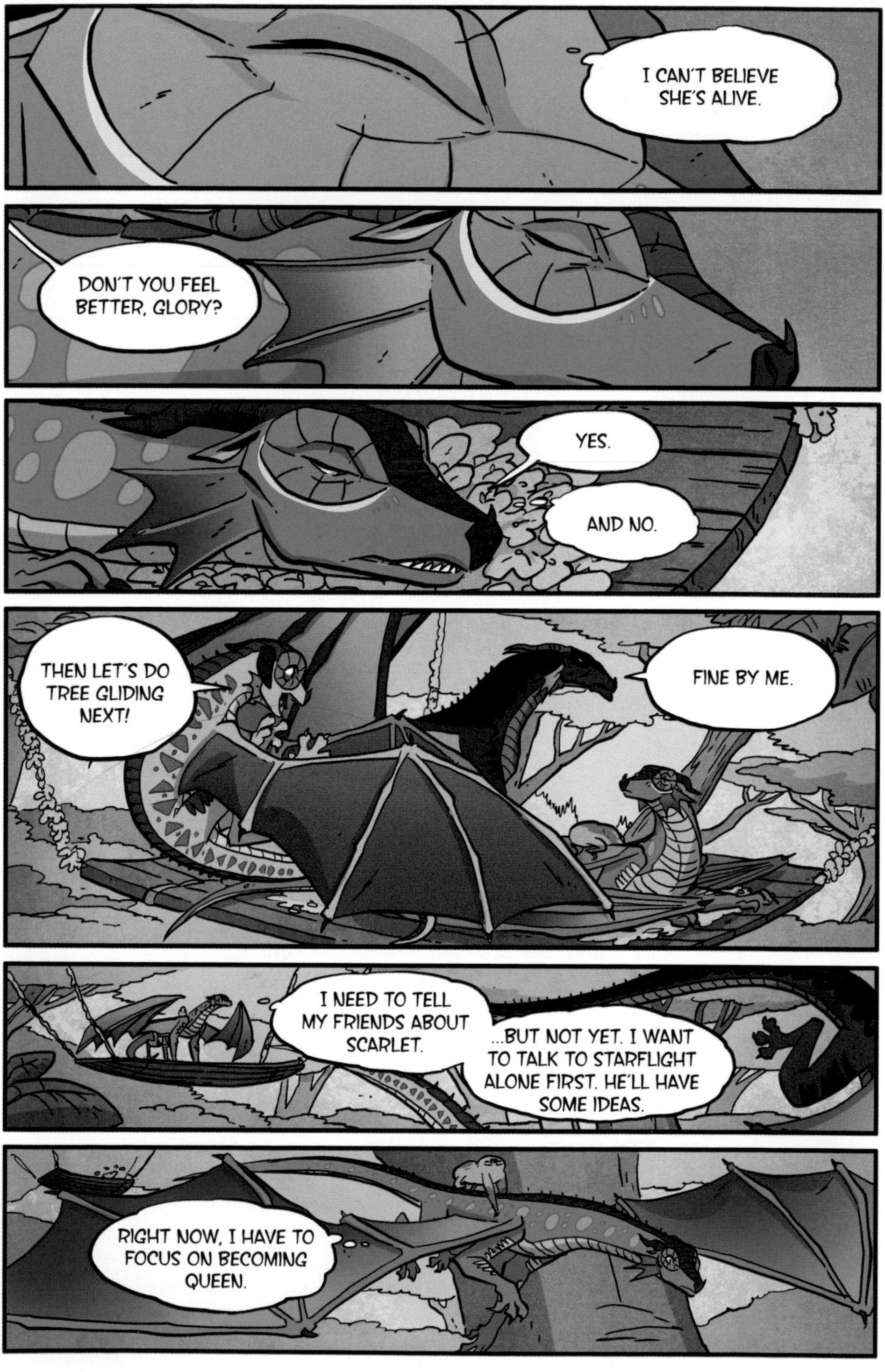
I CAN'T BELIEVE SHE'S ALIVE.
DON'T YOU FEEL BETTER, GLORY?
YES.
AND NO.
THEN LET'S DO TREE GLIDING NEXT!
FINE BY ME.
I NEED TO TELL MY FRIENDS ABOUT SCARLET.
...BUT NOT YET. I WANT TO TALK TO STARFLIGHT ALONE FIRST. HE'LL HAVE SOME IDEAS.
RIGHT NOW, I HAVE TO FOCUS ON BECOMING QUEEN.

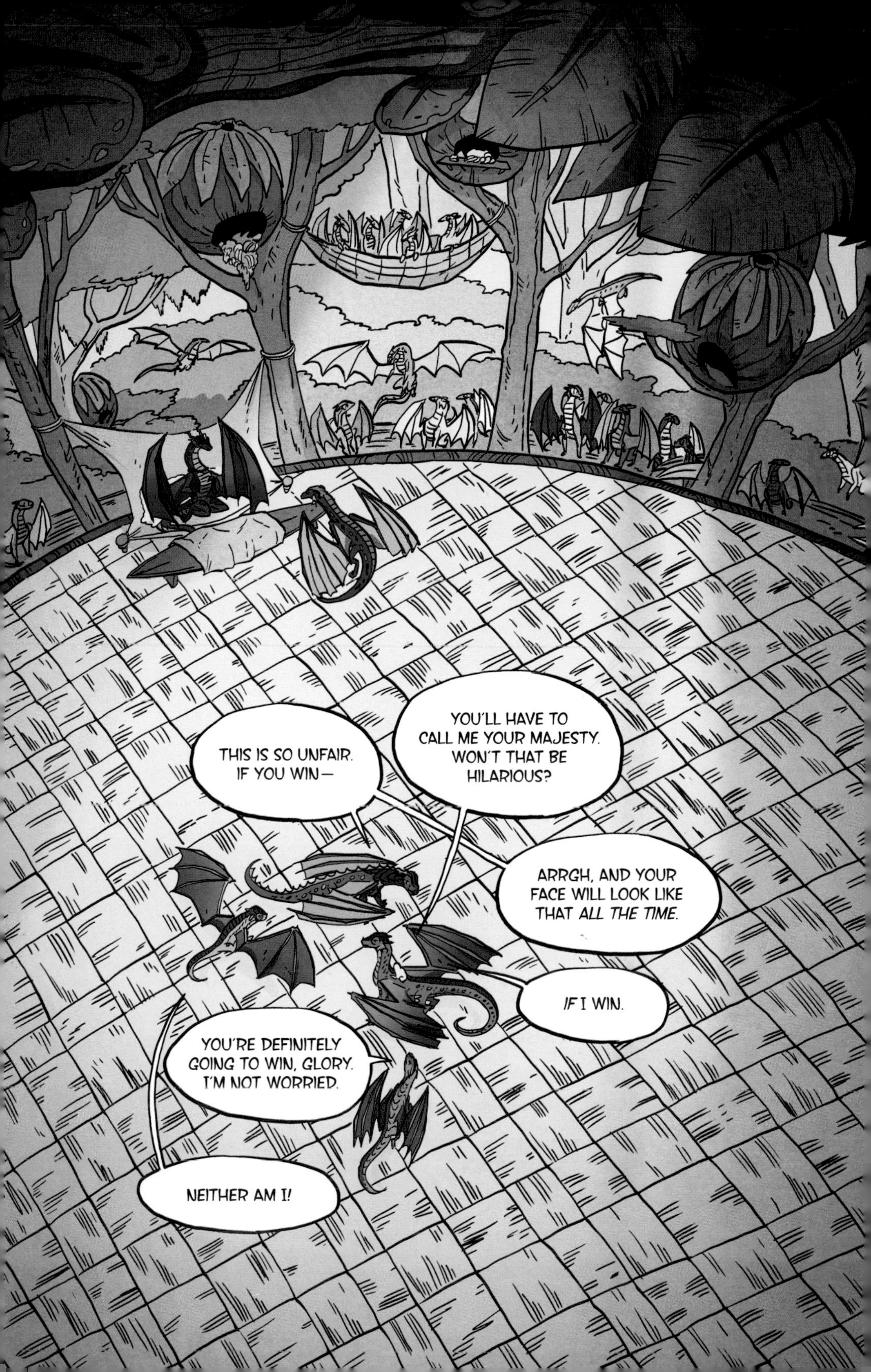
THIS IS SO UNFAIR. IF YOU WIN—
YOU'LL HAVE TO CALL ME YOUR MAJESTY. WON'T THAT BE HILARIOUS?
ARRGH, AND YOUR FACE WILL LOOK LIKE THAT *ALL THE TIME*.
IF I WIN.
YOU'RE DEFINITELY GOING TO WIN, GLORY. I'M NOT WORRIED.
NEITHER AM I!

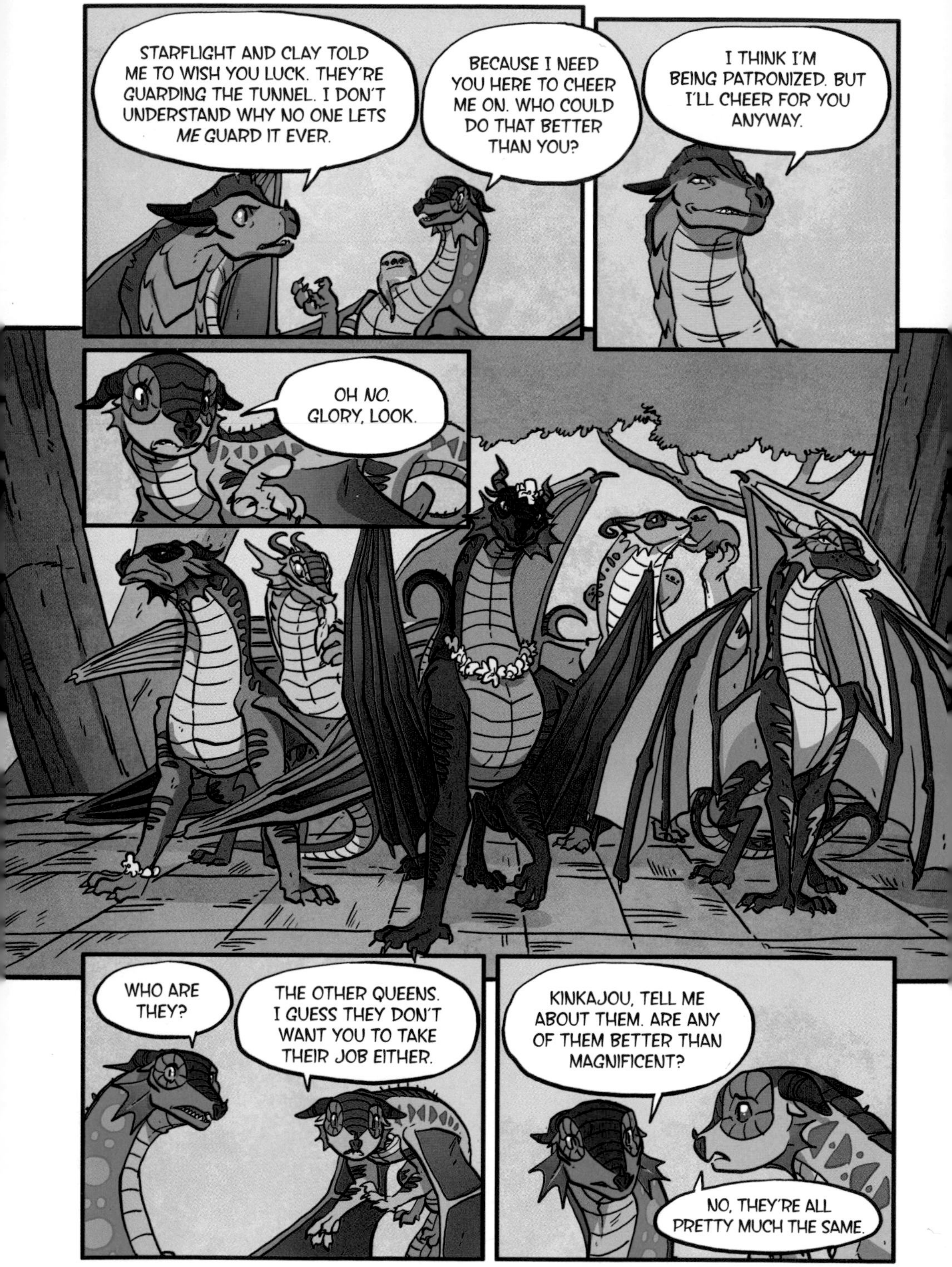
STARFLIGHT AND CLAY TOLD ME TO WISH YOU LUCK. THEY'RE GUARDING THE TUNNEL. I DON'T UNDERSTAND WHY NO ONE LETS *ME* GUARD IT EVER.
BECAUSE I NEED YOU HERE TO CHEER ME ON. WHO COULD DO THAT BETTER THAN YOU?
I THINK I'M BEING PATRONIZED. BUT I'LL CHEER FOR YOU ANYWAY.
OH NO. GLORY, LOOK.
WHO ARE THEY?
THE OTHER QUEENS. I GUESS THEY DON'T WANT YOU TO TAKE THEIR JOB EITHER.
KINKAJOU, TELL ME ABOUT THEM. ARE ANY OF THEM BETTER THAN MAGNIFICENT?
NO, THEY'RE ALL PRETTY MUCH THE SAME.

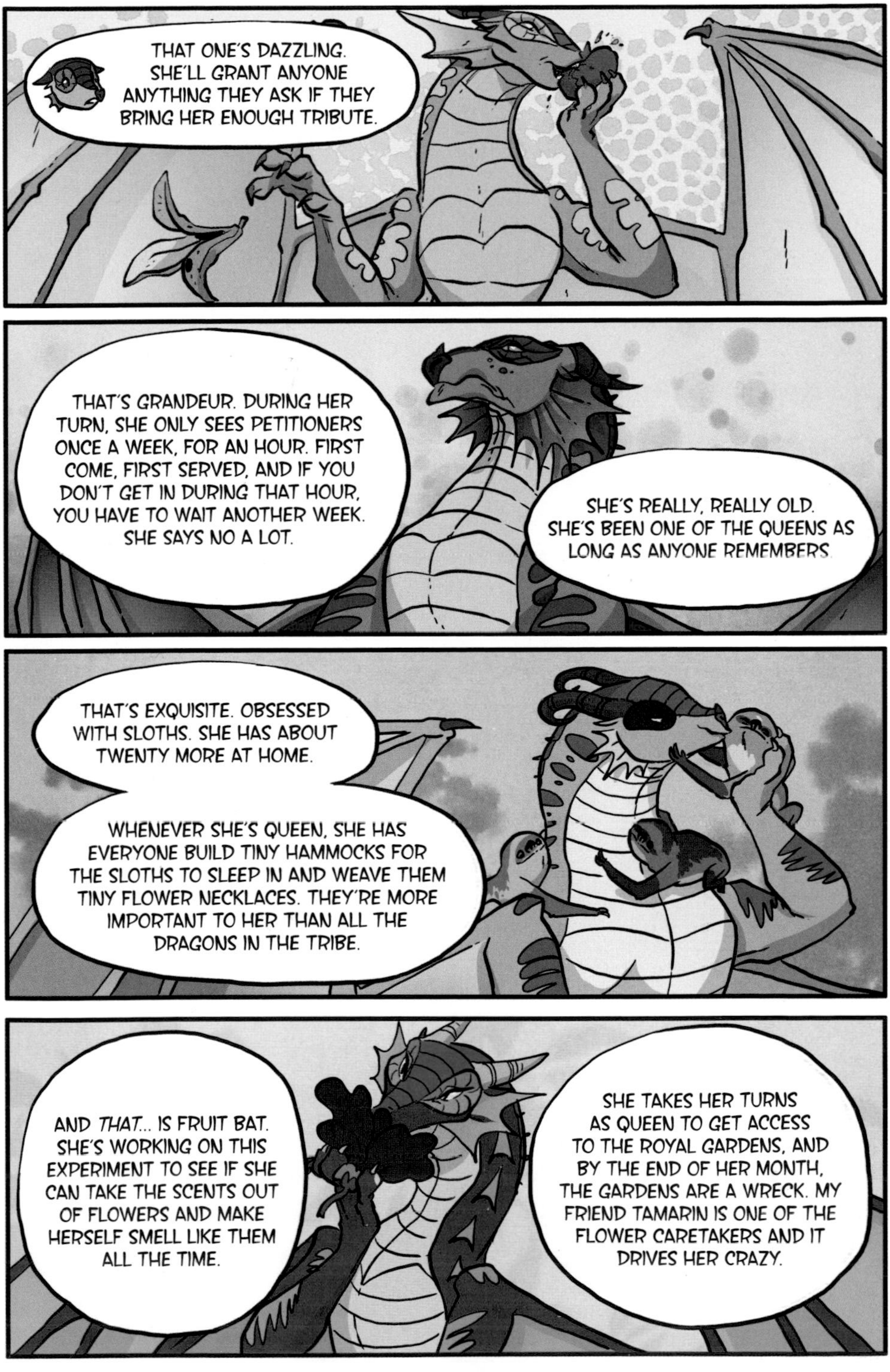
THAT ONE'S DAZZLING. SHE'LL GRANT ANYONE ANYTHING THEY ASK IF THEY BRING HER ENOUGH TRIBUTE.
THAT'S GRANDEUR. DURING HER TURN, SHE ONLY SEES PETITIONERS ONCE A WEEK, FOR AN HOUR. FIRST COME, FIRST SERVED, AND IF YOU DON'T GET IN DURING THAT HOUR, YOU HAVE TO WAIT ANOTHER WEEK. SHE SAYS NO A LOT.
SHE'S REALLY, REALLY OLD. SHE'S BEEN ONE OF THE QUEENS AS LONG AS ANYONE REMEMBERS.
THAT'S EXQUISITE. OBSESSED WITH SLOTHS. SHE HAS ABOUT TWENTY MORE AT HOME.
WHENEVER SHE'S QUEEN, SHE HAS EVERYONE BUILD TINY HAMMOCKS FOR THE SLOTHS TO SLEEP IN AND WEAVE THEM TINY FLOWER NECKLACES. THEY'RE MORE IMPORTANT TO HER THAN ALL THE DRAGONS IN THE TRIBE.
AND *THAT*... IS FRUIT BAT. SHE'S WORKING ON THIS EXPERIMENT TO SEE IF SHE CAN TAKE THE SCENTS OUT OF FLOWERS AND MAKE HERSELF SMELL LIKE THEM ALL THE TIME.
SHE TAKES HER TURNS AS QUEEN TO GET ACCESS TO THE ROYAL GARDENS, AND BY THE END OF HER MONTH, THE GARDENS ARE A WRECK. MY FRIEND TAMARIN IS ONE OF THE FLOWER CARETAKERS AND IT DRIVES HER CRAZY.

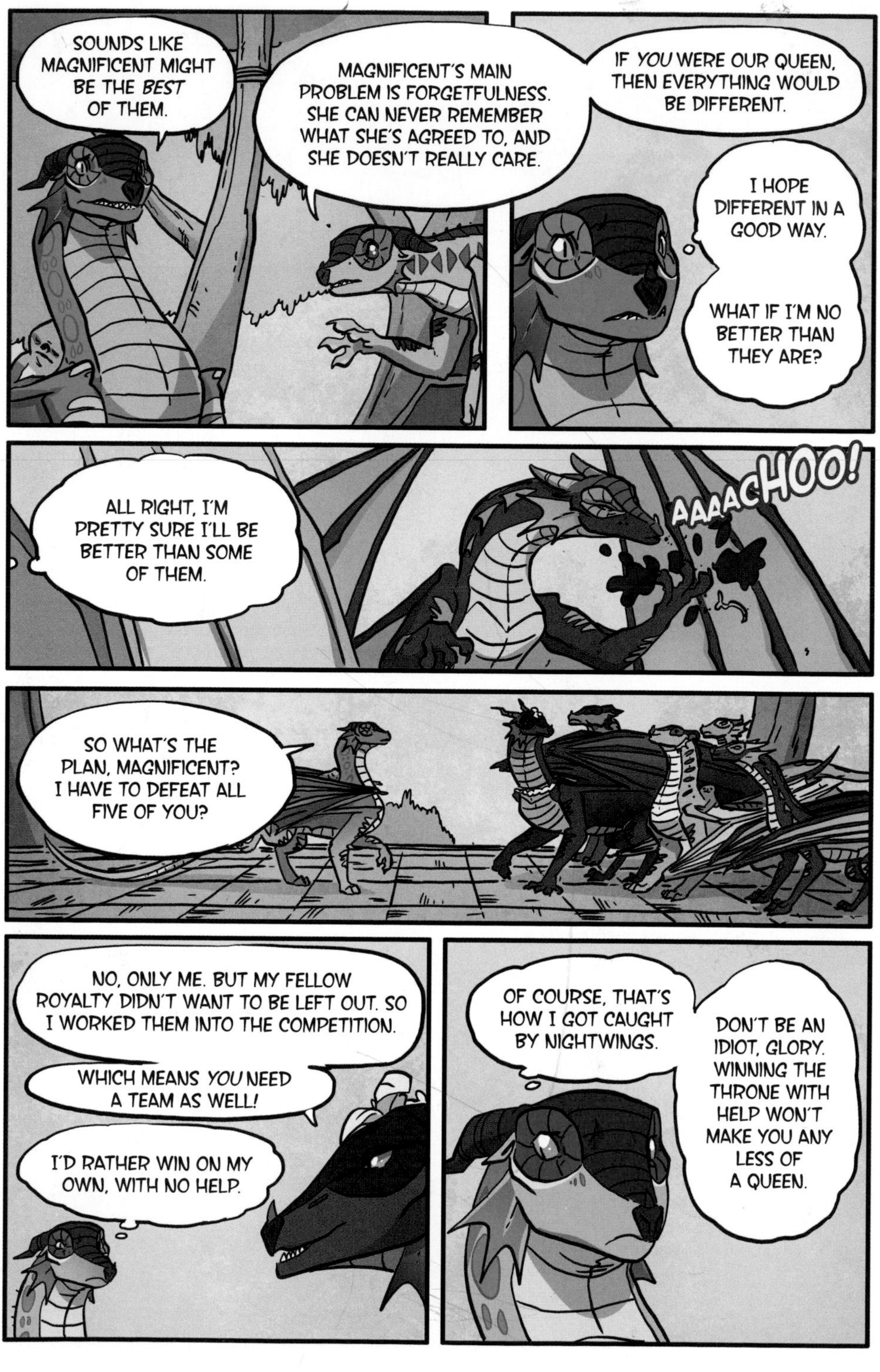
SOUNDS LIKE MAGNIFICENT MIGHT BE THE *BEST* OF THEM.
MAGNIFICENT'S MAIN PROBLEM IS FORGETFULNESS. SHE CAN NEVER REMEMBER WHAT SHE'S AGREED TO, AND SHE DOESN'T REALLY CARE.
IF *YOU* WERE OUR QUEEN, THEN EVERYTHING WOULD BE DIFFERENT.
I HOPE DIFFERENT IN A GOOD WAY.
WHAT IF I'M NO BETTER THAN THEY ARE?
ALL RIGHT, I'M PRETTY SURE I'LL BE BETTER THAN SOME OF THEM.
AAAACHOO!
SO WHAT'S THE PLAN, MAGNIFICENT? I HAVE TO DEFEAT ALL FIVE OF YOU?
NO, ONLY ME. BUT MY FELLOW ROYALTY DIDN'T WANT TO BE LEFT OUT. SO I WORKED THEM INTO THE COMPETITION.
WHICH MEANS *YOU* NEED A TEAM AS WELL!
I'D RATHER WIN ON MY OWN, WITH NO HELP.
OF COURSE, THAT'S HOW I GOT CAUGHT BY NIGHTWINGS.
DON'T BE AN IDIOT, GLORY. WINNING THE THRONE WITH HELP WON'T MAKE YOU ANY LESS OF A QUEEN.

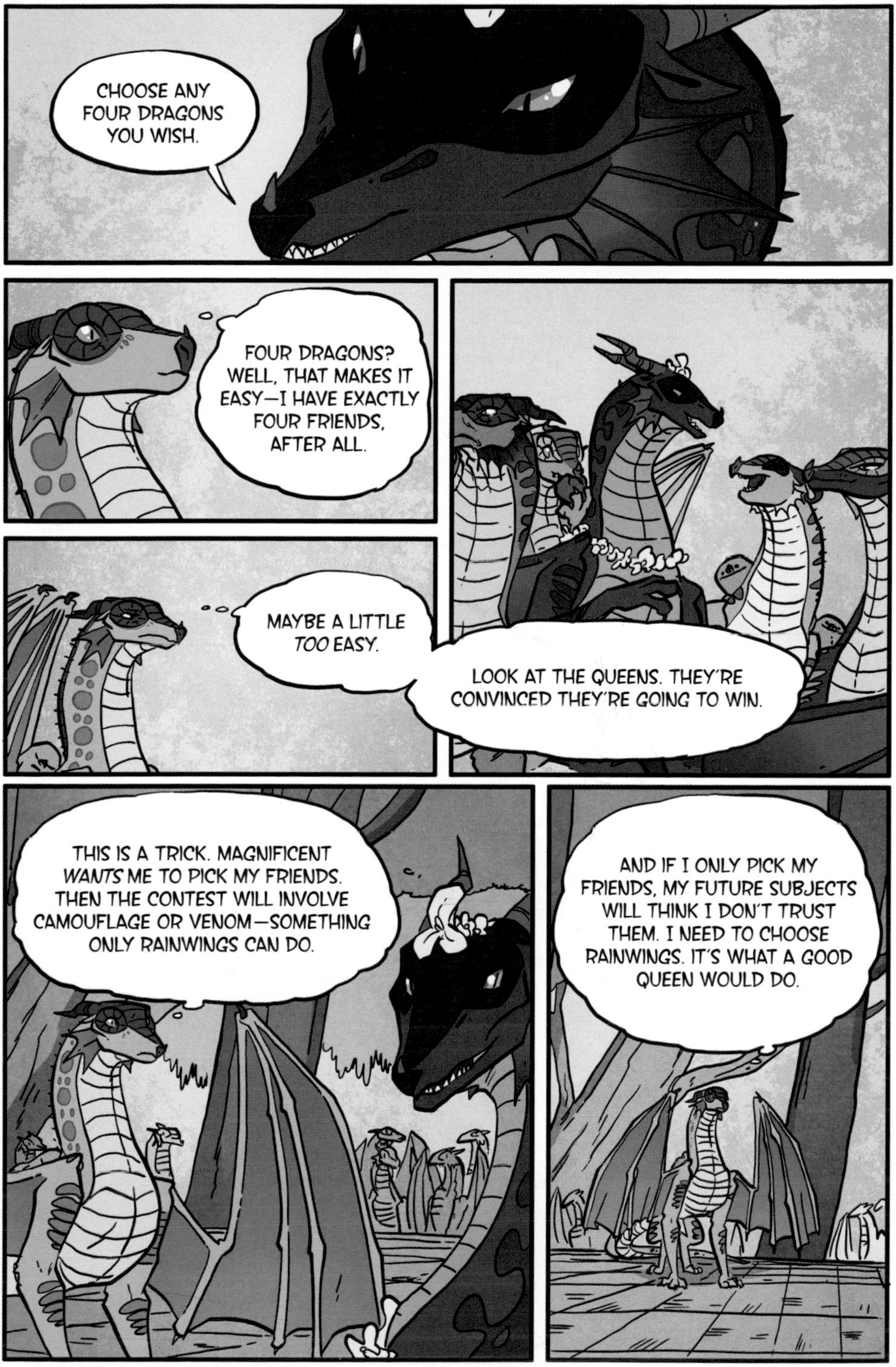
CHOOSE ANY FOUR DRAGONS YOU WISH.
FOUR DRAGONS? WELL, THAT MAKES IT EASY—I HAVE EXACTLY FOUR FRIENDS, AFTER ALL.
MAYBE A LITTLE *TOO* EASY.
LOOK AT THE QUEENS. THEY'RE CONVINCED THEY'RE GOING TO WIN.
THIS IS A TRICK. MAGNIFICENT *WANTS* ME TO PICK MY FRIENDS. THEN THE CONTEST WILL INVOLVE CAMOUFLAGE OR VENOM—SOMETHING ONLY RAINWINGS CAN DO.
AND IF I ONLY PICK MY FRIENDS, MY FUTURE SUBJECTS WILL THINK I DON'T TRUST THEM. I NEED TO CHOOSE RAINWINGS. IT'S WHAT A GOOD QUEEN WOULD DO.

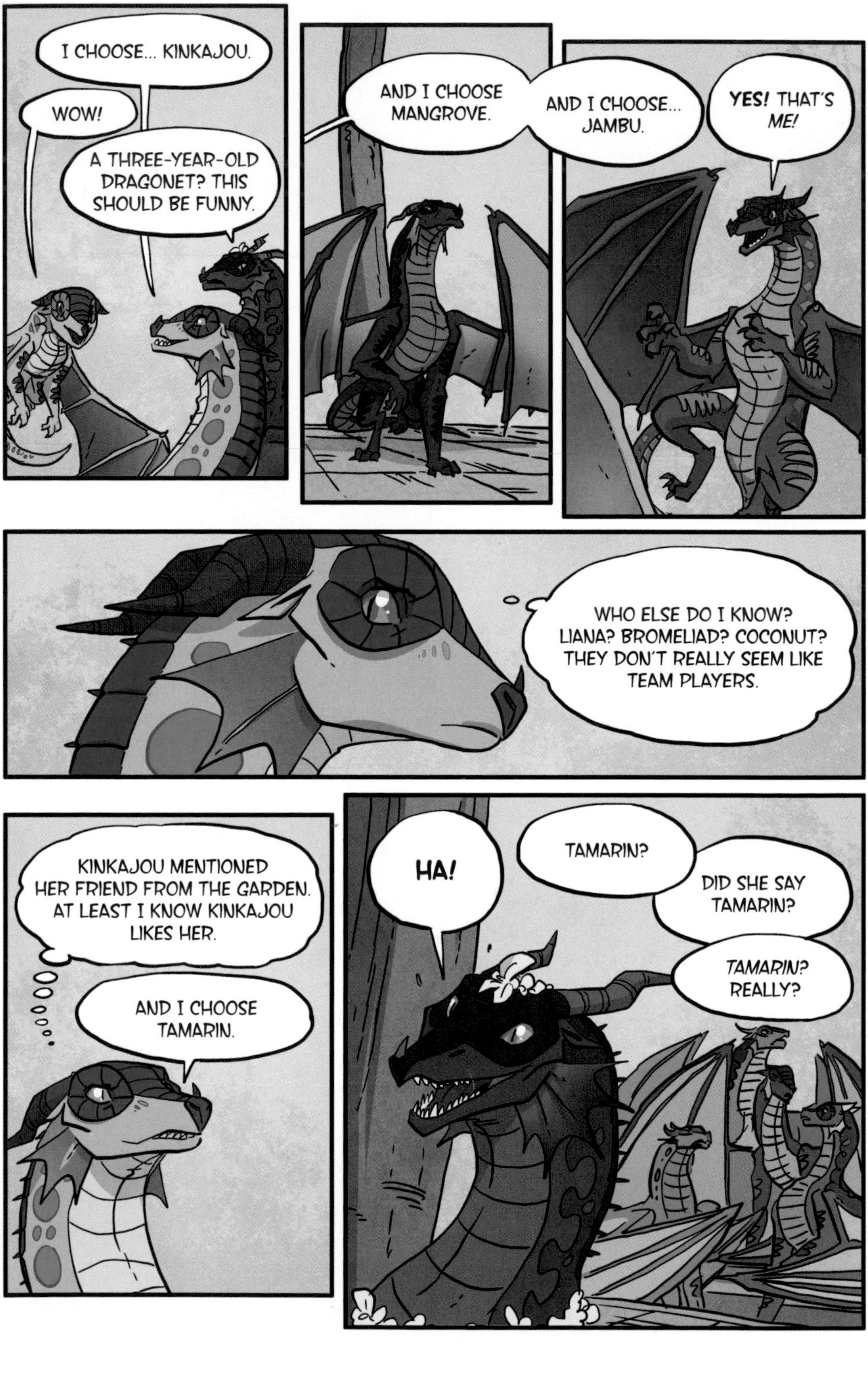
I CHOOSE... KINKAJOU.
WOW!
A THREE-YEAR-OLD DRAGONET? THIS SHOULD BE FUNNY.
AND I CHOOSE MANGROVE.
AND I CHOOSE... JAMBU.
YES! THAT'S ME!
WHO ELSE DO I KNOW? LIANA? BROMELIAD? COCONUT? THEY DON'T REALLY SEEM LIKE TEAM PLAYERS.
KINKAJOU MENTIONED HER FRIEND FROM THE GARDEN. AT LEAST I KNOW KINKAJOU LIKES HER.
AND I CHOOSE TAMARIN.
HA!
TAMARIN?
DID SHE SAY TAMARIN?
TAMARIN? REALLY?

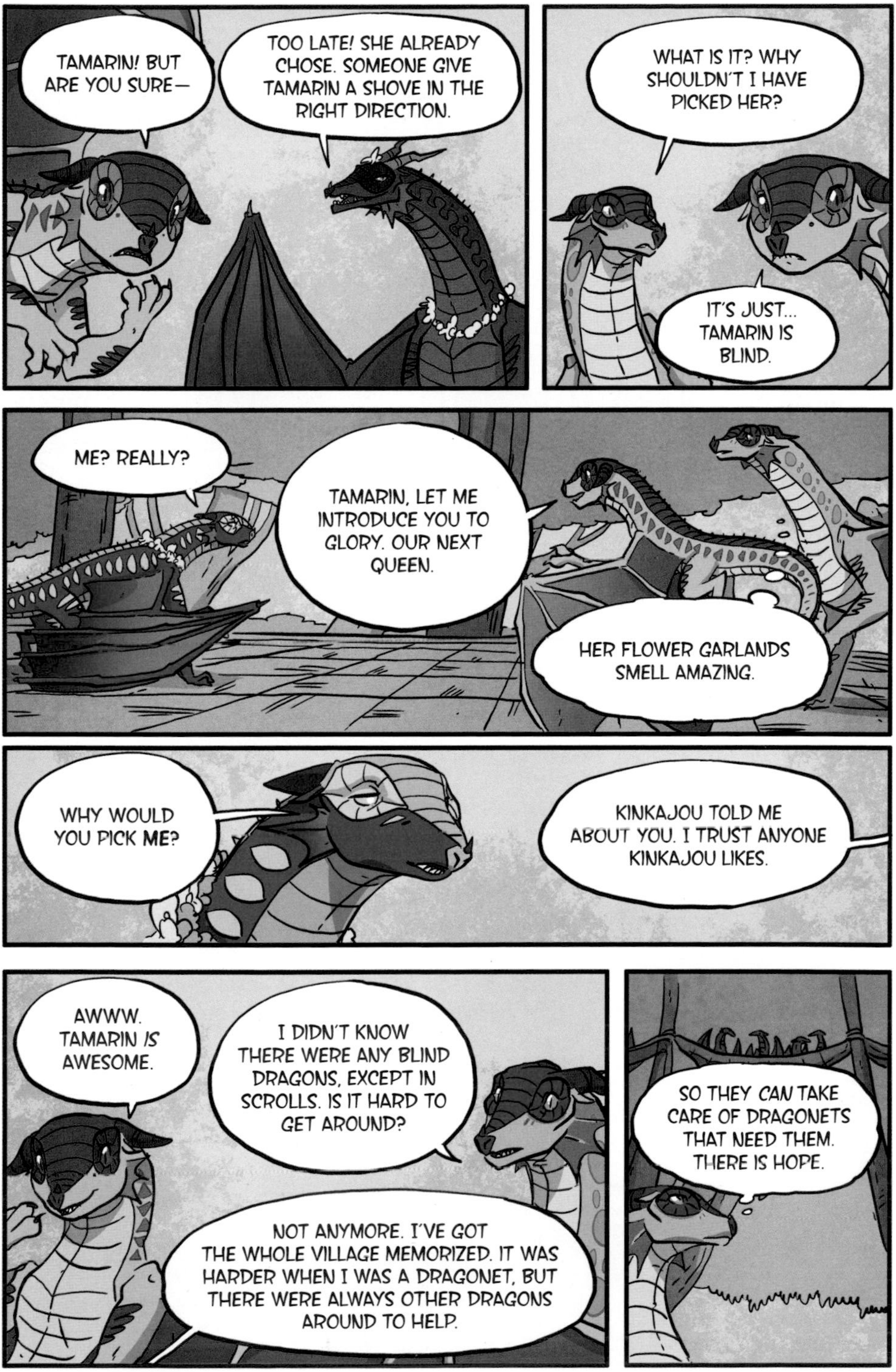
TAMARIN! BUT ARE YOU SURE—
TOO LATE! SHE ALREADY CHOSE. SOMEONE GIVE TAMARIN A SHOVE IN THE RIGHT DIRECTION.
WHAT IS IT? WHY SHOULDN'T I HAVE PICKED HER?
IT'S JUST... TAMARIN IS BLIND.
ME? REALLY?
TAMARIN, LET ME INTRODUCE YOU TO GLORY. OUR NEXT QUEEN.
HER FLOWER GARLANDS SMELL AMAZING.
WHY WOULD YOU PICK ME?
KINKAJOU TOLD ME ABOUT YOU. I TRUST ANYONE KINKAJOU LIKES.
AWWW. TAMARIN *IS* AWESOME.
I DIDN'T KNOW THERE WERE ANY BLIND DRAGONS, EXCEPT IN SCROLLS. IS IT HARD TO GET AROUND?
NOT ANYMORE. I'VE GOT THE WHOLE VILLAGE MEMORIZED. IT WAS HARDER WHEN I WAS A DRAGONET, BUT THERE WERE ALWAYS OTHER DRAGONS AROUND TO HELP.
SO THEY *CAN* TAKE CARE OF DRAGONETS THAT NEED THEM. THERE IS HOPE.

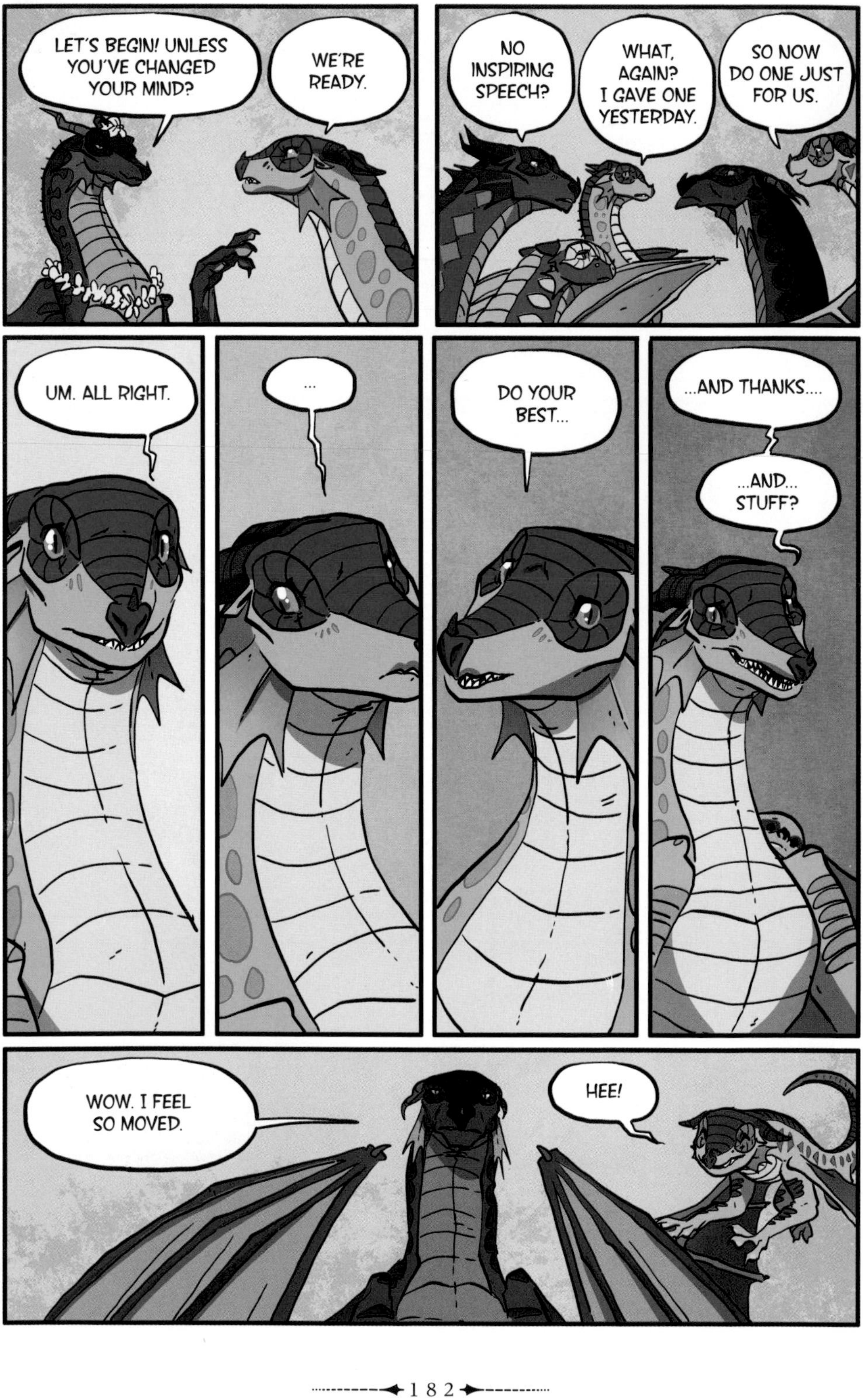
LET'S BEGIN! UNLESS YOU'VE CHANGED YOUR MIND?
WE'RE READY.
NO INSPIRING SPEECH?
WHAT, AGAIN? I GAVE ONE YESTERDAY.
SO NOW DO ONE JUST FOR US.
UM. ALL RIGHT.
...
DO YOUR BEST...
...AND THANKS....
...AND... STUFF?
WOW. I FEEL SO MOVED.
HEE!

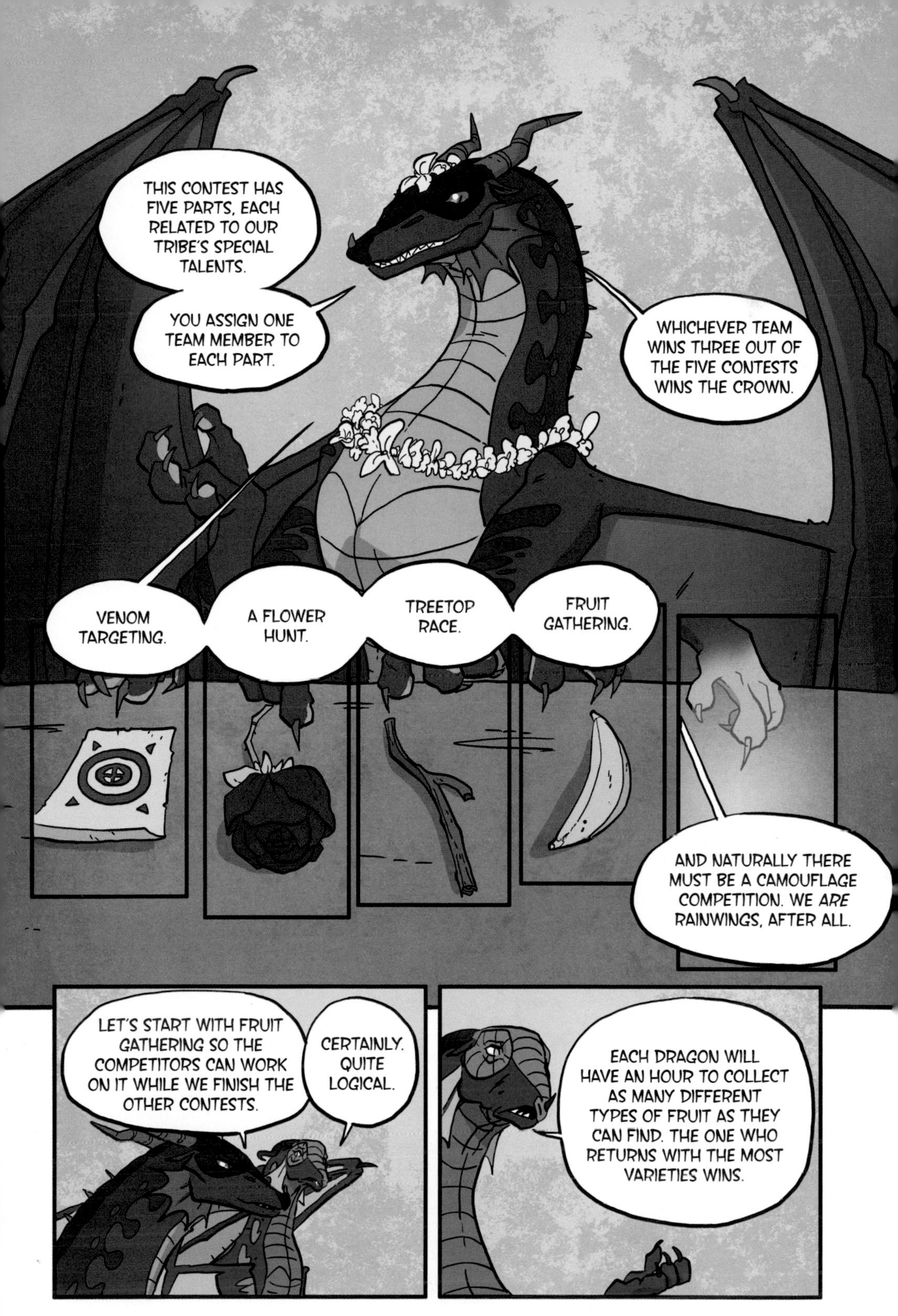
THIS CONTEST HAS FIVE PARTS, EACH RELATED TO OUR TRIBE'S SPECIAL TALENTS.
YOU ASSIGN ONE TEAM MEMBER TO EACH PART.
WHICHEVER TEAM WINS THREE OUT OF THE FIVE CONTESTS WINS THE CROWN.
VENOM TARGETING.
A FLOWER HUNT.
TREETOP RACE.
FRUIT GATHERING.
AND NATURALLY THERE MUST BE A CAMOUFLAGE COMPETITION. WE *ARE* RAINWINGS, AFTER ALL.
LET'S START WITH FRUIT GATHERING SO THE COMPETITORS CAN WORK ON IT WHILE WE FINISH THE OTHER CONTESTS.
CERTAINLY. QUITE LOGICAL.
EACH DRAGON WILL HAVE AN HOUR TO COLLECT AS MANY DIFFERENT TYPES OF FRUIT AS THEY CAN FIND. THE ONE WHO RETURNS WITH THE MOST VARIETIES WINS.

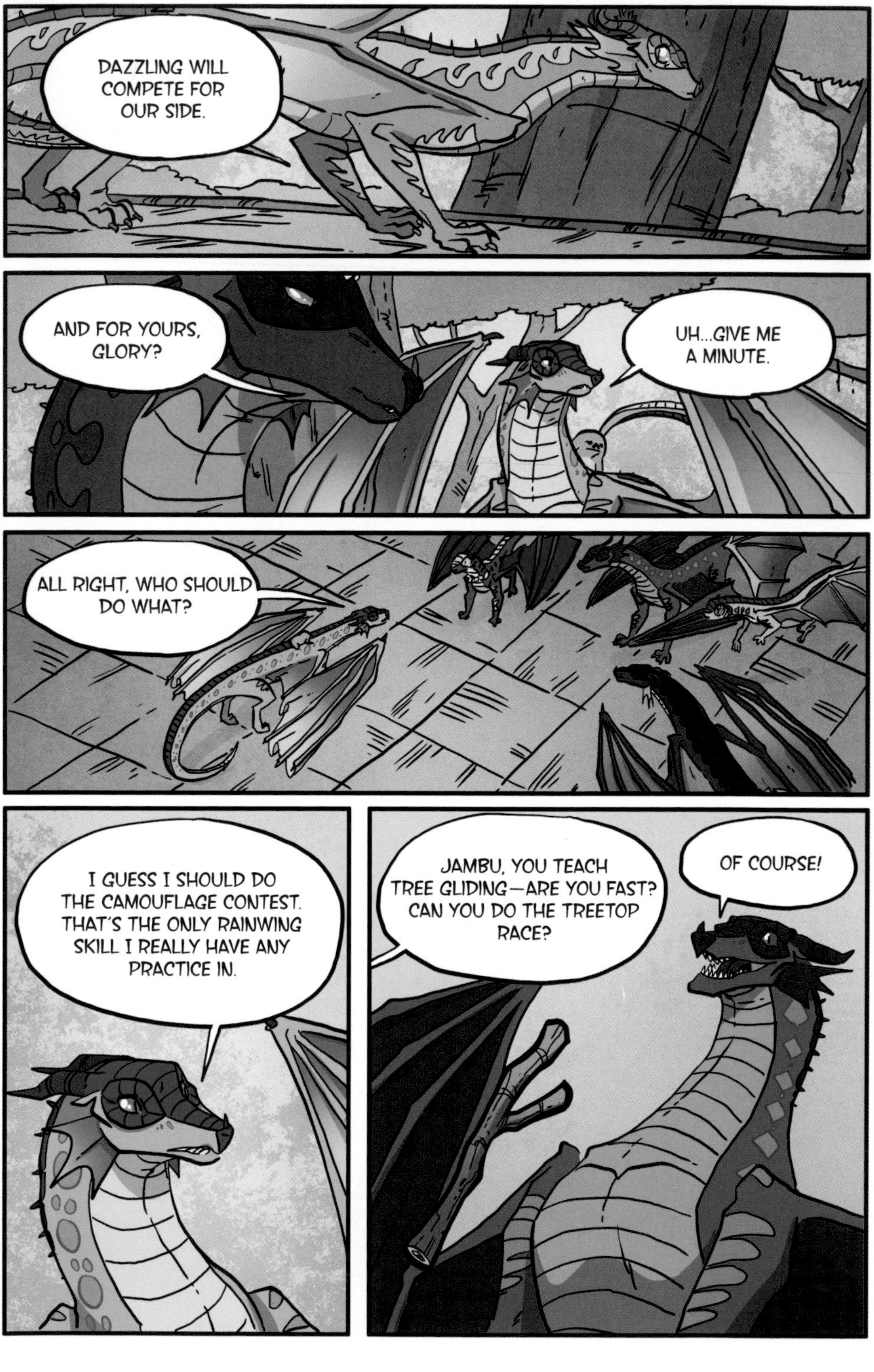
DAZZLING WILL COMPETE FOR OUR SIDE.
AND FOR YOURS, GLORY?
UH...GIVE ME A MINUTE.
ALL RIGHT, WHO SHOULD DO WHAT?
I GUESS I SHOULD DO THE CAMOUFLAGE CONTEST. THAT'S THE ONLY RAINWING SKILL I REALLY HAVE ANY PRACTICE IN.
JAMBU, YOU TEACH TREE GLIDING—ARE YOU FAST? CAN YOU DO THE TREETOP RACE?
OF COURSE!

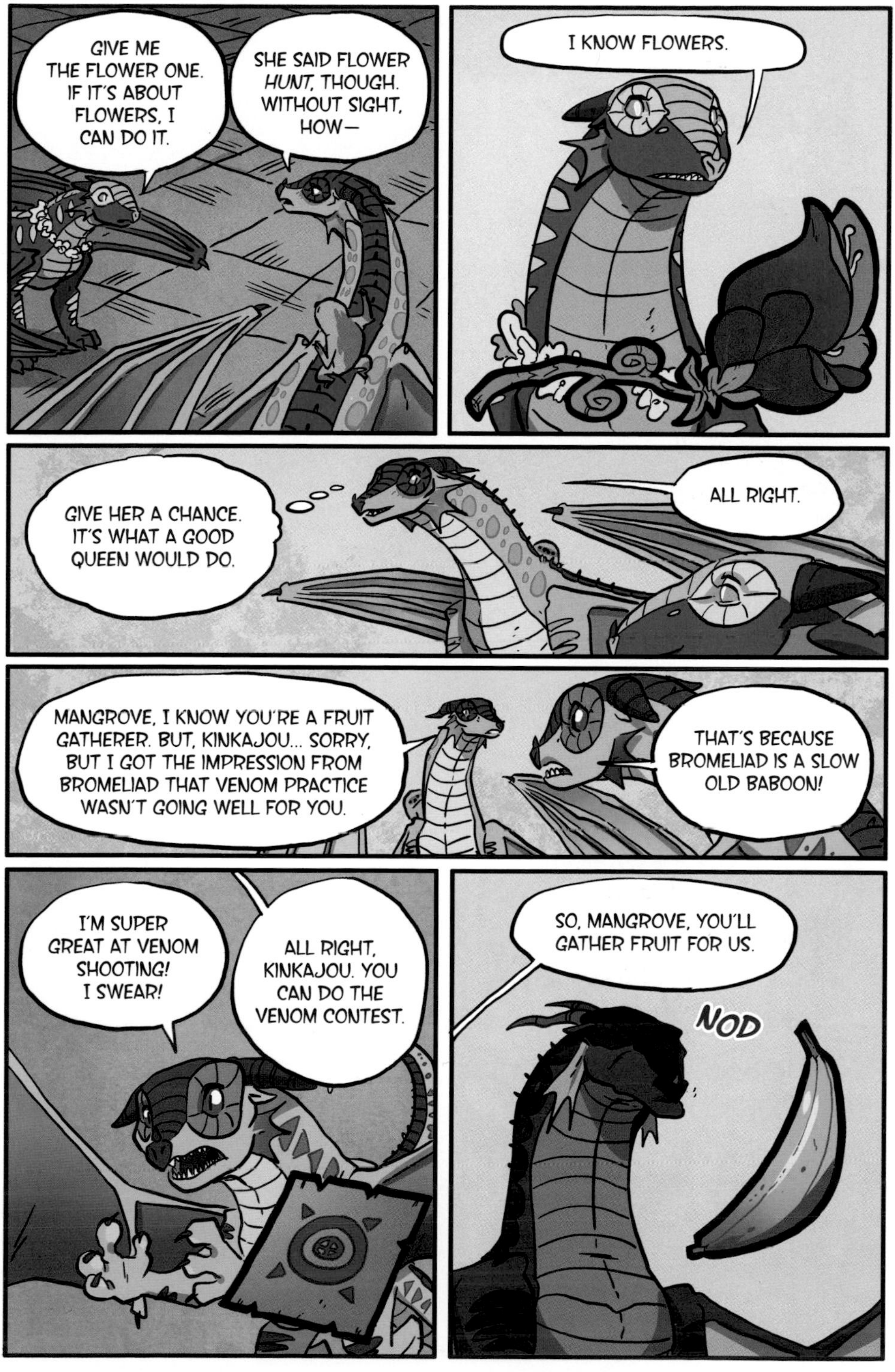
GIVE ME THE FLOWER ONE. IF IT'S ABOUT FLOWERS, I CAN DO IT.
SHE SAID FLOWER *HUNT*, THOUGH. WITHOUT SIGHT, HOW—
I KNOW FLOWERS.
GIVE HER A CHANCE. IT'S WHAT A GOOD QUEEN WOULD DO.
ALL RIGHT.
MANGROVE, I KNOW YOU'RE A FRUIT GATHERER. BUT, KINKAJOU... SORRY, BUT I GOT THE IMPRESSION FROM BROMELIAD THAT VENOM PRACTICE WASN'T GOING WELL FOR YOU.
THAT'S BECAUSE BROMELIAD IS A SLOW OLD BABOON!
I'M SUPER GREAT AT VENOM SHOOTING! I SWEAR!
ALL RIGHT, KINKAJOU. YOU CAN DO THE VENOM CONTEST.
SO, MANGROVE, YOU'LL GATHER FRUIT FOR US.
NOD

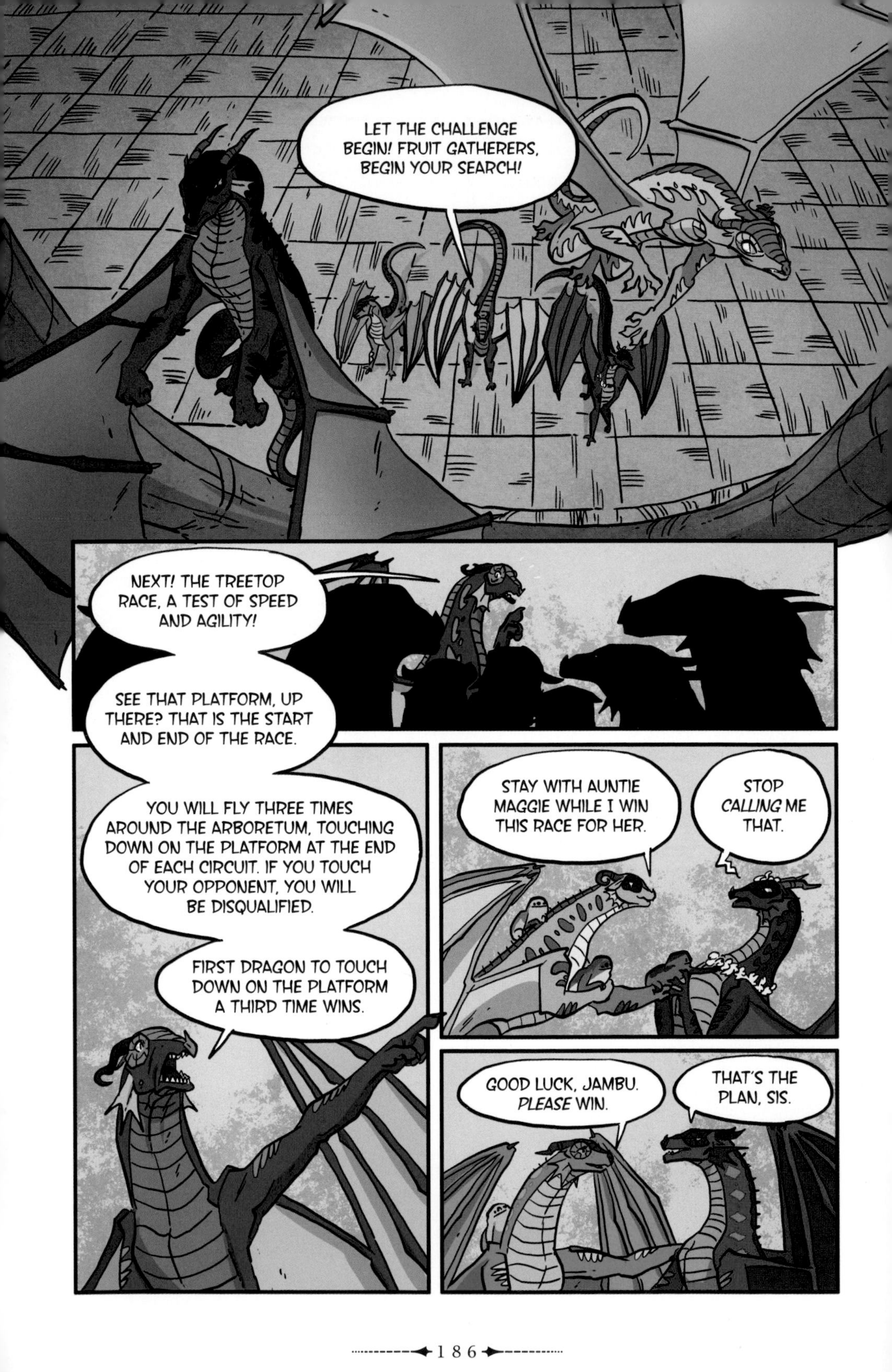
LET THE CHALLENGE BEGIN! FRUIT GATHERERS, BEGIN YOUR SEARCH!
NEXT! THE TREETOP RACE, A TEST OF SPEED AND AGILITY!
SEE THAT PLATFORM, UP THERE? THAT IS THE START AND END OF THE RACE.
YOU WILL FLY THREE TIMES AROUND THE ARBORETUM, TOUCHING DOWN ON THE PLATFORM AT THE END OF EACH CIRCUIT. IF YOU TOUCH YOUR OPPONENT, YOU WILL BE DISQUALIFIED.
FIRST DRAGON TO TOUCH DOWN ON THE PLATFORM A THIRD TIME WINS.
STAY WITH AUNTIE MAGGIE WHILE I WIN THIS RACE FOR HER.
STOP *CALLING* ME THAT.
GOOD LUCK, JAMBU. *PLEASE* WIN.
THAT'S THE PLAN, SIS.

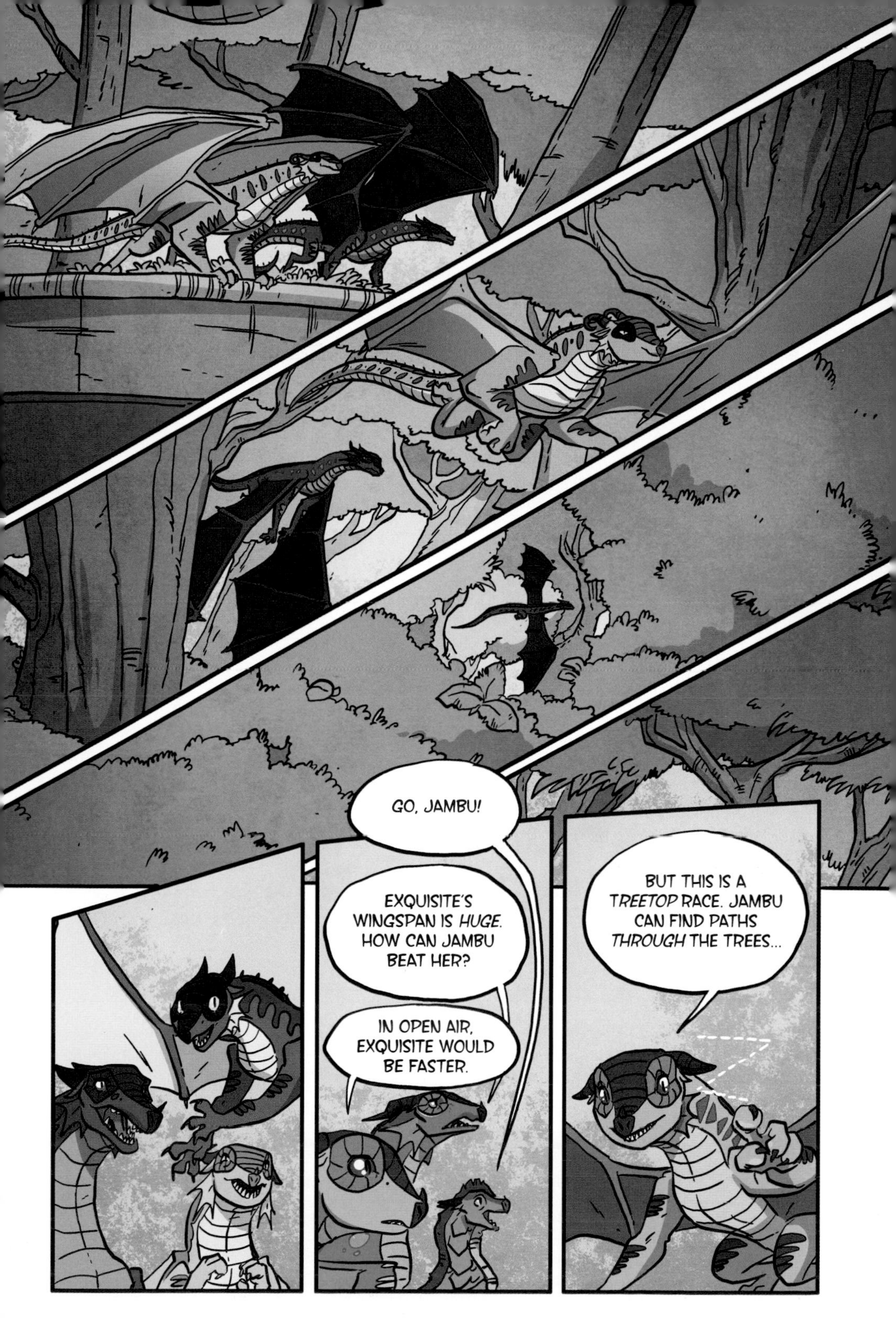
GO, JAMBU!
EXQUISITE'S WINGSPAN IS *HUGE*. HOW CAN JAMBU BEAT HER?
IN OPEN AIR, EXQUISITE WOULD BE FASTER.
BUT THIS IS A *TREETOP* RACE. JAMBU CAN FIND PATHS *THROUGH* THE TREES...

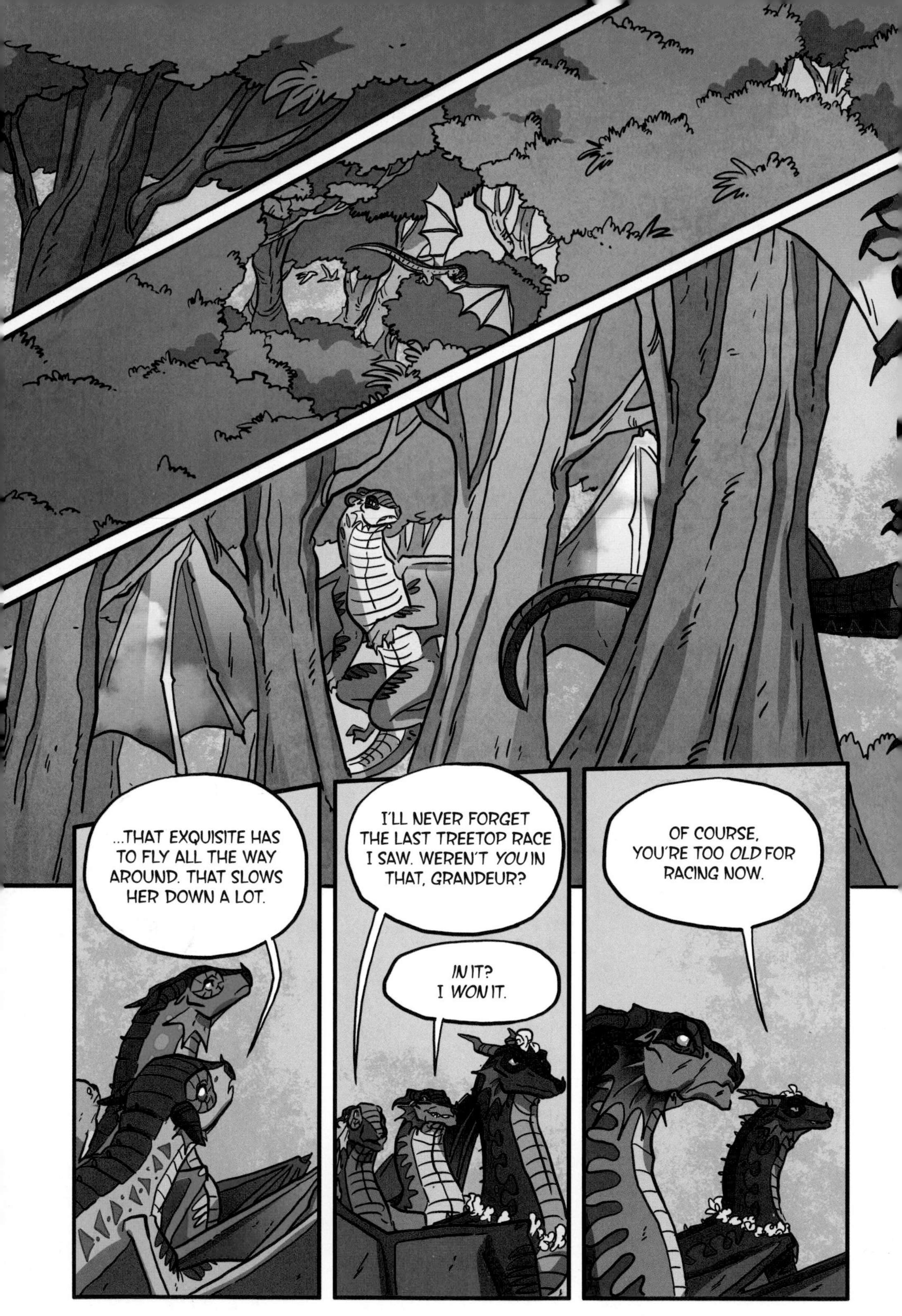
...THAT EXQUISITE HAS TO FLY ALL THE WAY AROUND. THAT SLOWS HER DOWN A LOT.
I'LL NEVER FORGET THE LAST TREETOP RACE I SAW. WEREN'T *YOU* IN THAT, GRANDEUR?
IN IT? I *WON* IT.
OF COURSE, YOU'RE TOO *OLD* FOR RACING NOW.

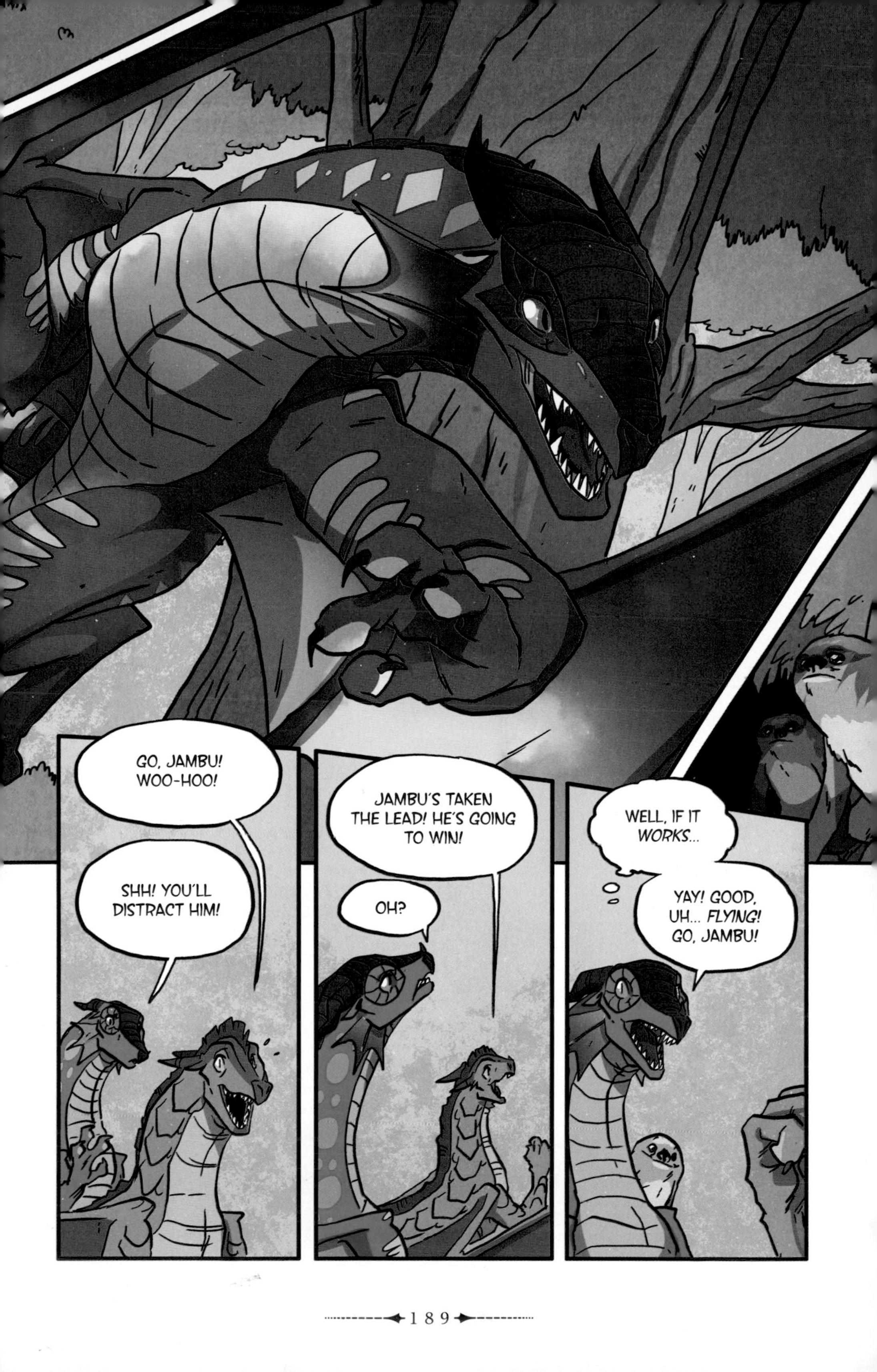
GO, JAMBU!
WOO-HOO!
SHH! YOU'LL DISTRACT HIM!
JAMBU'S TAKEN THE LEAD! HE'S GOING TO WIN!
OH?
WELL, IF IT *WORKS*...
YAY! GOOD, UH... *FLYING!* GO, JAMBU!

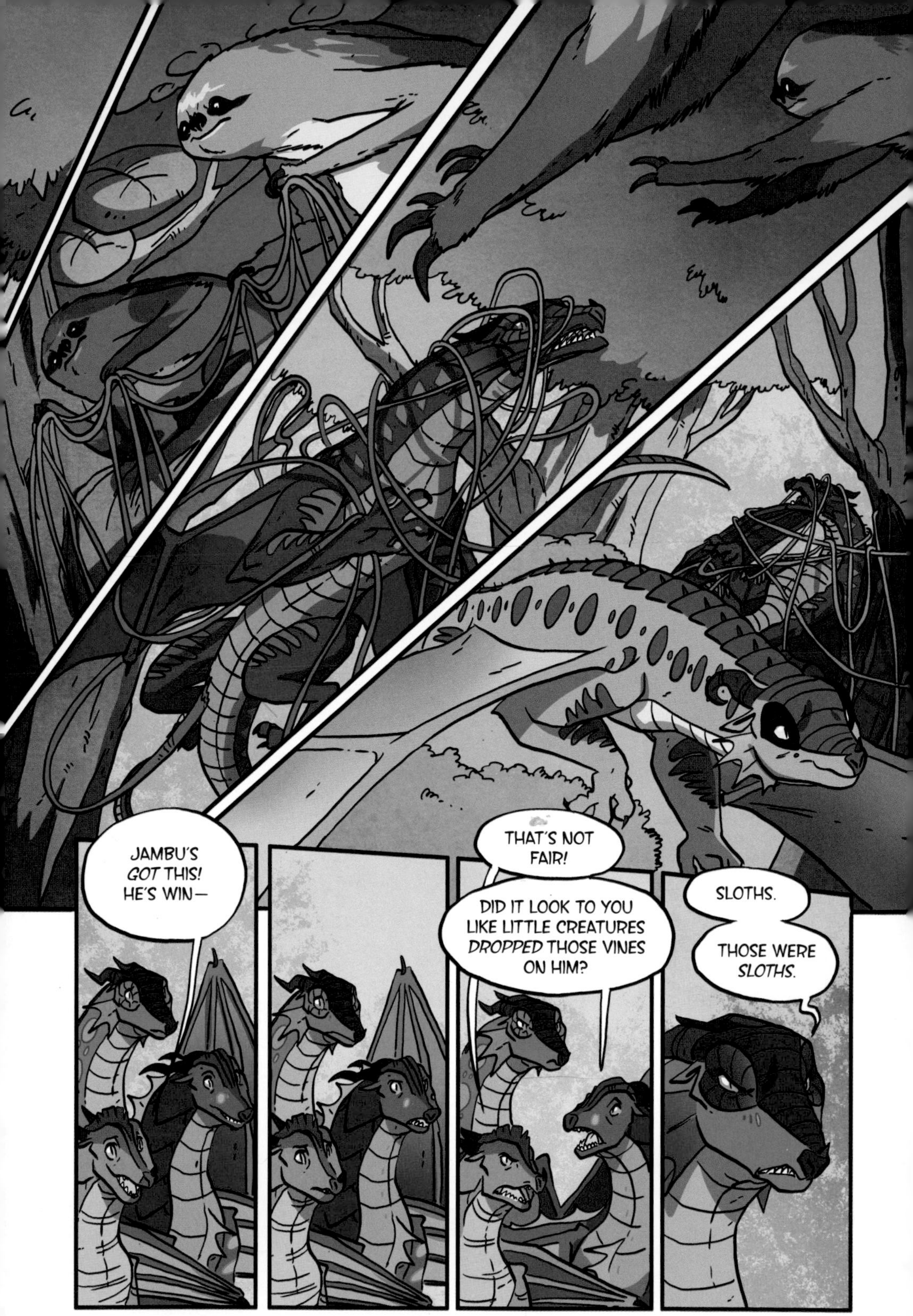
JAMBU'S *GOT* THIS! HE'S WIN—
THAT'S NOT FAIR!
DID IT LOOK TO YOU LIKE LITTLE CREATURES *DROPPED* THOSE VINES ON HIM?
SLOTHS.
THOSE WERE *SLOTHS*.

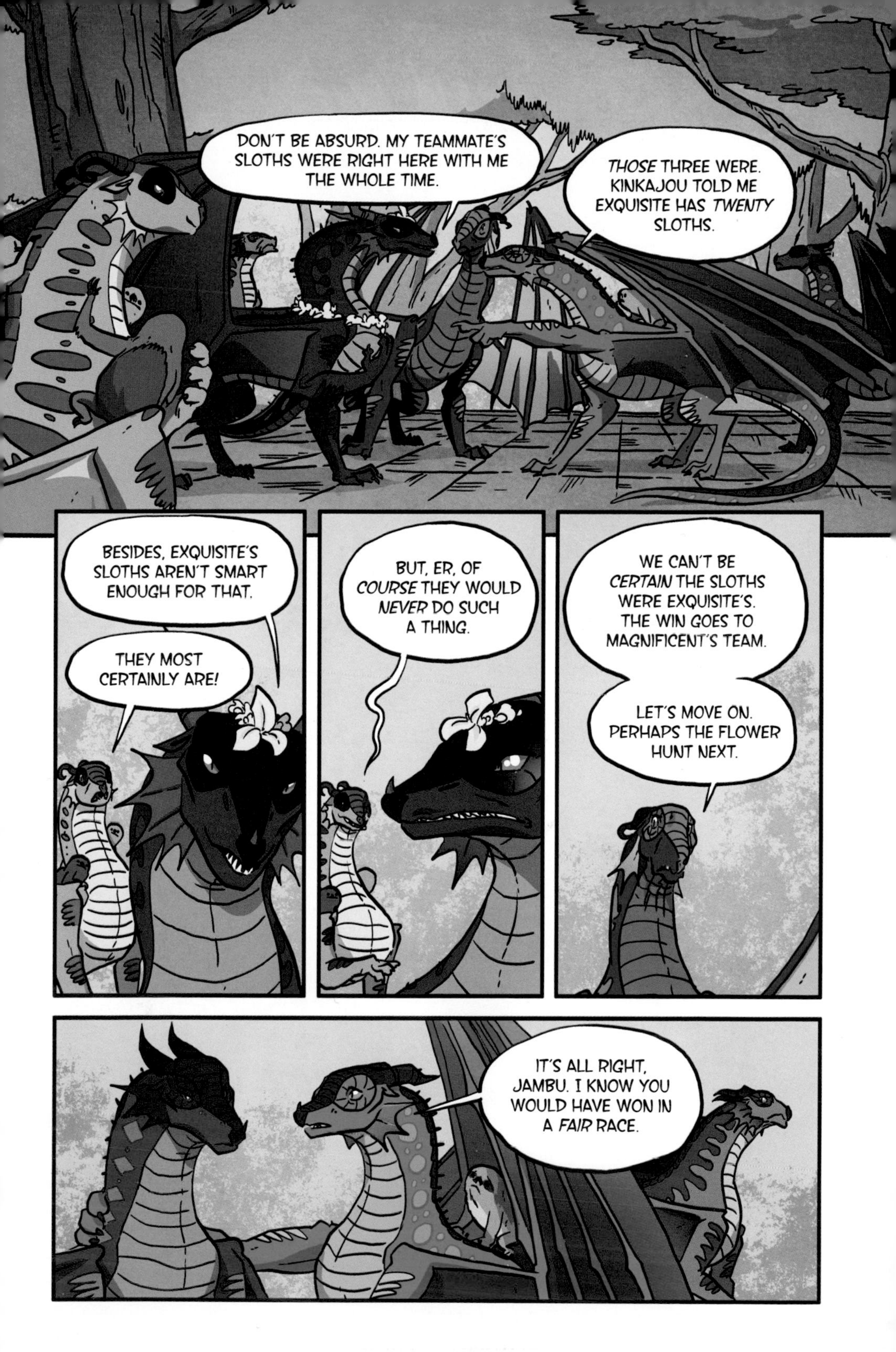
DON'T BE ABSURD. MY TEAMMATE'S SLOTHS WERE RIGHT HERE WITH ME THE WHOLE TIME.
THOSE THREE WERE. KINKAJOU TOLD ME EXQUISITE HAS *TWENTY* SLOTHS.
BESIDES, EXQUISITE'S SLOTHS AREN'T SMART ENOUGH FOR THAT.
THEY MOST CERTAINLY ARE!
BUT, ER, OF *COURSE* THEY WOULD *NEVER* DO SUCH A THING.
WE CAN'T BE *CERTAIN* THE SLOTHS WERE EXQUISITE'S. THE WIN *GOES* TO MAGNIFICENT'S TEAM.
LET'S MOVE ON. PERHAPS THE FLOWER HUNT NEXT.
IT'S ALL RIGHT, JAMBU. I KNOW YOU WOULD HAVE WON IN A *FAIR* RACE.

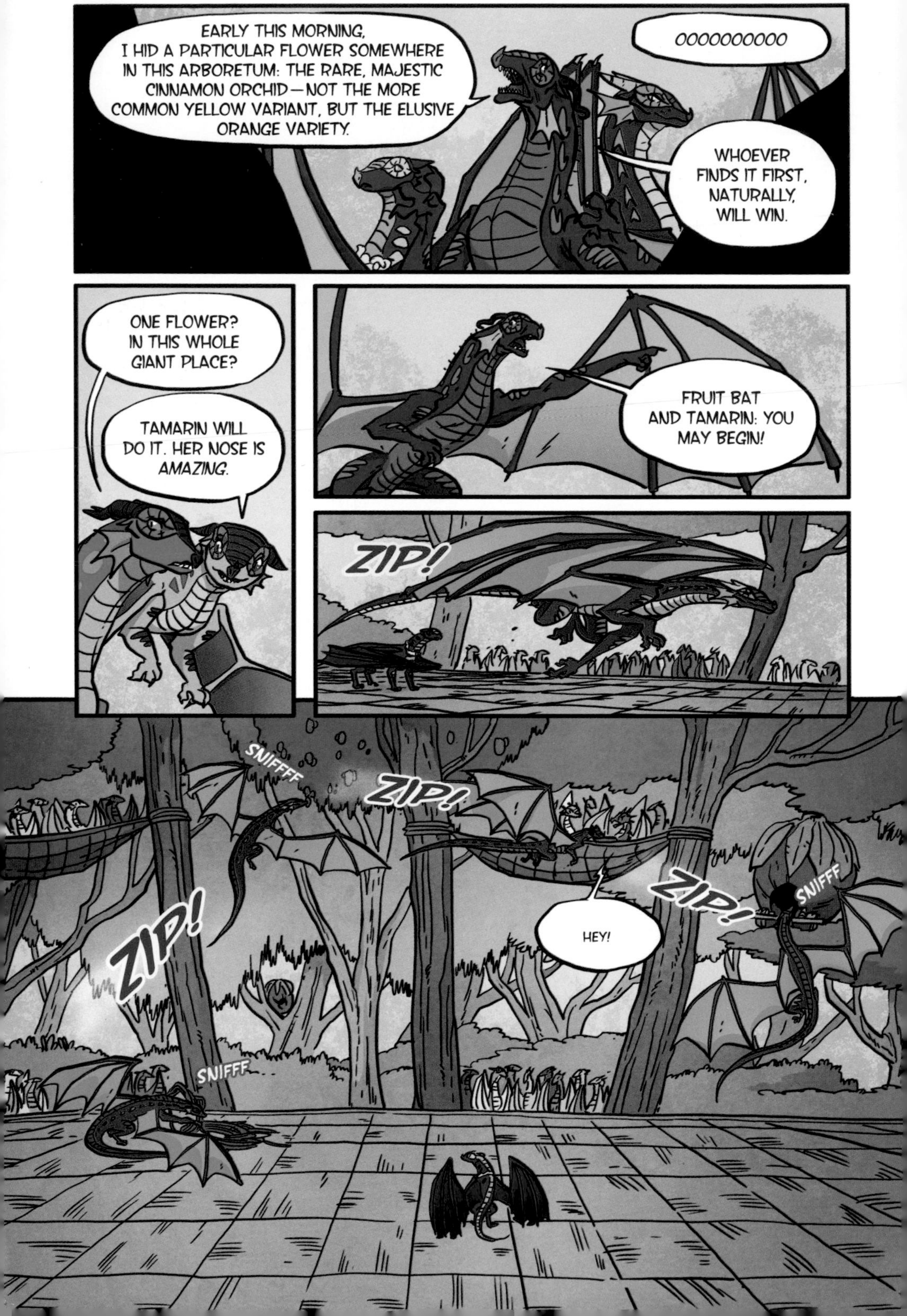
EARLY THIS MORNING, I HID A PARTICULAR FLOWER SOMEWHERE IN THIS ARBORETUM: THE RARE, MAJESTIC CINNAMON ORCHID—NOT THE MORE COMMON YELLOW VARIANT, BUT THE ELUSIVE ORANGE VARIETY.
OOOOOOOOOO
WHOEVER FINDS IT FIRST, NATURALLY, WILL WIN.
ONE FLOWER? IN THIS WHOLE GIANT PLACE?
TAMARIN WILL DO IT. HER NOSE IS AMAZING.
FRUIT BAT AND TAMARIN: YOU MAY BEGIN!
ZIP!
SNIFFFF
ZIP!
ZIP!
HEY!
ZIP!
SNIFFF
SNIFFF

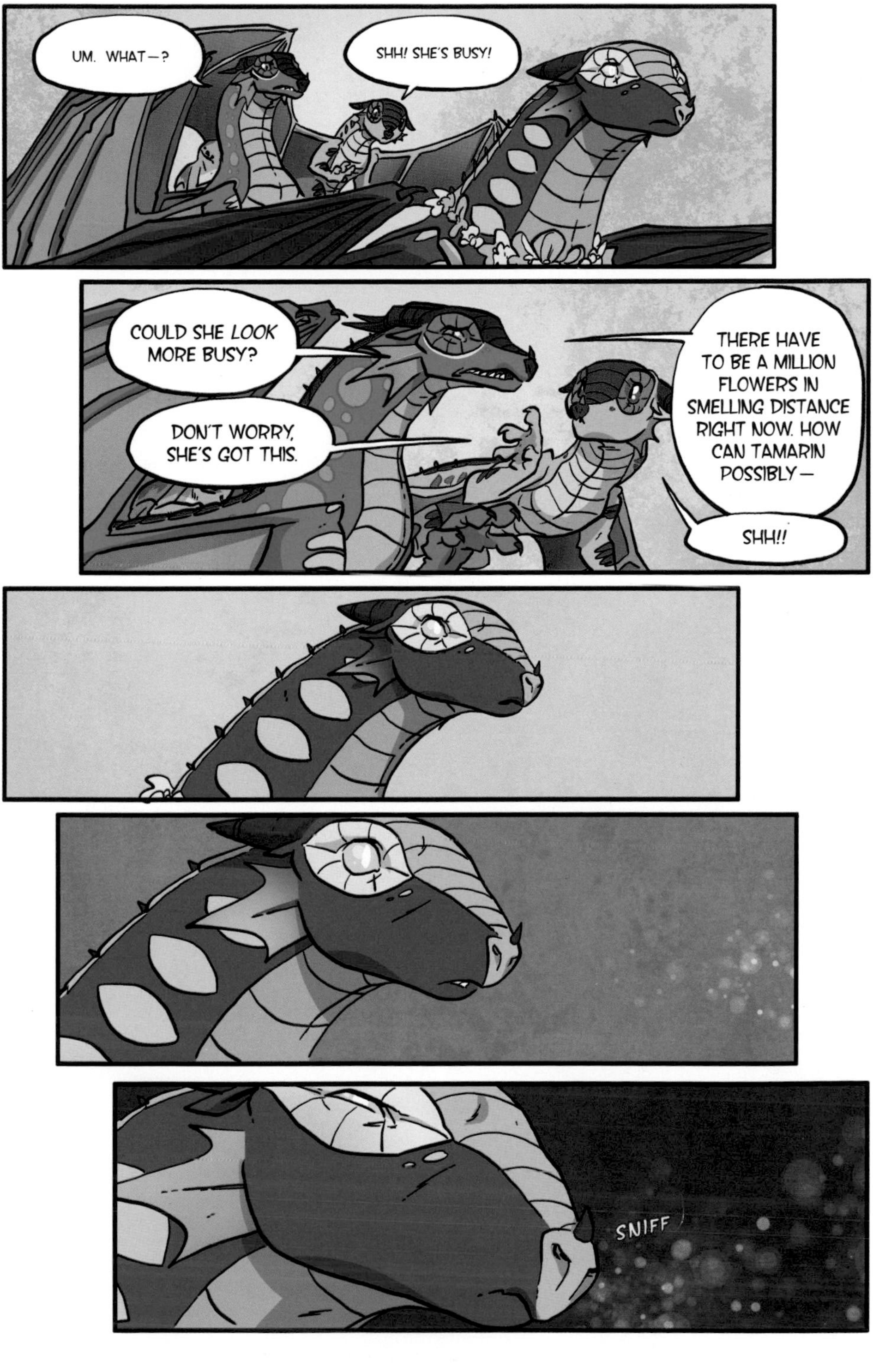
UM. WHAT—?
SHH! SHE'S BUSY!
COULD SHE *LOOK* MORE BUSY?
DON'T WORRY, SHE'S GOT THIS.
THERE HAVE TO BE A MILLION FLOWERS IN SMELLING DISTANCE RIGHT NOW. HOW CAN TAMARIN POSSIBLY—
SHH!!
SNIFF

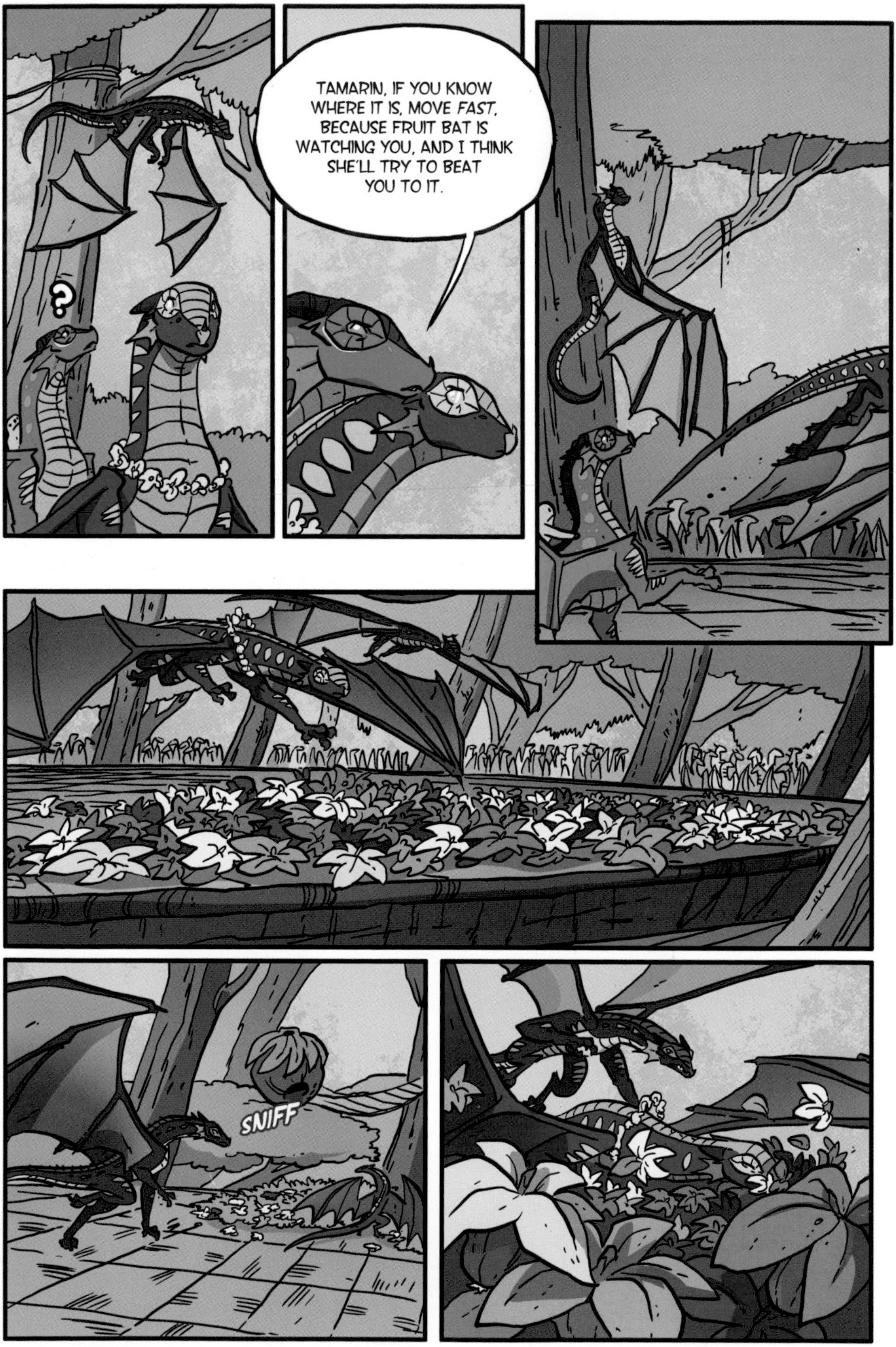
?
TAMARIN, IF YOU KNOW WHERE IT IS, MOVE *FAST*, BECAUSE FRUIT BAT IS WATCHING YOU, AND I THINK SHE'LL TRY TO BEAT YOU TO IT.
SNIFF

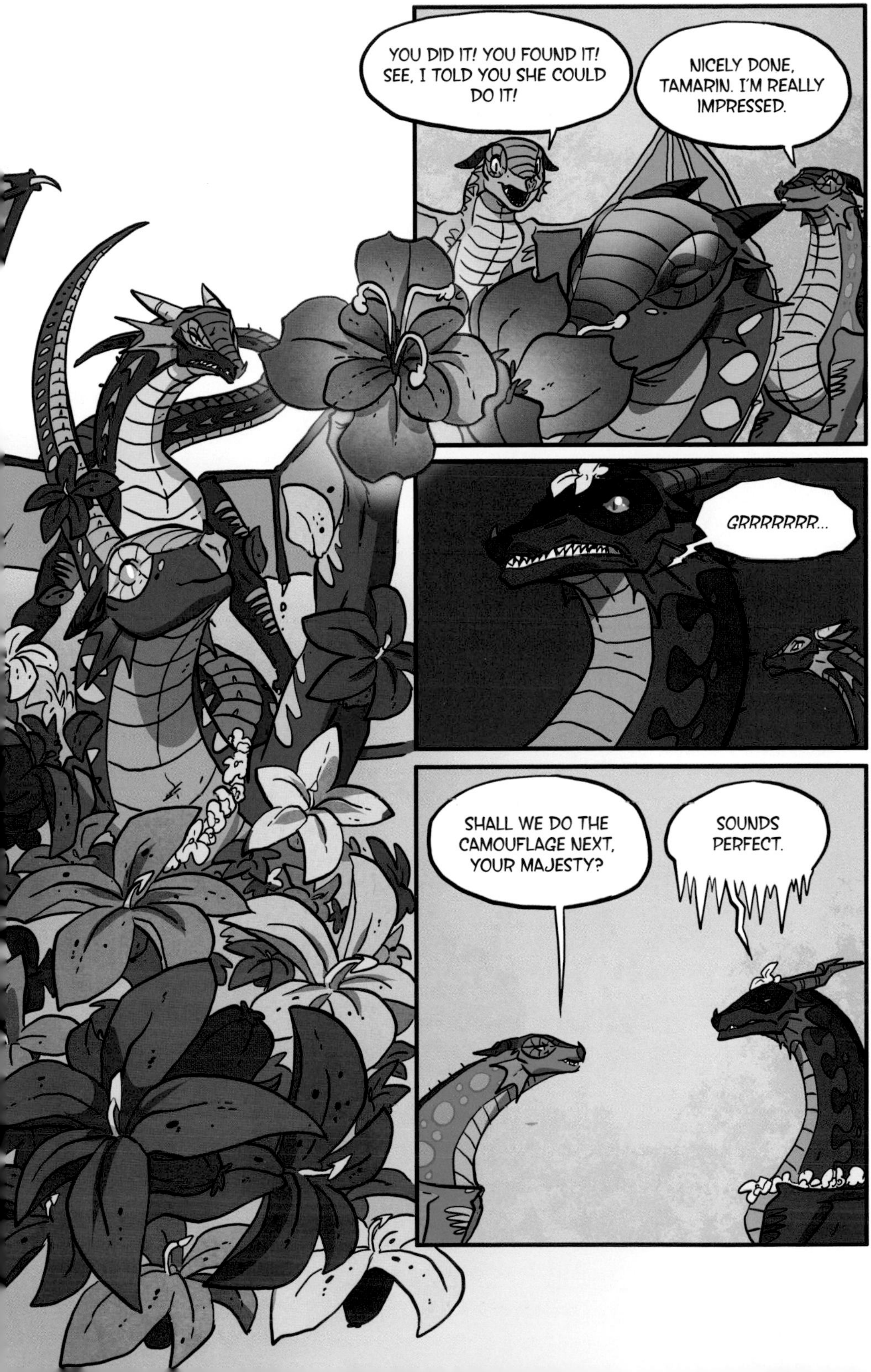
YOU DID IT! YOU FOUND IT! SEE, I TOLD YOU SHE COULD DO IT!
NICELY DONE, TAMARIN. I'M REALLY IMPRESSED.
GRRRRRRR...
SHALL WE DO THE CAMOUFLAGE NEXT, YOUR MAJESTY?
SOUNDS PERFECT.

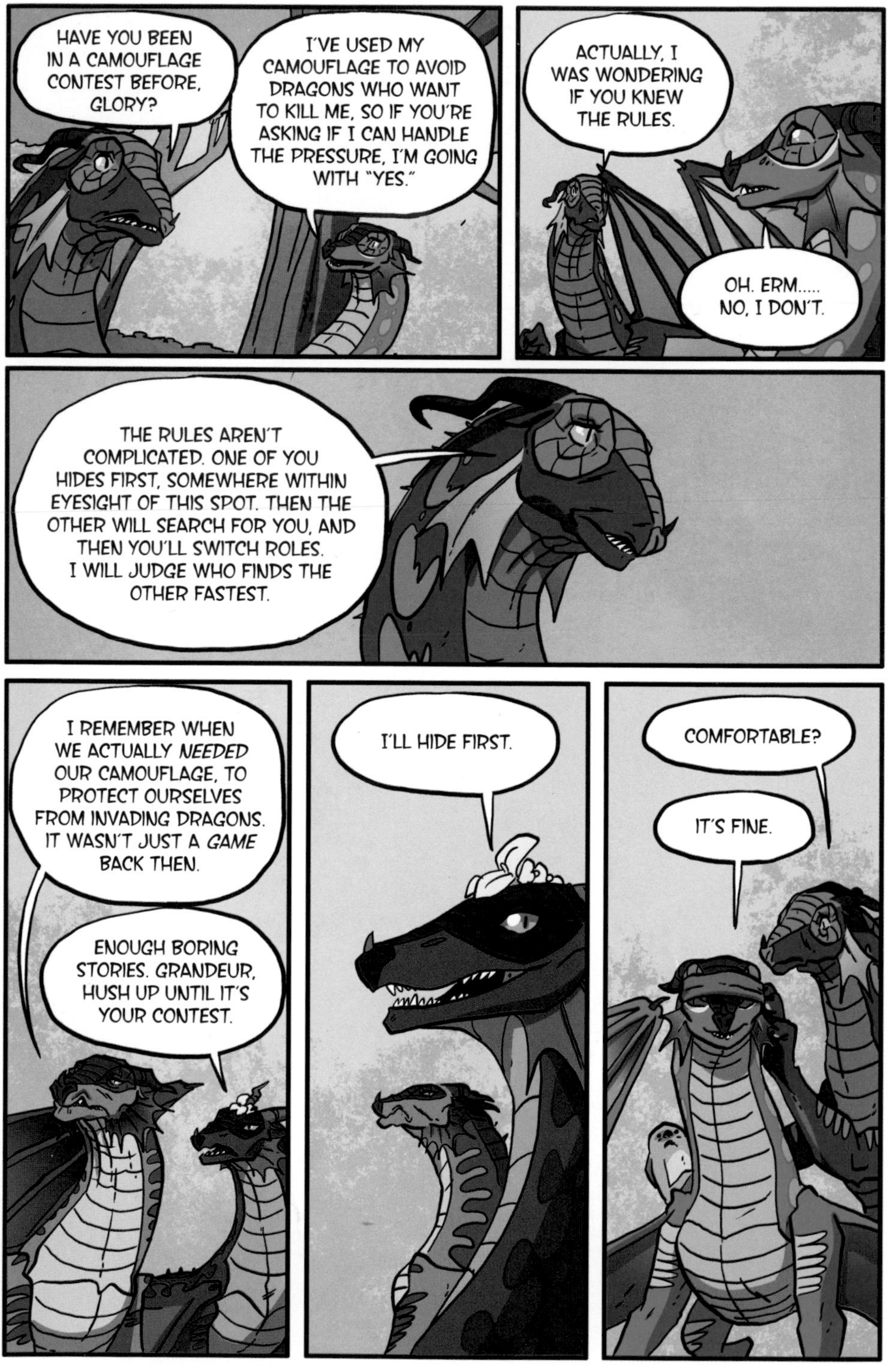
HAVE YOU BEEN IN A CAMOUFLAGE CONTEST BEFORE, GLORY?
I'VE USED MY CAMOUFLAGE TO AVOID DRAGONS WHO WANT TO KILL ME, SO IF YOU'RE ASKING IF I CAN HANDLE THE PRESSURE, I'M GOING WITH "YES."
ACTUALLY, I WAS WONDERING IF YOU KNEW THE RULES.
OH. ERM..... NO, I DON'T.
THE RULES AREN'T COMPLICATED. ONE OF YOU HIDES FIRST, SOMEWHERE WITHIN EYESIGHT OF THIS SPOT. THEN THE OTHER WILL SEARCH FOR YOU, AND THEN YOU'LL SWITCH ROLES. I WILL JUDGE WHO FINDS THE OTHER FASTEST.
I REMEMBER WHEN WE ACTUALLY *NEEDED* OUR CAMOUFLAGE, TO PROTECT OURSELVES FROM INVADING DRAGONS. IT WASN'T JUST A *GAME* BACK THEN.
ENOUGH BORING STORIES. GRANDEUR, HUSH UP UNTIL IT'S YOUR CONTEST.
I'LL HIDE FIRST.
COMFORTABLE?
IT'S FINE.

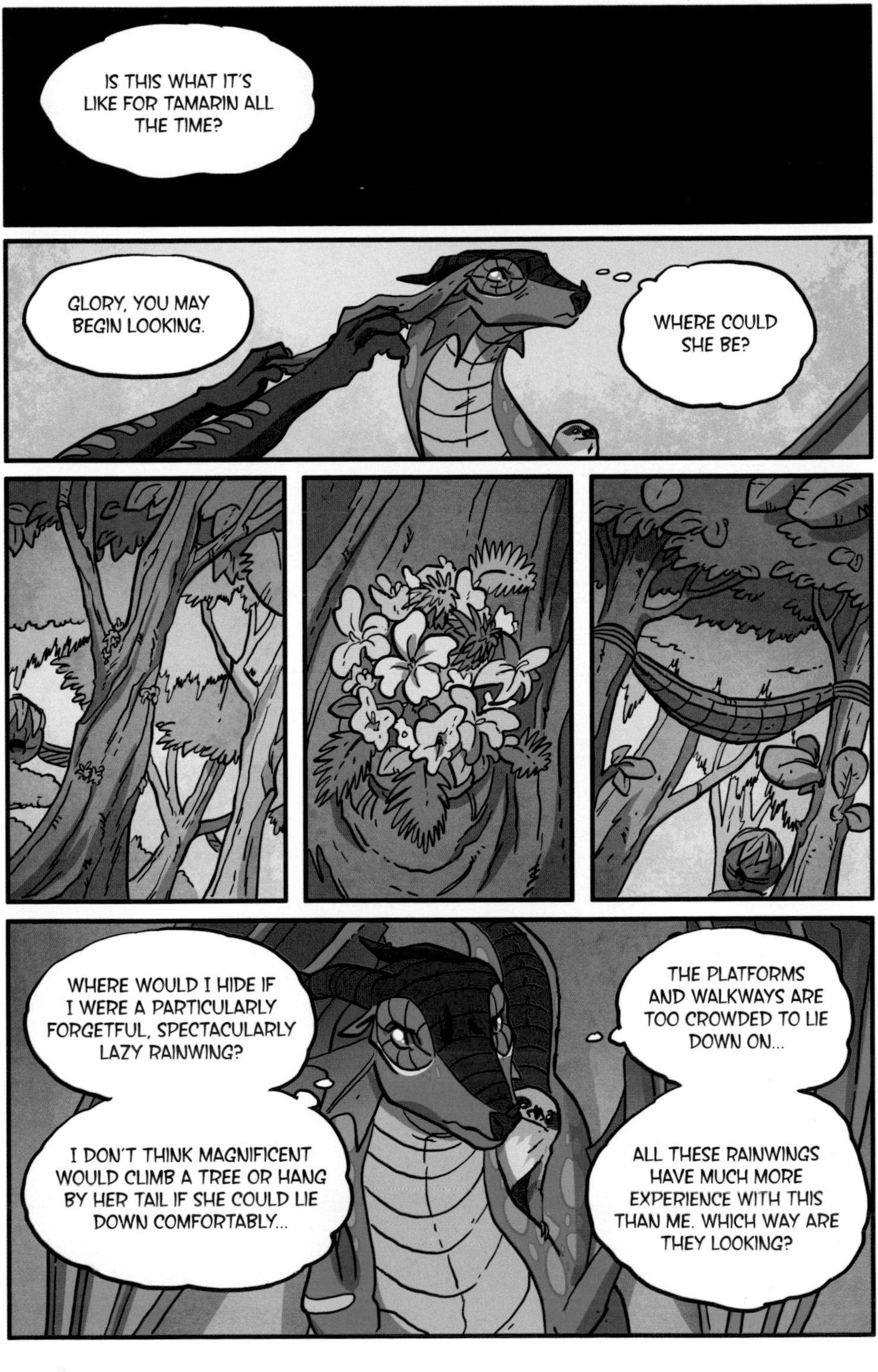
IS THIS WHAT IT'S LIKE FOR TAMARIN ALL THE TIME?
GLORY, YOU MAY BEGIN LOOKING.
WHERE COULD SHE BE?
WHERE WOULD I HIDE IF I WERE A PARTICULARLY FORGETFUL, SPECTACULARLY LAZY RAINWING?
THE PLATFORMS AND WALKWAYS ARE TOO CROWDED TO LIE DOWN ON...
I DON'T THINK MAGNIFICENT WOULD CLIMB A TREE OR HANG BY HER TAIL IF SHE COULD LIE DOWN COMFORTABLY...
ALL THESE RAINWINGS HAVE MUCH MORE EXPERIENCE WITH THIS THAN ME. WHICH WAY ARE THEY LOOKING?

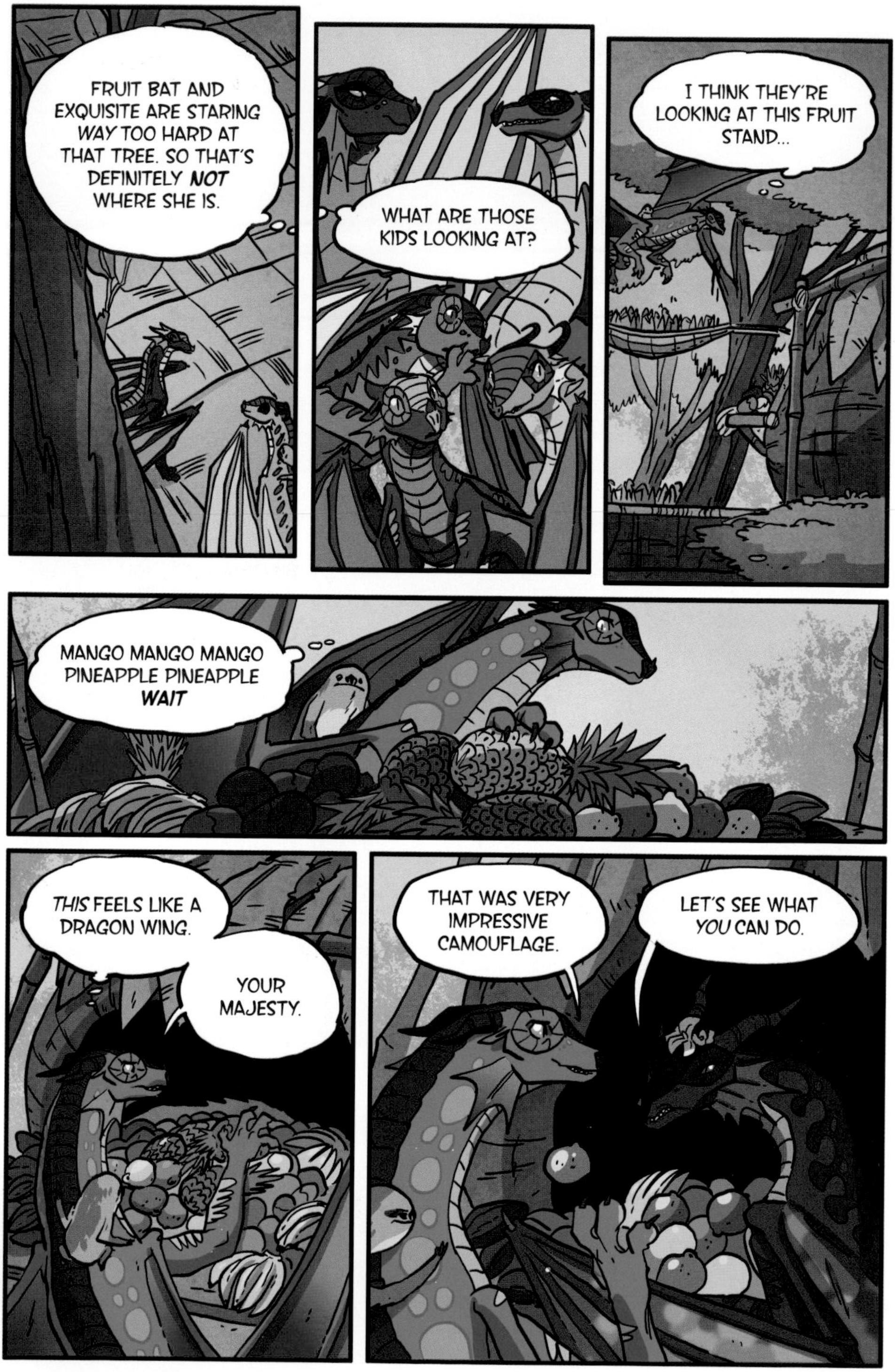
FRUIT BAT AND EXQUISITE ARE STARING *WAY* TOO HARD AT THAT TREE. SO THAT'S DEFINITELY ***NOT*** WHERE SHE IS.
WHAT ARE THOSE KIDS LOOKING AT?
I THINK THEY'RE LOOKING AT THIS FRUIT STAND...
MANGO MANGO MANGO PINEAPPLE PINEAPPLE ***WAIT***
THIS FEELS LIKE A DRAGON WING.
YOUR MAJESTY.
THAT WAS VERY IMPRESSIVE CAMOUFLAGE.
LET'S SEE WHAT *YOU* CAN DO.

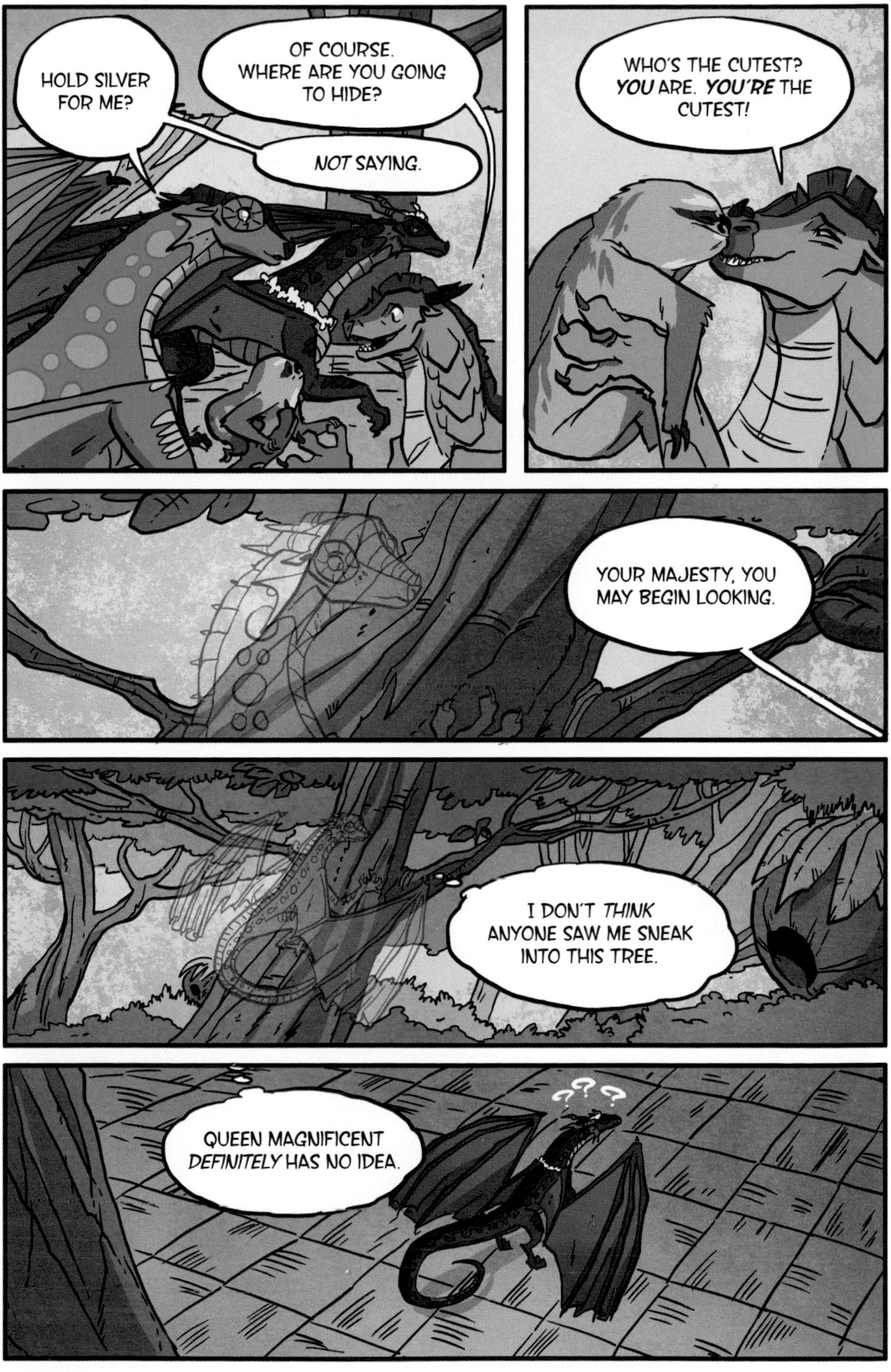
HOLD SILVER FOR ME?
OF COURSE. WHERE ARE YOU GOING TO HIDE?
NOT SAYING.
WHO'S THE CUTEST? YOU ARE. YOU'RE THE CUTEST!
YOUR MAJESTY, YOU MAY BEGIN LOOKING.
I DON'T THINK ANYONE SAW ME SNEAK INTO THIS TREE.
QUEEN MAGNIFICENT DEFINITELY HAS NO IDEA.
???

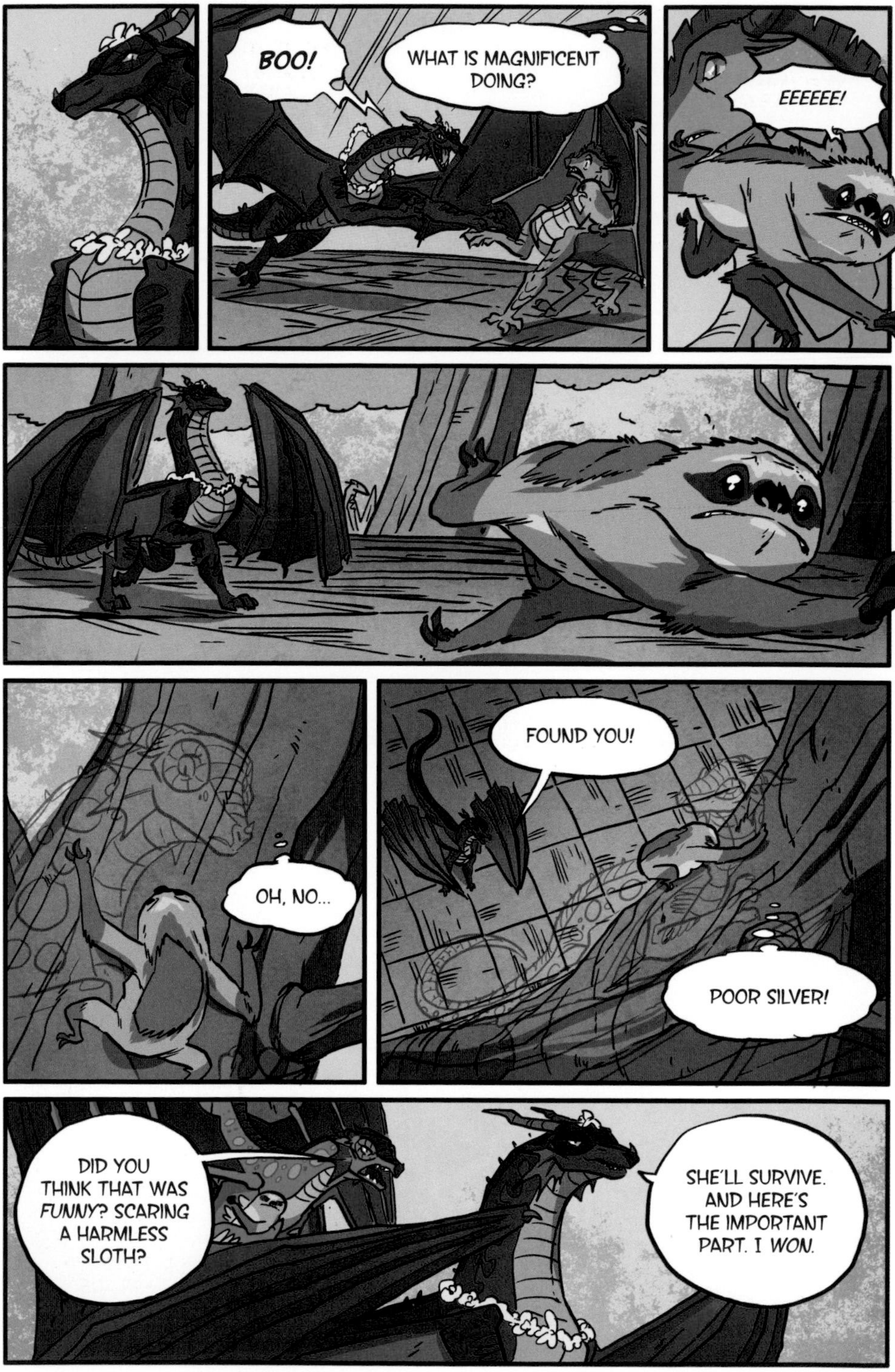
BOO!
WHAT IS MAGNIFICENT DOING?
EEEEEE!
OH, NO...
FOUND YOU!
POOR SILVER!
DID YOU THINK THAT WAS *FUNNY*? SCARING A HARMLESS SLOTH?
SHE'LL SURVIVE. AND HERE'S THE IMPORTANT PART. I *WON*.

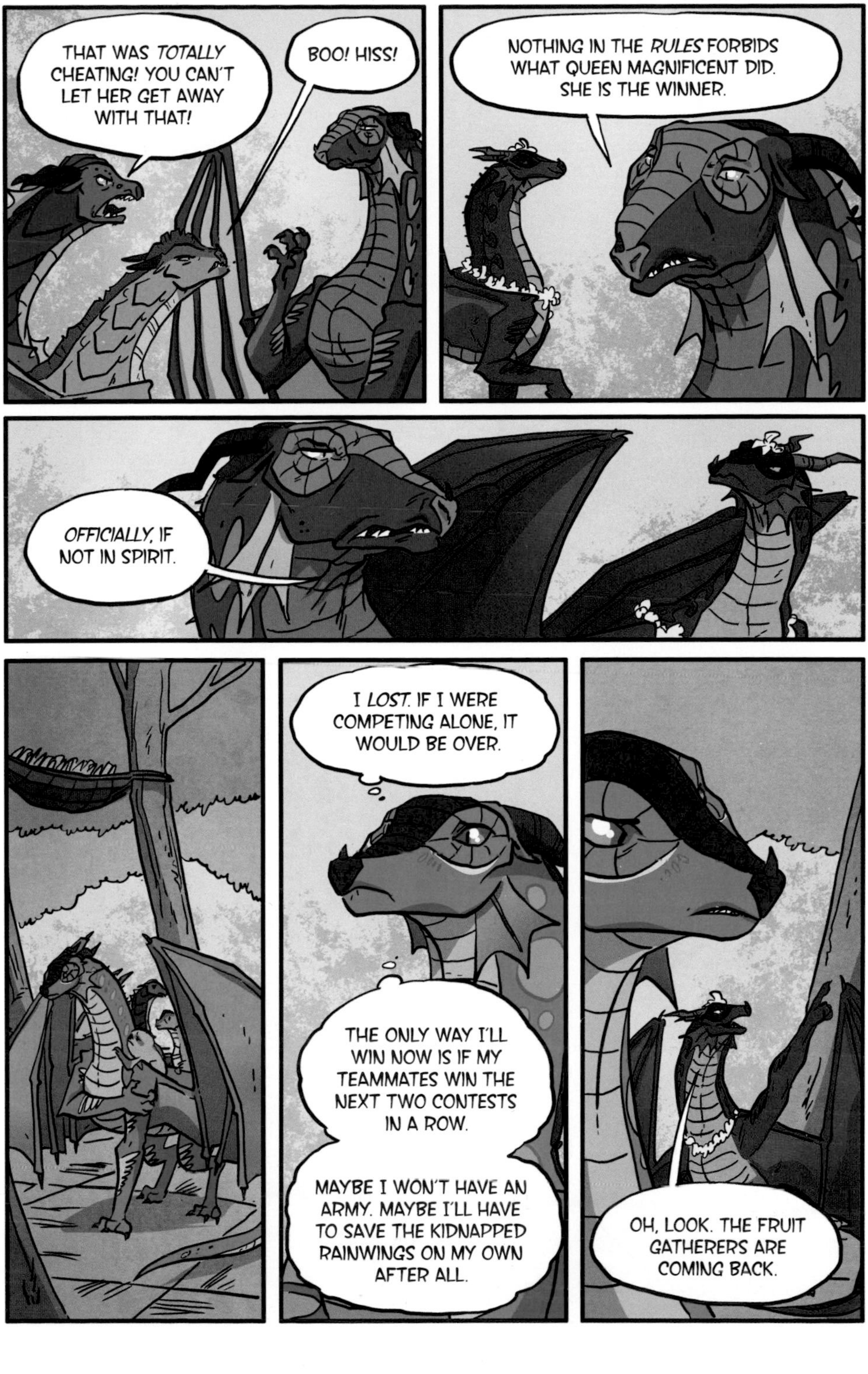
THAT WAS *TOTALLY* CHEATING! YOU CAN'T LET HER GET AWAY WITH THAT!
BOO! HISS!
NOTHING IN THE *RULES* FORBIDS WHAT QUEEN MAGNIFICENT DID. SHE IS THE WINNER.
OFFICIALLY, IF NOT IN SPIRIT.
I *LOST*. IF I WERE COMPETING ALONE, IT WOULD BE OVER.
THE ONLY WAY I'LL WIN NOW IS IF MY TEAMMATES WIN THE NEXT TWO CONTESTS IN A ROW.
MAYBE I WON'T HAVE AN ARMY. MAYBE I'LL HAVE TO SAVE THE KIDNAPPED RAINWINGS ON MY OWN AFTER ALL.
OH, LOOK. THE FRUIT GATHERERS ARE COMING BACK.

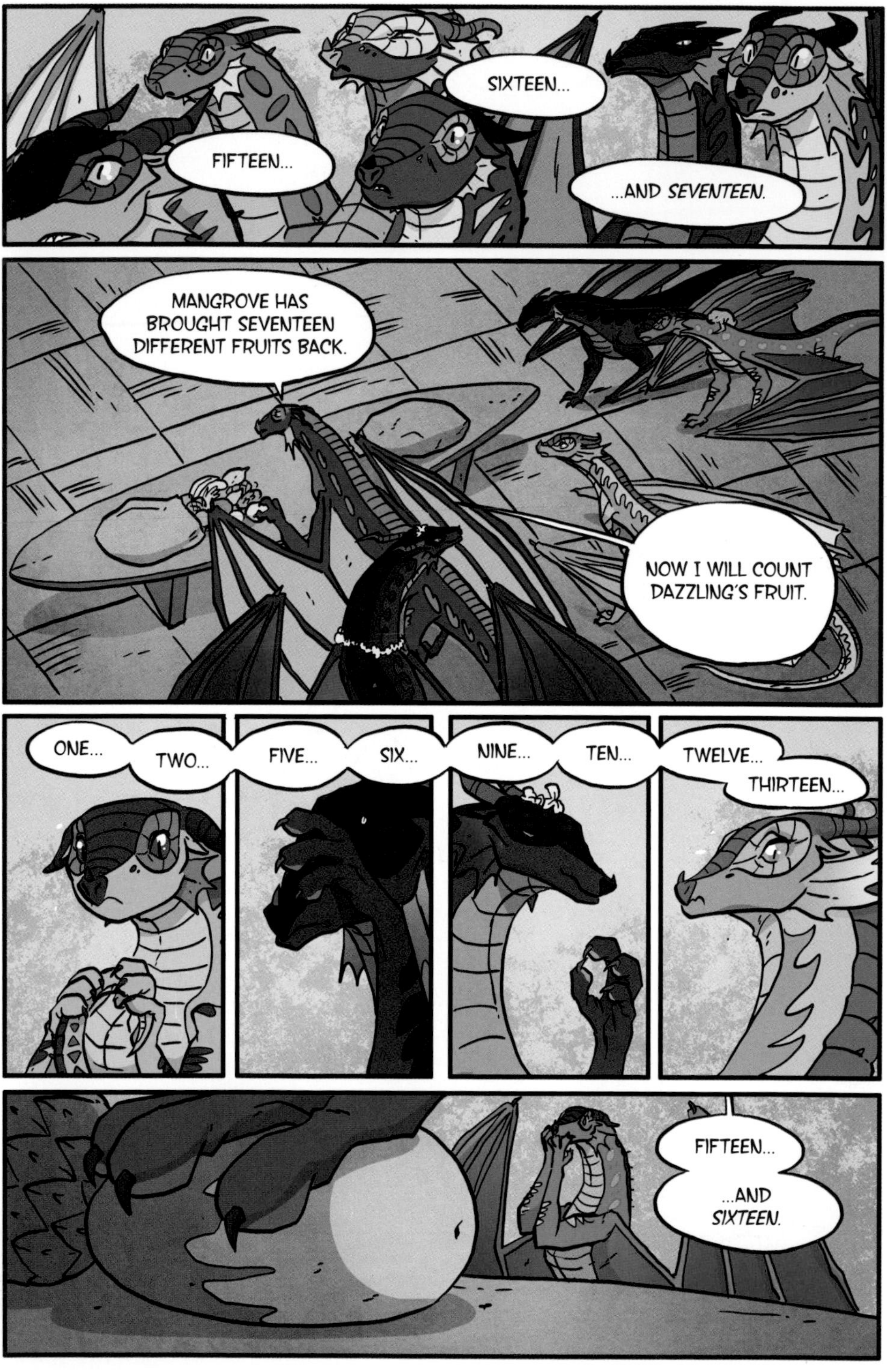
FIFTEEN...
SIXTEEN...
...AND *SEVENTEEN*.
MANGROVE HAS BROUGHT SEVENTEEN DIFFERENT FRUITS BACK.
NOW I WILL COUNT DAZZLING'S FRUIT.
ONE...
TWO...
FIVE...
SIX...
NINE...
TEN...
TWELVE...
THIRTEEN...
FIFTEEN...
...AND *SIXTEEN*.

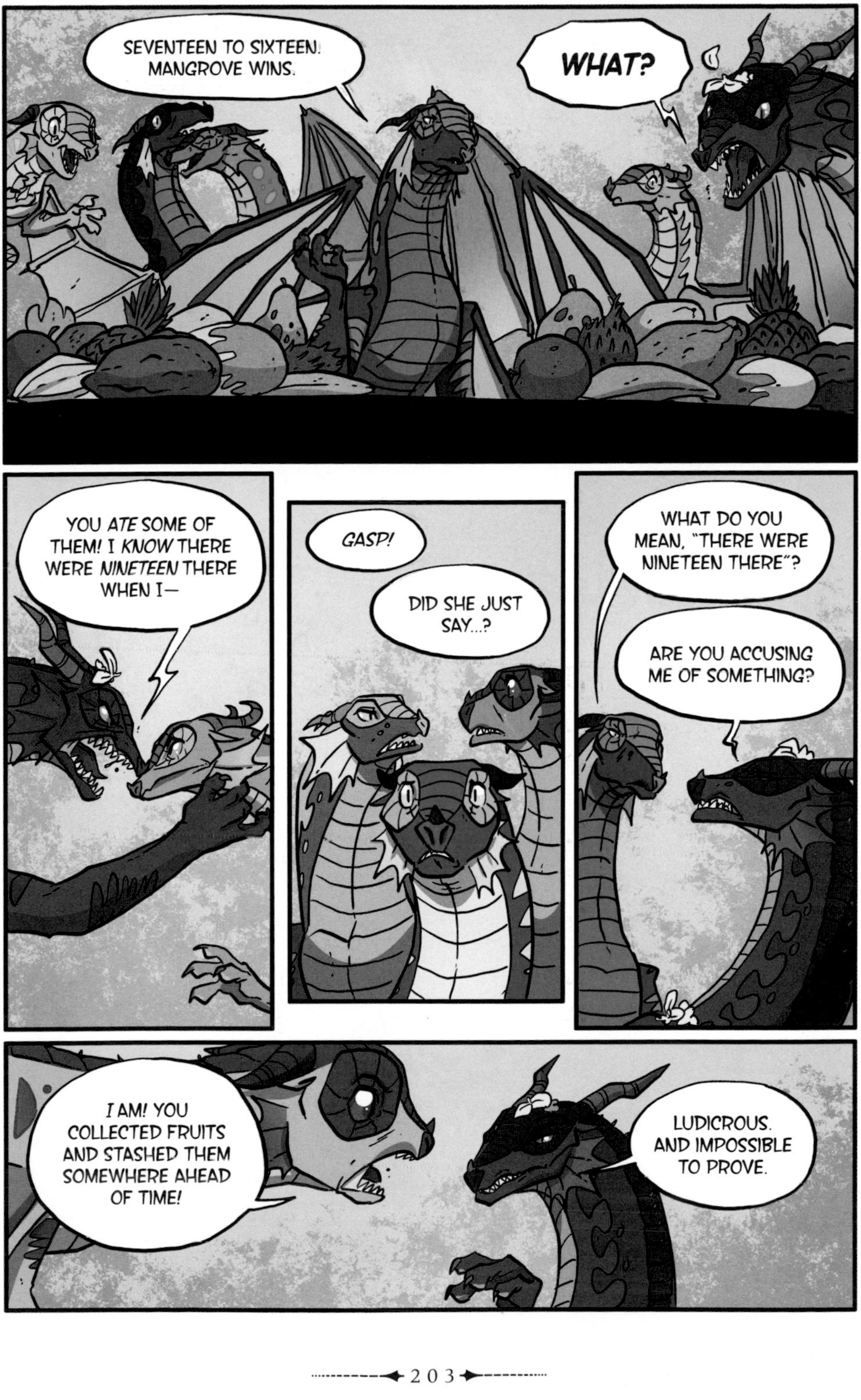
SEVENTEEN TO SIXTEEN. MANGROVE WINS.
WHAT?
YOU *ATE* SOME OF THEM! I *KNOW* THERE WERE *NINETEEN* THERE WHEN I—
GASP!
DID SHE JUST SAY...?
WHAT DO YOU MEAN, "THERE WERE NINETEEN THERE"?
ARE YOU ACCUSING ME OF SOMETHING?
I AM! YOU COLLECTED FRUITS AND STASHED THEM SOMEWHERE AHEAD OF TIME!
LUDICROUS. AND IMPOSSIBLE TO PROVE.

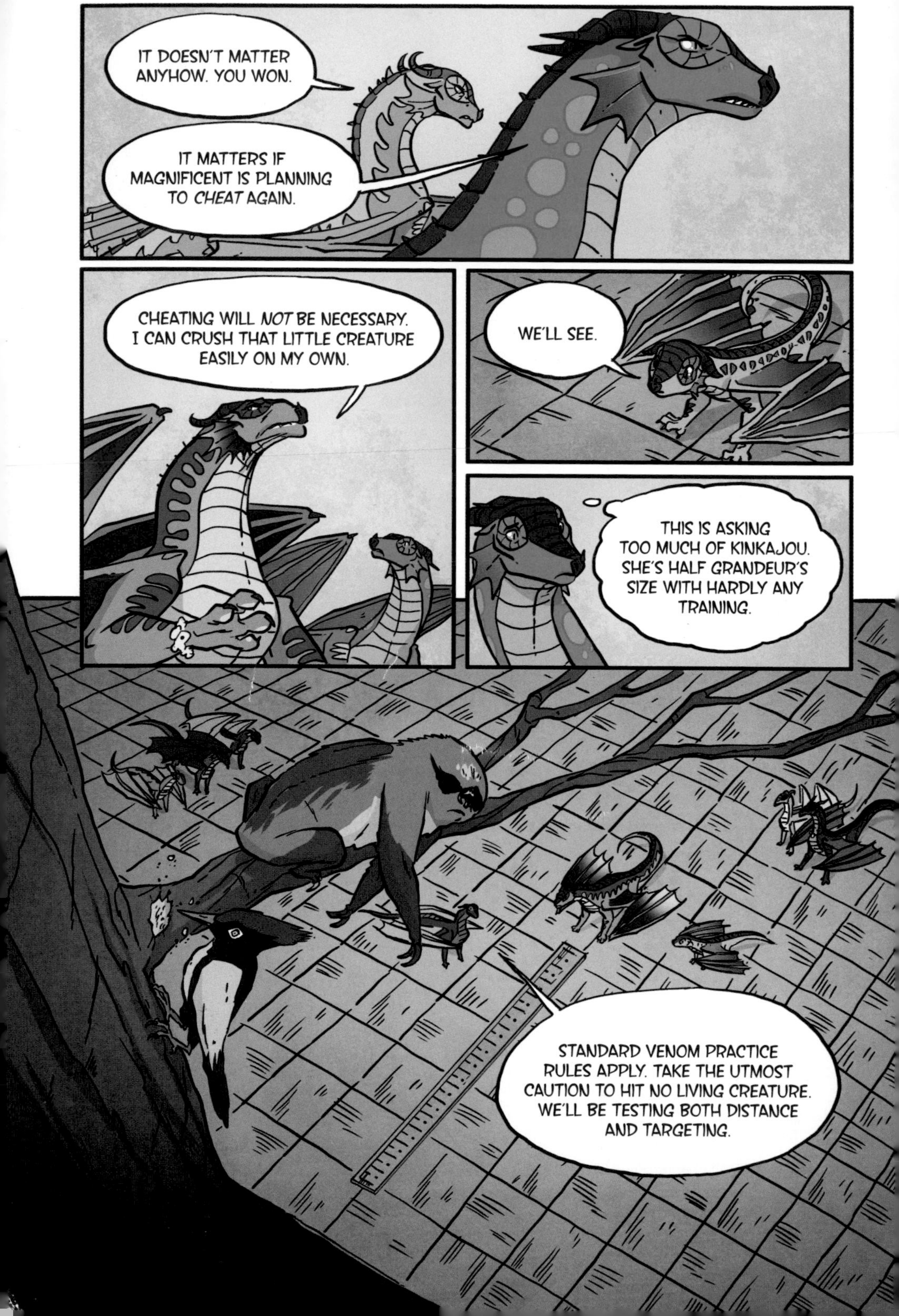
IT DOESN'T MATTER ANYHOW. YOU WON.
IT MATTERS IF MAGNIFICENT IS PLANNING TO *CHEAT* AGAIN.
CHEATING WILL *NOT* BE NECESSARY. I CAN CRUSH THAT LITTLE CREATURE EASILY ON MY OWN.
WE'LL SEE.
THIS IS ASKING TOO MUCH OF KINKAJOU. SHE'S HALF GRANDEUR'S SIZE WITH HARDLY ANY TRAINING.
STANDARD VENOM PRACTICE RULES APPLY. TAKE THE UTMOST CAUTION TO HIT NO LIVING CREATURE. WE'LL BE TESTING BOTH DISTANCE AND TARGETING.

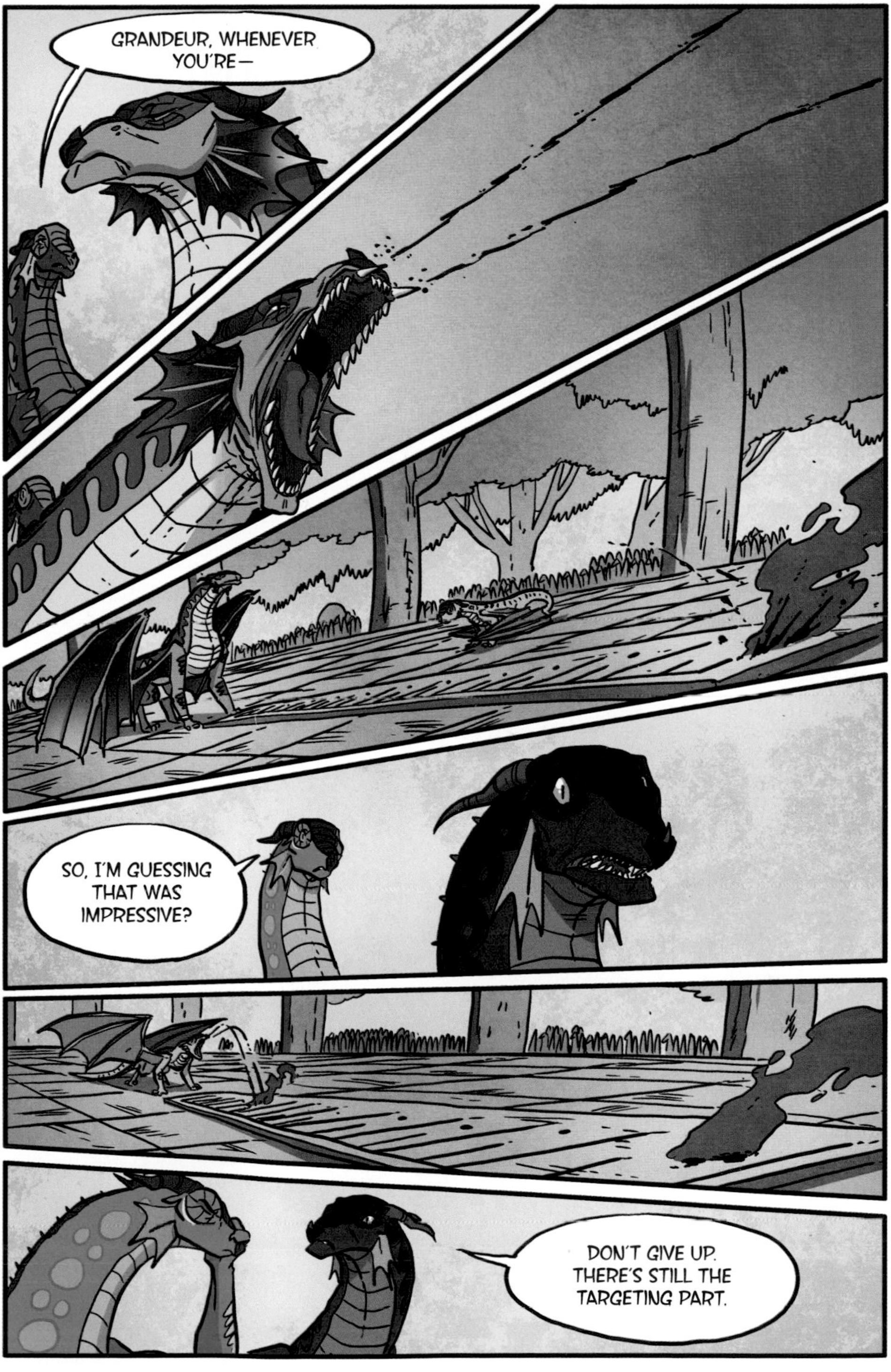
GRANDEUR, WHENEVER YOU'RE—
SO, I'M GUESSING THAT WAS IMPRESSIVE?
DON'T GIVE UP. THERE'S STILL THE TARGETING PART.

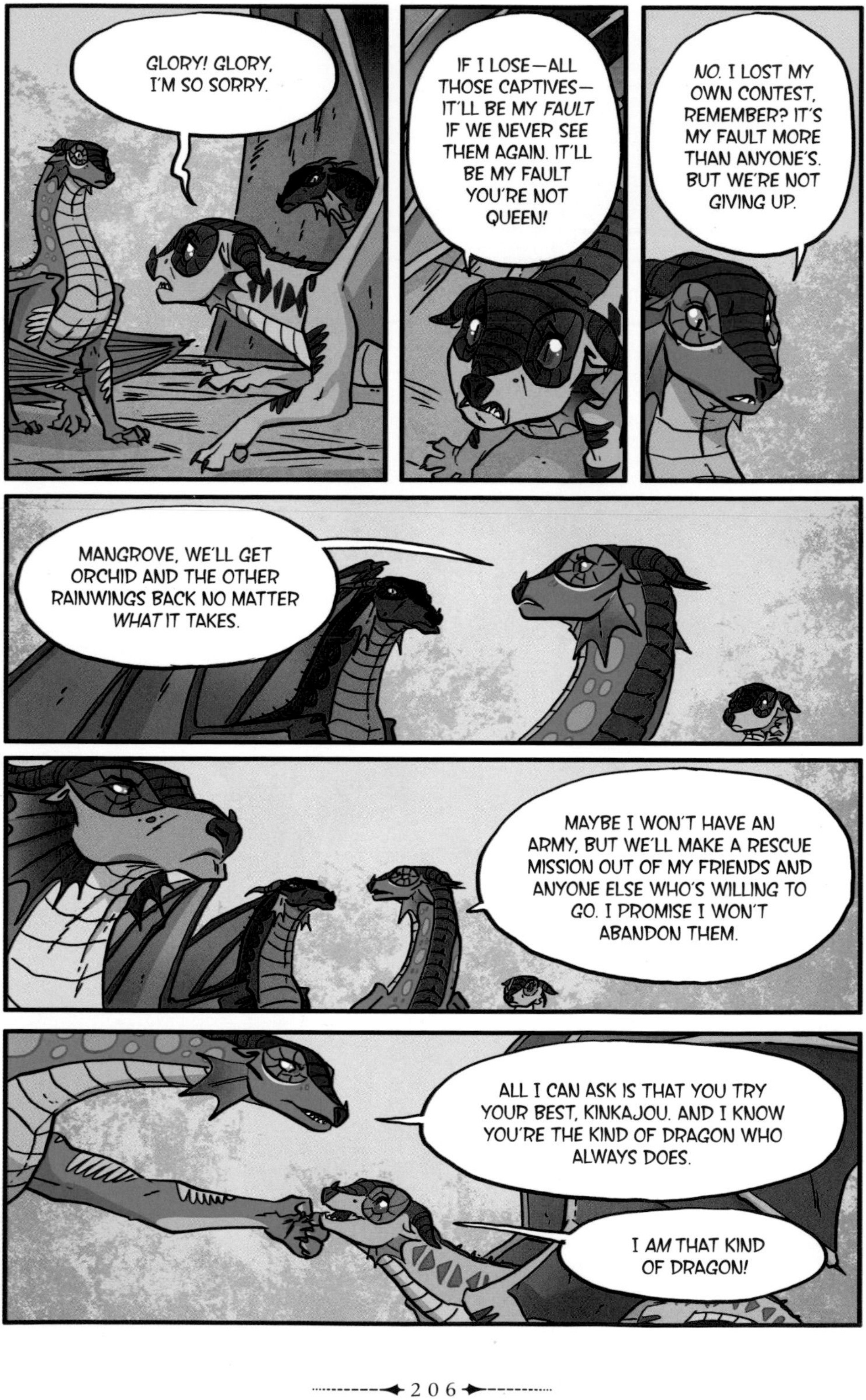
GLORY! GLORY, I'M SO SORRY.
IF I LOSE—ALL THOSE CAPTIVES—IT'LL BE MY *FAULT* IF WE NEVER SEE THEM AGAIN. IT'LL BE MY FAULT YOU'RE NOT QUEEN!
NO. I LOST MY OWN CONTEST, REMEMBER? IT'S MY FAULT MORE THAN ANYONE'S. BUT WE'RE NOT GIVING UP.
MANGROVE, WE'LL GET ORCHID AND THE OTHER RAINWINGS BACK NO MATTER *WHAT* IT TAKES.
MAYBE I WON'T HAVE AN ARMY, BUT WE'LL MAKE A RESCUE MISSION OUT OF MY FRIENDS AND ANYONE ELSE WHO'S WILLING TO GO. I PROMISE I WON'T ABANDON THEM.
ALL I CAN ASK IS THAT YOU TRY YOUR BEST, KINKAJOU. AND I KNOW YOU'RE THE KIND OF DRAGON WHO ALWAYS DOES.
I *AM* THAT KIND OF DRAGON!

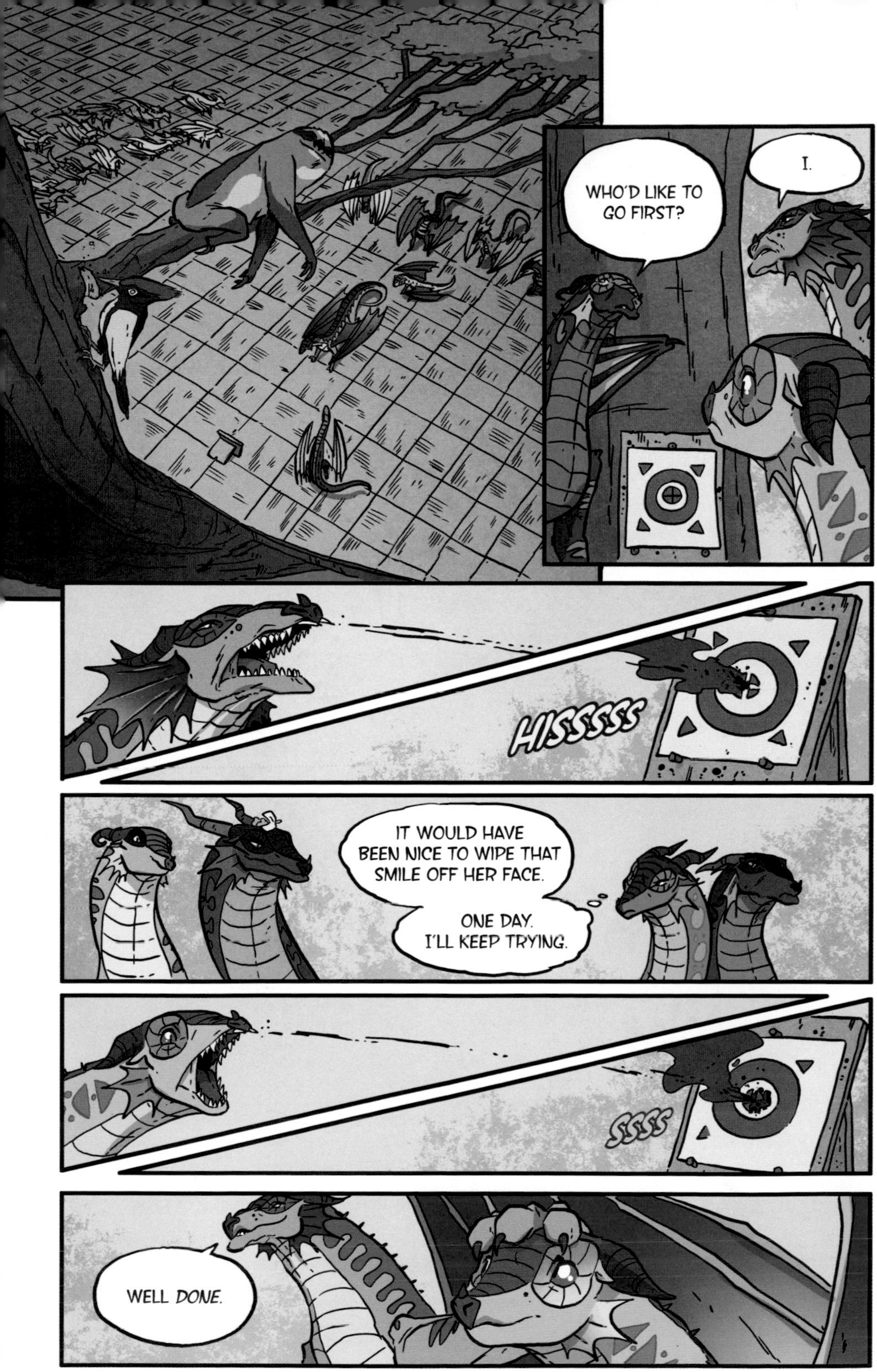
WHO'D LIKE TO GO FIRST?
I.
HISSSSS
IT WOULD HAVE BEEN NICE TO WIPE THAT SMILE OFF HER FACE.
ONE DAY. I'LL KEEP TRYING.
SSSS
WELL DONE.

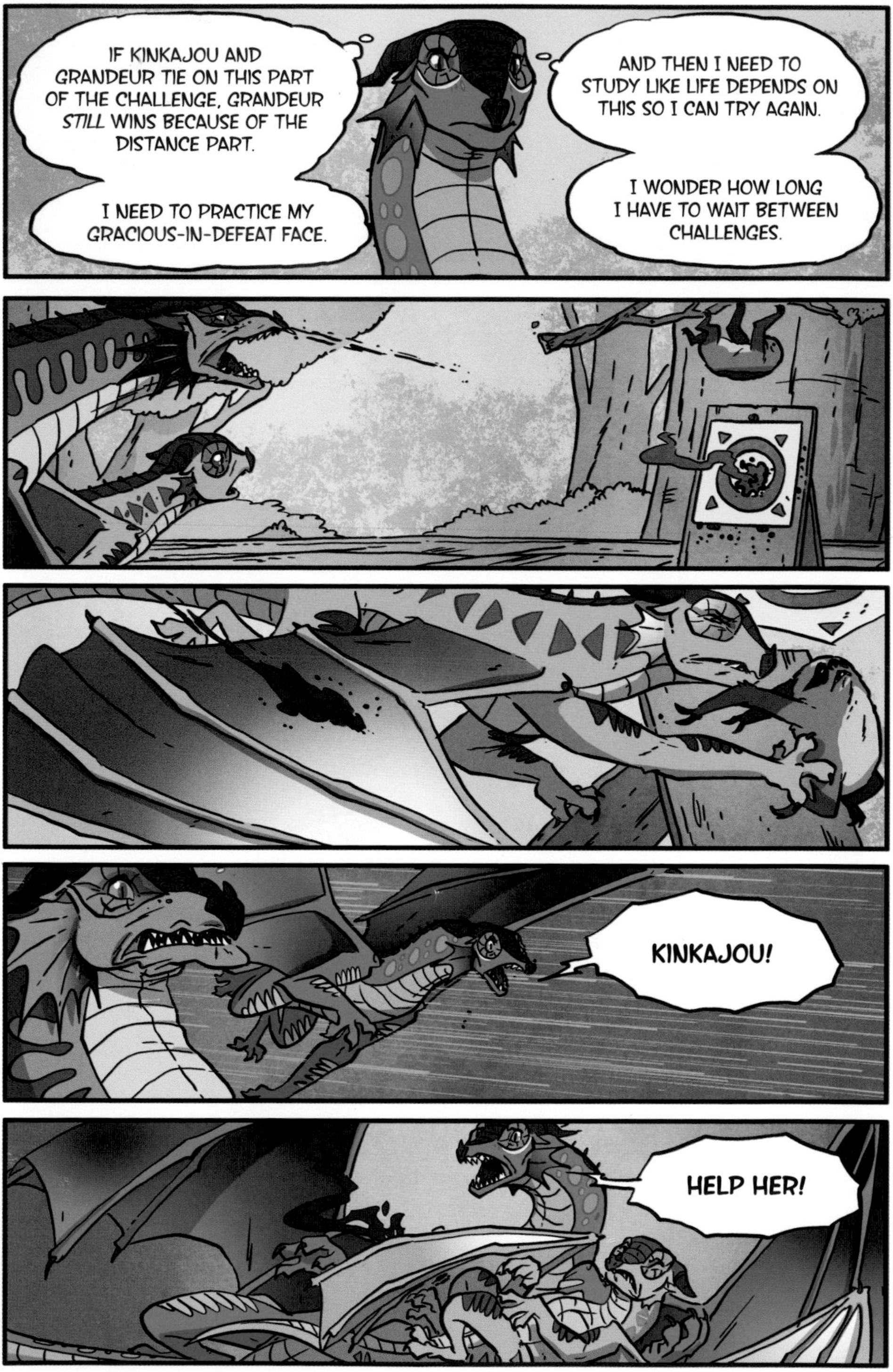
IF KINKAJOU AND GRANDEUR TIE ON THIS PART OF THE CHALLENGE, GRANDEUR *STILL* WINS BECAUSE OF THE DISTANCE PART.
I NEED TO PRACTICE MY GRACIOUS-IN-DEFEAT FACE.
AND THEN I NEED TO STUDY LIKE LIFE DEPENDS ON THIS SO I CAN TRY AGAIN.
I WONDER HOW LONG I HAVE TO WAIT BETWEEN CHALLENGES.
KINKAJOU!
HELP HER!

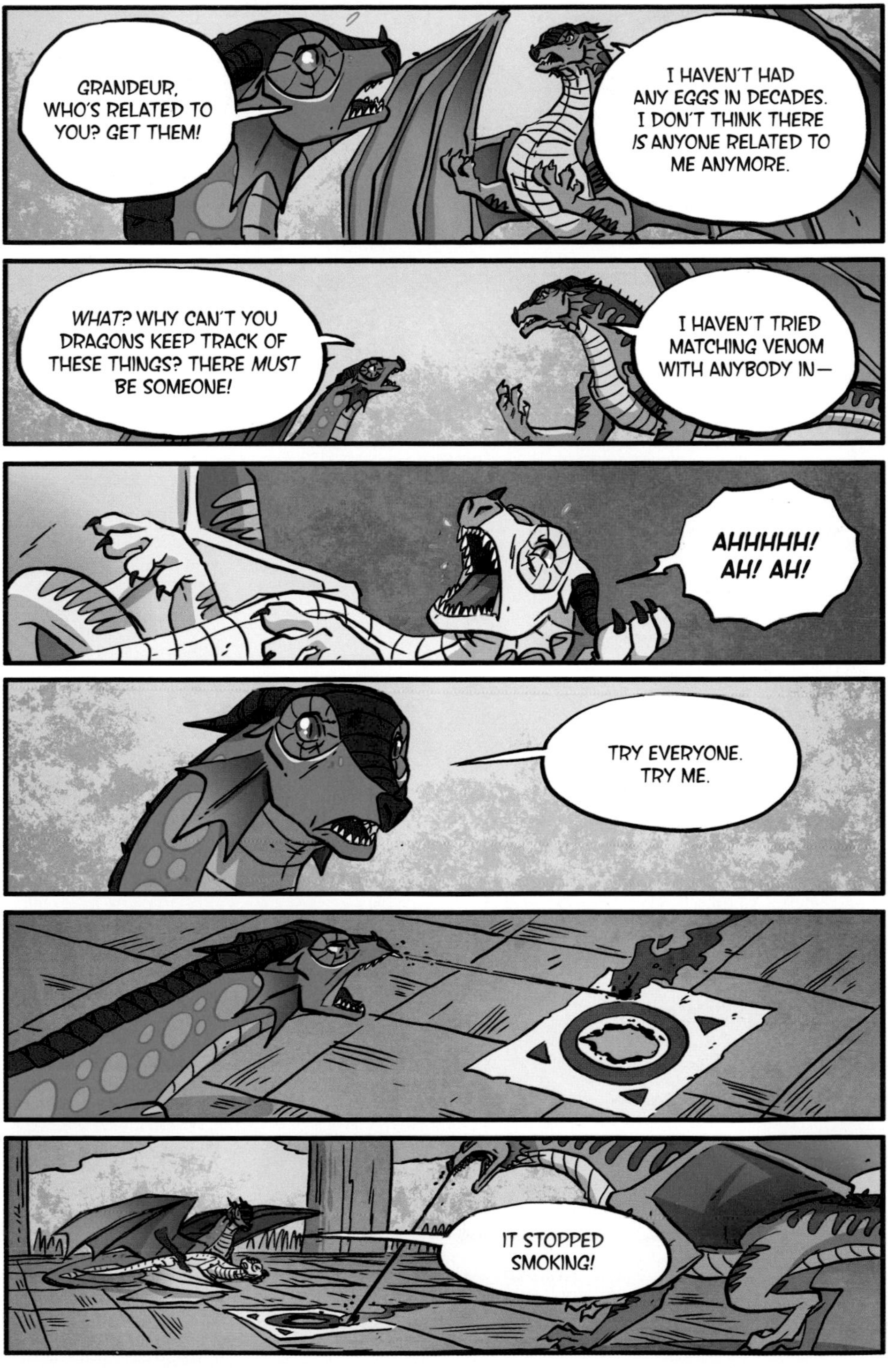
GRANDEUR, WHO'S RELATED TO YOU? GET THEM!
I HAVEN'T HAD ANY EGGS IN DECADES. I DON'T THINK THERE *IS* ANYONE RELATED TO ME ANYMORE.
WHAT? WHY CAN'T YOU DRAGONS KEEP TRACK OF THESE THINGS? THERE *MUST* BE SOMEONE!
I HAVEN'T TRIED MATCHING VENOM WITH ANYBODY IN—
AHHHHH! AH! AH!
TRY EVERYONE. TRY ME.
IT STOPPED SMOKING!

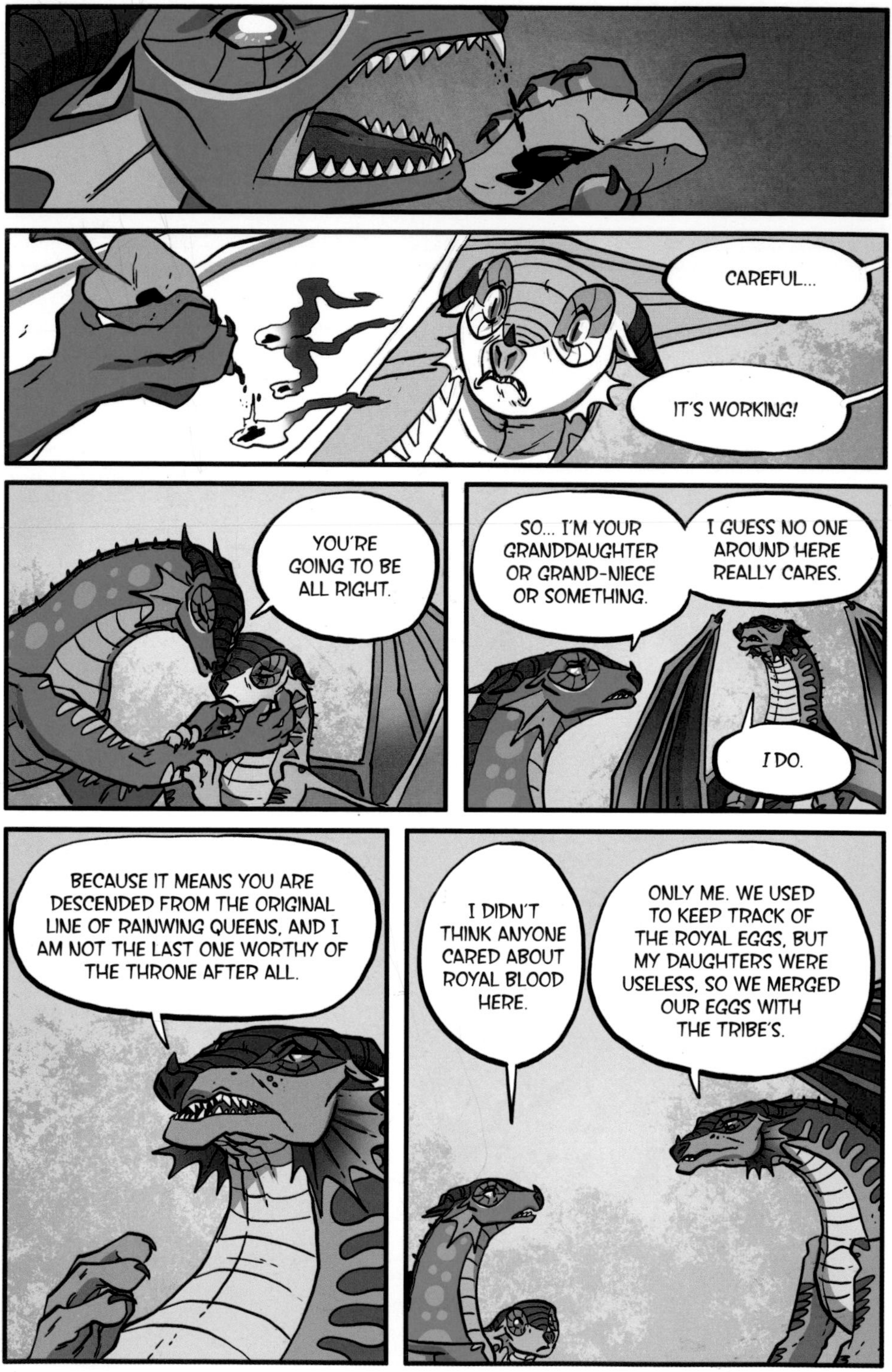
CAREFUL...
IT'S WORKING!
YOU'RE GOING TO BE ALL RIGHT.
SO... I'M YOUR GRANDDAUGHTER OR GRAND-NIECE OR SOMETHING.
I GUESS NO ONE AROUND HERE REALLY CARES.
I DO.
BECAUSE IT MEANS YOU ARE DESCENDED FROM THE ORIGINAL LINE OF RAINWING QUEENS, AND I AM NOT THE LAST ONE WORTHY OF THE THRONE AFTER ALL.
I DIDN'T THINK ANYONE CARED ABOUT ROYAL BLOOD HERE.
ONLY ME. WE USED TO KEEP TRACK OF THE ROYAL EGGS, BUT MY DAUGHTERS WERE USELESS, SO WE MERGED OUR EGGS WITH THE TRIBE'S.

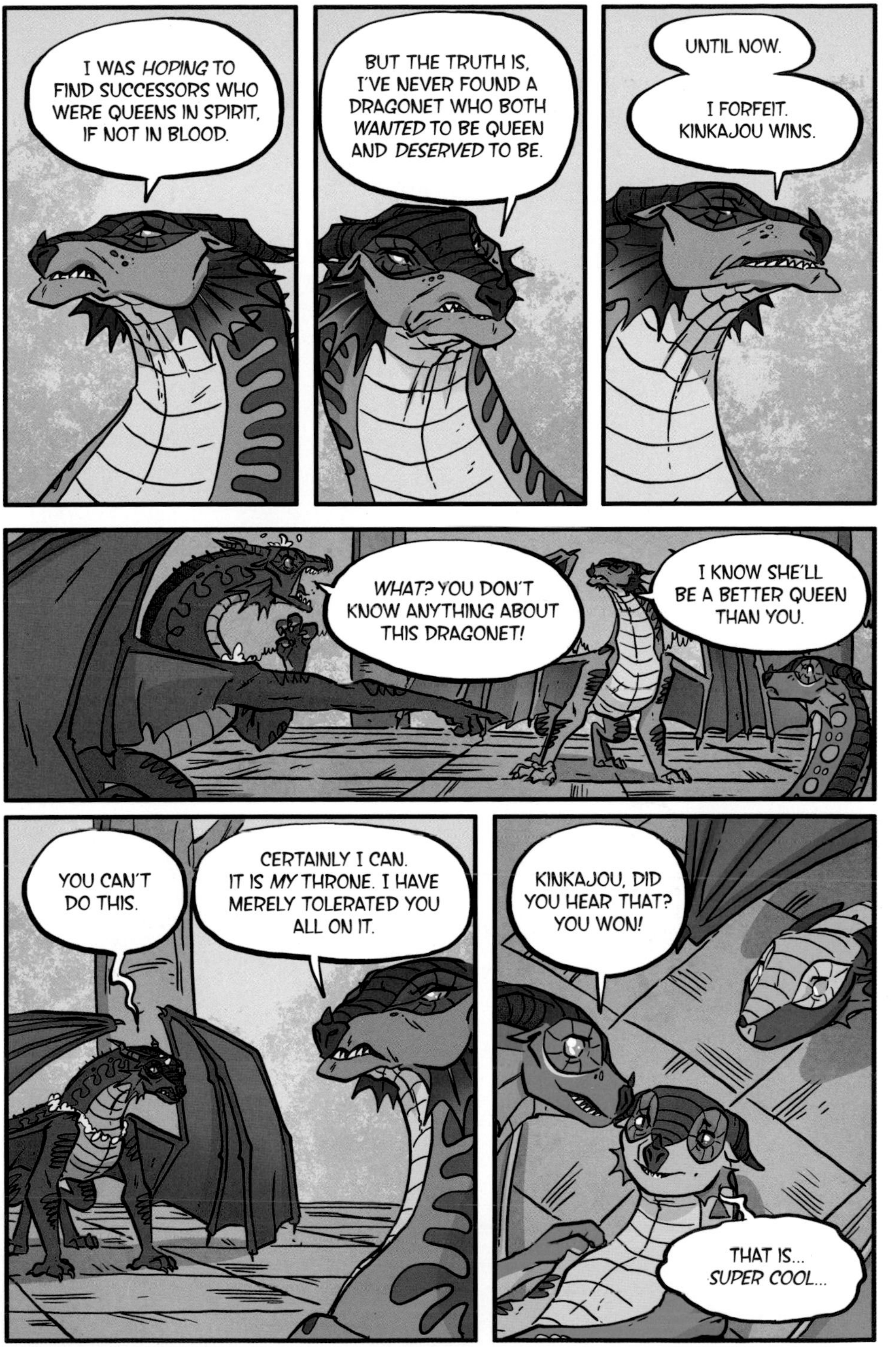
I WAS *HOPING* TO FIND SUCCESSORS WHO WERE QUEENS IN SPIRIT, IF NOT IN BLOOD.
BUT THE TRUTH IS, I'VE NEVER FOUND A DRAGONET WHO BOTH *WANTED* TO BE QUEEN AND *DESERVED* TO BE.
UNTIL NOW.
I FORFEIT. KINKAJOU WINS.
WHAT? YOU DON'T KNOW ANYTHING ABOUT THIS DRAGONET!
I KNOW SHE'LL BE A BETTER QUEEN THAN YOU.
YOU CAN'T DO THIS.
CERTAINLY I CAN. IT IS *MY* THRONE. I HAVE MERELY TOLERATED YOU ALL ON IT.
KINKAJOU, DID YOU HEAR THAT? YOU WON!
THAT IS... *SUPER COOL...*

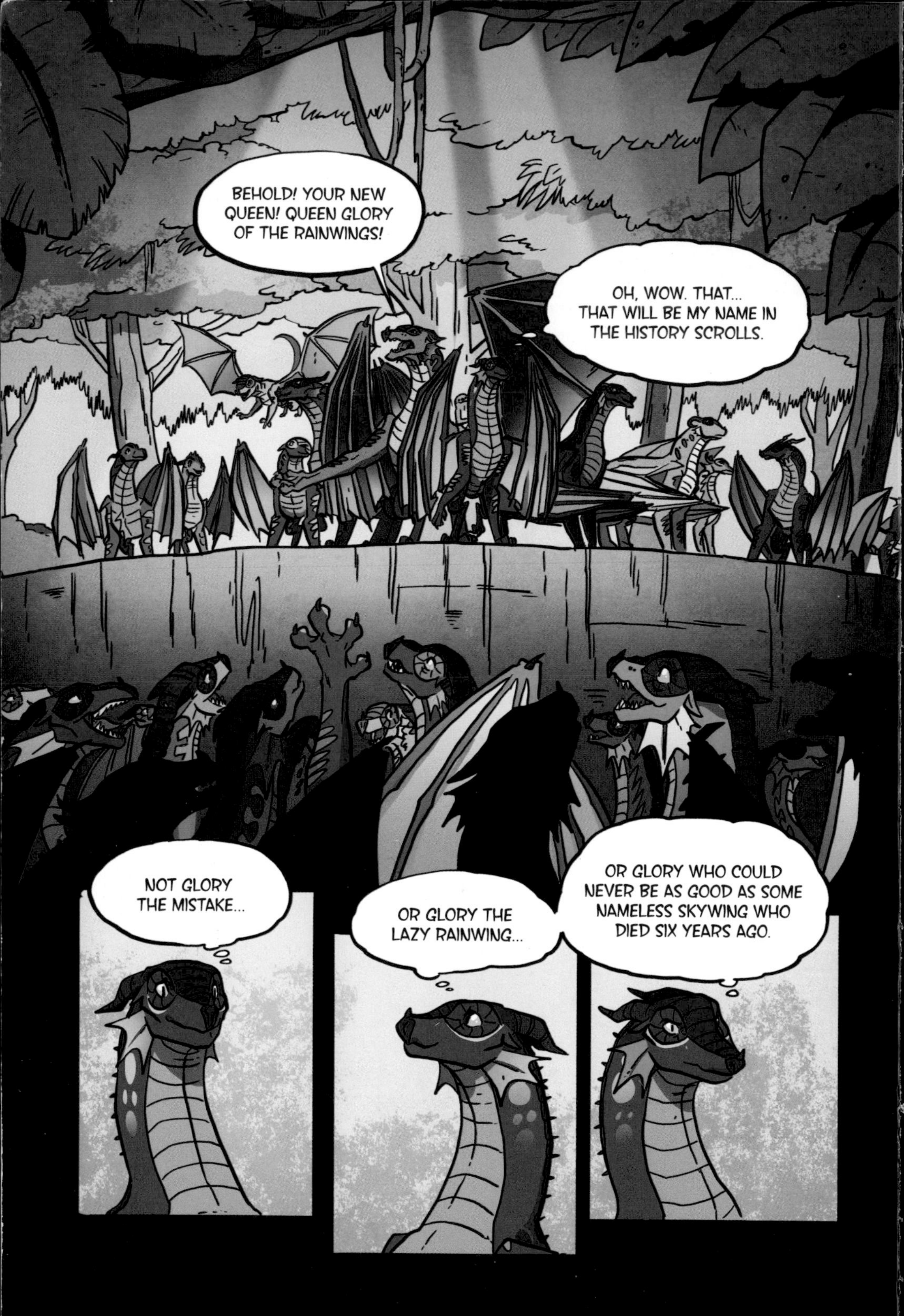
BEHOLD! YOUR NEW QUEEN! QUEEN GLORY OF THE RAINWINGS!
OH, WOW. THAT... THAT WILL BE MY NAME IN THE HISTORY SCROLLS.
NOT GLORY THE MISTAKE...
OR GLORY THE LAZY RAINWING...
OR GLORY WHO COULD NEVER BE AS GOOD AS SOME NAMELESS SKYWING WHO DIED SIX YEARS AGO.

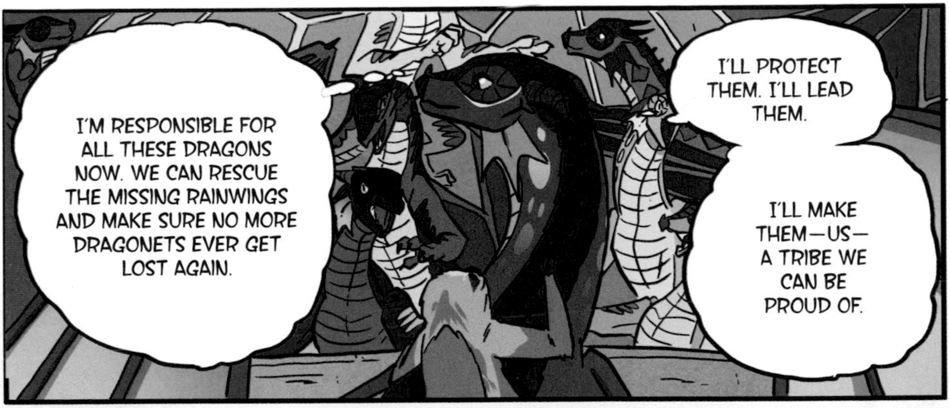
I'M RESPONSIBLE FOR ALL THESE DRAGONS NOW. WE CAN RESCUE THE MISSING RAINWINGS AND MAKE SURE NO MORE DRAGONETS EVER GET LOST AGAIN.
I'LL PROTECT THEM. I'LL LEAD THEM.
I'LL MAKE THEM—US— A TRIBE WE CAN BE PROUD OF.

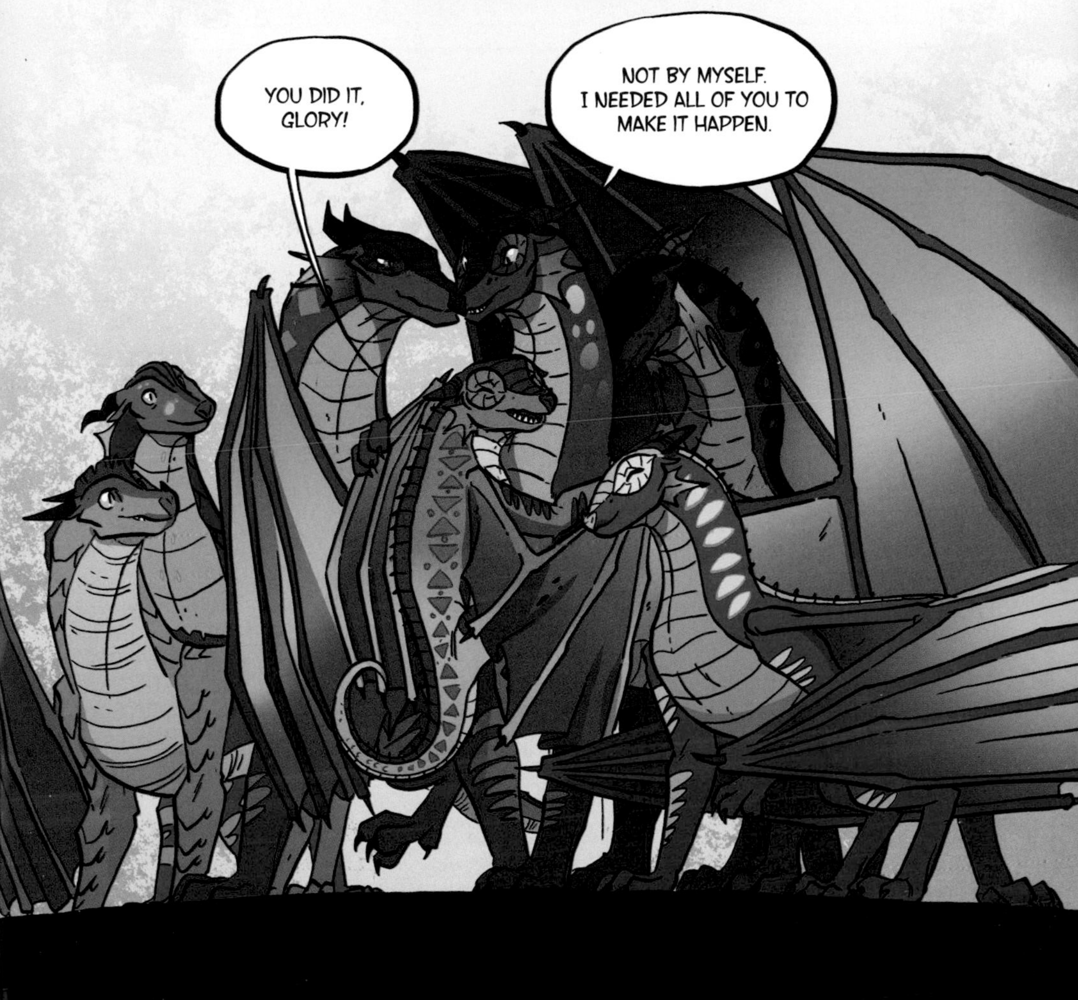
YOU DID IT, GLORY!
NOT BY MYSELF. I NEEDED ALL OF YOU TO MAKE IT HAPPEN.

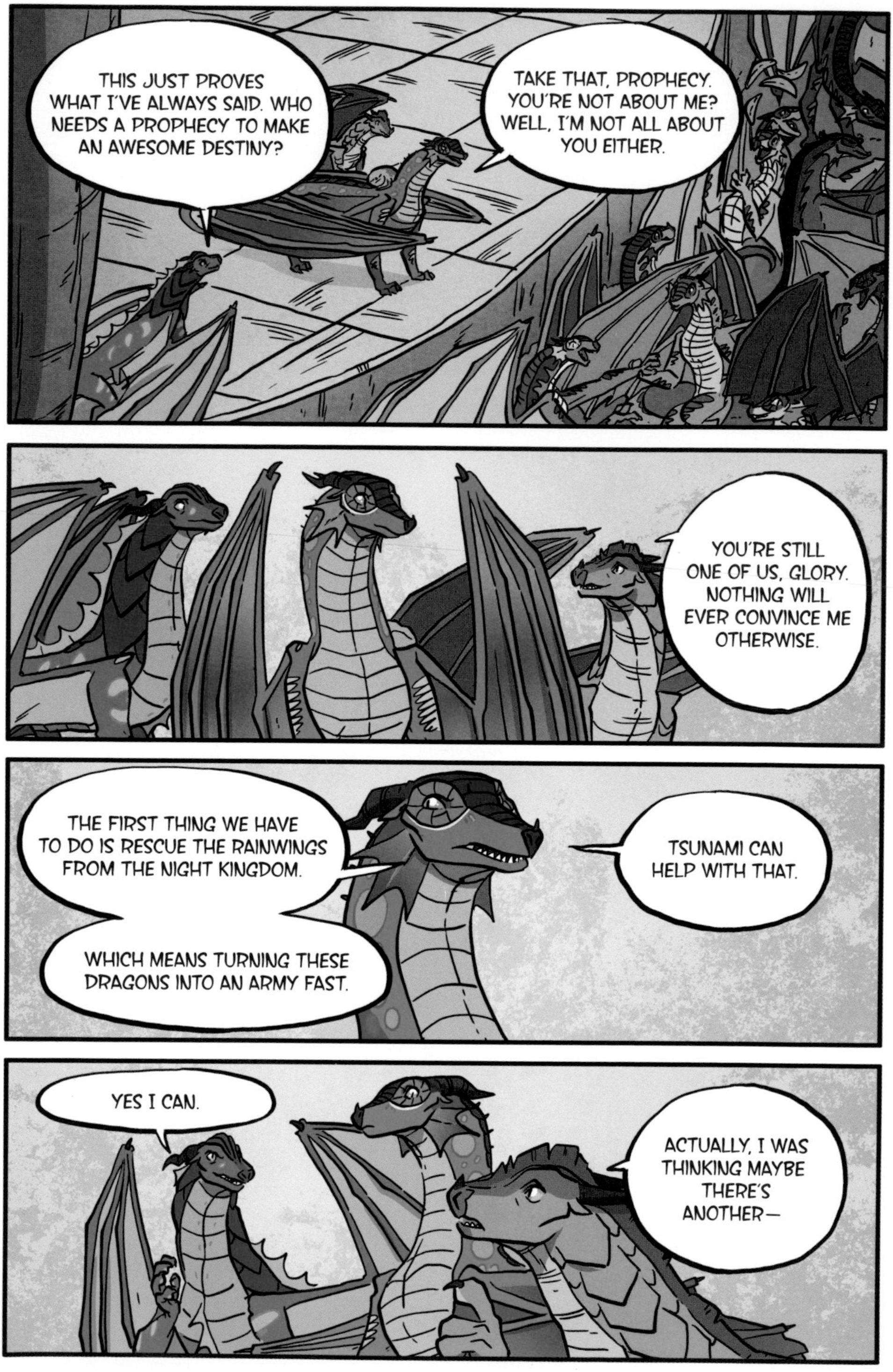
THIS JUST PROVES WHAT I'VE ALWAYS SAID. WHO NEEDS A PROPHECY TO MAKE AN AWESOME DESTINY?
TAKE THAT, PROPHECY. YOU'RE NOT ABOUT ME? WELL, I'M NOT ALL ABOUT YOU EITHER.
YOU'RE STILL ONE OF US, GLORY. NOTHING WILL EVER CONVINCE ME OTHERWISE.
THE FIRST THING WE HAVE TO DO IS RESCUE THE RAINWINGS FROM THE NIGHT KINGDOM.
WHICH MEANS TURNING THESE DRAGONS INTO AN ARMY FAST.
TSUNAMI CAN HELP WITH THAT.
YES I CAN.
ACTUALLY, I WAS THINKING MAYBE THERE'S ANOTHER—

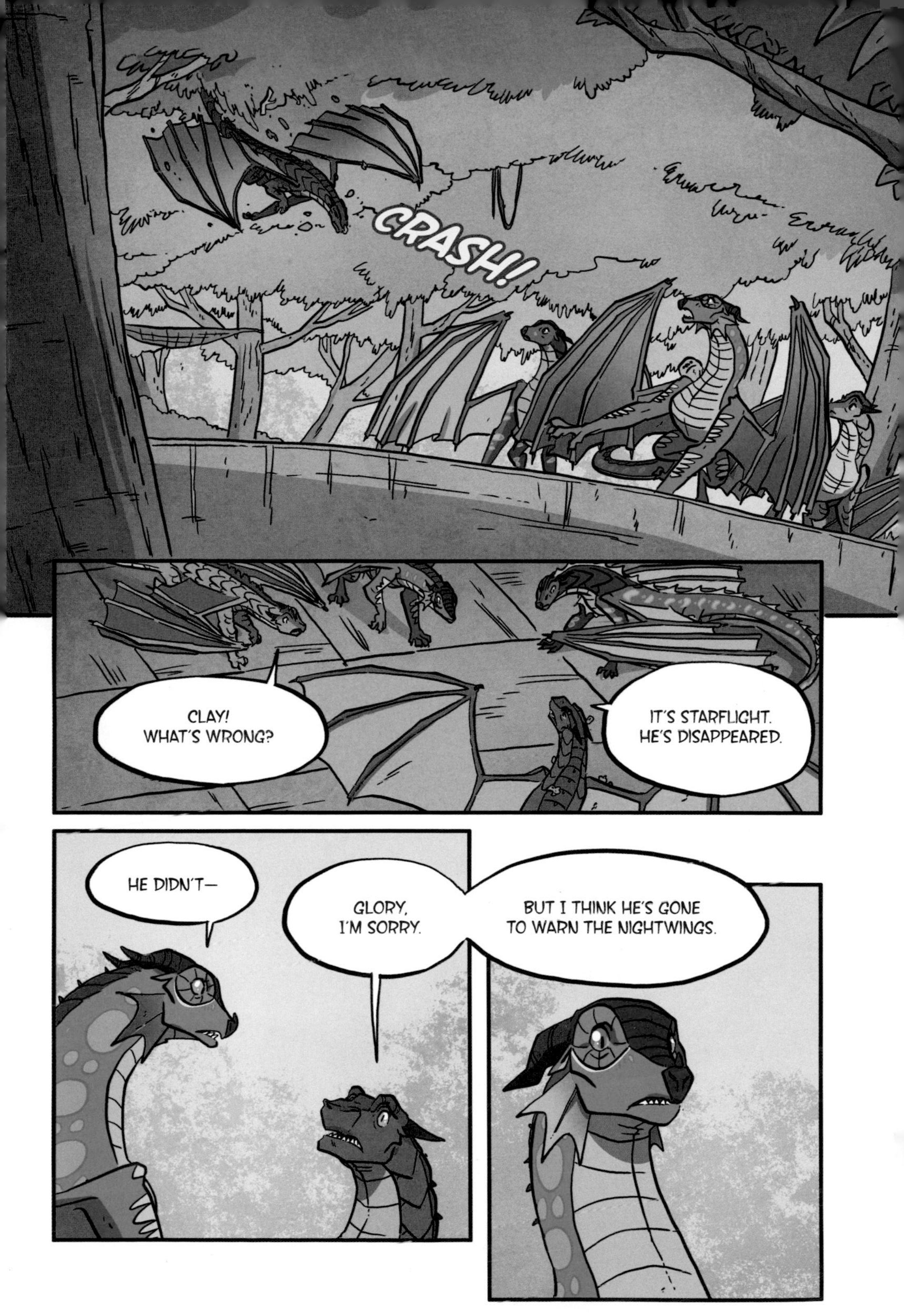
CRASH!
CLAY!
WHAT'S WRONG?
IT'S STARFLIGHT.
HE'S DISAPPEARED.
HE DIDN'T—
GLORY,
I'M SORRY.
BUT I THINK HE'S GONE
TO WARN THE NIGHTWINGS.

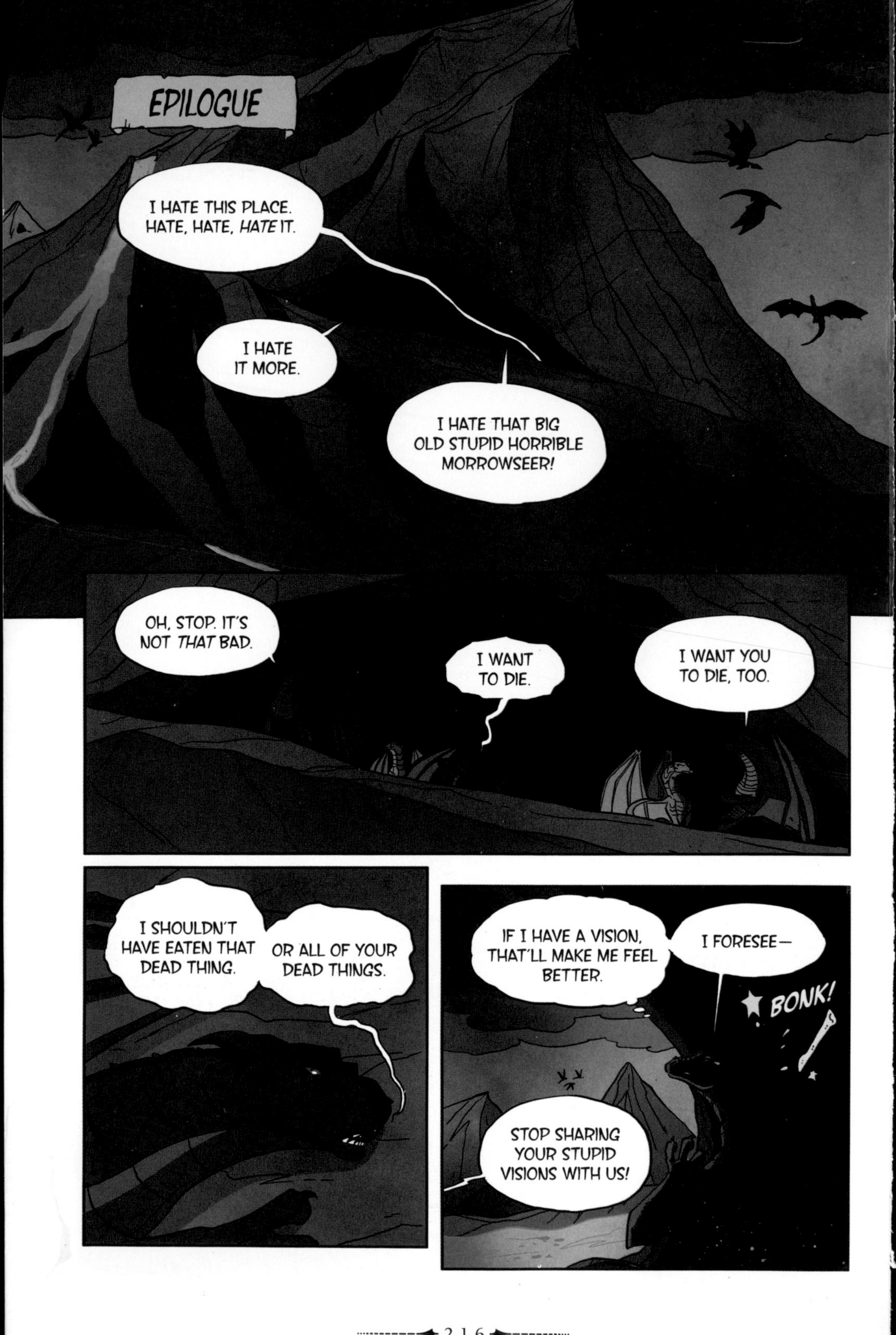
EPILOGUE
I HATE THIS PLACE. HATE, HATE, *HATE* IT.
I HATE IT MORE.
I HATE THAT BIG OLD STUPID HORRIBLE MORROWSEER!
OH, STOP. IT'S NOT *THAT* BAD.
I WANT TO DIE.
I WANT YOU TO DIE, TOO.
I SHOULDN'T HAVE EATEN THAT DEAD THING.
OR ALL OF YOUR DEAD THINGS.
IF I HAVE A VISION, THAT'LL MAKE ME FEEL BETTER.
I FORESEE—
BONK!
STOP SHARING YOUR STUPID VISIONS WITH US!

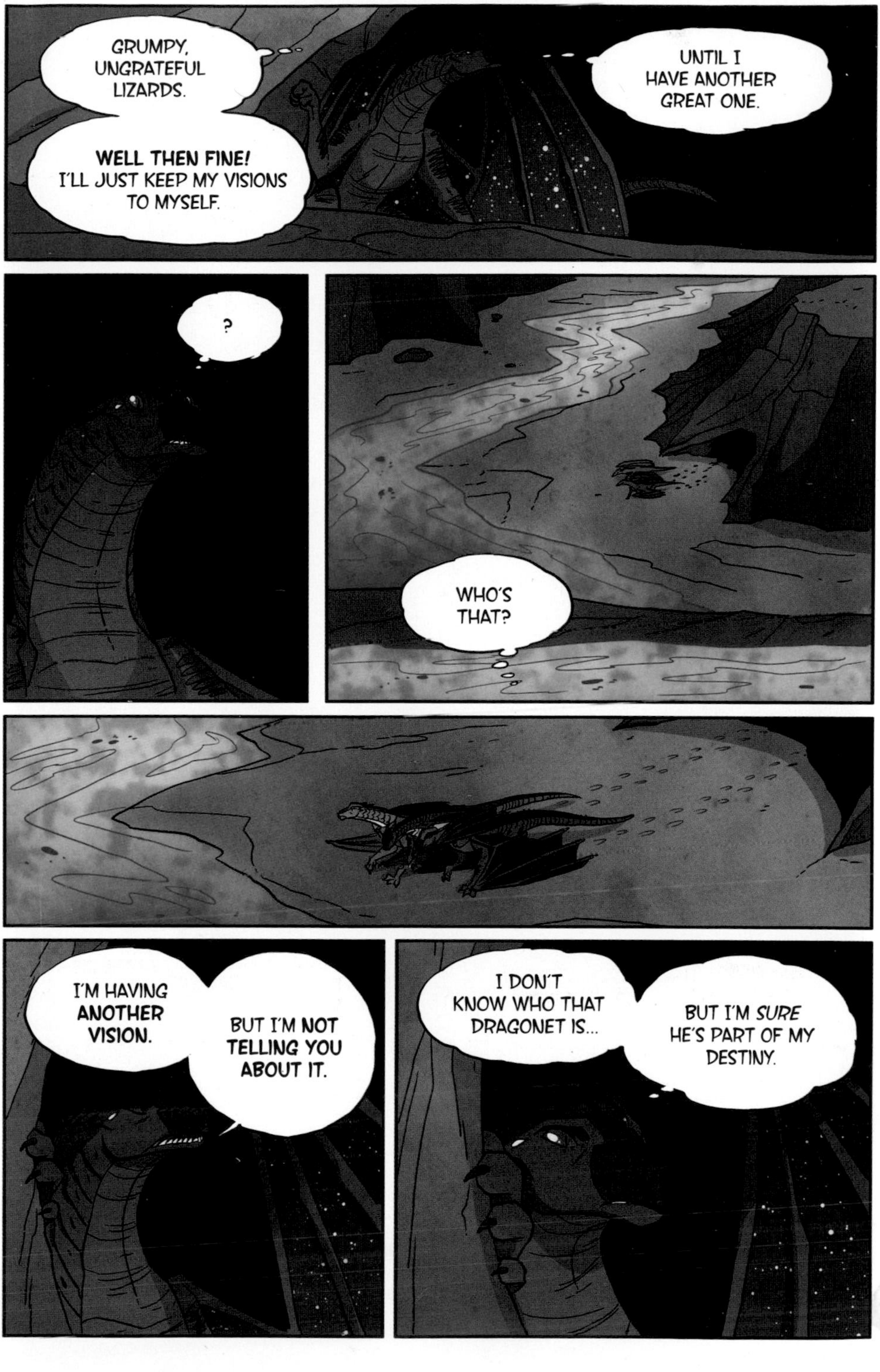
GRUMPY, UNGRATEFUL LIZARDS.
WELL THEN FINE! I'LL JUST KEEP MY VISIONS TO MYSELF.
UNTIL I HAVE ANOTHER GREAT ONE.
?
WHO'S THAT?
I'M HAVING **ANOTHER VISION.**
BUT I'M **NOT TELLING YOU ABOUT IT.**
I DON'T KNOW WHO THAT DRAGONET IS...
BUT I'M *SURE* HE'S PART OF MY DESTINY.

TUI T. SUTHERLAND is the author of the *New York Times* and *USA Today* bestselling Wings of Fire series, the Menagerie trilogy, and the Pet Trouble series, as well as a contributing author to the bestselling Spirit Animals and Seekers series (as part of the Erin Hunter team). In 2009, she was a two-day champion on *Jeopardy!* She lives in Massachusetts with her wonderful husband, two awesome sons, and two very patient dogs. To learn more about Tui's books, visit her online at www.tuibooks.com.

BARRY DEUTSCH is an award-winning cartoonist and the creator of the Hereville series of graphic novels, about yet another troll-fighting 11-year-old Orthodox Jewish girl. He lives in Portland, Oregon, with a variable number of cats and fish.

MIKE HOLMES has drawn for the series Secret Coders, Adventure Time, and Bravest Warriors. He created the comic strip True Story, the art project *Mikenesses*, and his work can be seen in *MAD* Magazine. He lives in Philadelphia with his wife Meredith and son Oscar, along with Heidi the dog and Ella the cat.

MAARTA LAIHO spends her days and nights as a comic colorist, where her work includes the comics series Lumberjanes, Adventure Time, and The Mighty Zodiac. When she's not doing that, she can be found hoarding houseplants and talking to her cat. She lives in the woods of Maine.